IF THE WEST FALLS...

Globalization, the End of America and Biblical Prophecy

BRIDGET S. HOWE

WestBow Press

Copyright © 2011 Bridget S. Howe

All rights reserved. No part of this book may be used or reproduced by any means, graphic, electronic, or mechanical, including photocopying, recording, taping or by any information storage retrieval system without the written permission of the publisher except in the case of brief quotations embodied in critical articles and reviews.

WestBow Press books may be ordered through booksellers or by contacting:

WestBow Press
A Division of Thomas Nelson
1663 Liberty Drive
Bloomington, IN 47403
www.westbowpress.com
1-(866) 928-1240

Because of the dynamic nature of the Internet, any web addresses or links contained in this book may have changed since publication and may no longer be valid. The views expressed in this work are solely those of the author and do not necessarily reflect the views of the publisher, and the publisher hereby disclaims any responsibility for them.

Any people depicted in stock imagery provided by Thinkstock are models, and such images are being used for illustrative purposes only.

Certain stock imagery © Thinkstock.

ISBN: 978-1-4497-2179-4 (e)
ISBN: 978-1-4497-2180-0 (sc)
ISBN: 978-1-4497-2181-7 (hc)

Library of Congress Control Number: 2011913129

Printed in the United States of America

WestBow Press rev. date: 10/24/2011

Contents

Acknowledgements		vii
Preface		vii
Facing Soldier's Field		x
1.	The Kingdom of the Khazars	1
2.	God	2
3.	The House of Rothschild	6
4.	The Minds of Men	9
5.	Freemasonry	21
6.	The Council of Foreign Relations, the Bilderbergers and the Trilateral Commission	22
7.	Dividing and Conquering America	30
8.	The House of Rockefeller	37
9.	The Bolshevik Revolution and the Third Reich	42
10.	History of a Terrible Secret	50
11.	The House of Rothschild and the Creation of Israel	57
12.	Establishing a Standard of Morality	60
13.	The National Security Act of 1947	63
14.	Operation Mockingbird	65
15.	Mind Control	69
16.	Spying on America and American Police State Part I	80
17.	Nothing Impossible	87
18.	Directed Energy Weapons	89
19.	Mind Control and Space Age Technology	108
20.	Give Us a King	112
21.	No Place for Our Children to Run	117
22.	America in Bondage	137
23.	Let Freedom Ring	148
24.	Operation Desert Storm	151
25.	Challenge to Your Thinking: Establishing Credibility	156
26.	The 9/11 Lie	161
27.	Afghanistan	183
28.	Operation Iraqi Freedom	187
29.	No Other Gods	196
30.	Imprisoned, Tortured and Tried	203
31.	The War on Terror	228
32.	The War on Drugs	238
33.	Adam Where Are You?	245
34.	Spying on America and American Police State Part II	246
35.	Organized Vigilante Stalking	261
36.	The Rule of Law	269
37.	Operation Zero Population Growth	273

38.	Global Agenda	278
39.	The Fourth Beast	281
40.	The Bohemian Grove, Washington and Witchcraft	289
41.	Whither the Church?	296
42.	Choose	306
43.	FEMA and Martial Law	316
44.	Hope	321
45.	The Fountain	331

Acknowledgements

When I was a child in the second grade, I did not have any real interest in academics. We had reading circle and we would be reading about Dick, Jane and Spot. I was the kid that was staring out the window and daydreaming. I never knew where we were when it was my turn to read. Our second grade teacher used to give us these Scholastic Readers flyers to take home that we could order books from. I never ordered any. But one day when my teacher was passing out the books she got in the mail, there was an extra book in the box. She asked me if I wanted it. I shrugged my shoulders and said, "Okay". I t was a story about a little boy who caught a magic fish. The fish promised him three wished if he would throw him back in the water. My teacher gave her students some time to read their books and I was surprised when I realized I could read the book I had. I had never tired to read on my own. That day I want home waving that little book in the air shouting, "Mommy, mommy, I can read!" My mother was so elated that I was taking an interest in something academic that from then on afterward she let me order as many books as I wanted. They were just pennies a piece then. So from that day forward, whenever my teacher got books in the mail that we ordered, there were two boxes. One box was for the rest of the class and one box was just for me. My mother's gift has been the most precious and valuable gift I have ever received from anyone. It has saved my life in more ways than one. Thanks Mom.

Fast forward about 10 years or so. I was sitting at my desk in my college dorm room. I had just purchased my text books for my first semester at Mt. Vernon Nazarene College, and I was sinking. I had never been an achiever in school. Though in my last three of years of high school I finally decided that it might be worthwhile for me to actually apply myself, I was staring at a stack of textbooks thinking that I had made a terrible error in not studying harder when I was in school. There was stuff I needed to know that I didn't because I hadn't studied, and I was sure I was not going to make it in my collegiate endeavor. Right at that moment into my darkness there came a shaft of light, a word from my Father in Heaven that lifted me out of my despair. He said, "What you need to know is in these books, and you can read." I made the Dean's list that first semester and finished my first year with a 3.7 GPA. (I didn't graduated with a 3.7 – more like a 3.2, but I graduated!) God is Abba, and I am his. He defines me. Thank you, Abba.

Preface

Anyone doing any kind of serious research pertaining to the subject matter of this book knows that they are walking through a mine field because research of this type is a search for truth – hard facts. Uncovering the truth can be dangerous. One begins such a search because they become aware that somebody is not telling the truth. That somebody has a vested interest in deceiving us. There are people that our government has paid to write books and deliberately sow disinformation. Of course, we all know that a lie becomes most believable if it is mixed in with some truth. And professional liars are cleverly disguised as virtuous persons. When a researcher beings to search for the truth, he or she has to be very diligent because the truth can be buried under a mound of lies. However, as one anonymous person quoted by Mark Phillips, co author of *Trance Formation of America* stated, "Truth lives a wretched life, but always survives a lie.[1]

When I was in college, in my introductory Psychology class, Dr. Randi Timpe's first lecture was about truth. He explained that truth can be represented by a capital "T" which stands for the whole truth in its most perfect and pure form. That is the truth represented by the word of God. Then there is little "t" which represents the portion of truth that we know. None of us has a monopoly on the truth, so the search for truth is continuous. Jesus said, "I am the way, the truth, the life. . . ."(John 14:6). In a search for pure truth we have a foundation in the scripture and in the person of Jesus Christ. In a world that has been filled with lies, knowing that you have truth in the word of God and in the person of Jesus Christ is a tremendously comforting feeling. It is something solid and sure. It is a rock under our feet. It is what gives us confidence when we are walking tediously through a mine field.

What I have to say in this book many of my brothers and sisters in Christ in America may find unbelievable. I would say to you that no one can force you to believe anything. It has been said that even God will not present us with so much evidence for his own existence that we can come to no other conclusion. He will always leave us with a choice. Faith therefore is a matter of choice. To believe in the truth is also a matter choice. I am not at all claiming to be error free. Knowing that much of what I have to say is very shocking, I attempted to verify every fact and every detail. Where I could not find a particular detail in more than one source, I used it if it were consistent with everything else I have read. Also, I have cited a few authors whose research where it pertained to factual data I felt was accurate, but I don't always agree with their interpretation of the facts. For example, Andrew Carrington Hitchcock is convinced that the conspiracy perpetrated by the New World Order is a Jewish conspiracy. Katherine Griggs, former wife of a mind controlled Green Beret involved in high level government corruption, tells us that it is a Zionist conspiracy. Zionism is a political movement not a religious one. There are wealthy Jews involved in this conspiracy, but I don't agree that all the players are Jewish or that the crimes they perpetrate are related to anything inherently Jewish. I Tim 6:10 tells us that the love is money is a root of all sorts of evil. It does not tell us that evil is associated with any particular ethnicity.

I would ask you to examine yourself as you read this book. In fact throughout this book I have written short chapters intended to challenge your status-quoness.

---

1   Cathy O'Brien & Mark Phillips, Trance Formation of America, (Frankston, Texas: Reality Marketing Inc., 1995) 2.

Please hear me when I say to you that truth is never convenient. Truth will set you free, but it is likely going to affront you first. It is uncomfortable. We humans have a terrible tendency to believe what is the most comfortable for us to believe. We don't want to be challenged. But to be committed to the truth is to accept challenge, to move from your comfort zones and to pick up your cross and follow Christ. People who sit in their easy chairs flipping channels and watching the news are not committed to the truth. They feel comfortable, safe and satisfied but are in fact in danger.

I began this project because I was jolted by an event in my own life that forced me to face that fact that people are not always what they present themselves to be, and the world is not what it appears to be on the surface. I was also faced with the reality that even "decent" people can be manipulated and deceived into complicity with the ugliest of criminal acts. In fact, people say "What you don't know can't hurt you." That is a "big fish" lie. What you don't know can kill you!

My Lord is always reminding me to be gentle. I have to work at being gentle when it comes to the subject of this book because I am greatly stressed by the complacency I find among my own countrymen. When you walk out your door you may not see dead bodies in the streets, blood on the ground or blown out buildings, and you may not be dodging bullets when you walk to your car. Because you don't see a war happening in your world doesn't mean there is not a war going on out there. It is an invisible covert war and an attack on innocent people. The war is hidden by those who are counting on the fact that if you don't see it you won't care is someone cries out to you, "Murder!". They are counting on the fact that you are too comfortable and satisfied in your world to even wonder why someone or many are telling you that something is wrong. The murderers have worked at making you complacent.

I and many others are witnessing the murder of a nation, nations and peoples. The murderer is the New World Order. The authors of the works I have cited are frustrated and many are very discouraged. They keep trying to tell us, and no one is responding. They are the weeping prophets of this generation.

Throughout this book as I point to cold hard facts, I also have to take sanity breaks every now and then. These chapters are time to contemplate the goodness of God. One cannot solely focus on the big, the bad and the ugly if one is to remain a sane rational person in an insane irrational world. You keep your balance in a storm by remaining focused. There are hopefully many who will read this who have not known a faith in Jesus Christ. I want to point them to the lifeboat. On that lifeboat is the one who spoke to the storm, "Peace, be still", and the storm obeyed. Jesus commands the storm. He is my hope and he gives my spirit peace in the storm. He is the one who helps me to overcome the murderer, the liar and the thief.

Facing Soldier's Field

I joined the U.S. Army in September 1981. After a three- month stint in basic training at Ft. Leonard Wood Missouri, extended because of a hospitalization, I was sent to the prestigious Defense Language Institute Foreign Language Center (DLIFLC) in Monterey, California. I arrived there in mid December. I was about twenty-three at the time.

Because of the coastal terrain, everything on the base was either up or downhill, and on my first day of actual duty I was heading downhill toward the medical clinic to turn in my medical records. It was a beautiful California day. The environment around me was green, green, green. The sky over the Monterey Bay was teal blue. The air was fresh and warm, and I could smell the salt from the bay as I listened to the lapping waves and the sound of barking seals on Seal Rock. I was in seventh heaven. This was definitely no hardship tour. I was to be a student of the Russian language there. Our classrooms were at the bottom of the hill in old buildings that smelled of old wood. There was a shortcut to the classrooms through the woods that was affectionately called the "Ho Chi Min" trail after the famous secret passageway the Viet Cong used in Viet Nam.

For one solid year, I learned to speak the language from native Russian instructors. Russia was at that time the big "threat". Nonetheless, our instructors taught us a very difficult language. We also heard the stories of life in a communist country. Russia was a place where one could stand in line all day to buy a loaf of bread only to find out that it was all sold out by the time you got to the head of the line. Russia was a place where you stood in line to buy shoes, and you bought whatever they had, even if they did not quite fit your feet. Russia was a country the natives wanted to escape from. And they tried, and if their petition to leave the country was denied they were labeled a "refusenik". Other people escaped by other than legal means. One of our instructors, Mrs. Caplan, was one of everybody's favorites. She and her family had escaped over the border. Her husband was killed in the process. She and her son survived. Mrs. Caplan of course became our instructor. Her son became an actor who became famous for his role as Cyrano de Bergerac in the Broadway stage production.

During my time in the military, I began to develop a deep appreciation of what a privilege it was to be an American and a Christian. While I was there in Monterey enjoying all the pleasures of living on the beach, I participated in what is called a "retreat" ceremony. My comrades and I were lined up rank and file on Soldier's Field facing the flag waiting for the sun to begin to set. When a soldier is standing in formation like that, her head and eyes are to be straight ahead standing stock still listening to the commands bellowed out by the unit commander. We waited and when the sun began to set, a soldier played "Taps" and the flag was slowly and lovingly lowered from the pole and folded ceremonially in a triangle. I was profoundly impressed, touched with the immensity of the privilege to be an

American citizen, a Christian and a soldier. I couldn't help it. Tears were streaming down my cheeks.

Facing Soldier's Field was the post chapel. It was the epitome of a little white church with a steeple. I later learned that a young army lieutenant who was the head of a satanic coven petitioned the post commander for the right to hold satanic worship services in that post chapel. His petition was granted because it was a government building, and he could not be denied. A post chapel has to be accessible to anyone of any faith. Therefore Christians, Muslims, Jews, and even Satanists all worship in the same building. I never worshiped in that chapel. It was not until years later that I learned just how infested and corrupted this nation has become because of the occult.

After completing all my training including more training at Goodfellow AFB in San Angelo, Texas, and another month of training at Ft. Devens Massachusetts in the spring of 1983, I traveled to West Germany for my first permanent duty assignment at the 108th Military Intelligence Battalion. It was a tactical assignment that involved a lot of guard duty and tromping around in the woods. I got to travel the world, and I got to hear from other people how they felt about America. Many Germans resented our presence in their country, but I met many people who were grateful to America for the assistance they received during the war.

While I was there I had to take many border tours. On my first tour with many of my comrades inside the "1 K zone", we learned the rules. The border is established by fences topped with concertina wire. Forward of the fences are black and yellow stripped cement poles that mark where the border actually sits. Behind the fence are towers of round cement disks piled up on another topped by a larger disk in which the guard watched from a window. We were told that if ever we saw someone trying to escape from East Germany that person had to be completely on the other side of the border before we could help. In other words, if I saw someone trying to escape, and he was being fired upon by East German soldiers, even if he had one big toe still on the east side of the border I was supposed to stand there and watch him die. I told myself that was probably a rule I would ignore. We were also told that we could not wave or communicate in any way with the guards because it could be misconstrued and cause an "international incident." I remember looking across the barbed wire fence at the guard towers and thinking, "There they are, guarding their own prison." I prayed silently for those guards.

On another border tour, we were in a small town on the boundary between East and West Germany. There was a road and a bridge that went to the other side. There was a wall across the road, and a barbed wire fence that went right down the middle of a creek that flowed under the bridge. Our tour guide had us standing on a platform so we could see on the other side of the wall. While he was talking, I observed an elderly gentleman walk up to the wall and stop. He was wearing a Fedora and a casual dress jacket. He stood there with his hands in his pockets and gazed at the wall. The tour guide noticed the man and told us his story. He said that after World War II, the man, who was a boy then, had left his house, which was on the other side of the wall, (I could see the roof) to go shopping in town. When he returned in the evening, there was a wall across the road and he could not go home. I felt for that man. I wondered who lived in that house with him. Did he have family there? Was he able to communicate with them? After the wall came down in 1989, I wondered if he went back to that house and what he found.

I performed a lot of guard duty while I was in Wildflecken. During one of those guard duty nights, I had a talk with another soldier in the unit who was guarding with me. He had been to Checkpoint Charlie, the passage between East and West Germany where tourists pass through in Berlin. He remarked about the difference in the atmosphere on either side of border at Checkpoint Charlie. On the west side people were milling about. There were bright colored lights on the buildings and people were running around in brightly colored clothing with their hair dyed weird colors. They were enjoying life. The east side was like a black and white photo. There were cameras on top of the buildings. No one wanted to stop and talk to anyone. People hurried to get inside because they were being watched. There was no spirit of frivolity in the air. No one was wearing brightly colored clothing or dyeing their hair. The buildings were all run down. The soldier said there is a rule that if you really wanted to leave East Germany, you could go on your sixtieth birthday, but you had to leave all your possessions behind. He was on his way back from a trip to East Germany at Checkpoint Charlie when he ran into a woman who had just turned sixty. She was going to the West. She had only a little change in her pocket, and she was as happy as a lark. Think about that for a moment. That woman was willing to let go of everything she had to gain her freedom.

While I was in Wildflecken, I attended the post chapel. This particular post chapel was not the typical generic church. There were three chaplains there at that time who were all very devout Christians, which is not always the case in a government-sponsored church. They preached the gospel with spiritual fervor. One of them followed me to Fort Meade when I left Germany. On a Wednesday evening service, I was privileged to listen to Mary Ann Hirschman who wrote *Hansi: the Girl Who Loved the Swastika*. In this book the main character was taken from her native Czechoslovakia and indoctrinated in Communist youth camps in Russia. She was told how horrible Americans were. During the war, in the midst of the foray she was on the run, scared and lost. She stumbled into an American military camp where she was "caught". However, the Americans were very kind to her, and ultimately they led her to a faith in Jesus Christ.

Mary Ann Hirschman now travels around doing speaking engagements. She told us that she had been in Yugoslavia speaking with a Catholic priest who was very concerned about the youth of his church. He felt they were too easily indoctrinated into the Communist way of thinking. He said to her, "Tell the Americans to hang on to their freedom. It is bad here, but we always have hope.

We can always run to the west. But if the west falls there will be no place left for our children to run."

Then I did not know just how precarious our freedom is. For very many reasons, as I hope you will see from reading this book, we are dangerously close to that place where there will be no place for our children to run.

1. The Kingdom of the Khazars

There is significant debate as to whether the large population of Jews living in Europe is actually descended from the Hebrews from Israel or rather from the Khazars who inhabited the territory. Robin de Ruiter indicates that they are of the Tartar and Mongol race which inhabited the Edomite territory [2]. According to David Icke the Khazars (also spelled Chasers) are descendants of the Hun tribe of Turkey whose blood line interbred with the Chinese and the Sumerians whose famous leader was Attila the Hun [3]. However, Yair Davidiy asserts that the Khazar kingdom is also said to occupy territory where the lost 10 tribes of Israel had been exiled. That would be in the area of the Don and Danaper rivers [4].

The Khazars were a warring nation and established the largest and most powerful kingdom in Eastern Europe. Their territory ran through the Danube River valley from Germany to Romania and into the Black Sea [5]. They were pagan and practiced phallic worship, human sacrifice and other forms of idolatry. The sexual practices of their worship reduced the nation to the most detestable sexual degradation which their 7th century King Bulan could not tolerate. Thus he chose to abolish phallic worship and establish a state religion. The three monotheistic religions in the area at the time from which he had to choose were Christianity, Islam and Judaism known then as Talmudism. The reason that King Bulan chose Talmudism over the other two faiths is also in debate. However the most logical reason would be that choosing Christianity would have subordinated the kingdom to the Roman Empire via the Roman Catholic church while choosing Islam would have subordinated it to the Caliph of Baghdad. King Bulan brought the Rabbi's from Babylon to the Kingdom of the Khazars to instruct them in their new state religion. Thus the Khazars were all circumcised on pain of death and the Rabbi's became their new spiritual leaders.

The Khazar language was Turkic or Asian, but it was not a written language. King Bulan took the characters of the Hebrew language and adopted them to the phonetic sounds of the Khazar language. This became known as "Yiddish". Though Hebrew and Yiddish use the same Hebrew characters there is nothing similar in the languages [6].

A small Slavic state North of the Khazar Kingdom was organized in 820 AD. They were Varangians from the Scandinavian Peninsula. This little nomadic

---

2   Robin de Ruiter, Worldwide Evil and Misery: The Legacy of 13 Satanic Bloodlines, (The Netherland: Mayra Publications, 2008) 147.
3   David Icke, Tales from the Time Loop, (Ryde, Iles of Wright, UK: David Icke Books, 2003) 93.
4   Yair Davidiy, "KHAZARS" an Overview: Israelite Tribes in Exile (January 29, 2011 - http://www.britam.org).
5   David Icke, Tales from the Time Loop, (Ryde, Iles of Wright, UK: David Icke Books, 2003) 263.
6   Robin de Ruiter, Worldwide Evil and Misery: The Legacy of 13 Satanic Bloodlines, (The Netherland: Mayra Publications, 2008) 149

state developed into the Russian empire and eventually swallowed up the Khazar Kingdom. While Russia was warring with her neighbors she sometimes had to give up some of her territory which was originally part of the Khazar kingdom. Those territories were in Poland, Bohemia, Lithuania, Rumania and Austria. Most Jewish Khazars settled in one of those countries.

These Khazars became known as the Ashkenazi Jews of Europe. When the Sephardic Jews (who can actually trace their ancestry back to Abraham) of Spain immigrated to the area some of them interbred with the Ashkenazi. It is strictly forbidden for Ashkenazim to interbreed with Sephardics in Israel today.

I think there might be some Jews who would be honestly shocked and dismayed to learn that they may not actually be descendants of Abraham. I know some Jewish Christians who are probably of Khazar descent who are also very proud of their Jewish Heritage who might be absolutely despondent at the thought that they may not truly descendants of Abraham. However, we do not despair. All Christians know that we are "engrafted branches" of that Abrahamic family tree. The scripture teaches that being Jewish is a state of the heart. "For he is not a Jew, which is one outwardly; neither *is that* circumcision, which is outward in the flesh: But he *is* a Jew, which is one inwardly; and circumcision *is that* of the heart, in the spirit, *and* not in the letter; whose praise *is* not of men, but of God" (Romans 2:28 – 29 NKJV). Jesus warned the Pharisees that God could raise up children of Abraham out of the rocks in the ground (Matt 3:9)

Jesus also warns us in the Book of Revelation about Jews who say they are Jews but are of the Synagogue of Satan. ". . . I *know* the blasphemy of they who say they are Jews, and are not, but *are* a synagogue of Satan" (Revelation 2:9 NKJV). What happens when people are forced to participate in a religion is that their usual practices simply go underground. The detestable idolatrous practices of the Khazars did not just simply go away. As we shall see they have surfaced again.

2. God

For since the creation of the world God's invisible qualities – his eternal power and divine nature have been clearly seen, being understood from what had been made, so that men are without excuse (Rom. 1:20 NIV).

I came home from work one day to find that somehow a bird had gotten trapped in my house. I don't know how it got in there, but this frantic frightened wild bird in my house desperately wanted out. The bird was really quite beautiful. It was black and it had small white dots evenly spaced all over its body. I marveled at this. Its body is covered with feathers that are made up of very fine threads. Yet when all these feathers are arranged on its body the white dots are lined up in perfect order. When the bird was born, of course it was pink and featherless. When it began to grown feathers it may have looked different until it matured. But in the maturation process, mother and father bird were not there with a paint brush and a measuring stick to make sure that it got its white spots all evenly spaced over its feathered body. This did not happen by accident either. I went downstairs and opened my front door and slowly cajoled the bird to fly out the door.

Let's consider for a moment the many varieties of birds in the air and their multicolored designs. How many species of birds are there? Does anybody know? And whose paint brush designed their colorful patterns? Or how about the fish in the sea? Like the birds, there are innumerable varieties of fish all with varied colors and patterns. And where is the artist that designed them? How about the flowers that grow over all the earth, the multiple different plant varieties, or the beautiful butterflies? An accident they say. A big bang!

If you had a black carpet in your home and handful of white paper hole punches and you let them go and fall to the floor, those hole punches would not accidently arrange themselves evenly about your carpet. In fact, if you wanted those hole punches to be evenly arranged on your carpet, you would be down on your knees with a measuring stick and a pair of tweezers for a good long time, depending on how important it was to you to accomplish the task. Let's take that one step further. Those white dots on the body of the bird were not solid white dots. They were comprised of white specks on the edges and tips of feather fibers that all came together in one spot to form a perfectly rounded white dot, in fact several of them perfectly spaced in a diamond pattern all over the body of the black bird. So now take your white hole punches and dump them in your shredder and grind them up. Then take all the fragments and toss them on your carpet and see how quickly they arrange themselves "by accident" in a pattern of white dots evenly spaced in a diamond pattern. So okay, you don't want to take the time to see if that will actually happen because you know of course it won't. If you left your house in the morning and it was a mess, you said to yourself, "I am really going to have to tear into this house when I get home." However, if when you returned home at the end of the day, and your house was all put in order and clean you would not say to yourself, "Wow! What happened? There must have been an accident!" Okay, you get the point.

There is something in mathematics called "P" or probability. It is a mathematical way of determining the probability that something can happen by chance. Usually a 1 in 20 "P" is enough to say that something did not occur by chance. If some mathematical genius had actually sat down and determined all the fine pieces of the puzzle of this intricately designed universe that functions with fine tuned precision and figured out the mathematical equation to determine the "P" value of it occurring by chance it would most likely be some astronomical figure like 1 in 6 bazillion. In other words mathematically the probability would be basically doo doo!

Let's look at something even more complicated. Prime numbers are a mystery. They are numbers that can only be divided by itself or by one. They do not occur at any discernable interval. Let's begin identifying them. They are 2, 3, 5, 7, 11, 13, 17, 19, 23, 29 etc. The occurrence of these numbers has no discernable mathematical pattern. However, if you put numbers on a grid beginning with the 1 in the middle and continuing from there in an Ulam spiral pattern with a white spot wherever a prime number occurs, a pattern begins to emerge. Modern day computers enable us to see things that were not possible before. What computers can do in seconds would be impossible for a man to complete in a lifetime. What does the computer reveal about prime numbers? There is a very discernable pattern. The Ulam spiral reveals a picture of a flower and the more prime numbers you have and the bigger your spiral gets the more detailed the flower becomes.[7]

Now here is something even more amazing. There are people in this world that will vehemently deny the existence of an intelligent being behind the creation of this planet. Yet those same people are among those who have been studying, testing and experimenting for how many thousands of years and spending how many man hours not to mention billions of dollars to try to figure out how to make it all happen just as the scripture says God made it happen. They have figured out how to control the weather and the human mind. They may even have figured out how to travel through time, and it may be possible some day in the near future for them to create matter and planets and stars. Nicola Tesla stated in 1908,

> Every ponderable atom is differentiated from a tenuous fluid, filling all space merely by spinning motion, as a whirl of water in a calm lake. It appears, then, possible for man through harnessed energy of the medium and suitable agencies for starting and stopping ether whirls to cause matter to form and disappear. At his command, almost without effort on his part, old worlds would vanish and new ones spring into being. He could alter the size of this planet, control its seasons, adjust its distance from the sun, guide it on its eternal journey along any path he might choose, through the depths of the universe. He could make planets collide and produce his [own] suns and stars, his heat and light, he could originate life in all its infinite forms. To cause at will the birth and death of matter would be man's grandest deed, which would make him the master of the physical creation, make him fulfill his ultimate destiny.

On January 7, 1958 Lyndon B. Johnson spoke these words to the Senate Democratic Caucus;

---

[7] Jeffery Satinover, M.D., Cracking the Bible Code, (New York: William Morrow, 1997) 248.

> Control of space means control of the world. . . . From space, the masters of infinity would have the power to control the Earth's weather, to cause drought and flood, to change the tides and raise the levels of the sea, to divert the Gulf Stream and change the climate to frigid. . . . There is something more powerful than the ultimate weapon. That is the ultimate position---the position of total control over the Earth that lies somewhere in outer space. . . . And if there is an ultimate position, then our national goal and the goal of all free men must be to win and hold that position.

It has taken a long time and a lot of money for some very intelligent atheistic people to get to the place where they think they might could just do what God has already done, but which they claim all happened by chance. When I stop to consider how hard some of the New World Order persuasion have tried to convince us that there is no God, it truly amazes me that these same people are driven to be able to control and do the same things that scripture clearly tells us are things that God has done – like creating stars and planets and controlling the weather. Though they insist that we have all descended from apes and there is no God here they are reaching to become gods themselves. And isn't it a wonder that what God was able to do in six days according to the scripture with the word of his mouth, science has had to spend billions of research dollars and billions of hours over generations of time to learn how to do – all the while insisting that the universe came into being by accident.

Now consider this. Whenever God spoke, something good happened. In the Genesis account of creation each time God spoke something into being, he stood back and saw that his work was good. He brought forth life when he opened his mouth. He created man from the dust of the ground. Then he breathed his breath of life into the man. This was good too. When Jesus walked upon the earth he spoke healing to the sick, the blind, the lame, the deaf. He even spoke life into lifeless bodies and they arose from the dead. God's creative energy has all been for the good of mankind. However we see another story when man begins to try to harness that kind of creative power himself. Mankind's scientific manipulations have created disease and disrupted the motion of this planet and the ecosystem so much so that the earth is now wobbling on its axis and sea turtles "forget" to migrate and freeze to death.[8] One would want to seriously consider the words of Jesus Christ when he said, "The thief does not come but to kill and steal and destroy. I have come that they might have life, and that they may have it more abundantly" (John 10:10 NKJV).

The proponents of globalization and the New World Order might want to consider the fate of the their Lord Lucifer which is predicted in the book of Isaiah;

---

8 Jerry E. Smith, HAARP: The Ultimate Weapon of the Conspiracy (Kempton, ILL: Adventures Unlimited Press, 1998) 109.

For you have said in your heart: "I will ascend into heaven, I will exalt my throne above the stars of God; I will also sit upon the mount of the congregation, on the farthest sides of the north; I will ascend above the heights of the clouds; I will be like the most High." Yet you shall be brought down to Sheol, to the lowest depths of the pit. Isa 14:13-15 NKJV

3. THE HOUSE OF ROTHSCHILD

Mayer Amschel Rothschild, an Ashkenazi Jew, is the patriarch of the Rothschild family clan. His name was originally Mayer Amschel Bayer and he lived in Germany in the 17th century. The family lived in the ghetto district of Frankfurt called Judengasse. Living conditions were not good there as there was an anti-Semitic bent in Europe at that time. Most Ashkenazi Jews at that time did not use sir names but had adopted the Chinese tradition of using symbols instead. These symbols were hung outside the family home and used like an address.[9] Some Jewish families chose sir names to fit in, and this family chose the name Bayer which means farmer, though they were not farmers but retailers.

When Mayer Amschel Bayer was 12 years old he was sent to school to become a Rabbi, but a year later his parents died. He was encouraged by his family to continue his schooling, but he loved coin trading. He moved to Hanover and went to work for the Oppenheimer Bank for seven years learning the ins and outs of money. He met General von Estorff who was a Numismatist who was impressed with the young Bayer's knowledge of the subject. Later Estorff joined the court of Prince William IX of Hesse-Hanau, a Freemason family. Mayer Amschel Bayer left the Oppenheimer bank after seven years and returned to Frankfurt making the best of his connections with Estorff and now the House of Prince William of Hesse.[10]

Later Mayer Amschel Bayer adopted the symbol that hung outside the family home as his family's name. That symbol was an occult symbol which was originally adopted by King Solomon when he became apostate and began worshipping Ashtoreth. The symbol was a red six pointed star which has become known as the Star of David. The name that Bayer adopted for his branch of the family was "Rothschild" which is German for "red shield". The symbol stands for '666' that is six lines, six angles and six points.[11] A blue six pointed star now adorns the flag of Israel. It is still the symbol of the Rothschild family, and it is a Rothschild descendent that now rules Israel behind the scenes.

Mayer Amschel Rothschild was not a cultured person and he did not even know the German language. He spoke Yiddish. He used his five sons to complete

---

9   Fritz Springmeyer, The Rothschild Bloodline (July 3, 2009 - http:// www.theforbiddenknowledge.com).
10 Andrew Hitchcock, The History of the House of Rothschild (Timeline of the Rothschild Family, May 7, 2001 -http://www.imthewitness.com).
11 Ibid.

transactions for him. Mayer Rothschild was devoutly Jewish, however it appears that his sons were later involved in the occult. One might wonder how someone growing up in an orthodox Jewish family ends up absorbed in the occult. The answer is probably found in the study of Jewish Mysticism, or Cabala. Not only have the Middle Eastern Jews a history in Baal worship, but the Khazars were originally idolaters involved in occultic practices such as human sacrifice and sexually perverted worship. Thus it is probably not a far stretch that Mayer Rothschild's sons could have wandered into the occult. Also Jewish Cabala is rooted in Egyptian mystery schools. Of course we know that the Jews were exiled in Egypt for 400 years and upon their exit from Egypt still were inclined toward Egyptian idolatry.

Mayer Rothschild became closely involved with Prince William of Hess who was only a year older than himself. They shared a love of coin trading. Prince William was a Freemason. Through him, Mayer Rothschild became involved with Freemasonry which is said to be based in Talmudic traditions. Those on the outer fringes of Freemasonry believe their organization is a nice fraternal organization. However, the core of Freemasonry is rooted in the occult.

Mayer Rothschild made his money by acting as an agent for Prince William of Hess. Prince William did not want anyone to know how much money he had so he used Rothschild as an agent. Mayer Amschel Rothschild eventually made enough money that he was able to establish his own bank. His five sons became the bankers in Europe. The Rothschilds five sons were Salomon, Nathan, Karl, James, and Amschel. Nathan established his bank in London, James in France, Salomon in Austria, Amschel in Germany and Karl (Kallmann) in Italy.

When the German princes of Thurn and Taxis wanted to open their own postal service between Brussels and Vienna, Mayer Amschel Rothschild loaned them money. The head office of the postal services was in Frankfurt and Mayer began to do business with them and became very close with them. The Postal service was in the habit of unsealing the letters and gleaning from them pertinent intelligence information which they gladly shared with Mayer Rothschild. In order to keep his own mail from being read, Mayer Rothschild established his own postal service. His network of secret routes and fast couriers was unrivaled. Of course the mail was opened up and Mayer Rothschild always knew in advance, for example when a war was being fought what the battle plans of both sides were going to be. The Rothschild couriers were the only merchants allowed to pass the English and French blockades which gave them an advantage. They used intelligence they gathered to help Nathan Rothschild make strategic moves on the stock exchange.[12]

Rothschild's sons would coordinate with each other through their respective banks in different European countries. Thus they loaned money to both sides of the war and benefited no matter who won. The fact that Napoleon would not

---

12   Andrew Carrington Hitchcock, The Synagogue of Satan (Austin, Texas: RiverCrest Publishing, 2007) 44 – 45.

borrow money from Rothschild because he did not want to be indebted to him did not make Nathan Rothschild happy. Unless he could get Napoleon in debt, he could not control him. Nathan Rothschild got his revenge however, when Napoleon was attempting to defend France against the Duke of Wellington and he was forced to borrow money from Nathan Rothschild's London Bank. However Nathan Rothschild also smuggled gold through France with the cooperation of his other family members and helped to equip Duke Wellington's army.[13] Napoleon was defeated.

Mayer Amschel Rothschild also established his own intelligence network. "By their own secret intelligence service and their own news network they could out maneuver any European government."[14] Nathan Rothschild learned of Napoleon's defeat at Waterloo from one of his own mail couriers. He used this information to gain the advantage in the stock exchange. Pretending to be despondent he sold all his stock at the London Stock exchange. All eyes on Nathan Rothschild who assumed that the Duke of Wellington has lost began madly selling off all their stock. Thus Nathan bought them up at a fraction of their real value. When the news reached the general populace the Duke of Wellington has defeated Napoleon, the stocks skyrocketed back up to their original value leaving Nathan Rothschild a return of 20 to 1 of his investment.[15]

The Rothschilds became adept at the art of ensnaring governments by lending them money. One of Mayer's sons, Amschel Rothschild, is now famous for his statement in 1838, "Permit me to issue and control the money of a nation, and I care not who makes its laws." The Rothschilds would, because of their powerful positions as European bankers, instigate conflict between ruling powers and then lend them money (on both sides) and thus nations became indebted to the Rothschild banking system. They were able to wield a considerable amount of power over European monarchies. Gary Allen in *None Dare Care it Conspiracy* remarks that once a King or President has borrowed money from a bank and the King or President does not cooperate with the banker's demands the banker can also loan money to the borrower's enemy and thus unseat that ruler.[16] Rothschild played this game well. Professor Stuart Crane studied the grouping of nations around the house of Rothschild. He was able to discern from examining who was in debt to Rothschild who was being punished.[17]

What can be seen from a careful look at world events, then, that this unseen hand was operating covertly to create conflicts in order to gain control over national

---

13 Jim Marrs, Rule By Secrecy (New York, NY: Perennial Harper Collins, 2000) 79.
14 Fritz Springmeyer, The Rothschild Bloodline (July 3, 2009 - http://www.theforbiddenknowledge.com)
15 Andrew Carrington Hitchcock, The Synagogue of Satan (Austin, Texas: RiverCrest Publishing, 2007) 45.
16 Gary Allen, None Dare Care it Conspiracy (Rossmoor, California: Concord Press, 1971) 38.
17 Ibid, 39.

governments. In fact it is also true that Mayer Rothschild also had his hand in the monetary affairs of the Roman Catholic church.[18]

On Sept. 19, 1812 Mayer Amschel Rothschild died. His will stipulated that only his five sons would inherit the family business. His daughters, whom he had married off to wealthy bankers' sons, were completely left out of his will.[19] His five sons were the bankers of Europe. When they passed, having gained considerable control over European governments, three cousins took over.

4. THE MINDS OF MEN

There have been some great thinkers in the world. I personally believe that Jesus Christ should top that list. It appears to me that what thoughts he shared lead to life and liberty for all peoples of the earth. He taught people to tell the truth, not to steal, lie, or commit murder or adultery. But Jesus also focused on the inward thoughts of men. People tend to focus on onward things, Jesus said, but God looks at the heart. Jesus taught on the commandments and added that though the commandment says "Thou shalt not commit adultery," even if you have a lustful thought toward a woman you have already committed adultery in your heart. Though the commandment says, "Thou shalt not murder," if you despise someone in your heart, you have committed murder. Jesus clearly taught in scripture that thoughts play an important role in who we are and what we become (Matt. Ch. 5). Indeed, there have been men in history whose thoughts and ideas, as harmful and as destructive as an atom bomb, have wreaked havoc on mankind. Their thoughts and influence are in fact still poisoning our world today.

JOHANN ADAM WEISHAUPT
1748-1830

Adam Weishaupt is one long dead but his thoughts, ideas and influence have perhaps led to the deaths of many innocent persons and are still doing so today. Johann Adam Weishaupt was born on February 6th, 1748 in Ingolstadt, Bavaria. His father was a professor of Law at Ingolstadt University and after his death young Weishaupt was nurtured by his godfather Johann Adam Freiherr von Ickstatt who was also a professor of Law at Ingolstadt. Ickstatt influenced young Weishaupt with the rational philosophy of Christian Wolf. He went to a school controlled by the Jesuits. He later went to the University of Ingolstadt and graduated at the age of 20 with a doctorate in law.

Weishaupt was studying to be a Jesuit Priest, and it has been said that he was angered when the Pope Clement XIV banned the order in 1773. However,

---

18 Fritz Springmeyer, The Rothschild Bloodline (July 3, 2009 - http:// www.theforbiddenknowledge.com)
19 Ibid.

he clearly did not favor the Jesuits. He rebelled against the Jesuit discipline.[20] He became a professor of Cannon Law at Ingolstadt University after the Jesuit order was banned by the Pope. This position was traditionally reserved for the Jesuits.

The Illuminati was officially established in Spain in 1530 with the writing of the Constantinople Letter. The plans in the letter pertained to world domination. This plan was further revised and fomented with consultation by the Rothschild banking company. Mayer Amschel Rothschild stated to the influential families of the Illuminati during a secret meeting, "If we combine forces we can rule the world." The goal of the Illuminati was to create a world dictatorship. The letter and the meeting provided the plan which included withholding information by manipulating the media, censoring the truth and restricting freedom. A few powerful families would dominate the economy, and politics of the world. "The ultimate goal was to reduce human interest to a point where they would agree to anything, therefore setting up the stage for a One-World Leader."[21] The Constantinople letter was thus placed in the hands of Adam Weishaupt and this became the basis for Weishaupt's plan to dominate the world. On May 1st, 1776, he established the Illuminati in Germany which was structured much like the Jesuit order but with radically opposed ideals. After he formed the Illuminati he refused the Jesuits entrance into his secret society and worked to eliminate them from Ingolstadt University.[22]

One other interesting fact about Weishaupt is that he was very interested in the occult and became obsessed with the great pyramid of Giza. He was convinced it was a prehistoric temple of initiation. After he made the acquaintance of Franz Kilmer, a Danish merchant who had resided in Alexandria Egypt, he began planning his secret society for the purpose of "transforming" the human race. "He devoted five years to thinking out the plan, borrowing from many different occult sources. His first name for the proposed order was the Perfectibilisen." This he may have gotten from the Cathars whose name means "perfect ones.'"[23] His reaction against the tyranny of the church is reflected in his statement, "Man is not bad . . . except as he is made so by arbitrary morality. He is bad because religion, the state, and bad examples pervert him. When at last reason becomes the religion of men, then will the problem be solved." [24] He was an influential visionary. He wanted to establish a New World Order, which included:

---

20 Joseph Trainor, Adam Weishaupt – The New World Order and Utopian Globalism (UFO Roundup, January 10, 2004- http:// www.illuminati-news.com.).
21 Robin de Ruiter, Worldwide Evil and Misery: The Legacy of 13 Satanic Bloodlines, (The Netherland: Mayra Publications, 2008)29.
22 Terry Melanson, Illuminati Conspiracy Archive Part One: A Precise Exegesis on Available Evidence (Illuminati Conspiracy Archive, August 5, 2005 - http://www.conspiracyarchive.com).
23 Joseph Trainor, Adam Weishaupt – The New World Order and Utopian Globalism (UFO Roundup, January 10, 2004 - http:// www.illuminati-news.com.).
24 Jim Marrs, The Rise of the Fourth Reich (New York, NY: Harper Collins, 2008) 13.

- Abolition of monarchies and all ordered governments
- Abolition of private property and inheritances
- Abolition of patriotism and nationalism
- Abolition of family life and the institution of marriage, and the establishment of communal education for children
- Abolition of all religion

He developed a plan, and the plan was kept secret within the Illuminati. It was so frightening that even those of the inner circle feared the outcome. Although attendees were sworn to secrecy, the Count de Virieu, a member of the Martinets Lodge at Lyons, was horrified of the secrets he learned while attending the Congress at Wilhelmsbad. When questioned about the secrets revealed there he replied, "I will not confide them to you. I can only tell you that all this is very much more serious then you think. The conspiracy which is being woven is so well thought out that it will be . . . impossible for the Monarchy and the church to escape from it."[25]

Weishaupt's plan included putting his handpicked "adepts" in positions of world leadership. A part of his plan also included ridding public institutions of anyone who would oppose him. He thus managed to push all the Jesuits out of Ingolstadt University. "Through the intrigues of the Brethren the Jesuits have been dismissed from all the Professorships; we have entirely cleared the University of Ingolstadt of them."[26] In addition to that the French Freemasons placed Illuminati into key government positions in France and eventually brought about the bloody French Revolution by deliberately undermining the Bourbon Dynasty of France.[27]

A respected British Historian, Professor John Robinson, who was also a Freemason, wrote in *Proofs of a Conspiracy*:

> I have found that the covert secrecy of a Mason Lodge has been employed in every country for venting and propagating sentiments in religion and politics that could not have been circulated in public without exposing the author to grave danger. I have observed these doctrines gradually diffusing and mixing with all the different systems of Free Masonry till, at last, AN ASSOCIATION HAS BEEN FORMED FOR THE EXPRESS PURPOSE OF ROOTING OUT ALL OF THE RELIGIOUS

---

25 Joseph Trainor, Adam Weishaupt – The New World Order and Utopian Globalism (UFO Roundup, January 10, 2004- http:// www.illuminatinews.com.).conspiracyarchive.com).

26 Terry Melanson, Illuminati Conspiracy Archive Part One: A Precise Exegesis on Available Evidence (Illuminati Conspiracy Archive, August 5, 2005- http://www.conspiracyarchive.com)

27 Pat Robertson, The New World Order (Dallas, Texas: Word Publishing, 1991) 68.

ESTABLISHEMENTS, AND OVERTURNING ALL THE EXISTING GOVERNMENTS OF EUROPE.[28]

The headquarters for Illuminated Freemasonry moved to Frankfurt Germany in 1782, which was controlled by the Rothschild family. It was in Frankfurt that Jews were first admitted to the Freemasons. This may be the link between the occult and high finance. "Remember, the Rothschilds financed Ceil Rhodes in Africa; Lord Rothschild was a member of the inner circle of Rhodes's English Round Tables; and Paul Warburg, architect of the Federal Reserve System, was a Rothschild agent."[29]

Weishaupt clearly intended to eradicate all religion. The first principle in which all Illuminees were educated states;

> I. The Illuminee who wishes to rise to the highest degree must be free from all religion; for a religionist (as they called every man who has any religion) will never be admitted to the highest degrees.[30]

However, Weishaupt made his illuminism a religion. Thus "European aristocrats transferred their lighted candles from Christian altars to Masonic lodges. The flame of occult alchemists, which had promised to turn dross into gold, reappeared at the center of new 'circles' seeking to recreate a golden age."[31] In 1871, Albert Pike wrote in *Morals and Dogma of the Ancient and Accepted Scottish Rite of Freemasonry*, a book intended for use by those of the Thirty-Third Degree of Masonic Councils, that the Masonic Temple is a religious temple. He states that all religions, including Christianity, gather around the Masonic alter where they pray to the one god who is "Balaam". He further states "Everything good in nature comes from Osiris," the Egyptian sun god whose symbol is the all Seeing Eye which is displayed on the back of the U.S. dollar. Pike asserts that Lucifer is the God of light who is struggling for humanity against Adonay the God of darkness and evil.

The Illuminati were aggressive recruiters to their order. An initiate was expected to proselytize or gain more recruits. He did this by keeping a diary and spying in his friends, family and associates to determine which of them would be appropriate for the order. He observed family, friends, enemies and strangers to determine their strong and weak points, as well as all their assets. This information was kept in a diary. They did not simply find members for their cult, they targeted

---

28 John Robinson, Proofs of a Conspiracy (New York: George Forman, 1978) 10.
29 Pat Robertson, The New World Order (Dallas, Texas: Word Publishing, 1991) 181.
30 Terry Melanson, Illuminati Conspiracy Archive Part One: A Precise Exegesis on Available Evidence (Illuminati Conspiracy Archive, August 5, 2005- http://www.conspiracyarchive.com).
31 Ibid.

them. They spied on a potential member so as to learn his habits, weaknesses and passions. They would gain the confidence of the target and engage him in conversation for the purpose of understanding what makes him tick. Amazingly, they actually went so far as to follow their prey into his bedroom, "where they will learn whether he is a hard sleeper, whether he dreams, and whether he talks when dreaming; whether he is easily or with difficulty awakened; and should he be suddenly, forcibly, or unexpectedly awakened from his sleep, what impression would it make of him?."[32] Because of their aggressive recruitment tactics Illuminism spread from Denmark to Portugal and even to New York City where the British Illuminists joined with Americans and founded the Columbian Lodge in New York City in 1782.[33]

Their members were kept under constant surveillance. Those who entered into the order were required to make confessions which were later used to control them, and they were sometimes manipulated into committing crimes which would later be used against them in gaining their cooperation. Tremendous control was maintained over members, as their minds were molded to suit the purposes of the order. Weishaupt wrote to his close associate Xavier Zwack, dated Mar 10 1778, "We cannot use people as they are, but begin by making them over". Those in the highest degrees of Illuminism were sworn atheists. However one of their members was apparently still holding on to his belief in God. Weishaupt wrote to Zwack, "Do put Brother Numernius in correspondence with me," he says, "I must try to cure him of his Theosophical ideas, and properly prepare him for our views."[34]

Another characteristic of Illuminism is typical of cults. No one was to ever question the character or actions of the leadership. "The Superiors of Illuminism are to be looked upon as the most perfect and the most enlightened of men; no doubts are to be entertained even of their infallibility." Their superiors in Illuminism were to be respected above civil authority.[35]

Weishaupt's philosophy has been used by tyrants such as Hitler and many others resulting in the senseless and macabre deaths of millions of innocents. "Behold our secret. Remember that the end justifies the means," he wrote, "and that the wise ought to take all the means to do good which the wicked take to do evil." In other words, says Marrs ". . .any means to gain their ends is acceptable, whether this includes deceit, theft, murder, or war".[36] This is also reflected in his statement, "Sin is only that which is hurtful, and if the profit is greater than

---

32 Ibid.
33 Joseph Trainor, Adam Weishaupt – The New World Order and Utopian Globalism (UFO Roundup, January 10, 2004- http:// www.illuminati-news.com.).
34 Terry Melanson, Illuminati Conspiracy Archive Part One: A Precise Exegesis on Available Evidence (Illuminati Conspiracy Archive, August 5, 2005- http://www.conspiracyarchive.com).
35 Joseph Trainor, Adam Weishaupt – The New World Order and Utopian Globalism (UFO Roundup, January 10, 2004- http:// www.illuminatinews.com.).
36 Jim Marrs, The Rise of the Fourth Reich (New York, NY: Harper Collins, 2008) 13.

the damage, it becomes a virtue."[37] Secrecy and covert activity characterized the Illuminati and is probably the reason for their continued proliferation. "The great strength of our Order lies in its concealment. Let it never appear in any place in its own name, but always covered by another name, and another occupation," stated Weishaupt. He not only deceived the public, but he reminded his top leaders they should hide their true intentions from their own initiates by "speaking sometimes in one way, sometimes in another, so that one is kept under constant surveillance to maintain and enforce absolute secrecy." This is also clearly reflected in his statement ". . . that one's real purpose should remain impenetrable to one's inferiors."[38] Members of the order were left with carrying out orders without really knowing the true purpose of what they were doing. Those who attempted to leave the order found themselves facing constant harassment to the point that their lives were nearly destroyed.[39]

Their activities caused considerable disruption for the civil authorities, and thus they were banned by the Duke of Bavaria, and anyone caught attempting to recruit would be put to death with the sword. Weishaupt went into exile thereafter and found protection in the court of Illuminati member the Duke of Saxe Gotha, Ernest Lewis. He enjoyed a salary and dignified life there as Honorary Counselor to the Duke.[40] Adam Weishaupt died on November 18th, 1830 in Gotha. The Roman Catholic Encyclopedia of 1910 says that he repented on his deathbed; while author Gary Allen claims that he was working on an essay on art magic when he suddenly dropped dead.[41]

GEORGE WILHELM FREDERICK HEGEL
1770 – 1831

George Wilhelm Frederick Hegel was a professor of philosophy at the University of Berlin. He believed that man is subordinate to the state and finds fulfillment in obedience to the state. He rejected religion and any sense of morality or notion of right vs. wrong. Hegel himself was a member of the Freemasons and likely also an Illuminist. He espoused the Freemason rationalist theology that reason is "the candle of the Lord". Hegel believed that history is determined by the resolution of conflict.

What became known as the Hegelian Dialectic was his theory that a force (thesis) dictates its own opposing force (antithesis). These forces in conflict result in

---

37 Joseph Trainor, Adam Weishaupt – Th e New World Order and Utopian Globalism (UFO Roundup, January 10, 2004- http:// www.illuminati-news.com.).
38 Jim Marrs, Th e Rise of the Fourth Reich (New York, NY: Harper Collins, 2008) 13.
39 Terry Melanson, Illuminati Conspiracy Archive Part One: A Precise Exegesis on Available Evidence (Illuminati Conspiracy Archive, August 5, 2005- http://www.conspiracyarchive.com).
40 Ibid.
41 Joseph Trainor, Adam Weishaupt – The New World Order and Utopian Globalism (UFO Roundup, January 10, 2004- http:// www.illuminati-news.com.).

the creation of a third force: a synthesis. Secrets societies, including the Illuminati as well as well known figures such as Karl Marx, Adolf Hitler, Meyer Rothschild, Wilhelm Wundt and Weishaupt came to believe that they did not have to wait for a crisis to present itself. They could create a crisis and use it to achieve their goals. "In other words, in the world of ruthless power politics, one can apply the Hegelian Dialectic in a perverse manner. Simply offer a draconian solution to a problem you have engineered, which, after compromises, still advances the secret agenda of those who created the problem in the first place."[42]

History reflects the outcomes of the use of the dialectic by the wealthy and powerful using it to advance their own agenda. Mayer Rothschild and his ilk were known to incite both sides of a conflict and then finance them both profiting greatly from it. The Reichstag fire is seen as the creation of a crisis to advance the NAZI agenda. Today, Hegel's dialectical theory can be seen clearly in the machinations of the U.S. Government and agencies of U.S. Intelligence especially the Central Intelligence Agency. The promoters of the New World Order in the United States have used the Hegelian Dialectic as a tool to promote their globalization ideals in the United States. "... again and again ... using the theory of the Hegelian Dialectic to bring it about. They are manipulating events, creating conflicts, creating wars, and destroying the lives of untold millions ... The New World Order is the desired synthesis of the controlling forces operant in the world today."[43]

WILHELM MAX WUNDT
1832- 1920

Another mind that shaped the thinking of the New World Order globalists was Wilhelm Max Wundt professor at the University of Leipzig in Germany. Wilhelm Wundt and his grandfather were Illuminists.[44] Wundt believed that experiences had to be scientifically quantified, and he reduced all human experiences down to bodily reactions. He funded the first experimental psychology laboratory in Leipzig in 1878. At Leipzig Wundt's studies in social psychology were focused on behavior control for controlling masses of people. The NAZI's adopted this point of view which permitted them to perform their experiments in the death camps of WWII.[45] Wundt redefined psychology as the study of the brain and nervous system, and declared that man was an animal without a soul which made it okay

---

42   Jim Marrs, The Terror Conspiracy: Deception, 911 and the Loss of Liberty (New York, NY: Disinformation, 2006)344 – 346.
43   Jim Keith, Mind Control, World Control (Kempton, Ill: Adventures Unlimited Press, 1997)p. 28
44   Terry Melanson, Illuminati Conspiracy Archive Part One: A Precise Exegesis on Available Evidence (Illuminati Conspiracy Archive, August 5, 2005- http://www.conspiracyarchive.com).
45   Jerry E. Smith, HAARP, The Ultimate Weapon of the Conspiracy (Kempton, ILL: Adventures Unlimited Press, 1998)126.

to treat people like animals. Essentially man was a machine, a robot and a cog in the greater machine of the state.

MILTON FREIDMAN
1912 – 2006

Milton Freidman was professor of Economics at the University of Chicago famous for his statement, "There are no free lunches". He promoted a theory of economic "shock therapy" that has become standard around the world with disastrous results. It is favored by the globalists because it promotes a free market economy and favors big business. He did not believe in government regulation of any kind and did not favor government supported institutions such as schools, hospitals, public utilities etc. "In his view, the state's sole functions were 'to protect our freedom both from the enemies outside our gates and from our fellow-citizens: to preserve law and order, to enforce private contractors, to foster competitive markets'". The three trademarks of a "Friedmanized" economy are 1.) privatization, 2.) government deregulation and 3.) deep cuts to social spending.[46] This typically results in loss of economic stability, rise in unemployment, a decrease in the quality of life for the citizenry and an increase in the suicide rate. Thus the populace usually revolts resulting in brutal crackdowns by dictatorships that employ Freidman's theory of economics. Thus people are murdered, tortured and "disappeared" in order to intimidate the populace and maintain the dictatorship in power. Dictators from around the world such as Chile's Pinochet employed consultants from the Chicago School of Economics when implementing this strategy. Pinochet was a ruthless dictator who actually was under house arrest waiting for trial being charged with war crimes when he died. [47]

NICOLA TESLA
1856 – 1943

Nicola Tesla was a physicist whose research and inventions were based on the concept that everything has wave properties including the earth, any physical structure such as a building, the atmosphere and even your mind. He believed that by synchronizing an artificial mechanical wave with a natural wave you could control the natural wave. He went bankrupt trying to prove that his inventions were applicable to providing wireless energy to communities and for use as powerful wireless weapons. He created earthquakes with his inventions, and it is suspected that his experiments resulted in the explosion of the French ship Ierna and the disappearance of whole Nomadic Villages in Siberia. The U.S. Military was not interested in his work so he took it overseas and the NAZIS and the Soviets got

---

46   Naomi Klein, The Shock Doctrine, The Rise of Disaster Capitalism (New York, NY: Metropolitan Books, 2007)5, 9.

47   Ibid

their hands on his notes after his death. His work is the foundation of a whole new brand of weaponry today called Directed Energy Weapons.

ALEISTER CROWLEY
1875-1947

Edward Alexander Crowley was born to a wealthy religious family at the height of the Victorian era on Oct. 12th, 1875.[48] His parents were members of the "Exclusive Brethren" a more radical branch of the "Plymouth Brethren". This was a particularly strict Christian group of which his father was a traveling preacher and author. According to one source he was particularly close to his father but according to another he changed his name to Aleister to avoid having the same name as his father. He was rebellious toward the family and their religion. His father died when he was age 11 years. His rebellious ways particularly concerned his mother who called him "The Beast", a label which he later proudly adopted calling himself "The prince-priest, the beast" in one of his published works.[49]

He gave up his virginity at age 14 with a housemaid and contracted gonorrhea at age 17 by a street walker.[50] His entire life was characterized by sexual promiscuity with both men and women. One of his published works was called *"White Stains"* in which he praised homosexual sex.

He attended Cambridge University studying mountain climbing and living a privileged life. He also began his work career as a diplomat and an ambassador. Crowley felt that being an ambassador would afford him short lived fame and he wanted to make more of an impression on the world. At the age of 23 he joined the Hermetic Order of the Golden Dawn which had heavy influence on western magical tradition. They synthesized the Kabala, alchemy, tarot, astrology, divination, numerology, Masonic symbolism and ritual magic into one system which was recognized for influencing many occult organizations to come. Crowley advanced quickly in rank under Alan Bennett his mentor. He completed the course of study for the rank of Adeptus Minor in 1900 but was not promoted in rank because the London controllers of the Order did not approve of his homosexual conduct. However, Crowley traveled to Paris and was promoted in a ceremony by Samuel Liddell Macgregor Mathers who led the Order. This served to alienate the London group.[51]

During a trip to Egypt he encountered an entity known as Aiwass which Crowley believed was his holy guardian angel. This came about when he and his wife encountered the Stele of Revealing painted with the image of Horus in a museum. The item was labeled with the number 666 in the museum catalog. It

---

48 Popculculture.com, Aleister Crowley, the Great Beast (The Biography Project, 1999 – 2004 - http://www.popculture.com).
49 Wikipedia, Aleister Crowley (http://www.wikipedia.en).
50 Popculculture.com, Aleister Crowley, the Great Beast (The Biography Project, 1999 – 2004. http://www.popculture.com).
51 Ibid.

was during this period that Crowley received either by dictation or by automatic writing the contents of what he published under the title *The Book of the Law*. This book contained the teachings of Thelema which is the Greek word for "the will". This concept which was central to all his teachings was represented in his statement, "Do As Thou Wilt Shall Be The Whole Of The Law." Crowley's religion, which is sometimes referred to as "Crowlianity", is a liberal mixture of elements of Christianity, Gnosticism and the Masons into its magical rituals.

Thelemites, or followers of the Law of Thelema, often greet one another with the shorthand "93", which is the numerical value of the phrase "Love is the law, Love under will." which is the proper response to the phrase "*Do As Thou Wilt* . . . " The meaning of the later is simply that one should do whatever your higher self dictates. To put it in modern vernacular, doing whatever your "higher self" dictates amounts to selfishly fulfilling every fantasy and every desire with absolute disregard for the rights of others or even the life of another.

This "doing what thou wilt" was the theme of the Abby of Thelema which Crowley established in Sicily with Leah Hirsig after WWI. It was called an "anti-monastery" and was characterized by the opposite of the disciplines one would find in a monastery. Those who lived there did whatever they pleased. The students studied magic but the main objective was to discover and manifest their true wills. While at the Abby, Crowley engaged in "no holds barred" sexual indulgences and drugs with anyone and everyone including children. The living conditions there were very unsanitary. His infant daughter Poupee died as well as one of his students Raoul Loveday. The wife of Raoul Loveday went back to England and exposed the Abby in the Press. The scandal that resulted ended in Crowley being expelled from Italy in 1923.[52]

His expulsion from Italy caused his life to take a turn for the worse. He was dubbed "the wickedest man alive" and his reputation was playing against him. He was not able to find a reliable publisher for his writing or a place to live.[53] In 1934 he filed a lawsuit against Nina Hammett for calling him a black magician in her book, *Laughing Torso*, published in 1932. Mr. Justice Swift addressed the Jury at the trial and said of Crowley "

> I have been over forty years engaged in the administration of the law in one capacity or another. I thought that I knew of every conceivable form of wickedness. I thought that everything which was vicious and bad had been produced at one time or another before me. I have learnt in this case that we can always learn something more if we live long enough. I have never heard such dreadful, horrible, blasphemous and abominable stuff as that which has been produced

---

52 Linda Blood, The New Satanist (New York: Warner Books, 1994) 52.
53 Popculculture.com, Aleister Crowley, the Great Beast (The Biography Project, 1999 – 2004. http://www.popculture.com).

by the man (Crowley) who describes himself to you as the greatest living poet.[54]

Crowley went bankrupt in the lawsuit which he lost. Aleister Crowley died December 1st, 1947 of a respiratory infection at age 72. Newspapers called his funeral a black mass, a very disturbing event which the Brighton counsel determined to never allow again.

Leo Strauss
1899 – 1973

Leo Strauss was born to an Orthodox Jewish couple, Hugo and Jennie Strauss on September 20th, 1899 in Kirchhain, Hesse, Germany. His Jewish upbringing entailed the strict observance of Jewish traditions without much knowledge of the Jewish faith. He was educated at the Gymnasium Philippinum in Marburg Easter where he was exposed to German Humanism. He also studied Schopenhauer, Nietzsche and Plato. At the age of 17 he converted to political Zionism absent of any religious commitment.[55]

In 1917 he was conscripted into the German army and served as an interpreter in the German occupation of Belgium until 1918. In 1919 he enrolled in the University of Marburg and later also at the Universities of Frankfurt am Main, Berlin and Hamburg where he studied philosophy, mathematics and natural sciences. He eventually earned a PhD. In 1931 he applied for a fellowship with the Rockefeller Foundation of the Social Sciences in Germany. By the end of 1932 he was in Paris France studying medieval Jewish and Islamic philosophy.[56]

For financial reasons he finally emigrated to the United States and in 1937 he was appointed research fellow at the Department of History at Columbia University in New York. He had left his wife and stepson behind in the United Kingdom. They joined him in the States in 1939. He went to the New York School of Social Research in 1938 to 1948. WWII began in September of 1939 and all of his family still living in Germany were deported to the concentration camps where they died. Strauss became a U.S. citizen in 1944. The war ended in 1945. In 1948 he was appointed a full professorship at the Department of Political Science at the University of Chicago. He was Professor of Political Philosophy from 1948 – 1968. From 1968 to 1969 he was professor of Political Science at Claremont Men's college in California. From 1969 to 1973 he was a Scott Buchanan Distinguished Scholar in Residence at St. John's College in Annapolis, MD. On October 18th 1973 Leo Strauss died of Pneumonia.[57]

---

54 Wikipedia, Aleister Crowley (http://www.wikipedia.en).
55 David McBryde, Leo Strauss (http://cato1.tripod.com).
56 Ibid.
57 Ibid.

Leo Strauss was a prolific writer and his students who were deeply influenced by his philosophy became key figures in American politics in this century. He was an atheist and a nihilist. That is, he believed that there was no God and there is no basis for any morality. There was in his view only one "natural right" that is the right of the superior elite to rule the inferior masses. He believed that societies should be hierarchal- divided between the ruling elite and the general public.

Perpetual deception was the core concept of the Straussian philosophy. This was necessary because the masses would not be able to cope with the truth that there is no God and no right or wrong. This would result in a state of anarchy. He also believed that people would be offended by the truth that there is no right other than the right of the superior to rule the inferior and that this knowledge would cause them to retaliate against the elite. Thus perpetual deception was necessary to protect the elite.[58]

In Straussian philosophy men are divided into three classes; The wise, or the ruling elite who are capable of coping with the harsh reality that there is no God and no right or wrong. "They are devoted above all else to their own pursuit of the 'higher' pleasures, which amount to consorting with their 'puppies' or young initiates"; the gentlemen are lovers of honor and glory. They believe in God, honor and moral values and are dedicated and motivated to acts of courage and self sacrifice at a moment's notice; the vulgar are selfish, slothful, indolent lovers of wealth and pleasure who can be manipulated to overcome their "brutish existence" by fear of impending death or catastrophe.[59]

Strauss believed that the rule of the wise was necessary but obtainable only by covert means which is facilitated by the "overwhelming stupidity of the gentlemen. The more gullible and unperceptive they are, the easier it is for the wise to control and manipulate them."[60] Thus Strauss believed in using the religious and their morality to control the masses. The ruling elite did not need to be bound by religious constraints. Thus his students, such as Paul Wolfowitz or George Bush may support religion and may even go to church but are not necessarily believers. Strauss believed, finally, that a perpetual state of war was necessary to maintain society. He believed the reason for this is that men tend to degenerate into a trivial sort of life dedicated to endless entertainment unless they were engaged in conflict. There has to be a threat to motivate men and woman to fight to the death. If there is no conflict then one had to be created.[61]

---

58 Danny Postel, Noble Lies and Perpetual War: Leo Strauss, the Neo-cons, and Iraq (Information Clearing House, 2003 - http://www.inforamtionclearinghouse.info).
59 Ibid.
60 Ibid.
61 Jim Lobe, Leo Strauss' Philosophy of Decpetion (Alertnet, May 19, 2003 - http://www.alertnet.org).

5. Freemasonry

On July 16th, 1782, an alliance between the Illuminati and Freemasonry was created in Wilhelmsbad (Germany) at a gathering of all Freemason Lodges. Adam Weishaupt was grateful for the support of the Masonic Protestant princes and rulers of Germany and Europe, but his goal of creating a one world dictatorship involved destroying the Monarchy so he limited the Princes and rulers of Germany to the lower degrees of the Illuminati and barred them from knowing the true purposes of the Order. The Illuminati spread over all of Europe and the United States. Before the states were united and the Constitution written there were 13 lodges established on American soil.[62]

Illluminized Freemasonry is characterized by secrecy. Their membership lists are not published nor are their objectives. Even within Freemasonry, which is structured by degrees like a pyramid, those at the outer ring of Freemasonry are denied certain information. Information is released to a member as he progresses through the different stages. Thus there is secrecy within the order itself.

On the surface, the Freemason lodge appears to be a fraternal organization and many Christians join. Though some of the language used by Freemasons sounds to a believer consistent with his Christian beliefs, one of the goals of Freemasonry is to destroy Christianity. Thus, a Christian is gradually and deliberately conditioned as he progresses through the degrees of Freemasonry to abandon his faith. A Christian's faith is gradually realigned so that he becomes a deist who believes in no supernatural intervention by God in human affairs. From that point he becomes an atheist, then a Luciferian. Journalist, William T. Still, indicates that Luciferians are distinguished from Satanists in that Satanists know they are doing evil, where Luciferians think they are doing good.[63] During their initiation the initiates make a symbolic journey from darkness to light during which they are hypnotized and demonized. As a result of this initiation they feel like a completely different person. They are rather glued to the order after this initiation and there is no way back once they have taken this road. They begin to refer to the demon that guides them as "the other person inside of me" which in the Bible would refer to Jesus Christ. The language is a deliberate attempt to mask the truth behind their initiation. However, the truth is exposed if the initiate attempts to resist the evil force inside of him. If he resists he is humiliated, agonized, tormented and tortured.[64]

What attracts people to Freemasonry may be the sense of belonging, but it also is certain that those involved in Freemasonry will be employed in some

---

[62] Robin de Ruiter, Worldwide Evil and Misery: The Legacy of 13 Satanic Bloodlines, (The Netherland: Mayra Publications, 2008) 32.

[63] Jim Marrs, Rule By Secrecy (New York, NY: Perennial Harper Collins, 2000) 161 - 162

[64] Robin de Ruiter, Worldwide Evil and Misery: The Legacy of 13 Satanic Bloodlines, (The Netherland: Mayra Publications, 2008) 45 – 46.

prominent position. Freemasons are very involved in politics and they have heavily populated political positions in the United States Government. George Washington was a Freemason. Edward Mandell House, Woodrow Wilson's advisor, was a Freemason. Henry Kissinger is a Freemason Allen Dulles, infamous Director of the CIA and his brother, Secretary of State John Foster Dulles who introduced the Scottish Rite of Free and Accepted Masons to the United States were also Freemasons. George W. Bush and at least nineteen former American presidents including Gerald Ford, Ronald Regan, George Bush Sr. and Bill (and Hillary) Clinton are also Masons.[65]

The most frightening aspect of Freemasonry is their commitment to one another regardless of the circumstances. They are thus obliged to protect and defend a fellow Freemason even if that one has committed murder. Thus a Freemason is under oath never to reveal the secrets that have been revealed to him and also to protect a fellow Freemason under any and all circumstances. Thus we have people in positions of power and authority who adopted Weishaupt's "end justifies the means" philosophy. He stated, "Behold our secret. Remember that the end justifies the means and that the wise ought to take all the means to do good which the wicked take to do evil." "So, for the enlightened or illuminated, any means to gain their ends is acceptable—whether this means lies, deceit, theft, murder, or war."[66]

When one begins to examine the corruption of the government of the United States of America, the U.S. intelligence community, Criminal Justice and Law Enforcement, we can now understand where it comes from. The attraction of Freemasonry is that those who participate are almost always guaranteed a position somewhere is society. They are heavily involved in politics and the intelligence community as well as Criminal Justice. Ruiter observes that most judges are Freemasons.[67]

6. The Council of Foreign Relations, the Bilderbergers and the Trilateral Commission

AKA the Illuminati

The Illuminati didn't go away after it was banned from Bavaria. It resurfaced again and again. You will not drive down any street in America and see a sign that says, "The Illuminati Club." You will see symbols of Freemasonry on buildings and on the car in front of you. The Church of Scientology doesn't hide itself, but it is

---

65 Ibid, 47.
66 Jim Marrs, Rule By Secrecy (New York, NY: Perennial Harper Collins, 2000) 237.
67 Robin de Ruiter, Worldwide Evil and Misery: The Legacy of 13 Satanic Bloodlines, (The Netherland: Mayra Publications, 2008) 40.

also Illuminati and its founder was also a Freemason. The Illuminati hides itself behind a veneer of respectability.

The Bilderbergers are a group that has no official name and no building or "mailing address". They were given a name by those who study their history. The Council of Foreign Relations publishes its news letter, "New World Vistas" and is available online to those who would care enough to read about what they are doing. The Trilateral Commission likewise has meetings where the press attends, but you never read about them in the paper or hear about them on the news. Had I not been researching I would never have known that there was such a thing as the Bilderbergers, the CFR or Trilateral Commission. But a careful study of each of these organizations reveals that their goals are the same as the original Illuminati;

- Abolition of monarchies and all ordered governments
- Abolition of private property and inheritances
- Abolition of patriotism and nationalism
- Abolition of family life and the institution of marriage, and the establishment of communal education for children.
- Abolition of all religion

The Council of Foreign Relations

Cecil Rhodes, a late 1800s gold and diamond magnate and founder of the nation of Rhodesia, was committed to a conspiracy to develop a one world government based on British rule. Between the ages of 24 and 46 he wrote a series of wills in which he designated his money to be used for the cause of the One World Government (the ultimate goal of the Illuminati). In his first will he states his purpose, "The extension of British rule throughout the world. . . . the foundation of so great a power as to hereafter render wars impossible and promote the interests of humanity." [68] He proposed a secret society based upon the Society of Jesus (the Jesuits) and the Masons. The secret society was formed with an inner circle and outer circles. In his third will he left all his money to Lord Rothschild who was his co-conspirator. In his final will his money was left to Rothschild's son in law Lord Rosebury. In this will he established the Rhodes scholarship. Rhodes' wills "centered on his desire to federate the English speaking peoples and to bring *the habitable portion of the world under their control.* For this purpose Rhodes left part of his great fortune to found the Rhodes Scholarships at Oxford in order to spread the English ruling class tradition (emphasis added)." [69]

Rhodes established the first Round Table in South Africa funded by Rothschild money dispossessing the South African Boers of the gold and diamonds in their

---

68 Gary Allen, None Dare Care it Conspiracy (Rossmoor, California: Concord Press, 1971) 80.
69 Pat Robertson, The New World Order (Dallas, Texas: Word Publishing, 1991)111.

soil. The Round Table was specifically established to maintain control over the country's wealth.[70]

The Round Table groups had branches in seven nations by 1915. After the death of Cecil Rhodes, Lord Alfred Milner, Lord Lionel Walter Rothschild, and their associates with the international bankers gained control of the Round Table groups which began expanding beyond the British Empire.[71] After WWI the Paris Peace Conference was held on May 30th 1919 at the Majestic Hotel in Paris France where it was proposed that a group be established to advise their prospective governments on international affairs. The group was to be called the Institute of International affairs. In 1921, it was decided that one group representing all nations was suspect, so a proposal resulted in the development of the English group called the Royal Institute of International Affairs (RIIA), the American sister organization the Council of Foreign Relations (CFR) and the Institute of Pacific Relations (IPR) to deal exclusively with far eastern affairs.[72] The Institutes of International Affairs became the umbrella organizations for the Round Tables.[73] The CFR was established in New York and became a front for J.P. Morgan and Co. and was dominated by Morgan associates.[74] At the Paris Peace conference, Woodrow Wilson was also tasked with forming the League of Nations. The Untied States was supposed to become absorbed into the World Government at that time; however the Senate would not approve of that decision.[75]

Lord Balfour was an inner circle member of the Round Table; Alfred Milner was the Round Table's official leader after the death of its founder, Cecil Rhodes; and the Round Table was funded by Lord Lionel Walter Rothschild. These were the very three people involved in the Balfour Declaration which paved the way to the establishment of the Nation of Israel.[76]

The Christian Science Monitor reports on the power of the CFR during six presidential administrations. "Because of the Council's single-minded, dedication to studying and deliberating American foreign policy there is a constant flow of its members from private to public service. *Almost half of the Council members have*

---

70   Jim Marrs, Rule By Secrecy (New York, NY: Perennial Harper Collins, 2000) 87.
71   Ibid, 88.
72   Jim Marrs, Rule By Secrecy (New York, NY: Perennial Harper Collins, 2000).
73   Fritz Springmeyer, The Rothschild Bloodline (July 3, 2009 – http://www.theforbiddenknowledge.com).
74   Gary Allen, None Dare Care it Conspiracy (Rossmoor, California: Concord Press, 1971) 81.
75   Warren B. Appleton, Politically Correct Treason (April 24, 2003. Illuminati Conspiracy Archives - http://www.conspiracyarchive.com).
76   David Icke, Tales from the Time Loop, (Ryde, Iles of Wright, UK: David Icke Books, 2003) 100.

been invited to assume official government positions or to act as consultants at one time or *another*" [emphasis mine].[77]

THE BILDERBERGERS

The Bilderberger, founded by Prince Bernhard of the Netherlands in May of 1954, was so named because of the site of the original meeting at the Hotel de Bilderberg in Oosterbeek, Holland. Bernhard was a former member of the NAZI *Schutzstaffel* (SS) and an employee of Germany's I.G. Farben in Paris. In 1937 he married Princess Juliana of the Netherlands and became a major shareholder and officer in Dutch Shell Oil along with Britain's Lord Victor Rothschild. After the Germans invaded Holland, the royal couple moved to London. It was here, after the war, that Rothschild and Retinger encouraged Prince Bernhard to create the Bilderberger group.[78] He was forced to resign as chairman in 1976 when it was revealed that he had accepted payoffs from Lockheed to promote the sale of its aircraft in Holland.

The secretive group meets once, sometimes twice a year, and the location of the meetings vary. Though the meetings are well attended by the press, no news of the meetings is ever published. One attends the meetings by invitation only. Those who attend include leading politicians and financial figures in the United States and Europe, such as the Rothschilds and the Rockefellers. In fact members of the Bilderbergs are often also members of the Council of foreign Relations and the Trilateral Commission. For example, Peter Rupert Lord Carrington, Chairman of the Bilderbergers, has been the director of Rothschild's Rio Tinto Zinc Corp, director of Barclay's Bank and is also a member of the Trilateral Commission.[79]

Those who are involved with the Bilderbergers are elected to political office. When the Bilderbergers decide they want someone in the office of the President of the United States, he will get elected to that office. In 1991 Bill Clinton, then governor of Arkansas was asked to be an honored guest at the Bilderberger meeting. The following year he ran for and was elected President of the United States. Others who have been elected to political office coinciding with Bilderberg attendance include Tony Blair who attended in 1993 and became Party leader in 1994 and Prime Minister in 1997; George Robertson who attended in 1998 and became NATO Secretary-General in 1999; and Romano Prodi who attended in 1999 and became President of Europe in September the same year. He became prime minister of Italy in 2006.[80]

---

77 Gary Allen, None Dare Care it Conspiracy (Rossmoor, California: Concord Press, 1971) 84.
78 Jim Marrs, Rule By Secrecy (New York, NY: Perennial Harper Collins, 2000) 41.
79 Fritz Springmeyer, The Rothschild Bloodline (July 3, 2009 – http://www.theforbiddenknowledge.com).
80 Daniel Estulin, The True Story of the Bilderberger Group (Walterville, OR: Trine Day LLC, 2007) 34.

Journalist Daniel Estulin, a former resident of Canada and the son of a former Soviet KGB officer, has followed the activities of the Bilderbergers for several years. Those he reported attending the Bilderberger meetings include: Henry Kissinger; David Rockefeller, CFR President; Richard Haas, President of the World Bank; James D. Wolfenson, one time President of the World Bank;; Rockwell A. Schnabel, U.S. Ambassador to the European Union; Heather Monroe-Blum, Principle and Vice Chancellor of Monroe University; Heir to the Belgium Throne, Prince Phillip; daughter of founder Prince Bernhard Queen Beatrix of the Netherlands; Head of the Policy Board for Donald Rumsfeld, Richard Perle; Martin Taylor, Honorary Chairman of the Bilderbergers and International Advisor of Goldman Saches; Deputy Secretary of Defense, Paul Wolfowitz; Former prime minister of Portugal, Pinto Balsemao; NATO secretary, General Jaap C. Hoop Scheffer; Peter Southerland; Doug Feith, Legal counsel to the White House; Donald Graham of the Washington Post; Indra Nooyi of PepsiCo; Jergen E. Schrempp, Chairman of the board of Management, DaimlerChrysler AG just to mention a few.[81]

Democracy is an obstacle to the elites of the Bilderberger which they are always challenged to overcome. "Democratic interference in foreign policy is avoided, in so far as possible,... When necessary, a consensus is engineered on issues which must get congressional/parliamentary approval, but wherever possible executive agreements between governments are used to avoid the democratic process altogether.[82] One of the main objectives of the Bilderbergers is to submit the sovereignty of the free nations of Europe to a Bilderberger-controlled British-American One World Government.[83] Daniel Estulin lists their agenda in detail in his book *The True Story of the Bilderberger Group.* [84]

- **One International Identity** - By empowering international bodies to completely destroy all national identity *through subversion from within*, [emphasis mine] they intend to establish one set of universal values. No others will be allowed to flourish in the future.
- **Centralized Control of the People** - By means of mind control, they plan to direct all humanity to obey their wishes.
- **A zero growth Society** - This is necessary in order to destroy general prosperity. Prosperity and progress go hand in hand and both have to be stopped in order to induce repression which is necessary in *order to divide society into owners and slaves.*

---

81 Ibid.
82 Peter Thompson, Bildergerg and the West (Book Sectionm, Trilateralism: Elite Planning for World Management, Editor Holly Sklar, Boston: South End Press, 1980) 158.
83 Daniel Estulin, The True Story of the Bilderberger Group (Walterville, OR: Trine Day LLC, 2007) 21.
84 Ibid, 41 – 43.

- **A State of Perpetual Imbalance** - They plan to create crisis to keep people in a continual state of psychological stress and keep them in perpetual imbalance. Thus "too tired and strung out to decide their own destinies, populations will be confused and demoralized to the extent that, 'faced with too many choices, apathy on a massive scale will result'."
- **Centralized Control of All Education** - This will allow them to rewrite history so that students will not be able to understand their true past.
- **Centralized Control of all Foreign and Domestic Policies** – What goes on in the U.S. affects the whole world. The Bilderbergers have control over the office of the President of the United States.
- **Empowerment of the United Nations** – Which will become the One World Government
- **Western Trading Block,** An American Union will be formed form the United States, Canada and South America.
- **Expansion of NATO** – NATO will become the world Army
- **One Socialist Welfare State** – *Obedient slaves will be rewarded and nonconformists will be targeted for extermination[emphasis mine].*

Estulin has an inside source at the Bilderberg meetings who does not agree with their agenda and who was influential in assisting him in exposing the plans of the 1996 Bilderberger conference to absolve the borders of Canada and the United States in 2000 and combine the two nations, minus French Speaking Québec, into one nation. Though the American press has been literally sold out to the Eastern Establishment, and they never tell the American Public about their agenda to absolve the borders of the United States and absorb this nation into a one world government, Mr. Estulin managed to inform the press in Canada about Bilderberger agenda that year. The Canadian press broadcasted the news to the Canadian public who rightfully acted with outrage and the Bilderbergers had to cease and desist.[85] This was not publicized in the United States. The Bilderbergers still have plans to combine not only the United States and Canada but also Mexico into one huge conglomerate. That of course would abolish the United States Constitution and the Bill of Rights.

What David Rockefeller hopes for is another Hegelian type crisis in order to bring about their desired ends. At the Annual Bilderberger Conference after the 9/11 attacks, David Rockefeller, announced, "We are on the verge of a global transformation. All we need is the right major crisis and the nations will accept the New World Order."[86]

---

85 Ibid, 5
86 Robin de Ruiter, Worldwide Evil and Misery: The Legacy of 13 Satanic Bloodlines, (The Netherland: Mayra Publications, 2008) 18.

The global elite have divided the world into ten different regions:[87]

- Region 1: The United States, Canada and Mexico
- Region 2: Western Europe
- Region 3: Japan
- Region 4: Australia and New Zealand
- Region 5: Eastern Europe
- Region 6: Latin America
- Region 7: North Africa and the Middle East
- Region 8: Central and Southern Africa
- Region 9: South and South-East Asia
- Region 10: Central Asia

The Trilateral Commission

The CFR became divided over the issue of the Viet Nam war and the inner core lost control of the group. Thus David Rockefeller envisioned another group that would supersede the CFR. Nixon had taken advantage of the division and managed to exert some control over wages and prices and imposed tariffs to check inflation. This enraged David Rockefeller and he determined to reign in the Nixon administration. Zbigniew Brzezinski offered a solution.

Zbigniew Brzezinski at the Brookings Institute had been researching the need for a closer cooperation between Europe, North America and Asia. He wrote in *Foreign Affairs*, a CFR publication, "A new and broader approach is needed— creation of a community of the developed nations which can ... address ... larger concerns confronting mankind.... A council representing the United States, Europe, and Japan, .., would be a good start". Later he published his book *Between Two Ages*, "National sovereignty is no longer a viable concept ... movement toward a larger community by the developing nations ... through a variety of indirect ties and already developing limitations on national sovereignty." He even envisioned a global taxation system.[88] He presented his vision for the Trilateral Commission at the Bilderberger meeting in 1972 in Knokke-Hiest, Belgium.

The Trilateral Commission began organizing on July 23-24, 1972, at the 3,500-acre Rockefeller estate at Pocantico Hills, New York. Participants selected by Rockefeller and Brzezinski included Brookings Institute Director of Foreign Policy Studies Henry Owen, McGeorge Bundy, Robert Bowie, C. Fred Bergsten, Bayless Manning, Karl Carstens, Guido Colonna de Paliano, Francois Duchene, Rene Foch, Max Kohnstamm, Kiichi Miyazawa, Saburo Ikita, and Tadashi Yamamoto.[89] In 1973, after a meeting with 300 influential friends of the Rockefeller brothers from Europe, North America and Japan, David Rockefeller

---
87 Ibid, 302
88 Jim Marrs, Rule By Secrecy (New York, NY: Perennial Harper Collins, 2000) 22- 23
89 Ibid, 23.

founded the Trilateral Commission. Founding members included Zibigniew Brzezinski, Jimmy Carter, George W. Bush, and Paul Volker who was later to be the Chairman of the Federal Reserve Board and Alan Greenspan, then a Wall Street banker. The Trilaterals were statesmen, businessmen, and intellectuals from Western Europe and Japan. The late senator Barry Goldwater in his 1979 book, *With No Apologies*, warned. "David Rockefeller's newest international cabal [the Trilateral Commission] ... is intended to be the vehicle for multinational consolidation of the commercial and banking interests by seizing control of the political government of the United States."[90]

The Trilateral Commission in headquartered in New York, Paris and Tokyo and meets every 9 months. It is funded by the Rockefeller Brothers Fund, The Ford Foundation, The Lilly Endowment, The German Marshall Fund, and corporations such as Time, Exxon, Bechtel, General Motors, Wells Fargo and Texas Instruments. Their total budget from 1976 – 1979 was $1,180,000.[91] This group exerts a tremendous influence on policy within the United States Government though the participants are not elected officials or are but are not acting in the capacity of elected officials at the meetings. For example, one of the authors of the Trilateral publication, *Crisis in Democracy*, published in 1975, Samuel P. Huntington argued that democratic institutions are incapable of responding to crises such as the Three Mile Island nuclear accident or the Cuban refugee boatlift operation and that leaders with specific expertise were needed to override the claims of democracy. Thus three years later Huntington was named the coordinator of security planning for the National Security Council under the Carter Administration. In this capacity he created the Federal Emergency Management Agency which is a civilian organization with the power to take absolute control of government functions in the event of an emergency.[92]

Like the Bilderbergers and the CFR, the membership list of the Trilaterals reads like the Who's Who of American government and Corporate VIPs. Current Federal Reserve Chairman Alan Greenspan is a member of the Trilateral Commission, the CFR and the Bilderbergers. Ronald Regan who initially expressed distrust for the commission ended up with several of their members on his cabinet along with several members of both the Bilderberger and CFR. However, concern over the influence that the Trilaterals wield over the supposedly democratic government resulted in investigations. "In 1980, the American Legion National Convention passed Resolution 773, which called for a congressional investigation of the Trilateral Commission and its predecessor, the Council on Foreign Relations. The following year a similar resolution was approved by the Veterans of Foreign Wars (VFW)."[93]

---

90 Barry M. Goldwater, With No Apologies (New York: William Morrow and Company Inc., 1979) 280.
91 Jim Marrs, Rule By Secrecy (New York, NY: Perennial Harper Collins, 2000) 24.
92 Ibid, 25.
93 Ibid, 28.

7. Dividing and Conquering America

The Illuminati were not a flash in the pan revolutionary group. Having been responsible for three bloody French Revolutions, having subdued the British Empire, the Illuminated Rothschilds were attempting to subdue America by gaining control of America's money. There were several attempts at establishing a central bank which finally ended in the establishment of the Federal Reserve System in 1913.

The first central bank in America was established in 1781 by Congressman Robert Morris called the Bank of North America. It was intended to be a model copy of the Bank of England which was under the control of Nathan Rothschild. It only lasted three years and was discontinued because of prevailing fraud and inflation caused by the creation of money with no base.[94]

The second central bank in America was created in 1791 by Secretary of Treasury Alexander Hamilton, former aide to Morris. This was the First Bank of the United States. Thomas Jefferson strongly opposed the establishment of the central bank. The bank had power to create money which was a power awarded solely to congress under the Constitution. This creating money out of nothing created inflation. This bank was created again on the model of the Bank of England and established a partnership between government and banking interests. "Twenty percent of the bank's capital was obtained through the federal government with the remaining 80 percent pledged by private investors, including foreigners such as the Rothschilds. The law records show that they [the Rothschilds] were the power in the old Bank of the United States," wrote author Gustavus Myers. It is clear that conspiring European bankers and their New World associates were trying to gain control over America's money supply.[95] The bank's charter came up for renewal in 1811 and was denied. However, on Nathan Rothschild's order, the British declared war on the United States funded by Rothschild money. The intent of the war of 1812 was to create a debt that would cause the United States to surrender to the British and renew the charter of the Bank of the United States. The British were unsuccessful in their assault on the United States, because they were also at war with Napoleon III. However, the debt incurred by the War of 1812 persuaded Congress to issue a twenty-year charter to the Bank of the United States in 1816.[96]

In 1832 president Andrew Jackson vetoed the congressional bill to extend the charter of the bank. This precipitated what became known as the Bank War. Jim Marrs writes "Jackson, the first president from west of the Appalachian Mountains and the hero of the Battle of New Orleans, denounced the central bank as unconstitutional as well as 'a curse to a republic; inasmuch as it is calculated to

---

94 Jim Marrs, Rule By Secrecy (New York, NY: Perennial Harper Collins, 2000) 67.
95 Ibid, 67 – 68.
96 Andrew Carrington Hitchcock, The Synagogue of Satan (Austin, Texas: RiverCrest Publishing, 2007) 48.

raise around the administration a moneyed aristocracy is dangerous to the liberties of the country.'"[97] President Jackson was taking steps to abolish the central bank, and on January 30th, 1835 there was an assassination attempt on his life. The assassin's pistols misfired. He was tried in court but was let of on the insanity plea. He later confessed that powerful people in Europe hired him and promised to protect him if he were caught. President Andrew Jackson was successful in abolishing the central bank in 1832. In 1838 he becomes the only president to have paid off the national debt. When he died he had the following inscription inscribed on his tombstone;

> "I killed the Bank."[98]

In 1837 a German born representative of the Rothschild banking system, August Schoenberg was dispatched to Cuba by Amschel Rothschild. Changing his name to August Belmont he went to New York Instead. The panic of 1837 became an opportunity for August Belmont and he bought government bonds during that time. He became so successful that he eventually became the financial Advisor to the President of the United States. His polices helped ignite tensions between the north and the south which eventually led to the civil war. Judah P. Benjamin and J.P. Morgan also acted as Rothschild proxies in the United States for creating conditions that resulted in the civil war. When the war broke out George Peabody and Julius Morgan raised money for the North. But Julius Morgan was also shipping supplies to the south to the confederate army. Both Peabody and Morgan were again Rothschild proxies in the United States.[99] The Civil War was instigated by the finance moguls of Europe. Otto Von Bismarck stated the following when he was Chancellor of Germany (1871- 1890);

> The division of the United States into federations of equal force was decided long before the Civil War by the high financial powers of Europe. These bankers were afraid that the United States if they remained as one block and as one nation would attain economic and financial independence which would upset their financial domination over the world.

Many people have thought that the American civil war was fought over slavery. Abe Lincoln clearly had no problems with people owning slaves. He stated "I have no purpose directly or indirectly to interfere with the institution of slavery in the states where it now exists. I believe I have no lawful right to do so, and I have no

---

97   Jim Marrs, Rule By Secrecy (New York, NY: Perennial Harper Collins, 2000) 68.
98   Andrew Carrington Hitchcock, The Synagogue of Satan (Austin, Texas: RiverCrest Publishing, 2007) 56.
99   Fritz Springmeyer, The Rothschild Bloodline (July 3, 2009 – http://www.theforbiddenknowledge.com).

inclination to do so.... My paramount objective is to save the Union and it is not either to save or destroy slavery. If I could save the Union without freeing any slave, I would do it". Lincoln knew that the conflict was an economic one, not an ethical one over the ownership of slaves.

Northern manufacturers had imposed stiff import tariffs on European products preventing the south from buying cheaper products. The North was also flooded with immigrants who were willing to work for a pittance while the southern cotton farmers were dependent upon human labor. The south was in fact willing to compromise on the issue of slavery but was not willing to give them up.[100] It was actually halfway through the civil war that Lincoln declared the emancipation proclamation. The freeing of slaves strengthened Lincoln's hand at home.

While the Civil War was being fought France had moved troops to the border of Mexico and Britain had moved troops to the Canadian border in the North. Should the South have won the civil war and the states had been divided the French and British would have moved in to take control of the divided nation. The Tsar of Russian, Alexander II, who was also having a problem with Rothschild, got wind of what the Illuminati were planning and moved his ships to both the east and west coasts of the United States in an effort to aid Lincoln in his quest to save the Union. Lincoln also would not borrow money from Rothschild banks to fund the war. The Constitution gave him the power to create money. Thus he created the "greenback" to fund the war effort to save the Union. He was resisting Rothschild efforts the put the nation in debt because he knew Rothschild would use debt to take control of the government.

Thus Rothschild's scheme was defeated. Hence Abraham Lincoln was assassinated, and on March 13th 1881 Tsar Alexander II was assassinated in St. Petersburg Sq in Russia following several attempts on his life that began in 1866 less than a year after Lincoln was assassinated.[101] President James A. Garfield was also assassinated in 1881 just two weeks after he publicly spoke out against the elite establishment attempting to control American through the corrupted banking system.[102]

Russia became a threat to the Rothschild's because of their favor towards America. Thus the Bolshevik Revolution was funded by Rothschild agents. Communism was a Rothschild creation. Socialism in Germany was also a Rothschild creation. History clearly displays a 'divide and conquer" mentality of the House of Rothschild. He created both communism and socialism and set Germany and Russian against each other. This fear of communism was later used in the United States by the elite to justify the multiple wars into which the American people were thrust.

---

100 Jim Marrs, Rule By Secrecy (New York, NY: Perennial Harper Collins, 2000) 208.
101 Andrew Carrington Hitchcock, The Synagogue of Satan (Austin, Texas: RiverCrest Publishing, 2007) 80.
102 Ibid, 79.

In 1907 J.P. Morgan, who had been in Europe traveling back and forth between the Rothschilds in France and England, returned to the United States and started the rumor that the Knickerbocker Bank of New York was insolvent. That started a run on the bank as people began a mass withdrawal of their deposits. This had a domino effect as the panic spread and people who had deposits in other banks also began massive withdrawals. Thus the American people were conditioned to accept the idea of a central bank to protect them from the abuses of Wall Street Banks. The panic also killed off rival banks and consolidated Morgan's preeminence in banking.[103] The Federal Reserve was established in 1913 on the recommendation of Colonel M. House advisor the President Woodrow Wilson. The Federal Reserve System is a privately owned network of banks under the control of the House of Rothschild.

President John F. Kennedy was the next President to challenge the Rothschild banking system. Historically we can see clearly that anyone who dared to resist the Rothschild owned central banks of America were prime targets. Abraham Lincoln refused to borrow money from the Rothschild bank for his war and he dared to use his constitutional power to create money. He was assassinated. Researchers, I believe, have correctly concluded that Lee Harvey Oswald, the lone gunman who allegedly assassinated President Kennedy, if he had any part in the assassination at all, most certainly did not act alone. Though the fingers are pointed at several possible suspects, it becomes clear by the actual facts surrounding the assassination who had the capacity and the motive to kill the president.

Four months before John F. Kennedy was assassinated he had signed executive order #11110 which restored the power of the U.S. Government to issue currency and took that power from the Federal Reserve. Kennedy placed the US Treasury Note under silver standard. Thus one U.S. note was issued for every ounce of silver in the U.S. Treasury. He then issued 4.3 billion dollars of U.S. notes. He was threatening to put the Federal Reserve out of business because the U.S. Treasury Note was based on silver. The Federal Reserve Note was based on nothing. Kennedy was also withdrawing troops from Viet Nam, systematically going after the MAFIA, cracking down on multinational businesses, making moves to halt segregation in the Deep South and attempting to reconcile American and Soviet relations. He was also blamed for the failed assassination attempt on the life of Fidel Castro.[104] John F. Kennedy had a lot of enemies, but he was the friend of the American citizen. He was not and would not be a puppet in the hands of the establishment that wanted to dictate and control the policy of the United States of America.

John Stockwell, a former CIA insider, notes that the assassination of John F. Kennedy could not possibly have been the work of one lone gunman. The FBI

---

103 Fritz Springmeyer, The Rothschild Bloodline (July 3, 2009 – http://www.theforbiddenknowledge.com).

104 John Stockwell, The Praetorian Guard: The U.S. Role in the New World Order (1991, Boston, MA: South End Press) 121.

has a systematic system of protecting the life of the president. They are very well practiced at it. "Numerous, almost routine, techniques are involved, like bringing extra security forces to blanket problem areas, moving in caravans of cars at a brisk 45 miles an hour, and using, whenever possible, unannounced routes that do not include sharp, slow turns". Yet on November 22, 1963, those normal protections were lifted. Texas guardsmen were not called out and Dallas Policemen were temporarily released from duty the day the President was passing through.[105]

The investigation by the Warren Commission "proved" that Lee Harvey Oswald was the killer. However, who should be on that investigative team, but Allen Dulles whom Kennedy had fired as director of the CIA. The evidence was tampered with and the body of the President had been altered along with photographs of the autopsy. In addition to that, 100 eyewitnesses of the assassination were subsequently murdered or died mysterious violent deaths. To this day there has never been a criminal investigation into the conspiracy behind Kennedy's assassination.[106]

It can be clearly seen in history how the established elite, which has been headed by the House of Rothschild has been controlling the United States from behind the scenes. The established elite gain control over a nation by putting the nation in debt. The object of the Federal Reserve was to put the nation under obligation and control of the bankers. One of the ways that the bankers of the world establish debt in a nation is by inciting wars. The sinking of the Lusitania was used as an excuse to get the American public to support the US entry into WWI. The Lusitania was a passenger ship. However, it was also carrying six million rounds of ammunition and military supplies destined for Great Britain which was at war with Germany. The passenger ship was sent on purpose at low speed directly into water that was patrolled by German U-Boats. The patrol ship that was supposed to protect the ship was withdrawn.[107] The Germans sent warnings to the ship which were ignored. Thus a ship with innocent civilian passengers was blown up by the Germans with the knowledge of the American President Woodrow Wilson that the ship was carrying military cargo.

The attack on Pearl Harbor is another prime example of this. Roosevelt needed an excuse to get American into World War II. In 1941 Japan was at war with China and the Japanese were buying steel scrap and oil from America to aid their war effort. President Roosevelt refused to sell them anymore steel or oil which he knew would provoke the Japanese to strike America.[108] British Intelligence, high U.S. Officials and President Roosevelt knew the Japanese had intentions of attacking Pearl Harbor and were tracking the Japanese fleet as it

---

105 Ibid, 122, 123.
106 Ibid, 124
107 Robin de Ruiter, Worldwide Evil and Misery: The Legacy of 13 Satanic Bloodlines, (The Netherland: Mayra Publications, 2008) 169.
108 Andrew Carrington Hitchcock, The Synagogue of Satan (Austin, Texas: RiverCrest Publishing, 2007) 142.

crossed the ocean. They did nothing to warn the military administration at Pearl Harbor of the impending attack. The Admirals of the fleet kept their silence until they retired and then they wrote a letter bitterly faulting Roosevelt for failing to inform them of the attack and leaving the U.S. fleet where it could be easily destroyed.[109]

Finally, the War in Viet Nam was also contrived. The CIA On July 30, 1964 attacked the North Vietnamese radar station on Hon Me Island and bombarded Hon Ngu in the Gulf of Tonkin. The North Vietnamese pursued their attackers on the US Maddox and the Maddox fired first and the Viet Namese responded by firing torpedoes. Of course the U.S. CIA coddled news media blamed the Viet Namese for the scuffle which was used by Lyndon Johnson to launch the Viet Nam war which had been planned in the United States for two years.[110]

When nations go to war they have to borrow money to pay for it. Thus the bankers loan money to all participants in the war at interest rates. Thus when the interest rate escalates the debt, the bankers can refuse to loan a country any more money unless they comply with certain conditions. Between 1928 and 1932 as a result of several wars, several countries declared bankruptcy including the United States. The bankers refused them any loans to get them out of the global depression that occurred at that time unless they declared bankruptcy. This meant that the bankers have owned those nations ever since.[111] The record of this bankruptcy is in the United States Congressional Record of March 17th 1933 (Vol. 33, page H-1303) which can be obtained at several web sites including http://www.gemworld.com/USA-Traficant.html. It states as follows;

> Members of Congress are official trustees presiding over the greatest reorganization of any Bankrupt entity in world history, the US Government. We are setting forth hopefully, a blueprint for our future. There are some who say it is a coroner's report that will lead to our demise. It is an established fact that the United States Federal Government has been dissolved by the Emergency Banking Act, March 9, 1933, 48 Stat. 1, Public Law 89-719; declared by President Roosevelt, being bankrupt and insolvent. H.J.R. 192, 73rd Congress m session June 5, 1933 Joint Resolution To Suspend The Gold Standard and Abrogate The Gold Clause dissolved the Sovereign Authority of the United States and the official capacities of all United States Governmental Offices, Officers, and Departments and is further evidence that the United States Federal Government exists today in name only.

---

109 John Stockwell, The Praetorian Guard: The U.S. Role in the New World Order (1991, Boston, MA: South End Press) 87.
110 Ibid, 81.
111 David Icke, Tales from the Time Loop, (Ryde, Iles of Wright, UK: David Icke Books, 2003) 61.

The receivers of the United States Bankruptcy are the International Bankers, via the United Nations, the World Bank and the International Monetary Fund. All United States Offices, Officials, and Departments are now operating within a de facto status in name only under Emergency War Powers. ***With the Constitutional republican form of Government now dissolved, the receivers of the Bankruptcy have adopted a new form of government for the United States. This new form of government is known as a Democracy, being an established Socialist/Communist order under a new governor for America*** [emphasis mine]. This act was instituted and established by transferring and/or placing the Office of the Secretary of Treasury to that of the Governor of the International Monetary Fund. Public Law 94-564, page 8, Section H.R. 13955 reads in part: "The U.S. Secretary of Treasury receives no compensation for representing the United States?'

It needs to be clarified that when the United States declared Bankruptcy in 1933 several congressmen spoke out. The one who was responsible for the words written above was Congressman Traficant. This is not the same Congressman Jim Traficant Jr. of Youngstown Ohio to whom many web sites attribute these words. He may be related to the original author whose words are also found at http://www.barefootsworld.net; however it was not he who authored those words which were spoken in Congress on March 17th 1933 and not March 17th 1993.

The bankruptcy occurred because the United States borrowed money from the Federal Reserve for the purpose of waging war which had to be paid back in gold. The problem was that what we owed to the Federal Reserve was more than all the gold that there was in the world and we only had four billion in gold. Therefore Congress turned over all the gold that the United States possessed in addition to this country and every citizen of the nation to the Federal Reserve in payment of the debt.[112]

There have been more definite and deliberate steps continuously since the establishment of the Federal Reserve to absolve the sovereignty of the United States and absorb it into a one world government system. Unfortunately, many of our elected officials who have sworn to protect and defend the Constitution of the Untied States have been all too willing to cooperate with the established elite. Thus 32 Senators and 92 Representatives signed the Declaration of **Interdependence** on January 30th 1976 in Washington D.C. The Declaration reads as follows: "Two centuries ago our forefathers brought forth a new nation: now we must join with others to bring forth a New World Order." This of course has been kept hidden from the American public. The NWO now has control of the government, but how will they control the people? They have a plan for this, and by the use of covert

---

112 James Montgomery, Treason in Government! Admiralty on Land (Knowledge is Freedom, BBS, August 27, 1995. http://www.barefootsworld.com).

means and modern technology they plan to control the lives of every single human being on this planet.

We have a Constitution that is supposed to protect us from abuses by government officials. However, those same government officials have to have respect for the Constitution of the United States. We can clearly see that they do not. Their illluminized minds have already determined that this government, "of the people by the people for the people" exists in name only.

8. The House of Rockefeller

The Rockefellers immigrated to America from Spain. John Davidson Rockefeller was the richest man of his time. Before he got into oil transport he made his money as a wholesaler of narcotic drugs.[113] The patriarch of the Rockefeller family, William Rockefeller started out selling "cancer cures" from a medicine wagon. The product called "Rock Oil," advertised as a diuretic medicine that guaranteed "All Cases of Cancer Cured Unless They Are Too Far Gone." Until recently this concoction was still being produced by a subsidiary of Standard Oil in New Jersey called Stanco. It was called Nujol and consisted mostly of petroleum and was peddled as a laxative.[114]

A story told by Nelson Rockefeller, John D. Rockefeller Sr.'s son, might give us some insight into the character of the Sr. Rockefeller. It is said that his father William Rockefeller, used to play a game with his son. He would have him jump off a high chair into his arms and catch him. But one day when little John jumped, his father stepped back and allowed his son to fall to the ground. William Rockefeller said to his son, "Remember, never trust anyone completely, not even me."[115]

When John D. Rockefeller wanted to expand into the oil business, he received capital from Rothschild through the National City Bank in Cleveland. With this came an agreement that Rockefeller would transport his oil using Rothschild railways, an illegal agreement for which the Rockefellers received a bonus concurrent with amount of oil they transported by train. This eliminated competition for the Rothschilds in transporting Rockefeller oil. The arrangement was facilitated by Jacob Schiff, of the company of Kuhn & Loeb that helped establish the Rockefeller foundation. When Rockefeller got into the oil business he set up the Standard Oil Trust, which now possesses ninety percent of the oil refineries in the United States.[116]

Raymond B. Fosdick, a leader in the American Eugenics Society who became the President of the Rockefeller Foundation in 1936 was the person to first

---

113 Robin de Ruiter, Worldwide Evil and Misery: The Legacy of 13 Satanic Bloodlines, (The Netherland: Mayra Publications, 2008)23.
114 Jim Marrs, The Rise of the Fourth Reich (New York, NY: Harper Collins, 2008) 187.
115 Jim Marrs, Rule By Secrecy (New York, NY: Perennial Harper Collins, 2000) 45.
116 Robin de Ruiter, Worldwide Evil and Misery: The Legacy of 13 Satanic Bloodlines, (The Netherland: Mayra Publications, 2008)22 - 23

convince John D. Rockefeller Jr. of the importance of birth control and eugenics. He was brother to the Rockefellers' pastor Harry Emerson Fosdick, for whom he built the Riverside church.[117]

John D. Rockefeller Jr. was in church every Sunday and he said in 1917, "I see the church molding the thought of the world, as it has never done before, leading in all great movements as it should. I see it literally establishing the Kingdom of God on earth."[118] It is interesting to note that the Rockefellers were Morano Jews. They attend a Baptist church. However as others have noted, the Rockefellers notion of "God" is not the same as the scriptures teach. He is Illuminati. To the Illuminati Lucifer is God.

John Rockefeller Jr. had five sons, John D. III, Nelson, David, Laurence and Winthrop. The Rockefeller family has been influential in US and global politics. They have established trusts by which they have funded and thereby manipulated American culture to satisfy the interests of the global elite.

David Rockefeller was the youngest of the five Rockefeller brothers. He earned a B.S. degree from Harvard, and then entered the London School of Economics, which is funded by the Rockefeller Foundation, the Carnegie United Kingdom Trust Fund, and the widow of J. P. Morgan partner Willard Straight. He was educated in the teaching of Ruskin and other socialists, including Harold Laski.[119]

The CFR was established in May, 1919 in an exclusive meeting at the Paris Hotel Majestic by leading representatives of the J.P. Morgan bank, Rockefeller Standard Oil group, Woodrow Wilson's advisor, Col. Edward House with Cecil Rhodes Roundtable Group. They met "to discuss establishing a private network of institutes to "advise" their respective governments on foreign affairs". The CFR was initially financed by J.P. Morgan, John D. Rockefeller, financiers Otto Kahn, Bernard Baruch, Jacob Schiff and Paul Warburg " … the most powerful men of their day in American Business."[120]

In 1941 David Rockefeller joined the Council of Foreign Relations and in 1950 he was elected vice President. He founded the Trilateral Commission in 1973. David Rockefeller was also chairman of the Board of the Chase Manhattan Bank from 1970 until recently.

It was David Rockefeller and Henry Kissinger who pressured Jimmy Carter to give political asylum in the United States to the Shah of Iran. This precipitated the hostage crisis. Iran threatened thus to take all their assets out of the Chase Manhattan Bank. Their assets were frozen and that decision that led directly to

---

117 F. William Engdahl, Seeds of Destruction (Canada: Global Research, Center for Research on Globalization, 2007) 83.
118 Jerry E. Smith , HAARP: The Ultimate Weapon of the Conspiracy (Kempton, Ill; Adventures Unlimited Press,1998) 217.
119 Jim Marrs, Rule By Secrecy (New York, NY: Perennial Harper Collins, 2000) 51.
120 F. William Engdahl, Seeds of Destruction (Canada: Global Research, Center for Research on Globalization, 2007) 103 - 104

the Iran hostage crisis. The removing of the Iranian assets from Chase would have caused the bank some considerable financial difficulty.[121] David Rockefeller's power is well noted by researchers. In 1973 he met with 27 heads of state including rulers of Russia and the United States. When in 1976 the president of Australia, Malcolm Fraser, visited the U.S. he conferred with David Rockefeller before meeting the President Gerald Ford. This is remarkable as the man was never appointed or elected to any government office.[122] He is powerful indeed. David Rockefeller, in Oct of 1964 took a vacation to the Soviet Union where he visited the Kremlin. After he departed Nikita Khrushchev was recalled from his vacation and notified that he had been fired.[123] He was absolute dictator of the Soviet Union and head of the Communist Party! Who had the power to fire him?

David Rockefeller is famous for his statement in his 2002 "Memoirs" in which he admits to being part of a global conspiracy. He states;

> For more than a century, ideological extremists at either end of the political spectrum have seized upon well-publicized incidents to attack the Rockefeller family for the inordinate influence they claim we wield over American political and economic institutions. Some even believe we are part of a secret cabal working against the best interests of the United States, characterizing my family and me as "internationalists," and of conspiring with others around the world to build a more integrated global political and economic structure—one world, if you will. If that's the charge, I stand guilty, and I am proud of it.

Laurence Rockefeller along with Lord Rothschild was behind the move to regionalize Europe and handpicked 100 of the world's elite for the purpose of doing so.[124] Laurence Rockefeller is also the single largest shareholder of Eastern Airlines. The Gambrell family was a major stockholder in Eastern Airlines and both Laurence and the elder Gambrell were on the board of directors. The Gambrels were closely connected the Carter Administration.[125]

Among others David, John D III, Laurence and Nelson Rockefeller created multinational agribusinesses. While David Rockefeller was busy with family finance, Nelson was busy with family politics. In 1940 under the Roosevelt administration he was appointed Co-coordinator of Inter-American Affairs. From

---

121 Murray N. Rothbard, Wall Street Banks, and American foreign Policy (http://www.lewrockwell.com).
122 Jim Marrs, Rule By Secrecy (New York, NY: Perennial Harper Collins, 2000) 53.
123 Gary Allen, None Dare Call it Conspiracy (Rossmoor, California: Concord Press 1971) 107.
124 Daniel Estulin, The True Story of the Bilderberger Group (Walterville, OR: Trine Day LLC, 2007) 24.
125 Laurence A. Shoup, Jimmy Carter and the Trilaterals (from Trilateralism, Elite Planning for World Management, Editor Holly Sklar, Cambridge,1980) 202.

this strategic position he worked at promoting family business interests in Latin America. John D. Rockefeller was busy with devising methods of purifying the "gene pool". Nelson went to work making food production in lesser developed countries "more efficient". It was called the "Green Revolution". He was thus funneling U.S. Government support to Rockefeller business allies in Latin America. Ostensibly he was protecting Latin America from NAZI infiltration. Considering that it was Standard Oil of New Jersey, a Rockefeller business, that fueled the German Luftwaffe, and it was the Rockefeller Foundation among others that funded Hitler's eugenics research, that is more than a little bit of an irony. When the British complained because they were being pounded by the Luftwaffe, Rockefeller rerouted his supply lines through the Panama Canal to avoid the British blockade.[126] Nelson was contributing to John D. III's "gene pool" cleansing efforts by promoting genetically modified food production in Latin America. GMO foods such as corn which contained a spermicidal agent were sold to Mexican farmers. The corn killed the sperm in the Mexican males who ate it.[127]

Nelson and David also instituted Operation Bootstrap for shipping production to Latin American countries where labor was cheaper. These were the sweatshops in Puerto Rico which were operated by slave labor and the employees were paid very little for their work.[128]

Nelson Rockefeller always wanted to be President of the United States but he was not acceptable to the vast majority of freedom loving Americans. That did not keep him from controlling the office of the president from behind the scenes. Even prior to the election which Nixon was sure to win, he was persuaded to meet with Nelson Rockefeller in his apartment in New York. The Pact of Fifth Ave' was established at this meeting and the Republican Platform was exchanged for Rockefeller's socialist plans.[129] Nelson Rockefeller assisted Nixon in appointing his cabinet members and he choose Henry Kissinger, whom he had never met, therefore to be his National Security Advisor and later Secretary of State.[130] Nelson is committed to the global conspiracy. In *The Future of Federalism* (1969) Nelson Rockefeller claims that current events compellingly demand a New World Order as the old order is crumbling, and there is "a new and free order struggling to be born." Rockefeller says: "There is a fever of nationalism .... The nation-state is becoming less and less competent to perform its international political tasks....

---

126 F. William Engdahl, Seeds of Destruction: The Hidden Agenda of Genetic Manipulation (Canada: Global Research, Center for Research on Globalization, 2007) 108..
127 Ibid, 272.
128 Ibid, 70.
129 Gary Allen, None Dare Call it Conspiracy (Rossmoor, California: Concord Press 1971) 109.
130 Pat Robertson, The New World Order (Dallas, Texas: Word Publishing, 1991) 100.

These are some of the reasons pressing us to lead vigorously toward the true building of a New World Order...."[131]

After Nixon's impeachment, Nelson Rockefeller, the four term Governor of New York, was appointed Vice President by Gerald Ford. As vice President, Nelson chaired the investigative committee ordered by Gerald Ford to investigate accusations of Central Intelligence Agency abuses. This was a little like setting the fox to guard the hen house. In the Rockefeller biography *Thy Will be Done*, Gerald Colby explores the CIA's mind control operation of which Nelson played no small part. Nelson Rockefeller combined the Federal Security Agency with the Department of Health, Education and Welfare. HEW became involved with Intelligence matters and became a conduit for MKULTRA and Project Artichoke. Thus HEW took over both projects with its subordinate office the National Institute of Mental Health (NIMH). The CIA had initiated mind control experiments under HEW during Nelson Rockefeller's tenure.[132]

John D. Rockefeller III became Senator of West Virginia. In 1974 the UN Population Conference failed to adopt the US position on population control. This position shaped by Rockefeller consisted of drastic global population reduction measures. Fierce resistance to the US position by the Catholic church and other UN nations convinced the US to adopt covert measures to implement their project. Henry Kissinger was left with developing the strategy.[133] It was John D. Rockefeller III who recommended to Nixon that he develop a national policy pertaining to worldwide population growth, food and strategic raw material. Thus Nixon appointed Henry Kissinger to the task. Henry produced the now famous National Security Services Memo 200 which was classified Confidential until the Catholic church forced it into open publication in 1989. "Global depopulation and food control were to become the U.S. Strategic Policy under Kissinger. This was the new 'solution' to the threats to U.S. global power and its continued access to cheap raw materials from the developing world."[134] The need for population control in poor developing countries was promoted by convincing Americans that overpopulation leads to hunger and more poverty which would lead to a community revolution. Laurence Rockefeller established the Conservation Foundation in 1958 which united with the Population council to promote the theme

> ... that natural resources must be conserved, but conserved from use by smaller businesses or individuals in order that select global corporations should be able to claim them thus establishing a kind

---

131 Robin de Ruiter, Worldwide Evil and Misery: The Legacy of 13 Satanic Bloodlines, (The Netherland: Mayra Publications, 2008)17.
132 Alex Constantine, Virual Government (Los Angeles, 1997) 29 - 30
133 F. William Engdahl, Seeds of Destruction: The Hidden Agenda of Genetic Manipulation (Canada: Global Research, Center for Research on Globalization, 2007) 56.
134 Ibid, 53.

of strategic denial policy masquerading as conservation. ... The population control lobby which would later shape Kissinger's NSSM 200 was consolidating around Rockefeller Foundation grants and individuals, preparing a global assault on "inferior peoples," under the name of choice, of family planning and of averting the danger of 'over-population' ---a myth their think-tanks and publicity machines produced to convince ordinary citizens of the urgency of their goals."[135]

Winthrop Rockefeller dropped out of Yale in 1934 and went to work at an oil field in Texas. In World War II he served as a combat infantryman and earned a Purple Heart, a Bronze Star and two Oak Leaf Clusters. After the war he returned to New York and enjoyed drinking, women and the New York City life. He grew tired of that and in 1953 he moved to Arkansas. In 1956 he was voted "Man of the Year" and in 1967 was elected Governor of Arkansas.[136] In Arkansas he was a businessman, philanthropist, and a rancher. He had a terrible problem with alcohol which lost him a third term as Governor of Arkansas. He died in 1973.[137]

The Rockefeller clan continues to exercise a controlling influence in American politics in the present day.

9. The Bolshevik Revolution and the Third Reich

With France and Britain coming dangerously close to both recognizing and aiding the South, it was Russia's pro-North Czar Alexander II who tipped the balance the other way. After receiving information that England and France were plotting a war to divide up the Russian Empire, Alexander ordered two Russian fleets to the United States in the fall 1863 to provide a protective presence to intimidate the British and the French who were waiting to take control of the United States should Lincoln lose the war and the States divide. This enraged Rothschild, and Alexander II was assassinated within a year of the Lincoln assassination.

Russia was a threat to the international bankers of the world because they were the largest untapped market on the planet and were becoming a superpower to rival the United States. Czar Nicholas the II was modernizing the Russian industry which was providing competition for Europe and United States. Unfortunately he was using basically slave labor to do it which did not make him popular in the

---

135 Ibid, 93.
136 Jim Marrs, Rule By Secrecy (New York, NY: Perennial Harper Collins, 2000) 50.
137 Holly Sklar, Trilateralism: Managing Dependence and Democracy - An Overview (from Trilateralism: Elite Planning for World Management, Editor Holly Sklar, Boston, MA: South End Press,1980) 55.

eyes of the people. In addition Russia was the world's number 1 oil producer. The Bolshevik Revolution crushed the oil competition for the United States.[138]

It was in 1905 that the initial assault on the rule of the Czars was challenged but the revolution failed. In November 1917 the revolution succeeded because of support from America and Great Britain. The Bolsheviks were the extremist wing of the Russian Social Democratic Party which advocated for the overthrow of capitalism. The Bolshevik revolution did not take place because the "downtrodden masses" rose up against the rule of the Czars, as has been popularly believed. It was the International Bankers who pulled the United States into the war which reversed the U.S. traditional policy of non involvement. In 1917 the United States, Russia and the British Commonwealth were involved in a battle against the Central Powers. Riots had broken out in Petrograd Russia because of breakdowns in transportation causing shortages in food supplies which led to the closing of factories. These riots were believed to have been incited by British agents.[139] Thus because of pressure from the United States, Czar Nicholas II abdicated. Most do not know that Czar Nicholas II had abdicated his throne seven months prior to the revolution. The provisionary government was led by Prince Lvov who was actually trying to pattern the Russian Government after the Democratic government of the United States. This of course would not suit the U.S. and European powers behind the revolution. The Lvov government was taken over by Aleksander Kerensky who was a so-called democratic socialist. He kept the war going against Germany on behalf of the elite while at the same time declared amnesty for communists and revolutionaries, 250,000 of whom returned to Russian and unseated the Kerensky government.[140]

Vladimir Ilyich Ulyanov, aka Lenin and Lev Davidovich Bronstein aka Leon Trotsky who were the catalysts behind the Bolshevik Revolution were nowhere in sight. They had been in exile since 1905 after an abortive attempt to dethrone the Czar. Lenin was in Switzerland and Trotsky was working for a communist newspaper in New York. They both returned to Russia at the behest of powerful men in Europe and the United States. It was Max Warburg (Brother of Paul Warburg who established the U.S. Federal Reserve System) of the German High Command and a displaced Russian living in Germany, Alexander Helphand AKA "Parvus", who put Lenin on a train with $5 to $6 million in gold and about 150 trained revolutionaries and sent him across Europe.[141] Trotsky left New York on board the S.S. Christina with 275 revolutionaries and headed for Nova Scotia where he and his money were impounded by the Canadian government. Trotsky had well voiced his intent to revolutionize Russia which would free German

---

138 Daniel Estulin, The True Story of the Bilderberger Group (Waterville, OR: Trine Day LLC, 2007) 169.
139 Jim Marrs, Rule By Secrecy (New York, NY: Perennial Harper Collins, 2000) 196..
140 Gary Allen, None Dare Call it Conspiracy (Rossmoor, California: Concord Press 1971) 67.
141 Ibid, 68 – 69.

soldiers to attack Canada. Thus the Canadian attempt to stop Trotsky was strategic. However Sir William Wiseman of Great Britain and Col E. Mandell House, advisor to Woodrow Wilson pressured the Canadian Government to let them go. Trotsky left Canada bound for Russia with an American Passport. He met up the Lenin and in November 1917, and by bribery, brutality and deceit they hired thugs and imposed their revolution of "more power to the people" on the Russian populace. They seized a few key cities but the revolution took place mainly in Petrograd. "It was as if the whole United States became Communist because a Communist-led mob seized Washington, DC. It was years before the Soviets solidified power throughout Russia."[142]

In 1915, the American International Corporation was formed to fund the Russian Revolution. The directors of the American International group represented the interests of the Rockefellers, Rothschilds, Du Pont, Kuhn, Loeb, Harriman, as well as Frank Vanderlipp of the Jekyll Island group which created the Federal Reserve and George Herbert Walker, grandfather of President George Bush. The financier of the Bolshevik Revolution included Jacob Schiff whose family lived with the Rothschilds in Frankfurt. Jacob Schiff of Kuhn, Loeb and Co. contributed an estimated $20 million. Warburg's attorney Elihu Root, a CFR member contributed another $20 million.[143] Others who contributed included Max Warburg and Olaf Aschberg of the Nye Banken of Stockholm, The Rhine Westphalian Syndicate, Jivotovsky, whose daughter later married Trotsky,[144] J.P. Morgan and Co. and the Rockefellers, and Lord Alfred Milner head of The Round Table and Alfred de Rothschild. Lord Alfred Milner contributed 21 million rubles. There is also evidence that President Woodrow Wilson also contributed $20 million dollars to the revolution from the war budget.

There were a number of British agents populating Petrograd at the time who helped incite the soldiers to mutiny.[145] Lenin and Trotsky were required to place MI6 (British Intelligence) operatives in key positions during the Russian Revolution, and these operatives were in turn controlled by the elite back in London, England. Lord Victor Rothschild, who also funded the revolution, had a key role in MI5.[146]

One of Lenin's first political acts upon seizing power was to nationalize the Russian banks. Thus a central bank was created in Russia - a key factor for

---

142 Gary Allen, None Dare Call it Conspiracy (Rossmoor, California: Concord Press 1971) 69.
143 Jim Marrs, Rule By Secrecy (New York, NY: Perennial Harper Collins, 2000) 192 – 193.
144 Gary Allen, None Dare Call it Conspiracy (Rossmoor, California: Concord Press,1971) 70.
145 Gary Allen, None Dare Call it Conspiracy (Rossmoor, California: Concord Press 1971) 72.
146 Fritz Springmeyer, The Rothschild Bloodline (July 3, 2009- http://www.thrforbiddenknowledge.com).

International bankers in controlling a nation.[147] The Bolshevik Revolution does not make sense on the surface because both Britain and America were at war with Germany and were allies of Czarist Russia. The Revolution freed German soldiers to continue their attack on Britain in which large numbers of British and American soldiers were killed. This is nothing short of treason. Gary Allen notes in *None Dare Call it Conspiracy* that Global conquest was the desire of the elite. Thus they began by establishing a central bank in Russia and thus the communist conspiracy gained a geopolitical foothold from which to launch their assault against the entire world. Russian then became the "enemy" of the West. Communist ideology centers on stripping the wealth of the rich. Therefore it is rather incongruent that wealthy men like the Rothschilds, Rockefellers, Schiffs, Warburgs, Morgans, Harrimans, and Milners would finance such a thing as the Bolshevik revolution unless of course they are controlling it to their own end. They control both sides of any conflict. They also gained "for themselves an enormous piece of real estate, complete with mineral rights, for somewhere between $30 and $40 million."[148]

Author David Icke observes a "multidimensional" aspect to the funding of the Bolsheviks. Lenin and Trotsky were being used to get Russia out of the war which benefited Germany, and communism created the division of fear and mistrust.[149] Now, the Insiders, as Gary Allen calls them, have an enemy to fight. Thus America has been propelled into war to fight the communists and make the world safe for democracy by the very same people who created communism in the first place. Marrs writes; "If there can be identified one single motivating factor behind the horror and tragedy experienced in the twentieth century, it is surely anti-communism. The animosity between the so-called democracies of the west and the communism of the east produced continuous turmoil from 1918 through the end of the century."[150] The bankers of the world understood the Hegelian Dialectic well and used it to their advantage. They created both communism and socialism and created fear and distrust on both sides thus inciting wars. The bankers were benefiting from both sides of the war and taking control of nation after nation as they drove them into debt in order to fund the wars. Thus America became indebted to the Federal Reserve with a national debt that she cannot pay. Therefore, she was compelled to declare bankruptcy. This decision turned this government of the people by the people for the people into a corporation owned by the international bankers. Thus the president elect of the Untied States of America is nothing more than a figurehead to maintain the illusion of democracy to pacify deceived Americans who have lost their freedom. In America they are

---

147 Daniel Estulin, The True Story of the Bilderberger Group (Waterville, OR: Trine Day LLC, 2007) 170.
148 Gary Allen, None Dare Call it Conspiracy (Rossmoor, California: Concord Press 1971) 73 – 75.
149 Jim Marrs, Rule By Secrecy (New York, NY: Perennial Harper Collins, 2000) 196.
150 Ibid,193.

also behind the creation of a bipartisan system in which the democrats blame the republicans who blame the democrats for the woes of this nation. Fear and distrust keep nations divided and thus they are unable to see who their true enemies are and unite to combat them.

The elites wanted Hegelian style conflicts so they ensured that the globe was never at peace. Harmony brings no profit. Thus they continued to create a system that was in conflict with itself to maximize profit. They ensured that there was conflict between the communists and socialists and this created a need for "peacekeeping" and wars to "make the world safe for democracy" which cost governments money which they borrow from the banking system. This puts the governments of the world in debt and thus liable to be controlled by the bankers. It also leaves the world in state of instability. When people are in an unstable environment they worry about surviving, not prospering. They are in a weakened state and are more likely to comply with the demands and wishes of those in power and control.

It was the treaty of Versailles after WWI that shamed Germany requiring them to make reparations after the war. Robertson writes, "It is one of the tragic ironies of history that the punitive terms of the Versailles treaty— which emasculated Germany's military power and forced it to pay $5 billion in war reparations— actually paved the way for the rise of Adolf Hitler and foreshadowed a second world war."[151]

Hitler was an impoverished high school dropout. He had been trying to make a living as an artist and was unable to do so. He eventually joined the military and was working in military intelligence when he was asked to infiltrate the German Workers Party. Hitler was later invited to join the German Workers Party. On orders from his superiors in the military he did join. It was there that he met his Thule Society mentor, Dietrich Eckert. A "secret doctrine" was imparted to Hitler by Eckert and University of Munich Professor Haushofer. According to this doctrine, non human entities who were visitors to earth produced by genetic manipulation a hybrid of their race and the human race. Something like this is actually reflected in the biblical account in Genesis 6 1:2 (NKJV) which says "Now it came to pass, when men began to multiply on the face of the earth, and daughters were born to them, that the sons of God saw the daughters of men, and they *were* beautiful; and they took wives for themselves of all whom they chose." This produced a giant race of which Goliath was one. According to the "secret doctrine" imparted to Hitler, the Aryan race was one of seven races that resulted from this interbreeding of human and non human races. The Giants spoken of in the Bible were a mutation. Hitler believed that the Aryan race was produced this way, and that they developed the mental and organizational abilities in humans by subjugating them. He believed that the conquerors continually intermarried with the inferior human race which resulted in the fall of their civilization.[152]

---

151 Pat Robertson, The New World Order (Dallas, Texas: Word Publishing, 1991) 51.
152 Jim Marrs, Rule By Secrecy (New York, NY: Perennial Harper Collins, 2000) 161 – 162.

Hitler eventually gained control of the German Workers Party, a labor union, through help form his military superiors and Eckert. In 1920 he changed the name of the party to the Nationalosozialistiche Deutsche Arbeiterpartei or NAZI which claimed 3000 members.

The Roundtable group was largely responsible for ensuring that Hitler was not stopped in Austria, the Rhineland and the Sudetenland. The Second World War was fought for the purpose of establishing a world government. Hitler was funded through the Warburg controlled Mendelsohn Bank of Amsterdam and the J. Henry Schroeder Bank with branches Frankfurt, London and New York. Legal counsel for the Bank was provided by Sullivan and Cromwell whose senior partners included John Foster and Allen Dulles. The Round Table did the work in Europe while the CFR, controlling the State Department, banked Hitler from the United States. [153]

The NAZI's saw themselves as a quasi religious group whose goals were the same as those of the Illuminati and Freemasonry. Hitler stated himself, "Anyone who interprets National Socialism merely as a political movement knows almost nothing about it. It is more than religion; it is the determination to create a new man."[154]

Hitler had acquired a book called the Protocols of the Wise Men of Zion from Alfred Rosenberg, a displaced Jew fleeing Russia during the Bolshevik revolution and one of the leaders of the NAZI party.[155] This book was originally written by a French Lawyer, Maurice Joly, in France in 1864 under the title of *Dialogue in Hell between Machiavelli and Montesquieu or the Politics of Machiavelli in the Nineteenth Century by a Contemporary*. It was political satire against the Machiavelli-inspired Napoleon III. It was later rewritten on orders of the Russian Ochrana, the czar's secret police with the intention of portraying the Russian Revolutionaries as pawns in the hands of an international Jewish Conspiracy to rule the world. The protocols are detailed instructions for covertly gaining control of the world. The Protocols explain how world domination is accomplished by controlling what the public thinks and hears, creating new conflicts, restoring old orders, spreading hunger, disease and destruction and seducing the youth. "By all these methods we shall so wear down the nations that they will be forced to offer us world domination."[156]

Hitler believed that the Protocols were real, and thus he began his campaign against the Jews. Hitler's mentor, Dietrich Eckert, was a member of the Thule Gesellschaft, or Thule Society, a cult of assassins. He also shared Eckert's interest in the occult. Eckert also introduced him to Peyote, a hallucinogenic drug. Hitler

---

153 Gary Allen, None Dare Call it Conspiracy (Rossmoor, California: Concord Press 1971) 85.
154 Jim Marrs, Rule By Secrecy (New York, NY: Perennial Harper Collins, 2000) 146.
155 David Icke, Tales from the Time Loop, (Ryde, Iles of Wright, UK: David Icke Books, 2003) p. 107
156 Jim Marrs, Rule By Secrecy (New York, NY: Perennial Harper Collins, 2000) 147.

became fascinated by the story of the "Spear of Destiny" which is on display in the Hofburg Museum in Vienna. This is the spear that was by legend thrust into the side of Jesus by a Roman Soldier. The legend has it that whoever controls that spear controls the world. Thus Hitler attempted to channel a spirit that was hovering near that spear and became inhabited by that spirit.

Hitler lost a popular election to an aging war hero, Field Marshal Paul Von Hindenburg, in 1932. However Business leaders such as Krupp, Siemens, Thyssen, and Bosch signed a petition in Hindenburg urging Hitler's appointment as chancellor of Germany. The petition was signed at a meeting of 39 such business leaders in the home of banker Baron Kurt Von Schroeder. At that meeting were also John Foster and Allen Dulles of New York's Sullivan and Cromwell law firm who represented Von Schroeder's bank. They cut a deal and encouraged Hitler to "stop the spread of communism" which of course included not attacking the bankers. Hitler was named Chancellor of Germany by President Hindenburg on January 30, 1993.

On February 27 1933, *the Reichstag* (Parliament) building burned in a fire blamed on the communists. A retarded youth, Marinus van der Lube, who was supposedly a card carrying communist, was taken into custody and eventually "confessed" to setting the fire. However, investigators later learned that the fire could not have been started by one person. In fact the incendiaries were brought into the building through a tunnel that led to the office Hitler's closest associate, Herman Goering. Nevertheless in another few days, Hitler was given dictatorial power with the passage of an emergency decree called the Enabling Act, euphemistically titled "The Law to Remove the Distress of the People and State" by which he assumed control of the government. This was another Hegelian style "crisis" created by the NAZI's themselves and blamed on the communists in order to offer a pretext for the eventual desired outcome – Hitler's absolute dictatorship over the German government. When President Hindenburg died on August 12, 1943, Hitler merged the offices of President and Chancellor and proclaimed himself commander-in-chief of the armed forces and absolute dictator of Germany.

Henry Ford believed that the Jews were involved in a conspiracy to bring on war for profits and he therefore was one of the funding sources for the NAZIs. That would have been an accurate assumption of Rothschild and his associates. Hitler was known to attack the Rothschilds for deliberately luring governments into debt and profiting from wars. In spite of this Hitler received considerable support from Britain even from the Bank of England dominated by Rothschild. On New year's day, 1924, Hjalmar Schacht, the new Reich Commissioner for National Currency, and Montagu Norman, governor of the Bank of England made a deal to open a German Credit Bank with half of the capital coming from the Bank of England based on pound sterling. The loan was approved and other London banks were encouraged to accept bills from the Germans which exceeded the loan. Joseph P. Kennedy, father of the future president of the United States and Ben Smith a Wall Street operator also contributed funds to Hitler's Germany. Sir Henri Detering, the powerful head of Royal Dutch-Shell Oil, who lived in London, provided funding.[157] and Prescott Bush, grandfather of President Bush, funded the NAZI Wehrmacht as steward of the Union Banking Corporation (UBC) owned by Harriman. The UBC was also involved with Fritz Thyssen whose factories built NAZI War Machinery. The German publishing Giant Bertelsmann owned by Thielens published Mien Kampf. They also published German NAZI Propaganda. Thielens were related to Fritz Theisen. President Bush gained a portion of his personal fortune from his affiliation with the UBC. Leading NAZI industrialists secretly owned the 'Harriman/Bush' bank and were transferring money into the UBC through a bank in Holland even after the US declared war on Germany. In 1951 when the bank liquidated, President Bush's grandfather and great grandfather received $1.5 million as a part of the dissolution. The Bush family fortune came from the Third Reich.[158]

It does not appear that the Rothschilds of Europe suffered much at all while Hitler was ravaging Europe because they fled to New York.[159] It is also strange that a number of Jews seemed to also be supporting Hitler. These were the wealthy elite associated with Rothschild who wanted a Jewish state. Thus the attack on the Jews created a "need" for a Jewish state. This is another application of the Hegelian "order out of chaos" mindset so prevalent among the Illuminati. Max Warburg, an Ashkenazi Jew, was head of I.G. Farben which made the Zyklon B gas that was used to kill the Jews in the gas chambers. I.G. Farben ran the concentration camp at Auschwitz. Max Warburg's Nephew used his influence in the United States to quash anti-NAZI/German boycotts. The B'nai B'rith anti defamation league, supposedly organized to fight anti-Semitism in the United States, also was involved in quashing anti-NAZI campaigns. Max Warburg controlled the American Jewish Community and his Kuhn, Loeb and Company had underwritten NAZI shipping.[160]

In fact many of the pro-NAZI supporters were Ashkenazi Jews of the Jewish Illuminati elite who turned on their own people. The major financial figures in the United States and Europe who supported the NAZI war machine were in fact Jewish. This is what has led some like Andrew Carrington Hitchcock to believe that this is a Jewish conspiracy to control the world. To understand this we must understand that the Illuminati see themselves as above everyone else, "Aryan", a pure bloodline.

---

157 Jim Marrs, Rule By Secrecy (New York, NY: Perennial Harper Collins, 2000) 166 – 167.
158 David Icke, Tales from the Time Loop, (Ryde, Iles of Wright, UK: David Icke Books, 2003) 106 – 107.
159 Jim Marrs, Rule By Secrecy (New York, NY: Perennial Harper Collins, 2000) 169.
160 David Icke, Tales from the Time Loop, (Ryde, Iles of Wright, UK: David Icke Books, 2003) 108.

However, Hitler committed the ultimate offense by refusing to allow his nation to become indebted to the Rothschild banking system. Hitler was very successful in turning the German economy around. He did this by breaking with the Jewish international bankers and reinstating a barter trading system. Thus he bartered the surplus of goods that Germany possessed with the surplus of another country and no debt was incurred by either side. He also issued money on the authority of the German Government backed by the productivity by the Germany labor force. The international banking system could not function in a country without debt.[161] This and the fact that public opinion in America was turning against Hitler as word of the Holocaust began to spread was creating bad publicity for Hitler in the United States which his US supporters could not afford so they ceased public support for Hitler and eventually America was drawn into the war to "rescue" Hitler's victims. America's role in the war, however, was not what it appeared to be.

10. History of a Terrible Secret

Few people in America know or understand that the roots of the Holocaust are here in the good old U.S. of A. Those who supported and financed Hitler's Third Reich were wealthy families of the Eastern Establishment. They are people who believe in a ruling class and adhere to ideals of Lock and Darwin that are all about genetics and the notion there are some who are fit to rule and some who don't even deserve to live they are so genetically flawed. They have established in America their own little NAZI underground fronted by the Midtown Sporting Club in New York City, financed by the Morgan family, several wall Street investment firms and the German General Staff. "'The penalty for betraying our secrets is death.' was the warning John Roy Carlson received upon infiltrating the group, 'We have men watching every one of you, men without mercy. Men who don't give a damn.'" Carlson swore not to reveal their secret, and he quotes an official at a "ritual war ceremony" he was invited to attend,

> You are Soldiers of Christ.... We are the trained body of Christian citizens who must give aid and defense to all Christian groups." Carlson states further, "A half dozen straight-backed chairs, several armchairs and a small round table with an open Bible laying on it composed the furniture. Across the pages of the Bible lay a bayonet. Several rifles leaned against the wall. I sat down facing the emblem of the Iron Guard, a large black circle and an inner circle of white. Within the circles was a red arm holding in its fist a flash of lightening. Herrmann Schmitt, the leader of the Guard, stood

---

161 Andrew Carrington Hitchcock, The Synagogue of Satan (Austin, Texas: RiverCrest Publishing, 2007) 137.

in the circle and blurted, 'We are FASCISTS, American fascists! Democracy is a tool to do away with Christianity. The time is ripe for something entirely new---fascism!"[162]

One of the trademarks of fascism is the control of the state by business giants. Thus they worked every so subtly and quietly behind the scenes in American government to put a ruling class in place. The fascist globalists promoted their own plan for population reduction and gene pool cleansing in American long before the Germans began their American inspired program. The idea of genetic selection grew from the writings of Sir Francis Galton, "who after study reached the conclusion that prominent members of British society were such because they had 'eminent' parents.[163]

David Star Jordan, President of Stanford University, wrote a book in 1902 called *Blood of a Nation* in which he stated that poverty and talent were both genetic traits that were inherited and not influenced at all by education. In 1904 Andrew Carnegie Founded the Eugenics Record Office in Cold Springs Harbor in New York where millions of index cards carrying information on the bloodlines of millions of Americans were gathered with the intent of planning the eventual removal of inferior bloodlines. The sponsors were out to eliminate those they deemed "unfit". The Harriman's provided more than $11 million dollars toward the establishment of the Eugenics Records Laboratory as well as eugenics studies at Harvard, Columbia and Cornell.[164] As early at 1911, Carnegie was funding an American Breeder's Association study on the "Best Practical Means for Cutting of Defective Germ-Plasma is the Human Population."[165]

In a landmark 1927 case, Buck vs. Bell, US Supreme Court Justice Oliver Wendell Holmes ruled that forced sterilization in the state of Virginia was Constitutional. Holmes wrote, "It is better for all the world, if instead of waiting to execute degenerate offspring for crime, or to let them starve for their imbecility, society can prevent those who are manifestly unfit from continuing their kind . . . Three generations of imbeciles are enough." The 1927 decision resulted in the forced sterilization of thousands of American citizens or persecution for being subhuman. Later, NAZI psychiatrist Dr. Ernst Rudin, head of the Racial Hygiene Society, in a Task Force on Heredity chaired by SS chief Himmler instituted a German sterilization law based upon the laws instituted in the Commonwealth of Virginia.[166] "Years later, the NAZIs at the Nuremberg trials quoted Holmes' words in their own defense. In a postwar world, not surprisingly, it was to no avail.

---

162 Alex Constantine, Virtual Government (Los Angeles, CA: Feral House, 1997) 32.
163 Jim Marrs, The Rise of the Fourth Reich (New York, NY: Harper Collins, 2008) 282.
164 Ibid, 283.
165 F. William Engdahl, Seeds of Destruction: The Hidden Agenda of Genetic Manipulation (Canada: Global Research, Center for Research on Globalization, 2007) 77.
166 Jim Keith, Mind Control, World Control (Kempton, Ill: Adventures Unlimited Press,1997) 23..

The Rockefeller propaganda machine buried the reference; the victors defined the terms of peace and the truth of war."[167]

Hitler wrote in Mein Kampf: "There is today one state in which at least weak beginnings toward a better conception of immigration are noticeable. Of course, it is not our model German Republic, but the United States." Hitler praised American Author Madison Grant for his 1916 book, *The Passing of the Great Race* in which Grant advocates "a rigid system of selection through the elimination of those who are weak or unfit---in other words, social failures (sic)." Grant was co-founder of the American Eugenics Society. By 1940 Germans had systematically gassed thousands Germans in old age homes and mental institutions. In 1940 Leon Whitney, Executive Secretary of the Rockefeller Funded American Eugenics Society had toured the German Eugenics institutes and said of the NAZI experiments, "While we were pussy-footing around . . . the Germans were calling a spade a spade."[168]

Psychiatry Professor, Dr. Ernst Rudin of the Kaiser Wilhelm Institute for Genealogy and Demography in Berlin was unanimously elected president of the International Federation of Eugenics Societies for its work in founding the German Society for Racial Hygiene. Rudin was funded by Rockefeller money. The Eastern Establishment and Hitler's eugenicists were determined to prove that "blacks were stupid, Jews were greedy, Mexicans were lazy, women were nutty, and so on---as well as the corollary: rich, white people with good table manners and glowing report cards were genetically superior."[169] Rockefeller also contributed $317,000 to the Kaiser Wilhelm Institute for brain research. In the 1930's they received batches of brains taken from victims of NAZI euthanasia program at the Brandenburg State Hospital where the NAZIs experimented on Jews, gypsies, the mentally handicapped and other "defectives."[170]

Psychiatrist Franz J. Kallmann, actually half Jewish, was a protégé of Dr. Ernst Rudin. Kallman had argued at the International Congress for Population Science in Berlin in 1935 that schizophrenics should be sterilized as well as their healthy relatives. Kallmann moved to New York after the war and became the director of research at the New York State Psychiatric Institute, an institution headed by the Freemason Dr. Lewis. He was funded by the Scottish Rite of Freemasonry to prove that mental illness was inherited genetically. This report was used for the justification of the murder of over 200,000 "mental defectives"

---

167 F. William Engdahl, Seeds of Destruction: The Hidden Agenda of Genetic Manipulation (Canada: Global Research, Center for Research on Globalization, 2007) 79.
168 Ibid, 81.
169 Jim Marrs, The Rise of the Fourth Reich (New York, NY: Harper Collins, 2008) 283 – 284.
170 F. William Engdahl, Seeds of Destruction: The Hidden Agenda of Genetic Manipulation (Canada: Global Research, Center for Research on Globalization, 2007) 80.

by the NAZI's T4 unit in Berlin.[171] The infamous NAZI T4 (Tiergartenstrasse 4) euthanasia program began in 1940. This became the prototype of the NAZI death camps. A fake shower was constructed which emitted carbon monoxide killing the victims. In April 1941the doctors of T4 began the 'Endlosung', or final solution in NAZI concentration camps.[172]

When the American public finally became aware of what was happening in the death camps in Germany, the tide of public opinion caused Rockefeller to cease funding Hitler's program. Frederick Osborn, a eugenics enthusiast supported the eugenics research of the Rockefeller Foundation. Both Osborn and Rockefeller publically denied knowing anything about the Auschwitz eugenics experiments and the horrors of the concentration camps, but they knew well where their money was going. It was Osborn who said the NAZI Eugenics program was the "most important experiment that has ever been tried." He later published in 1968 his book *The Future of Human Heredity: An Introduction to Eugenics in Modern Society*. At the same time John D III was preparing to head the Presidential Commission on the population problem. Osborn also praised Muller's proposal to develop sperm banks to make "good" sperm available.[173]

Hitler, the puppet of globalists in Europe did not like the fact that multinational businessmen, like Rockefeller, were attempting to control Germany. He attempted to form a treaty with England as he was engaging Russia in combat to avoid a war with both England and Russia at the same time. The attempt failed and he had no choice but to face a war on two fronts.[174] There is also evidence that he was planning an attack on New York.[175] Whether or not Rockefeller was aware of this is questionable, but Rockefeller, though he had to cease public support of Hitler's Reich, fueled the Luftwaffe through his Standard Oil.

Standard Oil of New Jersey, later named Exxon, is the largest oil company in the world controlling 84% of the petroleum market. Its bank was Chase Bank owned by the Rockefellers. The next largest stockholder in Standard Oil was I.G. Farben the huge petroleum trust of Germany and major supporter of the German war industry. Farben and the Rockefellers became connected in 1927 when Rockefeller began funding the German Eugenics research. So while Nelson Rockefeller was supposedly combating NAZI economic interests in Latin America, the Rockefeller family's Oil Company was shipping tetraethyl lead gasoline to the German Luftwaffe. When Great Britain objected because they were being

---

171 Jim Keith, Mind Control World Control (Kempton, ILL: Adventures Unlimited Press, 1997) 25, 27.
172 Jim Marrs, The Rise of the Fourth Reich (New York, NY: Harper Collins, 2008) 186-187.
173 F. William Engdahl, Seeds of Destruction: The Hidden Agenda of Genetic Manipulation (Canada: Global Research, Center for Research on Globalization, 2007) 90, 91.
174 Jim Marrs, The Rise of the Fourth Reich (New York, NY: Harper Collins, 2008) 48.
175 Ibid, 60.

pounded by the Germans. Rockefeller simply rerouted the shipments to avoid British search and seizures.[176]

Before America entered the war, The United States Military Intelligence unites had already been to Germany and in cooperation with the Vatican had established escape routes for the NAZIs, called "ratlines", every 40 mines along the German border. Some 5000 NAZIs escaped the allied forces. One of Hitler's right hand men, Martin Bormann, who was a financial mastermind, with the help of allies in the United States, Argentina and Switzerland created a financial foundation to support NAZI's fleeing Germany. Germany had lost the war. However, Martin Bormann had made plans to resurrect the Fourth Reich.

NAZI wealth came from the acquired treasures of Solomon's Temple that had originally been excavated from under Solomon's Temple by the Knights Templers, as well as gold that was confiscated from concentration camp victims. Heinrich Himmler dispatched Otto Skorzeny to a village in Southern France called Languedoc where the Templers were fabled to have hidden Solomon's treasure while they were fleeing persecution from the Catholic church. This fact has been disputed, but Jim Marrs notes that the Templers, after their "duty" of guarding the road near the temple was completed, were very wealthy people. The treasure was located by Skorzeny on Montségur in Languedoc. It has been estimated that the value of the treasure trove exceeded $60 billion.[177] Gold that had been confiscated from the concentration camp victims, private individuals and stolen from central banks and was melted into unmarked gold bars at the Reichsbank and sent to Rothschild's Bank of International Settlements (BIS). The BIS of Switzerland received a total of 13.5 tons of gold from NAZI Germany, a fourth of which was eventually stolen from the BIS.[178] This massive wealth confiscated by the NAZIs funded the NAZI underground after the war. Martin Bormann lead the SS to establish hundreds of corporations abroad. He also donated large funds of money to far-right political candidates. In this way he paved the way for the reconstruction of the Reich on foreign soil. The money was channeled through secret bank accounts. Bormann thus finances some 750 new companies to assist with the revival of the NAZI party and more than 100 of them were based in the United States.[179]

Hitler had friends in the White House going back to George H. W. Bush's parents. Prescott Bush, father of George H. W. Bush, was part owner of the Hamburg-American Shipping line. On October 20th, 1942 under the Trading with The Enemy Act, the U.S. Alien Property custodian seized shares of the Union

---

176 F. William Engdahl, Seeds of Destruction: The Hidden Agenda of Genetic Manipulation (Canada: Global Research, Center for Research on Globalization, 2007) 108.

177 Jim Marrs, The Rise of the Fourth Reich (New York, NY: Harper Collins, 2008) 103 – 105.

178 Robin de Ruiter, Worldwide Evil and Misery: The Legacy of 13 Satanic Bloodlines (The Netherlands: Myra Publications 2008) 205 – 206.

179 Alex Constantine, Virtual Government (Los Angeles, CA: Feral House1997) 7,8.

Banking Corporation (UBC) of New York City as well as Prescott Bush's holdings in the Hamburg-American shipping line because the bank was financing Hitler. They were ferrying arms and propaganda for the NAZI Party. Prescott Bush and father-in-law George Herbert Walker were on the board of Directors of UBC. Their attorney's were John Foster Dulles (later secretary of State under Dwight D. Eisenhower) and Allen Dulles (later Director of the Central Intelligence Agency). A company that was responsible for handling and distributing NAZI money was the Holland American Trading Company which was a subsidiary of UBC. Fritz Thyssen owned the Dutch branch. When the assets of this bank were sized he did not have to "transfer all his assets, all he had to do was transfer the ownership documents---stocks, bonds, deeds, and trusts---from his bank in Berlin through his bank in Holland to his American friends in New York city: Prescott Bush and George Herbert Walker". On November 17, 1942, U.S. authorities also seized the Silesian-American Corporation, managed by Prescott Bush and his father in law, George Herbert Walker with the charge that this company was supplying coal to NAZI Germany. The Grandfather of George W. Bush maintained more than a dozen relationships with the enemy as late as 1951. According to documentation recently released, Bush and his associates continuously tried to conceal their business dealings with the NAZIs from investigators.

General Reinhardt Gehlen, who was in charge of the Third Reich's military intelligence in Eastern Europe and the Soviet Union, two weeks after the war's end walked into an Army command center in Bavaria offering information to the U.S. Government. He was sent to a prison camp in Salzburg. Within a month he was taken to Augsburg for interrogation. It was not long after that that he was flown to the U.S. dressed in an American military uniform to confer with top American military officials. He was taken to Washington national Airport, and driven to Fort Hunt, outside Washington D.C. At Ft. Hunt, Gehlen, Allen Dulles and others made an agreement to combine the NAZI SS with the US Office of Strategic Services. This became the Central Intelligence Agency. Allen Dulles gave $200 million to fund Gehlen's intelligence organization which was working in a fortified stronghold in Bavaria and with little supervision gained control of the West German Intelligence service. Gehlen also provided 70 % of the intelligence for the Soviet Union and Europe to NATO. The NAZI's therefore infiltrated American Intelligence with the blessing of the Dulles brothers, Harriman, and George Bush.[180]

As many as 5000 NAZIs including scientists were brought into this country under Project Paperclip under the auspices of the Joint Intelligence Committee. President Harry S. Truman permitted the immigration of the German scientists on the stipulation that no one with a NAZI background guilty of war crimes would be among those given asylum in the United States. This project which began just after WWII continued into 1973 non-stop despite government claims

---

180 Jim Keith, Mind Control World Control (Kempton, ILL: Adventures Unlimited Press, 1997) 68 – 69.

that it ceased in 1947. The records of these NAZI scientists had been expunged of incriminating evidence of their criminal backgrounds. Of course it was Harry S. Truman who complied with a recommendation to make John Foster Dulles his Secretary of State and Allan Dulles Director of the CIA. These two men were instrumental in the Project Paperclip dealings. Project Paperclip was also supported by the globalist network rooted in the Council of Foreign Relations.[181]

Among the German imports to the U.S. was Karl Tauboeck, chief plant chemist at I.G. Farben's Ludwigshafen factory. He was the NAZI expert on sterilization drugs and had worked on the truth drug project that paralleled the project with the OSS and CIA. Also was Dr. Huburtus Strughold, who supervised the murder and torture of Dachau inmates, was later employed by NASA and lauded by NASA as the father of space medicine.[182]

Another infamous NAZI Scientist/war criminal given asylum in the United States was Werner Von Braun who came to the United States with most of his staff. Von Braun was the NAZI Scientist who developed the V-2 rocket that pounded England. As a high ranking SS officer, he was also responsible for the deaths of thousands of slave laborers at the NAZI advanced weapons facility in Peenemunende, Germany. The Office of Strategic Services forerunner of the CIA saved him from the Nuremberg Trial. He was transferred to the White Sands, New Mexico rocketry center in 1946 where he was made a technical advisor to the guided missile group and later the Army Ballistic Missile Group which he ran until his death.[183] For 20 years he designed weapons for the CIA and DOD. In the mid-1950s he joined the California Institute of Technology and jointed the science advisory board of the National Security Agency under Director John Samford.[184] Von Braun was named the Father of Rocket Science in the United States.

Dr. Joseph Mengele was known for his cruel experiments in mind control in which he tortured thousands of innocent victims at Auschwitz. He was tasked by Von Vershuer in 1943 to develop the technology to turn people into robots. At the end of the war, he supposedly fled to his hometown in Günzberg, Bavaria. In 1949 he allegedly traveled to Argentina and then fled to Paraguay. Researchers who were on the hunt for Joseph Mengele apparently got too close, and thus he "died" in a plane crash. In reality when Mengele disappeared from Auschwitz toward the end of the war, he was secretly flown to the United States where he continued to develop his knowledge of mind control for the profit of the New World Order.[185]

---

181 Jim Marrs, The Rise of the Fourth Reich (New York, NY: Harper Collins, 2008) 150 – 151.
182 Jim Keith, Mind Control World Control (Kempton, ILL: Adventures Unlimited Press, 1997) 70.
183 Jerry E. Smith, HAARP: The Ultimate Weapon of the Conspiracy (Kempton, ILL: Adventures Unlimited Press, 1998) 127.
184 Alex Constantine, Virtual Government (Los Angeles, CA: Feral House1997) 101.
185 Robin de Ruiter, Worldwide Evil and Misery: The Legacy of 13 Satanic Bloodlines (The Netherlands: Myra Publications 2008) 313.

The NAZIs were befriended in the United States and had a significant role to play in medicine, psychiatry, intelligence gathering, rocket science and mind control in the Cold War. We now have an infestation of NAZIs who have taken this nation on the sly while we slept.

11. The House of Rothschild and the Creation of Israel

In the 1880's Russian Jews were fleeing the Czar's pogroms. At that time Baron Edmond Rothschild began funding the emigration of Russian Jews to Palestine and their attempts to establish colonies there. "The Baron's money drained swamps, dug wells and built houses. It founded industries ranging from scent factories to glass works, from wine cellars to bottle manufacturers. The Baron established his own administration in Palestine and his overseers dictated to the farmers exactly what crops were to be grown and where". Theodor Herzl established the first Zionist congress but failed to gain the support of the Rothschilds who were not at that time Zionists. The British Rothschild's were happy with being British. Baron Edmond Rothschild wanted Jewish colonies but did not want Herzl in control. Edmond Rothschild maintained tight fisted control of the Jewish colonies in Palestine. The Jews sent a delegation to the Baron to ask him to relinquish such tight fisted control of the Yishuv. This upset the Baron. He replied: "I created the Yishuv, I alone. Therefore no men, neither colonists nor organizations, have the right to interfere in my plans."[186] Chaim Weitzman was the one who influenced Baron Edmond Rothschild to adopt a Zionist stance.

In 1907 Arthur Balfour was in a meeting with Henry White in which he declared that it might be necessary to go to war with Germany because she was building too many ships and infringing on British trade. To this Henry White replied; "If you wish to compete with German trade, work harder." Balfour responded, "That would mean lowering our standard of living. Perhaps it would be simpler for us to have a war." Balfour, noting White's shock, responded, "Is it a question of right or wrong? Maybe it is just a question of keeping our supremacy."[187] Thus World War I came about by Illuminati maneuvering. At the end of the war, impossible reparations payments were imposed on Germany, ensuring its collapse and creating the circumstances that brought Hitler and the NAZIs to power. At the Versailles Conference the Illuminati "front men" who were either a Rothschild by blood or were controlled by Rothschild agreed to support the creation of a Jewish homeland in Palestine.[188]

---

186 Fritz Springmeyer, The Rothschild Bloodline (July 3, 2009- http://www.theforbiddenknowledge.com).

187 Robin de Ruiter, Worldwide Evil and Misery: The Legacy of 13 Satanic Bloodlines (The Netherlands: Myra Publications 2008) 167.

188 David Ike, Tales from the Time Loop, (Ryde, Isle of Wright, UK: David Icke Books, 2003) 100.

The planning of the State of Israel began in 1917 when Lionel Walter Rothschild II, received a letter from British foreign secretary Arthur Balfour in reply to a letter asking for his support of the establishment of a Jewish state. Lord Balfour granted his approval. This became known as the Balfour Declaration. The Declaration read as follows;

Foreign Office
November 2nd, 1917
Dear Lord Rothschild,

I have much pleasure in conveying to you, on behalf of His Majesty's Government, the following declaration of sympathy with Jewish Zionist aspirations which has been submitted to, and approved by, the Cabinet.

His Majesty's Government views with favor the establishment in Palestine of a national home for the Jewish people, and will use their best endeavors to facilitate the achievement of this object, it being clearly understood that nothing shall be done which may prejudice the civil and religious rights of existing non-Jewish communities in Palestine, or the rights and political status enjoyed by Jews in any other country.

I should be grateful if you would bring this declaration of the knowledge of the Zionist Federation.

Yours Sincerely,
Arthur James Balfour

In 1922, the League of Nations approved the Balfour mandate in Palestine, thus paving the way for the later creation of Israel. The very people involved in the Balfour Declaration were Round Table associates including Lord Balfour Round Table inner circle member, Alfred Milner Round Table Leader and Lord Lionel Walter Rothschild who funded the Roundtable.[189] Sir Alfred Balfour was a British conservative, exiled Zionist and a Freemason,[190] "After World War I Britain ruled Palestine, and the Rothschilds ruled Britain. Also, a bulk of unpaid debts to the Rothschilds by the failed Ottoman Empire gave the family more control over Palestine. Then came Hitler." [191]

At a meeting of the International Chamber of commerce (ICC) held on July 12th 1937 in Berlin, Thomas J. Watson of IBM, Sir Arthur Balfour, F. H. Fentener

---

189 Ibid.
190 Robin de Ruiter, Worldwide Evil and Misery: The Legacy of 13 Satanic Bloodlines (The Netherlands: Myra Publications 2008) 159.
191 Fritz Springmeyer, The Rothschild Bloodline (July 3, 2009- http://www.theforbiddenknowledge.com).

van Vlissingen Chairman of ICC met with Adolf Hitler. IBM developed the punch card sorting machine that assisted the NAZIs in identifying and locating Jews throughout the empire. The Jewish exodus from Germany was planned in advance. However, the real children of Judea, the orthodox and Sephardic Jews, ended up in concentration camps and few of them survived.[192] The same people who funded the NAZIs also founded Zionism, the political movement that created a Jewish state. However, in 1939 Great Britain reneged on the Balfour Declaration when they issued the White Paper declaring that creating a Jewish state was no longer British policy. This White paper and change in policy prevented European Jews from escaping NAZI-occupied Europe.

At the end of WWII the push for a Jewish state became even stronger. In 1947, Zionist leader David Ben-Gurion turned to Nelson Rockefeller for his support in the United Nations to create a Zionist state. This was accomplished through blackmail. Rockefeller had funded the German Luftwaffe and had profited from it. Therefore Ben-Gurion had a large dossier full of blackmail material to use as leverage with Nelson Rockefeller. They had records of his Swiss Bank accounts with the NAZIs, his correspondence in setting up the German Cartel in South America, transcripts of his conversations with his NAZI cohorts and evidence that he had aided Allen Dulles in assisting NAZI war criminals to escape prosecution. An agreement was reached with David Ben-Gurion. In exchange for the support of the Latin Block in the NATO vote, the Zionists would abandon any attempts at bringing the NAZI war criminals to justice. The choice was simple, Rockefeller explained, "You can have vengeance, or you can have a country, but you cannot have both."[193]

Thus on November 29, 1947 the resolution recommending the partition of Palestine was approved by the UN General Assembly. The fact that Latin American countries switched their vote at the last minute shocked the Arab world. The Jews agreed to silence in exchange for their Israel, however western employers of NAZI refugees and war criminals continued to be blackmailed by the Jews. Thus the Jews gained nearly unconditional support for Israel and its policies.[194]

The symbol of the Rothschild family, the six pointed star that now adorns the flag of Israel, is a symbol of Ashtoreth originally adopted by King Solomon when he became apostate. The lower and upper stripes represent the Tigris and Euphrates rivers. It is blue, not red, but it is nonetheless the symbol of that family that now flies over the nation of Israel. The Rothschilds have been called Jewish Royalty and different leaders of the Rothschild clan have been called "King of the Jews" at various times.[195]

---

192 Robin de Ruiter, Worldwide Evil and Misery: The Legacy of 13 Satanic Bloodlines (The Netherlands: Myra Publications 2008) 198.
193 Jim Marrs, The Rise of the Fourth Reich (New York, NY: Harper Collins, 2008) 138 – 139.
194 Ibid.
195 Fritz Springmeyer, The Rothschild Bloodline (July 3, 2009, http://www.theforbiddenknowledge.com.

12. Establishing a Standard of Morality

It appears that proponents of globalization and the New World Order have decided to dispense with traditional Judeo-Christian values and substitute their own standard. This might be expected since the Judeo Christian value system does not suit their agenda. They have therefore decided that there is no such thing as right and wrong or good and evil. Those who believe in Judeo Christian values would tell them that it is wrong to destroy a country like Iraq and steal the country's wealth or make slaves out of anybody they choose or lie to the public about their actions or intentions or commit horrible acts of inhumane torture whenever it suits them or subvert the rule of law. Their belief structure begins with the premise that there is no divine being to whom they have to answer and that the 'state" is God. There is no such thing as freedom and dignity and no one has a right to a free will or to think for themselves and determine their own course in life. One might ask on what basis they think they have the right to make such assertions and do the things that they do. Who gave them the authority to do as such? It appears that their authority is based only on their ability to force their agenda on the populace. If they are resisted they put down that resistance by whatever means necessary to accomplish their goals.

One might consider how a standard is set. In the Judeo-Christian world there is a higher being who is perfect in every way and who has set a standard of perfect holiness against which all are measured. It would make logical sense that a being that is absolutely perfect might be the best place to start when establishing a standard of moral conduct. The opposite would be true of looking to anyone who is less than perfect to establish a standard of morality. But where do we get this notion that there is such a being in the first place? As the proponents of the New World Order have rejected the idea that there is such a divine being, on what basis do we insist that there is, indeed must be one? Defending the existence of God is not hard to do from a rational point of view. His existence is perfectly logical.

For a moment, let us stop and consider where we get such a notion that something called "perfection" even exists. How many times have you said yourself, "I'm not perfect" or even "No one is perfect"? We know instinctively we are flawed. But how do we know that? It would seem logical that we have an idea in our heads about what perfection is and we know we do not measure up nor does anyone else. But since we know no one who is perfect in this world, on what basis do we determine that we do not meet the standard? Somehow the idea of perfection is a part of our language and understanding even though we have never found anyone in this world to be just that. It would make sense then that we know that somewhere there is someone who is.

If this is indeed true, then it would explain why we find ourselves having to forgive others for imperfections. In other words, we seem to find it necessary to overlook the imprecations of others. They do not measure up to our standard, but we forgive because we have to admit that we too need forgiveness. It is also necessary to recognize that there are people in this world who are very unforgiving, exacting and demanding. They are not pleasant people to be around. They seem to be always demanding that everyone measure up to their standard. I have known such people. They are also people who seem to be absolutely blind to their own faults.

Let's examine something else for a minute. Let us think about opposites. There are word pairs in language that reflect again the notion that there is something that is called perfect. These are: good and evil, life and death, the truth vs. the lie, light and darkness. These are things that are much easier to discuss maybe because they do exist in our world. Light and darkness are easy to understand. We have day and night that we can all relate to. Life and death is easy to understand also. We have experienced life and we have seen loved ones die. So we know that there is such a thing as life and its opposite death.

The difference between truth and untruth or a lie might be a little harder for some to grapple with. In this day and age so many have decided that truth is "relative" and that those who advocate for absolutes in truth are "bigots", "overly religious", "politically incorrect", or "socially intolerant". But being one of those "overly religious" persons I would argue that no one really believes that truth is relative. That can be plainly seen the minute someone tells you a lie. Some will argue all day and all night that what is "true" for you may not be "true" for someone else. But the minute you tell someone a lie, suddenly truth is not relative anymore. Truth becomes very important. It can also be said that of all the Ten Commandments, the one that commands, "Thou shalt not lie" is the one that everyone has broken. So when you have lied to someone and they get very angry (and probably very self righteous about it) they are confessing that the notion that truth is relative is really not true. It is still against the law to lie in court, though there are those who do it and get away with it. That is called "testilying". In order for someone to hold you accountable for not telling the truth, they have to abandon the notion that truth is relative. Secondly, we have to consider for a moment on what basis anyone has the right to demand that you tell the truth. Where does anyone come up with the notion that they have the right to demand the truth from anyone? We immediately make a value judgment when we do that. We are saying it is right to tell the truth and wrong to tell a lie.

So let us look at a more complex issue, the notion of good and evil. If we look at this from a Biblical perspective our definition of good is easy. Jesus said it. Only God is good. "And Jesus said unto him, *'Why do you call me good? No one is good but One. That is God'*" (Mark 10:18 NKJV). There it is. From the biblical perspective, only one is good. Only one is perfect. Jesus challenged the man who spoke to him, a Pharisee named Nicodemus who called him good. What Jesus was saying to him was that only God was good, and therefore to call him good was to call him God. Elsewhere Jesus states, *"I and my Father are one"* (John 10:30 NKJV). God is good and God alone is good then God must also be perfect. From a Biblical perspective this is also true. *"Therefore you shall be perfect, just as your Father in heaven is perfect"*

(Mat 5:48 NKJV). From a Biblical perspective, God, personified in his son Jesus Christ, is perfect. In fact, he is the only one who is perfect. If from a biblical perspective the words "good" and "perfect" are synonymous, then the opposite of good, which is evil, is that which is opposite of God, less than perfect.

I think that many might object to that notion. We all know that we are not "perfect" but none of us would want to say that we are "evil". From a Biblical perspective however, this is precisely the case. In Matthew 7:11 Jesus tells us we are evil. How politically incorrect! How insulting! How dare he say such a thing in public!!!!! But then again, someone who is perfect must always speak the truth, however politically incorrect it may be. Something else here is worthy of note. Jesus declared that we are evil but are still capable of doing good. This is perhaps the thing which boggles our minds. We see ourselves in the most positive light because we seem to want to point to the "good" that we do. But from a biblical perspective even what we do that is "good" is far from the standard of perfection that God has established in himself.

In *People of the Lie* written by M. Scott Peck, the author attempts to find a definition for evil. He concludes that there are those in this world who instinctively know what the "public" expects of them and they try very hard to present themselves as being "respectable" people. However, they are deliberately deceiving the "public" and hiding behind a veneer of respectability. They are committing acts that are destructive to the lives of others, while at the same time defending that veneer of respectability with vengeance. In other words they know they are doing something wrong, but they make every effort to persuade the public that they are doing something good, and that if anything bad happens it is not their fault. He cited an example of a politician who had sent his son to him for counseling but really had no real desire for anything good to happen for his son, only to appear himself to be doing the right thing. This, says Peck, is evil.

Most of the time, evil is hiding behind a veneer of respectability. Evil wears a uniform and appears to be a public servant, a professional, even clergy. Evil organizations hide inside respectable organizations as can be clearly seen from the history of MKULTRA which hid its evil agenda inside hospitals, prisons, and even educational institutions. Evil agendas are hidden inside the intelligence community and other government organizations. They are all couched in language that makes them appear to be good. Evil wears a pin stripped suit, carries a briefcase, has a degree in some field of higher education. In fact, evil uses public office to perpetrate its evil agenda, all the while coming off as "respectable". Evil does not parade itself around for exactly what it is because it would be rejected outright, so it has to hide. This too is an aspect of anything evil. It is hiding in darkness. Again Jesus states, "For everyone practicing evil hates the light and does not come into the light, lest his deeds should be exposed" (John 3:20 NKJV). This may easily explain why those of the New World Order hid their evil agenda inside the secretive intelligence community.

So let us go back to our original notion – that there is something called perfection, that we know that nothing in this world measures up to that standard least of all ourselves. So on what basis then do we hold anyone accountable for anything at all. If there were no such thing as "perfection" than our standard would be very arbitrary. We would be always measuring people by ourselves. But we all have different standards. No one is exactly alike. No one demands the same things from everyone. Some of us are more easy going than others and some are very demanding – vigilante types. But if there is no absolute standard, we have no basis to hold anyone accountable for anything. If there is an absolute standard, we have to admit we are not it.

From a Biblical perspective, God is that standard. He is holy, righteous and perfect in all his ways. If he does not exist, then we have nothing left but anarchy to deal with. There is no basis for establishing laws and no basis on which to establish social order. There is no one who has the right to enforce any law on anyone or any basis for readjusting the laws. There is no one who has the right to exert his authority on anyone. In a world where we have rejected the absolute standard established by an absolutely perfect being, the only basis for social order is whoever is big enough and bad enough to force everyone to bend to his will. This is fascism. This is the New World Order.

"Our right lies in force. The word 'right' is an abstract thought and proved by nothing. The word means no more than: Give me what I want in order that thereby I may have a proof that I am stronger than you" Illuminati Protocol 1:13.[196]

13. THE NATIONAL SECURITY ACT OF 1947

The National Security Act was signed into law by Harry S. Truman shortly after WWII in 1947. With it came the formation of the CIA (a combination of the NAZI SS and the U.S. Office of Strategic Services). Many researchers mark the National Security Act as the beginning of the Shadow Government. The Shadow Government consists of the corrupted inner core of Congress, Senate and Executive Branch of the White House, the corrupted inner core of Law Enforcement nationwide, the corrupted inner core of the Military industrial Complex and the intelligence community and the controlling influence of the Eastern Establishment which steers the government from behind the scenes through the Bilderberger Group, the Council of Foreign Relations and the Trilateral Commission. The National Security Act became the virus that corrupted the entire nation and the conduit by which the corruption was spread around the world.

A study conducted by the Church Committee reads,

---

196 Robin de Ruiter, Worldwide Evil and Misery: The Legacy of 13 Satanic Bloodlines (The Netherlands: Myra Publications 2008) 203.

The National Security Act of July 1947 established the CIA as it exists today. Under the Act, the CIA's mission was loosely defined, since any efforts to flesh out its duties in specific terms would have unduly limited the scope of its activities. Therefore, under the Act, the CIA was charged to perform five general tasks. The first is to advise the National Security Council (NSC) on matters relating to national security. The second is to make recommendations to the NSC regarding the coordination of intelligence activities of the various departments. The third duty is to correlate and evaluate intelligence data and provide for its appropriate dissemination. Fourth, the CIA *is* to carry out "service of common concern". Finally, the CIA is authorized "to perform all other functions and duties related to Intelligence affecting the national security as the NSC will from time to time direct…

It is from this final directive that the wide-ranging power to do everything from plotting political assassinations and government overthrows to buying off local newspaper owners and mining harbors has come. The wording of that final directive has allowed presidents of the United States to organize and use secret armies to achieve covertly the policy aims that they are not able to achieve through overt means. It allows presidents both present and future to use the resources of the nation's top intelligence agency as they see fit.[197]

The National security act had the effect of centralizing the government – i.e. removing it from the hands of "We the People". Since the passing of the National Security Act of 1947, more and more power has been concentrated in the federal government while the president enacts laws by presidential orders rather than through the reasoned debate of elected officials. Thus the Act has created a national security state.[198] The National Security Act opened the door for the surveillance of American citizens who might be considered a threat. Problem was that the term "threat" was not clearly defined. The Supplementary Detailed Staff Reports on Intelligence Activities and the rights of Americans Book III final Report of the Select Committee to Study Governmental Operation With Respect To Intelligence Activities Untied States Senate April 23 (Under Authority of the Order of April 14), 1976 states the following;

---

197 United States Senate Select Committee to Study Governmental Operations With Respect to Intelligence Activities (Improper Surveillance of Private citizens by the Military, Supplemental Detailed Staff Reports on Intelligence Activities and the right of Americans, April 23, 1976).

198 Jim Marrs, The Terror Conspiracy: Deception, 9/11 and the Loss of Liberty (New York, NY: Disinformation, 2006) 396.

The National Security Act created the National Security Council which consisted of the President, the Vice President, the secretaries of state and defense. These positions are primarily dominated by members of the Council of Foreign Relations and the Trilateral Commission. The National Security Council dominates the U.S. Policy decision with regard to the use of armed force.[199]

The National Security Act was ostensibly created to protect military secrets, the exposure of which "could reasonably be expected to be detrimental to National Security." However this one piece of legislation has become the smokescreen behind which government entities hide crimes committed against innocent civilians. It does not in fact guard military secrets but shields criminals at the highest levels of government from being prosecuted for their crimes in the name of National Security. Cathy O'Brien writes, "Repeal of this Act and replacement with the established rules of military conduct concerning National Security that do not infringe upon the Constitutional rights of America's citizenry or the rights of its allies would result in compliance with the Constitution."[200]

Cathy O'Brien observes that the National Security Act opened the door for the CIA and others in government to cover up their crimes. Thus they have had card blanch to violate law and rights, practice psychological warfare intimidation tactics on anyone they chose, threaten our lives etc while they remain unaccountable to the law or the people of the United States of America. Keep in mind Cathy O'Brien's father was caught making kiddie porn films. He was not prosecuted because he agreed to cooperate with the CIA in allowing Cathy to become a project Monarch mind control slave. In addition to that he continued to impregnate his wife so those babies could be used for the Project. This is all kept secret under The National Security Act.[201]

14. Operation Mockingbird

In any fascist regime, the press has to be controlled. This is absolutely contrary to the ideals of a democratic nation. John Adams stated, "Liberty cannot be preserved without a general knowledge among the people." Thus, those who oppose liberty must also control the flow of information to the people. One of the key elements in the original Illuminati plan for world domination included controlling the flow of information to the people and censoring the press. Operation

---

199 The Supplementary Detailed Staff Reports on Intelligence Activities and the rights of Americans Book III final Report of the Select Committee to Study Governmental Operation With Respect To Intelligence Activities Untied States Senate April 23 (Under Authority of the Order of April 14), 1976 (http://www.icdc.com)
200 Cathy O'Brien & Mark Phillips, Trance Formation of America (Frankston, Texas: Reality Marketing,1995) 6.
201 Ibid 6, 82.

Mockingbird birthed by the Central Intelligence Agency was that program for controlling the press and destroying its ability to tell you the truth.

In 1948, Frank Wisner was appointed director of the Office of Special Projects (OSP). Soon afterwards OSP was renamed the Office of Policy Coordination (OPC). This became the espionage and counterintelligence branch of the Central Intelligence Agency. During the cold war undercover State Department Official, Frank Wisner, hired foreign students to influence European Labor Unions to combat communism. A short recap might be helpful here. Remember that the CIA was formed after WWII when the Office of Strategic Services combined with the NAZI SS. Also keep in mind that the same people who funded and brought Hitler to power as the leader of a labor union funded and created communism in Russia. Thus these same big business icons working behind the scenes of the United States Government deliberately created the fear of communism in order to manipulate the populace of the United States and other peoples around the world. Frank Wisner later established Mockingbird, a program to influence and control the information published by the press. He recruited Philip Graham publisher of *The Washington Post* and Army Intelligence alumni to run the project within the industry. According to Deborah Davis author of *Katharine the Great*, a book written about the owner of the Washington Post, Wisner "owned" members of the New York Times, Newsweek, CBS and other communications vehicles, in addition to 400 to 600 stringers. Katherine Graham gave a speech to senior CIA employees in 1988 in which she said, "We live in a dirty and dangerous world. There are some things the general public does not and need to know and shouldn't. I believe democracy flourishes when the government can take legitimate steps to keep its secrets and when the press can decide whether to print what it knows". Allen Dulles, Director of the CIA oversaw the network of Mockingbird infected press personnel. Allen Dulles had been a senior partner at the Wall Street firm of Sullivan and Cromwell, which represented the Rockefeller interests and other trusts, corporations, and cartels both German and American. These big business giants wanted their views represented in print.[202]

When Frank Wisner and Philip Graham both committed suicide, Allen Dulles, took over the direction of the operation. By 1955 the propaganda machine consisted of some 25 newspapers and wire agencies that consented to become forums for right wing propaganda. Some of these included William Paley (CBS), C.D. Jackson *(Fortune)*, Henry Luce *(Time)* and Arthur Hays Sulzberger *(N.Y. Times)*. Activists researching Freedom of Information Act (FOIA) documents pertaining to Mockingbird have been shocked to find that the CIA placed operatives inside every major news outlet in the country. In 1982 the CIA admitted for the first time that Journalists paid by the CIA were acting as case officers.[203]

---

202 Mary Louise, Operation Mockingbird: CIA Media PRISON PLANET.com ANALYSIS - http://www.prisonplanet.com).
203 Alex Constantine, Virtual Government (Los Angeles, CA: Feral House,1997) 37.

Henry Luce, owner of Life Magazine displayed his colors when he advocated for the creation of an "American empire" that would dominate the world in political power established through coercion including war or the threat of war "in which one group of people... would hold more than its equal share of power."[204]

Laurence Rockefeller was also instrumental in destroying the integrity of the Reader's Digest magazine. It was once founded by DeWitt Wallace as a tool for global education and uplift. They hired Laurence Rockefeller to protect their legacy but unfortunately he sabotaged and destroyed it instead. The Readers digest has become a propaganda tool in the hands of the CIA.[205]

A full third of the CIA's covert operations budget in the 1950's was dedicated to the propaganda campaign. American taxpayers paid $265 million yearly by 1978 to pay some 3, 000 salaried and contract CIA employees engaged in propaganda efforts. The budget was larger than the combined expenditures of Reuters, UPI and the AP news syndicates. In 1977 the Copely News Service admitted that 23 of its employees were full-time employees of the CIA.[206]

John Swinton, an eminent New York journalist and editor of the New York Times, at a banquet given in his honor in 1953 remarked after someone offered a toast to the independent press,

> *There is no such thing at this date of the world's history, in America, as an independent press. You know it & I know it... The business of journalists is to destroy the truth, to lie outright... We are the tools of rich men behind the scenes. We are jumping jacks, they pull the strings & we dance. Our talents, our possibilities & our lives are all property of other men. We are intellectual 'prostitutes'.*

This program was exposed during the Senate Hearings (Select Committee to Study Governmental Operations with Respect to Intelligence Activities) in 1975 by Frank Church and Otis Pike. The findings of the committee were so devastating that the House refused to release the report until it could be censored. The CIA special council threatened to destroy the careers of Frank Church and Otis pike as a result of the hearings. Thereafter both Frank Church and Otis Pike were defeated in their bids for re-election.[207]

In February 1976, Director of the CIA George H.W. Bush announced, "Effective immediately, the CIA will not enter into any paid or contract relationship with any full time or part-time news correspondent accredited by any U. S. news service, newspaper, periodical, radio or television network or station". He did add

---

204 Alex Constantine, Tales from the Crypt: The Depraved Spires and Moguls of the CIA's Operation Mockingbird (http://www.whatreallyhappened.com).
205 Alex Constantine, Virtual Government (Los Angeles, CA: Feral House,1997) 43.
206 Alex Constantine, Tales from the Crypt: The Depraved Spires and Moguls of the CIA's Operation Mockingbird (http://www.whatreallyhappened.com).
207 Alex Constantine, Virtual Government (Los Angeles, CA: Feral House,1997) 57.

that the CIA would welcome unpaid support of the news media.[208] However, CIA manipulation of the media continues unchecked.

> The ... CIA public affairs director Joseph Detrani ... touted what it saw as the accomplishments of the agency's existing media program. ... "PAO {public affairs office} now has relationships with reporters from every major wire service, newspaper, news weekly and television network in the nation" the report said. "This has helped us turn some 'intelligence failure' stories into 'intelligence success' stories, and it has contributed to the accuracy of countless others. In many instances," the report continues, "we have persuaded reporters to postpone, change, hold or even scrap stories that could have adversely affected national security interests or jeopardized sources and methods."[209]

Occasionally there will be a "leak" to the press and it will appear that the press is exposing some kind of government crime. However, what they actually do is called damage control. When a leak occurs, the press reports just enough information to allow the public to become righteously indignant. The government pretends to do something about it. A lamb may be crucified, such as what happened in the Iran/Contra affair when they decided to crucify Oliver North when in fact he was only one player. The U.S. arms-for-drugs trade kept weapons flowing to the CIA backed CONTRA army and cocaine flowing to U.S. markets. In 1986 the Christic Institute, an interfaith center for law and public policy, exposed the IRAN/CONTRA affair in a lawsuit. Leslie Cockburn published *Out of Control* in 1988 in which she exposed U.S. involvement in drug smuggling. The Washington Post countered by downplaying the charges of conspiracy and put forth false information about the U.S. involvement in drug smuggling presented to the Congress. Congress Committee Chairman Charles Rangel (D-NY) accused the Post of misleading reporting and the Post printed a partial correction and refused to print Congressman Rangel's letter.[210] What gets presented to the public in the damage control campaign is just enough to make the public think that "something was done" and the disinformation continues.

Naomi Wolf noted in her book *The End of America* that fascist dictators are afraid of authors and journalists. They tend to be arrested for ridiculous reasons. The Bush Administration has had several authors and journalists arrested who have published stories and books that are unsupportive of the Bush Administration. The U.S. Government has also published disinformation to distract the public

---

208 Wikipedia, Operation Mockingbird (February 2009- http://en-wikipedia.org).
209 Cheryl Welsh, U.S. Human Rights Abuse Report (Christians Against Mental Slavery, January, 1988 – http://wwww.mindjusttice.org).
210 Julian Holmes, CIA Disinformation in Action, Operation Mockingbird and the Washington Post (Educate Yourself, April 25th, 1992 – http://www.educate-yourself.org).

from the truth. Ms. Wolf noted that one of the reasons that a dictator floods the information highways with deliberate lies in that eventually there are so many untruths being propagated that people get weary trying to discern the truth from a lie. So people give up trying. The truth doesn't matter anymore.[211] Journalists who maintain a standard of integrity may find themselves looking at the world through a set of bars.

15. Mind Control

"We cannot use people as they are, but begin by making them over." Adam Weishaupt

The CIA began its investigation into what they called "behavior modification" when they learned of brainwashing techniques in Korea and the Soviet Union. The project which included some 175 subprojects was started in 1953 by Richard Helms then Director of the CIA and his good friend Psychiatrist Sidney Gottleib. MKULTRA consisted of a number of mind control research projects carried out on unconsenting subjects in 300 colleges, universities, prisons and other places. "The objectives were behavioral control, behavior anomaly production, and countermeasures for opposition application of similar substances. Work was performed at U.S. industrial, academic, and governmental research facilities. Funding was often through cutout arrangements."[212] The files containing the details of the research were destroyed by Richard Helms and Sidney Gottleib shortly before they both retired. The acronym MKULTRA is read by many to be a German acronym standing for "Mind Kuntrol". However, in an affidavit written by former CIA director William Casey, he referred to it as *Manufacturing Killers utilizing Lethal Tradecraft Requiring Assassination.*[213]

Mind control technology was first presented to the US government as a means of controlling the mind of the enemy. There are those in Washington DC with power and wealth to promote their own global agenda. Mind control in the hands of people who have no fear of God, who do not believe that "all men are created equal" and who believe that it is their right to create "a New World Order" or a utopian society have opted to use mind control for other than military concerns. At article by *Whiteout* reveals the stark reality of the CIA experiments and their connections to NAZI Germany.

> The bleak truth is that a careful review of the activities of the CIA and the organizations from which it sprang reveals an intense preoccupation with the development of techniques of

---

211 Naomi Wolf, The End of America (White River Junction, Vermont: Chelsea Green Publishing 2007). 127.
212 Jim Marrs, The Rise of the Fourth Reich (New York, NY: Harper Collins, 2008) 195.
213 Uri Dowbenko, Up Against the Beast, High-level Drug Running (Nexus magazine, 1999 – http://www.whale.to/b/dowbenko.html).

behavior control, brainwashing, and covert medical and psychic experimentation on unwitting subjects including religious sects, ethnic minorities, prisoners, mental patients, soldiers and the terminally ill. The rationale for such activities, the techniques and indeed the human subjects chosen show an extraordinary and chilling similarity to NAZI experiments. This similarity becomes less surprising when we trace the determined and often successful efforts of US intelligence officers to acquire the records of NAZI experiments, and in many cases to recruit the NAZI researchers themselves and put them to work, transferring the laboratories from Dachau, the Kaiser Wilhelm Institute, Auschwitz and Buchenwald to Edgewood Arsenal, Fort Detrick, Huntsville Air Force Base, Ohio State, and the University of Washington.[214]

MKULTRA involved the development of drugs to be used for behavior control which were administered to some subjects who had been misinformed of the project and some who were not asked to be subjects at all. It also involved the use of electrical implants and methodologies for "erasing" the human personality and "reprogramming" that personality to suit the agenda of the CIA. Their stated objectives were to override the human will and even to create a programmed assassin. They also used defenseless children and even infants in their experimenting and deliberately induced multiple personalities in minor subjects using sexual abuse, themes from Walt Disney productions and even religious language to program children to become slaves for the New World Order.

Dr. Carol Rutz author of *A Nation Betrayed* was also a victim of government abuse and mind control experimentation. One of the women that Carol interviewed for her book described "eye experiments" at a residential school. The experiments involved attempts change the eye color of the students at the school. As a child Dr Rutz knew Dr. Joseph Mengele as Dr. Black whose pet project was changing eye color. Dr. Mengele worked alongside Dr. Sidney Gottlieb, Dr. Ewen Cameron and others.[215] Dr. Mengele led the National Socialist Mind control program at the Kaiser-Wilhelm institute in Berlin and also at Auschwitz.[216] He also designed the MKUTRA project MONARCH.[217] Dr. Mengele perfected the "science" of inducing split personalities in children who were the subjects of Project Monarch. He perfected this concept on mass experimentation of inmates in concentration camps in Germany. Jennifer Greene was another one of his victims who changed

---

214 Whiteout, Project Paperclip and the Nuremburg Trials (Whitewash – http://www.bibilotecapleyades.net).
215 Jim Marrs, The Rise of the Fourth Reich (New York, NY: Harper Collins, 2008) 199.
216 Robin de Ruiter, Worldwide Evil and Misery: The Legacy of 13 Satanic Bloodlines (The Netherlands: Myra Publications 2008) 181.
217 Robin de Ruiter, Worldwide Evil and Misery: The Legacy of 13 Satanic Bloodlines (The Netherlands: Myra Publications 2008) 313.

her name to Arizona Wilder when her memories of her controller, Dr. Joseph Mengele, began to surface after his death. Among those who helped Joseph Mengele escape Germany at the end of WWII according to Arizona were the Senior *George* Bush, Henry Kissinger, Dick Cheney, the British royal family, the Rothschilds, and the Rockefellers to name a few.[218]

Dr. Albert Hoffman, a Swiss chemist working in Basal originally discovered the effects of LSD when he accidentally absorbed a chemical derived from the cereal fungus ergot into his fingers. He experienced a state of semi consciousness, kaleidoscope colors and visions. This chemical was being produced at Sandoz laboratories and was known as LSD-25. Psychiatrists began experimenting with this drug and gave it to staff members because they believed it produced a form of psychosis. They thought the doctors and staff taking the drug would be better able to understand the mental states of their patients.[219] The CIA was searching for a drug that would loosen the tongue or a truth drug that could be used during interrogations. Part of the experimentation was an effort to obtain a "truth drug" which was largely unsuccessful. However, cigarettes laced with marijuana had been given to a New York gangster, August Del Grazio, also called "Little Augie" with apparent success. Influenced by the drug, Augie revealed a generous amount of information about organized crime involving high-ranking government officials who took bribes from the mob.[220] The CIA carried out these experiments in collaboration with multiple NAZI scientists that have been given asylum in the United States under Project Paperclip.

The CIA would slip the drug into the drinks of their associates at parties. One of their associates was Dr. Frank Olson who eventually died because of a "bad trip." On November 27th 1953 Dr. Robert Lashbrook slipped 70 micrograms of LSD into Olson's drink at a conference without his knowledge. He shortly began exhibiting symptoms of paranoia and schizophrenia. He became deeply depressed and was taken to see Dr. Abramson for treatment. Later Abramson came to see Olson at his hotel room with a bottle of bourbon and a bottle of Nembutal. This would be an unusual combination for a doctor to give someone with symptoms like Olson's. The following day Olson was scheduled for a trip to Chestnut Lodge of Rockville, Maryland, staffed with psychiatrists with Top Secret CIA clearances. He leaped to his death the night before however through a closed window of the Statler Hilton in New York. Gottlieb and is team were verbally reprimanded for their part in the death of Frank Olson which was covered up for 22 years. In 1994, Forensic scientists exhumed the man's body and fond skull fractures that suggested homicide, rather than an accident.[221]

---

218 David Ike, Tales from the Time Loop, (Ryde, Isle of Wright, UK: David Icke Books, 2003) 281.
219 Jim Marrs, The Rise of the Fourth Reich (New York, NY: Harper Collins, 2008) 195.
220 Jerry E. Smith, HAARP: The Ultimate Weapon of the Conspiracy (Kempton, ILL: Adventures Unlimited Press, 1998) 134.
221 Jim Keith, Mind Control World Control (Kempton, ILL: Adventures Unlimited Press, 1997) 82 – 83.

Dr. Timothy Leary of Harvard University was paid through channels by the CIA to test LSD on prison inmates. This included 18 government grants paid through the National Institute of Mental Health, a CIA front Organization[222] and the Uris Brothers Foundation in New York.[223] The drug was administered to inmates of the Massachusetts Correctional institute at Concord. The results of the experiments were published in a 1962 paper entitled *How to Control Behavior*.[224] Leary was accused by state officials for inciting riots and was eventually fired.[225] It appears that Leary's behavior control techniques needed some tweaking.

Other subjects included 7,000 soldiers located at Edgewood Arsenal in Chesapeake Bay north of Baltimore Maryland between 1944 and 1976, a fact that was kept from the public.[226] These soldiers were told that they would be given drugs and that they would suffer from minor discomfort. They were not told what drugs they would be given and they were not told that several other subjects had died from the experiments. They were ordered to ride exercise bikes wearing oxygen masks while they were sprayed with a variety of hallucinogenic drugs including LSD, Mescaline, BZ and SNA (also known as "angel dust"). The objective of the research was to induce total amnesia which was obtained in many subjects. More than one thousand soldiers sustained serious psychological afflictions and epilepsy and many attempted suicide.[227] One of the soldiers who volunteered for the program wrote to Carol Rutz. He was 18 when he volunteered. He was 49 at the writing of his letter, and he is totally disabled as a result of the experiments. The VA denies culpability in the issue and refuses any assistance.[228]

Theodor Wagner-Jauregg and Freidrich Hoffman were other scientists at Edgewood who were from NAZI Germany. They studied the use of the deadly poison gasses of Abun and Sarin. US soldiers were exposed to these gasses in gas chambers akin to those used the NAZI death camps.[229]

Captain George Hunter White opened a Safe House in San Francisco where prostitutes administered LSD and other more potent drugs to unwitting patrons while White watched behind two way glass mirrors. This was called "Operation Midnight climax". These experiments continued through 1963. He is now famous for a statement that he wrote in a letter to a friend which was later published. He wrote, "I was a very minor missionary, actually a heretic . . . but I toiled wholeheartedly in the vineyards because it was fun, fun, fun. Where else could a

---

222 Alex Constantine, Virtual Government (Los Angeles, CA: Feral House, 1997)110.
223 Jim Keith, Mind Control World Control (Kempton, ILL: Adventures Unlimited Press, 1997) 99.
224 Ibid.
225 Alex Constantine, Virtual Government (Los Angeles, CA: Feral House, 1997)111.
226 Jim Marrs, The Rise of the Fourth Reich (New York, NY: Harper Collins, 2008) 200.
227 Whiteout, Project Paperclip and the Nuremburg Trials (Whitewash – http://www.bibilotecapleyades.net).
228 Jim Marrs, The Rise of the Fourth Reich (New York, NY: Harper Collins, 2008) 200.
229 Ibid.

red-blooded American boy lie, kill, cheat, steal, rape and pillage with the sanction and blessing of the All-Highest?"

Another MKULTRA CIA Psychiatrist was Dr. Ewen Cameron. His research conducted in Canada was funded by the Society for the Investigation of Human Ecology (a rather benign name for an organization that promoted eugenics and mind control for the established elite) to the tune of $60,000. His application for the grant proposed;

> a. The breaking down of ongoing patters of the patient's behavior by means of particularly intensive electroshocks (depatterning).
> b. During this period of intensive repetition the patient is kept in partial sensory isolation.
> c. Repression of the driving period is carried out by putting the patient, after the conclusion of the period, into continuous sleep for 7 – 10 days.[230]

His subjects were often not volunteers. He used "sleep treatment" developed by Hassan Azima and administered Thorazine and barbiturates continuously and put patients to sleep for 20 to 22 hours. He used the British Page-Russell electroconvulsive technique for drug induced coma for weeks and then waking them to administer electroshocks. Cameron's patients were often reduced to vegetables. In one study he placed his patients into sensory deprivation chambers for 65 days, doping them up with LSD and then using "psychic driving" to reprogram them. This involved the use of a repetitive phrase which Cameron acquired during interviews with the patient that contained emotionally charged material. This phrase would be played over and over again through a pillow with unmemorable earphones while the patient was in a drug induced sleep. His research on psychic driving was documented in research papers from 1961 – 1964 called "Study of Factors which Promote or Retard Personality Change in Individuals Exposed to Prolonged Repetition of Verbal Signals," and "The Effects upon Human Behavior of the Repetition of Verbal Signals."[231]

Naomi Kline records the interview of one of Dr. Cameron's victims in her book *Shock Doctrine*. Ms. Klein told Gail Kastner that she had been to Iraq and was writing a book about how the US government is trying to erase people. Gail replied, "You have just spelled out exactly what the CIA and Ewen Cameron did to me. They tried to erase and remake me, and it didn't work." Naomi knocked but the door was unlocked. Gail kept the door unlocked because it was too painful for her to get up to answer it. She sustained multiple tiny fractures down her spine from

---

230 Alfred W. McCoy, A Question of Torture: CIA Interrogation from the Cold War to the War on Terror (New York: Metropolitan Books, Henry Holt and Company, 2006) 43.
231 Jim Keith, Mind Control World Control (Kempton, ILL: Adventures Unlimited Press, 1997) 86.

the sixty-three times that the 150 -200 volts of electricity that shot through the frontal lobes of her brain while her body convulsed violently on the table, causing fractures, sprains bloody lips and broken teeth. Her back grows more painful with each passing day because of the arthritis that sets in. Kastner has no memory now. She keeps her memory in notes written on cardboard cigarette boxes that are piled up on her end table beside her chair.[232]

Cameron's depatterning experiments were about erasing the personalities of his victims and trying to reprogram them. Regression was the key element. Cameron sought to regress the personalities of his patients back to childhood. From that state he began the reprogramming. His patients did often regress. Many became incontinent and some sucked their thumbs. These people often died and many became vegetables.

Dr. Joseph Delgado specialized in the development of mind control devices for implanting in the brain. In the 1950's he locked the head of an animal or a person in a clamp and inserted a long needle into the brain through the skull through which he injected chemicals or electricity. Later "transdermal stimoceivers" or tiny radio broadcasting/receiving units were buried in the brain which carried electrical impulses to the brain, which would broadcast the subjects reactions to a computer. He was able to evoke or inhibit aggression using the implants.[233] Delgado progressed in his research toward the ability to interface the human brain and the computer as a method of behavior control. In this way he was able to override the human will. By destroying the frontal lobes he was further able to eliminate personal control. He was able to identify neuronal functions of the brain involved in spontaneity freedom and individuality and felt that these terms needed to be redefined in more concretely.[234]

Dr. Gordon Thomas, author of *Journey Into Madness, the True Story of CIA Mind Control and Medical Abuse* remarked in his book, "Dr. Gottlieb and behaviorists of ORD [Office of Research and Development], CIA, shared Dr. Jose Delgado's views that the day must come when the technique would be perfected for making not only animals but humans respond to electrically transmitted signals... Like Dr. Delgado (Yale University), the neurosurgeon (Dr. Heath of Tulane University) concluded that ESB [electronic stimulation of the brain] could control memory, impulses, and feelings and could evoke hallucinations as well as fear and pleasure. It could literally manipulate the human will at will."[235]

Dr. Delgado expressed his opinion to congress that it was appropriate to surgically alter someone's brain in order to make them conform. He states, "We

---

232 Naomi Klein, The Shock Doctrine: The Rise of Disaster Capitalism (New York: Metropolitan Books, Henry Holt and Company, 2007) 26 – 27.
233 Jim Keith, Mind Control World Control (Kempton, ILL: Adventures Unlimited Press, 1997) 127.
234 Ibid, 128 – 129.
235 Cheryl Welsh, U.S. Human rights Abuse Report (Christians Against Mental Slavery, January 1998 – http://www.mindjustice.org.).

need a program of psychosurgery for political control of our society. The purpose is physical control of the mind. Everyone who deviates from the given norm can be surgically mutilated. ... Man does not have the right to develop his own mind. ... We must electrically control the brain."[236]

Later Dr. Delgado shifted his research from brain implants to that of manipulating the atmosphere with electromagnetic fields thus electronically stimulating the brain without the use of implants. This kind of research is based on technology developed by Nicola Tesla which has become the foundation for a new breed of weapons called "Directed Energy Weapons" which are wireless and can be used to manipulated the human consciousness as well as all bodily functions. Researchers have found that the so called "UFO" abductions that have been reported by multiple victims have actually been CIA abductions where the victims were being kidnapped for mind control experimentation. Those abductees have found "alien implants" in various parts of their bodies which, having been removed, were found to be similar to those invented by Dr. Delgado in the 1950's.[237]

Dr. Elliot Barker of Oak Ridge Memorial Hospital in Ontario Canada developed a "treatment" that was called Defense Disruptive Therapy. It involved the use of heavy doses of narcotics like LSD, electric shock and physical torture and abuse. Steve Smith was arrested with a friend for stealing a used car from a used car lot. Eventually he ended up being a patient of Dr. Barker. Resistance resulted in Smith being stripped naked, injected and thrown into a cell or a twisted towel wrapped around his throat choking him to an unconscious state. He states, "After a week of this discipline I was a whipped animal, docile and cooperative. I followed Dr. Barker's dictates like a robot.[238] This is precisely the goal of CIA mind control operations – to turn humans into compliant robots. This is, remember, one of the goals of the Bilderbergers.

One of the main goals of the Bilderbergers was to produce a programmed assassin. Sirhan Sirhan, Robert Kennedy's Assassin, was but one such mind control victim. He had been diagnosed as Paranoid Schizophrenic. Dr. Diamond who examined him explained that paranoid schizophrenics do not hypnotize well and Sirhan Sirhan fell easily into a hypnotic trance. Under hypnosis Sirhan kept repeating "PRACTICE, PRACTICE, PRACTICE..." Dr. Diamond asked him what he was practicing. He replied "MIND-CONTROL, MIND-CONTROL, MIND-CONTROL, MIND-CONTROL..." using this repetitive phrase similar to Dr. Cameron's Psychic Driving.[239] A former army intelligence officer Charles McQuiston performed a Psychological Stress Evaluation on Sirhan and stated, "I

---

236 Jerry E. Smith , HAARP: The Ultimate Weapon of the Conspiracy (Kempton, ILL: Adventures Unlimited Press, 1998) 139.
237 Jim Keith, Mind Control World Control (Kempton, ILL: Adventures Unlimited Press, 1997) 279.
238 Alex Constantine, Virtual Government (Los Angeles, CA: Feral House, 1997) 193 – 201.
239 Alex Constantine, Psychic Dictatorship (Portland, OR: Feral House 1995) 12.

believe Sirhan was brainwashed under hypnosis by constant repetition of words like, 'you are nobody, you're nothing, the American dream is gone.'"[240] Other evidence indicates that Sirhan was brainwashed. He disappeared for three months in 1967 and when he returned he displayed a fascination with the occult. A man by the name of Walter Thomas Rathke trained Sirhan to hypnotize himself. McQuiston testified that he believed that Sirhan was programmed to shoot Kennedy.

Michael Sweeney, author of *The Professional Paranoid*, wrote about a man who showed up in a shopping mall with a small arsenal of weapons and ammunition. He was arrested by police. In his pocket were found scribbled notes with messages that were chant like and repetitious. An investigation did not reveal that he had any enemies and when questioned he seemed to lose contact with reality and could remember nothing.[241] The "remembering nothing" part is the whole point of programming a human to do something dirty. They can't remember what they did nor can they remember who programmed them to do it. Dr. George H. Estabrooks informed the Department of Psychology at Colgate University that it was possible to hypnotize a person without his knowledge or consent. He explained that it was possible for an enemy doctor to use hypnosis to control key military officers to follow his orders. He believed that the entire U.S. Army could be easily taken over in this way. Dr. Estabrooks demonstrated this by hypnotizing a military official to be a currier of intelligence documents. Only Dr. Estabrooks and the person who was to be the recipient of the documents could unlock the officials programming. The military official had absolutely no idea of what he was doing nor any memory of the act.[242]

A CIA memo uncovered in the investigation conducted by the Senate Hearing in 1975 stated the purpose of the project "to develop a capability in the covert use of biological and chemical materials… this field of covert … warfare gives us a thorough knowledge of the enemy's theoretical potential, ***thus enabling us to defend ourselves against a foe who might not be as restrained in the use of these techniques as we are***" [emphasis mine].[243] The CIA included in their MKULTRA project experiments with biological agents – disease. The US Army and US Navy experimented on human subjects using disease including swine fever, dingy fiver, and other deadly diseases. The CIA also gave whooping cough to all the children in a particular neighborhood. They placed light bulbs in the subway that gave people vertigo, and too bad if the children died or if someone fainted and fell on the train tracks.[244] Their

---

240 Ibid, 18.
241 H. Michael Sweeney, The Professional Paranoid, (Venice, CA: Feral House, 1998) 123.
242 Jerry E. Smith , HAARP: The Ultimate Weapon of the Conspiracy (Kempton, ILL: Adventures Unlimited Press, 1998) 128, 129.
243 United States Senate Ninety-Fourth Congress Hearings Before the Senate Select Committee to Study Governmental Operations With Respect to Intelligence Activities [Online] // - AARC Public Digital Library. -1976. - August 15, 2009. - http://www.aarchlibrary.org.
244 John Stockwell, The Praetorian Guard: America's Role in the New World Order (Boston, MA: South End Press, 1991) 98.

stated purpose, remember, was, "…enabling us to defend ourselves against a foe who might not be as restrained in the use of these techniques as we are". ?????!!!!!

The atrocities being committed by the CIA on human victims caught the attention of John K. Vance who acted as a translator at the Nuremburg trials. Vance, a graduate of Columbia University stumbled upon MKULTRA in the spring of 1963 while working on an inspector general's survey of the CIA's technical services division. Vance concluded his investigation with the statement, "The concepts involved in manipulating human behavior are found by many people both within and outside the agency to be distasteful and unethical." The upshot of Vance's discovery and the resulting report was that the agency began cutting back on the project which was supposedly to have ended in the 1960s.[245]

Alan W. Scheflin and Edward M. Opton, Jr. in their book "The Mind Manipulators" reviewed ten thousand pages of formerly Top Secret U.S. Army and CIA documents which revealed 25 years of the most extensive mind manipulation program in the history of the world conducted by U. S. Government agencies. This involved unwitting U.S. citizens as subjects used in experiments by psychologists, psychiatrists, physicians, prison officials, scientists, lawyers and politicians in public institutions such as universities, hospital laborites, mental institutions, medical offices, prisons and schools.[246] Much of the documentation was destroyed by Sydney Gottleib and his associates but what remained is quite revealing.

There has been mind control experimentation going on in the United States for 50 years and it has been covered up by our government "for reasons of national security". Publication of the documents found during the investigation revealed that those involved in the experiments knew that what they were doing was "distasteful and unethical". Sidney Gottleib throughout his proposal for the projects used the term "completely deniable" when describing the research. He states "Agency sponsorship of sensitive research projects will be **completely deniable**." And "…safe clinical conditions using materials with any Agency connection [that] must be **completely deniable** will augment and complement other programs recently taken over by TSS, such as [deletion]."[247]

Christina Welsh, President of Christians against Mental slavery notes that the CIA chose to cover up the research of MKULTRA even after the investigation revealed the extent of the atrocities committed by the CIA. The CIA's secrecy was also clearly aimed at the folks back home. As a 1963 Inspector General's report stated,

---

245 Jim Marrs, The Rise of the Fourth Reich (New York, NY: Harper Collins, 2008) 202.
246 Cheryl Welsh, U.S. Human rights Abuse Report (Christians Against Mental Slavery, January 1998 – http://www.mindjustice.org).
247 Shaffer Library of Drug Policy, Project MKUTRA: The CIA's Program of Research in Behavior Modification (Senate MKULTERA Hearing Appendix C, May 1 1953 - http://www.druglibrary.org).

Research into the manipulation of human behavior is considered by many authorities in medicine and related fields to be "professionally unethical"; therefore, openness would "put in jeopardy "the reputations of the outside researchers. Moreover the CIA Inspector General declared that disclosures of certain MKULTRA activities could result in "serious adverse reaction" among the American public.[248]

Because of the 1977 Church Committee investigation the CIA abandoned military instillations and laboratories for fear of exposure. They were ordered to stop but they did not. Their mind control simply moved into local commutes in cities across the country. One of their projects was the People's Temple run by Jim Jones whom researchers into CIA mind control have concluded was a CIA operative.

The People's Temple was moved from its location in the United States to Jonestown Guyana to cover its operation from prying eyes. The camp was 90% women and 80% black. They existed in slave labor conditions working up to 18 hours a day and were fed very little. "When Black members of the Temple arrived from the United States, they were bound and gagged before being taken to the compound. Once inside Jonestown, perceived infractions led to forced drugging, public rape, torture, and beatings." The Jonestown compound was guarded by all white males who were permitted to come and go as they pleased and were allowed to carry money. Some of them were mercenaries who had worked in Africa. The guards survived the Jonestown tragedy[249]. Elmer and Dianne Mertle, who had been blackmailed into joining the cult, were Jim Jones public relations officers. They left the group in 1975, changed their names to Al and Jeannie Mills and founded the "Concerned Relatives" support group and the Human Freedom Center in Berkley for those who survived the cult. Russell Taarg was their director. He was providing therapy though he was a physicist and not a psychologist or psychiatrist. Taarg was also employed by the CIA in their remote viewing program. Shortly after Taarg resigned from the center the Mills were assassinated. Witnesses say that they were assassinated by a therapist who used to work there.[250]

Al and Jeannie, however, were instrumental and persuading Congressman Leo Ryan to investigate the CIA ties to the cult. Unfortunately Congressman Ryan was murdered during his trip to Guyana along with 1,200 murder victims of Jonestown. In November of 1974 the U.S. Senate formed a Subcommittee on Constitutional Rights, one of whose members was Congressman Leo Ryan. He began investigation into federal funding of behavior modification programs.

---

248 Cheryl Welsh, U.S. Human rights Abuse Report (Christians Against Mental Slavery, January 1998 – http://www.mindjustice.org).
249 Jim Keith, Mind Control World Control (Kempton, ILL: Adventures Unlimited Press, 1997) 182.
250 Alex Constantine, Virtual Government (Los Angeles, CA: Feral House, 1997) 115.

Senator Sam Erwin, who headed the subcommittee, after interrogation of the head of the LEAA, Donald E. Santarelli, about the kind of projects that were being funded, announced that the organization would discontinue providing cash for psychosurgery and other forms of mind control. However, the CIA persisted. Subsequent to Leo Ryan's death, his aide, Joe Holsinger, exposed the formation of eccentric religious cults by the CIA. Joseph Holsinger had received an essay in the mail entitled *The Penal Colony* written by a Berkeley psychologist who indicated that the CIA had shifted its programs from public institution to private cult groups including the People's Temple rather than terminating MKULTRA experiments. Dr. Lawrence Laird Layton who was Chief of Chemical and Ecological Warfare Research at the Dugway proving grounds in Utah was the chief impetus behind the Johnstown project. His father in law had connections to the I.G. Farben and his Son in Law to the CIA.[251] Michael Meyers, author of *Was Jonestown a CIA Medical Experiment?*, researched The People's Temple for six years, concluding: "The Jonestown experiment was conceived by Dr. Lawrence Laird Layton, staffed by Dr. Layton and financed by Dr. Layton. It was as much his project as it was Jim Jones."[252] Dr. Layton's son Larry led the assault that murdered Congressman Leo Ryan. The African American cult had a Caucasian inner circle composed of Dr. Layton's family and in laws.[253]

Survivors of the Guyana experiments were able to determine that Jim Jones was an employee or operative of the CIA from 1963 until 1978. 1963 was the year the CIA turned to concealing MKULTRA mind control activity.

In October 1981 Johnstown survivors filed a $63 million dollar lawsuit in a US District Court in San Francisco against Secretary of State Cyrus Vance and former Director of the CIA, Stansfield Turner.

> The suit stated that the State Department and the CIA conspired to "enhance the economic and political powers of James warren Jones," conducting "mind-control and drug experimentation …." The suit was dismissed four months later for "failure to prosecute timely". All requests for appeal denied.[254]

Other mind control cults included The Process group founded by Robert DeGriffin Moore and the Final Church formed by Charles Manson. Both of these men had connections to CIA mind control specialists.[255] Of course these groups

---

251 Jim Keith, Mind Control World Control (Kempton, ILL: Adventures Unlimited Press, 1997) 181.
252 Robert A. Sterling, A Konformist Special: The Jonestown Genocide (The Konformist - http://www.io.com).
253 Alex Constantine, Psychic Dictatorship (Portland, OR: Feral House, 1995) 190.
254 Robert A. Sterling, A Konformist Special: The Jonestown Genocide (The Konformist - http://www.io.com).
255 Jim Keith, Mind Control World Control (Kempton, ILL: Adventures Unlimited Press, 1977).

were publically exposed as was the Jonestown group. The CIA had to find a way to further move their mind control agenda out into the wider community while concealing their intentions and methods.

16. Spying on America and American Police State Part I

Historically speaking, the "elite" have been grossly guilty of spying on Americans. They typically use the catch all excuse that it is in the interests of National Security. Of course using very loosely defined terms they could justify any kind of spying anywhere at any time.

During the Watergate Scandal, Hale Boggs was investigating Operation Octopus, a surveillance program from 1948 that turned any TV set into a transmitter with a 25 mile range. Boggs disappeared in the midst of his investigation. During the Nixon Administration the Office of Science and Technology made a recommendation to use TV sets for surveillance tools equipped with devices that would allow the government to remotely turn them on at will. Congressman William Moorhead nixed the project.[256] The Nixon administration persisted. The Law Enforcement Assistant Administration [LEAA], an arm of the U.S. Justice Department, met with Richard Nixon and various White House officials to discuss the development of a National Population Surveillance Computer System, for the purpose of monitoring American citizens and creating a national police force.[257] The plans were drawn up to merge police with the military and the National Guard. That year Senator Sam Ervin who headed a subcommittee on constitutional rights discovered that military intelligence had established a surveillance system capable of spying on thousand of American citizens who were mostly anti war protesters. It was code named Garden Plot (for controlling the people) and Cable Splicer (for controlling the government) and covered the states of California, Oregon, Washington and Arizona under the command of the Sixth Army. It was a plan adapted from procedures used in Viet Nam to dispel civil unrest. Rep. Clair Burgener of California and Subcommittee Chief Counsel Doug Lee after reviewing Cable Splicer training material determined that is was a plan for a takeover.[258] Another program for spying on Americans was Operation Shamrock which was uncovered in 1975 by the Senate Select Committee to Study Governmental Operations with Respect to Intelligence Activities, chaired by Idaho democrat Frank Church. President Lyndon Johnson and Richard Nixon used the NSA to gather files on thousands of American citizens and more than 1000 organizations mostly involved in protesting the Viet Nam war. The NSA collected nearly all international telegrams sent from New York. In 1945 the NSA,

---

256 Alex Constantine, Virtual Government (Los Angeles, CA: Feral House1997) 51.
257 Jim Keith, Mind Control World Control (Kempton, ILL: Adventures Unlimited Press, 1997) 111.
258 Jim Marrs, The Terror Conspiracy: Deception, 9/11 and the Loss of Liberty (New York: Disinformation, 2006) 269 - 270.

with the approval of President Harry S. Truman and Secretary of Defense James Forrestal, persuaded RCA Communications, Western Union, and ITT World Communications to hand over records of all incoming and outgoing international telephone calls and telegrams. The chief executives of these companies agreed to participate after they were reassured that they would be exempt from criminal liability or public exposure.[259]

In an operation called Minaret, the FBI submitted names of American citizens to the NSA that were considered a threat to state security which gave them information it had gleaned in the Shamrock data mining operation. The list of names included leftists and businessmen who had dealings with Cuba and progressed to include antiwar and civil rights activists. Some of them were Dr. Martin Luther King, Jr., Jane Fonda, Joan Baez, Dr. Benjamin Spock, and the Reverend Ralph Abernathy. Minaret was also exposed during the Church Committee review. President Ford, Donald Rumsfeld and Dick Cheney, clearly overstepping the bounds of executive authority, told the companies that were involved in Minaret not to show up for the hearings. However New York Representative Bella Abzug prevailed and these companies eventually had to show up for the hearings to testify and submit documentation of their involvement. During the hearings the Director of the CIA William Colby inadvertently informed the committee of the NSA surveillance of international communications. President Gerald Ford killed the Minaret program.[260]

A report issued April 23rd, 1976 by the Select Committee to Study Governmental Operations revealed that the United States Intelligence Committee and the United States Military had been involved in improper surveillance of private citizens and private organizations. The report which can be found on the web at http://www.icdc.com revealed the following;

> 1. Improper collection of information about the political activities of private citizens and private organizations in the late 1960s.
> 2. Monitoring of private radio transmissions in the United States. Section 605 of the Communications Act of 1934 prohibits anyone from intercepting and publishing the content of a private radio transmission. Despite this statutory prohibition the Army Security Agency, primarily a foreign intelligence-gathering agency, monitored and recorded domestic radio transmissions of U.S. citizens on six occasions in the late 1960s.
> 3. Investigations of private organizations considered "threats," by the military. ~ Although they are not expressly authorized by law, each of the military services investigates civilian groups, both within and without the United States, which it considers "threats" to its personnel, installations, and operations.

---

259 Tim Shorrock, Spires for Hire: The Secret World of Intelligence Outsourcing (New York: Simon & Schuster, 2008) 317.
260 Ibid, 319

4. Assisting Law Enforcement agencies in surveilling private citizens and organizations. - The Posse Comitatus Act (18 U.S.C. 1385) prohibits the military from "executing the law." Nevertheless, military intelligence has frequently provided assistance to civilian Law Enforcement agencies. In Chicago during the late 1960s, military intelligence agents turned over their files on civilians and civilian organizations to the Chicago police, were invited to participate in police raids, and routinely exchanged intelligence reports with the police. In Washington, D.C. Army intelligence participated in an FBI raid in a civilian rooming house and provided funds for the police department's intelligence division.

In 1971 the Department of Defense argued before congress that preemptive collection of intelligence data on civilian persons and organizations would be implied by sections 331-334 of title 110 of the United States Code in order to prevent insurrection. The Senate Subcommittee on Constitutional Rights rejected this assertion because it was unwilling to grant authority to DOD for political surveillance of civilians in the event of civil disturbances. It in essence determined that civil authorities should have the responsibility for gathering information on pending civil disturbances. It particularly stressed that the military *did not have the authority* to gather information on how American citizens exercised their First Amendment rights.

In March 1971, during congressional hearings on the Army's civil disturbance collection program, the Department of Defense announced the issuance of a new directive which as a matter of policy, prohibited the collection of any information whatsoever on "unaffiliated" persons and organizations, except for limited "military" purposes. It established that any information the military collected would not be through direct surveillance of civilians and organizations but would be obtained through liaison with Law Enforcement. It required the destruction of all current collection material held by the DOD that was found to violate the provision of the directive. Though the DOD Directive 5200.27 does prohibit the collection of intelligence pertaining to civilians and civilian organizations, loopholes are present with ambiguous terms so that "future surveillance activities in the civilian community might be undertaken consistent with the directive." The directive did not include a prohibition of surveillance of American citizens traveling or living in foreign countries.

Article IV, Section 4 of the United States Constitution provides that "the United States shall ... protect each [State] ... against domestic violence." In 1975 Congress passed a statute to implement Article IV, Section 4 which has been amended but still allows the President to use the militia of any state or the Armed Forces to "suppress insurrection."

In 1975, Senator Frank Church, who headed the Church Committee in charge of the senate hearings on improper surveillance of American citizens warned, "...

[the NSA] capability at any time could be turned around on the American people and no American would have any privacy left, such as the capability to monitor everything: telephone conversations, telegrams, it doesn't matter. There would be no place to hide."

President Ford issued an executive order in 1976 which prohibited the NSA from intercepting domestic telephone calls and telegrams. In 1978 Congress passed FISA, the Foreign Intelligence Surveillance Act, limiting NSA to spying only on foreign powers or their agents, including those engaged in terrorist activities. In order to surveil American citizens or foreigners living in the United States the government is supposed to apply to the FISA court for approval.[261]

COINTELPRO

J. Edgar Hoover became director of the Bureau of Investigation on May 10th, 1924. The Bureau of Investigation was later to become the FBI in 1935. He remained director until his death in 1972. While he was in charge of the FBI he executed a reign of terror in the United States by instituting what became known as the *Counter Intelligence Program*, or COINTELPRO. The stated purpose of COINTELPRO was to expose, disrupt, misdirect, discredit, or otherwise neutralize political dissidents. Political dissidents were defined as anyone who opposed government policy of any kind such as anti-war protesters, civil rights groups such as Martin Luther King's Southern Christian Leadership Conference, or other groups perceived as "hate groups" such as the Black Panthers. The American Socialist Party and the American Communist Party which were seen as threats to democracy were also targeted. The Democratic National Convention was also a target. Even though these groups were acting within the law of the United States and were not actually doing anything but exercising their rights to free speech, they were targeted by the FBI for harassment.

The COINTELPRO program was exposed to the public when anonymous persons broke into the FBI station at Media Pennsylvania and confiscated FBI COINTELPRO documents and handed them over the press. Carl Stern, a reporter for NBC invoked the Freedom of Information Act (FOIA) and filed a lawsuit against the FBI forcing them to release other documents related to COINTELPRO. The FBI decided to terminate COINTELPRO on April 27th 1971.[262] More than 20,000 pages of Bureau documents, depositions of many of the Bureau agents involved in the programs, and interviews of several COINTELPRO targets included information on more than 2,000 approved COINTELPRO actions. The investigation revealed the consequences of a government agency's

---

261 Tim Shorrock, Spires for Hire: The Secret World of Intelligence Outsourcing (New York: Simon & Schuster, 2008) 319 – 320.
262 Paul Wolf, Transcriber, COINTELPRO: The FBI's Covert Action Against American Citizens (Final Report of the Select Committee to Study Government Operations Book III April 23rd 1976 – http://www.icdc.com).

decision to take the law into its own hands based on its own perceived role for the "greater good" of the country. Tactics that were used were covert – in other words were designed to protect the perpetrators of their crimes from exposure. COINTELPRO tactics included planting fake evidence to implicate innocent persons and sending bogus letters accusing them of adultery deliberately intending to ruin their marriages. One letter called Martin Luther King an evil immoral beast and suggested he kill himself. Other tactics included exposing target's sexually transmitted diseases, and planting articles in the paper with slanderous material.[263] J. Edgar Hoover had a nasty habit of blackmailing anyone who opposed him or the established elite. He did not therefore favor President Kennedy, an honest man who was attempting to faithfully execute his duties and responsibilities as President elect of the United States of America. Hoover kept files on senators and congressman and any important person in Washington. Anyone who dared to cross him or investigate him would be threatened with exposure.[264]

There were several groups that were targeted including the Democratic Party, "black nationalist hate groups", the Communist Party USA, the Socialist Workers Party, Student Groups, Antiwar Protestors, groups such as Committee in Solidarity with People of El Salvador (CISPES) which opposed the US policies in South America. Any person who opposed the current administration was open to being targeted. The clearest examples of actions directly aimed at the exercise of constitutional rights are those targeting speakers, teachers, writers or publications, and meetings or peaceful demonstrations. Approximately 18 percent of all approved COINTELPRO proposals fell into these categories.[265] The Southern Christian Leadership Conference was identified as a "black nationalist hate group." These groups were targeted because of their "propensity for violence" or their "radical or revolutionary rhetoric [and] actions . . ." Revolutionary was defined as advocacy of the overthrow of the government. Field offices were directed "to exploit conflicts within and between groups; to use news media contacts to disrupt, ridicule, or discredit groups; to preclude "violence-prone" or "rabble rouser" leaders of these groups from spreading their philosophy publicly; and to gather information on the "unsavory backgrounds" ~ immorality, subversive activity, and criminal activity— of group members.[266]

---

263 Naomi Wolf, The End of America: Letter of Warning to a Young Patriot (White River Junction, Vermont: Chelsea Green Publishing, 2007) 85.
264 John Stockwell, The Praetorian Guard: America's Role in the New World Order (Boston, MA: South End Press,1991) 122.
265 Paul Wolf, Transcriber, COINTELPRO: The FBI's Covert Action against American Citizens (Final Report of the Select Committee to Study Government Operations Book III April 23rd 1976 – http://www.icdc.com).
266 UNITED STATES SENATE SELECT COMMITTEE TO STUDY GOVERNMEN ACTIVITIESTAL OPERATIONS WITH RESPECT TO INTELLIGENCE ACTIVIEIES, Improper Surveillance of Private Citizens by the Military, Arpil 23, 1976 – http://www.idcd.com).

The non-violent Southern Christian Leadership Conference was a concern to the FBI because of "communist infiltration". George C. Moore wrote in a memo, "As far as I know, there were not any violent propensities, except that I note ... in the cover memo [expanding the program] or somewhere, that they mentioned that if Martin Luther King decided to go a certain way, he could cause some trouble....".[267] The FBI plotted to drive King to suicide. They wanted to replace him with conservative Black lawyer Samuel Pierce (later named to Reagan's cabinet).[268] Agents' reports indicate that such FBI intervention denied Martin Luther King, Jr., and other 1960s activists any number of foundation grants and public speaking engagements.[269] Martin Luther King was planning a march on Washington in April 1968 in which he planned to bring the Nation's poor to the Capital in a massive protest demonstration. Dr. King was assassinated in Memphis on April 4th. Rioting erupted subsequently in Washington D.C.

One group targeted was the American Indian Movement (AIM) from South Dakota. The AIM group was protesting the massacre at Wounded Knee. The FBI's goal was to disrupt and discredit this group and to portray them as savages. The FBI waged a war against AIM from 1973 to 1976 killing 69 residents of the Pine Ridge reservation. The government also launched a program of psychological warfare to justify the mass murder. Their cruelty had no bounds. The FBI undercover operatives framed AIM members Paul "Skyhorse" Durant and Richard "Mohawk" Billings for the brutal murder of a Los Angeles taxi driver. The FBI pinned a bogus note from AIM taking credit for the murder and included a bundle of the victims hair pined to a signpost near the murder sight. The defendants were finally cleared of the spurious charges, but AIM lost financial support of many of its backers and its work among a major urban concentration of Native people was in ruin.[270]

The FBI had also infiltrated this group. In March 1975, it was discovered that AIM's national security chief, Doug Durham, was an undercover operative for the FBI. He regularly participated in strategy sessions with the FBI. He confessed to stealing organizational funds and set up the arrest of AIM persons for actions that he had organized. He authored documents that the FBI used as evidence to demonstrate the group's supposed violent tendencies.[271]

The FBI, state and local police attempted to crush this organization by murdering its leaders and members or sapping the organization of energy with continuous indictments on fabricated charges. "Russell Means has endured 13

---

267 Paul Wolf, Transcriber, COINTELPRO: The FBI's Covert Action against American Citizens (Final Report of the Select Committee to Study Government Operations Book III April 23rd 1976 – http://www.icdc.com).

268 Brain Glick, The War at Home: Covert Action Against U.S. Activists and What We Can do About It. (Boston, MA: South End Press, 1989) 16.

269 Ibid, 49.

270 Ibid, 22.

271 Ibid.

trials, and over thirty indictments, been shot twice and stabbed twice, and served time for a conviction on a phony riot charge; Clyde Bellecourt has been indicted 42 times". Multiple members such as Leonard Peltier, Dick Marshall, Ted Means and hundreds of others became political prisoners serving time on trumped up charges.[272]

Supposedly the Ku Klux Klan was a "white hate group" targeted by the FBI and infiltrated for the purpose of deterring violence. On December 19th, 1967, J. Edgar Hoover drafted a letter to Attorney General Ramsey Clark with a CC to Deputy Attorney General Warren Christopher pertaining to the FBI's KU Klux Klan COINTELPRO in which he states ". . . we conduct intelligence investigations with the view toward Infiltrating the Ku Klux Klan with informants, neutralizing it as a terrorist organization and deterring violence". There was no record of any reply to this letter and Clark did not remember ever receiving it. In addition he felt that such a program was criminal. He stated, "I think that any disruptive activities such as those you reveal regarding the COINTEL program and the Ku Klux Klan should be absolutely, prohibited and subjected to criminal prosecution."[273]

Brian Glick, however, reveals in *The War at Home*, that the Ku Klux Klan was actually on the FBI payroll. The FBI supplied intelligence information to the Klan so that they were able to brutalize freedom riders when they arrived at various places down south. Gary Thomas was the FBI operative that shot Viola Liuzo in 1963. He helped with the bombing that resulted in the deaths of four black children at a Birmingham Alabama church also in 1963. In 1965, 20% of the Kan members were on the FBI payroll and many had positions of power. FBI had positions of leadership in seven of fourteen groups and even started a splinter group that grew to nearly 200 members.[274] The Klan received only token harassment from the FBI so long as they cooperated in targeting FBI designated COINTELPRO groups.[275]

Since it was widely know that the government has informants literally "behind every bush" one of the covert tactics used to discredit a targeted leader of a targeted group is to spread rumors that the party is actually a government informant. This is called a snitch jacket. This can create distrust within a group and resulted in two persons actually being murdered by their own group members. This also has the effect of distracting attention from the party who is really the government informant. Although Bureau witnesses stated that they did not authorize a "snitch jacket" when they had information that the group was *at that time* actually

---

272 Michael Garitty, The U.S. Colonial Empire is as close as the Nearest Reservation: The Pending Energy Wars (book section, Trilateralism: Elite Planning For World Management, Holly Sklar Editor, Boston, 1980) 261.

273 Paul Wolf, Transcriber, COINTELPRO: The FBI's Covert Action against American Citizens (Final Report of the Select Committee to Study Government Operations Book III April 23rd 1976 – http://www.icdc.com).

274 Brain Glick, The War at Home: Covert Action against U.S. Activists and What We Can do About It. (Boston, MA: South End Press, 1989) 60.

275 Ibid,13.

killing suspected informants, they admitted that the risk was there whenever the technique was used. "It would be fair to say there was an element of risk there which we tried to examine on a case by case basis." Moore added, "I am not aware of any time we ever labeled anybody as an informant, that anything [violent] ever happened as a result, and that is something that could be measured." When asked whether that was luck or lack of planning, he responded, "Oh, it just happened that way, I am sure." However, there was indication that labeling someone a "snitch jacket" did result in the loss of life. One Bureau document stated that the Black Panther Party "has murdered two members it suspected of being police informants" (memorandum from FBI Headquarters to Cincinnati Field Office, 2/18/71).[276]

The 1960's program coordinated by the FBI was exposed in the 1970's and supposedly stopped, but covert operations against domestic dissidents have persisted and become an integral part of government activity justified as a means to combat terrorism and protect "national security". However, says Brian Glick, "They actually serve to foment violence and subvert democracy."[277]

17. Nothing Impossible

At the plane of Shinar the people of the earth all gathered together after the flood, determined to make a name for themselves and build a tower "to the heavens" to keep them from being scattered over all the earth.

> Now the whole world had one language and a common speech. As men moved eastward, they found a plain in Shinar and settled there. They said to each other, "Come, let's make bricks and bake them thoroughly." They used brick instead of stone, and tar for mortar. Then they said, "Come, let us build ourselves a city, with a tower that reaches to the heavens, so that we may make a name for ourselves and not be scattered over the face of the whole earth." But the Lord came down to see the city and the tower that the men were building. ***The Lord said, "If as one people speaking the same language they have begun to do this, then nothing they plan to do will be impossible for them.*** Come, let us go down and confuse their language so that they will not understand each other." So the Lord scattered them from there over all the earth, and they stopped building the city. That is why it was called Babel -- because there the Lord confused the

---

276 Paul Wolf, Transcriber, COINTELPRO: The FBI's Covert Action against American Citizens (Final Report of the Select Committee to Study Government Operations Book III April 23rd 1976 – http://www.icdc.com).

277 Brain Glick, The War at Home: Covert Action against U.S. Activists and What We Can do About It. (Boston, MA: South End Press, 1989) 6.

language of the whole world. From there the Lord scattered them over the face of the whole earth. (Genesis 11:1-9 NIV).

God made an awesome statement about mankind that day. God Almighty indicated that with man all things could be possible. In other words, God indicated that there was nothing he could do that man would not sooner or later figure out how to do. I often wondered why God saw this as a bad thing. One day, it dawned on me. We know that with God nothing is impossible. That is a good thing because "nothing impossible" kind of power in the hands of a Holy God means good things for his creation. But "nothing impossible" kind of power in the hands of corrupted human beings can only mean one thing, - the inevitable probability of unmitigated evil.

You have heard it said before that every action begins with a thought. Thoughts and ideas are the precursors to the development of modern technology. Machines were designed without brains or thoughts or consciences, but those that designed them had thoughts and ideas which go well beyond how to make the machine work. Scientists developed amazing things which they all perceived on some level to do something good for humanity. Some of those scientists might actually intend good, really good things out of their inventions. But far too many have thoughts behind their ideas and inventions that are created for the good of someone, but not necessarily for the good of all humanity. Those who have submitted their ideas and inventions to the will of the Almighty might be trusted to do some good. But there are far too many with no fear of God, or who have indeed created a god in their own image who they can manipulate like they manipulate their inventions for their own purposes. Psalms 14:1 says, "The fool has said in his heart, 'There is no god'. They are corrupt. They have done abominable works; there is none who does well" (NKJV). So the inventions of those who have no fear of God are corrupt, vile and used for corrupted purposes.

It is interesting for me to ponder the tree in the midst of the Garden of Eden which Adam and Eve were not to eat. The question of course is why he put it there if he didn't want them to eat of it. The answer is obvious to most evangelicals. God gave man a free will. He created us for relationship with himself. We had no choice about coming into being. We could not choose who our creator was. We had no say in the creation of the world. We were created for God by God for relationship with God. Have you ever thought about what it would be like to have a loving relationship with a robot? How would it be to have a relationship with a being that always does exactly what you want it do without question. It has no thoughts or designs of its own. It is a complete mirror of you. That is not exactly what God wanted. So he endowed his creation with a will. That is he gave us the ability to choose to do something other than obey him, love him, serve him and have relationship with him. We could choose him or not choose him. Ironically because human beings often throughout history and in this present day have chosen to do evil things which bring harm to others, we have questioned the goodness of God. In these pages I discuss how men and women have decided to create machines that will remove from mankind that thing which God gave them – the will. This is evil, and the logical progression of what happens in a society that ultimately rejects God. Somebody has to be in control. So when we ask, "Why does God allow bad things to happen?" we have to stop and think of what it would take for God to completely stop people from doing evil things. He would have to do what science has now chosen to do – annihilate the human will and force people into subjection. Instead he sent his son to the cross to die. He would rather die himself than make us all into slaves. There is joy in this thought. When we see what mankind has done with his "knowledge of good and evil", we realize that God in the end will be vindicated. When it is all done, and those who opposed God are finally defeated, no one will be left to question the goodness of God.

18. Directed Energy Weapons

On July 30th, 1908 a terrible catastrophe occurred in Siberia near the Stony River in Tunguska. "An explosion estimated to be the equivalent to 10 –15 megatons of TNT flattened 500,000 acres of pine forest . . . whole herds of reindeer were destroyed, and several nomadic villages were reported to have vanished. The explosion was heard over a radius of 620 miles". An investigation of the blast in 1927 did not reveal any evidence that the blast was caused by a meteor crash. There were no craters, no iron, stone or nickel down to 118 feet below the surface of the earth that would be typical of a meteor crash. However, several thousands of miles away on Long Island New York, Nikola Tesla was known to be attempting to demonstrate his wireless electromagnetic weapon "capable of releasing a destructive force of 10 megatons or more of TNT." Evidence indicates that it was his experiment that caused the catastrophe as he had both the capacity and the motive. It is believed that he was actually aiming for an uninhabited portion of the North Pole and did not intend harm. He simply missed his target.[278] Nikola Tesla was a frustrated genius and way ahead of his time. His research formed the basis of what are called Directed Energy Weapons (DEW) today.

We can all remember movies in which we watched someone get blasted with a "death ray." Star Wars and Star Trek all had amazing devices that could deter or destroy an enemy with an electrical ray. That is all science fiction according to Wikipedia. The definition of DEW according to Wikipedia is as follows,

> Directed-Energy Weapon refers to a type of weapon that emits energy in a particular direction by a means other than a projectile. It transfers energy to a target for a desired effect. Some of these

---

[278] Oliver Nicholson, Nichola Tesla's Radient energy System (Brooklyn Eagel,1995 – http://skepticsfiles.org).

weapons are real or practicable; some are science fiction. The energy is in various forms. Electromagnetic radiation (typically lasers or masers)... Particle with mass (particle beam weapons)... Fictional weapons often use some sort of radiation or energetic particle that does not exist in the real world.[279]

In 1908, the wireless device that evaporated 500,000 acres of forest, entire herds of reindeer and several nomadic villages was not science fiction. Scientists have been developing wireless DEW since before 1908 and today they can do amazing things... all from a distance... without leaving any evidence. They can do more than destroy things. They can direct and control things like your car, your mind and even the weather.

Nikola Tesla's work was not appreciated here in the United States, so he took his work overseas to Germany. The Germans were very interested in his work and so were the Soviets – both of whom got their hands on his notes after his death. The U.S. development of the atomic bomb in WWII motivated the Soviets to develop their own "wonder weapons" that they could use against the United States. The German scientists had the technology Stalin was seeking. Around 1950 they had developed electromagnetic machines that could influence the brain and nervous system directly. The United States was able to obtain one of these devices in the 1980s and the North Koreans has used the device successfully to brainwash U.S. prisoners in North Korea during the Korean War.[280]

The Soviets had also been aiming microwave energy weapons at the US Embassy in Moscow in the late 1950s. This device was an intelligence probe and a behavior control tool, and also a serious health hazard to the ambassadors. Two ambassadors had died of cancers and a third was diagnosed with a blood disease when the FBI and CIA began the investigation. It was substantiated that the Soviets had been aiming microwaves at the embassy. The post was declared a health hazard and the employees were given a %20 pay raise.[281] It was determined that the radiation was coming from a residential building across the street, and it stopped temporarily, when the building caught on fire.

The United States did begin researching electromagnetic technology to counteract the Soviets and to use against the "enemy." The weapons they developed are quite sophisticated and very dangerous. If the United States government officials had used the weapons for warfare purposes only as they purported to be "non-lethal," maybe they might not be such a problem. However, thoughts in the minds of men who believe that they have the power and the right to shape and design the world according to their own specifications have

---

279 Wikipedia, Directed-energy Weapons (http://en-wikipedia.org).
280 Lt. Col. T. E. Bearden (retd), History of Directed Energy Weapons (Christians Against Mental Slavery, 1990 – http://www.mindcontrolforums.com).
281 John J. McMurtrey, Inner voice Target Tracking and Behavioral Influence Technologies (Christians Agsinst Mental Slavery, 2003 – http://www.slavery.org.uk).

made the world of electromagnetic (EM) technology very, very dangerous and downright evil.

Let's take a look at the timeline of the development of this technology.

TIMELINE FOR THE DEVELOPMENT OF DIRECTED ENERGY WEAPONS

Between 1898 and 1938 Nicola Tesla made several advances in electromagnetic technology. In 1898 he had a device that would fit in his overcoat pocket that caused an earthquake in his neighborhood.[282] He was likely responsible for the fact that the French Ship Iena blew up in 1901.[283] and the Tunguska catastrophe in 1908.[284] By 1911 he had a device that would fit in a briefcase that would provide enough energy to power up an entire community. By 1938 he was able to extract energy from the cosmos to power machinery and by 1935 he announced that energy passing through the earth was sufficient to be used as a weapon from a great distance.[285] Nikola Tesla died in 1943 and his notes were confiscated from his hotel room by Stalin's agents. Stalin was intent on developing super weapons to counter the U.S. atomic weapons.[286]

The rest of the world was beginning to catch on the Nicola's ideas. In 1924 Grindell Matthews told the New York Times that he had developed a "death ray" that would put an army out of action and destroy a fleet of ships or airplanes with invisible electromagnetic power. That year Dr. TF Wall of Sheffield University in England applied for a patent for a wireless weapon capable of the same thing. Germany had also patented three weapons that would stop an airplane in midflight, stop tanks and bring an automobile engine to a standstill as well as destroy human life. The Soviet Union developed a death ray for destroying airplanes that same year.[287] In 1945 allies discovered that the Japanese had also developed a "death ray".[288]

In 1934 Dr. E.L. Chaffee & R.O. Light published A *Method of Remote Control of Electrical Stimulation of the Nervous System.*[289] Between 1950-1952 the Soviets developed EM machines that could influence the brain & nervous system

---

282 Lt. Col. T. E. Bearden (retd), History of Directed Energy Weapons (Christians Against Mental Slavery, 1990 – http://www.mindcontrolforums.com).
283 Jerry E. Smith, HAARP: The Ultimate Weapon of the Conspiracy (Kempton, ILL: Adventures Unlimited Press, 1998) 45.
284 Oliver Nicholson, Nichola Tesla's Radient energy System (Brooklyn Eagel,1995 – http://skepticsfiles.org).
285 Ibid.
286 Lt. Col. T. E. Bearden (retd), History of Directed Energy Weapons (Christians Against Mental Slavery, 1990 – http://www.mindcontrolforums.com).
287 Ibid
288 Judy Wall, Editor, Timeline: Electromagnetic Weapons (Resonance Newsletter, December 12, 2007 – http://www.raven.net).
289 Ibid

directly.[290] In 1953 the CIA, FBI and NSA petitioned Dr. Antoine Redmond to release information he had about remotely influencing the human brain from a distance without leaving any evidence and he refused.[291]

Between 1957 and 1958 the Soviets experimented with large Scalar EM Whitaker Beam weapons which may have been the cause of a huge nuclear accident that occurred in the Ural Mountains. Around this time anomalous radiation of the US Embassy in Moscow began and continues. By the early 1960's the Soviets were in the development stage of large scalar EM Beam weapons and used them to take down a U.S. U2 with their prototype. In late 1960's the Soviets had broken the genetic code of the human brain which is the first step in developing technology for influencing thought, vision, physical functioning, emotions and conscious states of the human mind.[292] That year News headlines announce that the Soviets have developed a "fantastic weapon" that will enable them to cut their armed forces by one third.[293] In 1963 Khrushchev destroyed the U.S.S. Thresher with their newly developed Scalar EM beam weapon.[294]

By 1965 the United States was experimenting with using microwaves for remotely controlling the behavior of monkeys in Project Pandora. By 1968, Dr. Gordon J. MacDonald, science advisor to President Lyndon B. Johnson, reports that human behavior can be influenced by Low Frequency E.M. waves. In 1970, Zbigniew Brzezinski writes his book, *Between Two Ages* that "technology is available for controlling the weather and impairing brain performance of large populations in selected regions over an extended period". By 1972 the U.S. Department of Defense announced the development of microwave weapons capable of producing 3rd degree burns on the human skin. Dr. Gordon J.F. McDonald testified before a House Subcommittee that electronic waves can be tuned to brain waves at 10 cycles per second that would enable external remote control of behavioral patterns. In 1972 Sharp and Grove had developed microwave transmission of voices through the human skull to the brain. Between 1975 and 1977 the U.S. Congress and other government officials are presented with research arguing in favor of using radar for remote control of the human brain.[295]

In July 1976 a worldwide communications blackout occurred because the Soviets were transmitting a communications band from 3-30MHZ which were

---

290 Lt. Col. T. E. Bearden (retd), History of Directed Energy Weapons (Christians Against Mental Slavery, 1990 – http://www.mindcontrolforums.com).
291 Judy Wall, Editor, Timeline: Electromagnetic Weapons (Resonance Newsletter, December 12, 2007 – http://www.raven.net).
292 Lt. Col. T. E. Bearden (retd), History of Directed Energy Weapons (Christians Against Mental Slavery, 1990 – http://www.mindcontrolforums.com).
293 Judy Wall, Editor, Timeline: Electromagnetic Weapons (Resonance Newsletter, December 12, 2007 – http://www.raven.net).
294 Lt. Col. T. E. Bearden (retd), History of Directed Energy Weapons (Christians Against Mental Slavery, 1990 – http://www.mindcontrolforums.com).
295 Judy Wall, Editor, Timeline: Electromagnetic Weapons (Resonance Newsletter, December 12, 2007 – http://www.raven.net).

dubbed "Woodpecker" signals and over the horizon radars by the U.S. intelligence community. This was an activation of giant E.M. weapons by the Soviets in accordance with their plan for world domination.[296]

On July 28 1976 a great earthquake destroyed Tangshan China killing 600,000 persons. Electrical beams associated with scalar EM weapons were seen in the sky prior to the event suggest scalar EM engineering of this disaster.[297]

On May 18th 1977 the Soviets and the U.S. signed the Environmental Modification Treaty (ENMOD), an agreement with 29 other countries promising not to attack each other by causing man made storms, earthquakes or tidal waves. The Soviets had been using weather manipulation against the United States for a year. However, in 1980 an anomalous uniform drought occurred across the entire U.S. artificially induced by the Woodpecker Interferometer grid established over the US by the Soviets.[298]

In 1978, a U.S. solar powered satellite was first proposed as a satellite born weapon to disable enemy missiles, but also as a psychological antipersonnel weapon capable of causing general panic. Congress refused to fund it because of the enormous cost. It resurfaced again in the Regan era as Star Wars and was funded under the DOD budget.[299]

In September, 1979 a US Cameraman finds evidence that there is at least one Scalar Em Howitzer/Interferometer in Afghanistan. There are indications popping up that other nations have developed Scalar EM weaponry.[300]

In 1981 the US Navy petitions Eldon Byrd of the Naval Surface Weapons Center to investigate the development of electromagnetic "non-lethal" weapons for use in crowd control, hostage removal, *clandestine operations*, etc.[301]

In January, 1982 1400 earth tremors registering 4.0 to 4.5 on the Richter scale were recorded in North Central Arkansas in an area where no tremors have previously occurred. These could have been stimulated by artificially induced scalar waves passing through the Ouachita fault zones.[302]

That same year Allen International developed EM Weapons for Law Enforcement use in Great Britain that have potential for causing permanent hearing impairment. These devices can also produce seizures, nausea, giddiness & fainting. The U.S. Air Force at the same time reviewed data on electro shock therapy which shows that electrical current is capable of interrupting mental functions for short periods and restructuring emotional responses over long

---

296 Lt. Col. T. E. Bearden (retd), History of Directed Energy Weapons (Christians Against Mental Slavery, 1990 – http://www.mindcontrolforums.com).
297 Ibid.
298 Ibid.
299 Ibid.
300 Ibid.
301 Judy Wall, Editor, Timeline: Electromagnetic Weapons (Resonance Newsletter, December 12, 2007 – http://www.raven.net).
302 Lt. Col. T. E. Bearden (retd), History of Directed Energy Weapons (Christians Against Mental Slavery, 1990 – http://www.mindcontrolforums.com).

periods and also able to modify & manipulate behavior and cause the heart to stop beating resulting in death.[303]

On April 9th 1984, a gigantic glowing mushroom cloud emerged from above the ocean off the cost of Japan representing the test of what is known as a "Tesla Shield" or an Antiaircraft, Antimissile shield which will dud all electronics, explode all high explosives, fuels and propellants and kill every cell of any living thing[304].

In April of 1985, Frank Golden discovered the sudden activation of 54 powerful EM frequencies transmitted into the earth as power taps used to stimulate the earth into forced electromagnetic resonance. The power taps are extracting energy from the molten core of the earth. In May the Soviets actuated 100 giant scalar EM weapons in a demonstration for newly elected leader Mikhail Gorbachev. Scalar EM command and control systems were also activated in an exercise that lasted several days. This was a fulfillment of Brezhnev's 1972 statement that by 1985 the Soviets would control 90% of the land mass of the entire planet. In December, the Soviets tested scalar EM weapons against an arrow DC-8 taking off from Gander Air force Base in Newfoundland. Two hundred and eighty-five members of the U.S. Marines and air crew perished when the plane come down. One eyewitness saw the crossed glowing beams form in the clouds and the beam of light that actually struck the plane.[305]

On January 1st 1986 Frank Golden detected and verified a metal softening signal added to the Woodpecker signals. On Jan 28th the Challenger and its crew perished. Seventeen pieces of evidence including the softening of the metal around the booster flame indicated that the Challenger and the crew perished due to Soviet Scalar EM attack. In the spring of that year a uniform drought occurring across the entire U.S. is attributed to Soviet Scalar EM weather engineering. On May 3rd a NASA Delta rocket carrying a critically needed weather Satellite failed with indicators of Scalar EM interference.[306]

In 1988 lawsuits filed by an environmental group forced the Pentagon to cease testing Electromagnetic Pulse Weapons at several locations.[307]

In 1993 the High Altitude Aural Research Project (HAARP) was activated with the capability to alter communication and surveillance systems. Using a 3.6 Gigawatt beam of effective radiated power, this project which has been extremely destructive to the upper atmosphere has the capability to deliver large amounts of energy comparable to a Nuclear bomb to any place on the globe via laser &

---

303 Judy Wall, Editor, Timeline: Electromagnetic Weapons (Resonance Newsletter, December 12, 2007 – http://www.raven.net).
304 Lt. Col. T. E. Bearden (retd), History of Directed Energy Weapons (Christians Against Mental Slavery, 1990 – http://www.mindcontrolforums.com).
305 Ibid.
306 Ibid.
307 Judy Wall, Editor, Timeline: Electromagnetic Weapons (Resonance Newsletter, December 12, 2007 – http://www.raven.net).

particle beams.[308] It also has the capacity to be used for weather control and mind control.[309]

February; BBC broadcast reveals that the FBI used EM pulse weapons against the Branch Davidians.[310]

What is Scalar Em Technology?

It might be helpful at this point to discuss the basic design of scalar EM technology. Nikola Tesla's basic theory was that sound waves, radio waves, microwaves or electromagnetic waves could all be manipulated by synchronization. That is, he believed that everything had its own natural vibration caused by waves inherent in creation. Scalar EM technology is based on the simple notion that by electronically synchronizing with the natural vibrations of anything, the atmosphere, the earth, a building, a human brain, you can manipulate and control it. For example, a building has a natural vibration. Tesla believed that he could cause the building to collapse by using his own device that synchronized a manmade wave with the natural wave of the building's vibrations. Once the wave from his little pocket sized device was synchronized with the building's wave, he could manipulate the strength of that wave by tuning it with his device. He actually created an earthquake while working in his laboratory this way, by accident.

> "… I was experimenting with vibrations. I had one of my machines going, and I wanted to see if I could get-in tune with the vibration of the building: I put it up notch after notch. There was a peculiar cracking sound. I asked my assistants where the sound came from: They did not know. I turned my machine up a few more notches. There was a louder cracking sound. I knew I was approaching the vibration of the steel building. I pushed the machine a little higher. Suddenly all the heavy machinery in the place was flying around. I grabbed the hammer and broke the machine. The building would have been about our ears in a few minutes: Outside in the street there was pandemonium…." [311]

Directed Energy Weapons also use the element of speed to strengthen the force of the charge. A wave signal sent to your television set creates a picture. However if that same wave is fired at your television at a much higher speed, it

---

308 Lt. Col. T. E. Bearden (retd), History of Directed Energy Weapons (Christians Against Mental Slavery, 1990 – http://www.mindcontrolforums.com).

309 Jerry E. Smith, HAARP: The Ultimate Weapon of the Conspiracy (Kempton, ILL: Adventures Unlimited Press, 1998).

310 Judy Wall, Editor, Timeline: Electromagnetic Weapons (Resonance Newsletter, December 12, 2007 – http://www.raven.net).

311 Oliver Nicholson, Nichola Tesla's Radient energy System (Brooklyn Eagel,1995 – http://skepticsfiles.org).

will cause the television to explode. Tesla's experiments caused some televisions to explode and the power being generated from Tesla's device destroyed the power company's generator.[312]

Types of Directed Energy Weapons

The following information about patented Directed Energy Weapons is available in open source material:

Laser weapons generate a brief high energy pulse and have the same effect when they hit a target as an explosive. It causes the surface of the target to evaporate. They are used in combat situations to intercept shells in flight or mortar rounds. The following are examples of laser weapons

- The Dazzler weapon generates a blinding light and bends, disorients or interferes with the human eye or an electric sensor which disorients or reduces human target activity and can potentially cause permanent blindness.[313] The rational of using this weapon is that it is more humane than killing the human target.
- Saber Shot: Weapon mounted or hand held weapon that "generates a blinding light, disorientation and reduces the human target's activity".[314]
- MARAUDER (Magnetically Accelerated Ring to Achieve Ultra High Directed Energy and Radiation)/MEDUSA (Mobile Energy Device U.S.A.): high powered microwave and laser weapons which are potentially lethal projectiles and able to "instantly destroy inorganic and organic material".[315]
- Ultraviolet Laser: This laser was developed by ISV Technologies in San Diego. It will paralyze animals and is being tested for use on humans.[316]
- The Star Wars program proposed by Ronald Regan was a Space Based Tray Laser capable of destroying ICBMs which was never officially approved. It was later funded under the DOD budget for black operations.[317]
- High Frequency Active Auroral Research Project (HAARP) has been approved and likely does everything the Star Wars program was designed to do. The HAARP sight situated in Anchorage Alaska is constructed of an antennae array which can be used as a

---

312 Ibid.
313 Douglas Pasternak, Non Lethal Wonder Weapons (http://mywebb.cableone.net).
314 Non Lethal Directed Energy Weapons (Defense Update, 2005 – http://defenseupdate.com.
315 Wikipedia, Directed-energy Weapon (http://en-wikipedia.org).
316 Ibid.
317 Ibid.

weapon capable of destroying anything it is aimed at as well as mind control of entire populations, weather control and earth penetrating topography.[318]

- Ground Wave Emergency Network (GWEN) was supposedly constructed by the U. S. Government in the 1980's for the purpose of maintaining defense communications in the case of a nuclear war. However, the agenda for GWEN has more to do with mind control than a nuclear threat. Experts agree that GWEN would easily be taken out by a nuclear blast.

The following are examples of Radio Frequency Weapons;

- Active Denial System (ADS): Vehicle mounted weapon that looks like a satellite dish and operates like a microwave oven. This weapon will raise skin temperature to about 130 degrees from up to 700 yards away.[319] It has not been determined that this weapon can actually produce skin burns or kill. However laser guided DEWs work like "artificial lightning to disable human targets or electronic circuits … This technology can be Lethal or Non Lethal".[320] William M. Arkin, "Senior Military Advisor to Human Rights Watch described it as a high powered microwave anti-personnel weapon which should be more carefully studied before it is used on crowds containing elderly people, children or pregnant women." Mr. Arkin also indicated that laser weapons have been determined to injure people. "Pentagon officials said scientists have been testing the weapon on animals and humans for more than three years without finding any evidence that it caused internal injuries, burns, and cancer or eye damage". However, when a tester programmed the weapon incorrectly it produced a nickel sized burn on his back.[321] The weapon was expected to be ready for use in 2006.
- CAPS: A microwave antipersonnel weapon developed by Rogations targets humans from a distance beyond what is possible with small arms. This is a vehicle and airborne mounted weapon.[322]

---

318 Jerry E. Smith, HAARP: The Ultimate Weapon of the Conspiracy (Kempton, ILL: Adventures Unlimited Press, 1998)
319 James Dao, Pentagon Unveils Plans for a New Crowd-Dispersal Weapon (New York Times, March 2, 2001 – http://www.commondreams.org).
320 Non Lethal Directed Energy Weapons (Defense Update, 2005 – http://defense-update.com).
321 James Dao, Pentagon Unveils Plans for a New Crowd-Dispersal Weapon (New York Times, March 2, 2001 – http://www.commondreams.org).
322 Non Lethal Directed Energy Weapons (Defense Update, 2005 – http://defenseupdate.com.update.com).

- Electric Beam in a Vacuum: This is an electric discharge that can travel unlimited distances at a speed slightly slower than the speed of light.[323]

Plasma weapons fire a beam of excited matter consisting of electrons and protons or nuclei which is what makes up plasma.[324]

Some DEWs use sound waves. Acoustic DEW weapons create a "flash-bang" effect which can incapacitate people for a few seconds when aimed at a crowd.[325] The following are examples of acoustic DEWs:

- LRAD: Long Range Acoustic Device used by US Soldiers in Iraq. This device blasts sounds in a narrow beam at 150 decibels which is 50 times the human threshold for pain. When firing short bursts of intense acoustic energy it can incapacitate people within 300 meters.[326]
- Another acoustic weapon developed for crowd control by Premix Physics International operated by a single person blasts acoustic pressure of up to 165 db at a distance of 15 meters.[327]
- Acoustic Phase Array: Consists of 36 horns which can focus acoustic output at the target which can incapacitate and disorient humans from a standoff distance.[328]
- The Scientific Applications & Research Associates inc. (SARA) has built an acoustic weapon that "will make internal organs resonate: the effects can run from discomfort to damage to death." Used as acoustic fences these devices would make intruders increasingly uncomfortable as they draw closer and are viable today. Acoustic rifles are also in development.[329]
- Shockwave: Uses a vortex system generates a high powered shockwave which can inflict considerable damage on a target.[330]

The Pentagon has not authorized the Department of Defense to use acoustic weapons because of the potential harm to pregnant women, children, the disabled and the elderly. However, the research to develop acoustic weapons is underway including the Vortex project.[331]

The Marine Corp was petitioned by scientist Clay Easterly from the Health Sciences Research Division of the Oak Ridge National Laboratory about a study

---

323 Wikipedia, Directed-energy Weapon (http://en-wikipedia.org).
324 Ibid.
325 Non Lethal Directed Energy Weapons (Defense Update, 2005 – http://defense-update.com.
326 Ibid.
327 Ibid.
328 Ibid.
329 Douglas Pasternak, Non Lethal Wonder Weapons (http://mywebb.cableone.net).
330 Non Lethal Directed Energy Weapons (Defense Update, 2005 – http://defenseupdate.com.
331 Douglas Pasternak, Non Lethal Wonder Weapons (http://mywebb.cableone.net).

he had conducted for the National Institute of Justice for Research on Crime Control. One of the projects he suggested was an electromagnetic gun that would induce epileptic seizures and another was a thermal gun that would heat the body (not just the skin) to 105 to 107 degrees Fahrenheit which would cause discomfort, fevers or even death.[332]

Microwaves can stimulate the body's peripheral nervous system to such an extent that the body shuts itself off producing a stun effect. This can only be achieved from short distances. Microwave weapons which are potentially more dangerous long term because of obvious health risks includes the Pulse Wave Matron which works on direct contact, is a cigarette pack sized device that can paralyze a person for several minutes. This device scrambles signals from the cortex and voids voluntary but not involuntary muscle movement so vital functions are maintained.[333]

Weapons that disable electronic equipment such as missiles and radio frequencies can be modified to do the same on human beings because the human body is also an electrical system, and therefore it is also possible to electrically disrupt body functions, the central nervous system and the human brain. Weapons that can "vibrate the insides of humans to stun them, nauseate them or even liquefy their bowels and reduce them to quivering diarrheic messes" have also been tested. Weapons in development are electromagnetic waves to put people to sleep, heat them up and knock them down. One potential project being reviewed was a device called "Put the enemy to sleep, Keep the Enemy from Sleeping" which seeks to use acoustics, microwaves and brain-wave manipulation to alter sleep patterns. Radiofrequency antipersonnel weapons research is in progress. The budget for such weapons is over 110 million over the next six years[334].

Directed Energy Weapons that are specifically developed for mind/behavior influence called Psychotronic Weapons are listed below.[335]

- Lowery patent # 6052336 is "an apparatus and method of broadcasting audible sound using ultrasonic sound as a carrier". It projects sound inside a person's head so that it will appear that they are hearing voices as no one else will hear the sound.
- Monroe Patent #5356368" Method of and apparatus for inducing desired states of consciousness" replicates brainwave patterns also causing a person to hear what no one else can hear. This device can be temporarily incapacitating and cause intense discomfort.
- Norris patent # 5889870" acoustic hearing device & method "produces sound within cavities such as the ear canal.

---

332 Ibid.
333 Ibid.
334 Ibid.
335 John J. McMurtrey, M.S. Inner voice Target Tracking and Behavioral Influence Technologies (Christians Agsinst Mental Slavery, 2003 – http://www.slavery.org.uk).

- The Burton patent # 4877027 "Hearing System" converts speech from a remote point into the head of a target.

Devices developed for reading the thoughts of a target include System and method for predicting internal condition of live body which is patent #5785653 and also Mardirossian Patent # 6011991for brain wave analysis and/or use of brain activity.[336]

Directed Energy Weapons also include implant devices that can turn a person into a robot. These devices can be readily inserted with a hypodermic needle and the result is that the person can be remotely controlled with a radio. Scientist Han Moreover who studies robotics reported that "Within the near future it will be possible to put a person's personality into a computer and a computer personality into a person".[337] Microchip implants have been in use since the late 1960's. Examples of microchip implants are listed below.[338]

- Intelligence-manned interface (IMI) biotic is injected into people, was used in the Iraq war was invented by Dr. Carl Sanders.
- The Rambo chip was injected into U.S. Soldiers in Vietnam and the National Security Agency was able to "see and hear" what soldiers experience in the battlefield with a remote monitoring system (RMS).
- A chip the diameter of a strand of hair is placed into the optical nerve of the eye and "it draws neuroimpulses from the brain that embody the experiences, smells, sights and voice of the implanted person. Once transferred and stored in a computer, these neuroimpulses can be projected back to the person's brain via the microchip to be reexperienced. Using a RMS, a land based computer operator can send electromagnetic messages (encoded as signals) to the nervous system, affecting the target's performance. "With RMS, healthy persons can be induced to see hallucinations and to hear voices in their heads." These microchips can also be used to induce severe muscle cramps experienced as torture by the victim.

Microwave hearing was first documented by Allen Frey in 1969. Microwave hearing causes the person targeted to hear something that no one else can hear and the person's thoughts can also be remotely influenced. The CIA calls this voice synthesis co-synthetic telepathy. This kind of influence can "shift the direction of group decisions in large populations". The Department of Defense has a small

---

336 John J. McMurtrey, M.S., Though Reading Capacity (Christians Against Mental Slavery, September 12, 2005 – http://www.slavery.org.uk).
337 Cheryl Welsh, U.S. Human Rights Abuse Report (Christians Against Mental Slavery, January 1998 – http://www.mindjustice.org).
338 Rauni-Leena Lukanen-Kilde, Microchip Implants, Mind Control, and Cybernetics (December 6, 2000 – http://www.conspiracyarchive.com).

business contract for the study of remote thought influence which is classified but a New World Vista's report states that "covert suggestion and psychological manipulation are a possibility. . . . Thus it may be possible to stalk selected adversaries in a fashion that would be most disturbing to them". Nobel Peace prize nominee Roberto Becker who specializes in biological electromagnetic fields research speaks of the use of radiofrequency voice transmission, "Such a device has obvious applications in covert operations designed to drive a target crazy with 'voices' or deliver undetectable instructions to a programmed assassin."[339]

The U.S. DOD has plans for using mind control technology against terrorists, but this technology is also in the hands of local Law Enforcement. In fact the FBI used these devices against the Branch Davidians. C. B. Baker reported that when the FBI used their flame throwing devices on the building in which the Branch Davidians were hiding, some of the members of the church attempted to run out of the burning building. However, "They suddenly turned around and ran back INTO the fire which demonstrated an extreme mental disorientation of the type created by Psychotronic Mind Control Weapons. The few victims who survived were visibly confused and unable to talk coherently or move".[340]

The Soviets began researching remote thought influence in 1925 and at the end of 70 years Psychotronic Weapons started to come off the conveyors of assembly lines in the secret factories [such as the famed N 11] for use against the population on a mass scale. These weapons can kill at a distance, cause or imitate chronic illness, create irresponsible or criminal personality changes, cause auto, train or airplane accidents, destroy any structure, create weather or natural catastrophes, control the behavior of a human or an animal (or make a human behave like an animal) and change the world view of entire populations.[341]

The Russians developed a technique which they call psycho-correction, and Janet E. Morris and husband Christopher C. Morris have developed psycho-correction technology which they demonstrated to U. S. Intelligence officers which can be used in the form of hand held weapons to influence a target's thoughts and behaviors. Researchers at Yale and Tulane university concluded that electronic stimulation of the brain could control memory, impulses, feelings and could evoke hallucination as well as fear and pleasure and absolutely allow total manipulation of the human will.[342]

---

339 John J. McMurtrey, Inner voice Target Tracking and Behavioral Influence Technologies (Christians Agsinst Mental Slavery, 2003 – http://www.slavery.org.uk).
340 C. B. Baker, New World Order and Psychotronic Tyranny (Youth Action News Letter, December 1994 – http://www.angelfire.com).
341 N. I. Anisimov, Psychotronic Golgotha (Christians against Mental Slavery, 1999 http://www.mindjustice.org).
342 Cheryl Welsh, U.S. Human Rights Abuse Report (Christians Against Mental Slavery, January 1998 – http://www.mindjustice.org).

Human Rights Issues Arise

With all these new weapons being tested the obvious question might be, on whom are they testing these weapons? Supposedly these weapons were developed to be used by the military in combat situations and by Law Enforcement in crowd control. That is how they are being presented to the public. Dr. John H. Gibbons, assistant to the President for Science and Technology and Director of the Office of Science and Technology Policy White House Science Advisor presented at a conference on Nov 5th 1994 that application for EM technology included dealing with terrorist groups, crowd control, controlling breeches of security at military installations and antipersonnel techniques in tactical warfare. However, for the past 50 years there has been consistent evidence that the US government has tested and used these weapons against innocent civilians. This has been a covert operation which the US government refuses to comment on "because it can be reasonably be expected to be damaging to the interests of national security." Since the 1960's there have been complaints that the U.S. and other governments have been experimenting on their citizens without their consent. This was the subject of the MKULTRA Senate Hearings in the early 70's. Cheryl Welsh, President of Citizens against Mental Slavery indicates, "Proof in support of the allegations is growing… Most scientists have agreed that mind control is theoretically possible in this lifetime and many sign national security oaths which prevent them from discussing their research in this area".[343]

Government projects involving this type of technology are typically Top Secret or funded under the "black budget" because they are dangerous, disturbing, and tend to infringe on human rights. These weapons, called non-lethal by the US government, can be lethal. In fact President Clinton called them "soft kill" weapons.[344] These weapons are being presented as non lethal, humanitarian and bloodless. Anisimov in his book *Psychotronic Golgotha* states that the scientists who developed them, and I might add the politicians who want to employ them, adorn themselves in respectability, however there is nothing respectable about what they do. The general populace is convinced through mass media swaying the minds of uninformed citizens and thus, by deception, criminals who employ these weapons are shielded from being prosecuted for their crimes. "Today non-lethal weapons do not come under even one of the international conventions which would prohibit the development, accumulation, and application of such types of weapons"[345].

The Red Cross Human Rights Watch is leading the fight against antipersonnel lasers. In 1995 The U.S. signed a treaty that prohibits the development of lasers

---

343 Ibid.
344 C. B. Baker, New World Order and Psychotronic Tyranny (Youth Action News Letter, December 1994 – http://www.angelfire.com).
345 N. I. Anisimov, Psychotronic Golgotha (Christians against Mental Slavery, 1999 - http://www.mindjustice.org).

that cause permanent blindness.[346] However there is concern over who may have purchased these weapons from the Russians.[347] These "non lethal" weapons have come up before regulatory bodies like The U.N. However, the U.S. draft law prohibiting weapons that use electromagnetic behavioral influence and sound technologies for the purpose of information war, emotional manipulation or mind control has not been passed though use of these devices in Michigan is a felony.[348] The fact that these weapons are in the hands of local Law Enforcement should cause us concern, but they have also placed these weapons in the hands of local civilian groups who are targeting persons who have committed no crimes but might be considered a "threat" to national security. These civilian groups have become modern hit squads and are available to large corporations or anyone who has the money to hire them to take out persons they just want to get rid of.[349] As Law Enforcement has released these weapons into the hands of local citizenry, it should not surprise us that they have been mishandled. However, some of these devices are being marketed to the average citizen via the internet. The International Union of Radio Science has recognized that there is criminal use of DEWs.[350]

I have read numerous cases of this kind of harassment going on all over the United States. With more than 3,000,000 victims in the United States alone it is hard to imagine how this could have been kept quiet for so long. It has to do with an imbalance in power. The U.S. Government is able to hide the crimes they commit behind the veil of national security. They are therefore exempt from being held accountable for their actions. They are also good at manipulating the media so that it does not get reported in the news. Law Enforcement, the FBI and the CIA are all a part of the structure that is perpetrating the abuse. Judges, attorneys and the legal system are also locked in to covering this abuse so that victims are denied justice. Indeed psychologists, psychiatrist and physicians have also become a part of the web either willingly, or because they have been deceived or threatened with the loss of their careers.[351]

In fact the biggest problem with informing the American public about the abuses pertaining to Directed Energy Weapons and mind control experimentation are related to the fact that our government has a policy of deliberate deception. It is not an accident that this kind of technology has fallen under the U. S. intelligence community. It is kept secret because publication of this information about Directed Energy Weapons and Mind Control "can be reasonable expected to cause damage to national security." Usually, this kind if cover is used because there is something that the U. S. Government wants to hide from other world

---

346 Ibid.
347 Douglas Pasternak, Non Lethal Wonder Weapons (http://mywebb.cableone.net).
348 John J. McMurtrey, Inner voice Target Tracking and Behavioral Influence Technologies (Christians agsinst Mental Slavery, 2003 – http://www.slavery.org.uk).
349 Mark Rich, The Hidden Evil, (May 5, 2006 – http://www.thehiddenevil.com).
350 John J. McMurtrey, Inner voice Target Tracking and Behavioral Influence Technologies (Christians agsinst Mental Slavery, 2003 – http://www.slavery.org.uk).
351 Mark Rich, The Hidden Evil, (May 5, 2006 – http://www.thehiddenevil.com).

governments. But considering that every major government in the world also has and is experimenting with Directed Energy Weapons and mind control, not to mention the fact that the Soviet Union gave their mind control technology to the United States Government, the only people left to hide this from would be from the general populace, and for obvious reasons. The U. S. Government wants to use it to control us. As there is virtually no system of accountability for U. S. Intelligence activities. They can literally get away with murder.

The U. S. Government is quite comfortable with deceiving people. The group of wealthy elites in Washington who dictate government policy from behind the scenes feels that deception is a necessary and normal part of governing a nation. In 1975 Samuel Huntington wrote a report entitled *The Crisis of Democracy* in which he bemoaned the fact that hundreds of American citizens were protesting government policy. The elite were threatened by this. Huntington warned "The effective operation of a democratic political system usually requires some measure of apathy and non-involvement on the part of some individuals and groups." He also insisted that "secrecy and deception ... are ... inescapable attributes of government".[352] In the published documents which record the Senate hearing in the MKULTRA scandal, Dr. Sydney Gottleib states repeatedly in his proposals for the project that they would be "completely deniable".[353] In addition to that the U. S. Government is still manipulating the News Media. Project Mockingbird still chirps.

Cheryl Welsh, herself a victim, states, "Two points are critical to remember. One, the government is torturing U. S. citizens with this technology & two the U.S. public has the right to have a say in the U.S. development of this technology". These human rights violations have been actively covered up by the U. S. Government for the last 50 years, and have been classified under the National Security Act according to government policy. The U.S. Public has a right to review the factual and documented information about this kind of experimentation and targeting of U.S. and citizens and have a say in government policy pertaining to such.[354]

Martin Cannon, author of *Mind control and the American Government* reported that many of our representatives have a 'waive' file, which contains pleas for help by victims of clandestine bombardment with non-ionizing radiation or microwaves. Many Ann Dufrense of Senator Glenn's office in particular has received volumes of mail from victims of electromagnetic harassment and illegal experimentation. Senator Glenn is the sponsor of S193, the Human Research

---

352 F. William Engdahl, Seeds of Destruction: The Hidden Agenda of Genetic Manipulation (Canada: Global Research, Center for Research on Globalization, 2007) 41.
353 Schaffer Library of Drug Policy (Project MKULTRA, the CIA's Program of Research in Behavior Modification. Senate MKULTRA Hearing Appendix C. – http://www.druglibrary.org).
354 Cheryl Welsh, U.S. Human Rights Abuse Report (Christians Against Mental Slavery, January 1998 – http://www.mindjustice.org).

Subject Protections Act of 1997, which has been stalled in the Labor and Human Resources committee.[355]

Victims of Directed Energy Weapon Assault

A person may or may not know that they are being externally influenced by some sort of Psychotronic weapon. Those who do know and complain are typically labeled "mentally ill" to discredit them. This technology has been kept secret because the U.S. intelligence community has worked with the American Psychological Association in the development and revision of the Diagnostic and Statistical Manual (DSM). "This psychiatric 'bible' covers up the secret development of MC [Mind Control] technologies by labeling some of their effects as symptoms of paranoid schizophrenia".[356] Victims of mind control experimentation are thus labeled mentally ill because their doctors learned their list of symptoms from the DSM. Most psychologists, psychiatrists and physicians have not been educated on the trauma experienced by mind control victims, let alone the fact that there is such a thing.

In addition, persons who are targeted by these weapons are generally under constant surveillance, so anyone that they try to report this abuse to can also be remotely influenced by the same weapons so that they will not believe the victim who is being targeted. This can include Law Enforcement, physicians and attorneys. It is estimated that there were more than one million victims of Psychotronic terror in the Soviet Union.[357] There have been numerous reports of this kind of harassment and experimentation in which American citizens have been targeted by the United States Government. It is estimated that there are more than 3,000,000 victims in the United States alone, and this is a global problem. Julianne McKinney, Director of the Electronic Surveillance Project Association of National Security Alumni as of the publication of her 1992 report had personally investigated hundreds of reports of this kind of abuse being inflicted on American citizens.[358]

While the problem has not been widely publicized, the problem is so wide spread that it will inevitably become public knowledge. The use of these weapons causes irreversible health consequences for victims including but not limited to blindness, deafness, cancer, kidney and liver damage and damage to the central nervous system. The list of illnesses and side effects of electromagnetic irradiation include tightness and sharp head pains; dizziness; pressure on the ear drums; vibrating of the wall of the peritoneum, rib cage and muscle groups; dry mouth; pain in the teeth and gums; difficulty swallowing; sweating palms; tumors;

---

355 Ibid.
356 Rauni-Leena Lukanen-Kilde, Microchip Implants, Mind Control, and Cybernetics (December 6, 2000 – http://www.conspiracyarchive.com).
357 N. I. Anisimov, Psychotronic Golgotha (Christians against Mental Slavery, 1999 http://www.mindjustice.org.
358 Mark Rich, The Hidden Evil, (May 5, 2006 – http://www.thehiddenevil.com).

painful sensations in the sex organs and anus; spontaneous arousal of sex organs; fluctuating blood pressure; decrease in visual acuity; coughing; fluctuating body temp.; coma; itching; uncoordinated speech; fear; anxiety; malignant new growths; damage to the cardiovascular system; coagulation or disintegration of the blood; illnesses of the brain, central and peripheral nervous system; eye illnesses; illnesses involving the sex organs; a deterioration of the movement-support apparatus; a breakdown of the ribcage; damage or the rupture of organs; muscle atrophy; a destruction of the endocrine system; damage to the skin; hair loss; brittleness of nails etc. Statistics from the former Soviet Union where this kind of abuse was rampant indicate there is literally not one person who did not suffer from some kind of chronic illness related to this list of symptoms.[359]

The Soviets made heavy use of implant devices by which they could control people with a radio. Nearly 30% of the population of the former Soviet Union carries in their bodies these implant devices. Therefore, the person with one of these devices becomes a puppet in the hands of the terrorist who torments them. This is called "psycho programming" and is "… conducted along the following schemes: computer operator-victim and in the reverse sequence: victim-computer operator".[360]

Victims of this kind of harassment include whistleblowers, anyone who opposes globalization, minorities, family members of targeted individuals, war protesters, single women, the disabled, the elderly, school children or anyone considered undesirable.

I am currently experiencing microwave harassment, and my research began because there was evidence that something was very wrong in my environment. I was baffled by the fact that Law Enforcement was ignoring physical evidence that something foul was going on. I was told by a detective at the local Sheriff's Dept. that the Sheriff's Deputy had spoken to all my neighbors, and no one said they saw or heard anything unusual. I did some investigating of my own. I spoke with my neighbors and they did not report seeing or hearing anything unusual, but neither did I find one of my neighbors who could say that the Sheriff had ever been bye to ask them any questions. This is a typical pattern in covert harassment cases.

People who have been targeted include:
- Seneca Women's Peace Encampment in New York. They were able to file an injunction at the Newbury County Court and the EM zapping stopped but their homes and cars were broken into and their mail pilfered.[361]
- Delores Hejazi wrote a letter of complaint to the IRS and her problems began. She was systematically discredited and became suicidal. She was unable to get an investigation of her claim which was reported in the

---
359 N. I. Anisimov, Psychotronic Golgotha (Christians against Mental Slavery, 1999 http://www.mindjustice.org).
360 Ibid.
361 Cheryl Welsh, U.S. Human Rights Abuse Report (Christians against Mental Slavery, January 1998 – http://www.mindjustice.org).

Cleveland Plain Dealer newspaper "of being repeatedly attacked and tortured by government agencies beam weaponry and laser technology". She refused treatment for her throat cancer and died recently.[362]

- One woman was being electronically harassed and actually killed one of her children to protect her from further torture. Lasers were being used against her. She contacted the Soviet Embassy to report the harassment which she believed to be U.S. Government sponsored. She was then hospitalized in a Midwestern facility where the harassment continued.[363]

- An individual who had been publically opposing the installation of high power lines in her neighborhood was threatened by an employee of the local power company. "Since receiving the threat, the individual's 11-year old daughter has been reduced to extremes of pain, resulting in her recurrent hospitalization for treatment of illnesses which cannot be diagnosed. It is also apparent to this individual that her three-year-old son is on the receiving end of externally-induced auditory input".[364]

- Cheryl Welsh, Director of Christians against Mental Slavery, described her own experience like being in an electronic prison. She states, "Any and all electrical systems in her environment, including the brain are targeted, controlled and manipulated 24 hours a day. The technique of stimulus, response as in a psychology experiment are used to find weaknesses and a breaking point".[365]

- Rex Niles, a successful businessman and a Former FBI whistleblower cooperated with investigators who prosecuted and convicted 19 industry buyers and supervisors on tax evasion and kickback charges amounting to millions in under the table payments to electronics contractors. He participated in the Federal Witness Protection program but has subsequently documented proof that he was harassed with microwave radiation, resulting in lack of sleep aggravating his conscious and unconscious mind. Though he had physical proof of high radiofrequency levels, he was discredited as being mentally ill and his claim was not investigated.[366]

- Brian Wronge, a prison inmate who had been illegally used for experimentation with implant devices attempted to file a lawsuit. In 1991 lab reports revealed the implants. The Judge instructed him to find a surgeon to remove the implants as evidence in his trial. He was

---

362 Ibid.
363 Julianne McKinney, Microwave Harassment and Mind Control Experimentation (December, 1992 – http;//www.xs4all.nl).
364 Ibid.
365 Cheryl Welsh, U.S. Human Rights Abuse Report (Christians against Mental Slavery, January 1998 – http://www.mindjustice.org).
366 Ibid.

unable to do so. The surgeons he sought assistance from who refused cited threats of FBI retaliation as the reason. Even the Physicians for Human Rights (PHR) Board, which has a large membership and a documented mandate to stop torture committed by a government refused to assist.[367]

19. Mind Control and Space Age Technology

When Dr. Aldrich took over the Office of Research and Development he birthed Operation Often which was an investigation into the methods of occult behavior control. Sorceress Sybil Leek Houston was their consultant. They investigated space age technology [Directed Energy Weapons] and its application to mind control.[368] Julianne McKinney, director of the National Security Alumni, an agency that opposed covert activity by the U.S. intelligence community, investigated numerous claims by individuals who felt they were being electronically harassed by the U.S. Government. They investigated the claims of individuals who were scattered throughout the United States most of whom indicated that their problem began in 1989. She states,

> Reactivation of surveillance/harassment/mind-control operations in the United States generally suggest that the KGB, as an institution, was never the real threat. A KGB "mentality," which is underlying pragmatic contempt for civil liberties, appears instead, to have been the driving force behind MKULTRA, MHCHAOS and COINTELPRO, and the operations now being reported to us[369].

The US Military and Law Enforcement have been in search of weapons that could incapacitate people without killing them since the end of the cold war. Eldon Byrd working for the Marine Corp with the Radiology Research Institute studied the influencing of electrical activity in the brain. Byrd was able to determine that brainwaves would move into sync with waves impinging on them from the outside, and was thus able to induce the brain to release behavior regulating chemicals with Very Low Frequency electromagnetic radiation. Thus the research team was working on weapons for influencing thoughts and behaviors of a target.

---

367 Ibid.
368 Alex Constantine, Psychic Dictatorship in the U.S.A. (Portland: Feral House, 1995) 5.
369 Julianne McKinney, Microwave Harassment and Mind Control Experimentation (December, 1992 – http://www.xs4all.nl).

The Agenda for Mind Control

The goal of mind control is the absolute annihilation of the person physically, emotionally and mentally. The target may be killed or the personality reshaped. Julianne McKinney quoted William Sergeant author of *A Battle for the Mind: A Physiology in Conversion and Brainwashing* in her report, *Microwave Harassment and Mind Control Experimentation:*

> By increasing the prolong stress in various ways, or inducing physical debilitation, a more thorough alteration of the person's thinking process may be achieved if the stress or physical debilitation, or both, are carried one stage further, it may happen that patterns of thought and behavior, especially those of recent acquisition, become disrupted. New patterns can then be substituted, or suppressed patterns allowed reasserting themselves; or the subject might begin to think or act in ways precisely contradict his former ones.... If a complete sudden collapse can be produced by prolonging or intensifying emotional stress, the cortical slate may be wiped clean temporarily of its more recently implanted patterns of behavior, perhaps allowing others to be substituted more easily.[370]

This diabolical kind of thinking is very Hegelian and comes straight from the pit of hell. Those who want to reprogram your mind are people who have erased in themselves any form of conscience or moral or ethical code and may first target people who continue to have a conscience or an ethical code, such as people they perceive to be "homo phobic" or anyone who dares to challenge their evil agenda.

Current reports indicated that victims of mind control have experienced what would be described as sheer torture by the use of electromagnetic energy. The purpose of torture is the same, the breaking of the human personality to reshape it. "It is a fact that nobody likes to admit but torture is an ancient and well established institution of socialized human behavior. As reported in New York Times Magazine, Dec. 28, 1997 in the article *To Hell and Back* 'The primary purpose of torture is ... to break the victim's personality. In this torture is wildly successful'"[371].

The Secret Soviet Directed Energy Weapons factory, N11's, agenda for the development of these weapons included but was not limited to:[372]

---

370 Julianne McKinney, Microwave Harassment and Mind Control Experimentation (December, 1992 – http://www.xs4all.nl).
371 Cheryl Welsh, Human Rights Abuse Report (Christians against Mental slavery, January 1998 – http://www.mindjustice.org).
372 N.I. Anisimov, Psychotronic Golgotha (Christians against Mental slavery, 1999 – http://www.mindjustice.org).

- Distant control of the thought processes and behavior of human beings and the use of implant devices and pharmacologicals to do both.
- Psychotropic apparatuses for distant modification of the human body
- Distant control of human beings by means of radio & T.V.
- The creation of a bio-robot.
- Technology for erasing the human brain.
- Distant control of the environment of 3rd world nations.
- "Distant influencing of populations with the aim of creation of a law abiding society loyal to the existing governmental order and political system".
- Distant control of the health of whole populations specifically persons with mental health issues.
- "Distant alteration of individuals at the *genetic & psychophysical* level [Emphasis Mine]".
- Controlling populations from outer space.
- Controlling of agriculture by controlling the weather and cataclysms.

Jane's Radar & Electronic Warfare Systems list 13 tracking systems for tracking humans purchased by the Militaries of 27 countries.[373] The United States Government's agenda includes being able to track and monitor the activities of every American citizen. The National Security Agency has an electronic surveillance system that can simultaneously monitor millions of people implanted with microchips.[374] The U. S. appears to want to target specific groups of people for monitoring and mental manipulation. A conference held recently at John Hopkins University in Maryland which included Attorney General Janet Reno, numerous scientists and weapons experts, intelligence officials from state and local police departments was designed to prepare Law Enforcement officials for the use of Psychotronic mind control weapons. Groups to be targeted with these weapons include "non-traditional foes" such as gun collectors, unorganized militia and "church cult groups". The Clinton Administration included Christians, patriots, pro-gun groups, right to life groups and so called cults as potential targets of these weapons.[375] The Pentagon issued a directive which states, "...the term 'adversary' is used in its broadest sense including THOSE WHO ARE NOT DECLARED

---

373 John J. McMurtrey, Inner Voice Target Tracking and Behavioral Influence Technologies (Christians against Mental slavery, April 6th, 2003 – http://www.slavery.org.uk).

374 Rauni-Leena Lukanen-Kilde, Microchip Implants, Mind Control, and Cybernetics (December 6, 2000 – http://www.conspiracyarchive.com).

375 C. B. Baker, New World Order and Psychotronic Tyranny (Youth Action News Letter, December, 1994 –http://www.anglefire.com).

ENEMIES, BUT WHO ARE ENGAGED IN ACTIVIES WE WISH TO STOP. THIS POLICY DOES NOT PRECLUDE ... DOMESTIC USE OF NON-LETHAL WEAPONS BY U.S. MILITARY FORCES IN SUPPORT OF LAW ENFORCEMENT."[376] The Council of Foreign Relations and Trilateral politicians foresee the use of Psychotronic weapons to modify *the ionosphere* for the purpose of mass behavior control. Zibigniew Brzezinski, founder of the Trilateral Commission and the Federal Emergency Management Agency that is specifically designed to force U.S. Citizens to comply with world government mandates wrote in his book Between two Ages, that technology will be made available to the government to conduct secret warfare including control of the weather and behavior of U.S. Citizens. He states,

> It is possible—and TEMPTING—to exploit, for strategic-political purposes, the fruits of research on the brain and on human beings with ... accurately timed, artificially excited electronic strokes ... could lead to a pattern of oscillations that produce relatively high power levels over certain regions of the earth ... In this way, one could develop a system that would SERIOUSLY IMPAIR THE BRAIN PERFORMANCE OF A VERY LARGE POPULATION IN SELECTED REGIONS, OVER AN EXTENDED PERIODS.

The Ground Wave Emergency Network (GWEN) was supposedly constructed by the U. S. Government in the 1980's for the purpose of maintaining defense communications in the case of a nuclear war. However, the Clinton Administrations agenda for the GWEN towers were quite different. These devices are actually designed to transmit signals via the ground to specific targeted populations in order to soften them up to submit to U.N. occupation forces. "Expected resistance to U.N. occupation forces, from militias of loyal Americans will be significantly reduced by having GWEN system in targeted areas transmit specific Psychotronic signals that encourage depression and submission".[377] HAARP is designed to do the same thing. Both of these systems are designed to target specific locals with specific frequencies all across America. The GWEN system was also designed for weather control. Therefore the government can orchestrate drought, or flood, or weather catastrophes at will to force the American populace into submission. GWEN uses the 10 Hz frequency which is the same frequency used by the Soviet Woodpecker grid system which has been used for weather zapping against America since July 4th, 1976. That frequency is also the same frequency upon which the human brain operates. It should be noted that the ENMOD treaty which the U.S. singed prohibits the U.S. from using weather as a weapon against other nations but not against her own population. These weapons suite the agenda of the established

---
376 Ibid.
377 Ibid.

elite to control the universe which includes control of the weather and control of your mind. They can cause draught, floods, "natural" disasters and use this power to punish those who will not submit. They can control your thoughts and manipulate you to suite their own agenda – and that is what they plan to do.

20. Give Us a King

*Then all the elders of Israel gathered together and came to Samuel at Ramah, and said to him, "Look, you are old, and your sons do not walk in your ways. Now make us a king to judge us like all the nations." But the thing displeased Samuel when they said, "Give us a king to judge us." So Samuel prayed to the Lord. And the Lord said to Samuel, "Heed the voice of the people in all that they say to you; for they have not rejected you, but they have rejected me, that I should not reign over them. According to all the works which they have done since the day that I brought them up out of Egypt, even to this day—with which they have forsaken me and served other gods—so they are doing to you also. Now therefore, heed their voice. However, you shall solemnly forewarn them, and show them the behavior of the king who will reign over them." So Samuel told all the words of the Lord to the people who asked him for a king. And he said, "This will be the behavior of the king who will reign over you. He will take your sons and appoint them for his own chariots and to be his horsemen, and some will run before his chariots. He will appoint captains over his thousands and captains over his fifties will set some to plow his ground and reap his harvest, and some to make his weapons of war and equipment for his chariots. He will take your daughters to be perfumers, cooks, and bakers. And he will take the best of your fields, your vineyards, and your olive groves, and give them to his servants. He will take a tenth of your grain and your vintage, and give it to his officers and servants. And he will take your male servants, your female servants, your finest young men, and your donkeys, and put them to his work. He will take a tenth of your sheep. And you will be his servants. And you will cry out in that day because of your king whom you have chosen for yourselves, and the Lord will not hear you in that day." Nevertheless the people refused to obey the voice of Samuel; and they said, "No, but we will have a king over us, that we may also be like all the nations, and that our king may judge and go out before us and **fight our battles** [emphasis mine]." And Samuel heard the words of the people, and he repeated them in the hearing of the Lord. So the Lord said to Samuel, "Heed their voice, and make them a king"* (I Sam 4 1-22 NKJV).

Now Samuel said to all Israel: "Indeed I have heeded your voice in all that you said to me, and have made a king over you. And now here is the king, walking before you; and I am old and gray headed, and look, my sons are with you. I have walked before you from my childhood to this day. Here I am. Witness against me before the Lord and before his Anointed: Whose ox have I taken, or whose donkey have I taken, or whom have I cheated: Whom have I oppressed, or from whose hand have I received any bribe with which to blind my eyes. I will restore it all to you."

And they said, "You have not cheated us or oppressed us, or have you taken anything from any man's hand."

Then he said to them, "The Lord is witness against you, and his anointed is witness this day, against you, and his anointed is witness this day that you have not found anything in my hand."

And they answered, "He is witness."

Then Samuel said to the people, "It is the Lord who raised up Moses and Aaron, and who brought your fathers up from the land of Egypt. Now therefore, stand still, that I may reason with you before the Lord concerning all the righteous acts of the Lord which he did to you and your fathers: "When Jacob had gone into Egypt, and your fathers cried out to the Lord, then the Lord sent Moses and Aaron, who brought your fathers out of Egypt and made them dwell in this place. And when they forgot the Lord their God, he sold them into the hand of Sisera, commander of the army and Hazor, into the land of the Philistines, and into the hand of the king of Moab; and they fought against them. Then they cried out to the Lord, and said, 'We have sinned, because we have forsaken the Lord and served the Baals and Ashtoreths; but now deliver us from the hand of our enemies, and we will serve you.' And the Lord sent Jerubbaal, Bedan, Jephthah, and Samuel, and delivered you out of the hand of your enemies on every side; and you dwelt in safety; And when you saw that Nahash king of the Ammonites came against you, you said to me, 'No, but a king shall reign over us,' when the Lord your God was your king.

Now therefore, here is the king whom you have chosen and whom you have desired. And take note, the Lord has set a king over you. If you fear the Lord and serve Him and obey His voice, and do not rebel against the commandment of the Lord, then both you and the king who reigns over you will continue following the Lord your God. However, if you do not obey the voice of the Lord, but rebel against the commandment of the Lord, then the hand of the Lord will be against you; as it was against your fathers.

Now therefore, stand and see the great thing which the Lord will do before our eyes: Is today not the wheat harvest: I will call to the Lord, and he will send thunder and rain, that you may perceive and see that your wickedness is great, which you have done in the sight of the Lord, in asking a king for yourselves."

So Samuel called to the Lord, and the Lord sent thunder and rain that day; and all the people greatly feared the Lord and Samuel.

And all the people said to Samuel, "Pray for your servants to the Lord your god that we may not die; for we have added to all our sins the evil of asking a king for ourselves."

Then Samuel said to the people, "Do not fear. You have done all this wickedness; yet do not turn aside from following the Lord, but serve the Lord with all your heart. And do not turn aside; for then you would go after empty things which cannot profit or deliver, for they are nothing. For the Lord will not forsake his people, for his great name's sake, because it has pleased the Lord to make you his people. Moreover, as for me, far be it from me that I should sin against the Lord in ceasing to pray for you; but I will teach you the good and the right way. Only fear the Lord, and serve Him in truth with all your heart; for consider what great things he has done for you. But if you still do wickedly, you shall be swept away, both you and your king" (I Sam 12: 1-25 NKJV).

It was Lord Acton that said, "Power corrupts. Absolute power corrupts absolutely". How long did it take us to figure out what God warned the Israelites about long ago? Why did they want a King? What was wrong with what they had? In the book of Judges we read "In those days *there was* no king in Israel, *but* everyone did *what was* right in his own eyes" (Jud 17:6 NKJV). We read that verse and we think, "Total anarchy!" But we never stop to consider that God had not willed for there to be a king in Israel. He set up Israel with a system of civil laws and a system of accountability among the people. He did not appoint them a king. Problem was that the Jews, who were human and sinners like we all are, did not obey God's laws, and the people began to slide into immorality. Then God would send in the rebellious idolatrous nations around them to occupy them, hound them until they cried out to their God for deliverance. They would have to repent of course of their rebellion against God and then God would deliver them. This is not anarchy. This is freedom, divine freedom. This was God's way. He did not want to put his people under the bondage of a king. In other words he did not want them to have a *centralized government*.

But they got tired of the marauders and invaders and decided that they wanted a king to fight their battles for them. In other words, they did not want to take responsibility for the moral climate of the nation and hold each other accountable to being obedient to God. They wanted to go home and tend their gardens, and redecorate their houses and tend their flocks. If they had been diligent and had been obedient to God, they would not have had any battles to fight.

God told them they had asked of him a wicked thing. They thought if they had a king they would not have to worry about so much. They could leave governing to the "government". Had they the foresight to see what would become of them as a result of their request, they might have decided to hold on to their freedom by being obedient to God. Of all the kings of Israel and Judah, only a handful were actually obedient to God. The rest "did what was evil in the sight of the Lord." Even those who were "good" kings, David, Josiah, Hezekiah, Asa, all made fatal errors that resulted either in their deaths or the deaths of a multitude of innocent people in the nations of Israel and Judah. The Jews ended up in exile twice, and were occupied by the time Jesus came to earth.

So let's rethink this government thing again. Do we really want a king? Do we really want a government – a president? Our problem in American is that we have all disassociated ourselves from the government. This is supposed to be a government "of the people, by the people, for the people". However, we don't think of ourselves as the government. That's "them" up there in Washington. And you know, that is just what they want you to think. They want you to disassociate yourselves from the government of the nation so they can literally get away with murder without you knowing about it.

We want to go home and tend our gardens and redecorate our houses, do the laundry and sit on the back patio and drink sweet tea. We don't want to have to fight. We push ourselves to go to the poles 2 or 3 times a year but that is about as much government as the average American wants to get into. But, do you know how to run for office? Do you know how to get a measure put on the ballet? No. "They" do that. Then how is this going to be a government of the people by the people for the people if you and I are going to be nothing more than passive participants?

Our government is talking about "privatizing". It's all about "choice" they say and saving money. Keep in mind, the U.S. Government regularly deceives you in order to gain your cooperation. Whatever they have been presenting to you is designed to get you to cooperate with something that, if you understood the real implications, you would not. For example they are cutting the police force. Saving money. They did not tell us that they were spending our tax money to hire private mercenary firms, like Blackwater, to patrol our streets and monitor situations in an emergency; did not tell us that they are paying billions of tax dollars to private surveillance companies to spy on us. Those are cost plus contracts. That is they cost more than paying the local police to do their jobs. So what's the point? The point is that in "privatizing" they take the governing of the nation out of the hands of "we the people" and put it in the hands of the globalists whose goal is to make money first and foremost. They do not have your best interests at heart. Not only that, you have no say in a "privatized" government. Eventually all the "privatized" government services end up in the hands of the established elite who want to rule the world. They want to eliminate the middle class. Their stated intentions are to reduce the world population down to slaves and owners, eliminate national boundaries etc. That is your privatized government. God warned the Israelites about this. We have to get used to the idea that when God warns us about something there is a very good reason for it.

So, you don't "feel led" to run for office. You don't feel qualified. So you leave that to someone else who is probably not led and whose philosophy is that it is okay to lie, cheat, steal and commit murder to accomplish their tasks. Think not? "They" in Washington have lying down to an art form. They put it in manuals. That is they have manuals like *Revolution in Military Affairs* that specifically tells their selected audience how to deceive the public into accepting the changes "they" want to make. It doesn't mean that there aren't good people in government offices, but they are losing ground because of lack of support. They are fighting a battle that you and I don't see. They are fighting to maintain a standard of morality and integrity in an environment where their values make them a target. Congressman Leo Ryan is a good example. He was murdered while investigating the criminal activity of the CIA associated with the People's temple in Jonestown Guyana. Ted Gunderson was an FBI Chief Special Agent who investigated among other things the Franklin scandal in Omaha Nebraska and also Satanic Ritual Abuse in America. He eventually became "discredited". There is a pattern here. Anyone who honestly cares about being decent moral upright people working anywhere in the secular world or sometimes even in the church, sadly, becomes a target. The Shadow Government is fighting to keep its stranglehold on this nation *and they are winning*!

They are winning because too many very decent Americans are too content with their lives to pick up a sword and fight. Decent people can also be very complacent. "I voted today" reads the sticker on your lapel. By refusing to do more than go to the poles and vote, we are voting for the destruction of this nation and we are acquiescing to the crimes being committed by our government against innocent people in this nation and around the world.

"But what do I do?" you ask. Maybe you really don't feel like you can run for office. But you can get together with your family, friends and neighbors and organize an effort to become informed about what you government is really doing. You can assist someone else to run for office. You can get a measure put on the ballet in your community – to, say, get Directed Energy Weapons banned in your communities and gangstalking outlawed. You can make people aware of the atrocities being committed by our government. You can educate your community. You can stick up for the victims who have been stalked into the ground by gangstalkers, the hundreds of Middle Eastern persons who were imprisoned on false charges and brutally abused, the thousands of infants who never had a name or a birth certificate because they were bred to be sacrificed on satanic alters, and you can support and defend those children who were sexually abused by government officials and therefore never got justice. You can be educated yourself by reading what the journalists and authors are telling you about our country and turn off the television, the government's propaganda machine.

Finally, you can get down on your knees and pray. This nation has never been in worse condition morally. By fighting back we are no longer complicit in its crimes. We can make a difference when we decide that it is our job to run the government. We don't need a king or a president. We need Jesus Christ to be the Crowned King of our nation and the world. He created this universe. Only he can run it.

As Christians we have been waiting for Christ's return. During a particularly anointed prayer session, I heard the voice of the Holy Spirit say to me, "He will return when you [the people] declare him King." Jesus will not rule over people who do not want him to rule over them. He will indeed return when we declare him King. When we stop looking to someone else to do it for us and we are ready to be accountable to God for how this nation is run, he will return and be our king. Keep in mind, however, that the deceivers will try also to pretend to be him as well. Jesus warned us that this will also occur in the last days (Matt 24:5). We need to be diligent and watchful and careful that we are also not deceived.

21. No Place for Our Children to Run

Children at Risk

In America we must be acutely aware that there is a significant problem with missing and exploited children which is why we have an organization that is dedicated to finding and protecting those children. The faces of missing children are plastered on the walls of grocery stores and department stores where we shop. They come on coupons that we get in the mail. We hear news of missing children on the news all the time. We have the Amber Alert system to inform us when a child has gone missing in a particular area. We even see the faces of missing children on milk cartons. One would then think that this nation is dedicated to protecting children.

The most at risk kids for exploitation and abduction are children in the foster care system. An article printed by Massnews.com in June 2002 reported that Florida and Massachusetts could not account for a large number of children on their roles. Massachusetts looses about 400 foster children per year according to the Legal Services Reporter. Two of those children, 17 year old Latasha Cannon and Kelly Hancock 14, were found murdered. In the state of Florida there were more than 1000 children missing who were on the roles of the Department of Children and Families when Governor Jeb Bush, brother of George W., ordered them found. He declared the investigation a success when all but 88 of them were finally located. The report also indicated that many of them are running away from abuse in the foster care homes where they are placed, however the DSS/DCF do not report them missing because they continue to collect the money they receive for providing their care. When children have to be removed from the home they are placed in foster care environments where they are not safe. "Twelve billion a year in federal money, plus billions more in state funding is being poured into this system under the guise of protecting children from abuse and neglect in their homes."[378]

Scandal at the Texas Youth Commission

So while we have a foster care system that is supposed to protect children from abuse in their homes, we have public officials who regularly engage in prostitution of minors and legislators are turning their heads the other way. A 2007 article written by Wayne Madsen reports that 10 underage males housed at a youth detention facility in West Texas were sodomized by the faculty and the Justice Department refused to prosecute. Texas Ranger Brian J. Burzinski filed charges on behalf of the boys implicating two employees of the school, Ray Brookings and John Hernandez. Bill Bauman, assistant to the West Texas U.S. Attorney General

---

378 Nev Moor, Lost Children of Florida and Massachusetts (MassNews.com – June 17, 2002 – http://www.caiga.org).

declined to prosecute because the boys who claimed that they had been raped did not sustain bodily injury or bodily harm. He stated he did not believe the boys were forced to have sex, (in other words they willingly complied). He was apparently looking out for the interests of the National Man Boy Love Association, whose motto is "Sex before eight or it's too late". Thus he declared that sex between staff and underage boys at the facility was okay as long as it was consensual.[379]

State Senator John Whitmire (D Texas) and republican Governor Rick Perry however were outraged and determined that the school should be in receivership status. The Texas Youth Commission (TYC) investigated and found that there were other incidents of inappropriate sexual harassment at other TYC facilities. State Senator Juan Hinojosa learned that youth detained at another South Texas district in 2005 were held longer then their sentence required if they refused to consent to having sex with staff members. Another staff member at Brownwood in Central Texas was accused of having sex with a 15 year old girl. The Brownwood police covered up the incident. Mr. Nichols the acting director of the TYC investigated 1300 cases of wrong doing in 2006 which included 98 cases of reported sexual abuse. In 78 of the cases the staff members were either fired or resigned but not prosecuted.[380]

Hernandez and Brookings did go to trial. John Paul Hernandez was acquitted on Monday February 21, 2011 of 14 counts in 11 indictments of alleged sexual abuse of five inmates in 2004 and 2005. A police officer on the jury influenced the jury by stressing that the man could be convicted only if there was no reasonable doubt that he was guilty[381]. The reasonable doubt was raised by a former corrections officer who testified that she heard two of the youth say in a hallway conversation that they were going to accuse Hernandez of molesting them so they could get out of the facility[382]. Hernandez attorney, Albert G. Valdez, told prosecutors in his arguments that there was no DNA, no fingerprints, no crime scene photos and no witnesses to the acts.[383] However witnesses against Hernandez besides the youths themselves included Training Specialist Randy Foster who reported that both Brookings and Hernandez were taking youth to places where they could be alone with them after hours. Also Assistant Principle Monroe Elms found Hernandez alone with youth in darkened classrooms, behind locked doors on multiple

---

379 Wayne Madsen, WH/Justice Department Coverup Pedophilia Cases (March 27, 2007- http://www.rense.com).
380 Ralph Blumenthal, Texas Calls for Takeover of States Juvenile Schools (New York Times, February 28, 2007 – http://www.nytimes.com).
381 The Associated Press, Jurors felt youth prison official was guilty but were swayed by ex-cop, lack of physical evidence (http://www.dallasvoice.com)
382 Betsey Blaney, Jury acquits Hernandez: Ex-principle not guilty of all charges (Odessa American Online, February 22, 2011 – http://www.oaoa.com).
383 Betsey Blaney, Texas youth prison abuse case ends in acquittal (Seattle Times, February 22, 2011 – http:seattletiems.nwsource.com).

occasions in the spring and summer of 2004.[384] Ray Brookings was sentenced in April 2006 to 10 years in prison for sexual abuse of prison inmates.[385]

A number of other Washington political figures have been charged with similar crimes involving White House Page Boys. Career Justice Department officials and the FBI leaked the information to ABC news because Attorneys General John Ashcroft and Alberto Gonzales covered up the scandal for political reasons. "The back story of Pagegate is that there was a criminal conspiracy by the top political leadership of the Justice Department to cover up the predatory activities of [Mark] Foley and other GOP members of congress since at least 2003 and likely as early as 2001". Children at Guantanamo and Abu Ghraib were also similarly sodomized while Donald Rumsfeld and other White House officials covered it up.[386]

Trance Formation of America

The *Trance Formation of American*, co-authored by Cathy O'Brian and CIA Insider Mark Phillips, is a shocking testimony of the corruption of Law Enforcement, the intelligence community and the White House. Though this book would be extremely hard to read for anyone because of the sexual content, it is unfortunately the true life testimony of Cathy O'Brian who was a project Monarch mind control slave. Her training took place in multiple places around the country but her basic Monarch programming took place in a Catholic School, St François De Sales in Muskegon Michigan. She was born into a third generation occult family and had been molested from the time she was an infant in her family. Her father had used her and her siblings to make kiddie porn films which he sold to make money. The films were discovered and someone turned her father in to the authorities. However, instead of rescuing her and her siblings, government officials made a deal with her father to not prosecute him if he would let Cathy become a part of the CIA Monarch program. He agreed. She was molested by a CIA operative, Father James Thaylen, who was head of the school. Cathy pulled no punches in her testimony about how as a child she was physically abused, deliberately traumatized in order to induce her to disassociate, and programmed to be a "White House Presidential Model Sex Slave". I read about half way through her book and had to put it down because the sexual content was so contaminating. However, her testimony implicated U.S. Public officials such as Bill and Hillary Clinton, Gerald Ford,

---

384 Tish Elliot-Wilkins, Summery Report for Administrative Review, Texas Youth Commission (Office of the General Council, February 15, 2007 – http://www.dallasnews.com).

385 Betsey Blaney, Texas youth prison abuse case ends in acquittal (Seattle Times, February 22, 2011 – htp:seattletiems.nwsource.com.)

386 Wayne Madsen, WH/Justice Department Coverup Pedophilia Cases (March 27, 2007- http://www.rense.com).

Dick Cheney, Ronald Regan, Senator Robert C. Byrd just to name a few. She and her daughter were rescued by Mark Phillips who was contracted by the CIA to perform mind control research on primates. Together they documented their attempt to get the criminal justice system to prosecute those she charged with criminal offences against her and her daughter – to no avail. Not only was the White House involved but also the National Security Agency, NASA and the Catholic School where she was being "programmed" by CIA operatives working in the school. That fact that elected officials and Law Enforcement were guilty of sodomizing and raping a child should be of extreme concern to this nation and to our churches. The fact that these people were never charged, let alone indicted is indication that our criminal justice system is completely defunct. The very people whose job it was to protect her were responsible for criminal exploitation and for covering it up.

Interestingly, in *Mind Control World Control*, author Jim Keith reviewed Cathy O'Brien's testimony and indicated that he did not think it was true. I have cited Jim Keith's work in this book, and I was surprised at his analysis of her testimony. Jim Keith is now deceased. Having spent now 4 years researching the "conspiracy" and having read numerous testimonies of abuse by various victims as well as many other conspiracy authors, I believe the attempt at discrediting the testimony of Cathy O'Brien was not the work of Jim Keith. I believe that the CIA, in a desperate attempt to discredit Cathy O'Brien as well as Mark Phillips who rescued Cathy, edited Jim Keith's work to cover up their crimes. The remarks made about Mark Phillips in *Mind control, World Control* were not at all objective nor based on any facts contradicting what Phillips stated in the book. They were simply insulting. That is not the work of an experienced author nor a professional journalist. That would be more like something the CIA would do to cover up a heinous crime. Cathy's testimony is very consistent with the testimonies of other victim witnesses as we shall see. I also don't believe that any serious researcher familiar with the "conspiracy" would be willing to put anything at all past the CIA. That would include those who used to work for them and are now speaking out, such as John Stockwell and Mark Phillips.

Cathy O'Brien was taken to Offutt Air Force Base in Nebraska, to a Top Secret NASA/Military Instillation where she was further "conditioned". She writes in *Trance Formation of America;*

> The "you can run, but you can't hide" conditioning was deeply ingrained in my mind there through a technique that was later used on Kelly [her daughter], as well as on other mind-control slaves. I was taken underground to a so-called 'secret' circular room where the walls were covered with numerous screens showing satellite pictures from around the world. These satellites are referred to as "Eye in the Sky"- An Air Force official explained to me that my every move could be monitored via satellite. On a separate four screen

viewer, he demonstrated what, in retrospect, was a contrived pre-recorded slide show, with the scenes changing as rapidly as he spoke and typed it into the computer. "Where will you run?" he asked me. "To the Arctic? The Antarctic? Brazil? The mountains? The desert? The prairies? The hills of Afghanistan? The city of Kabul? Devil's Tower (Wyoming)? Would you try to run to Cuba and live among our enemies? We can find you there. There is truly no place to run and no place to hide. The U.S. Senate (the picture was of Byrd)? The White House? Or to your own backyard? (My father was depicted waving from his front door, cupping his hands over his mouth saying, "Come back" just like Aunt Em in *The Wizard Of Oz*.) "The moon? We got you covered. You can run, but you can't hide." This had been sufficient to convince me in my suggestive state that my every move could be monitored.[387]

The Franklin investigation and the Washington Pageboy Scandal

Child abuse associated with Offutt Air Force Base in Nebraska surfaced in yet another scandal now known as the Franklin cover up. The Franklin scandal began when the Manger of the Franklin Federal Credit Union, Larry King was investigated for Fraud. In Oct. 1988 the FBI and the IRS determined that there was $40,000,000 missing from the FFCU. The investigation eventually led to allegations by several Nebraska children that they were being used in a child prostitution ring also managed by Larry King whose business partner was former ABC reporter and Washington socialite Craig Spence. Several Nebraska political figures were eventually implicated in the scandal including former Police Chief Charles Wadman, Fort Calhoun Superintendent of Schools Deward Finch and Fort Calhoun High School principal Kent Miller as well Jarrett Webb who worked for the Omaha Public Power District and was a board member of the Franklin Federal Credit Union. Mrs. Webb was a cousin to Larry E. King Jr. who managed the credit union. Paul Bonacci, one of the child victims in the Franklin scandal reported that King sent Limousines to Offutt AFB to get CIA officials for King's parties..[388]

Foster children in the custody of the Webbs accused them of physically beating them with a belt and a railroad iron as well as sexually abusing them. The Webb's natural son Joey also complained of abuse. There were nine total children in the care of the Webbs. The Sheriff's Department of Washington County Nebraska handling the case contacted the Nebraska Department of

---

387 Cathy O'Brien & Mark Phillips, Trance Formation of America (Frankston, Texas: Reality Marketing Inc.,1995) 117.
388 John DeCamp, The Franklin Cover-up (Lincoln, Nebraska: AWT, 1992) 175.

Social Serivces on June 10, 1985. The children also repoted that the Webbs were suppleid with kiddie porn films by Larry King.[389]

Several children reported being taken by plane to Washington for sex parties at the White House. Larry King's business partner, Gregg spence, ran a male child prostituion ring. The page boy scandal involved high level government officials and was therefore covered up. Howerver, Washington Times reporters examined hundreds of credit card vouchers charged to Spence's escourt business, Professional Serivces Inc. and other escourt services implicating several former White House colleagues of US Attorney General J.B. Stephens who were among the clients of the prostitution ring. Those who confessed to using the services include Charles K. Dutcher, former associate Director of Presidential Personnel in the Regan Administration and Paul R. Balach, Labor Secretary and Elizabeth Dole's personal liaison to the White House. Mr. Dutcher was congressional aide to former Rep. Robert Baumann who resigned from the White House after having admitted to engaging in sex with teenage male prostitutes. Ted A Blodgett, White House staffer who prepared President Regan's daily news summery denied the charges to his credit card.[390] Reporters from the Washington Times found that some of the credit card vouchers from Spence's escort service were signed by US military personnel using Depart of Defense credit cards. Top level Pentagon officials expressed concern that the KGB had infiltrated the "homosexual nest" in the top of the Regan administration and was using male prostitutes to compromise and blackmail US Intelligence personnel.[391] Investigation of Larry E. King Jr. revealed his involvement in child prostitution. He had confiscated money from the Credit Union to throw lavish parties for governing officials, many of who were from Washington DC including George H. W. Bush. Pres Bush was implicated in at least one sexual encounter with a 19 year old African American named Brent.[392] Larry King was eventually charged with misappropriation of funds and sentenced to prison. However, though there were multiple victim witnesses to the child sexual and ritual abuse, child pornography and prostitution of children, the Grand Jury denied the evidence and refused to prosecute Larry King for child sexual abuse.

The investigation revealed that King had several close connections with the US intelligence community, the military and the White House. In fact the CIA frequently borrowed money from the Credit Union without a contract or any formal agreement for repayment. An informal agreement for repayment within

---

389 Ibid, 5-10.
390 Paul M. Rodriguez & George Archibald, Homosexual prostitution inquiry ensnares VIPs with Regan, Bush (Washington Times on Franklin Affair, June 29, 1989 – http://www.wanttoknow.info).
391 Paul M. Rodriguez & George Archibald, Homosexual prostitution inquiry ensnares VIPs with Regan, Bush (Washington Times on Franklin Affair, June 29, 1989 – http://www.wanttoknow.info).
392 Wayne Madsen, WH/Justice Department Coverup Pedophilia Cases (March 27, 2007- http://www.rense.com).

30 days was frequently not honored.[393] Cathy O'Brian's entertainer and former mind controller husband, Alex Houston who worked with the CIA, went to Boy's Town on "business" "...where the wayward boys were being traumatized and sexually abused in accordance with the Catholic churches involvement in Project Monarch." Paul Bonacci, who had been at Boys Town, named Cathy's husband as one of his abusers at that location.[394]

A photographer who was arrested on child pornography charges said that he was recruited by King to photograph children at White House Child sex parties. Although he stated that he did shoot some pictures for King, he refused to do anything involving pornography. But he testified that while he was attending a function at the White House, he saw another photographer there who looked exactly like him. The double was even carrying the same camera and wearing the same clothes, same hair doo and the like. Rusty also refused to do a snuff film.

> Recently arrested photographer Russell E. "Rusty" Nelson- who according to U.S. District court testimony [2-5-1999] was impersonated by another photographer at Capitol Hill child sex parties during the Reagan and Bush presidencies, told us last week that in 1988 he refused Hunter Thompson's offer of $100,000 to film a graphic child sex "snuff" movie to be sold to wealthy private clients where a young boy would be murdered as a sacrifice.[395]

Rusty was out of jail but in hiding at the time of the interview. His story of seeing a double of himself at the party at the Capitol is not farfetched. It is speculated that Hitler may have had a double and it may have been his double that was shot and not himself. Hitler's aid Rudolf Hess also had a double.[396] Lee Harvey Oswald, John Hinckley, Timothy McVey and Patty Hurst may have also had doubles.[397] Howard Hughes had a double.[398] It is not an uncommon thing for the CIA, the government and the intelligence community to use doubles to accomplish their purposes.

Paul Bonacci, Alisha Owen, Daniel King and Troy Boner were among 80 victim child witnesses in the Franklin case which involved Larry King, Omaha Chief of Police Robert Wadman, the Webbs and a few others with links to the

---

393 John DeCamp, The Franklin Cover-up (Lincoln, Nebraska: AWT, 1992) 172.
394 Cathy O'Brien & Mark Phillips, Trance Formation of America (Frankston, Texas: Reality Marketing Inc.,1995) 148.
395 Tom Flocco, Amber Alert on Capitol Hill (Truth in Government in Our Lifetime, March 28, 2005 – http://www.tedgunderson.com).
396 Jim Marrs, The Rise of the Fourth Reich, (New York. NY: William Morrow of Harper Collins, 2008) 2, 47.
397 Jim Keith, Mind Control World Control (Kempton, ILL: Adventures Unlimited Press, 1997) 165, 177.
398 Robin de Ruiter, Worldwide Evil and Misery: The Legacy of 13 Satanic Bloodlines, (The Netherland: Mayra Publications, 2008)26.

White House. John W. Decamp represented Alisha Owen who testified that Chief Wadman made her pregnant and is the father of her daughter. He also represented Paul Bonacci who was accused of perjury for testifying against King and others associated with him in a child pornography scandal that involved sadism, ritual abuse, murder and the **kidnapping and selling of children**.[399] A raid initiated because of reports of blackmail and credit card fraud was conducted at 6004 34th place NW in Washington DC. In the raid a switchboard was found operating several homosexual escort services. "In addition to credit-card fraud, the investigation is said to be focused on illegal interstate prostitution, abduction and use of minors for sexual perversion, extortion, larceny and related illicit drug trafficking and use by prostitutes and their clients."[400]

Paul Bonacci met a man named Walter Carlson in 1979 at an Independence Day picnic. He went home with Carlson and watched cartoons, pornographic films and eventually had sex. Paul was eleven years old. He met *World-Herald* columnist Peter Citron at a public park. "Bonacci says that he was flown to California, Colorado, New York, Minnesota and elsewhere at the behest of the mercurial Larry King, and prostituted to politicians and wealthy businessmen."[401] Alisha Owen witnessed sexual encounters between adult males and minor males at parties involving public officials. Usually present at these parties were Larry King, Robert Wadman, former Game and Parks Commissioner Eugene Mahoney, Alan Baer, an official of J. T. Brandels & Sons, a local department store, Peter Citron, Harold Anderson, and the superintendent of a school Deward Finch. Alisha Owens also named a judge Theodor Carlson as a perpetrator.[402]

In a complaint filed at the U.S. District Court of Nebraska Bonacci testified that at the age of 12 he was forced to attend sex parties, and sadistic rituals that were attended by influential Citizens of Nebraska. He estimated that he had attended 25 – 30 group sex rituals between 1979 and 1984. At one these parties he was beaten for refusing to participate in a sadistic ritual and burned with a cigarette. Bonacci testified in court to being witness to and forced participant in a gruesome murder. He stated that he and another boy named Nicholas were taken by helicopter to a place in California near a Kern River and a bridge with a name on it. They had a naked little boy in a cage. Bonacci and Nicholas were warned that they had better cooperate.[403]

---

399 John DeCamp, The Franklin Cover-up (Lincoln, Nebraska: AWT, 1992) 233.
400 Paul M. Rodriguez & George Archibald, Homosexual prostitution inquiry ensnares VIPs with Regan, Bush (Washington Times on Franklin Affair, June 29, 1989 – http://www.wanttoknow.info/).
401 Alex Constantine, Psychic Dictatorship in the U.S.A. (Portland, OR: Feral House, 1995)156.
402 John DeCamp, The Franklin Cover-up (Lincoln, Nebraska: AWT, 1992) 71.
403 Alex Constantine, Psychic Dictatorship in the U.S.A. (Portland, OR: Feral House 1995)157.

In a taped interview with investigator Gary Caradori on March 14, 1990[404] Paul Bonacci gave a more detailed description of that encounter. They watched while adult men sodomized the little boy who was crying and screaming and bleeding from his anus. The adult male shot the little boy in the cage and forced Paul and Nicholson to bite his genitals off and later put those genitals in their mouths. They watched the men dispose of the body in a clearing. The entire incident had been filmed. Paul Bonacci told Caradori that after the incident they were hosed off and later taken to a hotel where they were instructed to shower and dress up in "Tarzan things" and then in shorts, socks and a shirt. They were taken to a house where they met with some others who sat around and watched the film of Paul Bonacci and Nicholas sodomizing the little boy in the cage. While the men watched the film they sodomized Bonacci and Nicholas. Bonacci states that he and Nicholas were required to sodomize each other and watch the film where they were forced to perform oral sex on the little boy in the cage. Paul was at sex parties for five days. He didn't remember much about those parties except that he cut his own wrists. He was taken to the hospital by one of the men who gave him a different name. He was in the hospital for two days and one of the men paid the bill.[405]

Paul made two trips to Washington, D.C. with Larry King where he had sex with other people. Larry King was trying to earn favor with the Republican Party and Paul believed the men he had sex with were republicans. One of those was a man named Frank who he thought might be a senator or governor or other state official.[406]

On June 21, 1991, 21-year-old Alisha Jahn Owen was pronounced guilty by a jury in Douglas County, Nebraska, on eight counts of felony perjury. On August 8, 1991, she was sentenced to serve nine to twenty-seven years in prison. Owen was indicted for telling a grand jury, before which she testified in 1990, that she was sexually abused as a juvenile by a Nebraska district court judge, by the chief of police of the city of Omaha, by the manager of the Franklin Community Federal Credit Union, and others. Alisha Owen also witnessed, she said, the abuse of other children by figures in Nebraska's political and financial establishment whom she named, among them the publisher of the state's largest newspaper, the *Omaha World-Herald*. She testified that she was in a group of Nebraska children who functioned for years as illegal drug couriers, traveling nationwide, for some of Nebraska's wealthiest, most powerful and prominent businessmen.[407]

A local and a federal jury with a mandate to consider the charges of child abuse connected with the Franklin Credit Union *indicted the victim-witnesses for perjury instead*. Paul Bonacci was also indicted but the charges were dropped, but not before he spent a good deal of time in prison. The Grand Jury made the

---
404 John DeCamp, The Franklin Cover-up (Lincoln, Nebraska: AWT, 1992) 103.
405 Ibid, 104
406 Ibid, 102.
407 Ibid, xvii

decision that the child witnesses were lying and though they determined that the children had been previously abused, would not concede that they had been abused by the people the children testified about. Two other children, Danny King and Troy Boner, recanted after being threatened by the FBI. The FBI had actually threatened to kill members of Troy's family if he did not recant.[408] Fritz Springmeyer, states in *The 13 Satanic Bloodlines* that ex-Satanists were trying to warn the public that the FBI had been involved in selling them children for sacrifice. "When the Illuminati was beginning to get exposed in the Franklin Saving & Loan case in Lincoln, NE the FBI was part of the dirty actors and was part of the cover up".[409]

Gary Caradori had managed to confiscate enough evidence to convict all those implicated by the child witnesses of the Franklin investigation, however before he could get this evidence to the proper authorities, Caradori's private airplane exploded mid flight killing both he and his 8 year old son.[410]

Kathleen Sorenson who had been fostering the Webb girls after they had been removed from the Webb's home had fostered a number of children who had been ritually abused. She was interviewed about what she had learned from the children on live television. She was killed in a head on collision that FBI investigator Ted Gunderson determined was not an accident.[411]

The press, in particular the Omaha World Herald did not do the job of unbiased reporting. Instead they attempted to discredit the victim witnesses and those that were trying to help them. Their final analysis was that the allegations were a "carefully crafted hoax".[412] Alisha Owen and Paul Bonacci who refused to recant their testimonies were charged with perjury and sentenced to prison. Though the charges against Paul Bonacci were dropped, Alisha Owen spent more time in solitary confinement than any women in history. Experts who had worked with Paul Bonacci including Dr. Judianne Densen-Gerber, New York-area psychiatrist, lawyer, child abuse expert and Dr. Beverly Mead, psychiatric consultant to the Omaha Police Department concluded that he could not possibly be lying. John Decamp was a witness himself that Paul Bonacci was not lying. John Decamp also attended several functions at the White House. He was not participating in child prostitution nor was he aware that those things were happening at the time. However, he heard Paul Bonacci's descriptions of those functions that he also attended and knew that he had to have been there.[413] Alisha Owens also passed a lie detector test as well as two other victim witnesses. Alisha Owen named Police Chief Wadman as the father of her child. Wadman claimed that DNA tests

---

408 Alex Constantine, Psychic Dictatorship in the U.S.A. (Portland, OR: Feral House 1995)158.
409 Fritz Springmeyer, The 13 Satanic Bloodlines (July 3, 2009, www.theforbiddenknowledge.com).
410 John DeCamp, The Franklin Cover-up (Lincoln, Nebraska: AWT, 1992) 2-3.
411 Ibid, 210 – 211.
412 Ibid, 106.
413 John DeCamp, The Franklin Cover-up (Lincoln, Nebraska: AWT, 1992) 167.

proved that he was not the father. However, an Omaha reporter who had been following the case indicated that the DNA tests never happened.[414]

During the Franklin investigation, a congressional investigation was initiated into a homosexual sex and drug ring operating out of the White House. It was squashed because it involved kids. The ring originated during the J. Edgar Hoover era. Hoover wanted to find ways of blackmailing congressmen to keep them under his thumb. The CIA hired call boy networkers to entice congressmen into living out their sexual fantasies with little boys and capturing them of tape. The tapes were thus used to blackmail the congressmen.[415] In fact Craig Spence, Larry King's business partner, was said to be operating a CIA blackmail ring. Spence had a Victorian Mansion on Wyoming Ave. that he planted with bugs and video equipment that was used to make incriminating tapes of political elites engaging in sex with male child prostitutes. The parties at his mansion were attended by the likes of William Casey, Ted Koppel, John Mitchell and Eric Severide. Four months after the story broke Craig Spence was found dead at the Ritz Carrolton Hotel in Boston of an apparent suicide.[416] Cathy O'Brien described a situation that would confirm that this is still going on. In Icke's book *The Biggest Secret* Cathy details an incident in which Bill Clinton was sexually exploiting her and her minor daughter at the same time while Sr. George Bush, his boss, was filming the incident. Bill remarks, "You don't have to do that. I am already one of you. My position does not need to be compromised".[417]

Project Monarch and U.S. Government Involvement in Missing and Exploited Children

I have already discussed the fact that Hitler found support for his eugenics and mind control research from American businessmen and politicians. We already are now familiar with Operation Paperclip – shocking though it may seem to us. One of those scientists who was given asylum in America whom I have already mentioned was famous Auschwitz Doctor Joseph Mengele. Joseph Mengele was thought to have been killed in Venezuela, but victim witnesses tell a different story.

A company known as IG-Farben-Chemiekartell, with funds it received from Rockefeller and government ministries, provided support to Hitler. This company was supervised by the ruling elite in the United States. The company was part of the National-Socialist mind control project led by Dr. Joseph Mengele at the

---

414 Alex Constantine, Psychic Dictatorship (Portland, OR: Feral House 1995) 154.
415 Ibid, 180 – 181.
416 The Franklin Credit Union Child Sex Ring Scandal (http://www.francesfarmersrevenge.com).
417 David Icke, The Biggest Secret (Wildwood, MO: Bridget of Love, 1999) 338.

Kaiser-Wilhelm institute in Berlin and later at Auschwitz.[418] Joseph Mengele, after WWII was the mastermind behind the secret CIA project Monarch. The goal of the Monarch program was designed to transform humans into robots. The victims are subject to "controllers" who are Illuminati. The Monarch slaves are placed in high positions in government, the church, educational institutions, scientific community, and financial institutions so they influence all aspects of civilian life. These human robots do their work without revealing any Illuminati secrets and without them there would be no NWO.[419] Mengele's method involved inducing trauma with children and even infants which would cause the child's mind to split off into another personality. This is commonly called Multiple Personality Disorder and more recently called Dissociative Identity Disorder. At an Air force base in California which was built ostensibly for testing new weapons, children and infants were robotized in this way in a horrific program sponsored by the CIA. A hanger where the programming took place contained 2000 to 3000 electrified cages just big enough to contain one infant stacked to the ceiling. After the infants spent a great deal of time being treated with kindness and tenderness they were then placed in the cages. Thus the infant became cruelly bonded to the same doctor who was abusing them. This prevented them from disassociating themselves from the abusive person. David Icke calls this "love bombing".[420] The electrified cages called "woodpecker grids" shocked the babies at the whim of the doctor. The infants were also subjected to flashes of bright light which were used to hypnotize them. After several days in the cages they would be brutally raped. This is deliberately induced trauma which causes the infants personality to split even before the core personality can be developed.

And where did they get 3000 infants to fill those cages? In *Tales from the Time Loop*, David Icke details eyewitness reports of the underground tunnel system in America that was built by nuclear underground blasts. Children from all over the world were kidnapped and taken into this underground system.[421] One of these systems is Dulce AFB. About one million children per year were snatched off of America's streets. These were Mengele's mind control subjects. Some of them were turned into mind controlled sex slaves and some assassins. Others were slaughtered in front of the other children for the purpose of terrifying them. Montauk Island and about 25 other similar facilities were used to turn about 250,000 young boys into mind controlled slaves. They became journalists, radio and TV personalities, businessmen, lawyers, judges and prosecutors.[422]

---

418 Robin de Ruiter, Worldwide Evil and Misery: The Legacy of the13 Satanic Bloodlines (The Netherlands, Myra Publications, 2008) 181.
419 Ibid, 312.
420 David Icke, The Biggest Secret (Wildwood, MO: Bridget of Love Publications, 1999) 350.
421 David Icke, Tales from the Time Loop, (Ryde, Iles of Wright, UK: David Icke Books, 2003) 293.
422 Ken Adachi, Mind control – The Ultimate Terror (Educate Yourself – http://www.bibilotechapleyades.net.

The fact that the U.S. intelligence community is involved in child ritual abuse, sexual exploitation and even selling of children into slavery is well documented. Gordon Thomas writes in *Enslaved* (1991) that a worldwide slavery underground involved the CIA in kidnapping Latin American children who were ". . . sold to child sex rings, or sold so their organs could be used in transplants." Some of the pilots ". . . made two or three flights a day. ... The majority of the fliers were mercenaries who had flown for the CIA".[423] Cathy O'Bryan's father was actually promoted at his place of employment because of his connections with the Pentagon. He was busy impregnating his wife so they could sell their babies to the "Project". He was also prostituting Cathy to officials of the Muskegon Coast Guard while transporting drugs to and from the base.[424] According to an article by Tom Flocco children were abducted by pedophile members of congress and abused at child sex parties. "Witness says abducted children-23 now dead-abused by 20-30 pedophile members of congress at child sex parties held at Embassy Row mansion where Secret Service secured presidential limo was seen parked outside".[425]

Another public official implicated by Cathy O'Brien was Lt. Col. Michael Aquino. The Army Lt. Col. was responsible for Cathy's mind control behavior programming which took place at Ft. Campbell Kentucky. He held a Top Secret security clearance in the Defense Intelligence Agency's Psychological Warfare Division. Aquino describes himself as a neo-NAZI and is founder of the Himmler inspired Temple of Set. He was responsible for the programming of many child slaves of the CIA's project Monarch. He used the usual sleep, food and water deprivation as well as sexual assault and high tech high voltage electricity to accomplish mind control programming on both Cathy and her daughter Kelly, who had not ever had a chance to develop her base personality before mind control tortures created in Kelly multiple personalities.[426]

The Advisory Committee on Human Radiation Experiments is a 14-member committee of experts of various sciences and law. Therapist Valerie Wolf testified before this committee that those who have been victims of mind control research as children were intimidated as adults so that they would not talk about their victimization. Dr. Colin Ross, a psychiatrist who treats dissociative identity disorder wrote that he became interested in mind control research when he had multiple patients suffering from D.I.D. who reported being victimized on military bases across the U.S.[427]

---

423 Gordon Thomas, Enslaved (New York: PHAROS BOOKS, 1991) 158.
424 Cathy O'Brien & Mark Phillips, Trance Formation of America (Frankston, Texas: Reality Marketing Inc.,1995) 93.
425 Tom Flocco, Amber Alert on Capital Hill (Truth in Government in Our Lifetime, March 28, 2005 – http://www.tedgunderson.com).
426 Cathy O'Brien & Mark Phillips, Trance Formation of America (Frankston, Texas: Reality Marketing Inc.,1995) 110 – 112.
427 Cheryl Welsh, U.S. Human Rights Abuse Report (Christians against Mental Slavery, January, 1998 – http://www.mindjustice.org).

In 1987 the military base of the Presidio of San Francisco Child Development Center was scandalized because of multiple allegations from children and their parents that they were being ritually and sexually abused there. One three year old told her mother that she had been taken to the home of Lt. Col. Michael Aquino and his wife Lilith and "subjected to bizarre satanic ritual abuse".[428]

Attorney Cynthia Angell was representing the father of two small children whose mother was accusing him of molesting them. The mother was attempting to revoke his visitation rights. However, the attorney learned from the children that the abuse had not occurred in the father's home but had in fact occurred at the Presidio Child Development Center where the children's mother left them during the day. The Attorney was meeting with a witness on February 2nd 1989 when she was kidnapped from her car by two strongmen for three hours. She was blindfolded and threatened with physical harm if she did not drop the custody case. She was then made to listen to a tape of children and adults chanting and screaming. She was released after three hours back to her car. She immediately went to the police and gave a description of one of the men who made no effort to cover his face. The man she described was a dark haired Latin with a mustache who had been reported to police before. The description would fit Lt. Col. Michael Aquino. Lt. Col. Aquino subsequently failed to show up for the hearing of the child molestation charges that had been filed. There had been numerous allegations against the Day Care center involving child molestation beginning in 1987 when the three year old girl reported the abuse to her mother. "Indeed, much of the evidence for the abuse of children at the Presidio facility is compelling. It includes medical documentation of sexual abuse, accurate descriptions of places claimed to have been used for rituals, and the indirect evidence of the children's continued nightmares and adjustment problems".[429]

Eventually there were 60 children that were coming forward and testifying that they had been sexually abused while attending the Day Care. However, the abuse was not limited to sexual fondling. "Mr. Gary" had urinated and defecated on the child victims and forced them to do the same to him. He had also forced them to drink urine and eat feces and had smeared blood and feces on their bodies. The children had also been threatened with guns and were warned not to tell what happened or they and their parents would be killed. "In several cases, there was physical evidence to support the allegations. Medical examiners discovered that five of the children had Chlamydia, a sexually transmitted disease".[430]

Gary Willard Hambright, a Southern Baptist preacher, was arrested on child molestation charges on January 5th 1985. He had no apparent connections to Satanism

---

428 Linda Blood, The New Satanist (New York: Warner Books, 1994) 15.
429 Ibid, 162-163.
430 Linda Goldston, Army of the Night (San Jose Mercury News, July 24, 1998 – http://www.whale.to).

so the prosecution was pursuing a simple case of pedophilia. Michelle and Larry Adams-Thompson heard of the reports of sexual abuse at the preschool and took their daughter, Lisa, to a therapist at the Letterman Army Medical Center. However Lisa Adams-Thompson who had been in Hambright's classroom had described ritual abuse that had been performed by a "Mikey" and Shamby" at their home in San Francisco. Later, while the child was with her parents at the Post Exchange, she saw "Mikey" and "Shamby" and pointed them out to her parents. The parents recognized Lt. Col. Michael Aquino and his wife Lilith.[431] The FBI was contacted and Lisa was interviewed. The FBI report stated the victim was driven with Mr. Gary to his house where he photographed her naked. Mikey and Shamby were also present. Mikey, (Lt. Col. Aquino) put his penis in the victim's mouth bottom and vagina. Mikey was dressed in women's clothing and Shamby was dressed in men's clothing.[432]

Other children would also later describe "Mikey" and "Shamby" and described their San Francisco home. "Michael Aquino is just one of several mind-control programmers who have gone by the name of Micky. Because Mickey Mouse is substituted for being the programmer at different points in programming, this scene will tie in well with other standard programming sessions which are based on Disney films".[433] Cathy O'Brien also testified that Monarch programmers use characters and language from Disney films to trigger and program alters.[434]

Parents of the victims eventually learned that these kinds of allegations against the Presidio Child Development Center were nothing new and that such allegations had turned up in other Military bases across the country including West Point, Fort Dix, Fort Leavenworth, and Fort Jackson in South Carolina totaling fifteen day care centers in all including two U.S. Air Force day care centers and at a facility run by the U.S. Navy in Philadelphia. Reports of satanic activities, satanic graffiti and other occult symbols "have been found behind the military intelligence building in a concrete bunker that appeared to have been used as a ritual chamber".[435] Reports of a possible child abduction led Presidio MP's to the gardener's shack on the grounds of a park that was adjacent to a Presidio housing area. Kicking down the door they found a bed, a manikin holding a gun, a pentagram drawn on the floor and a collection of doll's head's decorating the ceiling. However, the MP's were ordered by the Magistrate to cease the investigation.[436]

The McMartin Preschool Scandal

---

431 Linda Blood, The New Satanist (New York: Warner Books, 1994) 170.
432 Linda Goldston, Army of the Night (San Jose Mercury News, July 24, 1998 – http://www.whale.to).
433 Frits Springmeyer, The Disney Bloodline (July 3, 2009 – http://www.theforbiddenknowledge.com).
434 Cathy O'Brien & Mark Phillips, Trance Formation of America (Frankston, Texas: Reality Marketing Inc.,1995) 84.
435 Linda Goldston, Army of the Night (San Jose Mercury News, July 24, 1998 – http://www.whale.to).
436 Ibid.

Mind control research at Langley in the 1960's consisted of "Auschwitzian behavior modification research funded by the government". The CIA feared exposure thus they left the laboratory and hid themselves in the community in plain sight. They developed religious cults in which to work their mind control agenda. These mind control cults created by the CIA included the People's Temple (Jonestown, Guyana), the Symbionese Liberation Army (Patty Hearst's kidnappers) Ordo Templis Orientis (OTO, of which Aleister Crowley was chief in the England Branch), Finders, Solar Temple and the Bhagwan Shree Rajneesh Movement. Also Charles Buckey, an engineer for Hughes Aircraft built the McMartin preschool mind control operation in Manhattan Beach California in 1966. Hughes Aircraft is known to be a CIA front.[437]

In the McMartin Preschool molestation case, 389 toddlers were interviewed — nearly all of whom described abuse at the preschool. Of those 389 toddlers, 80 percent had physical symptoms, including blunt force trauma of sexual areas, scarring, rectal bleeding and STDs. "The McMartin disclosures to parents and psychologists are identical to those of children victimized in the formative years of the CIA's mind-splintering laboratory experiments".[438]

The children reported that there were tunnels under the school " . . .by which they could be secretly transported to and from the school, and in which they were subjected to horrific abuse in a secret room". Because the investigation commissioned by the District Attorney's office found no evidence of tunnels and during the trial and Buckey said there were no tunnels under the preschool, this was frequently cited as "proof that the children's stories were fabrications. It was universally accepted that the tunnels did not actually exist . . ." This was what got reported in the Media. However, during the trial, in April 1990, the preschool was sold. The parents of the preschoolers got permission from the new owner to excavate under the preschool and they hired Gary Stickle, Ph.D., a highly regarded archeologist who was recommended by the Chair of the Interdisciplinary Program of the Archeology Department at UCLA. Several other technical specialists assisted in the excavation. They discovered two tunnel complexes under the preschool just as the children had described.

> Both the contour signature of the walls and the nature of recovered artifacts indicated that the tunnels had been dug by hand under the concrete slab floor after the construction of the building... Not only did the discovered features fulfill the research prequalifications as tunnels designed for human traffic, there was also no alternative or natural explanation for the presence of such features...[439]

---

437 Alex Constantine, Virtual Government (Los Angeles, CA: Feral House, 1997) 152.
438 Ibid, 152-153.
439 David McGowan, the Pedophocracy, Part IV: McMolestation (Child Sexual Abuse at the McMartin Pre-School, August 2001 – http://www.the7thfire.com).

Ray Buckey was indicted twice on charges of child molestation and the juries were unable to reach a verdict each time because they said there was not enough evidence to prove that Ray Buckey, son on Charles Buckey, was the one responsible for the abuse. Although all the jurists stated that they believed the children had been abused.[440] The children named seven teachers (six women and one male) as having molested them. They were charged with 209 counts of child molestation. There were others who were also named and other unidentified strangers who were not charged.[441]

The children described sexual abuse that occurred on school grounds as well as at a local market, churches, a mortuary, various homes, a farm, a doctor's office, other preschools and other unknown locations. Victim witnesses reported being photographed in the nude, drinking a red or pink liquid that made them sleepy and animal sacrifices some of which occurred in churches. They reported sticks put in their vaginas and rectums and being defecated and urinated on. They also reported that the adults dressed in black robes formed a circle around them and chanted.[442]

The attempt to sway public opinion was again the project of the public news media in the McMartin case. Lost Angeles Times Reporter David Shaw described the behind the scenes role played by a screen writer, Abby Mann, to tilt public opinion in favor of Ray Buckey. Noel Greenwood, also of the Lost Angeles Times shared David Shaw's opinion. "Noel Greenwood, an *LA Times* editor, has described the wall of pro-Buckey PR thrown up by Mann and friends as "*a mean, malevolent campaign* conducted by people… whose motives are highly suspect and who have behaved in a basically dishonest… and dishonorable way". Abby Mann characterized the McMartin Preschool trial as a witch-hunt. He convinced Mike Wallace to run the special episode totally favoring the Buckey's. Mike Wallace, of 60 minutes, portrayed those defending the children and their parents as "nattering lunatics". During the 60 minutes episode, however, no police or even DA's investigators were interviewed or even mentioned. The episode was filmed in Abby Mann's living room.[443]

California and Disneyland

California may not be the "place you wanna be" if you intend to raise children. Susan Warmsley and her assistant, Pamela Harris, were investigating a place called the Ranch in the dessert of California near San Diego where "something almost unspeakably evil continued to happen out in the desert, where those babies

---
440 Alex Constantine, Virtual Government (Los Angeles, CA: Feral House, 1997) 153.
441 David McGowan, the Pedophocracy, Part IV: McMolestation (Child Sexual Abuse at the McMartin Pre-School, August 2001 – http://www.the7thfire.com).
442 Ibid.
443 Alex Constantine, Psychic Dictatorship (Portland, OR: Feral House, 1995) 88 – 89.

were being bred and other fearful things were going on".[444] It had been reported to her that catholic priests were involved in what was happening at the Ranch. Pamela gathered information about the place from children she treated for abuse at the center that she and Susan ran. It was described as a compound like structure surrounded by a chain-link fence topped with barbed wire that is patrolled by armed guards in trucks. They also used a helicopter. In that place high-ranking government, military and civilian personnel sexually exploit children in any way they please. The children are also murdered there for sexual gratification. "This is a place where children are held as slaves, where they are abused and put through every form of pornography. They are filmed, tortured, and finally murdered".[445]

Paul Bonacci may have visited the Ranch. The experience he described included a trip in a helicopter to the place where they were forced to sodomize the boy in the cage. Susan and Paula did not meet Paul Bonacci but they met several other children who described experiences much like his. In fact they had little or no success getting the police or the FBI to investigate the place described as the Ranch. Their office was invaded and their files full of testimonies from multiple children about the place were stolen. The thieves left behind their Styrofoam coffee cups. The cups contained urine.[446] Pamela Harris eventually left California. It was not a place where she wanted to raise her children.

Another hot spot for CIA Illuminati mind control abuse of children is Disneyland. Springmeyer reports that American's Most Wanted has a large file of children who have been kidnapped while at Disneyland. According to an inside source the Disney Police are a part of those involved in the kidnap and abuse of children.[447]

Satanism, Pedophiles and the CIA

There are a number of people and organizations that are attempting to discredit those who are pressing the case for justice for ritually abused children. The False Memory Syndrome Foundation (FMSF) is one and Victims of Child Abuse Laws (VOCAL) is another one. The FMSF board is almost exclusively composed of former CIA and military doctors currently employed by major universities. None have backgrounds in ritual abuse--their common interest is behavior modification.[448] The members of FMSF have been accused of child abuse themselves including Executive Directors Peter and Pamela Freyd. Their statistics relating to the number of victims falsely accused of ritual child abuse fluctuates

---

444 Gordon Thomas, Enslaved (New York: PHAROS BOOKS, 1991) 41.
445 Ibid, 81.
446 Ibid, 105.
447 Fritz Springmeyer, The Disney Bloodline (July 3, 2009 – http://www.theforbiddenknowledge.com).
448 Alex Constantine, Psychic Dictatorship in the U.S.A. (Portland, OR: Feral House, 1995) 58.

remarkably though they accuse the press of not reporting accurate figures. The FMSF ignores statistics that do not support their agenda, such as the fact that only 5% of all child abuse cases ever reach a courtroom half of which result in the child remaining in the custody of the abusive parent.[449]

Martin T. Orne is a senior CIA researcher and original board member of the Foundation and a psychiatrist at the University of Pennsylvania's Experimental Psychiatry Lab in Philadelphia. He studied hynoprogramming of anti-social behavior and mind subduing techniques as well as erasing memory in 1962 at Cornell University funded by the CIA. Martin Orne was called upon by the CIA to support Ray Buckey in the McMartin Case. He is also a veteran of the CIA's pedophile/blackmail ring.[450]

Michael Sweeney, author of *The Professional Paranoid* notes that a number of CIA fronts and CIA contractors have ties to the FMSF. He cites more than 100 such organization. "Laughably, some of the principle players drifting in and out of CAN, FMSF, and the original MK Ultra experiments are often the same people, and these groups often work together".[451]

The Founder of FMSF, Ralf Underwager, director of the Institute of Psychological Therapies in Minnesota, founding member of VOCAl and former Lutheran Pastor, was forced to resign from the FMSF for stating that he felt it was "God's will" for adults to engage in sex with children. His remark was published in an Amsterdam Journal for Pedophiles, *Pedika*. When members of the Children of God cult were being arraigned on charges of child molestation in France in 1992, he ran to their defense. "In the interview, he prevailed upon pedophiles everywhere to shed stigmatization as 'wicked and reprehensible' users of children". In 1994 Underwager told British reporters that %60 of all women who had been molested as children reported that the experience was good for them.[452] He frequently appeared as a well-paid expert witness for the defense in child sexual abuse cases. "He contends that children are natural liars, and that investigators and therapists are the real child abusers, subjecting children to the equivalent of North Korean-style brainwashing tactics".[453]

The FMSF has asserted that false memories are an established fact. However, researchers at Carrolton University were unable to find any evidence of false memory pathology. Connie Kristiansen, professor of psychology at Carleton University examined the statistical claims of the FMSF who claim that 25% of all recovered memories of child abuse are completely false. This was compared to another "Ottawa" study in which half of the subjects remembered abuse and half recalled other buried memories. "The responses of the two groups were evaluated.

---

449 Ibid, 63.
450 Alex Constantine, Virtual Government (Los Angeles, CA: Feral House1997) 153.
451 H. Michael Sweeney, The Professional Paranoid (Venice, CA: Feral House, 1998)131.
452 Alex Constantine, Psychic Dictatorship in the U.S.A. (Portland, OR: Feral House, 1995) 65.
453 Linda Blood, The New Satanist (New York: Warner Books, 1994)122 – 123.

Only two of the 51 women with recovered memories had symptoms that met the false memory criteria, leading the researchers to conclude that the syndrome does not exist as defined by the Foundation and may not exist at all".[454]

Daughter of FMSF directors Peter and Pamela Freyd, Jennifer Freyd, professor of Psychology at the University of Oregon, openly accused her parents of abuse at a Mental Health conference in Ann Arbor Michigan in 1993. Her father was a victim of sexual abuse as a child and graduated to adult male prostitution. He repeatedly sexually abused Jennifer when she was a child. Her father told people that she was brain damaged, which is highly unlikely given her career. Jennifer Freyd was a graduate student on a National Science Foundation fellowship. She was a professor at Cornell and the recipient of numerous research awards.[455] Pamela Freyd said that her daughter's memories were confabulations and used her own Psychiatrist, also a FSMF board member, to back up her statements.

Dr. Catherine Gould is chairwoman of the Ritual Abuse Task Force, and a licensed Clinical Child Therapist who has spoken out about the news media's "pattern of biased and inaccurate reporting" and the tendency to side with SRA perpetrators when it comes to ritual child abuse. There is a concerted effort by the press and SRA perpetrators to discredit therapists who are trying to help ritually abused children. Because there is a strong alliance between cults who ritually abuse children and the CIA, therapists who are threatening to expose them are often harassed. Several therapists of the Task Force began to experience strange symptoms which were diagnosed by their physicians as organophosphate poisoning. One therapist got a pesticide poisoning test kit and discovered that several food items in her refrigerator were laced with pesticide poison. The therapist also reported multiple home invasions reported by eyewitnesses during the day when they were not at home. Neighbors also report nighttime surveillance. The interior of their home has been splattered with blood on three occasions. They have been followed by a variety of vehicles. Two pet birds also mysteriously died. SRA survivors on the task force have experienced organophosphate poisoning and have received threats as well, though the news media poo pooed the reports by multiple therapists treating SRA survivors and ignored the medical reports.[456]

There are many babies that are bread within the Satanist cults which never see the light of day and never have a name. They are birthed specifically for ritual sacrifice. I personally knew a woman, diagnosed with MPD with over 300 personalities, who grew up in the occult and was impregnated for the purpose of birthing sacrificial babies. She gave birth to 12 children who were thus sacrificed. She was horribly emotionally traumatized with having to witness the slaughter of her babies. I was with her during a group meeting while she was reliving the agony of watching her children die. She cried out in agony over and over again, "They

---

454 Alex Constantine, Virtual Government (Los Angeles, CA: Feral House 1997) 179.
455 Alex Constantine, Psychic Dictatorship in the U.S.A. (Portland, OR: Feral House, 1995) 66.
456 Ibid, 100-101.

cut off my baby's head! They cut off my baby's head!" The members of her cult also tried to kill her several times but she survived.

Where will our children run?

How are we going to protect ourselves and the children of this nation if public officials are being blackmailed and compromised to such a degree that they are clay in the hands of the NWO? If our public officials are being compromised and Law Enforcement is also involved and the Judges who are Freemasons are all obliged to protect the culprits of abuse, how are we as American citizens going to protect the children? The American evangelical church if very Pro-Life, but they are focused on the lives of only one population of people – the unborn. I do not want to detract from the importance of that issue in any way. I am prolife and I volunteer at a prolife clinic. However, I have not heard pastors stand behind the pulpit and speak out against Satanism or stand up for those who have endured Satanic Ritual Abuse. Evangelicals went *nuts* over the publication of the children's book series by J.K. Rawlings, *Harry Potter*. Could we get that fired up about the real thing? Could we push for legislation that maximizes the penalties for SRA and could we push to put the bite back into Law Enforcement so they can actually do their jobs? If we don't are we justified in believing that at least the people close to us are safe? If I can't protect my neighbors' children where will they run? I am reminded of the words of a Yugoslavian Priest,

"Tell the Americans to hang on to their freedom. It is bad here, but we always have hope. We can always run to the West. But if the West falls, there will be no place for our children to run."

22. America in Bondage

We're Talking Slavery

You will recall from reading the chapter about the Bilderbergers that their intentions are to enslave the entire world's population. "The Bilderbergers envision a socialist welfare state, where obedient slaves will be rewarded and non-conformists targeted for extermination".[457] The enlightened (?!) elite seem to concur that this is the way things ought to be. Jose Delgado, one of the famed CIA mind control scientists who used ESB (Electrical Stimulation of the Brain) to control human behavior, had this notion that societies ought to be controlled and that freedom and individuality were rather nebulous concepts. What we call the "will" are mere neuronal functions and that technology should be able to control

---

[457] Daniel Estulin, The True Story of the Bilderberger Group (Waterville, OR: Trine Day LLC., 2007) 43.

those functions so that the terms "freedom" "individuality" and "spontaneity" should have to be redefined in more scientific terms. He also believed that slaves could be happy being slaves.

> In some old plantations slaves behaved very well worked hard and were submissive to their masters and were probably happier than some of the free blacks in modern ghettos. In several dictatorial countries the general population is skillful, productive, well behaved, and perhaps as happy as those in more democratic societies[458]

Aldous Huxley described in the preface to *Brave New World* a totalitarian state in which slaves do not have to be coerced because they love their servitude. To make them love it was the job of "ministries of propaganda, newspaper editors and school teachers...".[459] In 1961, at a lecture to the California Medical School in San Francisco Huxley stated:

> There will be in the next generation or so a pharmacological method of making people love their servitude and producing dictatorship without tears so to speak, producing a kind of painless concentration camp for entire societies so that people will in fact have their liberties taken away from them, but will rather enjoy it, because they will be distracted from any desire to rebel - by propaganda, or brainwashing, or brainwashing enhanced by pharmacological methods. And this seems to be the final revolution.

B. F. Skinner, chairman of the Psychology Department at Harvard University, in his book entitled *Beyond Freedom and Dignity* said, "We can no longer afford freedom, and so it must be replaced with control over man, his conduct and his culture."[460] B.F. Skinner used all his behavior control techniques on his own daughter Debbie who committed suicide in her 20s. Also "little Albert" was the illegitimate son of John Watson who used him for his experiments. He also committed suicide in his 20's.[461]

It should be clear to us that the biggest threat to our freedom is not the military might of another nation, but the warped thinking of people in our own nation who have the power and the wealth to use us to further their private agenda. We have

---
458 David McGowan, Lies My Psychology Professor Taught Me (The Konformist – http://www.konformist.com).
459 Sklar, Holly, Overview: Managing Dependence and Democracy (book section,Trilateralism: Elite Planning For World Management, editor Holly Sklar, Boston, MA: South End Press, 1980) 47.
460 A. Ralf Epperson, The New World Order (Tucson: Publius Press, 1990) XVII.
461 David McGowan, Lies My Psychology Professor Taught Me (The Konformist – http://www.konformist.com).

been warned of this. Writing in 1971, Gary Allen listed 14 sign posts to slavery including but not limited to detention of individuals without judicial process (This is occurring under the US Patriot Act and the Military Commissions Act); government monitoring of private financial records (It is now a requirement that banks report all major monetary transactions to the US government and hold your funds until the government has given a release); putting legal restrictions on the attendance of private schools (a law pending passage in 2010 is a law that holds private schools to stricter requirements than public schools which is perceived by some as an attempt to close private schools); compulsory psychological treatment for non-government workers or public school children (frequently used as a way to control or discredit dissidents); placing legal restrictions on the number of people permitted to meet in a private home (this occurred in California recently when a pastor was told he had to have a Major Use Permit to have a Bible Study in his home); wage and price controls; compulsory registration with the government of where you work (your place of business reports your wages to the IRS every year); any attempt to restrict freedom of movement within the United States (such as no-fly lists); and making new laws by executive decree (President George W. Bush signed more executive orders than any president in the history of the United States).[462]

Slavery Statistics

The Bilderbergers made their intentions clear. The established elite intend to make slaves out of all of us and reduce this nation to the status of a third world nation. Considering that that is their intention, it follows that the current statistics on slavery reflect the fulfillment of their agenda. There are more people in slavery now than in any other time in history. According to UNICEFF there are 12 million men, women and children enslaved worldwide [463] while an organization called *Free the Slaves* estimates that the number of people enslaved today is 27 million. Three out of four of them are women and half of them are children.[464] Estimates by the US State Department suggest up to 17,500 slaves are brought into the US every year, and 80% are estimated to be female and 50% are minors. The U.S. Department of Justice estimates that there are 200,000 U.S. citizens, mainly children and young women, who are at high risk of being trafficked throughout the U.S for sexual purposes.[465]

Former Secretary of State, Madeline Albright, stated that human trafficking is the largest growing criminal enterprise in the world. The UN estimates that

---

462 Gary Allen, None Dare Call it Conspiracy (Rossmoor, California: Concord Press 1971) 132 – 133.
463 The Barnaba Institute against Modem-bay Slavery & Exploitation (http://www.barnabainstitute.org).
464 www.yeeeeee.com, 10 Shocking Facts about Global Slavery in 2008 (June 7, 2008 – www.yeeeeee.com).
465 The Barnaba Institute against Modem-bay Slavery & Exploitation (http://www.barnabainstitute.org).

human trafficking generates about 7 billion dollars per year. The United Nations Office of Drugs and Crime believes that human trafficking is the world's most lucrative crime next to drugs and arms dealing. Many drugs and arms dealers are now also dealing in human trafficking because you can sell a boy or a girl several times in one night whereas you can only sell drugs and arms once.[466]

The Trafficking in Victims Protection Act

A web site called Humantrafficking.org reports;

> The US government is strongly committed to combating trafficking in persons at home and abroad. The Trafficking Victims Protection Act of 2000 enhances preexisting criminal penalties, affords new protections to trafficking victims and makes available certain benefits and services to victims of severe forms of trafficking. It also establishes a Cabinet-level federal interagency task force and establishes a federal program to provide services to trafficking victims. The U.S. Government recognizes the need to sustain and further enhance efforts in order to achieve the goals and objectives of the Act.[467]

The TVPA of 2000 mandated the creation of the Office to Monitor and Combat Trafficking in the State Department also referred to in the article as the G/TIP office. This office has provided millions of dollars in grants to organizations worldwide to combat trafficking. In November 2003 Congress reauthorized the TVPA. It was reauthorized again in 2005 and signed into law in January 2006. The 2007 report states;

> These programs include disseminating information on the dangers of trafficking; strengthening the capacity of non-governmental organizations to protect those groups from abuse and violence, and outreach and economic opportunity programs for those most at risk of being trafficked. The U.S. has assisted countries to enact anti-trafficking legislation, trained Law Enforcement officials, prosecutors, border guards and judicial officers on detecting, investigating, and prosecuting traffickers and protecting victims and provided start up equipment for new anti-trafficking police units.[468]

It looks good on paper, but it does not appear that the TVPA is really helping. The Bush administration launched a $5 million dollar ad campaign against human

---

466 Ibid.
467 http://www.humantrafficking.org, (2007).
468 Ibid.

trafficking which promised health care, housing, food and even citizenship to victims of human trafficking. However, the ad did not say that the victims were required to cooperate with the criminal investigation of their abusers. This may not be a viable option for most victims. "Those who cooperate may face retaliation from their exploiters or risk harm to their loved ones in their homelands." Victims who do come forward have to prove that they are survivors of "a severe form of trafficking" and they have to demonstrate that returning to their native country would result in severe hardship. The risk is so great and the requirements are so stringent that few victims are actually able to take advantage of government assistance. The Trafficking Victims Protection Act promised 5,000 temporary visas each year for survivors who could later apply for permanent residency, but only about 450 victims have received benefits from the TVPA since its passage in 2000 out of an estimated 14,500 to 17,500 persons trafficked annually.[469]

There are more reasons why trafficked victims are not being helped by anti-trafficking legislation. Local Law Enforcement responsible for identifying victims may not identify them properly or many simply arrest them for being illegal immigrants. Victims come from countries where they have learned not to trust Law Enforcement officials who are brutally corrupted. Children are often too traumatized to be able to tell someone what has happened to them and children represent 50% of all trafficking victims. Emphasis is placed on sex trafficking and not enough on labor trafficking.[470]

Stark Reality

Is the U.S. Government really trying to combat human trafficking, or are they just pretending for the sake of the uninformed public? A report entitled *10 Shocking Facts about Global Slavery in 2008* at http://www.yeeeeee.com states, "According to the CIA, more than 1,000,000 people are enslaved in the US today. Thousands of cases go undetected each year and many are difficult to take to court as it can be difficult to prove force or legal coercion". The testimonies of multiple others indicate that the CIA is actually carrying out the Bilderbergers agenda. Mark Phillips reports that the CIA has a huge worldwide invisible slave trade operation.[471] We already know that they have taken children and traumatized them in order to use them as sex slaves. It should not surprise us then that Law Enforcement officials and other professionals whose job it is to protect and defend us from sexual exploitation are actually supporting sex slave trafficking in the United States. A U.S. federal agency provided condoms to the child victims of sex

---

469 Pueng Vongs, Gov't Effort to Stem Human Trafficking Helps Very Few (New America Media. - Pacific News Service, December 16, 2004 – http://www.news.pacificnews.org).
470 Ibid.
471 Cathy O'Brien & Mark Phillips, Trance Formation of America (Frankston, Texas: Reality Marketing Inc.,1995) 13.

trafficking in San Diego County California for years. A Latin American doctor employed by the agency was threatened with legal action by her supervisors if she spoke out or tried to organize a rescue effort.[472] Another physician with a fictitious name of Patricia testified that Federal Agents participated in the sexual exploitation of minors.

> A lot of money is involved in this business, thousands and thousands of dollars. I have seen myself how U.S. INS agents have sex with these minor girls for free, in exchange for protection; these agents even enter the houses of prostitution in uniform. May a lightning-bolt split me in half if I am lying?[473]

Katherine Griggs experienced abuse from her ex husband U.S. Marine Corps Col. George Raymond Griggs. She went public in 1996 after receiving death threats. She sought help from William Colby, former Director of the CIA who mysteriously turned up dead a few weeks later. She was finally rescued by former White House press corps staff, Sarah McClendon, who gave her shelter and helped her to go public with her story. That was how she met Pastor Rick Strawcutter, a preacher and owner of a 500 watt private FM station 99.3 on the dial in Lenawee County Michigan. He produced two extended interviews which he released in 2000. One was a two hour filmed interview called *Sleeping with the Enemy* and the other was the unedited 8 hour version. She stated that her husband was a trained assassin who was involved in a group called The Firm or The Brotherhood.

> I learned about how he was sexually molested by homosexual teachers at the elite Hun School, where a lot of the others in this small elite group also attended, including the members the Saudi Royal family. He told me how sex is used to control, intimidate and groom boys into this type of military service from a young age. He mentioned how many of The Brotherhood, as he liked to call them, are members of the "Cap and Gown" Princeton group or the "Skull and Bones" Yale crowd and how they performed sexually perverted induction ceremonies with anal and oral sex performed inside coffins.[474]

The Strawcutter tapes reveal how members of The Brotherhood operate in a world of treachery, deceit, lies, murder, drug running, sex slavery and illegal weapon sales. This is done for the purpose of accomplishing the agenda of the secret societies and forming a one world government. People who are a part of this

---

472 About the Child Rape Camps of San Diego County, California - A Crime Against Humanity inside the U.S.A. (http://www.libertadlatina.org).
473 Ibid.
474 Greg Szymanski, The Evil Lurking Within (July 31, 2005 – http://www.rense.com).

elite group consider themselves above the law and literally get away with murder. It is all about psychological operations and sexual perversion is used to control those who become a part of the group through the Skull and Bones and Cap and Gown sororities at Yale and Princeton. The group was formed by Germans who have strong connections with people in Europe and in war colleges. Paul Wolfowitz is the head of the group which includes Donald Rumsfeld, George H. W. Bush, Dick Cheney, Henry Kissinger and Andy Fine. The goal of the group is to destroy America. They will do anything to get what they want including murder and crashing planes into buildings notwithstanding.[475]

Mind control slavery is at the core of the NWO operation which is fueled by the CIA. Cathy O'Brien speaks of the "Most Dangerous Game" in her book Trance Formation of American that involves high level government officials, such as presidents and vice presidents, who send human beings running through the woods so that they can hunt them down for sport. Cathy was a victim in this game more than once. On one particular occasion an Italian soldier, a mind controlled slave, was sent running through the woods while George H. W. Bush and Bill Clinton hunted them down in a black helicopter. Cathy and her daughter Kelly were loaded onto the helicopter with the Italian soldier in uniform. In flight George Bush opened the door of the helicopter and gave the soldier an order, "Free Fall. That's an order". The soldier replied, "Yes Sir" and jumped from the helicopter without a parachute. Cathy watched in horror as he landed on the water, splattered and sank.[476]

Lauren Stratified described her experience at "the Ranch" near San Diego where she was raped by people whose job it was to protect her from being sexually exploited. One policeman used to rape her wearing only his gun. For more than a year Lauren was sexually violated by "doctors, lawyers and men in the highest levels of major corporations. They were judges, politicians, and entertainers."[477]

A few isolated cases you think? Guess again. Cathy O'Brien and Mark Phillips contacted not less than 43 officials in a professional capacity including Law Enforcement about those in government positions in Washington including but absolutely not limited to Dick Cheney, Ronald Regan, Senator Robert C. Byrd, George H. W. Bush and both Bill and Hillary Clinton who had sexually exploited her and her daughter and used them as drug couriers. To my knowledge not one of them has ever been charged let alone tried or convicted for the crimes they committed against her and her daughter.[478]

Law Enforcement and the criminal justice system failed Cathy O'Brien and she is not the only one. Jill Leighton ran away from home when she was a teenager

---

475 Ibid.
476 David Icke, The Biggest Secret (Wildwood, MO: Bridger of Love Publications, 1999) 341.
477 Gordon Thomas, Enslaved (New York: PHAROS BOOKS, 1991) 60.
478 Cathy O'Brien & Mark Phillips, Trance Formation of America (Frankston, Texas: Reality Marketing Inc., 1995).

because of abuse in her home. She ran into a man named Bruce who was very kind to her and offered her a job. With sweet words he persuaded her to come to his office and being an adolescent with nowhere to go, she willing went with this man. For three years he used her as a sex slave whereby he prostituted her to others for profit. Three years into her captivity the police came to her captor's home and arrested him. However, they did nothing to help her. Her captor, Bruce, was arrested on unrelated charges. They found her handcuffed and gagged in a closet but did nothing to support her. She asked to speak with a female officer and was denied. In fact that told her that they were executing a warrant and at that if she didn't shut up she could also be arrested. Jill was still under age at the time.[479]

I'm going to speculate. It was Law Enforcement's job to respond to that young woman, which they did not do. That is a serious act of negligence on their part. However, knowing the state of Law Enforcement in this nation which is being hindered by NWO corruption, it is highly possible that Law Enforcement was given a "stand down" order and was actually not permitted to do what we actually pay them to do. I have to think for a moment. If Law Enforcement is not allowed to help a minor who is being held captive as a sex slave, what would be the point of arresting her perpetrator on "unrelated charges"? I have to believe that someone in that mess was a daddy. Someone wearing a uniform had the capacity to think, "What if that was my baby girl?" Maybe that someone had enough compassion and enough integrity to find a way to do his job even though he was told not to. She was rescued but not directly. We have to ask ourselves, however, why could they not do what they are paid to do, what they put on that uniform to do? Could it be because sex slavery is encouraged and acceptable to the NWO? Could it be because there were public officials who availed themselves of her "services" via her pimp? If that were the case and the guy was arrested, Jill's testimony in court could have resulted in a few public officials being exposed, their careers damaged not to mention the fact that they might have had to spend time in jail. But I'm just speculating.

Sex slavery is not the only kind of slavery plaguing the planet. Other forms of slavery exist which include chattel slavery (the traditional meaning of slavery), bonded labor, forced labor, and forced marriage (white slavery), amongst others. A Chattel slave is actually owned by another person. Bonded labor is a form of slavery that chains a person to another person or organization for life. Forced marriage also called "white slavery" is the forced marriage of a woman to another or sale as a concubine. Cathy O'Brien experienced both sexual exploitation and forced marriage. She was also owned by Senator Robert C. Byrd.[480] Cathy O'Brien has also stated that children who were traumatized and mind controlled in the

---

479 Jill Leighton, My Life as a Slave in America (Enslaved; True Stories Of Modem Day Slavery I ed., Editors Jesse Sage and Liora Kasten, New York: Palgrave, McMillan, 2006) 78.
480 Cathy O'Brien & Mark Phillips, Trance Formation of America (Frankston, Texas: Reality Marketing Inc., 1995).

United States were sold into slavery in Saudi Arabia.[481] There is also indication that gangstalkers are pushing women into prostitution and sex slavery.[482] Then of course there is mind controlled slavery.

Children in third world countries are also commonly sold by their parents who are experiencing extreme poverty. In Africa poor families often send their daughters to the city to work for extra money. They may think they are doing their child a favor by sending them out of their village dead end life. They often work for free because their parents think they will be better fed in the homes of their employers. These well to do Africans who practice this form of slavery immigrate to the United States and bring the practice with them. "Around one-third of the estimated 10,000 forced laborers in the United States are servants trapped behind the curtains of suburban homes, according to a study by the National Human Rights Center at the University of California at Berkeley and Free the Slaves, a nonprofit group."[483] They are easily disguised behind the walls of gated communities where they appear to be another child busy doing chores. However they never go to school and they work up to 20 hours a day for work that they may or may not get paid for.

Shyima was 10 when a wealthy Egyptian couple, the Ibrahims, brought her from a poor village in northern Egypt to work in their California home in August of 2000. Shyima worked as a slave for the family and their five children cleaning their house doing their laundry and ironing their clothes. She worked 20 hours a day and got paid $45 a month. She lived in the garage and was not allowed to attend school. A neighbor got suspicious and called the police in April 2002. A detective showed up at the home and confiscated home videos showing Shyima doing the chores in the home and also the contract that was signed by Shyima's father and mother who sold their daughter to the Ibrahim's for money and in payment of medical bills.[484]

It took several months after Shyima was taken from the home of the Ibrahim family to finally tell officials what had happened to her there. The case was brought to trial and the couple successfully prosecuted. The Ibrahims pleaded guilty to the charge of forced labor and slavery. They were required to pay Shyima $76,000 for the labor she had performed for them. The husband was sentenced to three years in prison and his wife 22 months. The couple was deported. However, the woman was released from prison two years later and found another child slave to take care of the chores. She returned to the same gated apartment complex in California. Shyima was adopted by a couple in California who sent her to school and then to college. She decided she wanted to become a police officer.[485]

---

481 Ibid, 205.
482 Mark Rich, The Hidden Evil (May, 5 2005 – http://www.thehidenevil.com).
483 AP News, Child maids now being exported to US (Ap News, Zimbio, December 28, 2008 – http://www.zimbio.com).
484 Ibid.
485 Ibid.

Adult men and women are often lured by scouts called "touts" to the United States with a promise of a better life. Typically they become victims of debt bondage or sex slavery. A single mother, Mary Louise, living in Manila Philippines was lured by such a person. She was promised a better job in the United States and she would be able to earn enough money eventually to bring her children to the U.S. with her. During her screening however, she was required to be photographed in her underwear. A one way ticket was purchased for her that she would be required later to repay. She eventually reneged much to the wrath of her tout. The problem occurred when one of Mary Louise's children became ill and died. She became concerned that if this occurred with her other two children and she were in the US she would not be able to care for them. Her tout was found murdered a few days after Mary Louise changed her mind.[486] Many like her were not so lucky. They are often lured into debt that they can never repay. Those that enslave them will pay them a salary but then charge them for the use of silverware and toilet paper besides room and board, for example, so that they can never repay the debt. Thus they are enslaved for life.

Many illegal immigrants are in this country being used as slave labor. They are making very little and working long hours in the fields of places like Orange Country California. They experience abuse but don't report it because they are in the country illegally. And they are susceptible to other forms of exploitation because of their immigrant status. Children often disappear from those fields and are never seen again.[487]

Catching and prosecuting the criminals just might be Law Enforcement's worst nightmare. Law Enforcement as an agency is snared in the NWO's wicked agenda. Though there are countless Law Enforcement officials who have enslaved themselves by staying awake all hours of the night, drinking too much coffee, eating too many donuts and smoking too many cigarettes while on stakeouts trying to gather enough evidence to put the criminals behind bars, there are doubtless people in their own units who are working against them and likely tipping off the criminals who often escape. Police in Atascadero Southern California raided the home of Rodney and Linda Phelps who had already fled their home. The police were intending to question them about 15 Mexican children whom the couple had allegedly sexually abused and killed while filming. They found film making equipment but did not find the snuff films. It is likely the Phelps has taken them with them when they fled. The films would likely be sold for a substantial sum of money. Witnesses said they saw the couple fleeing with foreign looking children but the police did not pursue further investigation.[488] Since Police are very quiet when engaged in such investigations such that the only people who would know about the investigation would be their own people, it is highly possible that the couple was tipped off by someone inside the police department. Considering that

---

486 21 – 33.
487 Ibid, 80.
488 Ibid, 64,

nothing further was done about the Phelps, it would seem logical that this was the case. They call it speculation. But when we have pedophile presidents and sadomasochistic vice presidents who are not prosecuted for their crimes, even though there have been multiple testimonies of their culpability, that would lead to the conclusion that the criminal justice system is corrupted to the point that it is actually protecting criminals from being prosecuted. And there is money involved. "Follow the money honey."

Law Enforcement officials and social workers who actually care about the victims they are trying to get justice for have slaved long hours very carefully gathering evidence to convict a criminal who is too frequently let off on some technicality or given a very light sentence. FBI investigator, Jack O'Malley spent months collecting evidence setting a trap for a pornographer from Germany who was trapping and victimizing children in his trade. When he finally caught him the man was charged with three counts of exporting pornography from Germany to the United States. He was sentenced to four months in jail and when he was released he paid his own fair back to Germany.[489] Social workers and therapists have to prepare child witnesses to take the stand only to watch their witnesses being torn about by the accused party's attorney. The therapists get charged with putting ideas into their heads. The children get accused of lying. One has to marvel at the integrity and dedication of those professionals in Law Enforcement and social services who refuse to give up the fight.

There are Freemason lodges in every city in America. There are Freemasons in every public office who have a sworn oath to protect any of their members even if they have committed murder or sexually exploited a child or adult. That means a Freemason Judge is going to have to find a way to get that child pornographer off or least get him a really light sentence. It should not surprise us that Law Enforcement is literally being diluted to the point that they cannot do their jobs. Is it probable that those in power actually are deliberately handicapping Law Enforcement? It is my firm conviction that Law Enforcement is being chained as well as gagged. I believe that Law Enforcement is equally frustrated with the situation.

The facts are these; The United States Government is being controlled behind the scenes by wealthy powerful people who have an agenda for world domination; they perceive themselves to be a superior brand of human being and the rest of us are just a bunch of dumb klutzes; they have no ethical code as they operate with situational ethics which allows them to change the rules so that they always win the game; they have every public institution in America under their thumb including Law Enforcement, the American Bar Association, the National Educators Association, the Better Business Bureau, the American Psychiatric Association, the American Medical Association, the American Psychological Association, the National Institute of Mental Health etc. The U.S. Government is involved in drug trafficking, slave trading, child prostitution, and making mind controlled robots out of as many American citizens as they can. We as American

---

489 Ibid, 257.

citizens can effect change by facing the issues and challenging ourselves to address them.

23. Let Freedom Ring

The little ferret was in a glass encasement at the pet store. She was white and had pink eyes, an albino. I picked her up and played with her while she explored me. I think she was a whole $99 dollars. I had to buy a ferret cage of course. When I brought her home, I put her cage together and then took her out of her box and put her in the cage with all the accessories that I had purchased for her. Then I watched. She was a tiny thing, still an infant. Yet the fury that poured out of her as a result of being put in a cage was absolutely amazing. She clamped her jaws around those bars and yanked and pulled with all her might. When the bars did not budge she moved to another spot and tried the same thing. She moved to the second story of the cage and tried again and again and again until she just gave up and fell exhausted into the little sleep sack that I had hung at the top of the cage. If I could describe the language that she was speaking by her behavior, she was saying, "NNNO, NNNO, NO I will not be caged. No I won't! NOOOOOOO!"

She eventually succumbed to the cage. However, she and her playmate which came later really enjoyed being let out of the cage. When I let them out they would scamper all over my apartment turning over trash cans, crawling under couch cushions and of course exploring me. But when they were in the cage they slept, ate and pooped. Eventually my landlord nixed the ferret idea and they were given away.

Later, after I moved to a place that was ferret friendly I got two more ferrets. I was into ferrets. I read all the ferret literature which told me that I should get the biggest cage I could find so that the ferrets would have plenty of room to play. So one day when I was in Pet Smart I found a giant ferret cage that was the floor model on sale. I bought it and brought it home. I was really excited. This thing was 36 inches square and it was as tall as I was. It was on wheels too. I cleaned it up and put it together and put tunnels in it and even a rope that hung from the top of the cage to the floor. I thought they would have fun climbing on that. After I got the cage all put together I introduced them to their new "home". This was great I thought, they will have plenty of space to play. But I discovered to my chagrin that all they did in that cage was eat and sleep and poop. They never touched the rope. They only climbed through the tunnels if they were going between the bed, the food and the litter box.

So I got them leashes. They make special ferret leashes that you strap on and take your ferrets for walks. So when I took them outside on their little leashes, do you know what they did? They flattened their little bodies on the sidewalk and refused to budge. They looked up at me, side by side they were, with looks on their precious little faces that said, "Ummm, no." Like the other two, the only time they actually played was when they were uncaged and unleashed.

If you go to the zoo and watch the animals there on display in their respective cages, they do pretty much the same; eat, sleep and poop. I've watched the lions and big cats. They are either sleeping or pacing. I watched the sharks in the shark tank swimming around in circles. Monkeys do a little better – they like bars. They can hang from them and jump around on them. Elephants seem just to sway back and forth a lot. But all in all, I don't think that caged animals really do a lot of living.

I have watched the Lord of the Rings probably sixteen times and have just about got the script down pat. One part of that film that I find pretty memorable is the part where Aragorn finds Lady Aowen practicing her swordsmanship. He confronts her and says to her, "You have some skill with the blade." She replies, "The women of my country learned long ago that those who don't use them can still die by them. I fear neither pain nor death," she says defiantly. Aragorn asks, "What do you fear, my Lady?" She replies, "A cage and to stay behind bars till use and old age accept them and all chance of valor is beyond recall or desire." Aragorn looks at her and says very gently, "You are a daughter of kings, a shield maiden of Rohan. I don't think that will be your fate."

Our creator created us for freedom. It is in our blood. He did not create children or adults for cages and he did not create animals for cages either. There are no cages on earth that occur naturally. There are boundaries. The sea creatures are bound to remain in the water because they are created for water. The birds of the air know their domain. They can land, but they are more at risk on the ground then they are in the air. Likewise land animals drink water, and some of them can also traverse the water, and they have boundaries too but there are no bars. In fact, in the whole nation of Israel when God originally designed it, there were not even jails for criminals. If you committed a crime you made restitution. If you committed murder, you died. If you committed murder accidentally there were "cities of refuge" where you could run and had to remain until the priest of that city died (Numbers 35). But there were no bars.

Since God created neither people nor animals for cages, it might explain why neither adjusts well to such an environment. Our God is a God of freedom. We have freedom built into the very fabric and fiber of our beings. We even resist relationships with people who cling too tightly. It has been said, "If you love something let it go. If it comes back to you it is yours. If it does not, it never was." We run from people who bind us. We die emotionally, spiritually and even physically when we are caged physically or psychologically. God did not create us for cages.

The New World Order insists that they want a society in psychological bondage. They have to control us. They fear our freedom because they are afraid they will lose something they want. Psychologically they are not healthy people. In fact, people who want to control others around them are people who live lives of fear. Abusers are cowards. They have to control everyone around them or they fear they will lose something they desperately want and think they can't live without. So they control people with physical and psychological intimidation. They themselves are not free. They are bound by fear.

Our God has no fear. He created us and then set us free. Those of us who came back to him are his. Those who refuse him never were. But we are all free. We are not his slaves. We are his children. We serve him out of love. He refuses to force us into submission. Which means that those who he created for freedom, choose to sometimes steal the freedom of others and he will not violate their desire to do so. So he says to us who they are trying control, "Will you fight? Will you resist? Will you throw off their bars and chains? Will you pick up your sword and trust me to win this battle for you? Or will you succumb to your cage?"

A wild bird caught and confined to a cage will refuse to eat. It would rather die than be confined. A wild animal in a trap will chew its leg off before it surrenders its freedom. Do the wild beasts of this world have more respect for their freedom than we humans do?

The Steward of Ministereth looked over the wall down upon the hoard of Sauerman's evil army. The cowardly ruler of Ministereth turned and looked at his soldiers on top of the wall and cried out, "Run for your lives!!" Right at that moment Gandolf, the wizard, wacked him in the head with his staff and knocked him unconscious. Gandolf bellowed out to the frightened army, "Man the towers!" and the battle was on. Throughout the entire film series of Lord of the rings, it is very plain that the good people of Middle Earth are outnumbered. But they fight anyway because there is something worth fighting for. It's slavery or freedom. Take your pick. They laid down their lives for one another. They fought for those they loved. If they had had to fight only for themselves, they would not have had the strength to do so. But there were others whose lives they weren't willing to surrender to an evil domination.

The Lady Aowen was defending her uncle, Théoden King of Rohan, who had fallen and was about to be consumed by a dragon. The Lady cut off the head of the dragon. Then she took on the Witchking of Agmar, the dragon's rider. He was cloaked in black and his head was a hideous looking helmet with a black hole where his face should have been. There was fear in her eyes as he swung at her with a barbed steel ball on the end of a chain. It hit her shield and sprained her wrist. She was knocked to her knees, but she did not quit. She was defending someone else's life besides her own. Aowen stood facing the Witchking. He looked at her and laughed. "No man can kill me!" he said. At that defining moment in the battle Aowen pulls off her helmet to reveal her golden tresses. She smiles when she says, "I am no man!" and then with a shout she drives her sword into that black hole, and he whom no man could kill lay at the Lady's feet, a pile of rubble.

A movie with a powerful message was Lord of the rings. The people who made this nation a free nation had much in common with the Lady. They were willing to fight for their freedom. They paid a price and some sacrificed their lives to give it to us. Why are we letting three hundred wealthy powerful bullies steal from us what is rightfully ours? Will you fight? We used to sing this little song when we were school children.

My country tis of thee
Sweet land of Liberty
Of thee I sing
Land where my fathers died
Land of the Pilgrims pride
From every mountainside
Let freedom ring

What kind of song do you want your children to sing?

"It is for freedom that Christ has set us free. Stand firm, then, and do not let yourselves be burdened again by a yoke of slavery"(Gal 5:1NIV).

24. Operation Desert Storm

President Kennedy helped to orchestrate the violent coup by the Ba'th party in Iraq in 1969. At that time Saddam Hussein, who had been a member of the Party since 1957, became acting vice Chairman of the Revolutionary Command. He succeeded the State and Party leader, Ahmed el-Bakr in all his capacities in 1979.[490] From September 23rd 1980 forward Saddam Hussein was the ally of the United States in his eight year war against the Khomeini regime in Iran. Thus both the United States Government and the British supplied Saddam with chemical and biological weapons in the fight against Iran. A U.S. State Department document declassified in 2002 revealed that the U.S. supplied anthrax and bubonic plague cultures, arms supplies and nerve gas to Saddam.[491] The U.S. also supplied crop dusting helicopters which Saddam used to gas the Kurds.[492] Elements of the nerve gas that Hussein used came from an American company called LaFarge. George Bush Sr. was once owner of this company and Hillary Clinton was at that time CEO.[493]

The U.S. looked the other way while Saddam gassed the Kurds in his nation and the Iranian soldiers because Saddam was furthering U.S. interests in the Middle East. On May the 16th, 1988, Hussein killed more than 5000 Iraqis with chemical weapons in one day which lead to worldwide condemnation. The U.S. looked the other way.[494] The Untied States had publically condemned the use of

---

490 Robin de Ruiter, Worlddwide Evil and Misery: The Legacy of 13 Satanic Bloodlines (The Netherlands, Myra Publications, 2008) 226.
491 David Icke, Tales from the Time Loop, (Ryde, Iles of Wright, UK: David Icke Books, 2003) 134.
492 Jim Marrs, The Terror Conspiracy: Deception, 911 and the Loss of Liberty (New York: Disinformation, 2006) 357.
493 Robin de Ruiter, Worldwide Evil and Misery: The Legacy of 13 Satanic Bloodlines (The Netherlands, Myra Publications, 2008) 228.
494 Ibid.

lethal chemical weapons; however they did not sanction Hussein for their use in any way. On 11/21/1983, Lawrence Eagleburger of the State Department instructed U.S. staff in Bagdad, "... We do not want to help Iran's cause by encouraging their propaganda against Iraq." Eagleburger stated that maintaining the U.S. Iraqi relationship was important when mentioning Iraq's use of chemical weapons. "We do not mention the issue of chemical weapons to confront you, but also not to support the opinions of others. The reason that we do so is that it has been America's long-standing policy to denounce the use of lethal chemical weapons". When Iran accused Iraq of violating the 1925 Geneva Protocol which prohibits the use of chemical weapons, this became a political problem for the United States and had the potential to make relations between Iraq and the United States more difficult. When in 1984 Hussein's use of chemical weapons became obvious, the US had no choice but to condemn it publically. Hussein reacted to this with outrage even though the United States went to great pains to convince him that their statement was "for public consumption only." Publically the U.S. downplayed Hussein's use of chemical weapons while they continued to support Hussein in his war against Iran. Thus they provided secret service information to Hussein and made sure that he was well supplied with weapons.[495]

Saddam Hussein had also purchased Directed Energy Microwave weapons from a British company called Marconi. He was supplied with troposcatter weapons which gave him the ability to have wireless communication with his troops on the southern front, but they also had mind control capacity. The Troposcatter is a machine that talks to the brain. This would give Saddam's forces the ability to wipe out entire officer corps, division and battalions.[496] The United States could not have been happy about microwave weapons with their mind control capacity in the hand of Saddam Hussein. The United States used these weapons in the Gulf War which might partly explain why entire units of Hussein's forces were surrendering en mass. Imagine what a war would be like if both sides of the war were employing mind control technology on each other's troops. The objective of psychological warfare is to convince the enemy that they cannot win the war and thus surrender is in their best interest. If microwave weapons are used in a war in this capacity by two sides of the same war, soldiers on both sides of the front could be surrendering at the same time.

The Bush Administration began looking for an excuse to go to war with Iraq. In fact declassified documents reveal that the U.S. had plans for the destruction and rebuilding of Kuwait before the invasion. One month before our December 15, 1990 declaration of war, Secretary of State James Baker signed a report which detailed the destruction of Kuwait including setting the oil wells on fire, and how Kuwait will be rebuilt "with despotism instead of democracy". The report included

---

495 Ibid, 227 -228
496 Alex Constantine, Psychic Dictatorship in the U.S.A (Portland, OR; Feral House, 1995) 43.

a list of US corporations that would be assigned the task of rebuilding Kuwait and extinguishing the oil fires and the Arabs who would be in control.[497]

The eight year long war between Iraq and Iran had sapped Hussein of financial resources. Kuwait was also contributing to Hussein's financial woes. John Stockwell writes, "During the Iran/Iraq war of the 1980's, Kuwait advanced its border further north and seized valuable Iraqi oil reserves. Kuwait cost Iraq billions of dollars in revenues by manipulating oil prices."[498] Hussein was out of money and could not pay his bills to the international bankers. OPEC refused to allow him to raise oil prices. He needed cash so he turned to Kuwait which was the third largest producer of oil in the world. Kuwait was once a possession of Iraq that was carved out of Iraq by the British in 1914 and became a British protectorate in 1961 when Iraq sought to reclaim it.[499] Hussein once again sought to reclaim Kuwait as a part of Iraq. He began to mass his forces at the border of Kuwait. Before the invasion he sought the approval of the United States, and he got it. He was assured by several State Department officials including John Kelly, Assistant Secretary of State, State Department Spokeswoman Margaret Tutwiler, and April Glaspie, U.S. Ambassador to Iraq that the United States had no treaty with Kuwait.[500]

April Glaspie met with Saddam Hussein on July 25th 1990. She made reference to the fact that Hussein was massing troops along the border of Kuwait and asked why. At that time Saddam revealed that he intended to reclaim Kuwait as an Iraqi possession.[501] April Glaspie clearly indicated to Saddam that her instructions from Secretary of State, James Baker, were to work at improving relations with Iraq. She then went on vacation. When the crisis escalated on August 2nd and Iraqi troops moved into Kuwait, Bush froze all Hussein's assets. Hussein was shocked by the reaction of the United States. Furthermore, April Glaspie who was equally surprised by the Presidents reaction to the crisis was prohibited from speaking out publicly about the obvious betrayal.[502]

"With the Iraq invasion and conquest of Kuwait, Bush was handed his much-needed war on a silver platter. Hussein, columnists have noted, was surprised by Bush's all-out reaction. But the U.S. war fever was predictable. At this point, even an all-out war would be in Bush's political interests, presuming the United States could win."[503] However, convincing the American public of the necessity of

---

497 David Icke, Tales from the Time Loop, (Ryde, Iles of Wright, UK: David Icke Books, 2003) 137.
498 John Stockwell, The Praetorian Guard: America's Role in the New World Order (Boston, MA: South End Press,1991)13.
499 Jim Marrs, The Terror Conspiracy: Deception, 911 and the Loss of Liberty (New York: Disinformation, 2006) 358.
500 Pat Robertson, The New World Order (Dallas, Texas: Word Publishing, 1991) 10 -11.
501 Jim Marrs, The Terror Conspiracy: Deception, 911 and the Loss of Liberty (New York: Disinformation, 2006) 358.
502 Ibid, 359.
503 John Stockwell, The Praetorian Guard: America's Role in the New World Order (Boston, MA: South End Press,1991) 25.

going to war was important. The president can't just decide to throw the nation into a conflict. Only congress can declare war and the American people influence congress. Thus the media becomes involved in the strategy. A little "spin" was needed. So on October, 10th 1990 a 15 year old girl named Nayirah testified before Congress that she had been volunteering in a Kuwaiti hospital when she witnessed babies being dumped from their incubators onto the floor by Hussein's soldiers. George Bush later even stated the exact number of babies that had been dumped on the floor and died – 312.[504] Afterward it came out that the girl was in fact the daughter of the Kuwaiti ambassador to the U.S., that her name was not Nayirah and that the girl had not in fact witnessed any such atrocity. Yet her testimony was used to justify the first war with Iraq.

One can conclude from available sources that Bush Sr.'s purpose for betraying Hussein had to do with the embarrassment over Saddam's use of chemical weapons supplied by the United States and Britain, Saddam's acquisition of DEW non-lethals and a premeditated desire on the part of the United States to invade Kuwait having to do with the oil assets of that nation. Pat Robertson has also noted that President Bush Sr. spoke publicly of the New World Order for the first time while addressing the invasion of Kuwait. Establishing the long planned for (or shall we say long conspired) New World Order may have been the bottom line for the invasion. George Bush declared publicly that launching the New World Order was the main issue and not the invasion of Kuwait. He told Congress and the nation on July 29th, 1991

> What is at stake is more than one small country, it is a big idea—a New World Order, where diverse nations are drawn together in common cause to achieve the universal aspirations of mankind: peace and security, freedom and the rule of law. Such is a world worthy of our struggle, and worthy of our children's future . . . . [505]

On February 1st, 1991 at a Fort Gordon Georgia, President Bush stated in a address, "When we win and we will, we will have taught a dangerous dictator, and any tyrant tempted to follow in his footsteps, that the United States has a new credibility and *that what we say goes* [italics mine], and that there is no place for lawless aggression in the Persian Gulf and in this New World Order that we seek to create."[506] If Kuwait was actually the objective, it would explain why Bush Sr. did not at that time complete a full blown invasion of Iraq.

The picture that the American public was presented of Desert Storm was a much sanitized picture of the war. It seemed to be over in the blink of an eye. We

---

504 Robin de Ruiter, Worlddwide Evil and Misery: The Legacy of 13 Satanic Bloodlines (The Netherlands, Myra Publications, 2008) 229.
505 Bush George H. W. George H. W. Bush's State of the Union Address, Envisioning One Thousand Points of Light (January 29, 1991 -http://www.infoplease.com).
506 Pat Robertson, The New World Order (Dallas, Texas: Word Publishing, 1991) 40.

were assured they did everything they could to protect the civilian population. However, US bombs had a nasty habit of hitting the wrong things. Seventy percent of the bombs that rained down on Iraq "missed" their targets. Civilian facilities such as a civilian bomb shelter, and a milk factory, were hit because they were supposedly military targets. However, with the sophisticated surveillance technology in the possession of U.S. forces such mistakes would be impossible.[507] In fact not only did U.S. planes hit civilian structures, they also hit the wrong country. Some of their bombs went to Syria and Turkey. There was another problem. Sadaam was attempting to use civilians as a human shield so he planted his artillery inside schools and hospitals. This made it pretty amazing that most civilian structures were still standing when the bombing ceased.[508] The United States was also guilty of war crimes of the kind for which German and Japanese soldiers had been condemned to death. UN forces used bulldozers to fill in trenches occupied by Iraqi troops burying the soldiers alive. In fact the Iraqi army was in retreat heading out of Kuwait across the border of Basra with prisoners and civilians. The US pilots disabled the vehicles both in front of and in the rear of the convoy bringing the convoy to a dead stop on the open road. Then they continued to systematically bomb the convoy frozen in place and flew back and forth to the aircraft carrier to reload. This was simply mass murder, "and thousands died at the hands of the very people who now 'fight terrorism' and promote themselves as morally superior to those they target."[509]

The fire power unloaded on the Iraqi troops was grossly disproportioned to the ability of the republican Guard to respond. The Iraqi military had a limited fleet and no submarines, and the Iraqi soldiers were few and poorly motivated. Hundreds of US fighter planes bombed the civilian population every night. More than 150,000 Iraqi civilians and as many soldiers were killed with Napalm *even though they were running away or towards American troops waiving white flags.*[510]

U.S. army documents reveal that about 315 tons of depleted uranium was dropped on Iraq and Kuwait. This indiscretion on the part of the US military resulted in a huge increase on the number of cancer patients and deformed children in Iraq including deformities that no doctor has ever seen in any medical handbook. Babies were born without eyes, a brain or genitalia or with a cleft palate or monstrous heads. Most infuriating is the fact that the United Nations imposed sanctions on Iraq which prohibited the supply of medicines needed to treat uranium poisoning. Iraqis were not the only ones to suffer from the unrestrained use of depleted uranium. In more than 10 years since the war more

---

507 David Icke, Tales from the Time Loop, (Ryde, Iles of Wright, UK: David Icke Books, 2003) 139.
508 Aaron Glantz, How America Lost Iraq (New York: JEREMY P. TARCHER/PENGUIN, 2005) 14, 16.
509 David Icke, Tales from the Time Loop, (Ryde, Iles of Wright, UK: David Icke Books, 2003) 139.
510 Robin de Ruiter, Worlddwide Evil and Misery: The Legacy of 13 Satanic Bloodlines (The Netherlands, Myra Publications, 2008) 230.

than 90,000 U.S. soldiers are suffering illnesses related to depleted uranium contamination. British soldiers have also higher instances of deformities in their children like the ones found in Iraqi children. The United States and their allies did know the risk of using depleted uranium and willing subjected even their own people to contamination.[511]

Palestinians, Sudanese, Egyptians, Filipinos and other imported laborers also got killed while fleeing Kuwait. The mass murder and subsequent burial of Iraqi soldiers that had actually surrendered along with the murder of civilians fleeing in their private cars was in gross violation of the Hague and Geneva conventions. Michael Ratner, former director of the Center for Constitutional Rights stated "This was a well planned, systematic killing of a defenseless population, murdered by a powerful Air force that was yet to set food on Iraqi soil."[512] The bombing by US and British forces continued more than 10 years after the end of the war!

For the ten years following the first war with Iraq the U.N. imposed sanctions on Iraq that literally brought that nation to its knees. The White House justified sanctions against Iraq because Saddam Hussein was stockpiling "weapons of mass destruction" and biological weapons which were in fact funded and supplied by the US and British governments and their allies. Icke states, ironically "Only one nation has dropped nuclear weapons on another country at the time of this writing . . . the United States". The United States Military is guilty of stockpiling deadly chemical weapons all across America in spite of a treaty in which the U.S. agreed to destroy them.[513]

Another war, a few more thousand lives destroyed, and we go on talking about how "our troops" are over there defending our freedom. I don't have anything against "our troops". We so easily adopt the party line. "Our troops", in fact, are not over there defending our freedom. Let's be honest. They are being used to further a diabolical agenda for world domination. I was one of "our troops" once. I was grateful for the opportunity to serve my country, and I was proud of that uniform. Right now I really wish that there were more Americans who were willing to fight the battle for our integrity and refuse to defend the lie.

25. Challenge to Your Thinking: Establishing Credibility

We do not give thought enough to how it is that we determine someone to be credible or not. More like breathing, it happens without conscious thought. However, considering that we are now swimming in the soup of deception in this country, it is time we took a careful look at how it is that we determine someone to be credible. What makes someone believable to us?

---

511 Ibid, 231.
512 Ibid, 230.
513 David Icke, Tales from the Time Loop, (Ryde, Iles of Wright, UK: David Icke Books, 2003) 143.

We of course would never believe someone who lies. Therefore truth is at the core of the credibility issue. Whether we like it or not, we have to also consider that everyone lies. Those of us who choose to be truthful find that a commitment to truthfulness is challenged on a daily basis. Being truthful requires vigilant thought because the truth is sometimes inconvenient.

Knowing that truth is at the core of the credibility issue, we would of course not have relationships with people we could not trust to be truthful. Thus, when it comes to establishing credibility we begin with the people who are closest to us – those with whom we have intimate relationships. Therefore in a conflict of information we would believe those closest to us before a careful examination of the facts. If a careful examination of the facts revealed that the one we are closest to was not truthful, it would injure the relationship. But most likely, we would choose to trust our intimate associates before examining the facts and in fact may choose not to examine the facts if we have so trusted someone.

We have a tendency to indiscriminately trust authority. Rightly or wrongly we assume that persons in positions of authority are credible people. Considering the evidence against those now in power in this country, that would probably not be a healthy assumption. Nevertheless, we do it before a careful examination of the facts. It may be that even after a careful examination of the facts reveals something unbelievable about the one in authority we might assume that there was an error. In fact, our desire to trust authority has much to do with our desire to feel safe and secure. If we can't trust authority, then we can feel insecure. This is uncomfortable because authority has power. Power in the hands of people we can't trust is dangerous. This is a danger that we might not want to face unless circumstances demands it of us.

Credibility is established by position, education and wealth. All of those things make us assume that such a person is credible apart from a careful examination of the facts. In fact when someone of position, education or wealth is more knowledgeable of the facts than we are and they have access to information that we do not, we may choose to abdicate our ability to examine the facts. This too is a dangerous thing to do.

We establish credibility by appearance. A person in uniform is suddenly a vitreous person, without a careful examination of the facts. However, persons in uniform have committed violent crimes. Uniforms can be acquired without virtue. They can be bought, stolen or simply worn unfaithfully, and a badge does not necessarily glitter with virtue. Mark Rich notes in his work, *The Hidden Evil* that someone wearing a lanyard and carrying a clipboard is believable even without any evidence. We want to believe that we can trust the clergy. Cathy O'Brien however, can tell us a different tale. We also believe a person who is physically attractive before we believe someone who is not. That has been demonstrated by scientific research time and time again. However, as I have heard a young single woman lament, "There are a lot of good looking jerks in the world".

We can even be made to doubt ourselves if we do not learn to question those credibility props. In fact, those who are closest to us can doubt us if they have been beguiled by them. Remember Eve in the Garden of Eden. A perfect woman, in a perfect world, with a perfect husband and a perfect marriage and a perfect relationship with God was beguiled by something as incredible as a snake. He didn't even attempt to disguise himself as something more credible than that, and Eve was beguiled by him. Even those who are closest to us who have earned our trust cannot always be trusted without question because they can also be deceived.

Of course we know we are not perfect. No one is faultless. We make mistakes and we can be fooled. It is not a comfortable thing to do maybe, but we have to be on our guard. The basis on which we establish credibility is really very flimsy. It can be demonstrated that we have been very gullible. It does not in fact take much to deceive us. So maybe we had better learn to be more discerning. Any stalking victim can tell you that even the people closest to them have betrayed them because they were fooled, bribed, or intimidated into doing something they otherwise would not have done.

An old song sung by Evi Tournquist says, "The things we can depend upon grow fewer every day. When that number gets to one, the one is gonna show the way." That one she is talking about is Jesus Christ. That one when he came to this earth absolutely divested himself of all the things that would normally have made him credible to us, absolutely all of them.

He was not good looking. He could have come as the most handsome man in the world, but he chose not to be. Isaiah 53:2 says, "He grew up before him like a tender shoot, and like a root out of a dry ground. He had no beauty or majesty to attract us to him, nothing in his appearance that we should desire him" (NIV). He was not born into a wealthy or influential family. Matthew 13 and Mark 6 tell us that he was a carpenter's son. He also did not have a "degree". John 7:15 (NIV) tells us, "The Jews were amazed and asked, 'How did this man get such learning without having studied?'" He was called Rabbi by his followers, but he did not complete the rabbinical training required to bear that title. He did not come with a title or position. If he had the Jews would not have been amazed at his learning. They would have expected it. He was a king but he did not come wearing kingly vestments. The only thing he wore that was unusual was a seamless undergarment (John 19:23). Jesus slipped quietly into this world without any props. He had no name, no fame and no fortune, but he was indeed a king. The star, which shown so brightly when Jesus was born, was understood by the astrologers of the day. Everyone, whether they believed in God or not, knew the star was a sign that a king had been born.[514] He came as the Word of God. His only prop was the truth of his word and the works he performed. The people were either going to take him at his word or by his works or they were not going to take him at all.

---

514 Ernest L Martin, The Star That Astonished the World (Portland: Ask Publications, 1996) 15.

People have been trying to discredit him ever since. Is it not ironic that those who have something to hide are always trying to discredit those who dare to tell the truth? Jesus had that problem when he walked on this earth. Jesus was accused of being demon possessed (John 8:49). His family thought he was out of his mind (Mark 3:21). He said in John 8:46-47 (NIV), "If I am telling the truth, why don't you believe me? He who belongs to God hears what God says. The reason you do not hear is that you do not belong to God."

Credibility according to Jesus is established by what you do. Jesus said, "Watch out for false prophets. They come to you in sheep's clothing, but inwardly they are ferocious wolves. But by their fruit you will recognize them. Do people pick grapes from thorn bushes, or figs from thistles? Likewise every good tree bears good fruit, but a bad tree bears bad fruit. A good tree cannot bear bad fruit, and a bad tree cannot bear good fruit" (Matthew 7:15 – 18 NIV). Jesus established his credibility by the things that he did. He raised the dead (John 11:43-44); He gave sight to the blind and made the lame to walk (Matthew 21:13); He made the deaf to hear and the mute to speak (Matthew 7:32 – 35); He healed the sick (Matthew 8:14 – 15); He cast out demons (Luke 4:41); He fed the hungry (Matthew 14:19-20). Jesus said, "The words I say to you are not just my own. Rather, it is the Father living in me, who is doing his work. Believe me when I say that I am in the Father and the Father is in me, or at least believe on the evidence of the works themselves" (John 14:10 – 11).

Finally, he established his credibility by his resurrection from the dead. He clearly told his disciples that he was going to be killed and on the third day he would be raised (Matthew 16:21). He was in the grave three days and on the third day he rose from the dead (Matt 27:59 – 28:6). In *Image of the Risen Christ* the only member of the Shroud of Turn Research Team who was actually a Christian, Dr. Kenneth Stevens, details the results of the research of this scientific inquiry into the validity of the claims about the Shroud. It was a fascinating study. The scientists on the team were not Christians except for the author of the book. They looked at the shroud from a completely scientific point of view and tried with all their might to avoid the religious implications of their findings. What they learned, having tested the shroud with the most modern of research tools, is truly fascinating. They did first conclude that the shroud was not a forgery. In other words, it really was a burial cloth that had covered a dead man. It was not painted or scorched. They determined that the man who was covered with that shroud had suffered and died in exactly the same way that the Bible says that Jesus Christ suffered and died. They found that the body that had been buried in that cloth had come out after three days. This they were sure of because there were signs that the body had been in rigor mortise but had not been in decay. If the body had been in the cloth longer than three days there would have been signs of decay. They also concluded that when the body came out of that cloth it did so *without disturbing the cloth!* In other words, the body *came through* the cloth. They also concluded that the power that caused the negative image (like the image of a camera film) to be imprinted on that cloth was so strong that it would have destroyed any normal human body. Finally, the evidence presented in the shroud brought them to the place where they could find no better explanation than that the man who had been in that cloth had been resurrected from the dead. The evidence was enough that at least one other scientist became a believer in Jesus Christ at the conclusion of the study.[515] Jesus established his own credibility.

Most of us are concerned about telling lies. We care about being honest truthful people because we want to be trusted, though we all have to admit that we have all lied about something. What we need to be equally concerned about is knowing the truth. The reason why it is important that we be concerned that we are not deceived is that we will act on what we believe to be true. In believing and acting on a lie we can actually do harm to innocent people and be harmed ourselves. We can even become complicit in committing a crime. We don't want to think of ourselves as criminals, but to embrace a lie is to become criminal. In this way, even the Christian church in Germany committed crimes against the Jews because they believed and acted on lies.

The book of Daniel tells us what to expect in the last days. He tells us that the antichrist will deceive people. In fact the words are chilling.

> In the latter part of their reign, when rebels have become completely wicked, a stern-faced king, a master of intrigue [read *"covert activity"*], will arise. He will become very strong, but not by his own power. He will cause astounding devastation and will succeed in whatever he does. He will destroy the mighty men and the holy people [read "the saints of God"]. *He will cause deceit to prosper, and he will consider himself superior* [like the Illuminati do]. When they [the holy people] feel secure, he will destroy many and take his stand against the Prince of princes. Yet he will be destroyed, but not by human power (Dan 8:23 – 25 NIV).

---

515 Dr. Kenneth E Stevenson, Image of the Risen Christ (Canada: Frontier Research Publication Inc., 1987).

There is no passage of scripture in the Bible that more clearly depicts what is happening in our world today. The Illuminati clearly perceive themselves as superior to the rest of us. They are committed to a profoundly destructive, wicked agenda for world domination. They will and have taken as many lives as they have to in order to accomplish their tasks and they continue to deceive everyone in the process. It is therefore very important that we become very discerning people. It is important also that we put our faith in Jesus Christ and not in governing officials. They are being controlled and manipulated by a very deceitful and destructive manipulator who in the Bible is referred to as the Antichrist. It doesn't mean that there are not honest trustworthy people in government. There are, and they need our prayers, but they can also be deceived and manipulated.

Jesus said, "For my Father's will is that everyone who looks to the Son and believes in him shall have eternal life, and I shall raise him up at the last day" (John 6:40 NIV). You know, there is a reason why I threw my lot in with Jesus. He raised the dead when he was living on this earth. He said he was going to be killed and then he would be raised on the third day. It happened just as he said. The facts about his life and his death bear consistent witness that he was exactly who he said he was. He promised me that if I believed him he would raise me up on the last day also. I believe him.

26. The 9/11 Lie

On the morning of September 11, 2001, I was in a department meeting at work. That morning, just at the close of the meeting, a young woman rushed into the meeting room and announced to us that the World Trade Center had been hit by an airplane. Moments later she again came to tell us that a bomb went off at the Pentagon.

The official story that we received about the 9/11 events was that Muslim hijackers had hijacked four planes and deliberately crashed two them into the World Trade Center, the Pentagon and one in Pennsylvania which had been bound for the Whitehouse. The evidence, we were told, came from phone calls made from cell phones and onboard telephones by passengers and crew members to family and friends. We are told that this band of hijackers from a terrorist group known as al-Qaida was headed by Osama Bin Laden. Later we were told that the Afghanistan government was harboring Osama and that his escapade was funded by none other than Sadaam Hussein.

A careful examination of the facts would indicate that this is not really what happened. Piece by piece researchers have taken this scenario apart. A lie, like a house of cards, comes tumbling down with the wind of truth. FBI director Robert Mueller speaking in San Francisco in April 2002 stated, "In our investigation we have not uncovered a single piece of paper either here in the United States or in the treasure trove of information that has turned up in Afghanistan and elsewhere that mentioned any aspect of the September 11th plot."⁵¹⁶ In fact the FBI has no evidence at all linking Osama Bin Laden to the 9/11 events.

What is true is that the technology that made it possible to make cell phone calls in flight, called a Pico Bell, was not developed until 2004 and was not installed on any aircraft until 2007. Otherwise the altitude and speed of the aircraft made it impossible for the cell signal to connect with the cell tower long enough to complete a call. How then do we explain the fact that friends and relatives reported that they received calls from those hijacked planes? Modern technology provides the answer. By using a ten minute recording of anyone's voice, experts are able to clone any voice and develop a facsimile. Technology also exists that makes it possible to fake a caller ID number.⁵¹⁷ Evidence pertaining to those calls also indicates that the calls were faked. Ted Olson, the husband of flight attendant Barbara Olson, reported that his wife made a collect call to him from the plane to tell him that the airplane had been hijacked by Muslims. He first reported that she had used an onboard phone to call him and must have called collect because she did not have her purse. However, onboard phones cannot be activated without a credit card. He then said she used a cell phone. That is also not possible because we know that onboard cell phone calls were not possible until the year 2007 and if she were using a cell phone she would not have had to call collect.⁵¹⁸

The most famous of those calls came from Tom Burnett to his wife Deena Burnett. There are problems with this as well, not to mention again that cell phone calls from the air were not possible at that time. The other obvious problem was that "Tom" only mentioned Deena's name on the call. When his wife asked him if he wanted to speak to the children, he declined saying he would talk to them later. He never mentioned their names. It would seem improbable that he would have declined speaking to his children knowing that the plane was on a suicide mission and that he might not have a "later" moment to speak with his children. Another caller, Mark Bingham, who reportedly called his family from the air on a cell phone, when speaking with his mother greeted her by saying, "Hi mom, this is Mark Bingham". It is not plausible that someone talking to his mother would have to identify himself by his first and last name. Another telltale sign is that those who received those calls reported that they heard no commotion in the background. It was calm. There was no shouting and no screaming. This also makes the cell phone story quit implausible considering the circumstances.⁵¹⁹ Jim Marrs also asks in *Terror Conspiracy*, "And why did news outlets describe the throat cutting and mutilation of passengers on Flight 93 with box cutters when *Time* magazine on September 24 reported that one of

---

516 9/11 Hard Facts (2009 http://www.911hardfacts.com).
517 David Ray Griffin, The New Pearl Harbor Revisited: 9/11, The Cover-Up, and the Expose (Northampton: Olive Branch Press, 2008) 118.
518 Ibid, 60-62.
519 Ibid,118- 119

the passengers called home on a cell phone to report, "We have been hijacked. They are being kind'?"[520]

WTC Towers & Flights 11 and 175

On the morning of 09/11 at 08:10am American Airlines flights 11 and 175 took off from Boston Logan Airport both en route to Los Angeles. Air Traffic Controllers lost contact with American Airlines flight 11 at 08:14am. At 8:21 Flight 11 was observed going off course. At that time Air Traffic Controllers would have notified the FAA that Flight 11 was at least experiencing some kind of in flight emergency. There is an emergency protocol for such situations and those who participate are well practiced at it. Though it might take some time to determine that an aircraft which has gone off course is actually being hijacked, the FAA learned the flight had been hijacked at 08:25am. At that time the fighters from Andrews Air force Base should have been scrambled and they would have had plenty of time to intercept flight 11 before it hit the WTC. This kind of thing happens routinely and in fact between September 2000 and June 2001 the Pentagon launched fighters on 67 occasions to escort wayward aircraft out of forbidden air space.[521] However, according to military officials the F-15 pilots flew "like a scalded ape, topping 500 mph but were unable to catch up to the airliner." This is an obvious distortion because an F15 can fly four times faster than a Bowing 757. William Thomas states in his online article *911 Commission Cover-UP*, "Launched per regulations as soon as radio and transponder contact was lost with Flight 11, with both sets of throttles hammered to the stops the fastest fighters on earth would have intercepted Flight 11 over the Hudson River at least six minutes from Manhattan."[522]

Flight 11 struck the north face of the 110-story North Tower of the World Trade Center (WTC) at the 96th floor at 8:46 am. If standard procedure had been followed, the FAA would have notified the North Eastern Defense Sector (NEADS) at 08:22, nine minutes before AA flight 11 hit the North Tower. Even launching as late as they did - on the FAA's first officially acknowledged phone call to NORAD at 08:40 - the Mach 2.5 fighters could have reached Flight 175 before it reached the World Trade Center. Though the F15's were just lifting off just as Flight 11 hit the North Tower, Flight 175 was still 20 minutes out. The F15s were given instead faulty coordinates and "fighters outside of NYC were kept in unexplained holding patterns over Long Island while flight 175 slammed into the South Tower."[523]

---

520 Jim Marrs, The Terror Conspiracy: Deception, 911 and the Loss of Liberty (New York: Disinformation, 2006) 27.
521 William Thomas, 911 Smoking Gun - The Story (December 14, 2003 – http://www.rense.com).
522 William Thomas 911 Commission Coverup (June 21, 2004 – http://www.rense.com).
523 9/11 Hard Facts (2009 http://www.911hardfacts.com).

What is the official explanation for this not so funny comedy of errors? According to *NORAD's Response Times*, an official document put out on September 18, one week after 9/11 by the North American Aerospace Defense Command (NORAD) the FAA didn't notify NEADS that flight 11 had been hijacked until 08:40. Normal procedures had been radically violated with disastrous consequences but, amazingly, no one was fired or charged with dereliction of duty. However, witnesses contradict the official explanation. Robin Hordon, former employee of the FAA's Boston center, citing testimony of an employee on duty that day, stated he believes the FAA was notified by 08:20 of the in-flight emergency of flight 11. This controller has stated, according to Robin Hordon, that "the FAA was not asleep and the controllers . . . followed their own protocols." On the basis of this testimony as well as his own familiarity with procedures, Hordon believes that the FAA had actually contacted NEADS by 08:20." [524] Reliable reports indicate that the FAA had notified NORAD at 08:25 am of the hijacking of flight 11. NORAD Official Lt. Col. Dawn Deskins of the Air National Guard states that the military had received the information by 08:30am. The 9/11 Commission Report states that the military was not contacted till 08:37am[525] which is 23 minutes longer than standard operating procedure would have allowed.[526] Investigative reporter Tom Flocco who attended the 9/11 Commission hearing also reported that Laura Brown, the deputy in public affairs at FAA headquarters, stated that the National Military Command Center had initiated a teleconference at about 08:20 or 08:25 that morning. However she changed her story after she consulted with her superiors and sent another email to Mr. Flocco. Flocco felt that her original statement was more accurate and was changed to suite her superiors.[527] Two F15's were not scrambled from Otis Air Force Base until 08:46 am "…thirty-two excruciating minutes after existing standard operating procedures explicitly instructed regarding the scrambling of military jets on the morning of September 11th."[528] The author of *911 Hard Facts* writes,

> This wild deviation from standard protocol has been glossed over by official reports as a simple case of confusion, chaos, faulty communication, ineffective response training, etc. But 32 minutes of delay is not chaos and confusion. It is a systematic failure at so many levels of so many interlinked individuals and departments to perform their most basic responsibilities that it defies the laws

---

524 David Ray Griffin, The New Pearl Harbor Revisited9/11, The Cover-Up, and the Expose (Northhampton: Olive Branch Press, 2008) 4.
525 The National Commission on Terrorist Attacks Upon the United States The 9111 Commission Report (New York) 20.
526 9/11 Hard Facts (2009 http://www.911hardfacts.com).
527 Tom Flocco Rookie in the 9-11 Hot Seat? (June 18, 2002 – http://www.tomflocco.com).
528 9/11 Hard Facts (2009 http://www.911hardfacts.com).

of probability to suggest that they all failed at the same time on the same day in the exact same coordinated manner. At the least their behavior was gross, criminal incompetence that should have led to the dismissal and trial of people up and down the chain of command in the FAA and NORAD. Their 'chaos and confusion' resulted in the deaths of 3000 people, yet not one of them was fired or tried. Why?[529]

Monte Belger, Acting FAA administrator on 9/11 testified that in his 30 year history with the FAA that military persons were present with the FAA at all times and had access to real time information and all parties involved knew what to do. Other witnesses who included employees of United and American Airlines, family members of those that perished, media reps who had access to classified material pertaining to 9/11, the FBI and the firemen involved have been officially restricted from talking to Congress and the press. One very interesting note is that as of June of 2001 Donald Rumsfeld rewrote a 50 year standing policy which then dictated that from that date any response to a hijacked aircraft had to be cleared first through his office.[530] To call the 9/11 events a conspiracy is almost an understatement.

WTC Collapse

Careful examination of the collapse of the World Trade Center buildings 1 and 2 and WTC 7 also reveals some interesting and disturbing facts, which of course contradict the official story. We are told that the fires caused by burning jet fuel weakened the steel supports of the WTC which caused the buildings to collapse. WTC 7 which was not hit by airplanes also collapsed supposedly from fires caused by falling debris from the other two burning buildings. First of all no steel structured building has ever collapsed due to fire. Secondly, witnesses inside the towers on 9/11 testified to hearing explosions *before* the airplanes hit the tower. In fact, as in the incident at the Pentagon which will be discussed further on, witnesses inside the towers smelled cordite which is a main ingredient used in explosives. Experts in demolition who witnessed the collapse of the towers stated that there are many factors that would indicate the buildings fell because of explosives such as would have happened in a controlled demolition. The buildings fell at nearly free fall speed into their own footprint. A burning building does not come down that way. A burning building would fall apart one section at a time because fires do not burn a building uniformly. Also, fires from jet fuel do not burn hot enough to melt steel. '...steel does not begin to melt until it reaches about 2,700°F (1,480°C), and an open, diffuse fire fed by hydrocarbon material (including jet fuel) could never, even under the most ideal conditions, get much

---

529 Ibid.
530 Ibid.

above 1,832°F (1,000°C)."[531] Kevin Ryan was the site manager of Environmental Health Laboratories, a division of Underwriters Laboratories which had certified the steel components used in construction of the WTC towers for their ability to withstand fires. Ryan wrote a letter to the National Institute of Standards and Technology (NIST) to Dr. Frank Gayle in November of 2004 challenging conclusions that the building collapsed due to burning Jet fuel. He stated,

> [S]teel components were certified to ASTM E119.... [T]he steel applied met those specifications. The time temperature curves for this standard require the samples to be exposed to temperatures around 2,000°F for several hours.... [E]ven un-fireproofed steel will not melt until reaching red-hot temperatures of nearly 3,000°F.... [T]he buildings should have easily withstood the thermal stress caused by pools of burning jet fuel."[532]

Brigham Young University Professor of Physics Dr. Steven Jones, who specializes in the fusion of metals, also contested the official story that WTC 7 collapsed from fires caused by falling debris from the North Tower. He referenced the Windsor building that caught fire in Madrid Spain in February 2005 which burned for several hours and when the fire was finally out the building was still standing. That 32 story building burned for 20 hours gutting the entire building. However, as would be typical of any burning structure, though parts of the building did collapse, the structure remained standing when the fire had finally burned out.[533]

Strategically planted explosives are what weaken steal and cause a steel structure to fall symmetrically. This is the way demolition experts bring down high rises in areas where they have to protect other buildings and pedestrians from falling debris. There was molten steel found in the debris of the collapsed WTC buildings and demolition expert, Brent Blanchard, told Professor Steven E. Jones of Brigham Young University (BYU) that he had never seen molten steel at a demolition sight where thermite explosives had not been used.[534] Thermite has "a highly volatile and potentially explosive reaction in which aluminum metal is oxidized with other metals to create an incredibly hot and potent reaction that can cut through metal as thick as steel and iron in fractions of a second."[535] This material is used by the military in antitank weapons and also for the destruction

---

531 David Ray Griffin, The New Pearl Harbor Revisisted: 9/11, The Cover-Up, and the Expose (Northampton: Olive Branch Press,: Olive Branch Press, 2008) 31 – 32.
532 Kevin Ryan Text of Email Letter from Kevin Ryan to Frank Gayle (November 11, 2004 - http://911review.com).
533 9/11 Hard Facts (2009 – http://www.911hardfacts.com).
534 Steven E. Jones, 2006, Why Indeed Did the WTC Buildings Collapse? (Book Section, David Ray Griffin and Peter Dale Scott, 9/11 and American Empire: Intellectuals Speak Out, Vol. 1, Northampton: Olive Branch Press, 2006) 36.
535 9/11 Hard Facts (2009 – http://www.911hardfacts.com).

of buildings and bridges. It is also used by professional demolition crews as cutter charges to sever steel beams in buildings being intentionally demolished. Dr. Steven Jones tested debris found at buildings near the WTC where they would have fallen or been blown from the WTC towers disasters. He found "compounds wholly consistent with thermite reactions – Abundant Iron, Zinc, Sulfur, Manganese, Fluorine, and, perhaps most suspiciously, Barium, a highly toxic substance found in military grade explosives, not in building material, airplanes, or office supplies."[536]

According to the official story the building collapsed the way it did because the fires weakened the steel structure and the floors falling one at a time onto the floors beneath caused the building to come down the way it did. However, the North Tower was hit on the 90th floor. Since fire travels up and not down there should have been no damage to the 89 floors underneath which were already bearing the weight of all the above floors. Likewise the South Tower was hit at the 80 floor so the 79 floors beneath the 80th floor would have been unaffected by the fire above. Witnesses inside the WTC testified to hearing explosions going off in the lower levers of the Towers *before* the planes crashed. William Rodriguez was one of them. "WTC janitor William "Willy" Rodriguez, the last person to leave the WTC alive on 9/11, has testified that he was in the first *basement* 1 of the WTC when an immense explosion went off *below* him in the yet deeper subbasement level (s) of the building a few seconds *before* the plane hit the tower high above."[537] Firefighter Edward Cachia and others with him also witnessed what they thought were explosions at the WTC, "[We] thought there was like an internal detonation, explosives, because it went in succession, boom, boom, boom, boom, and then the tower came down.... It actually gave at a lower floor, not the floor where the plane hit."[538]

FLIGHT 77

The official story stated that AA flight 77, being hijacked by Muslim terrorists, crashed into the Pentagon. Allegedly the pilots and crew and passengers were herded to the rear of the plane by the hijackers. However, information gained from the NTSB through a FOIA request backed up by an Australian computer programmer reveals that the flight deck door, that is the door of the cockpit, was never opened. The information came from the Flight Data Recorder (FDR) which was allegedly found inside the Pentagon. The FDR makes a recording every four seconds. In order for the hijacker to enter the cockpit and get everyone out without it being recorded on the flight data recorder he would have had to know which second the recorder

---

536 Ibid
537 Jim Marrs, The Terror Conspiracy: Deception, 9/11 and the Loss of Liberty (New York: Disinformatin, 2006) 444.
538 Steven E. Jones, Why Indeed Did the World Trade Center Collapse (Book Section, 9/11 and American Empire: Intellectuals Speak Out, Vol. 1, book Editors Griffith David Ray and Peter Scott, North Hampton: Olive Branch Press2006) 45.

was recording and timed it perfectly to get in and out of the cockpit within the four seconds. And what would be the point of that? Would they be trying to hide the fact that they were hijacking the plane? The alleged hijackers did not try to hide that fact. If the door was never opened the hijackers would not have been able to gain access to the cockpit to remove the pilots nor navigate the plane. It has also been determined that the FDR could not have come from the plane that crashed. The FDR that was alleged from flight 77 was most likely planted making it anyway a fake piece of evidence. Anyway you look at it, it doesn't wash.[539]

The alleged flight path of flight 77 has presented some significant issues. There was a Virginia Department of Transportation pole and several light poles in its path which it supposedly struck during its decent. However in another article written by Rob Bolsamo et al. in The Canadian National Newspaper, other interesting facts are revealed. The FDR reveals that there was no impact of the craft; that the plane was 300 feet too high to have struck the light poles and 100 feet too high to have struck the Pentagon; that the FDR reveals that the flight path was several degrees north of the light poles that it supposedly hit and this is corroborated by eyewitness reports including the Pentagon Police.[540]

Eyewitnesses saw a missile, not a bowing 757, hit the Pentagon. "Tom Seibert said, 'We heard something that made the sound of a missile, then we heard a powerful boom.' Mike Walter excitedly told CNN, 'A plane, a plane from American Airlines. I thought, 'That's not right, it's really low.' And I saw it. I mean, it was like a cruise missile with wings.'"[541] French author Thierry Meyssan reported that he had been on the highway just in front on the Pentagon where traffic was moving very slowly when he heard a whooshing sound which began behind him and then and stopped suddenly in front of him to his left. A fraction of a second later he witnessed the explosion at the Pentagon. "The next thing I saw was the fireball. I was convinced it was a missile. It came in so fast it sounded nothing like an airplane". David E. Edwards, professor of anthropology at Salisbury University in Maryland who was on his way to the Capital for a 10:00 am meeting on the subway when a young couple boarded and reported breathlessly that they had just seen a missile hit the pentagon. Charles Lewis who was at the LAX listening to Walkie Talkie chatter also reported hearing that the Pentagon had been hit by a "rocket."[542] Others reported that physical evidence supporting the official story that flight 77 crashed into the Pentagon was absent. The available physical evidence did support the notion that the Pentagon was hit by a missile.

---

539 Pilots for 9/11 Truth Forum 911: Pentagon Aircraft Hijack Impossible (November 27, 2009 – http://pilotsfor911truth.org).
540 Rob Balsamo et al., Pilots say Official account of 911 contradicted by U.S. Government's own data (The Canadian National Newspaper - April 5th 2011 - http://www.agoracosmopolitan.com).
541 Jim Marrs, The Terror Conspiracy: Deception, 9/11 and the Loss of Liberty (New York: Disinformatin, 2006) 35.
542 David Ray Griffin, The New Pearl Harbor Revisited: The Cover-up and the Expose (Northampton: Olive Branch Press, 2008) 105-106.

Donald Rumsfeld, the secretary of defense, in an apparent slip of the tongue said the aircraft that slammed into the Pentagon was a "missile". Karen Kwiatkowski who was present inside Pentagon on the morning of the attack also stated that the damage that she witnessed was what she would have expected to see from a missile attack, not from a Bowing aircraft. The hole was not larger than 20 feet in diameter and did not immediately cause the façade of the building to collapse.[543]

Air traffic controller Danielle O'Brien told ABC News, "The speed, the maneuverability, the way that he turned, we all thought in the radar room, all of us experienced air traffic controllers, that that was a military plane. You don't fly a 757 in that manner. It's unsafe". The agility of vessel and the "high-pitched" noise it made along with the small hole it produced led many researchers to conclude that it was a missile painted to look like an American Airlines plane. Photos of crash site did not reveal evidence that a plane had crashed there. There was evidence that a missile had crashed there. "Several photos of what appears to be part of a jet engine cannot be matched with the 757 engine, but more like that of a missile jet engine."[544] The official explanation for the lack of visible evidence of a plane crash was that plane disintegrated upon impact. However, this explanation does not hold water. One very telling reason is that he FBI claimed that it was able to identify passengers on the plane by fingerprints. If the fires were hot enough to disintegrate an airplane, how is it that fingers with fingerprints survived? Debris found on the lawn at the crash site was from an A-3 Sky Warrior, a much smaller aircraft than a bowing 757.[545]

April Gallop, an Army employee with a Top Secret clearance, on site on the morning of the crash testified that she did not see any plane parts inside or outside the building.[546] She also did not smell jet fuel, but she did smell cordite, a key ingredient in the manufacture of bombs. She stated, "Being in the Army with the training I had, I know what a bomb sounds and acts like, especially the aftermath, and it sounded and acted like a bomb."[547] April also testified that while she was in the hospital men in suites who refused to identify themselves visited her. They told her to take the compensation money and shut up about what she had seen. They told her a plane hit the Pentagon, but she never saw any plane. In addition when she logged on to her computer there was an explosion which threw her backwards out of her chair. Her watch and the clock on the wall stopped from the explosion at 9:30 to 9:31 am. The Pentagon was allegedly struck by flight 77 seven minutes

---

543 Karen Kwiatkowski, Assessing the Official 9/11 Conspiracy Theory ([Book Section] 9/11 and American Empire, Intellectuals Speak Out, Vol. I, book Editors, Griffin David Ray and Peter Dale Scott. - Northampton: Olive Branch Press, 2007) 28.
544 Jim Marrs, The Terror Conspiracy: Deception, 9/11 and the Loss of Liberty (New York: Disinformatin, 2006) 34 – 35.
545 Ibid, 446.
546 PR Newswire 2011 Amidst Growing World Doubts About 9/11, Career Army Officer Takes Bush Administration Officials to Court April 5th Represented by Center for 9/11 Truth (March 23, 2011 – http://news.yahoo.com).
547 Jim Marrs, The Terror Conspiracy: Deception, 9/11 and the Loss of Liberty (New York: Disinformatin, 2006) 440.

later at 09:38 am.[548] Also Karen Kwiatkowski noted that all uniformed personnel were ordered to report to the area of the crash for stretcher duty but there were no bodies to load on stretchers so they disbanded.[549]

There were those who testified that they saw the plane hit the Pentagon, but a careful examination of their testimony reveals some telling inconsistencies. Jerry Russell, who has advanced degrees in both engineering and psychology, examined testimonies of those who claimed to have seen the plane hit the Pentagon. Of the testimonies that he examined only 31 of them could provide any realistic details. Then he found that 24 of the 31 "witnesses" either worked for the Federal Government or the mainstream media (in other words Mockingbird) and 21 of the testimonies contained "substantial errors or contradictions". For example Steve Anderson, Director of communications for USA today said the plane drug its wing on the ground before it struck the Pentagon. That would have left a huge gash in the lawn which photographs showed was not present. Allen Killsheimer reported holding a section of tail in his hand, but no one else reported seeing the tail section and no photographs show parts of the aircraft. Retired Army Officer Frank Probst reported that the plane was flying so low that he dove to the ground to keep from being hit by it. He reported that one of the plane's engines passed by him within about six feet. "Dave McGowan, who has studied the effects of wind turbulence from large airliners, pointed out that if a Boeing 757 going several hundred miles a hour had come that close to him he would have been a victim, not a witness."[550]

One other interesting fact is that the Pentagon does have a sophisticated anti-aircraft (AA) defense system, though the Pentagon denied this was the case because it was too costly. However the Capital Building is installed with an AA defense system. If Washington could afford the expense of installing AA defense for the Capital building, it would not make sense that the Pentagon would not to have one. French author Thierry Meyssan indicates that French officials given a tour of the Pentagon were shown the anti-aircraft system at the Pentagon.[551] Considering that the Pentagon would undoubtedly be a primary target in any attack on the Untied States, we would expect the Pentagon to have an antiaircraft defense system. Others familiar with the Pentagon such as April Gallop and comptroller's office supervisor Paul Gonzales testified that it was the best defended and safest building in the world. However the system was not activated on the morning of the attack. Why was it not activated? An antiaircraft defense system sends out a signal to an approaching craft called "Identification Friend or Foe?

---

548 PR Newswire 2011 Amidst Growing World Doubts About 9/11, Career Army Officer Takes Bush Administration Officials to Court April 5th Represented by Center for 9/11 Truth (March 23, 2011 – http://news.yahoo.com).
549 Karen Kwiatkowski, Assessing the Official 9/11 Conspiracy Theory ([Book Section] 9/11 and American Empire, Intellectuals Speak Out *I* book auth. Griffin David Ray and Peter Dale Scott. - Northampton: Olive Branch Press, 2007) 20.
550 David Ray Griffin, The New Pearl Harbor Revisited: The Cover-up and the Expose (Northampton: Olive Branch Press, 2008) 73.
551 Ibid,106.

(IFF)". If the approaching craft is on the proper frequency, and a friendly aircraft would be, it would respond to the signal, "Friend". Thus the antiaircraft system would not intercept the approaching aircraft. If the craft that was approaching the Pentagon was indeed an American military vessel it would have responded to the IFF with the appropriate signal which would explain why the AA system did not intercept the incoming craft. If on the other hand, it was not a friendly vessel then the only way the Air Defense system would not have responded would have been if someone in the Pentagon had turned it off.

One very telling indication that the attack on the Pentagon was an inside job was the fact of missing money. The day before the attack, Donald Rumsfeld announced that the Pentagon was missing 2.3 trillion dollars. The area of the building that was hit was the Army auditors' offices. The auditors were searching for the missing money and their computers which contained the data from their investigation were destroyed. The area of the Pentagon that was hit would have been the least likely target area for a terrorist. The offices of the Secretary of Defense and other key officials were on the opposite side of the building. The morning of the attack April Gallop had returned to work after being away on maternity leave. She was taking her infant son to the daycare but was told upon entering the building that there was some important paperwork that needed to be completed immediately and that it was okay for her to take her son with her. She went to her office and logged onto her computer and that is when the explosion happened burying her and her infant son in debris. She was able to get herself and her son to safety, but she reported that her computer was on fire. She believed that her logging on to her computer had triggered a bomb.[552]

Flight 93

The official story about Flight 93 was that it was hijacked by Muslim terrorists and that passengers on board the plane fought back and hence the plane crash landed in Pennsylvania. The phone calls are the only evidence that we have that there were terrorists on the plane. We have already discussed the fact that cell phone calls could not have been made from the plane in-flight. There is therefore no evidence that there were terrorists on board the plane. There are multiple other problems with the story of flight 93. There is evidence that Flight 93 did not crash, but was instead shot down. Since we do not have any evidence that there were terrorists on board the plane, the story about the passengers who fought back has also been debunked. Whitehouse Counter Terrorist Chief, Richard Clark, states that he received the authorization from Dick Cheney shortly after 09:45 to shoot down any airliners that were still airborne.[553] Also an eight mile line of debris

---

552 Ibid, 100 – 101.
553 David Ray Griffin, et. al, 911, The American Empire and Common Moral Norms (Book Section, 911 and American Empire, book editor David Ray Griffin & Peter Dale Scott Peter, North Hampton: Olive Branch Press, 2007) 8.

from the plane suggests that the plane was shot down while it was still airborne.[554] Pennsylvania state police officials reported that plane fragments were found twelve kilometers away from the crash site. On September 13, Reuters also reported that plane fragments had fallen from the sky. This of course would only have happened if the plan exploded in mid air, and not if it had crashed.[555] Apparently in 2004 in another "slip of the tongue" Donald Rumsfeld on a visit to troops in Iraq also referred to the plane in Pennsylvania being shot down.[556] Officials at NSA were aware that United Flight 93 was shot down by an Air Force air to air missile, but the 9/11 Commission never spoke to them about it.[557]

Witnesses at the crash site also report, as in the crash at the Pentagon, the absence of evidence that a plane had crashed there. Flight 93 would reportedly have had 37,000 gallons of fuel left when it crashed yet tests of the soil did not reveal the presence of fuel and there was no smell of fuel at the crash site. Other witnesses who included a television reporter, a newspaper photographer and a paramedic all said that they did not observe anything that would indicate that a plane had crashed there. There were no suitcases, no recognizable plane parts, no body parts and no patients.[558]

Shanksville Mayor Ernie Stull stated in March 2003 on a German TV show that the crash site was devoid of evidence that a plane had crashed there. County Coroner Wallace Miller said that it looked like the passengers had been let out at another location and had not been in the plane when it crashed. In fact no one seems to know where the bodies from flight 93 ended up.[559] Miller, who was required by law to establish the cause of death of the victims, wrote down "murdered" for the 40 victims on the plane and "suicide" for the four hijackers. Miller told a reporter that he did not have any way of proving what had happened.[560]

Finally witnesses reported that there were actually two crash sites for flight 93. They were 6 miles apart. Witnesses at Indian Lake reported seeing the plane fly directly over Indian Lake coming from the East. But other reports from the Shanksville area reported that the plane came from the North. This is confirmed by the information gained from the FDR which 9/11 Truth Organization acquired

---

554 Jim Marrs, The Terror Conspiracy: Deception, 9/11 and the Loss of Liberty (New York: Disinformatin, 2006) xvi.
555 Robin de Ruiter, Worldwide Evil and Misery: The Legacy of 13 Satanic Bloodlines (The Netherlands, Myra Publications, 2008) 283.
556 Jim Marrs, The Terror Conspiracy: Deception, 9/11 and the Loss of Liberty (New York: Disinformatin, 2006) 142.
557 David Ray Griffin, The New Pearl Harbor Revisited: The Cover-up and the Expose (Northampton: Olive Branch Press, 2008) 127.
558 Ibid, 120.
559 Robin de Ruiter, Worldwide Evil and Misery: The Legacy of 13 Satanic Bloodlines (The Netherlands, Myra Publications, 2008) 284.
560 Jim Marrs, The Terror Conspiracy: Deception, 9/11 and the Loss of Liberty (New York: Disinformatin, 2006) 143.

from the NTSB by an FOIA request.⁵⁶¹ Witnesses in the area reported seeing a second airplane flying close to the first one and this was confirmed by CCN broadcast showing radar images to two planes flying closely together.

The question that remains to be answered is what happened to the bodies from flights 93 and 77. Since we can conclude that flight 77 did not crash into the Pentagon, where did it go? Where were the bodies from flight 93? Since we have no bodies, should we assume that those passengers are actually dead? It is quite apparent by all evidence that something is being covered up by our government and if those "bodies" were still alive they could probably tell us something the real perpetrators of this crime don't want us to know. Are they dead or are they just "Lost"?

Remote Control?

A most disturbing fact relates to the remote control capability of the aircraft involved in 9/11. This technology was first installed in the Global Hawk. Thus this would preclude the possibility of a highjacker flying the airplane into a building. As soon as air traffic controllers determined that the plan had been highjacked it could be remotely captured and safely landed on the ground. This technology was also installed on the bowing 757 and 767 that were involved in the 911 events. Though the US government made statements to indicate that it had not yet happened and made overtures to the effect that it would be in the future to preclude anything like 9/11 ever happening again, the technology already did exist. It is highly likely that the 9/11 events could have been orchestrated from a command center from the ground using remote control. The fact that WTC 7 collapsed though it was not hit by a plane suggests that the command center could have been inside that building. This might also explain why flight 97 was shot down. It is possible that somehow the remote control short circuited and the pilots were able to gain control of the plane again. If the pilots were able to land the plan safely, they would be able to testify that the control of the plane was taken out of their hands and not by hijackers.⁵⁶²

Evidence of Prior Knowledge of the 9/11 Events

Researchers around the world and within the United States have concluded that there was U.S. Government complicity in the 9/11 events. Two basic theories about that day have emerged. One is called the "Let it happen on purpose" or LIHOP theory. The other is the "Made it happen on purpose" or MIHOP theory. The LIHOP's believe that government officials knew what was going to happen

---

561 David Ray Griffin, The New Pearl Harbor Revisited: The Cover-up and the Expose (Northampton: Olive Branch Press, 2008) 121.
562 Robin de Ruiter, Worldwide Evil and Misery: The Legacy of 13 Satanic Bloodlines (The Netherlands, Myra Publications, 2008) 287.

and did nothing to prevent it. That would make it a mirror incident of Pearl Harbor which was discussed earlier in which the President of the United States deliberately provoked the Japanese into aggression and did nothing to stop them when he received warnings that the Japanese were going to attack. I am in the MIHOP camp. I believe the 9/11 incidents were more similar to the Reichstag fire which was shown to be caused actually by a member of the NAZI Party. In either case the government used the 9/11 incident as justification for gross infringements on the liberties of American citizens and as justification for two illegal wars. This is clearly another demonstration of the Hegelian Dialectic at work.

A very telling incident is the collapse of WTC building 7 which was not hit by any aircraft but also collapsed. It reportedly was burning from fires caused by debris falling from the North Tower. Amazingly, A BBC broadcast shows reporter Jane Stanldly telling the audience that the WTC 7 has collapsed. However, in the background behind the reporter WTC building 7 is seen still standing! This would indicate that they had foreknowledge that the building was going to collapse. Larry Silverstein took over ownership of WTC 7 and the North and South Towers just before 9/11. In July 2001, he took out an insurance policy on those buildings which had a clause in it to insure them in case of terrorist attacks. This might not be surprising in light of the 1993 attacks. He made this statement on a PBS broadcast, "I remember getting a call from the, er, fire department commander, telling me that they were not sure they were going to be able to contain the fire, and I said, 'We've had such terrible loss of life, maybe the smartest thing to do is pull it. And they made that decision to pull and we watched the building collapse." The term "pull" is a demolition term which means to bring the building down using, of course, explosives. This takes weeks of preparations so Larry Silverstein had to have know in advance of the 9/11 events. He was embarrassed about his statement and 2 years later stated that he meant to pull the firefighters out of the building. However, the firefighters had been pulled out of the building several hours before. In fact the man pocketed $1 billion and $500 million in profits from the insurance on those buildings. The author of 9/11 Hard facts also states, "It is worth noting that on the morning of 9/11, all of the buildings making up the WTC complex not owned by Larry Silverstein managed to remain upright, despite equally heavy fire and structural damage."[563]

To be sure, we can conclude that the WTC buildings did not collapse from fires caused by burning jet fuel as the official story indicated. We can conclude from eyewitness testimony that there were explosions inside the building on the lower levels even before the planes hit. Expert testimony indicates that the collapse of the building could have only been caused by the presence of explosive devices. Here is the telling fact. To bring a building down in that way using cutter charges to weaken the steel beams takes weeks of planning and preparation. In other words someone had access to those buildings for an extended period prior to September 11th to plant those explosives. One cannot simply walk in off the street and plant explosive devices in the WTC, particularly since there was a terrorist attack on

---

563 9/11 Hard Facts (2009 – http://www.911hardfacts.com).

those buildings in 1993. How did that occur? Interestingly, George Bush's younger brother, Marvin Bush, was a principal for Securacom which is the company that provided security for the WTC, United Airlines and Dulles International Airport. George Bush's Cousin, Wirt Walker III, was the Company's CEO until January 2002. In fact in the weeks leading up to September 11th there were multiple security drills in which everyone had to evacuate the building.[564] This of course would be excellent cover for insiders to plant those explosives.

Other suspicions have been raised due to the fact that there was a sizable purchase of "put options" just prior to the 9/11 events. To purchase a put option is a bet that the stock prices will go down. The put options that were purchased were for United and American airlines, which were the two involved in the 9/11 crisis, and for the occupants of 22 stories of the WTC, Morgan Stanley Dean Witter. The prices did plummet as a result of the 9/11 crisis which resulted in a profit of tens of millions of dollars to the investors which would raise suspicions that the investors had advanced knowledge of the 9/11 events.[565]

Though the Bush administration denies any prior knowledge of the attacks, there are witnesses to the contrary. On July 10 2001, CIA Director George J. Tenet and counterterrorism Chief J. Cofer Black met with Condoleezza Rice and warned of an impending attack involving al Qaeda. Tenet reported that Ms. Rice was polite but brushed them off. When the meeting was made public knowledge Rice initially denied that the meeting had taken place. However, Tenet's testimony of the meeting was reported to the 911 Commission and reporters acquired transcripts of the testimony. Rice had to backtrack on her denial. Public records reveal that Rice did in fact ask Tenet and Black to make the same presentation to Secretary of Defense Donald Rumsfeld and Attorney General, John Ashcroft . It would be highly unlikely if 911 was in fact an inside job that the CIA Director was not in on the act. The CIA has been from the beginning the hub of New World Order activity. It is more likely that Tenet was lying along with Condoleezza Rice. George Bush indicated in a statement that he made to the press on August 25th, 2001 that there had been a meeting at his ranch on August 24, 2001 involving himself, George Tenet, Condoleezza Rice, Donald Rumsfeld and Vice Chairman of the Joint Chiefs Richard Myers. This meeting lasted for 6 hours. "Is it reasonable to think that Tenet simply forgot about the meeting? It appears that he lied in an attempt to keep it secret."[566] If in fact that meeting lasted 6 hours it is highly unlikely that George Tenet did not have an opportunity to discuss with George Bush and those present his

---

564 Jim Marrs, The Terror Conspiracy: Deception, 9/11 and the Loss of Liberty (New York: Disinformatin, 2006) 50.
565 David Ray Griffin, et. al, 911, The American Empire and Common Moral Norms (Book Section, 911 and American Empire, book Editors, David Ray Griffin & Peter Dale Scott Peter, North Hampton: Olive Branch Press, 2007) 6.
566 Mark H. Gaffney, The 911 Mystery Plane and The Vanishing of America (Walterville: Trine Day LLC, 2008) XXIV.

"concerns" about the impending attack by al Qaeda on U.S. soil. If this was an inside attack then George Tenet most certainly was a part of the operation. If it was not, then he did in fact have opportunity to discuss it with George Bush. Why did he lie about it? Why did Condoleezza Rice lie? The logical explanation is that they knew about the impending attack, but George Bush had denied that there was any warning about the attack. Why deny it unless it was because they did nothing to stop it? If they did nothing to stop it then they must have been complicit with it. If they were complicit then they could not admit that they knew about it. In fact it was Mark Gaffney's conclusion that they used al Qaeda as patsies for a covert operation that was being planned before George Bush came into office.[567]

A legitimate U.S. military counter-terrorist operation known as Able Danger operating out of Ft. Belvoir, was tracking Mohammad Atta and company as early as January or February of 2000. In May of 2000 the officers in charge were ordered to shut down Able Danger and destroy all data. The officers were threatened with prison sentences if they refused. The Pentagon attempted to prevent the 2005 Senate Judiciary Committee from investigating Able Danger and when that failed refused to allow staff knowledgeable about Able Danger to testify. Lt. Col. Anthony Shafer testified anyway and was thereafter targeted for harassment. In fact Shaffer and others involved in investigating Able Danger knew that Mohamed Atta was a terrorist threat and Shaffer attempted to contact the FBI three times. Three meetings with the FBI were canceled by high level Pentagon attorneys.[568]

Shaffer still managed to bring the existence of Able Danger to the attention of the 911 commission. In Afghanistan Philip Zelikow, Executive Director of the Commission, and several commission staffers who were then on tour gathering firsthand information about the U.S. war on terrorism, asked him to contact him later about Able Danger but when he did three months later he was told the Commission was not interested. Lt. Col. Shaffer notified his commander of the contact he had made with Zelikow and "all hell broke loose." Shaffer's security clearance was revoked. He lost access to his files on Able Danger and he later learned that all the data on Able Danger had been destroyed. His testimony before congress was dismissed because of a lack of evidence, which of course had been deliberately destroyed. His career was trashed.[569] Tenet told a 2002 Joint House-Senate panel investigating 911 that al Qaeda began planning the 9/11 attacks as early as 1998. If this is the case the CIA had to have been tracking bin Laden at least as early as 1998. In 1998 he told the Senate Intelligence Committee that the CIA was recruiting al Qaeda operatives in order to defeat them. In fact Tenet writes in his memoirs; "... the [9/11] commission failed to recognize the sustained comprehensive

---

567 Ibid, 120.
568 Ibid, 120 – 21.
569 Ibid, 118 - 119

efforts conducted by the intelligence community prior to 9/11 to penetrate the al Qaeda organization."⁵⁷⁰

In fact the truth is that the CIA had a well established relationship with al Qaeda. For 20 years the United States has been involved in aggressive covert programs in order to gain control over the Persian Gulf and to gain access to Central Asia for development by US oil companies. The US has used "Arab-Afghan" terrorists associated with al Qaeda as assets since the 1990s, "who, in country after country, were involved in trafficking Afghan heroin".⁵⁷¹ The 911 Commission denied the CIA al Qaeda connection. The Commission report stated that "Bin Laden and his comrades had their own sources of support and training, and they received little or no assistance from the United States."⁵⁷² However, al Qaeda received a great deal of support indirectly from the US government beginning in Afghanistan until 1992 and afterwards in other countries such as Azerbaijan between 1992 and 1995. They received lots of money from the CIA station in Islamabad. They were trained in urban terrorism by Pakistani ISI operatives who received their training from the CIA. Members of the al Qaeda network including Mohamed Atta were granted visas to enter the US in spite of the fact that they were suspected of terrorism, and soldiers of al Qaeda were also admitted to the US for training purposes. At Ft. Belvoir, Virginia, an al Qaeda operative was given a list of Muslims who would be potential al Qaeda recruits, and al Qaeda operative Sergeant Ali Mohamed who was in the US Army Special Forces, trained al Qaeda personnel while in the US. The FBI repeatedly protected members of al Qaeda from prosecution. All of this may have been done because the US did not want to offend al Qaeda's two primary supporters, Saudi Arabia and Pakistan, because of US oil interests in Central and South Asia, "and oil led to US coexistence with both al Qaeda and the world-dominating Afghan heroin trade."⁵⁷³

There is considerable reason to believe that neither al Qaeda nor Osama bin Laden had anything to do with the 9/11 "terrorist" attack. The deceased were taken to the morgue in Dover Delaware. The Pathologist who examined the bodies, Thomas R. Olmstead, was able to identify all the bodies but did not find any bodies with the names of the hijackers.⁵⁷⁴ Olmstead found no Arab bodies present in the

---

570 Ibid, 119 – 120.
571 Peter Dale Scott, The Background of 9/11: Drugs, Oil, and US Covert Operations (Book Section, 911 and American Empire I book editors Griffin David Ray and Peter Dale Scott, Northampton: Olive Branch Press, 2009) 73.
572 The 9/11 Commission Report: Final Report of the National Commission on Terrorist Attacks upon the United States (New York) 56.
573 Peter Dale Scott, The Background of 9/11: Drugs, Oil, and US Covert Operations (Book Section, 911 and American Empire I book editors Griffin David Ray and Peter Dale Scott, Northampton: Olive Branch Press, 2007) 74.
574 Robin de Ruiter, Worldwide Evil and Misery: The Legacy of 13 Satanic Bloodlines (The Netherlands, Myra Publications, 2008) 271.

morgue.[575] That was for the crash at the Pentagon. There is the other problem that many of the supposed hijackers named by the FBI are still alive. For example the hijackers from flight 93 were supposedly Ziad Jarrah, Ahmed Alhaznawi, Saeed Alghamdi and Ahmed Alnami. "But the BBC reported later that Saeed Alghamdi was still alive. His driving license and car registration showed his address as 10 Radford Blvd., on the US Navy's Pensacola base in Florida. Another report showed Ahmed Alnami to be alive".[576] Also hijacker suspect Waleed al-Shehri was also reported by the BBC to be alive and living in Morocco on September 22, 2001. Brothers Ameer and Adnan Bukhari were identified as hijackers but CNN later reported that Ameer had died the year before (not on 9/11, 2001) and Adnan Bukhari was still alive. Wail al-Shehri and the supposed brother of Waleed al-Shehri were substituted for the Bukhari's when it was discovered that they were alive, but of course both al Shehris are alive as well.[577]

In addition though Osama bin Laden is listed on the FBI's Most Wanted List he is not listed as being wanted for the 9/11 attacks. The reason being according to the FBI is that they have no hard evidence linking bin Laden to the 9/11 attacks. Bin Laden was actually heard on television denying any involvement with the 9/11 attacks. On September 16th, on an Arabic television broadcast Al Jazeera, bin Laden categorically denied any involvement. He stated, on September 17, 2001: "I would like to assure the world that I did not plan the recent attacks, which seems to have been planned by people for personal reasons. I have been living in the Islamic emirate of Afghanistan and following its leaders' rules. The current leader does not allow me to exercise such operations." [578] He repeated this denial during an interview with the Pakistani newspaper *Ummaut*. Bin Laden made yet another statement denying involvement with the 9/11 attacks on November 3, 2001 reported by Al-Jazeera. During this last statement he also accused the Bush administration of "waging a crusader war" against Muslims. The only evidence presented by the U.S. Government linking bin Laden to the 9/11 attacks was a video tape which turned up "by chance" in Afghanistan by U.S. military forces in Jalalabad on December 9, 2001 shortly after the U.S. invasion. The film depicts bin Laden and several al Qaeda operatives celebrating the attacks. It was released December 13, 2001 along with an English translation and a DOD press release with a statement by Donald Rumsfeld, "There was no doubt of bin Laden's responsibility for the September 11 attacks before the tape was discovered."[579] The

---

575 Greg Szymanski, Family Members Of Doomed911 Flights 'Strangely Silent About Irregularities & Inconsistencies Of Official Government Story (November 18,2005 - http://www.rense.com).
576 Rowland Morgan, Flight 93 Revealed (New York, CAROLL & GRAF PUBLISHERS, 2006) 47 – 48.
577 David Ray Griffin, The New Pearl Harbor Revisited: The Cover-up and the Expose (Northampton: Olive Branch Press, 2008)158.
578 9/11 Hard Facts (2009 – http://www.911hardfacts.com).
579 Mark H. Gaffney, The 911 Mystery Plane and The Vanishing of America (Walterville: Trine Day LLC, 2008)114.

film shows Bin Laden writing with his right hand, but he is left handed. The man identified as Bin Laden in the video has darker skin, fuller cheeks, and a broader nose than other videos portray him. He also appears healthier and heavier than the way he appears in other videos. An article in the Guardian pointed out that in the video Bin Laden is wearing a ring on his right hand, whereas in other videos he has never worn any jewelry other than a watch.[580] The English translation of the Arabic from the film rather adlibbed information that was not actually on the tape. "Gernot Rotter, professor of Islamic and Arabic Studies at the University of Hamburg, stated, 'The American translators who listened to the tapes and transcribed them apparently wrote a lot of things that they wanted to hear, but that cannot be heard on the tape no matter how many times you listen to it.'"[581]

More disturbing are the myriad of contradictions between the official story, the 9/11 Commission Report and eyewitness testimony. One blaring and disturbing example is the testimony to the 9/11 Commission Hearing given by Transportation Secretary Norman Mineta pertaining to Dick Cheney's entrance to the Presidential Emergency Operations Center (PEOC) and the stand down order that he gave. Cheney reported that he did not arrive at the PEOC until 9:58 or shortly before 10:00 am.[582] However, Norman Mineta testified that he arrived at 09:20 and Dick Cheney was already there and fully in charge. In addition to that, according to Mineta's testimony Cheney gave a stand down order pertaining to the aircraft approaching the Pentagon. That stand down order was to *prevent* military fighter jets from intercepting flight 77 allegedly heading toward the Pentagon. Mineta's statement to the Commission reads as follows,

> During the time that the airplane (Flight 77) was coming into the Pentagon, there was a young man who would come in and say to the Vice President "...the plane is 50 miles out...the plane is 30 miles out"....and then it got down to the plane is 10 miles out. The young man also said to the vice president "Do the orders still stand?" And the Vice President turned and whipped his neck around and said "Of course the orders still stand, have you heard anything to the contrary!??"[583]

Norman Mineta's testimony was omitted from the 9/11 Commission report. The author of 9/11 Hard Facts make explicit his accusation.

---

580 David Ray Griffin, The New Pearl Harbor Revisited: The Cover-up and the Expose (Northampton: Olive Branch Press, 2008) 209.
581 Mark H. Gaffney, The 911 Mystery Plane and The Vanishing of America (Walterville:Trine Day LLC, 2008) 115.
582 The 9/11 Commission Report: Final Report of the National commission on Terrorist Attacks Upon the United States (New York) 40.
583 Gregor Holland, The Mineta Testimony: 911 Commission Exposed (July 22, 2005 - http://www.911truth.org).

Mineta's testimony proves that Cheney, and other top military officials in the bunker with him at that time, not only knew about Flight 77's whereabouts and approach, they were giving *direct orders* as to how to engage and deal with it. And since Cheney has admitted numerous times that orders to shoot down planes were not given until after 10:10 a.m., clearly Cheney's orders referred to in Mineta's testimony were to not shoot down AA77. Meaning, the Vice President of the United States, the ranking government official in Washington that morning, ordered that the airplane be allowed to freely enter D.C. airspace, line up the Pentagon, and slam into its West wing. That Cheney did not even evacuate the White House bunker in which he was himself sitting, even though it was surely a potential target only furthers the suspicion of the VP's full knowledge of AA77 intentions. And while the media refuses to connect the dots, Cheney's deliberate order of non-action in regards to the flight, and his refusal to evacuate the Pentagon, are nothing less than high treason and mass murder. Any reasonable investigator would put Cheney into an interrogation room, and hammer at him over and over and over to explain his comments, his whereabouts, his meaning, his contradictions, and the highly suspicious nature of his behavior.[584]

Still more ironic is that on the morning of September 11th the President of the United States was on a well publicized visit to a second grade classroom when the attacks occurred. Upon learning of the attacks he did not immediately spring into action and assume his role as Commander in Chief of the Armed services. He sat for another 10 minutes. His location was publicized on television so any terrorists would have known where he was making him of course a target. If the Secret Service did not know in advance of the attacks they would have had no way of knowing how many hijackers there were and they would by procedural necessity have to assume that the President would be a likely target. Yet, when the normal protocol would have been for the Secret Service to whisk the president to immediate safety, they did not that morning follow procedure.

Here is another interesting fact pertaining to the demolition of the WTC buildings. Contrary to federal law regarding crime scenes, the debris from the WTC were carted off and shipped overseas to be melted down and reused before any investigator had a chance to examine the debris for evidence of the actual causes of the collapse of the WTC buildings. The 911 Commission and NIST had to work from computer models to determine the cause of the collapse of the buildings and what they did was take the official explanation and work backwards to find a computer model that fit the official description which is also contrary to accepted standards of scientific investigation. Both the 9/11 Commission

---

584 9/11 Hard Facts (2009 – http://www.911hardfacts.com).

and NIST ignored eyewitness testimony and other evidence that would have contradicted the official story.

One telling piece of evidence indicates that government officials, including the President also seem to have known about the anthrax attack prior to the first outbreak. A public interest group, Judicial Watch responsible for investigating and prosecuting government corruption, was investigating the fact that White House officials including President Bush were on a regime of Cipro, a powerful antibiotic which is effective against anthrax, one month *before* the first anthrax attack.[585] The strain of anthrax which was used was a military grade that was not available outside of the United States. The type of anthrax used was a highly controlled "Ames strain developed by the U.S. Army at Ft. Detrick, Maryland and at the University of Iowa in Ames, Iowa. It is a military grade weaponized anthrax developed by William Patrick, former Ft. Detrick bioweapons expert. The FBI listed him as a "person of interest" in the anthrax investigation.[586]

There is yet another coincidence that would indicate complicity and/or foreknowledge of the 9/11 attacks by top level US officials. Attorney Stanley Hilton, graduate of Harvard Law School and former senior advisor and lead counsel for Bob Dole attended the University of Chicago as an undergraduate in the 1960's. While he was a student of Leo Strauss, known as the father of neo-conservatism, he and his peers Paul Wolfowitz and Richard Perle "…fabricated a 'Pearl Harbor-like incident'. He further states that he, Perle, Wolfowitz, and other students of Straus discussed an array of different plots and incidents 'like September 11th' and 'flying airplanes into buildings . . .."[587] In fact Hilton led a lawsuit after the 911 attacks in which he represented 400 people in the suit against George W. Bush, Condoleezza Rice, Cheney and Rumsfeld. Hilton accused Bush of national treason and mass murder and also claimed that Bush, Rice, Cheney, Rumsfeld and J. Tenet planned and supported the 9/11 events.[588] In late 2004, William Rodriguez, the World Trade Center Employee who testified that he heard bombs exploding inside the WTC before the planes hit, filed suit against George Bush, Dick Cheney, Donald Rumsfeld and others in a Philadelphia federal court under the Racketeer Influenced and Corrupt Organizations (RICO) act. He accused them of either planning or having foreknowledge of the 9/11 attacks and exploited them in order to launch the preplanned war against Afghanistan and Iraq.[589] In addition to that he made hundreds of allegations including

---

585 Robin de Ruiter, Worldwide Evil and Misery: The Legacy of 13 Satanic Bloodlines (The Netherlands, Myra Publications, 2008) 291.
586 Jim Marrs, The Terror Conspiracy: Deception, 9/11 and the Loss of Liberty (New York: Disinformatin, 2006) 458.
587 9/11 Hard Facts (2009 – http://www.911hardfacts.com).
588 Robin de Ruiter, Worldwide Evil and Misery: The Legacy of 13 Satanic Bloodlines (The Netherlands, Myra Publications, 2008)278.
589 Jim Marrs, The Terror Conspiracy: Deception, 9/11 and the Loss of Liberty (New York: Disinformatin, 2006) 46.

...that FEMA is working with the US government's plan to create an "American Gulag" concentration camp which FEMA will run once the federal government's plan to impose martial law is in place; that phone calls made by some of the victims, as reported by their family members, were not actually made but were "faked" by the government using "voice morphing" technology; that a missile, not American Airlines flight 77, struck the Pentagon; that United Airlines flight 93 was shot down by the U.S. military; that the defendants had foreknowledge of the attacks and actively conspired to bring them about; that the defendants engaged in kidnapping, arson, murder, treason, conspiracy, trafficking in narcotics, embezzlement, securities fraud, insider trading, identity and credit card theft, blackmail, trafficking in humans, and the abduction and sale of women and children for sex. ....[590]

Philadelphia lawyer Phil Berg who filed the suit on his behalf has been traveling and raising support for the lawsuit which our Mockingbird infected press has refused to publicize. The 237 page complaint was filed in Philadelphia, but the Judge referred the case to New York after the defendants' attorneys filed a motion to dismiss the case on the grounds of national security in 2005.[591] In January 2006 Mr. Rodriguez filed a 51 page affidavit in opposition to the dismissal. On June 26th, 2006, the court dismissed Rodriguez's claims against the USA, DHS, and FEMA, and gave him until July 7th to show why the lawsuit should not be dismissed against 153 other defendants named in the suite. Mr. Rodriguez failed to do so.[592]

Might it be time for the people of the United States file a class action lawsuit? Might it be time for the citizens of this deceived nation finally put their foot down and join William Rodriguez and say very loudly, "No! Absolutely not! Um! Nope, not gonna stand for this!" I was just wondering what would happen if the rest of us got some fight in us and were willing to do what a janitor from the World Trade Center was willing to do.

To be sure, evidence would indicate that the 9/11 events were in fact an inside job, not the act of a Muslim cleric and a band of extremists. This act of treason against the United States was used as an excuse to invade Afghanistan, Iraq and as a justification for the passing of the Patriot act which was a gross infringement on the civil liberties of American citizens. It is clearly another Hegelian type crisis used to accomplish the agenda of the NWO.

---

590 Wikipedia, William Rodriguez(November 12, 2010 - http://en. wikipedia.org).
591 Greg Szymanski, 9/11 Conspiracy, AFP Talks to Man Behind the September 11 RICO Suite (July 2, 2005 – http://www.americanfreepress.net).
592 Wikipedia, William Rodriguez (November 12, 2010 - http://en. wikipedia.org).

27. Afghanistan

The events of 9/11 were the apparent impetus for the invasion of both Afghanistan and Iraq because allegedly Afghanistan was harboring al Qaeda terrorists and Sadaam Hussein was funding their operation. What researchers have revealed is that al Qaeda was actually formed by the CIA to fight the Soviet occupation of Afghanistan. The group was originally a conglomerate of Arab NAZIs known as the Muslim Brotherhood based in Egypt that was attacking the infant state of Israel. When they were expelled from Egypt by Egyptian President Gamal Abdal Nasser in 1954 they went to Saudi Arabia. In the 1950s the CIA evacuated them from Saudi Arabia. In 1979 the CIA sent them to Afghanistan to fight the Soviets. In Afghanistan they were renamed "Makrab al Khidimar al Mujahideen" or MAK because "Muslim Brotherhood" sounded too "Naziish". Osama Bin Laden was one of the students involved with them at that time.[593] The Afghan leader Jallaladin Haqqani organized the group of Arab and Afghan leaders into a group called as-Qaeda. They received considerable financial support from the CIA station in Islamabad. The volunteers were trained in urban terrorism by Pakistani ISI operatives who were also trained by the CIA.[594] Al Qaeda activists were trained by a CIA operative and FBI informant, Egyptian Ali Mohamed. He was at the same time a reserve officer in the US Army Special Forces and he was in Afghanistan with U.S. backing.[595]

Our house of cards continues to crumble. Particularly since we know that after the actual invasion of Afghanistan, the capture of Bin Laden was apparently and likely deliberately botched and eventually the hunt for him was abandoned. CIA operative Gary Bernstein was the CIA's field commander in the joint CIA—US Armed Forces hunt for bin Laden in Afghanistan. The moment when they had Osama Bin Laden surrounded except for one avenue of escape, the U.S. military refused to supply the 800 rangers that were needed to block his escape stating that they were going to allow the Afghans to capture Osama Bin Laden. Bernstein had relayed to the U.S. Military that the Afghan military leaders were not interested in capturing bin Laden and might actually prefer that he escape. "So why," he asked, "was the US military looking for excuses not to act decisively? Why would they **want** to leave something that was so important to an unreliable Afghan army?" The fact was that the U.S. military had been instructed to capture bin Laden "dead or alive". Allowing him to escape therefore does not make sense if that was really their

---

593 Jim Marrs, The Rise of the Fourth Reich (New York: William Morrow of Harper Collins Publishers, 2008) 208-209.
594 Peter Dale Scott, The Background of 9/1l: Drugs, Oil, and US Covert Operations (Book Section, 9/11 and American Empire, Vol. I., book Editors, David Ray Griffin and Peter Dale Scott. – Northampton: Olive Branch Press, 2007) 74.
595 Ola Tunander, The War on Terror and the Pax Americana (Book Section, 911 and American Empire, Vol. 1, book Editors, David Ray Griffin Peter Dale and Scott, Northampton: Olive Branch Press, 2007) 155.

intention. If in fact they were actually supposed to let him get away, then it makes sense that they actually let him escape.[596] This makes sense particularly in light of the fact that the FBI has stated that they had no hard evidence linking Osama bin Laden to 9/11, that the bin Laden family and the Bush family were long time friends and that at a press conference on March 13th 2002 President Bush stated that they were not actively pursuing Osama bin Laden, that he was no longer a security threat because of the U.S. occupation of Afghanistan.[597]

So why then did we actually invade Afghanistan? There are three very obvious reasons revealed by those with a nose to dig. One not quite as obvious at the others would be the lack of a Rothschild controlled central bank in both Afghanistan and Iraq.[598] Muslim nations have not been willing to partake in the practice of usury. Afghanistan and Iraq were two of seven nations left in the world that do not have a central bank.

The other two reasons for the invasion would be the more obvious ones, oil and the production of heroin. In 1991, a US run oil company, MEGA oil, established itself in Baku and though it never found any oil there was instrumental in removing Azerbaijan from Soviet Russian influence. The company was actually run by Richard Secord, Heinie Aderholt, and Ed Dearborn who were three veterans of US operations in Laos and Nicaragua. They did manage to bribe the government and set up an airline company similar to Air American which had been used by the CIA for covert operations. The new airline was shuttling Afghan mercenaries into Azerbaijan to fight against the Armenians and their Russian allies. Heroin was also being transported from Afghanistan through Baku into Chechnya, Russia and North America. It is highly likely that MEGA was also involved. By 2000 nearly 20% of the Heroin being seized in the United States that had come from Afghanistan being distributed by Kosovar Albanians was double from what had been seized in 1996.[599] The author of 9/11 Hard Facts states unequivocally that capturing bin Laden was not the reason for the invasion of Afghanistan. The real reason was gaining access to the huge reserves of natural gas and energy in Central Asian countries like Turkmenistan and Uzbekistan and linking the pipeline through Pakistan, India, Iran and Iraq to the Persian Gulf and then to the west for the benefit of certain allies of multi-national corporations competing on the market. This of course does not justify war.[600]

---

596 David Ray Griffin, The New Pearl Harbor Revisited (Northampton: Olive Branch Press, 2008)205 – 206.
597 Mark H Gaffney, The 911 Mystery Plane and The Vanishing of America (Walterville: Trine Day LLC, 2008) 116.
598 Andrew Carrington Hitchcock The Synagogue of Satan (Austin, Texas: RiverCrest Publishing, 2007) 251.
599 Peter Dale Scott, The Background of 9/11: Drugs, Oil, and US Covert Operations (Book Section, 9/11 and American Empire, Vol. I., book Editors, David Ray Griffin and Peter Dale Scott. – Northampton: Olive Branch Press, 2007) 75-76.
600 911 Hard Facts (2009- http://www.91Ihardfacts.com).

Americans were also presented with the idea of liberating the Afghanistan people from the oppressive rule of the Taliban. The 9/11 Commission did acknowledge that the US war in Afghanistan was aimed at producing "regime change."[601] The Commission asserted that the United States wanted to change the regime because the Taliban were incapable of providing peace and ending the civil war, were perpetrating human rights abuses and providing a safe haven for al Qaeda. The Commission ignored all evidence that the United States wanted to get control of Central Asia which is what Zbigniew Brzezinski recommended in *The Grand Chessboard*.[602] In 1997, six international companies and the government of Turkmenistan formed Central Asian Gas Pipeline, Ltd. (Ceil Gas) to build a 790-mile-long pipeline to link Turkmenistan's natural reserves with Pakistan and perhaps on to the New Delhi area of India. America's Unocal Corporation, a Texas based Oil Company, headed up this consortium. Other companies involved were Delta Oil Company Limited of Saudi Arabia, Indonesia Petroleum Ltd. of Japan, ITOCHU Oil Exploration Co. Ltd. of Japan, Hyundai Engineering & Construction Co., Ltd. in Korea, and the Crescent Group of Pakistan.[603]

Prior to the 2001 invasion the United States was protecting the Taliban and attempting to gain their cooperation in a pipeline deal between UNOCAL and the Afghan government. It was during this period that the worst Taliban abuses occurred and al Qaeda led by bin Laden was admitted to Afghanistan.[604] Originally, it was hoped that the Taliban would stabilize the country enough to facilitate the building of the pipeline; however they did exactly the opposite. The Taliban, following a *Strategy of Tension*, were turning various groups against each other, destabilizing the country so that they could continue to control it. This is a traditional illluminized strategy. Creating factions within the nation that are constantly fighting amongst themselves makes the country unstable and controllable. This, however, defeated the purpose for putting the Taliban in power in the first place. The Bush Administration wanted the Taliban to work for a unified government. When that in fact failed, invading the country and toppling the Taliban regime fixed the problem. Three days after the invasion of Afghanistan, the plans to build the pipeline from the landlocked Caspian Sea to Pakistan was resumed.[605] In fact, the man that the US installed as a leader in Afghanistan, Hamid Karsai, is reported to be a former advisor to UNOCAL. Nine

---

601 Final Report of the National commission on Terrorist Attacks upon the United States, The 9/11 Commission Report) 203.
602 David Ray Griffin, The New Pearl Harbor Revisited (Northampton: Olive Branch Press, 2008)197.
603 Jim Marrs, The The Terror Conspiracy: Deception, 9/11 and the Loss of Liberty (New York: Disinformatin, 2006) 176.
604 Richard Falk, Global Ambitions and Geopolitical Wars: The Domestic Challenge (Book Section, 9/11 and American Empire, Vol. I, book editors David Ray Griffin & Peter Dale Scott, Northampton: Olive Branch Press, 2007) 123.
605 David Ray Griffin, The New Pearl Harbor Revisited (Northampton: Olive Branch Press, 2008)198.

days later Bush appointed Zalmay Khalilzad as Karsai's special envoy. Khalizad was an American born in Afghanistan, also a former employee of UNOCOL, who studied political science at Columbia University. He had worked with Zbigniew Brzezinski and had been a longtime supporter of the Taliban.[606]

Drug trafficking also was a key element in the invasion of Afghanistan. The United States Government, contrary to what they have presented to the American public, is not fighting drug trafficking, but facilitating it. Opium grown in Afghanistan produces a cash crop that is important to the Shadow Government. CIA Director William Casey launched covert operations in the Persian Gulf for gaining control of oil reserves. Drug laundering and trafficking was a part of funding those operations which were not financed by a congress. US sponsorship of drug trafficking began with the Afghan war of 1979 – 1989 with CIA links to the Bank of Credit and Commerce (BCCI).[607] CIA assets controlled the heroin trade. Mujahedeen guerrillas who were seizing control of territory in Afghanistan induced peasants to plant the opium " . . . as a revolutionary tax. Across the border in Pakistan, Afghan leaders and local syndicates under the protection of Pakistani Intelligence operated hundreds of heroin laboratories". In the spring of 2001 the Taliban had destroyed 95% of the poppy crop. In 2002 the Afghanistan opium production was 74 tons as compared to 3656 tons the year before. Under the Taliban no more than 185 tons of opium was harvested. After the invasion the crop soared to 3,400 tons again. *US News & World Report noted* that there was almost 500,000 acres of poppies being cultivated. Even under the occupation of US and allied forces, in 2005, Afghanistan earned $2.7 billion exporting opium, which is 52% of the country's $5.2 billion gross domestic product.[608] The United States Drug Enforcement Agency in Islamabad would not make seizures or arrests that would impact the drug trafficking because this was secondary to maintaining the production of the oil pipeline. According to the United Nations the profit from the drug trade is about $700 billion tax free US dollars per year which is money that has to be carefully laundered.[609]

That the invasion of Afghanistan was already planned prior to 9/11 is understood by researchers and others worldwide. It is truly amazing that the American people were completely bamboozled by government officials using the "terrorist threat" after 9/11 as an excuse to invade Afghanistan when foreign news agencies and other internationals knew of the invasion prior to 9/11. In February of 1998 the House International Relations Committee's Sub-Committee on Asia

---

606 Jim Marrs, The The Terror Conspiracy: Deception, 9/11 and the Loss of Liberty (New York: Disinformatin, 2006) 177.
607 Peter Dale Scott, The Background of 9/11: Drugs, Oil, and US Covert Operations (Book Section, 9/11 and American Empire, Vol. I., book editors, David Ray Griffin and Peter Dale Scott. – Northampton: Olive Branch Press, 2007)73.
608 Jim Marrs, The The Terror Conspiracy: Deception, 9/11 and the Loss of Liberty (New York: Disinformatin, 2006) 220 – 221.
609 Daniel Estulin, The True Story of the Bilderberger Group (Waterville: Trine Day LLC, 2007) 371.

and the Pacific discussed removing the government of Afghanistan from power. In June of 2001 the US government told India that there was going to be an invasion of Afghanistan in October. *Jane's Defense News* in March 2001 reported on the US plans to invade Afghanistan that year. The BBC also reported that Pakistani foreign secretary was informed by the US prior to 9/11 that there was going to be an invasion of Afghanistan in October.[610] MSNBC also reported that the plan to invade Afghanistan and pursue al Qaeda and Bin Laden was already sitting on George W. Bush's desk on the morning of September 11th. This was a presidential directive waiting for his signature that had been developed by the CIA.[611] Former Pakistani Foreign Secretary, Niaz Naik, told BBC on 09/14/01 that senior American officials told him in mid July 2001 at a UN sponsored international contract group on Afghanistan in Berlin that the US would invade Afghanistan by mid October 2001. He predicted that the attack would be launched from Uzbekistan and Tajikistan. This is yet more indications that US officials knew of the 9/11 events before they occurred.[612] Officials from the Clinton administration told journalist Steve Coll that the Pentagon was looking at a possible invasion of Afghanistan in the spring of 1998.[613] Zbigniew Brzezinski had also called for America to take control of Central Asia in his audacious book *The Grand Chessboard*. Thus, in 2004 the Bush administration established long-term bases in Afghanistan and made arrangements to establish bases in Pakistan, Kyrgyzstan and Uzbekistan.[614]

Of course we were not told. We were told that the US was invading Afghanistan in an effort to hunt down bin Laden who allegedly planned the 9/11 incident. Chirp, Chirp, Mockingbird.

28. Operation Iraqi Freedom

The second invasion of Iraq, Operation Iraqi Freedom, was planned in advance just at the first invasion. The excuse for the invasion of Iraq the second time was that Saddam Hussein had weapons of mass destruction and chemical weapons and that he was behind the attacks on the World Trade Center. Suffice it to say that not only did Saddam Hussein not have anything to do with the 9/11 attacks, neither did Osama Bin Laden or al-Qaida. The Baath party clearly indicated that it had no part in the 9/11 attacks and in fact al Qaeda and the Iraqi Baath party

---

610 Pete Phillips, Bridget Thornton and Celeste Vogler, Parameters of Power in the Global Dominance Group: 9/11 & Election Irregularities in Context (Book Section, *9/11 and American Empire Vol. I.*, book editors, David Ray Griffin and Peter Dale Scott, Northampton: Olive Branch Press, 2006) 185.
611 Mark H Gaffney, The 911 Mystery Plane and The Vanishing of America (Walterville: Trine Day LLC, 2008)111.
612 Ibid, 112.
613 Ibid.
614 David Ray Griffin, The New Pearl Harbor Revisited (Northampton: Olive Branch Press, 2008)199.

were enemies and took public pot shots at each other.[615] The United States has more WPM than Saddam ever had, and the United States had supplied him with chemical weapons.

A memo released in 2005 by the UK Sunday Times called the "Downing Street Memo" was a report written by British National Security Aid Matthew Rycroft pertaining to a meeting in July 2002 between British Prime Minister Tony Blair and Richard Dearlove, head of the MI6 intelligence service, who had just returned from a meeting with Bush administration officials. The contents of this memo which were not reported in the United States clearly indicated that Bush had not considered any other action but military where Saddam Hussein was concerned, and that the intelligence revealing the WPM was very flimsy. The intelligence facts were "cooked" to support Bush's policy. "Bush wanted to remove Saddam, through military action, justified by the conjunction of terrorism and WMD. But the intelligence and facts were being fixed around the policy. ... It seemed clear that Bush had made up his mind to take military action, even if the timing was not yet decided. But the case was thin. Saddam was not threatening his neighbors, and his WMD capability was less than that of Libya, North Korea or Iran."[616] The Memo also mentioned the need for legal justification for an invasion. The memo states, "We should work up a plan for an ultimatum to Saddam to allow back in the UN weapons inspectors. This would also help with the legal justification for the use of force. The Attorney-General said that the desire for regime change was not a legal base for military action."[617]

Another British document pertaining to a January 31, 2003 meeting between Bush and Blair indicated that Blair was solidly behind Bush's decision to invade Iraq. This memo mentioned that Bush was considering provoking Saddam into firing on UN aircraft or flying U2 reconnaissance aircraft painted with UN colors because he had no hard evidence against Saddam. If Saddam took the bait he would be in breach of UN resolutions.[618]

The point of invading Iraq had nothing whatsoever to do with WPM or with 9/11. The Illuminati agenda for world domination was at the core of this war. The agenda included the desire to open the whole block of Arab nations up to the free trade agenda of the Friedman globalists. They wanted to incorporate Iraq as a model nation of their free market experiment. The war was about conquering the Arab would. They could not accomplish this task all at once so they had to choose one Arab country to serve as a catalyst. The invasion of

---

615 Robin de Ruiter, Worldwide Evil and Misery: The Legacy of 13 Satanic Bloodlines (The Netherlands, Myra Publications, 2008) 293.
616 Matthew Rycroft, The secret Downing Street memo (The Sunday Times, May 1, 2005 - htttp:llwww.timesonline.com).
617 Ibid.
618 Jim Marrs, The The Terror Conspiracy: Deception, 9/11 and the Loss of Liberty (New York: Disinformatin, 2006) 197.

Iraq would become the model in the Arab-Muslim world which would initiate a chain reaction for turning Arab countries into a Friedman style globalized free market. "Joshua Muravchik, an American Enterprise Institute pundit, forecast a 'tsunami across the Islamic world' in 'Tehran and Bagdad,' while the archconservative Michael Ledeen, advisor to the Bush administration, described the goal as 'a war to remake the world.'"[619]

To implement the reconstruction strategy one must have a Hegelian style crisis. In Illuminati thinking one does not have to wait for one to happen naturally. It can be created. Thus 9/11 was the created crisis. Then the psychological devastation of the nation of Iraq on the tails of the physical attack puts the people of the nation in a state of disorientation so that they cannot fight back. They are worried about surviving, not resisting. Under these circumstances the nation was ripe for reconstruction.

The free market model would include privatizing public institutions such as schools, health care, public utilities etc. It would also include selling contracts for these institutions and private businesses to multinational businesses such as Halliburton, Bechtel, etc, companies in which American businessmen in politics had a controlling interest such as Cheney, Bush, Rumsfeld and Rockefeller. Yes, the banks were up for sale also. What the United States intended to do was destroy the nation, wipe out its memory and national heritage and remake it according to a New World Order model.

The second invasion of Iraq was characterized by the same senseless bombarding of civilians and soldiers who were not fighting. The Iraqi army did not have the fire power to resist the American Army and there was not the need for the extreme use of armaments used on the Iraqi people. A Belgian news photographer, Laurent Van der Stoct, working for an agency under contract with the New York Times Magazine, reported "The Iraqi army was like a ghost, it barely existed." The Iraqi army responded to the invasion with minimal fire power. The trenches were deserted and the journalist observed a dead Iraqi soldier lying next to a piece of bread and some equipment. "There was nothing that really made him feel that there was a real confrontation going on, nothing comparable to the 'massiveness of the means at the Americans' disposal.'"[620]

US officials said they were doing all they could to protect civilians however this did not appear to be the case at all. For example, US troops exploded an arms dump near Haj al-Muallimin on April 26th 2003 killing 12 civilians. The US claimed that they were being fired on by Iraqis. This would be quite suspect since they had been exploding arms dumps all over the country and the people in that area had already asked them to move the arms dump because of the imminent danger it presented to the civilian population. Another 13 civilians were killed

---

619 Naomi Klein, The Shock Doctrine: The Rise of Disaster Capitalism (New York: Metropolitan Books, Henry Holt and Company, 2007) 328.
620 David Icke, Tales from the Time Loop (Ryde, Isle of Wright,UK: David Icke Books, 2003)164.

and many more were injured when US troops fired on a group of protestors in Fallujah demanding that the military leave the school so the children could return to learning. The military again claimed they had been fired on but witnesses only saw two stones thrown by the civilians. The following day two more civilians were shot who were protesting the deaths of the previous day.[621]

When the US invaded Iraq under the Bush administration and took over the government, he also took over the economy. Paul Bremer was put in charge of the Coalition Provisional Authority (CPA). He instituted what has become known as Bremer's 100 orders. His first act was to fire 500,000 state workers in Iraq. Most were soldiers, but there were doctors, teachers, and engineers as well. The excuse was that they were riding the government of Hussein sympathizers. He reduced the corporate tax rate from 40% to 15% which severely depleted the revenue of the Iraqi government. He thus began the process of siphoning off Iraqi assets to foreign businesses. "Order 39 allowed foreign companies to own 100 percent of Iraqi assets outside the natural-resource sector. This insured unrestricted foreign business activities in the country".[622] Investors were permitted to take 100% of the profit out of the country without any requirement to reinvest or without any taxation. The Iraqis had been under a U.S. sponsored sanction for ten years and their resources were already sapped. "With its economy and banking system devastated by war and more than a decade of US-led economic embargo, Iraqis were in no position to buy their privatized state companies. Foreign multinationals were the only possible actors who might benefit from Bremer's grand economic recovery scheme."[623]

The nine national museums were among the public institutions that were destroyed. It is also apparent that the U.S. military had no intention to protect those museums as they did nothing to stop the looting and may have actually encouraged it. Soldiers stood outside the museums cheering the looters on and actually may have deliberately caused destruction to the structures themselves. "'Not since the Taliban embarked on their orgy of destruction against the Buddha's of Bamiyan and the statues in the museum of Kabul—perhaps not since World War II have so many archaeological treasures been wantonly and systematically smashed to pieces,' reported British newsman Robert Fisk, who toured the museum shortly after the incident."[624] The looting of the Iraqi museums of their ancient history was another method of dehumanizing the people of Iraq. Their memory was erased.

The national library, which contained copies of every book and doctoral thesis ever published in Iraq, was a blackened ruin. Thousand-year-old illuminated

---

621 Ibid, 163.
622 F. William Engdall, Seeds of Destruction: The Hidden Agenda of Genetic Manipulation (Canada, 2007)199
623 Ibid.
624 Jim Marrs, The The Terror Conspiracy: Deception, 9/11 and the Loss of Liberty (New York: Disinformatin, 2006) 216.

Korans had disappeared from the Ministry of Religious Affairs, which was left a burned-out shell. A high school teacher lamented the loss of their national heritage. A merchant lamented the destruction of the museum. "It was the soul of Iraq. If the museum doesn't recover the looted treasures, I will feel like a part of my own soul has been stolen." University of Chicago archeologist called it a lobotomy. "The deep memory of an entire culture, a culture that has continued for thousands of years, had been removed."[625]

More than three thousand artifacts were lost in the burning and looting of the museums in the aftermath of the war. Later in April 2003 more than 50,000 priceless artifacts were taken from the Bagdad museum by what appeared to be professional thieves. The thieves had keys to the museum and the vaults and glass cutters that were not available in Iraq. There also had to have had knowledge of the layout of the museum and where certain artifacts would be stored. A huge bronze bust weighing hundreds of pounds was missing which would have required a fork lift to move.[626]

These museums may have been one of the real reasons behind the Iraqi invasion. There were many rare antiquities and ancient technologies contained in those museums. In 1999 there were nearly 400 ancient Sumerian artifacts in the southern Iraqi town of Basmyia 100 miles south of Bagdad dating to about 2500 B.C.E. More discoveries were made in 2002 and 2003 by German & French archeologists that had excavated with permission from Saddam Hussein.[627] The Sumerian treasures contained information about ancient technology such as early aircraft that flew, anti gravity technology and time travel. Remember the NAZI's were involved in research into antigravity technology and time travel. They are offshoots of the early Illuminati. Ancient Summer is the original site of the Tower of Babble where God first confounded the language of the people.

Only the Ministry of Oil was left standing after the invasion, and Bush had plans to privatize this as well. One of the trademarks of Freidman Economics is the attempt to take national resources and invite multinational businesses to invest in them, thus removing the national resources from the nation and putting it in the hands of foreign investors. This was the only recommendation of the Iraq Study Group fronted by James Baker that the Bush Administration agreed to. The new oil law for Iraq would allow companies like Shell and BP to sign 30 year contracts allowing them to keep tens or even hundreds of billions of dollars in profits. Oil was 95% of country's revenue. This would impoverish the country. Only one of 20 elected Iraqi officials knew the law was being drafted and they did not have any say in its development. Greg Muttitt, of the oil-watch group *Platform*, stated that if the law passed Iraqis would lose a great deal because they don't have the

---

625 Naomi Klein, The Shock Doctrine: The Rise of Disaster Capitalism (New York: Metropolitan Books, Henry Holt and Company, 2007) 336.
626 Jim Marrs, The The Terror Conspiracy: Deception, 9/11 and the Loss of Liberty (New York: Disinformatin, 2006) 215 – 216.
627 Ibid, 214.

capacity because of the devastation of Iraqi industry and financial decimation to take part in bargaining for a good deal on the oil production of their own nation.[628] The law that finally passed eliminated the Iraqis from having any say at all in who was to gain the contracts for the Iraqi oil assets. It placed no limits in the amount of profits the contactors could take from the country and they were not required even to hire Iraqis to work the oil fields. "It's hard to overstate the disgrace of this attempted resource grab. Iraq's oil profits are the country's only hope of financing its own reconstruction when some semblance of peace returns. To lay claim to that future wealth in a moment of national disintegration was disaster capitalism at its most shameless."[629]

The Iraqis began to resist the occupation when they witnessed the CPA actually attempting to steal their country from them. Only 15,000 Iraqis were hired in the reconstruction, a brazenly low figure.[630] Not putting the Iraqis to work reconstructing their own nation was a huge mistake. One employee of a plant that was pending privatization said to Naomi Klein, "'There are two choices,' he said smiling kindly, 'Either we will set the factory on fire and let the flames devour it to the ground, or we will blow ourselves up inside it. But it will not be privatized.' It was an early warning—one of many—that the Bush team had definitely overestimated its ability to shock Iraqis into submission."[631]

Naomi Klein detailed the disastrous reconstruction project and the brazen mismanagement in detail in her 2007 book, *The Shock Doctrine*. It is worth reading because it is a very clear picture of the New World Order and their global domination agenda. In six months the Iraqis were not drinking clean water from Bechtel pipes, their homes were not lit up with GE lights, their Parsons-built hospitals were not sanitary, and their streets were not being safely patrolled by DynCorp-trained police. If that had occurred, the Iraqi people might not have been so upset at not having any say in the reconstruction of their homeland. As it was, the Iraqis began systematically targeting reconstruction sights. Because of the free-for-all approach of the globalists with contracts that promised them a profit plus the cost of the work they scammed like mad. Thus U.S. citizens paid for air conditioning and what the Iraqi's got was a fan in a room. "More to the point, all this time Iraqis watched their aid money stolen as their country boiled."[632]

Another institution important to the Iraqi people was its agriculture. This too was destroyed. Under Bremer's 100 orders Iraqi's farmers were required to purchase GMO products from American agribusinesses like Monsanto and they

---

628 Naomi Klein, The Shock Doctrine: The Rise of Disaster Capitalism (New York: Metropolitan Books, Henry Holt and Company, 2007) 376.
629 Ibid, 377.
630 Ibid, 355.
631 Ibid, 353.
632 Ibid, 356- 357.

were prohibited from saving seeds from the harvest to be replanted. This would have resulted in fines imposed by the seed supplier.[633] To ensure Iraqi dependence on US Agribusiness for seeds, the national seed bank which contained samples of seed varieties located in Abu Ghraib disappeared. "Following the US occupation of Iraq and its various bombing campaigns, the historic and invaluable seed bank in Abu Ghraib vanished, a further casualty of the Iraq war." Iraq could still request assistance from the International Center of Agricultural Research in Dry Areas in Syria which was a part of the network of international seed banks. However, under Bremer Iraq was not permitted to access this resource.[634]

An interesting fact that ads to the ire of the Iraqi situation was that prior to the Gulf War Iraq had suffered a severe drought for three years which severely depleted their wheat crop. Considering that the US had the capability to control the weather and since it was discussed as a method of imposing the will of the US on other nations (reference US military strategy document *Weather as a Force Multiplier*), might it not be conceivable that the US did indeed create the drought prior to the invasion to strengthen its hold on the Iraqi economy? Under Bremer's 100 orders Iraq's farmers were required to purchase GMO products from American agribusinesses like Monsanto and they were prohibited from saving seeds from the harvest to be replanted. This would have resulted in fines imposed by the seed supplier. To ensure Iraqi dependence on US Agribusiness for seeds, the national seed bank which contained samples of seed varieties located in Abu Ghraib disappeared. Iraq could still request assistance from the International Center of Agricultural Research in Dry Areas in Syria which was a part of the network of international seed banks. However, under Bremer Iraq was not permitted to access this resource.[635]

Iraqi farmers were promised that the GMO seeds that they were required to plant would produce higher yields for them. This was flat out lie. The seeds were designed to resist the Monsanto produced herbicides but other weeds required more herbicides than normal seeds that had grown in the region which cost more to the farmer. This in turn sapped the soil of nutrients which required more fertilizer and an additional financial burden to the farmers. Of course they couldn't afford it. The returns did not cover the cost and the yields of the seeds progressively decreased from year to year. Thus Iraqi farmers had to be subsidized by US Agribusiness.[636]

There is amidst the atrocity committed by the United States Government against the Iraqi people, the relief of some very decent people who dared to tell the truth. Jessica "I'm not a hero" Lynch is one of those voices of truth and sanity. The

---

633 F. William Engdall, Seeds of Destruction: The Hidden Agenda of Genetic Manipulation (Canada, Global Research, Center for Research on Globalization 2007) 200.
634 Ibid, 202.
635 Ibid, 200 – 202.
636 Ibid.

United States used Jessica Lynch as a media manipulating tool to urge American support of the war. They turned this young woman into a war hero by fabricating a story which she later had enough integrity to tell us all was not true. She was traveling with a supply unit, the 507th Ordinance Maintenance Co., when she and her traveling companions took a wrong turn while making a delivery. They ran into Iraqi troupes and the vehicle she was traveling in overturned. According the media "spin" on the story she opened fire on Iraqi assailants picking them off one by one till she ran out of ammunition. She even continued to shoot after she had been shot and stabbed several times. However, Icke notes that it is rather odd that she ran out of ammunition in a supposed fight to the death, but her Iraqi assailants didn't kill her.[637] Her Iraqi doctors indicated that she suffered fractures to her arms and lower limbs and had a small wound in her skull. Iraqi Dr. Harith a-Houssona said, "I examined her, I saw she had a broken arm, a broken thigh and a dislocated ankle. … There was no [sign of] shooting, no bullet inside her body no stab wound – only road traffic accident."[638] American doctors confirmed the testimony of the Iraqi doctors. Her father, Greg Lynch reported that she did not have any penetration wounds. Dr. Haitham Gizzy said, "'She was given special care, more than the Iraqi patients.' Harith al-Houssona, another doctor who treated Lynch, said: 'She was very frightened when she woke up and she kept saying: 'Please don't hurt me, don't touch me.' I told her that she was safe, she was in a hospital and that I was a doctor, and I never hurt a patient.'" The doctor actually went outside the hospital during the bombing putting himself at risk to get supplies of her favorite drink, orange juice, and struggled to persuade her to eat.[639] The Iraqi Intelligence attempted to have Jessica delivered to an American outpost by ambulance, however when the ambulance arrived carrying Ms Lynch, the Americans opened fire.

Here's the spin. The next day American troops invaded the hospital in a "daring rescue" operation. The Iraqi doctors testified that they made a big show of it. The media story indicated that the hospital was crawling with Iraqi troops. There were no Iraqi soldiers or militiamen in at the hospital when the US Special Operations forces arrived in their helicopters. The only people in the hospital when American troops arrived were doctors and patients. The rescue was videotaped but scenes that would incriminate the US military were omitted such as doctors with stethoscopes around their necks being interrogated. There was no one at the hospital that had a weapon to fire on US soldiers. U.S. soldiers, on the other hand had weapons and, to add effect to the dramatic media production, they were firing blanks.[640] To add insult to injury the US troops damaged the bed that Jessica was

---

637 David Icke, Tales from the Time Loop (Ryde, Isle of Wright,UK: David Icke Books, 2003)179.
638 John Kampfner, Saving Private Lynch story 'flawed' (BBC NEWS. - May 15, 2003 - http://news.bbc.co.uk).
639 David Icke, Tales from the Time Loop, (Ryde, Iles of Wright, UK: David Icke Books, 2003) 179.
640 John Kampfner, Saving Private Lynch story 'flawed' (BBC NEWS. - May 15, 2003 - http://news.bbc.co.uk).

using. It was a bed specifically designed for patients with bed sores. Dr. Harith said, "It was the only bed like it that we have, the only one in the governorate." The doctor was happy that Jessica was going back to her people but was saddened at her departure.[641]

Another US Marine reservist, Stephen Eagle funk, age 20, refused to be sent to Iraq because he believed it was "immoral because of the deception involved by our leaders." He said, "I would be going in knowing that it was wrong and that would be hypocritical." He faced a possible court martial and time in a military prison. He joined the military for the purpose of having his college fees paid. He warns younger kids who have no idea of what is involved. He reported on his combat training "Every day in combat training you had to yell out 'Kill! Kill!' and we would get into trouble if you didn't shout it out, so often I would just mouth it so I didn't get into trouble." Stephen spoke to young people about the manipulations of the military and encouraged them to find other ways to fund their college educations.[642]

There were a few journalists who protested the way the war in Iraq was being portrayed by the media. One Katy Weitz resigned her job out of a sense of integrity. She stated, "I want to be proud of the work I help to produce, not shudder in shame at its front page blood lust." Another reporter for MSNBC, Ashleigh Banfield, angered her employers when she gave a lecture at Kansas State University on April 24th 2003. "She described what the global audience was not allowed to see. Nobody witnessed the real horrors of what happened, she said, and so people could not 'seriously revisit the concept of warfare the next time we have to deal with it'". There have been a lot of dissenting voices before the conflict about the horrors of war, but she was very concerned that the 'three week TV show' may have changed people's opinions. 'It was very sanitized', She said."[643]

I remember watching the invasion on the news. At the time, as a U.S. veteran, I was still remembering the tears I cried during that retreat ceremony. I was remembering stories about what good American soldiers had done during WWII and the respect she had gained around the world. I believed when I watched Hussein's army surrender to the United States in whole units that they trusted us more then they trusted their own leader. I did not know that DEW could influence them to give up. I did not know how many lies we, the American people, had believed. If I had known I would have told the Iraqi's "Fight! Don't surrender! You have no idea what they will do to you! Don't give up!" I don't believe that most American soldiers really understood the agenda of the Bush administration or the NWO. I don't believe if they did they would have been willing to do what they did. The average American isn't a monster and I don't believe that the soldiers who were sent to Iraq were all monsters either. The fact is that decent people can be

---

641 David Icke, Tales from the Time Loop, (Ryde, Iles of Wright, UK: David Icke Books, 2003) 180.
642 Ibid, 171.
643 Ibid, 152.

misled and when that happens they are capable of doing monstrous things. The fact that we have been misled does not eliminate our culpability. What we did to Iraq was monstrous.

What I really don't like is the propaganda that we were all fed that made us think that Arab peoples are all insane jihadists. They show up a picture of a two year old with dynamite wrapped around his waist and that's all it takes! Nobody told us that %60 of the population of Iraq is their children. I guess they really are not blowing them up, are they? They love their children. Could we grieve for them? Can be have enough heart to grieve with them for the loss of the children who perished in Iraq because of an insane war fought by people who believe that people are disposable? Could we have enough heart to at least try to make reparations? Not that we ever could. Maybe we could do the Christian thing and humble ourselves and ask for forgiveness.

29. No Other Gods

Perhaps it is now a good time to consider the first of the Ten Commandments found in Exodus chapter 20 which says, "Thou shalt have no other gods before me." This commandment sometimes gets lumped together with anther which says "Thou shalt not make for thyself any graven image," but they are two separate commandments. The latter refers to a physical representation of deity which is forbidden. The other refers to the concept of divine authority. The commandment clearly indicates that God intends to be the highest authority in our lives. There shall be no other authority higher than his. In America now the state is pushing to usurp God's divine right to rule. This is nothing new. It has happened throughout history. We as believers would not ever bow down to a graven image. For one thing we know that nothing made by the hands of man can possibly do us any good or harm. It is an image and nothing more. However, I am concerned that we as believers have been bowing down to the god of the State when we should be putting up much resistance. Let me explain.

Every believer knows that God requires us to be respectful of people in authority, but he did not ever tell us that they were saints. When he spoke to his disciples of the Pharisees and the Experts in the Law Jesus said, "The teachers of the law and the Pharisees sit in Moses' seat. So you must obey them and do everything they tell you. But do not do what they do, for they do not practice what they preach. They tie up heavy loads and put them on men's shoulders, but they themselves are not willing to lift a finger to move them" (Matt 23:2 – 4). Clearly scripture tells us that God ordains all authority. Romans 13: 1 – 7 tells us that God expects us to be obedient to governing authorities because he has ordained them. However in Hosea 8:4 God also says, "They set up kings without my consent. They chose princes without my approval" (NIV). This would indicate that God did not choose every person in authority. However, as he told to Israelites when they asked for a king, "Since you asked for it, you got it, but now you're going to have to live with it." Whether or not God actually put a person in authority is not the issue. The fact is, they are and we must treat them with respect.

Now here is where the conflict happens. Devoted believers who are doing exactly what God would have commanded them to do by being obedient to authority may also be at the same time violating his commandment to have no other gods. As believers in today's world, we are being lured into moral compromise by indiscriminate obedience to authority. I want to carefully examine this issue because it is a delicate one.

There are clearly times in scripture when persons resisted authority and did so wisely with positive results. In the book of Esther, Mordecai refused to comply with an edict from the King to bow down to the King's assistant Haman. This was clearly to Mordecai a violation of the first and second commandments. It amounted to paying homage to a human that was due only to God. This is found in Esther 3:1&2. This enraged Haman who prepared a gallows upon which to hang Mordecai, and he persuaded the King to issue an edict that would have destroyed all the Jews living in Persia at that time. Mordecai did disobey an edict from the King, but he also had saved the Kings life. It was not in spirit of rebellion against authority, but in a spirit of obedience to God that Mordecai resisted. In the same spirit he honored the King when he learned of a plot to assassinate the King in Chapter 2 and via Esther warned the King. The King's life was thus spared. The end result was that Hayman and his sons were hanged on the gallows that he had prepared for Mordecai, and the Jews were permitted to defend themselves on the day the King had decreed that they would be annihilated. God showed Mordecai favor because of his obedience to him.

In the book of Daniel, chapter 1, Daniel and his three companions in exile, Shadrach, Meshach, and Abednego, were given meat to eat that had been sacrificed to idols. This is something that God commanded the Jews not to do. Thus they resisted, but they didn't just refuse. They negotiated. They reached an agreement. They were given vegetables to eat and those in authority over them determined that they were actually in better health then the other servants who ate what they gave them. Thus they found favor in the eyes of those in authority over them.

It is not always possible to negotiate. There are some things that are not negotiable. King Nebuchadnezzar ordered that everyone bow down and worship the golden image he had created (Daniel 3:5). Shadrach, Meshach and Abednego did not comply with this edict. It would have been in violation of the commandment to have no other gods before the God of Heaven. King Nebuchadnezzar was requesting that everyone pay homage to an idol which God said was only due to himself. The King had to throw them in the fiery furnace even though he did not want to. Because of their obedience to God, they were rescued and God was glorified.

Some of the ruling officials who were jealous of Daniel tried to set a trap for him. In Daniel chapter 6 we learn that they persuaded the king to decree that anyone who prayed to any other god but the King would be thrown into the lions' den, knowing full well that Daniel would disobey the edit. Thus he was thrown into the lions' and God rescued him, to the great relief of the King who actually favored Daniel. Daniel was not at all resentful to the King either. His attitude toward the King did not change. King Nebuchadnezzar actually was hoping that Daniel's God would rescue him as well. King Nebuchadnezzar was learning something about the God of the Jews in all these situations.

In the New Testament Peter and the apostles were ordered not to preach anymore in the name of Jesus, and they respectfully told those in authority over them, they should obey God rather than men (Acts 4:18 – 19). Thus in Acts 5: 28 and 29 those same authorities demanded an explanation because they had expressly forbidden them to teach anymore in the name of Jesus. And Peter and the other apostles insisted that they would obey God rather than men. The authorities thus began to seek a way to kill them but did not at that time proceed to do so because of the warning of Gamileel.

Every soldier in the Army is told that they cannot get away with committing crimes even if they are ordered to do so. Soldiers are required to obey *lawful* orders. This is stressed because during Viet Nam soldiers, in obedience to those in authority over them, committed some heinous crimes which resulted in the death or injury of innocent people. In the Book of Kings, David orders Joab, his General, to conduct a census of all the fighting men in Israel and Joab, understanding the motive behind the order resisted David, but David insisted so Joab obeyed. Had Joab refused to obey this order, 70,000 people in Israel would not have perished.

Every person in a position of authority is going to make a mistake every now and then. It becomes a real problem when those who are barking out orders do so without concern for the loss of human life and those following those orders just blindly, even robotically obey! Considering that the elite establishment has no real concern for the loss of human life, it disturbs me greatly that they are so willing to use even decent people who actually have a conscience to do very indecent, horrible things. What is very wrong is that in a state of apathy even decent people can become complicit in the act of murder.

In MyLai Army intelligence had reported that the villagers at MyLai were harboring Vietcong. Task Force Baker C Company, 1st Battalion, 20th Infantry of the 11th light Infantry Brigade was sent to MyLai. They were given ambiguous instructions about engaging enemy combatants and they were not given a clear definition of what an enemy combatant really was. The soldiers were all clear about the Geneva Convention which makes it a crime to do harm to a non-combatant or even an enemy combatant who had laid down his arms. They should have also been familiar with the Law of Land Warfare from the US Army Field Manuel which specifically states that they cannot obey an unlawful order. However, Charlie Company found not one single enemy combatant in the villages of MyLai. They found not one armed Vietnamese. No Vietnamese fired on them. They found unarmed women, children and old men. Nevertheless the soldiers of Charlie Company stood at the doors of those village huts and sprayed them with bullets or blew them up with hand grenades killing between five and six hundred unarmed villagers including children. The killing spree lasted the entire morning.[644] A helicopter pilot, Hugh Thompson, could see what was happening from the air. He landed the helicopter and began to rescue Vietnamese survivors and ordered his machine gunner to open fire on any soldiers who continued to shoot villagers. During his rescue operation he pulled a three year old out of a ditch who was almost smothered in blood but not injured. "After he radioed for help from other helicopters, an enraged Thompson reported to his section leader and in graphic detail told of what he had seen. Soon afterward, Charlie Company was ordered to stop killing civilians.[645] They were *following orders*. It is also possible that they were being directly influenced by Directed Energy Weapons. I have already discussed that DEW can be and has been used to influence the behavior of whole groups of people.

Abu Ghraib is another example of people blindly following orders. People give in to doing things that ought not to be done when they think they have the support of people in superior positions and when "everybody else is doing it". Occasionally, someone like MP SP4 Joseph M. Darby, who decided that what he was seeing was wrong both legally and morally, will speak up. A lot of people don't realize it, but those who spoke out against the abuses of Abu Ghraib suffered for it. The problem is that there are too few people who have enough sense of self confidence that they are willing to do so. So few who choose to think independently that is. To be able to think differently from everybody else, even your superiors, is a tremendous gift.

When God says to us "Thou shalt have no other God's before me" he isn't being arrogant, controlling and self centered. God understood that power corrupts. He understood that those in authority would not always honor him or his commandments. There are those who believe that they are above the law, and those who believe they are above the laws of God. God does not therefore command his children to blind obedience of authority. He set himself above all authority and commanded us to have no other gods before him because this was his way of holding power in human hands in check. When persons in authority refuse to honor the authority of God almighty, they become gods unto themselves. When they do this, they adopt an "end justifies the means" mentality and they become utterly corrupt. Thus God's way of keeping authority on earth from walking all over people and enslaving them was to place himself as the highest authority in everyone's life. This was also his way of holding society in check even in a world where not everyone would choose to obey him. Thus by commanding

---

644 Peck M. Scott M.D., People of the Lie (New York, NY: Touchstone, 1983) 213- 214.
645 David Wallechinsky, My Lai Massacre (Morgana's Observatory- http://www.dreamscape.com).

us to have no other gods before him, he was protecting us and protecting society at large.

We live in a world of bullies who have no fear of God at all. Bullies like to be in control of everyone and everything, and they desire to make slaves of everyone. They are sinners. God does not authorize rebellion. He permits us to answer to him directly in matters of morality. When I was in the military there was on occasion that someone with a little rank got a little full of himself or herself. In the military anyone who has one more stripe than you has authority over you. However, I found myself often in the favor of my commander who on more than one occasion corrected those who were attempting to use their authority like a bit in my mouth. My commander knew how to command his troops, but he also knew that there were soldiers out there who liked to throw their weight around. He would thus say, "You are taking your orders from me, okay?" He offered protection from overzealous leaders.

When God said to us, "Thou shalt have no other God's before me" he was putting his protective wings around us. If we choose to listen to the voice of God when we have authority demanding that we compromise our principles we are honoring God and we are acting as protectors of our world. Unfortunately, we of the church have not been willing enough to challenge authority on that basis. I fear that Christians in the work place are complacent enough to comply with orders that would violate the law of God. They want to protect that paycheck, and they want to please their bosses, but in so doing are contributing to the moral corruption of our world and the unraveling of the moral fabric that God designed to protect us.

None of our bosses are going to demand that we bow down to a golden image, but they might demand that we bow down to the state. They may inch by inch push you to compromise your values until you are absolutely violating God's commandments. One woman I know who went to work for a facility for the mentally retarded was asked to compromise her beliefs in a deplorable way. She was told that if those who she cared for who had cerebral palsy wanted to have sex and were physically incapable of executing the act, she had to assist. Not married mind you, just residents in the same facility. She did not say that she ever actually had to do that, but I can tell you what I would have said. "Sorry, I can't do that." I was told the same thing at a facility that I worked at in Loudonville Ohio that was supposed to be a Christian Facility! Because they got funding from the state they could not refuse to allow unmarried persons to engage in sex with one another in their facility.

Being faithful to God's commandments in a secular environment where those in authority do not have any respect for God is a challenge. To do so in the proper attitude is equally challenging. But to shrink back and simply comply when being asked to compromise moral principles in a faithless act. There were times when I had to take a deep breath and do something that I knew would bring disfavor, but I was not at all comfortable with the thought of refusing to face the challenge, although there were times when it was taxing me and I just gave in. It is sometimes tiring, mostly because there are too few Christians in the work world who are willing to resist immorality in the work place. There is really very little support. Even Christians are "programmed" to simply follow orders.

An experiment conducted by Stanley Milgram at the Interaction Laboratory at Yale University revealed that even very decent ordinary people can be induced to do monstrous things to other people just because a person adorned in a white coat told them to do it. Forty New Haven Connecticut residents were persuaded to induce shock of up to 450 volts of electricity on victims (pretending) who were obviously suffering from the voltage. They were compliant 100 percent of the time though the victim was screaming in agony and even after the screaming stopped and the victim appeared to have passed out continued to follow orders. John Conroy, author of *Unspeakable Acts, Ordinary People* studied incidents of torture occurring in three environments, Israel, Northern Ireland and the United States. He believed that those who committed horribly indecent acts of torture were probably monsters. Then he interviewed them and found out that they were really very ordinary people who were just following orders. Several of the victims reported meeting their torturers later in life in a different situation. One of them asked his victim to give his son a job. He agreed to do so. Later they went to a bar and had some drinks and danced. They did not mention the torture. They were "both ashamed."[646]

When the government wants to persuade principled people to participate in something they would otherwise consider to be unethical, they do it by compartmentalization. When I worked for the National Security Agency I had a Top Secret Security clearance. However, I did not have access to all information that was classified Top Secret. I had to have a "need to know". So when the government, manipulated by the NWO, wants to do something and they want your participation they may decide not to tell you exactly what you are doing because you do not have a "need to know". This follows the Illuminati practice of giving people orders while those who follow them may not actually know why they are doing what they are doing.

There are those who have not shrunk back. The state says you cannot bring your religious beliefs to work with you, thus a teacher in the High School in Mt. Vernon Ohio was fired because he kept a Bible on his desk (Radio Broadcast WCVO 104.9, Columbus OH). I was harassed because I would not promote a safe sex agenda with my clients when I worked for the Country Board of MR DD. A friend of mine who was a very good teacher was fired from her position on trumped up charges. She honestly believed it was because she was a Christian. A judge in Alabama was removed from his position because he insisted on displaying a monument to the Ten Commandments on the lawn of the Courthouse. A teacher in New York who is a gangstalking victim was "mobbed" out of two jobs

---

646 John Conroy, Unspeakable Acts ,Ordinary People; The Dynamics of Torture (Berkley, UNIVERSITY OF CALIFORNIA PRESS, 2000)176.

in the public schools because of her beliefs. A Pastor in Nebraska was sentenced to prison because he opened a school to educate the children in his congregation and refused to have the school licensed. Under the Law, he was entitled to do so. He was finally released from prison in his eighth month and the Supreme Court ruled in his favor. This was in 1977.[647] No telling what they would say now.

We live in a world that has been overrun with people who worship Satan. They are Illuminati, Freemasons and Scientologists. They have been given positions of authority in exchange for loyalty to those they serve in these secret societies. They have an "end justifies the means" ideology. Thus it is okay to lie, cheat, steal and even commit murder to accomplish their goals. They are protected from prosecution for criminal activity by those in those secret societies who have people in positions of authority in every office in the land. God commands us to respect authority, but to have no other gods before him at the same time. If we will as a body of believers face these challenges in faith and obedience to God, we can overcome this darkness.

One more word is worth considering here. Before Jesus formally entered into his ministry, he was led into the wilderness to be tempted of the Devil for 40 days and 40 nights. During that time he neither ate nor drank, so he was in a physically weakened state. The final temptation was one we need to carefully consider. Satan took him to the highest pinnacle of the temple and said, "I will give you all the Kingdoms of the world if you will bow down to me." Wow! This was the temptation of power and wealth. A lust for power and wealth is precisely what it is that corrupts earthly authority. It is precisely this temptation to which the New World Order has surrendered itself. It is the antichrist that is behind the New World Order. But Jesus said to Satan, "It is written, Worship the Lord your God and serve him only" (Matt 4:10 NIV). This is precisely the response we need to give to those who are attempting to usurp the authority of Jesus Christ on earth. This is precisely the temptation we are faced with when we are being asked to compromise moral principles by those who hold our paychecks.

In the beginning of this book, I explained how Adam Weishaupt managed to get all the Jesuits removed from Ingolstadt University which he did by covert activity. This is an old Illuminati trick. It is still in use today, and we need to think about the true danger it poses to our civilization. The Illuminati oppose Christianity. Earlier I discussed how many Christians have lost jobs because of harassment or discrimination because of their Christian beliefs. It disturbs me that too many Christians simply accept this kind of blatant discrimination. The reason why this concerns me is that when we accept this kind of ruthless immoral discriminating what we are doing is one, bowing to a false god, and two, we are slowly, job by job, surrendering this nation to the immoral agenda of those who want to be in power at any cost. We should fight back. So when a teacher in your community gets fired from his job because he is keeping a bible on his desk, it

---

647 A. Ralf Epperson, The New World Order (Tucson, Arizona: PUBLIUS PRESS, 1990) 225 – 228.

is the responsibility of the church to get behind him and hold those responsible for this perversion of justice accountable. If we do not, we are all going to find ourselves out of work and our nation completely in the hands of those with an immoral agenda.

Human rights activists are speaking out against slavery. We are doing our best to stop the trafficking in human persons. So we buy back the slaves. But did anyone tell you the CIA is being funded by the money that you used to buy back the slaves? Did you know that the CIA has a worldwide slave trafficking business? Do you know what products you purchased that were brought to you by slave labor?

You were created in God's image. That God who created you brought the entire universe into being in six days by the word of his mouth. He gave you the ability to think and reason. There is not a computer on this planet that can do even half of what your brain can do. The New World Order does not want you to use that brain, because if you do you just might decide to speak out against something you see or hear that you know in your heart of hearts is very wrong. You might just decide to run for office and you might get elected. If that happens you might make it difficult for the NWO to accomplish their wicked agenda. Think!

30. Imprisoned, Tortured and Tried

The Prisoners

The 9/11 incident opened the door for the contrived war on terror. This is not a war against any nation in particular and it has no end. There are many around the world who are looking at America with a "What on earth are you doing!?" kind of shock. They are speaking out. Can we hear what they have to say?

The United States invaded Iraq in the wake of the 9/11 lie. If we have in fact determined that 9/11 was a lie, then there was absolutely no basis for the invasions of Afghanistan or Iraq. Thus, it should not surprise us to know that those who were captured and taken prisoner were not actually war criminals nor were they in any way responsible for acts of terror against the United States or anyone else. In fact the U.S. military dropped leaflets all over Afghanistan offering rewards for $50 to $5000 for anyone suspected of terrorism or being involved with al Qaeda. The Northern Alliance of Afghanistan along with Afghan warlords turned in as many as 40,000 people. Even $50 U.S. dollars for an Afghan warlord is a huge sum of money. Thus they turned in their enemies, people they didn't like or anyone they could pick up including Taxi drivers and even a 90ish year old Shepherd.[648] There were some leaflets offering rewards of even a million dollars.[649] Their detention was also a violation of the Geneva Conventions.

---

648 Edward Spannaus, Bush and Hitler: What the 'Torture Memos' Reveal (June 27, 2004- http://www.informationclearinghouse.info).
649 Wikipedia, Guantanamo Bay detention camp (January 2, 2010 - http://en.wikipedia.org).

There were also children kept at Guantanamo which is absolutely illegal under international law. London lawyers estimated that there were 60 detainees held at Guantanamo who were under the age of 18 when they were captured. "They include at least 10 detainees still held at the US base in Cuba who were 14 or 15 when they were seized - including child soldiers who were held in solitary confinement, repeatedly interrogated and allegedly tortured."[650] One of those children, Mohamed el Gharani, is accused of a 1998 al Qaeda terrorist plot in London. He was actually 12 years old at the time and living with his parents in Saudi Arabia. A Canadian-born boy, Omar Khadr, the son of a known al Qaeda commander, was arrested in 2002 at the age of 15 and has been kept in solitary confinement. He allegedly killed a US soldier with a grenade in July 2002. Clive Stafford Smith, a legal director of Reprieve and lawyer for a number of detainees, said it broke every widely accepted legal convention on human rights to put children in the same prison as adults - including US law. In fact minors can be tried for crimes they have committed, however it is not acceptable to hold minors without a trial in shocking conditions and try them by military commissions that are rigged. There is also a UN convention against the use of child soldiers.[651]

The Guantanamo Bay Detention Center, where much abuse of detainees took place, was established in Cuba under a special agreement between the United States and the Cuban Government in which the United States leased the facility. The Cuban government signed an agreement that they would not hold the Guantanamo facility or its operation accountable under the laws of Cuban or the Cuban judicial system. The United States maintained that because Guantanamo was not on U.S. soil it was not also subject to U.S. law. It was therefore a law free zone. It was not originally, however, supposed to be a detention center. It was supposed to be used for other purposes. According to the Geneva Convention of 1949, as a detention center it is flatly illegal. Prisoners at the Guantanamo Bay Detention Center were held in isolation, subjected to physical and, psychological stress that could easily be defined as torture. Those detained there were denied legal representation or any opportunity to challenge their detention in any court. They were tried under special military tribunals which allowed for evidence to be submitted which was obtained under duress and for hearsay evidence. Detainees could be convicted with such evidence that is normally not permitted in any court of law.[652] This same lawless system was applied at Baghram or Abu Ghraib under the Coalition Provisional Authority.

Washington wanted intelligence from somewhere. The military had prisoners. The New York Times reported in June 2004 that only two dozen of nearly 600 detainees were actually linked with al Qaeda and they had only limited information

---

650 Severin Carrell, The Children of Guantanamo Bay (The Independent UK, January 2, 2010 - http://news.independentminds.livejournal.com).
651 Ibid.
652 Edward Spannaus, Bush and Hitler: What the 'Torture Memos' Reveal (June 27, 2004- http://www.informationclearinghouse.info).

to offer in questioning.[653] The United States wanted intelligence material from these people. Interrogators were under pressure to extract something of value from these prisoners who actually know probably nothing. The interrogator is under pressure from superiors to perform, and there is no intelligence to be gleaned from the people they have to interrogate who were captured and detained under false pretenses.

The Laws and the Pathway to Abuse

Every soldier in the United States military is instructed on the details of the Geneva Convention. Basically every soldier knows that the United States does not torture prisoners of war. In fact not only do U.S. military personnel know not to torture prisoners of war, they know they are required to provide them with needed medical care, food and shelter. In the case of a nuclear, biological or chemical attack, for example, U.S. soldiers are instructed to don their personal NBC equipment and then assist a prisoner of war in donning their own equipment. In addition to that every soldier knows that he can be prosecuted for war crimes even if he committed a crime while obeying orders. In other words, he cannot be ordered to do something that is in violation of the law or the Geneva Convention. Thus he or she is required to obey all *lawful* orders. These are things a soldier learns in basic training.

During interrogation training, which I took at Ft. Bragg North Carolina in the summer of 1989, our instructor, Chief Warrant Emanuel Rodriquez, a former NYPD police detective, reiterated the dictates of the Geneva Convention. He also told us that torture does not produce good intelligence. Law Enforcement experienced in interrogation know that information gained while torturing a suspect is not reliable and is therefore not admissible in court because when people are being tortured they will say anything just to stop the pain.

The Geneva Convention was designed to prohibit the kinds of things that occurred during WWII in NAZI Germany from ever happening again. Nations around the world convened and developed the Convention with the common understanding that torture is degrading, inhumane, and *morally reprehensible*. The United States of American signed and agreed to abide by the Geneva Convention.

In addition to the Geneva Convention, the United States has had its own laws regarding torture.

Statute Title 18, U.S.C. § 2340 of U.S. law reads as follows;

(1) "torture" means an act committed by a person acting under the color of law specifically intended to inflict severe physical or mental pain or suffering (other than pain or suffering incidental to lawful sanctions) upon another person within his custody or physical control;

---

653 Wikipedia, Guantanamo Bay detention camp (January 2, 2010 - http://en.wikipedia.org).

(2) "severe mental pain or suffering" means the prolonged mental harm caused by resulting from—

(A) The intentional infliction or threatened infliction of severe physical pain or suffering;

(B) The administration or application, or threatened administration or application, of mind-altering substances or other procedures calculated to disrupt profoundly the senses or the personality;

(C) The threat of imminent death; or

(D) The threat that another person will imminently be subjected to death, severe physical pain or suffering, or the administration or application of mind-altering substances or other procedures calculated to disrupt profoundly the senses or personality; and

(3) "United States" means the several States of the United States, the District of Columbia, and the commonwealths, territories, and possessions of the Untied States.

This law also specifies the punishment for the crime of torture.

(a) Offense. *Whoever outside the United States commits or attempts to commit torture shall be fined under this title or imprisoned not more than 20 years, or both, and if death results to any person from conduct prohibited by this subsection, shall be punished by death or imprisoned for any term of years or for life* [emphasis mine].

(b) Jurisdiction. There is jurisdiction over the activity prohibited in subsection (a) if—

(1) The alleged offender is a national of the United States; or

(2) The alleged offender is present in the United States, irrespective of the nationality of the victim or alleged offender.

(c) Conspiracy. A person who conspires to commit an offense under this section shall be subject to the same penalties (other than the penalty of death) as the penalties prescribed for the offense, the commission of which was the object of the conspiracy.

FM 34-52 was also very explicit about the treatment of POW's. The military's Filed Manual on the proper procedures for field interrogations was updated in 1992 just after the first Gulf War. The manual detailed strict adherence to the Uniform Code of Military Justice, the Geneva Convention and International law in the process of acquiring reliable intelligence. The FM 34-52 expressly prohibits the use of force, including acts of violence or intimidation, including physical or mental torture, threats, insults or exposure to inhumane treatment in the process of interrogation. These were considered illegal and would not be condoned by the U.S. The reasons for this prohibition was that the results were unreliable and because they damaged the reputation of the United States. Inhumane treatment by the U.S. military would also put U.S. service members at risk of similar abuses if they fell into enemy hands.

Given this understanding, then it should greatly disturb us that somehow there was a severe lapse of moral integrity as well as a respect for the law at Abu Ghraib and Guantanamo. When I saw the news broadcast about the Iraqi prisoners of war who had been sodomized by U.S. Army Soldiers in a prison that was managed by the United States Military, I believed that someone local to that prison had a lapse of moral integrity. "We have laws. . ." I thought and I assumed that those involved would be prosecuted. But in a world where the Shadow Government is slowly overtaking the legitimate government of "we the people", things are not at they should be. The problem at Abu Ghraib did not happen because somebody in Iraq lost their mind, but because someone in Washington lost their mind. And in fact though there were some low level prosecutions for the crimes committed against the Iraqi prisoners of war, those who were actually responsible absolutely escaped prosecution altogether. Those who were prosecuted were token patsies designed to satisfy the American people that "something was done" but the real criminals escaped. There were 800 investigations of primarily low-ranking U.S. Soldiers. There were a total of 89 convictions. Of 34 soldiers suspected of being responsible for a prisoner's death, only 14 were sentenced. The toughest sentence for being responsible for a prisoner's death was five months in jail. Not one single military intelligence officer was ever court marshaled as of July 23rd, 2006.[654]

When we talk of abused prisoners of war, we understand that those prisoners were sodomized, but the abuse went much deeper. The legal pathways that lead to the abuse are rooted in 911. If 9/11 was an inside job committed by officials high up in the United States Government, and I concur with many writers and elements of the 9/11 truth movement that it was, and the second war in Iraq was justified by a contrived terrorist attack, those who are really responsible have to find a "Patsy" to take the blame. Here it might be a good idea to define the term "Patsy". The United States Government is frequently involved in covert operations. Of course there are undercover cops out there who are trying to catch the covert criminals. They are actually trying to do something good and putting their own lives at risk in the process. They would not be doing what they are dong if it weren't for covert operations that are illegal and *morally reprehensible* justified by covert criminals "for reasons of national security". When covert operators decide that they want to take someone out, for example President Kennedy, they have to find someone to take the blame because that will give direction to the "investigation", provide a "perpetrator" to "prosecute" and a sacrificial lamb to crucify. It would be typical in a crime involving high level government officials that the "Patsy" is identified sometimes within hours of the actual perpetration of the crime. This usually involves complicity on the part of intelligence community and Law Enforcement. Since the perpetrators usually known in advance who they are going to blame for the crime, almost no investigation is required. Thus, once the lamb is crucified, the investigation will cease and those who really committed the crime are off the

---

654 Naomi Wolf, The End of America: Letter of Warning to a Young Patriot (White River Junction, Vermont: Chelsea Green Publishing, 2007) 67 – 68.

hook. Basically prosecution of a "Patsy" causes people to stop looking for the perpetrator.

So if United States Government officials have once again been involved in a criminal covert operation, of course they need a "Patsy". They have pegged Osama Bin Laden and al Qaeda being responsible for the crime they committed themselves. However they need a conviction. They know that neither the Taliban, al Qaeda, Osama Bin Laden, the Iraqi nor Afghani people are guilty, but they assert that they are. If however they interrogate prisoners of war who are not in any way connected to the 9/11 events they are not going to get the needed "intelligence" because they are innocent. They also know that torture will cause an innocent party to confess to things *they did not do* just to get the pain to stop. Isn't that exactly what they wanted?

But we have this inconvenient Geneva Convention, the Torture Statute, the Field Manual for military interrogations and international laws that prohibit them from doing what they wanted to do. But that is not really a problem. There are always ways of finding loopholes in any law that gets in the way. And that is exactly what they did. Objections to the application of the Geneva Convention came from Secretary of Defense Donald Rumsfeld; Jim Haynes, General Counsel for the Secretary of Defense; Dick Cheney's attorney David Addington; and Bush's legal Council Alberto R. Gonzales. The issue was sent to the Office of Legal Council at the Justice Department to John Yoo, and Robert Delahunty prepared an opinion for Jim Haynes. They wrote a draft memo dated January 9th 2002 stating that the Geneva Convention did not apply to al Qaeda or Taliban. On January 19th 2002 Rumsfeld and Haynes directed General Richard Meyers, the Chairman of the Joint Chiefs of Staff, that Taliban and al Qaeda detainees did not qualify as POW's. ". . . but that they should be treated humanely and *to the extent appropriate to military necessity,* in a manner consistent with the Geneva Convention."[655] Resistance came from Colon Powel and his Council William Taft but they were overruled.

Alberto R. Gonzales Legal counsel to the White House signed a memo on January 25th, 2002 written by Dick Cheney's attorney David Addington arguing that al Qaeda and Taliban prisoners were not subject to the provisions of the Geneva Convention because

> ...it is not the traditional clash between nations adhering to the laws of war that formed the backdrop for GPW[Geneva Conventions for Prisoners of War]. The nature of the new war places a high premium on other factors, such as the ability to quickly obtain information from captured terrorists and their sponsors in order to avoid further atrocities against American civilians, and the need to try terrorists for war crimes such as wantonly killing civilians. In

---

655 Phillip Sands, The Torture Team: Rumsfeld's Memo and the Betrayal of American Values (New York: Paulgrave/MacMilliian, 2008) 31.

my judgment, this new paradigm renders obsolete Geneva's strict limitations on questioning of enemy prisoners and renders quaint some of its provisions...[656]

The Gonzales memo further states that neither al Qaeda nor the Taliban qualify as nations. It also stated that Afghanistan is a "failed state" because the Taliban failed to take complete control of the state and that the Taliban had not been recognized internationally as the formal government of Afghanistan. Therefore since they are not nations with which the United States is as war, detainees of al Qaeda or the Taliban do not qualify as prisoners of war. This memo was sent to George W. Bush who on February 7th 2002 made the decision that the Geneva Convention did not apply to al Qaeda and Taliban detainees.

The Geneva Convention however does not state that it is limited to conflict between nations nor does it apply only to certain types of detainees. The Convention Common Article 3 reads as follows;

In the case of armed conflict *not of an international character* [italics mine] occurring in the territory of one of the High Contracting Parties, *each Party to the conflict shall be bound* to apply, as a minimum, the following provisions:

(1) Persons taking no active part in the hostilities*[which would include most of the 40,000 plus detainees who were illegally captured and imprisoned]*, including members of armed forces who have laid down their arms*[such as the Iraqi soldiers who were running away from the combat and waiving white flags who were assassinated from the air by the U.S. military]* and those placed hors de combat by sickness, wounds, detention, or any other cause, shall in all circumstances be treated humanely, without any adverse distinction founded on race, color, religion or faith, sex, birth or wealth, or any other similar criteria. To this end the following acts are and shall remain prohibited at any time and in any place whatsoever with respect to the above-mentioned persons:

(a) violence to life and person, in particular murder of all kinds, mutilation, cruel treatment and torture;

(b) taking of hostages;

(c) outrages upon personal dignity, in particular, humiliating and degrading treatment;

(d) the passing of sentences and the carrying out of executions without previous judgment pronounced by a *regularly constituted court* [*not military commissions which acted against all standard due process procedures*] affording all the judicial guarantees which are recognized as indispensable by civilized peoples.

(2) The wounded and sick shall be collected and cared for [*not buried alive as U.S. forces did to Iraqi soldiers who were legal combatants*].

---

656 Edward Spannaus, Bush and Hitler: What the 'Torture Memos' Reveal (June 27, 2004- http://www.informationclearinghouse.info).

Article 4 of the Geneva Convention further specifies what constitutes a Prisoner of War;

A. Prisoners of war, in the sense of the present Convention, are persons belonging to one of the following categories, who have fallen into the power of the enemy:
(1) Members of the armed forces of a Party to the conflict, *as well as* members of militias or volunteer corps forming part of such armed forces.
(2) *Members of other militias and members of other volunteer corps, including those of organized resistance movements, belonging to a Party to the conflict and operating in or outside their own territory, even if this territory is occupied, provided that such militias or volunteer corps, including such organized resistance movements, fulfill the following conditions:*
(a) that of being commanded by a person responsible for his subordinates;
(b) that of having a fixed distinctive sign recognizable at a distance;
(c) that of carrying arms openly;
(d) that of conducting their operations in accordance -with the laws and customs of war [emphasis mine].

It would appear that the Taliban and al Qaeda would qualify as POWs under common Article 4 (2) as long as they have a recognizable sign that can be read at a distance and that they conduct their operations "in accordance –with the laws and customs of war". There are two problems here. It might be a worthwhile to examine CIA covert operations to determine if their operatives would qualify as POWs and thereby be subject to the provisions and protections of the Geneva Convention considering that the CIA rarely posts a sign identifying itself for what it is and considering that they rarely if ever subject themselves to any law let alone the laws of war. But that is another discussion. The problem is compounded by the fact that they determined that the Taliban and al Qaeda did not qualify as "POWs" under the Geneva Convention, but those that were captured and tortured and tried were for the most part *not* either of those! *They were innocent civilians who had done nothing to hurt any American, had not participated in any terrorist act of any kind and who knew absolutely nothing about what was happening!!*

The convention further states "No physical or mental torture, nor any other form of coercion, may be inflicted on prisoners of war to secure from them information of any kind whatever. Prisoners of war who refuse to answer may not be threatened, insulted, or exposed to *unpleasant or disadvantageous treatment of any kind.*" And Article 130 of the GPW states

> Grave breaches to which the preceding Article relates shall be those involving any of the following acts, if committed against persons or property protected by the Convention: willful killing, torture or inhuman treatment, including biological experiments,

willfully causing great suffering or serious injury to body or health, compelling a prisoner of war to serve in the forces of the hostile Power, or willfully depriving a prisoner of war of the rights of fair and regular trial prescribed in this Convention.

Article 131 of the GPW would apply to the President of the United States when it states, "No High Contracting Party shall be allowed to absolve itself or any other High Contracting Party of any liability incurred by itself or by another High Contracting Party in respect of breaches referred to in the preceding Article." Nevertheless, based on the opinion of Gonzales and others in February 2002 Bush decided that the Geneva Convention did not apply to the Taliban and al Qaeda and that they did not qualify as Prisoners of War and were designated "illegal combatants". On March 22, 2002 Bush requested assistance from his legal counsel in finding legal loopholes for exempting al Qaeda and Taliban from protection under the Geneva Convention and for allowing interrogation techniques that would include torture. These extreme measures were needed because of the need for "timely intelligence" in the contrived "war on terror.[657] That started White House attorneys, the Justice Department and the Department of Defense on a journey which resulted in the inhumane treatment of persons detained at Guantanamo, Abu Ghraib, and elsewhere in prisons managed by the U.S. Military.

In August 2002 a Justice Department memo written by Assistant Attorney General Jay S. Bybee was issued explaining that laws prohibiting torture of prisoners do "not apply to the President's detention and interrogation of enemy combatants". Bybee's fifty page memo, interpreting the UN antitorture convention and USC §§ 2340-2340A, concluded that federal law addressing torture is only limited to acts that are specifically intended to inflict "severe pain or suffering, whether mental or physical". It further stipulated that physical pain had to be equivalent to the pain experienced in serious physical injury such as "organ failure, impairment of bodily function, or even death." Thus Bybee found grounds for exculpating CIA developed interrogation practices depending on the agent's intention. "Thus, an interrogator who tortured but later claimed that his aim was to gain information rather than inflict pain, was not, in Bybee's twisted logic, guilty of abuse". He did not determine that sensory deprivation met this qualification. "More broadly, he concluded that any limitation on commander-in-chief's powers to order interrogations would 'represent an unconstitutional infringement of the President's authority to conduct war.'"[658]

On December 2nd 2002 Donald Rumsfeld signed another memo. This one was called "Counter-Resistance Techniques" written by William J. Haynes II, the General Counsel at the Defense Department. To this memo was attached a

---

[657] Naomi Wolf, The End of America: Letter of Warning to a Young Patriot (White River Junction, Vermont: Chelsea Green Publishing, 2007) 57.

[658] Alfred W. McCoy, A Question of Torture: CIA Interrogation from the Cold War to the War on Terror (New York: Henry Hold and Company, 2006) 121 – 122.

legal opinion written by Lieutenant Colonel Diane Beaver, Staff Judge Advocate at Guantanamo; a request for approval for new more "forceful" interrogation techniques from Beaver's boss Major General Mike Dunlavey, head of interrogation at Guantanamo; another memo from General Tom Hill, Commander of U.S. Southern Command, requesting a new list of interrogation techniques; and a new list of 18 techniques divided into three categories in a three page memo from Lieutenant Colonel Jerald Phifer. Category I included yelling and deception. Category II included humiliation and sensory deprivation; stress positions such as standing for a maximum of four hours; falsified documents; isolation for up to thirty days; interrogation outside the standard interrogation booth; deprivation of light and auditory stimuli; hooding during transportation and questioning; twenty-hour interrogations; removal of religious and all other comfort items; switching from hot rations to "meals, ready-to-eat" (MREs); removal of clothing; forced grooming, such as shaving of facial hair; and the use of individual phobias, like fear of dogs, to induce stress. Category III included the use of "mild, non-injurious physical contact," like grabbing, poking and light pushing; the use of scenarios designed to convince the detainee that death or severely painful consequences were imminent for him or his family; exposure to cold weather or water; the use of a wet towel and dripping water to simulate drowning also called "waterboarding".[659]

The Victims

They wanted intelligence and they got it. That is they got what they were most likely seeking – confessions. But of course they were false confessions. The conditions that the detainees were subjected to included being in isolation from family and friends for two years, under the control of U.S. military personnel who may or may not feed him, turn the lights off during the day or on at night, allow him to exercise at their whim, let him shower if they want to, let him wear clothes if they want to, keep him in solitary confinement if they wanted to, have him beaten and deprive him of sleep. Eventually he is going to confess to anything though none of it is true.[660] So much for timely intelligence. Consider that one of the excuses that the "torture team" used for using illegal torture techniques was the need for timely intelligence to prevent further loss of American lives. So what if it takes them two years to extract the information from them!

David Hicks and Mamdouh Habib were two detained at Guantanamo who were citizens of England picked up by the Northern alliance in Afghanistan. "Defense Secretary Rumsfeld claimed that Hicks, an alleged Australian Taliban fighter, was someone who had threatened to kill Americans, one of the 'worst

---

[659] Phillip Sands, The Torture Team: Rumsfeld's Memo and the Betrayal of American Values (New York: Paulgrave/MacMilliian, 2008) 3 – 4.

[660] Michael Ratner and Ray Ellen Guantanamo: What the World Should Know (White River Junction: Chelsea Green Publishing Company, 2004) 44.

of the worst.'"⁶⁶¹ Hicks had been detained at Guantanamo Bay as an "unlawful combatant" for more than two years without being charged. Neither hicks nor Mamdouh confessed to anything but, according to Ratner, Rumsfeld was lying. Though Rumsfeld referred to these people as the "worst of the worst" who tried to kill tens of thousands of Americans, their own internal documents reveal that U.S. Officials knew that this was not the case.⁶⁶²

Then Director of the Center for Constitutional Rights, Michael Rater, was defending detainees who had been tortured and "confessed". The confessions were false. His clients were shown video tapes which supposedly depicted them with Osama bin Laden. Initially they insisted that it was not them in the videos, but due to coercion they eventually confessed. These were actually citizens of Great Britain and the British Government was forced to investigate and prove to the American Government that the individuals were actually in the United Kingdom at the time the video's were shot.⁶⁶³ There were more; On August 4th 2004 three other residents of the United Kingdom detained by the United States filed reports of "severe abuse" of themselves and others while in custody. They were tortured into making confessions. They also reported that conditions grew worse upon the arrival of General Geoffrey D. Miller. They claimed that military intelligence officials were fully aware of the abuse. The British government did investigate.⁶⁶⁴

One of the top terrorists is reportedly Mohamed al-Kahtani (also spelled *al-Qahtani*) who was also identified as the "20th" hijacker, from Saudi Arabia who is believed to have planned to participate in the September 11 attacks in 2001.⁶⁶⁵ He had apparently been trained to resist interrogation. Or maybe he was not spewing forth intelligence information because he really didn't have any. Nevertheless it was because of him that Dunlavey felt that tougher interrogation techniques were needed. He was thus placed in an isolation facility separate from other detainees.⁶⁶⁶ Mohamed al-Kahtani was forced to wear a bra, dance with another man and threatened with dogs.⁶⁶⁷ After long and abusive interrogations Al Kahtani supposedly said he knew Osama Bin Laden and that his best friend's name was Zaid and that he had been sent to the United States by Khalid Shekh Mohammed. Allegedly he also provided key information about people such as Jose Padilla, the dirty bomber, and the shoe bomber Richard Reid. No details were given and the claims could not be checked. The interrogation log provided very little support for these claims.

---

661 Ibid, 55.
662 Ibid, 56.
663 Ibid.
664 Wikipedia, Guantanamo Bay detention camp (January 2, 2010. - http://en.wikipedia.org).
665 Ibid.
666 David Ray Griffin, The New Pearl Harbor Revisisted: 9/11, The Cover-up and the Expose (Northampton: Olive Branch Press,2008) 44.
667 Wikipedia, Guantanamo Bay detention camp (January 2, 2010. - http://en.wikipedia.org).

Phillip Sands interviewed those who were present for the interrogation of al-Qahtani and asked if anything they had produced during the interrogation was of any value. No one indicated that they had. Mike Dunlavey was asked the same question and refused to answer.[668]

Another detained in connection with 9/11 was Khalid Sheikh Mohammed (KSM) who had reportedly confessed to numerous acts including planning an attack on the Plaza Bank in Washington State. However, he was captured in 2003. The bank was not built until 2006.[669] Mohammed was reportedly the mastermind behind the 9/11 attacks. However, the 9/11 commission report which details Mohammed's involvement is based on secret CIA interrogations which have never been independently confirmed. KSM allegedly stated that he assigned Hani Hanjour to the Pentagon mission because he was their most experienced pilot. Reports were that Hanjour was a terrible pilot and that instructors didn't even want to give him a license. One would therefore wonder where this "confession" came from.

At the Trial of Moussaoui, the FBI presented a photo of Mohamed Ata with another alleged hijacker, al Omari, at the Jetport gas station at 8:28:29PM on November 10th, 2001, two months *after* he supposedly hijacked one of the doomed planes from 9/11.[670] A Minnesota flight school warned the bureau that Moussaoui appeared to be the type of person who might fly a plane loaded with fuel into a building and thus Moussaoui was arrested by the FBI.[671] Zacarias Moussaoui, who became known as the "20th" hijacker, in April 2005 pleaded guilty to terrorism charges but denied having anything to do with the 9/11 attacks. He stated that he was to be a part of a second wave of attacks. At his trial he claimed that he was supposed to be on a 5th plane that was supposed to hit the White House. After his trial he stated that his guilty plea was a complete fabrication and filed a motion to withdraw it and was denied. A Minneapolis FBI agent who filed the warrant to search Moussaoui's belongings testified that he told the Department of Justice Inspector General that the FBI was guilty of "obstructionism, criminal negligence and careerism" in the handling of evidence pertaining to Moussaoui.[672] Moussaoui was actually sitting in a jail cell for almost one month *before* the September 11th attacks because the FBI had arrested him "under desultory investigation as a

---

668 Phillip Sands, The Torture Team: Rumsfeld's Memo and the Betrayal of American Values (New York: Paulgrave/MacMilliian, 2008) 144 – 145.
669 David Ray Griffin, The New Pearl Harbor Revisisted: 9/11, The Cover-up and the Expose (Northampton: Olive Branch Press,2008) 216 - 217
670 Ibid,160.
671 Jim Marrs, The Terror Conspiracy: Deception, 9/11 and the Loss of Liberty(New York: Disinformation, 2006) 97.
672 David Ray Griffin, The New Pearl Harbor Revisisted: 9/11, The Cover-up and the Expose (Northampton: Olive Branch Press, 2008) 227

possible "suicide hijacker," because the FBI, lacking omniscience, did not have precise foreknowledge of Al Qaeda's plot or Moussaoui's possible role."[673]

Abu Zubaydah, chief recruiter for Al Qaeda, was captured in Pakistan in April 2002. He was flown to a secret base in Thailand for interrogation. He had been shot in the groin and had been denied pain killers during his interrogation by the CIA. Zubaydah allegedly identified Khalid Sheikh Mohammed as a lead agent in the 9/11 attacks while he was being tortured. He also reportedly provided information about the alleged "dirty bomb" plot in Chicago perpetrated by Jose Padilla.[674] In addition he reportedly stated the names of three members of the Saudi Royal Family who knew in advance of the 9/11 attacks. Those three individuals reportedly died within days of each other subsequent to Zubaydah's testimony.[675] Zubaydah revealed an interesting relationship between the Saudi Royal Family, al Qaeda and Pakistan Intelligence which surprised the CIA.[676] Interestingly, while the CIA was using "enhanced interrogation techniques" such as water boarding while interrogating Zubaydah, and they allegedly taped these interrogations where they gained "valuable intelligence" the tapes were destroyed.[677] Zubaydah also testified that another Pakistani, Rajaa Gulum Abbas, also seemed to know in 1999 about the destruction of the twin towers. Interestingly, George Bush increased aid to Pakistan even after knowledge of this testimony.[678]

Resistance from Within

Major General Geoffrey Miller, who was head of interrogations at Guantanamo, stated that three quarters of his prisoners had confessed to something. These are coerced confessions. Therefore they are not admissible in court. But these "unlawful combatants" weren't tried in regular courts with traditional laws. They were tried by military commissions that are subject to specialized rules and therefore coerced confessions were acceptable as well as hearsay evidence.[679]

The FBI was also involved in interrogation of suspected terrorists and they provided resistance to the use of these techniques. Senior Law Enforcement

---

673 Alfred W. McCoy, A Question of Torture: CIA Interrogation from the Cold War to the War on Terror (New York: Henry Holt and Company, 2006) 193.
674 Ibid, 120.
675 David Ray Griffin, The New Pearl Harbor Revisited: 9/11, The Cover-up and the Expose (Northampton: Olive Branch Press, 2008) 140.
676 Jim Marrs, The Terror Conspiracy: Deception, 9/11 and the Loss of Liberty(New York: Disinformation, 2006) 28.
677 Mark H Gaffney, The 911 Mystery Plane and The Vanishing of America (Walterville: Trine Day LLC, 2008) xix.
678 David Ray Griffin, The New Pearl Harbor Revisisted: 9/11, The Cover-up and the Expose (Northampton: Olive Branch Press, 2008) 223.
679 Michael Ratner and Ray Ellen Guantanamo: What the World Should Know (White River Junction: Chelsea Green Publishing Company, 2004) 75.

agents with the Criminal Investigation Task Force began to complain inside the Defense Department in 2002 that the interrogation tactics used "were unproductive, not likely to produce reliable information and probably illegal". Not satisfied with the response they were getting from the Army commanders running the prison camp, they consulted with David Brant, director of the Naval Criminal Investigative Service (NCIS) who consulted Navy General Counsel Alberto J. Mora. Mora and Navy Judge Advocate General Michael Lohr believed techniques being used and the treatment of the POWs to be illegal and petitioned the Defense Department to investigate and provide standards prohibiting these coercive tactics. Therefore on January 15, 2003, Donald Rumsfeld temporarily suspended these tactics at Guantanamo until a new set of guidelines could be produced.[680] The Defense Department working group began their defense of their techniques by submitting a draft document with a narrow definition of torture and a broad interpretation of executive power not much different from Bybee's original memo of August 2002. Mora and his group responded. Military lawyers advocated for strict adherence to the law and the treaty. Major General Jack Rives, Deputy Judge and Advocate General for the Air Force stated that the extreme interrogation techniques were violations of domestic criminal law and the UCMJ. Further the techniques placed interrogators at risk for prosecution at home and abroad. The techniques also risked damaging the reputation of the United States which had once suffered greatly due to atrocities committed during the Vietnam conflict. The reputation of the United States was repaired by reestablishing solid standards for moral conduct. They determined that even if "unlawful belligerents" might not be entitled to protections under the Geneva Conventions, it may result in a breakdown of military discipline and could be seen as a green light for all forms of abuse. It would further damage the reputation of this nation and put our own troops at risk of harm if captured. Other top military legal officials expressed concern that American people would not approve of techniques that were in violation of America's most fundamental values, and that soldiers would run the risk of prosecution. They expressed concern that it would risk portraying the United States as a lawless nation. These concerns from seasoned military leadership were ignored by the Bush administration.[681]

The Scandal

In 2004 the scandal broke. On January 13, 2004, an MP guard, SP4 Joseph M. Darby, slid a compact disk with the notorious photographs under the door of the Criminal Investigation Division at Abu Ghraib. This set in motion the

---

680 Wikipedia, Guantanamo Bay detention camp (January 2, 2010. - http://en.wikipedia.org).
681 Alfred W. McCoy, A Question of Torture: CIA Interrogation from the Cold War to the War on Terror (New York: Henry Hold and Company, 2006) 128, 129.

Taguba investigation in February 2004.[682] The Taguba report submitted by Major General Antonio Taguba notes favorably the actions of Sp4 Darby and Master-at-Arms First Class William J. Kimbro, a US Navy Dog Handler, who refused to participate in improper interrogations "despite significant pressure from the MI personnel at Abu Ghraib" as well as 1LT David O. Sutton, 229th MP Company, who immediately stopped the abuse and reported the incident to the chain of command.[683] The Taguba report states;

> ...between October and December 2003, at the Abu Ghraib Confinement Facility (BCCF), numerous incidents of sadistic, blatant, and wanton criminal abuses were inflicted on several detainees. This systemic and illegal abuse of detainees was intentionally perpetrated by several members of the military police guard force (372nd Military Police Company, 320th Military Police Battalion, 800th MP Brigade), in Tier (section) 1-A of the Abu Ghraib Prison (BCCF). The allegations of abuse were substantiated by detailed witness statements (ANNEX 26) and the discovery of extremely graphic photographic evidence.[684]

The Taguba report further details the abuses as follows:

6. (S) I find that the intentional abuse of detainees by military police personnel included the following acts.
   a. (S) Punching, slapping, and kicking detainees; jumping on their naked feet;
   b. (S) Videotaping and photographing naked male and female detainees;
   c. (S) Forcibly arranging detainees in various sexually explicit positions for photographing;
   d. (S) Forcing detainees to remove their clothing and keeping them naked for several days at a time;
   e. (S) Forcing naked male detainees to wear women's underwear;
   f. (S) Forcing groups of male detainees to masturbate themselves while being photographed and videotaped;
   g. (S) Arranging naked male detainees in a pile and then jumping on them;
   h. (S) Positioning a naked detainee on a MRE Box, with a sandbag on his head, and attaching wires to his fingers, toes, and penis to simulate electric torture;
   i. (S) Writing "I am a Rapist" (sic) on the leg of a detainee alleged to have forcibly raped a 15-year old fellow detainee, and then photographing him naked;

---

682 Ibid, 142.
683 Maj. General Antonio Taguba, The Taguba Report (The Agonist. - THE 800th MILITARY POLICE BRIGADE. - December 23, 2009. - http://www.agonist.org).
684 Ibid.

j. (S) Placing a dog chain or strap around a naked detainee's neck and having a female soldier pose for a picture;

k.(S) A male MP guard having sex with a female detainee;

1. (S) Using military working dogs (without muzzles) to intimidate and frighten detainees, and in at least one case severely injuring a detainee;

m. (S) Taking photographs of dead Iraqi detainees.

The Science of Torture

A careful examination of the Taguba report from Iraq and the written directives from White House Officials reveals a striking extremism in the actual conduct of the interrogators and military police in contract to what was actually prescribed by the White House. Alfred McCoy examined the pictures from Abu Ghraib and Guantanamo and noted that the techniques that were actually being used were not what were prescribed by the Whitehouse, though these were obviously questionable techniques. There was nothing in the written material from Washington authoring stronger techniques that authorized sodomizing detainees, attaching electrical wires anywhere on their bodies let alone on genital organs, forcing them to wear women's underwear or forcing male and female detainees to engage in intercourse while filming them. The techniques that were used were from the CIA's Kubark Manuel.[685]

The Central Intelligence Agency studied torture and all its possible uses and effects during the MKULTRA period. Experienced interrogators had discovered that physical torture produced heightened resistance, however the CIA had perfected the use of psychological torture. The CIA used "sensory disorientation" and "self-inflicted pain" in combination causing the victims to feel responsible for their suffering making them more likely to give in to their torturers. This complete assault on all senses including auditory, visual , tactile, and temporal (confusing the detainee about time) in addition to temperature extremes, sexual humiliation and violation of cultural norms has been refined by the CIA over years of research to become al all out systematic assault on the fundamentals of personal identity. The photos of the hooded POW standing on a box with arms extended and wires attached to his hands is this no touch torture from the Kubark manual. The hood provides sensory deprivation. The electrical wires attached to fingers would bring electrocution if the detainee dropped the extended arms position resulting in "self inflicted" pain. This kind of torture leaves no physical scars and no evidence that abuse has occurred. "Applied under the pressure of actual field operations after 1963, psychological methods soon gave way to unimaginable cruelties, physical and sexual, by individual perpetrators whose improvisations, plumbing the human capacity for brutality, are often horrifying."[686]

---

685 Alfred W. McCoy, A Question of Torture: CIA Interrogation from the Cold War to the War on Terror (New York: Henry Hold and Company, 2006) 136 – 137.

686 Ibid, 7 - 9

The CIA's years of research into torture were published in the Kubark manual in 1963. The training manual was disseminated around the world. The 128 page manual is based on the years of research conducted under the MKULTRA project by scientists such as Ewen Cameron and Donald Hebb. 1963 was the year MKULTRA came to a close and two years after Ewen Cameron's research was finished. The resulting KUBARK manual is a guide to dismantling personalities. The manual describes how techniques such as sensory deprivation and the disruption of time cause regression of the personality and causes the subject to look upon his torturer as a "father figure." Thus the CIA sought to turn adults into dependent compliant children who are very open to suggestion. The Kubark method is designed to induce and sustain shock, thus prisoners are captured in late night or early morning raids meant to be jarring and disorienting. They are hooded, blindfolded, stripped, beaten, and subjected to sensory deprivation and "... from Guatemala to Honduras, Vietnam to Iran, the Philippine to Chile, the use of electroshock is ubiquitous."[687]

Joshua Key, a soldier who came home on leave and never returned to Iraq described the raids he was required to perform on the homes of Iraqis. He was interviewed by Peter Laufer in *Mission Rejected; Soldiers who said "No" to Iraq*. He describes the raids that were conducted in Iraq in which doors of private residences were blown off with C4 explosives. Six man teams would go in and invade the home at night and grab men and children, and load them on a truck. The trauma is compounded by the fact that there is a language barrier. The soldiers speak English. The Iraqis speak a dialect of modern Arabic (Iraqi). The Iraqis are being yelled at in English. They don't understand. They yell back in Iraqi. The U.S. Soldiers don't understand.[688] There is an invisible wall that keeps both sides from seeing each other as human beings.

Steven Casey, another soldier who was disgusted with the duty he'd been ordered to perform during his fifteen months in Iraq, also described similar raids to the ones described by Joshua Key. "You go in their house, you completely disrupt their house, all their drawers are inside out." The occupants are crying and screaming. "We tear things up, things that they probably can't afford to fix. Broken mirrors. You're throwing stuff around trying to find things."[689] He actually filmed one of the raids on the house. Peter Laufer viewed the video and described the scene.

> It's chaos as a woman's voice, in accented English, pleads, terrified, "What's happened?" And then, "My children! My children! What's happened?" She cries out over and over, "What? What?"
> And from the soldiers, running footfalls and "Let's go! Let's go!"

---

687 Naomi Klein, The Shock Doctrine: The Rise of Disaster Capitalism (New York: Metropolitan Books, Henry Holt and Company, 2007) 39 – 41.
688 Peter Laufer, Mission Rejected: Soldiers Who Said No to Iraq (White River Junction: Chelsea Green Publishing, 2006)8 -9.
689 Ibid, 170.

> The confusion is clear in the cacophony of soldiers' voices . . . [690]

The CIA published anther manual twenty years after The Kubark Manual on counter intelligence was published. The *Human Resource Exploitation Training Manual* published in 1983 contained material from the original Kubark manual. It was used in 1987 in Latin America by the CIA and Green Berets as an instructional tool in what was called "Project X", the Army's Foreign Intelligence Assistance Program for training counterinsurgents. Material in this manual revealed that Americans were violating their own laws against torture as well as the Geneva Convention. Intelligence material uncovered in an investigation revealed that the U.S. military had violated its own rules. Defense Secretary Dick Cheney was aware of the violations because he received a report detailing the use of improper training material in March 1992 that was contained in Spanish-language manuals prepared by SOUTHCOM and the U.S. Army School of the Americas which had been distributed in Latin American between 1987 and 1991. The materials violated law and policy pertaining to the handling of human intelligence sources by the use of techniques such as fear, beatings, false imprisonment, executions and the use of truth serum. "The investigation found that the 'offensive and objectionable material' undermined U.S. credibility, although it found no evidence of a deliberate and orchestrated attempt to violate DOD or Army policies."[691]

Shamefully, America has been conditioned to accept sexual perversion for decades. However, Muslim culture has not acquiesced to such perversion, and for a "Christian" nation to sodomize a Muslim people who are morally conscientious is extremely damaging to their tender psyches. Muslims look upon America as the "Great Satan" while our government has portrayed Muslims as a bunch of violent terrorists. If you agree that 9/11 was an inside job perpetrated by the Bush Administration, then this assault on the Iraqi people which was for furthering the agenda of the established elite in Washington is morally reprehensible. Who are we calling a terrorist?

The CIA has spread their torture filth all over America and South America and Law Enforcement is not a stranger to torture. Dan Mitrione, a former Indianapolis, Indiana, police chief who served seven years in Brazil and three in Uruguay in the Office of Public Safety was kidnapped by the Tupamaro guerrillas and held until they had drawn international publicity to their cause. After they had exposed him, they killed him. Researchers and international tribunals investigated his activities and former associates testified. He was an expert in the art of torture. He taught torture to the Uruguay police. There were training films and manuals and lectures, but of course the trainees had to have hand's on practice. Thus Mitrione grabbed beggars off the streets to use as guinea pigs. They weren't guilty of anything so they could not give their torturers any information to make the pain stop. " All they

---
690 Ibid, 171
691 Phillip Sands, The Torture Team: Rumsfeld's Memo and the Betrayal of American Values (New York: Paulgrave/MacMilliian, 2008) 53.

could do was lie there and scream. When they would collapse, doctors would be brought in to shoot them up with vitamins to rest them up for the next session. When they would eventually die, their bodies would be mutilated and dropped in the streets to strike fear in the peoples' hearts."[692]

Mitrione's deputy in the Public Safety office was William Cantrell, a CIA agent. His torture techniques bore all the trademarks of the CIA mind control menu. His motto was "The right pain in the right place at the right time." A Cuban double agent Manuel Hevia Cosculluela who had joined the CIA and had worked with Mitrione published a book eight years after Mitrione's death. He witnessed the beggars being tortured to death and he wrote, "The special horror of the course . . . was its academic, almost clinical atmosphere. . . He said he considered interrogation to be a complex art . . . The objective was to humiliate the victim, separating him from reality, making him feel defenseless. No questions, just blows and insults. Then silent blows."[693] A woman who had been one of his victims sued. The woman was held and tortured in Brazil for two-and a-half years before she was released because of international protest. Testifying before tribunals, she explained that her torturers did not behave like raving psycho-paths. She remembered during one session one of the American's called his wife and had a chit chat about being home in a couple of hours and picking up the children on the way home. All this time she was lying naked on a table while half a dozen men were doing horribly painful and degrading things to her body.[694]

U.S. Concentration Camps Around the World

What is also clear is that the CIA was involved in the interrogations in both Guantanamo and Abu Ghraib. The photographs we saw would indicate that the CIA "was both the lead agency at Abu Ghraib and the source of systematic tortures practiced in Guantanamo, Afghanistan, and Iraq."[695] Late in 2001 Rumsfeld began building a network of secret prisons around the world with the help of the CIA in a tightly classified "special-access program" (SAP) to pursue the leadership of al Qaeda. The SAP program was known only to a few top officials who were barred from admitting that it even existed. In 2002 president Bush signed Pentagon legislation for the SAP which stated, "Situations may arise especially in wartime in which the President must promptly establish special access controls on classified national security information."[696] For this program Rumsfeld approved prior

---

692 John Stockwell The Praetorian Guard: The U.s. Role in the New World Order (Boston, MA: South end Press, 1991) 75.
693 Alfred W. McCoy, A Question of Torture: CIA Interrogation from the Cold War to the War on Terror (New York: Henry Holt and Company, 2006) 72 -73.
694 John Stockwell The Praetorian Guard: The U.s. Role in the New World Order (Boston, 1991)75 - 76
695 Alfred W. McCoy, A Question of Torture: CIA Interrogation from the Cold War to the War on Terror (New York: Henry Holt and Company, 2006) 5 -6.
696 Ibid, 116.

authorization for kidnapping, assassination, torture, the use of Navy Seals and Army Delta Force troops, and the establishment of a network of CIA detention centers. At the request of George Tenet, CIA Director, many of these detainees were "ghosted", that is they were held without registration at Guantanamo and Abu Ghraib and elsewhere so no one knew where they were. In addition they were denied legal representation, and some detainees, under what is known as "extraordinary rendition" were sent to other nations for interrogation such as Egypt where there is no law against torture and where the George Bush and others in the Bush administration knew they would be tortured. A 2006 article published by the ACLU (http://www.aclu.org/human-rights-national-security) discussed the abuses associated with the SAP program which was being actively covered up. The ACLU acquired some 90,000 documents pertaining to detainee abuse through FOIA requests which are being used in a lawsuit being handled by Lawrence Lustberg and Megan Lewis of the New Jersey-based law firm Gibbons, Del Deo, Dolan, Griffinger and Vecchione, P.C. Among the abuses listed were confining detainees in a metal box. This was not one of the authorized techniques.

Military Tribunals

Khalid Sheik Mohammed (KSM) and, Ramzi Binalshibh were the only available key witnesses with any inside information on the 9/11 plot. However, the 9/11 Commission was denied permission to question either of these two detained in connection with 9/11 by the CIA.[697] KSM had also been subjected to waterboarding, a technique that induces a sense of drowning in the victim, 183 times before the technique was banned.[698] This of course would indicate that any confessions that were made by KSM would not be admissible in court. But KSM was tried by a special Military tribunal which allowed for hearsay and coerced confessions. In February 2008 George Bush was calling for the death sentence of KSM, Abu Zubaydah and other members of al Qaeda who were allegedly involved in the 9/11 attacks. This has caused concern, as well it should. Lieutenant Commander Charles D. Swift of the Judge Advocate General's (JAG) Corps of the US Navy contends with the use of coerced evidence being used in the prosecution by military tribunals. The other problem was that the Jury was not permitted to hear KSM's testimony but were given a document entitled "Substitution for the Testimony of Khalid Sheikh Mohammed" which allegedly contained his confession. These military commissions were so questionable that several prosecutors resigned from the commissions. They in fact violate normal due process for several reasons. One prosecutor was told that it was not necessary to have any evidence to get a conviction. Even the chief prosecutor, Colonel Morris

---

697 David Ray Griffin, The New Pearl Harbor Revisited: 9/11, The Cover-up and the Expose (Northampton: Olive Branch Press, 2008) 212 - 213.
698 BBC NEWS WORLD, Profile: Khalid Sheikh Mohammed - al-Qaeda 'kingpin' (BBC NEWS WORLD. - April 4 2011 – http://www.bbc.bo.uk).

Davis, resigned when he learned that Depart of Defense General Counsel William Haynes, who insisted that they could not acquit anyone, had been put over him in the chain of command.[699] Besides allowing confessions made under torture, prosecutors were not under obligation to inform defense attorneys of evidence against those they defended; hearsay evidence was allowed in obtaining a conviction and the alleged witnesses were not available for cross examination; the presiding officers and jurors are picked by the same party who approved the charges and the same official has the power to overrule any motion for dismissal; witnesses for the defense have to be approved by the same presiding official; defense attorneys could not share the prosecutors evidence with the defendant.[700]

The Saudi Royal Family is close business partners with George Bush. However, it is also known that Saudi Arabia was on the Bush Administrations list of countries to be invaded by the United States. On the day of the 9/11 attacks however, the Bin Laden Family and members of the Saudi Royal family were allowed to leave the United States by air, during the period when all other air traffic had been grounded by executive order. Saudi Arabia was the birthplace of most of the hijackers and yet while the WTC burned, Saudi Arabia received exclusive and preferential treatment from the White House.[701] Zubaydah during interrogation allegedly revealed the connection between Pakistan Intelligence, al Qaeda and the Saudi Royal Family who was allegedly funding al Qaeda. This makes it doubly hard to accept the fact that George Bush was calling for the death sentence for Zubaydah and other "suspected" 9/11 perpetrators. It also raises serious questions as to why the tapes of Zubaydah testimony were destroyed.

On August 28th, 2004, the Supreme Court had assembled to hear arguments pertaining to the detainee rights and had been assured by the U.S. Solicitor General that the government could be trusted not to torture. Hours later, a 60 Minutes broadcast aired the story of the abuses of the detainees at Abu Ghraib. Then the press published leaked secret documents produced by the Bush administration, including Bybee's August 2002 memo. The pictures from Abu Ghraib began circling around the world on the internet. The Pentagon had to issue 24 death certificates for detainees who had died while incarcerated, 12 of which had been ruled homicides. Donald Rumsfeld called it "abuse" but it was not "torture". In closed door hearings however, Congress determined that Rumsfeld's assertion that the "abuse" was not "torture" was not accurate. "On May 10, after the Senate condemned the violence against detainees by a 92 to 0 vote, Bush offered an oblique apology, noting that there would be "a full accounting for the cruel and disgraceful

---

699 David Ray Griffin, The New Pearl Harbor Revisisted: 9/11, The Cover-up and the Expose (Northampton: Olive Branch Press, 2008) 215 -218.
700 Ibid, 217.
701 Jim Marrs, The Terror Conspiracy: Deception, 9/11 and the Loss of Liberty(New York: Disinformation, 2006) 240.

abuse of Iraqi detainees"[702]. Bush attempted to shut down the prison, but an Army Judge ordered it to be left intact as a crime scene. For two succeeding months Bush continued to obstruct the investigation. The U.S. Supreme Court ruled that war was not a valid reason to deny detainees basic rights and that they could not be held indefinitely. Thus the Pentagon was facing the reality that all their detainees could be transferred to federal courts. They quickly sent up a military commission which of course denied the detainees at Guantanamo and Abu Ghraib representation. Their jailers became judge and jury and they were hastily tried and all but 33 of 558 of them convicted. However the proceedings were stopped when U.S. District Judge James Robertson ruled that the military courts had violated the defendants' rights under the Geneva Conventions. The Bush administration was also challenged by attorneys of 100 detainees who filed writ of habeas corpus petitions. District Court Judge Joyce Hens Green reviewed 50 of those petitions and affirmed the right of habeas corpus and ruled the evidence from the military tribunals were likely tainted by torture.[703]

A court of appeals ruling in July 2005 reversed Judge Robertson's ruling. The U.S. Supreme Court ruled in *Harridan v. Rumsfeld* on June 29, 2006 that the detainees were entitled to the minimal protections listed under Common Article 3 of the Geneva Conventions. The Department of Defense subsequently issued a memo on July 7 2006 stating that those designated "enemy combatants" being detained by the United States would be afforded the protections of the Geneva Convention.

So what should become of all the violations of the Geneva Convention and the U.S. Torture Statute and other laws pertaining to torture? You know, they never quit. It might be worth considering why we have to have laws that say we can't torture people. Why do people even have to be told that? Is it not common sense? Actually your average Joe on the street probably isn't thinking about torturing anyone. You and I probably don't think about torturing people or have ever been tempted to do so. For whom were these laws against torture created? Those in power, that's who. Those laws were written for those who are so determined to get what they want that they would be willing to torture someone and even kill someone to get it. In November 2006 President Bush signed the Military Commissions Act (MCA) which gave any president the authority to establish a separate justice system for trying alien unlawful enemy combatants. The MCA justice system eliminated the basic protections afforded defendants in our domestic system of laws, in our military justice system, or in the system of laws used to try war criminals and anyone accused of being alien unlawful enemy combatants are exempted from the protections of the Geneva Conventions. The United States has signed the Geneva Conventions and agreed to abide by them, but the Military Commissions act repudiates the

---

702 Alfred W. McCoy, A Question of Torture: CIA Interrogation from the Cold War to the War on Terror (New York: Henry Holt and Company, 2006) 146.
703 Ibid, 149.

United States commitment to the Geneva Convention. The MCA authorizes the use of "coerced" interrogation to obtain evidence and denies detainees the right to challenge the legitimacy of their confinement or treatment. In addition, and this should raise alarm bells across America, Bush and his attorneys now assert that they can designate any American citizen as an "enemy combatant". They now claim the authority to knock on your door, seize you at anytime in anyplace, and essentially subject you to the same kinds of treatment that the detainees at Abu Ghraib and Guantanamo were subjected to including keeping you in indefinite isolation, delaying your trial indefinitely, inhibiting your communication with your attorney, threatening you in interrogations and using things you confessed under coercion in your trial. The president claims the right to do this to any American citizen at any time even if you have committed no crime on his say so alone because he has deemed you "enemy combatant". It is a status offense which means that you are one if the president says you are one.[704] The Military Commissions Acts specifically refers to "non citizens" when discussing "enemy combatants". However, the Patriot Act essentially gives the President or his representative card blanch to do as he pleases in absolute violation of the Constitution and Bill of Rights.

U.S. citizens are absolutely at risk of arbitrary arrest and imprisonment. Jose Padilla, United States Citizen and former gang member, was arrested in May 2002 at Chicago's O'Hare airport and accused of "intending to build" a dirty bomb. He was classified an enemy combatant and denied his rights as a U.S. citizen. He was imprisoned at a U.S. Navy facility in Charleston, South Carolina and given the Ewen Cameron style torture treatment intended to erase one's personality. That is he was injected with a drug which was either LSD or PCP and subjected to sensory deprivation in a cell with blacked out windows and no clock or calendar. He was shackled and his eyes were covered with blackout goggles and his ears covered with headphones whenever he left the cell. He was kept in these conditions for 1,307 days. He had no contact with an attorney or anyone else except for his interrogators. He was also subjected to loud noises and bright lights. He was not tried until December 2006 by which time he had regressed to a childlike state. The damage was permanent. The original charges were dropped. He was finally allowed legal representation and he was examined by a psychiatrist who determined that he could not assist in his own defense. The judge determined that he was nonetheless fit to stand trial.[705]

Dr. Al-Badr Al-Hazmi, a 34-year-old- radiology resident at the University of Texas Health Science Center was rudely awakened at 5 am in his San Antonio,

---

704 Naomi Wolf, The End of America: Letter of Warning to a Young Patriot, (White River Junction: Chelsea Green Publishing, 2007)16.

705 Klein Naomi, The Shock Doctrine: The Rise of Disaster Capitalism (New York: Metropolitan Books/ Henry Hold and Company, 2007) 44.

Texas home, on September 12th, 2001 by heavily armed federal agents. Without a search warrant his home was ransacked, his wife and children were held at gunpoint, and he was arrested and thrown naked into a cold cell. He was beaten repeatedly during interrogations and when he was finally allowed to speak to an attorney, it was discovered that his very common middle-eastern name sounded like the names of two of the suspected 9/11 hijackers. Al-Hazmi was released and allowed to return home after a week without having been charged with any crime.[706]

Addressing a decision made by the Supreme Court that a Saudi American Yasser Esam Hamdi who was arrested in Afghanistan, was entitled to due process, Sandra Day O'Connor stated, "indefinite detention for the purpose of interrogation is not authorized." And, extending these concerns to foreigners held at Guantanamo, she warned that "an unchecked system of detention carries the potential to become a means for oppression and abuse of others."[707]

Ostensibly the MCA was supposed to prohibit the use of torture; however, there were "holes which allowed the CIA and their contractors to continue to use Kubark sensory deprivation, sensory overload and waterboarding." Bush also used a signing statement asserting his right to "interpret the meaning and application of the Geneva Conventions" as he saw fit. The New York Times called this a unilateral rewriting of more than 200 years of traditional law.[708] Researchers saw in the MCA a reflection of the military tribunals set up by the NAZI's in Germany to prosecute those who resisted the NAZI regime. These courts gradually took over the duties of the ordinary justice system. Experts estimated that the court of Hanover, Germany alone eventfully sentenced 4000 defendants, and about 170 of them to death.[709] Journalist and attorney Phillip Sands, author of *The Torture Team*, who researched the legal pathway of the abuses at both Abu Ghraib and Guantanamo, decided to speak with a judge and prosecutor of an international criminal court under the auspices of NATO. They agreed that creating immunity would allow the crime to be covered up which was almost an admission that a crime had occurred. The Judge called it *"pactum scaelaris"* or an evil pact. The Judge determined that the facts of the case obligated him to investigate.[710]

In the case of the abuses of the Bush Administration, Democracy may have actually triumphed. The Bush administration expired and a new president was

---

706 Jim Marrs, The Terror Conspiracy: Deception, 9/11 and the Loss of Liberty(New York: Disinformation, 2006) 305 - 306
707 Alfred W. McCoy, A Question of Torture: CIA Interrogation from the Cold War to the War on Terror (New York: Henry Holt and Company, 2006) 148.
708 Klein Naomi The Shock Doctrine, The Rise of Disaster Capitalism (New York: Metropolitan Books/ Henry Hold and Company, 2007) 43.
709 Jim Marrs, The Rise of the Fourth Reich, (New York. NY: William Morrow of Harper Collins, 2008) 335.
710 Phillip Sands, The Torture Team: Rumsfeld's Memo and the Betrayal of American Values (New York: Paulgrave/MacMilliian, 2008) 208.

elected to office. Barak Obama issued an order as of January 22 2009 to close all the detention facilities including Abu Ghraib, Guantanamo and the network of prisons that were planted throughout the United States under a Special Access Program established by Rumsfeld. He also declared that the standards of the Geneva Convention would be upheld which suspended the Military Commissions Act of 2006 for 120 days. A military judge at Guantanamo, however, on January 29, 2009 rejected the White House request in the case of Abd al-Rahim al-Nashiri. Then On May 20, 2009, "The United States Senate passed an amendment to the Supplemental Appropriations Act of 2009 (H.R. 2346) by a 90-6 vote to block funds needed for the transfer or release of prisoners held at the Guantanamo Bay detention camp. In November 2009, 215 prisoners remained at the Guantanamo Bay detention camp."[711] President Barack Obama responded with a memorandum on December 15, 2009 closing the detention facility and transferring all detainees to the Thomson Correctional Center, in Thompson Illinois. However a recent article published by the NY Daily news reports that Obama has reopened the military trials at Guantanamo Bay and that KSM will be tried there.[712]

A 2004 inspector General's report released in August 2009 indicated that there were numerous possible violations of the felony torture statute prohibiting both "the intentional infliction or threatened infliction of severe physical pain or suffering" and "the threat of imminent death". The report detailed the unauthorized use of techniques which "warranted criminal investigations." One of those cases involved a CIA officer who repeatedly choked a shackled detainee until he almost passed out and other cases of mock executions. Former vice President Dick Cheney in an interview with fox News objected to the fact that the Obama Administration is threatening to disbar the lawyers who gave the legal opinions that paved the way for the abuse in the first place.[713]

What can we learn from this? Dan Mitrione was reportedly a devout Catholic, a family man. He had all the hallmarks of "respectability". Yet according to one of his students he believed that torture was science and not sadism.[714] McCoy rightly noted that permitting people to torture other people gives them an inflated ego which perpetuates abuse that escalates to a horrifying level. Lord Acton said, "Power corrupts, absolute power corrupts absolutely." Why is that so? Why is it that when people are given power over other people it degenerates into something ugly and abusive and does not

---

711 Wikipedia, Guantanamo Bay detention camp (January 2, 2010. - http://en.wikipedia.org).
712 Michael Mcauliff, Obama reopens military trials at Guantanamo Bay: 9/11 suspects less likely to see civilian court (March 7, 2011 - http://www.nydailynews.com).
713 Muriel Kane, Cheney 'Ok' With Violating Felony Torture Statute. (August 29, 2009 - http://www.prisonplanet.com).
714 Klein Naomi The Shock Doctrine, The Rise of Disaster Capitalism (New York: Metropolitan Books/ Henry Hold and Company, 2007) 92.

become something positive? People are sinful. Without the constraints of law, human nature will degenerate and even those charged with upholding the law will fall if not held accountable. What we have to learn from this is that in order for civilized nations to remain civilized, laws must be in place and they must be defended. No one, but no one can be excused from being held accountable to the law, not Law Enforcement, not law makers, not the military, not even the intelligence community nor U.S. Government officials, not anyone. The Constitution of the United States can only protect us if we protect it. Allowing the President to eliminate anyone from protections under the Geneva Conventions is just a hole in the dike which will eventually consume every American.

31. THE WAR ON TERROR

AKA THE WAR ON DEMOCRACY

The events of 9/11 opened the door for the Bush Administration to make sweeping changes in foreign and domestic policy that resulted in essentially gutting the Bill of Rights and severely depleting this nation's civil liberties. We now have this nebulas war on terror which justifies this serious infringement on the democratic process in this nation. You phone is being tapped, your bookseller has to surrender the list of books you have been reading to "authorities" without a warrant, your computer hacked and monitored, you can even be stalked and harassed by government sponsored terrorist gangs because you are suspected of something all because of the "war on terror". You can be arrested and detained on the whim of the President of the United States or one of his designees, held without being charged, abused during interrogation, denied legal representation, forbidden to speak on your own behalf should you even be tried, convicted on hearsay evidence and a coerced confession – because of this nebulas war on terror.

However, by this time we have established that 9/11 was not the work of al Qaeda terrorists. In fact the events of 9/11 has the signature not of an al Qaeda operation, but of an illuminated Hegelian contrived crisis invented by those in government with an agenda that is wholly un American. In fact, a careful examination of "terrorist" attacks around the world also have the distinct markings of the Hegelian style crisis contrived in order to justify draconian changes to government policy that severely limit the civil liberties of the residents of that nation where the attack occurred. I will examine a few of these "terrorist attacks" which demonstrate the active deception by the Illuminati perpetrators.

The Hegelian Dialectic and Zionism

One of the signatures of the Illuminati is to create a crisis to accomplish their agenda. In the process of creating a crisis they also create an enemy. There has to be a "villain" to blame. Over the years the Illuminati created communism and thus created a fear of the communist takeover. They created the NAZIs and with it a fear of socialism. Then in a perceived attempt to save the world from communism and/or socialism they lured people into all kinds of wars and conditioned people to accept draconian changes in government policies that effectively stamped out not communism or socialism but democracy. The modern enemy is no longer communism but "radical Islam".

Researchers have determined that the war between the Arabs and the Jews has also been a war created by Zionist Jews executing Hegelian crises for the purpose of furthering their agenda. Zionist Jews have actively persecuted the Sephardic Jews and have been in control of the Nation of Israel. Zionists, most of whom are Ashkenazi Jews, are not truly religious. They are primarily secular and many are occultists. In a 2007 article Ismail Salami notates an interview with Allen Hart, author of *Zionism, the Real Enemy of the Jews*. He declares there is a grand difference between Judaism and Zionism. He states, "ZIONISM is a secular, colonialist ideology which makes a mockery of, and has contempt for, the ethical principles and moral values of Judaism. The evidence which supports this statement begins with the fact that Israel was created mainly by Zionist terrorism and ethnic cleansing." [715]

In 1941, pro British supporters decided to arrange a little skirmish in Basra to make a pretext for British intervention. Thus they sent a message to the Jews of Iraq that the Brittish appointed Regent wanted to see them. As was their custom, the Jews brought flowers for the Regent. However, the cars that brought the Jews for the meeting, contrary to custom, dropped them off in an area where there was a heavy concentration of British forces. Thus the newspaper headlines the next day said, "Basra Jews Receive British Troops with Flowers." This of course sparked resentment among the Iraqis which resulted in an unarmed conflict that day between Iraqi Jews and Iraqis living in Basra. As it turns out the Brittish appointed Regent was not in Basra that day. The rioting created a pretext for British intervention which resulted in more British troops entering Basra and the surrounding area, more riots, homes and shops being looted etc. The riots continued from May through June with the death toll as high as 500 Jews. Naeim Giladi, himself a former Zionist, writing for *Jews Against Zionism* in 2002, was convinced that the riots were orchestrated by the British for geopolitical reasons, - that is to create a pretext for British intervention and to create an atmosphere that would persuade the Jews to flee from Iraq to Israel. It also created a pretext for the establishment of a Zionist underground in Iraq. This was confirmed to

---
715 Ismail Salami, Redefining the war in Iraq: Interview with Alan Hart (October 9, 2007 - http://payvand.com).

him by four other individuals who would have known that that was the case. One of them was David Kimche, who had been with British Intelligence during WW II and with the Mossad after the war and later became Director General of Israel's Foreign Ministry. It was in this position in 1982 when speaking for the British Institute of International Affairs that he confirmed that British Gurkha units participated in the slaughter of Jews in Baghdad in 1941.[716]

In 1951 it was Ashkenazi Jews that perpetrated terrorist attacks that they blamed on the Palestinians in order to stir up support for Zionism. The Sephardic Jews lived among the Arabs peacefully for years. They were hurt in the terrorist attacks as the real targets of Ashkenazi Jews who are politically connected to Rothschild. Edmond De Rothschild is controlling the Nation of Israel from behind the scenes. Zionist propagandists, for example, blamed anti-Jewish Iraqis for bombs that were set off in Iraq. While Islamic Jihadists' were blamed for the grenades that killed and maimed Jews living in Iraq and causing property damage, they were actually thrown by Zionist Jews. Former senior CIA officer Wilber Crane Eveland explains in his book *Ropes of Sand: America's Failure in the Middle East* that Zionists planted bombs in the U.S. Information Service Library and in synagogues in attempts to portray the Iraqis as anti-American and to terrorize the Jews in order to persuade them to flee to Israel. The Iraqi police investigated and provided information to the American Embassy showing that the bombings were in fact the workings of an underground Zionist organization motivated by a desire to increase the Jewish population in Israel.[717] Giladi confirmed that the anti-American and anti Jewish leaflets were typed on the same stencil machine as the Zionist leaflets that were dropped encouraging Jews to flee to Israel. He also confirmed that the explosives used in one attack at Belt-Lawi were traced to a suitcase of a Zionist Jew named Yosef Basri who executed the attack with Jew Shalom Salih. "Both men were members of Hashura, the military arm of the Zionist underground. Salih ultimately confessed that he, Basri and a third man, Yosef Habaza, carried out the attacks."[718]

Likewise the Zionists in Israel went on ruthless campaign to expel the Palestinians from Israel. The Zionist committed a series of massacres against the Palestinian Arabs forcing them by the millions into exile. American taxpayers footed the bill for the weapons and large amounts of TNT used by the Zionist terrorists against Palestinian Arabs. One such Zionist terrorist attack involved the use of a British police vehicle loaded with TNT which was exploded in a crowd of Arabs at the Hebron Gate Market place in Jerusalem killing twenty and wounding seventy Arabs.[719]

---

716 Naeim Giladi, The Jews of Iraq (April 16, 2011 - http://www.jewsagainstzionism.com).
717 Robin de Ruiter, Worldwide Evil and Misery: The Legacy of 13 Satanic Bloodlines (The Netherlands, Myra Publications, 2008) 161.
718 Naeim Giladi, The Jews of Iraq (April 16, 2011 - http://www.jewsagainstzionism.com).
719 Latheef Farook , Zionist Jews- Godfathers of Terrorism (January 18, 2009 - April 9, http://www.rense.com).

After the Zionists expelled 750,000 Palestinians from their land and acquired the property they moved Ashkenazi Jewish farmers and settlers from Europe in to occupy the land. In fact while the Israeli government sent European Jews to solids housing, 82% of the Jews of Middle Eastern origin were housed in tent encampments.[720] Zionists have an agenda that is completely incompatible with the true Jewish faith not to mention the Christian faith. Christians have rightfully embraced the Jews but true Jews do not embrace Zionist terrorism. Keep in mind that before the Zionist movement took root, Jews and Arabs lived peacefully side by side in the Middle East. In fact, Giladi notes that in Iraq during the rioting and looting perpetrated by Zionist Jews against the Jews of Iraq the Muslim neighbors of those Jews fought to defend them.[721]

Gladio and Hegelian Crises

Another now familiar "false flag" orchestrated in Italy by NATO working with right wing organizations and guided by the CIA and the Pentagon was "Operation Gladio" intended to dissuade voters from voting for communists. One attack which involved an explosion in a waiting room in a railway station in Bologna killed 85 people and wounded another 200. Italian Judge Felice Casson researched the involvement of Italian Military Intelligence with the Gladio Operation which was designed to weaken the communist movement in Italy. Cason reported his findings to a much surprised Italian Senate who ordered an investigation by Prime Minister Giulio Andreotti on August 2nd 1990. Giulio handed his report to the Senate on October 24, 1990. High ranking officials in the Italian government were implicated and were forced to testify including Francesco Cossiga, a former prime minister (1978-1979), who in 1990 was acting president. He testified that the secret army within the intelligence branch had been kept secret for 45 years. It was part of a stay behind army that was tasked with perpetrating a resistance movement operating behind enemy lines in case of a Soviet invasion. He further testified that "the Italian branch of a secret stay-behind army . . . had been set up after World War II by the CIA and SIFAR as part of an international network of clandestine resistance within NATO countries..."[722] This was called a Strategy of Tension, and Gladio bomber Peteano Inciguerra had testified in 1984 that absent of any Soviet invasion the secret army had functioned in the capacity of discouraging a "slide to the left" in Italian politics. Further investigation by the Italian parliament revealed that the secret Gladio army, the CIA, the Italian Military Intelligence Service, and selected Italian neo-fascists fought the Italian

---

720 Robin de Ruiter, Worldwide Evil and Misery: The Legacy of 13 Satanic Bloodlines (The Netherlands, Myra Publications, 2008) 161 - 162)
721 Naeim Giladi, The Jews of Iraq (April 16, 2011 - http://www.jewsagainstzionism.com).
722 Daniele Ganser, The "Strategy of Tension" in the Cold War Period (Book Section, 911 and American Empire: Intellectuals Speak Out, Vol. I, book Editors, David Ray Griffin & Peter Dale Scott, Northampton: Olive Branch Press, 2006) 88.

Communists and Socialists due to fears that they would betray NATO from within. Massacres, bombs and military actions had been organized, supported or promoted by men within the Italian State institutions and by men linked to United States Intelligence.[723]

The Gladio operation had its roots in the P2 Masonic Lodge which was connected to a secret society called the Knights of Malta, a modern recreation of the Knights Templar. And who do we find cavorting in these secret societies? CIA directors John McCone and William Casey who along with Reagan's first secretary of state, Alexander Haig had association with a Knight named Licio Gelli, "…who during the 1980s turned a little-used Italian Masonic lodge into what was termed a 'worldwide fascist conspiracy' with the help of the Mafia, the Vatican Bank, and the CIA". Gelli became a Freemason in 1963 and took over the *Propaganda Masonica Due* (P2) lodge in 1966. He increased the membership from 14 to 100 with the help of funding from the CIA according to Italian reporter and P2 member Mino Pecorelli and CIA Contract Agent Richard Brenneke. The P2 Lodge also had connections to the Mafia and the Italian Military. "Gelli also claimed to be on friendly terms with former CIA director and President George Bush, who some claimed was an 'honorary' P2 Lodge member."[724]

By covert operations Gelli was able to literally control the Italian government. Members of the P-2 lodge included the elite of Italian society including one hundred and ninety five military officers, two serving Ministers, three ex-Ministers, one Party Secretary, sixteen Magistrates, four hundred and twenty two State officials, thirty six M.P.s as well as Secret Service heads and various bankers and capitalists.[725] In addition they found a document entitled *The Strategy of Tension* which was a carefully designed plan to fabricate leftist terrorism in order to motivate the Italians to demand an authoritarian and even fascist government. This was the plan that evolved into "Operation Gladio" that came to fruition following WWII by the workings of CIA official James Jesus Angleton with the intended goal of preventing a communist takeover of Italy. The Gladio operation involved creating alliances between the Mafia, the Vatican, the CIA and the Knights of Malta.[726]

P2 was implicated in the 1980 bombing of the Bologna train station which killed eighty-five persons.[727] P2 was possibly implicated the December 1988 bombing of Pan Am Flight 103 over Lockerbie, Scotland.[728] Among the victims were CIA team members carrying evidence to Washington of CIA involvement with drug smuggling and CIA gun running in the Middle East. The CIA was at

---

723 Ibid, 91.
724 Jim Marrs, Rule by Secrecy (New York: Perennial/ Harper Collins, 2000) 257.
725 Steven, The Strategy of Tension in Italy (September 17, 2006 – http:libcom.org)
726 Jim Marrs, Rule by Secrecy (New York: Perennial/ Harper Collins, 2000) 257.
727 Laura Picci, A Massacre to Remember -The Bologna Train Station Bombing, Twenty-Five Years Later (July, 2005 - http://www.threemonkeysonline.com).
728 Jim Marrs, Rule by Secrecy (New York: Perennial/ Harper Collins, 2000) 257.

the crash site and confiscated all evidence.[729] Like Iran/Contra, these activities were being run from Washington and involved high ranking officials including President George H. W. Bush. P2 was also likely responsible for the assassination of Italian Prime Minister Aldo Moro who was told by Henry Kissinger that he should "halt his stabilizing policies" or he would pay for it.[730] Alarmingly Gladio operations were actually standardized in a United States Field Manuel, FM 30-31B which describes the methodology for launching terrorist attacks in nations that are not aggressively resisting communist subversion. The manual specifically warns that danger is present when leftist groups "renounce the use of force" and begin to adhere to the democratic process. Thus special operations, aka terrorist attacks, are launched by the U.S. Intelligence to convince the governments of those countries and the public of the danger of insurgents. The manual warns that these operations must remain secret.[731]

The mass bombings, kidnappings and assassination in Italy struck terror into the general populace with the goal of weakening left-wing political parties. The investigation eventually uncovered 139 secret weapons caches buried in meadows, forests, churches and cemeteries. And this was not limited to Italy. In the fall of 1990 the investigation revealed that post WWII the American CIA and British MI-6 had established operations similar to Gladio in every nation of Western Europe ostensibly for the purpose of providing resistance in the event of a Soviet Invasion. There were thousands of parliamentary forces that the CIA and MI-6 had armed and trained. The forces were composed of conservatives, Catholics and also extremist groups, right wing elements and criminal drug traffickers. The German groups included former NAZI SS. All the secret networks were organized separately and controlled by NATO.[732]

The Soviet invasion never materialized so the groups became involved in other things. They participated in the Coup in Greece and Turkey and the attempted Coup in Italy and France. In 1958, the French President Charles de Gaulle made a decision to grant independence to the French colony of Algeria. The CIA opposed this decision and joined elements of the French Army in an attempt to assassinate de Gaulle and overthrow his government. The attempt failed, de Gaulle was outraged and henceforth pulled France out of NATO. Subsequently, the U.S. military was forced to relocate NATO headquarters from Paris to Brussels, Belgium.[733]

The Gladio Scandal erupted in Europe on the Eve of Sadaam Hussein's invasion of Kuwait. Because GHW Bush was afraid it would negatively impact

---

729 Joel Skousen, Government Cover-ups: Pan Am l03 April 9, 2011 - http://www.worldaffairsbrief.com).
730 Jim Marrs, Rule By Secrecy (New York, NY: Perennial Harper Collins, 2000) 258.
731 Chris Floyd, Sword Play: Attacking Civilians to Justify "Greater Security". - February 18, 2005. http://www.globalresearch.ca).
732 Mark H. Gaffney, The 911 Mystery Plane and The Vanishing of America (Walterville: Trine Day LLC, 2008) 278.
733 Ibid.

the first Gulf war, the agreement was made between the Bush Whitehouse and the Press the keep the Gladio scandal from the American people. It just would not do for the American public to know just how much U.S. intelligence had been involved in subverting democracy around the world, thus the Mockingbird was asked not to sing that song.

The "Strategy of Tension" was applied in Bologna as well as Central America by the Reagan and Bush administrations. "During the 1980s, right-wing death squads, guerrilla armies and state security forces — armed, trained and supplied by the United States — murdered tens of thousands of people throughout the region, often acting with particular savagery at those times when peaceful solutions to the conflicts seemed about to take hold."[734] This pattern of criminal activity repeated in South America was called Operation Condor. It involved right-wing elements in Argentina, Chile, Paraguay, Brazil and Uruguay.[735] "Under Condor, the intelligence agencies of the Southern Cone shared information about "subversives" —aided by a state-of- the-art computer system provided by Washington—and then gave each other's 'agents safe passage to carry out cross-border kidnappings and torture, a system eerily resembling the CIA's 'extraordinary rendition' network today."[736] The same "strategy" was at work in South East Asia in Operation Phoenix which involved the assassination of some 35,000 Viet Namese and the overthrow of Cambodia's Prince Sihanouk in March 1970. Gaffney writes, "This was followed by a U.S. invasion of Cambodia, plunging that country into a bloody civil war that culminated in the Pol Pot reign of terror. For years, Sihanouk had pursued a policy of neutrality, but this was unacceptable to U.S. leaders fixated on the Cold War".[737] The "Strategy" was also applied in Iraq to convince the Iraqi people of the necessity of keeping American military forces indefinitely.[738]

The United States Government has a well developed propaganda machine for getting Americans to support socialist causes. During the Iran/Contra scandal, the American news media reported that the Sandinistas were guilty of terrorism in Central America. In reality that was not the case according to former CIA case officer John Stockwell. Any crimes committed by Sandinista Soldiers were dealt with through the normal judicial process with severe sentences. But the United States funded armed forces and death squads to the tune of billions of dollars who were slaughtering people in El Salvador and Guatemala. "The country is miserable and it was never the fault of the Sandinistas; misery was the stated purpose of the

---

734 Chris Floyd, Sword Play: Attacking Civilians to Justify "Greater Security". - February 18, 2005. http://www.globalresearch.ca/.
735 Mark H. Gaffney, The 911 Mystery Plane and The Vanishing of America (Walterville: Trine Day LLC, 2008) 279.
736 Naomi Klein, The Shock Doctrine: The Rise of Disaster Capitalism (New York: Metropolitan Books/Henry Holt and Company, 2007) 91.
737 Mark H. Gaffney, The 911 Mystery Plane and The Vanishing of America (Walterville: Trine Day LLC, 2008) 280.
738 Chris Floyd, Sword Play: Attacking Civilians to Justify "Greater Security". - February 18, 2005.

U.S. *Contra* destabilization program. One can only imagine what schools and clinics and irrigation projects could have been built with $1 billion."[739]

We're Singing the Same Song!

In order to establish this "Strategy of Tension" the NWO has to villanize someone. When I was a soldier, Russia was the villain. The propaganda machine incited the fear of a communist "Russian" takeover. However, since the Soviet Union has dissolved, and relations with Russian and the United States has softened, because they have the same agenda, the NWO has to pick a new enemy. Thus they have villianized *radical Islam*.

One of the books I read, or should I say attempted to read, while researching this book was written by an American Muslim who went to Central Asia to assist his fellow Muslims in their Holy War. I put the book down at about page 96 because the gruesomeness of the Islamic vengeance upon their enemies was more than I could stomach. Yes they are radical and yes it is gruesome. However, I wonder just how outraged you would be if someone from the other side, your enemy, raped your teenage daughter, publically executed her and left her with a wooden stake between her legs?[740] This happened in Chechnya where Russian Soldiers were repeatedly raping men women and children in the name of looking for terrorists. That is what these Radical Islamic Mujahedeen were fighting. Aukai Collins, in his book *My Jihad* describes in detail how they beheaded the Russian soldiers who were responsible for terrorizing their villages.[741]

An American soldier, Joshua Key, who had been to Iraq and refused to go back, described a scene that turned his stomach. He has a recurring nightmare of an experience he had in March 2003 just after the U.S. invasion of Iraq. What he saw were Iraqi soldiers, plural, decapitated. He saw no evidence of a firefight. He saw American soldiers kicking the detached heads around on the ground.[742] Let's think about this a minute. In normal combat it is possible for soldiers to have a leg or an arm blown off or even loose a head. They can get their guts blown out. That would be what one would normally expect to see after a firefight. However, an entire group of Iraqi soldiers with their heads cut off is not the result of a normal firefight. For that to have happened, those soldiers either already had to have been dead or they had to have already surrendered. In either case, what Joshua Key witnessed was the evidence of a terrorist act and/or a war crime.

---

739 John Stockwell, The Pratorian Guard: America's Role in the New World Order (Boston, MA: South End Press, 1991) 68.
740 Aukai Collins, My Jihad (Guilford: The Lyons Press, 2002) 61.
741 Ibid, 88 – 89.
742 Peter Laufer, Mission Rejected: Soldiers Who Said No to Iraq (White River Junction: Chelsea Green Publishing, 2006) 1.

Every solider is trained to come running out to formation in the morning shouting an anthem. The Mujahedeen in Collins unit did the same.⁷⁴³

> We lined up on the road in front of the house as the last stragglers ran out. Once everyone had assembled, Ulbi did a quick head count.
> *"Tickbird"* he yelled.
> *"Allah-u-Akbar"* everyone roared back, *God is great.*
> *"Sabilallah! Sabilallah!"* one of the men shouted. *What is Allah's way?*
> *"Al jihad! Al jihad!"* they yelled back. *Jihad is the way.*
> *"Tarianah! Tarianah!" What does Allah say?*
> *"Al kital! Al kital!" Kill! Kill!*

Stephen Eagle Funk, a 20-year-old US marine reserve who refused to be sent to Iraq described his experience in training. "Every day in combat training you had to yell out, 'Kill! Kill!' and we would get into trouble if you didn't shout it out, so often I would just mouth it so I didn't get into trouble . . ."⁷⁴⁴ Funny, the Mujahedeen and the U.S Marines were singing the same song! Who taught them that song? Could it be a puppeteer inciting both sides against each other? The puppeteer is the NWO, the global elite using us all in a game where we get sacrificed, and they take all the plunder – from both sides. Chris Floyd, who authored an article called *Sword Play: Attacking Civilians to Justify "Greater Security"*, asks a very provocative question,

> Perhaps it's just a coincidence. But the U.S. elite's history of directing and fomenting terrorist attacks against friendly populations is so extensive — indeed, so ingrained and accepted — that it calls into question the origin of every terrorist act that roils the world. With each fresh atrocity, we're forced to ask: Was it the work of "genuine" terrorists or a "black op" by intelligence agencies — or both? While not infallible, the ancient Latin question is still the best guide to penetrating the bloody murk of modern terrorism: Cui bono? Who benefits? Whose powers and policies are enhanced by the attack. . . ?⁷⁴⁵

Considering the mentality of the Washington elite pertaining to running the world, it should not be difficult for us to then grasp the reality that 9/11 was another "Gladio" operation designed to entice American's into accepting

---

743 Aukai Collins, My Jihad (Guilford: The Lyons Press, 2002) 71 – 72.
744 David Icke, Tales from the Time Loop (Ryde, Isle of Wight, UK, 2003) 171.
745 Chris Floyd, Sword Play: Attacking Civilians to Justify "Greater Security". - February 18, 2005.

changes in policy that have severely impacted our freedoms, our privacy and our peace of mind. We have established the fact that al Qaeda was fostered and nourished by the CIA. That their al Qaeda operatives were involved in terrorist attacks sponsored by the CIA is well established. For example Ali Mohamed, an Egyptian trained by the CIA and enlisted in the United States Army, was Osama Bin Laden's mentor. He was an FBI informant as well, and he "clearly enjoyed US protection. In 1993, when detained by the police in Canada, a single phone call to the United States secured his release. This enabled him to play a role, in the same year, in planning the bombing of the US embassy in Kenya in 1998."[746]

The War on Terror is also a perfect solution to the Straussian ideal of keeping a nation in perpetual military conflicts in order to keep them from "trivializing life" in the search for endless entertainment. It doesn't matter if there is tremendous loss of life. There is no right or wrong. So if there is no right or wrong, how many of us would choose entertainment to the wonton slaughter of innocent lives for the purpose of furthering the globalists' agenda? So what's wrong with entertainment? Nobody has to die!

This war on terror just as the contrived fear of communism and socialism is allegedly making the world safe for democracy. Barry Goldwater observed in that by the end of WWII more than 50% of the people on the planet were ruled by governments that promoted individual freedom. However by 1967 there was only 30% of the planet's population enjoying any freedom. As of the writing of his book published in 1979 only 17 percent of the world's population had any personal liberty. He also observes that every president since Roosevelt had advocated for expansion in government at the cost of liberty.[747]

We have been deceived. If we now know the truth, how then shall we respond? As an American Soldier I took an oath to defend America against "all enemies foreign and domestic". I am wondering when the U.S. Military, that is those who still care about our Constitution and still have a conscience, are going to take a stand to defend this nation against the abuses of the "illluminized" elite in Washington. Let us keep in mind that when we defend our freedom, we are also defending the freedom of a world that has had enough of the deception, terror and harassment propagated by the United States Government "in the interest of National Security."

> *For thus says the LORD, who created the heavens (he is God!), who formed the earth and made it (he established it; he did not create it a chaos, he formed it to be inhabited!): I am the LORD, and there is no other. I did not speak in secret, in a land of darkness; I did not say to*

---

746 Peter Dale Scott, The Background of 9/11: Drugs, Oil, and US Covert Operations (Book Section 9/11 and American Empire, Vol. I, book editors David Ray Griffin and Peter Dale Scott – Northampton: Olive Branch Press, 2007) 77.

747 Barry M. Goldwater, With No Apologies (New York: William Morrow and Company Inc., 1979) 153 – 154.

the offspring of Jacob, "Seek me in chaos." I the LORD speak the truth, I declare what is right (Isaiah 45:18 – 19, NRSV).

32. THE WAR ON DRUGS

AKA FUNDING THE WAR ON DEMOCRACY

It was tempting to skip writing this chapter because by now the fact that the United States Government, AKA the Illuminati, AKA the NWO, has been involved in drug trafficking has already been established by multiple witnesses not the least of which were the children who testified in the Franklin investigation that they were used as drug couriers. We have this D.A.R.E program developed by Law Enforcement which is designed to keep kids from being involved in the use of illicit drugs. We have criminal courts to prosecute those who traffic in drugs and use them complete with prison sentences. We have drug rehabilitation programs to help people get clean of drug use. We have funerals for people who get lost in the maze of drug addictions. And we have the United States Government working against all of this.

When or where did we begin to slide into this pit? America has been sponsoring drug trafficking Muslim warriors including al Qaeda since the Afghan War of 1979-1989 via the CIA's link to the drug laundering Bank of Credit and Commerce International (BCCI) otherwise known as the Bank of Crooks and Criminals International. This was William Casey's strategy for launching covert operations that were not approved of or funded by Congress.[748] In the 1980's drug profits funded the Iran/Contra affair when Congress denied more funding under the Boland amendments. Congressman Lee Hamilton, who later became the chair of the 9/11 Commission, played a role in the massive cover-up. It should not surprise us then that Lee Hamilton as the chairman of the 9/11 commission, experienced in cover-up operations, worked exhaustively to hinder the 9/11 Commission from accomplishing its intended purpose.

America's support of al Qaeda already spoken of in the chapter on 9/11 was rooted in the need to maintain working relationships with the Saudi and the Pakistani intelligence networks. United States oil companies were able to access oil rich Azerbaijan through US organized covert operations using Arab-Afghan operatives associated with bin Laden. "Oil was the driving force of US involvement in Central and South Asia, and oil led to US coexistence with both al Qaeda and the world-dominating Afghan heroin trade". Drug trafficking was a source of income for al Qaeda contrary to what was reported in the 9/11 Commission. This has been established by the governments of Great Britain and other European

---

748 Peter Dale Scott, The Background *of 9/11*: Drugs, Oil, and US Covert Operations (Book Section, *9/11 and American Empire*, Vol. I, book editors, David Ray Griffin and Peter Dale Scott, Northampton: Olive Branch Press, 2007) 73.

countries.⁷⁴⁹ It was U.S. support of al Qaeda that increased heroin trafficking to Western Europe and the United States.

Three veterans of US operations in Laos and Nicaragua, Richard Secord, Heinie Aderholt, and Ed Dearborn, in 1991 turned up in Baku and established the MEGA oil company which never found any oil. This was a cover operation for drug trafficking. They established an airline specifically to support US covert operations and transport of Mujahideen mercenaries in and out of Afghanistan. President Carter and CIA Director Stansfield Turner started the largest covert operation in terms of money spent run by the CIA called the "Golden Crescent" in Afghanistan in the 1980's. Hundreds of millions of dollars were spent in CIA air transports hauling arms and inevitably drugs. Within the first five years of its operation it became the world's largest source of Heroin.⁷⁵⁰ In Kosovo in 1998, al Qaeda-backed Islamist jihadists of the Kosovo Liberation Army received support from the United States Government. "Meanwhile by 2000, according to DEA statistics, Afghan heroin accounted for almost 20 percent of the heroin seized in the United States—nearly double the percentage taken four years earlier. Much of it is now distributed by Kosovar Albanians."⁷⁵¹

Drug smuggling was a routine during the Viet Nam war when drugs were smuggled in the cadavers of fallen U.S. soldiers who were being shipped back to the United States. An Opium gang of United States Army soldiers who settled in Thailand called the Black Masonic Club was led by Leslie "Ike" Atkinson, nicknamed "Sergeant Smack." Atkinson was also linked to the murder of Dr. Jeffery McDonald's wife and two daughters by witness Helena Stoeckley one of the doctor's patients. Dr. McDonald was the drug counselor at Fr. Bragg, North Carolina. He became disturbed by the increase in the number of soldiers he was seeing for drug rehabilitation therapy and began to investigate in an attempt to stem the tide of drug addictions he was seeing. Unfortunately, he got too close to the truth about the government sponsored drug trafficking at Ft. Bragg where soldiers' dead bodies were used to smuggle the drugs into the states. The heroin was delivered to Ft. Bragg and Johnson-Seymour Air Force Base in the cadavers of deceased U.S. military. It was stuffed into coffins, body bags and even internal organs. From there it was distributed to eastern and southeastern states.⁷⁵²

In an attempt to silence McDonald on February 17th, 1970 people from Atkinson's group brutally murdered McDonald's wife, his two daughters and stabbed him as well. Collette Macdonald and five year old Kimberly and two year old Kristen were bludgeoned and stabbed to death. Dr. McDonald also sustained

---

749 Ibid, 75.
750 John Stockwell, The Pratorian Guard: America's Role in the New World Order (Boston, MA: South End Press, 1991)119.
751 Peter Dale Scott, The Background of 9/11: Drugs, Oil, and US Covert Operations (Book Section, 9/11 and American Empire, Vol. I, book editors, David Ray Griffin and Peter Dale Scott, Northampton: Olive Branch Press, 2007)75 – 76.
752 Alex Constantine, Psychic Dictatorship in the U.S. A. (Portland: Feral House, 1995) 124.

multiple stab wounds one of which resulted in a collapsed lung. Jeffery McDonald was hospitalized for 10 days. Shockingly, the government determined that the stab wounds on Dr. McDonald were "superficial" and "self inflicted". He was charged with the murder of his wife and two daughters and after being acquitted twice he was finally convicted by a 1982 Supreme Court decision and sentenced to three life terms in a medium security prison in Sheridan, Oregon.[753]

Ted Gunderson independently investigated the MacDonald Murders and submitted evidence in defense of Dr. MacDonald which was ignored by the court. He listed 42 elements including the botched investigation, evidence that would have vindicated Dr. McDonald that had been "lost" or destroyed and the disallowing of testimony of 47 witnesses who observed the real culprits of the crime at the crime scene. In addition to this, though Dr. MacDonald had submitted to several psychiatric evaluations by Dr.'s who testified at two previous trials that he could not have committed the murders, Judge Dupree requested another evaluation and an 80 year old Psychiatrist, Dr. Brussels, who displayed signs of obvious dementia in court, was asked to evaluate Dr. MacDonald. Dr. Brussels' assessment contradicted the previous evaluations. Thus Judge Dupree disallowed all of the psychiatric evaluations to be used as evidence in court. What was also ignored by the FBI was the confession of one of the real assailants, Gregg Mitchell. Ted Gunderson, who is experienced in investigating occult related crimes, saw evidence of occult involvement in the murders which was of course ignored. What actually happened is that the members of a cult, who murdered MacDonald's wife and children in a satanic ritual, were also being used as drug runners for the illegal operation at Ft. Brag. Officials involved in that operation were afraid that if the cult members who committed the murder were investigated and prosecuted it would lead to the exposure of the CIA sponsored drug running operation.[754]

Bill Tyree was another party caught in the snare of CIA illegal drug running operations. An imprisoned former Green Beret, Tyree sued the CIA, George Bush and others in an attempt to bring to light their complicity in government sanctioned drug trafficking and cover-up. Tyree was also framed for his wife's murder in an attempt by the CIA to conceal drug trafficking at Ft. Devens. Tyree states that drugs were flown into Panama and were subsequently shipped to Mena, Arkansas under Operation Watchtower.[755] Researchers assert that Bill Clinton squashed the investigation into drug smuggling at Mena. In an affidavit signed by William Casey, former director of the CIA, he states that Bill Clinton helped the drug running operation in Mena by "containing" the local Law Enforcement investigations. He also states that Bill Weld, as Assistant United States Attorney, was in charge of the Criminal Division of the Department of Justice and in that

---

753 Ibid, 121.
754 Ted Gunderson, Ted Gunderson's "brief' summery of the investigation of the Jeffery MacDonald Murder case (http://www.thejeffreymacdonaldcase.com).
755 Uri Dowbenko, Up Against the Beast: High Level Drug Running (1999- http://www.whale.to/b/dowbenko.html).

capacity controlled the investigations by federal Law Enforcement in a deliberate attempt to conceal the drug running operation and U.S. Government officials involved in it. He also discussed the role that Oliver North played in the drug running operation in his affidavit which was signed December 9th, 1986 in McLean Virginia. The affidavit is also signed by Richard Nixon. A copy of the affidavit with signatures is available at http://www.takeoverworld.info/Casey_affidavit_CIA_drugs.html. Casey makes a chilling statement in that affidavit.

> My actions may be recorded as criminal condemning countless [Americans] to drug dependency. I don't care. All wars produce casualties. Generally the more violent the war, the shorter the length. My choice was either to stare down a protracted cold war guerrilla insurgency in Latin America or use the mean's available to finance and wage a violent war of short duration for democracy. I stand by my decision. The tool is cocaine. The trick is to understand that the drug user had the freedom to make a choice. They chose the drug. I chose to use their habit to finance the democracy that all [Americans] enjoy. To keep those [Americans] safe from the communist threat knocking on our back door in Latin America. For a change the drug user will contribute to society.

Keeping the world safe for democracy was the excuse he used for committing a crime. Let us be reminded that the CIA was created by people who oppose democracy and created communism in the first place. So he speaks a lie to defend a lie. Dr. MacDonald's wife and children did not make that choice and neither did Bill Tyree's murdered wife.

The children of the Franklin investigation testified that they were used as drug couriers. Caradori, the private investigator in the Franklin investigation found evidence that Police Chief Bob Wadman was involved in drug trafficking.[756] John DeCamp who defended the children in the Franklin investigation was actually good friends with former Director of the CIA William Colby. He consulted with him about the investigation. He did not know, maybe, that William Colby headed up the American terrorist Phoenix Operation. He probably did not know that the CIA was involved in drug trafficking as well as physical and mental abuse of children under the MKULTRA program. He was therefore shocked when the former CIA director advised him to walk away from the Franklin investigation.[757]

Journalist Daniel Hopsicker interviewed Mohammed Atta's girlfriend Amanda Keller who testified that Mohammed Atta was involved in drug trafficking and had connections in the underworld. Hopsicker reported that former Assistant Attorney General Michael Chertoff had stated to the Senate Banking committee, "Frankly, we can't differentiate between terrorism and organized crime and drug

---

756 John W. DeCamp, The Franklin Cover Up (Lincoln, Nebraska: AWT, 1992) 240.
757 Ibid, xii, xiii.

dealing."⁷⁵⁸ Barry Seal, one of America's most successful drug smugglers and a CIA agent, had been implicated in the CIA drug smuggling connected to the airport at Mena, Arkansas which was linked to Bill Clinton when he was Governor. Cathy O'Brien reported that she was used to make a cocaine drop to Bill Clinton which was a gift from Senator Ben Johnston. She watched him snort two lines of cocaine at that encounter. She had been forced to marry Grand Ol'Opery performer Wayne Cox who was also a serial killer. Cox was also involved in cocaine deliveries in Texas, Arkansas, Mississippi, Tennessee and Florida.⁷⁵⁹ She accompanied him on numerous cocaine deliveries. She was with Cox on numerous cocaine and gun runs. He also was activating mercenaries for operations ordered by Senator Johnston. She saw the numerous underground stashes of weapons that were not on military installations.

The former CIA agent and drug smuggler, Barry Seal, was connected even to the office of the president of the United States. He ran into some legal problems related to drug smuggling and Vice President George H. W. Bush failed to lend his assistance in getting him out of trouble. In retaliation he arranged a sting operation in which brothers George W. and Jeb Bush were caught receiving cocaine shipments at a Florida airport in 1985. The two were caught on video receiving the shipment. Barry Seal stepped in and got them out of trouble but held onto the video tape for insurance. Apparently his "insurance" ran out and he was machine-gunned in Baton Rouge, Louisiana, on February 19, 1986, less than a year after his sting operation. His video tapes disappeared. The turboprop King Air 200 used in the sting was also linked to several members involved in the Iran-Contra affair.⁷⁶⁰

In a curious article entitled *THE SOUND OF LOONIES FROM THE GRASSY KNOLL TO THE BIRTHERS*, John Camp makes some rather unbelievable statements such as, "The CIA asked permission from drug enforcement officials to install a camera on the plane in order to gather evidence that Nicaragua had become a trans-shipment point for cocaine processed in Colombia". We already know that the CIA is absolutely involved in drug trafficking. That they would even actually ask the Drug Enforcement Agency permission to do anything at all is rather dubious. He goes on to indicate that Barry Seal was only involved in one CIA drug running operation and that the Mena drug trafficking operation was a myth. As we have eyewitness testimony from Cathy O'Brien who delivered a shipment of cocaine to Bill Clinton herself as well the as the sworn affidavit from former CIA Director William Casey there can be no doubt that Mena was

---

758 Jim Marrs, The Terror Conspiracy: Deception, 9/11 and the Loss of Liberty, (New York: Disinformation, 2006) 27.
759 Cathy O'Brien and Mark Phillips, Trance Formation of America (Frankston, Texas: Reality Marketing Inc., 1995) 103.
760 Daniel Hopsicker and Michael C. Ruppert, The Bush Drug Sting, The Sins of the Father, The Sins of the Son and — The Smoking Airplane (http://www.rromthewilderness.com).

a drug trafficking hub central for the CIA. John Camp professes to be have been a personal friend of Barry Seal.[761]

There is also evidence linking Vice President George H. W. Bush, then in charge of the Nation's anti-drug task force, to drug trafficking in the United States. When Noriega refused to cooperate with the CIA's plan to invade Nicaragua, the Contra arms supply line was shifted to the Ilopango airbase in El Salvador, and Felix Rodriguez was put in charge. The Medellin cocaine cartel was making payments through Felix Rodriguez, giving them access to the Contra air transport program. Telephone records reveal that Felix Rodriguez was making visits to Vice President Bush's office several times a week.[762] Another associate of Vice President George Bush was a man named Donald Aronow who built speed boats for drug traffickers. Aronow was gunned down Feb. 3rd 1987. The week prior to that, he had had several conversations with Vice President Bush. Aronow had been questioned by police about cocaine trafficking and was scheduled to testify in court and turn states evidence.[763]

Vietnam veteran Col. James "Bo" Gritz who was working to locate American POW's was told by Burmese General Kuhn Sa, the head of the Golden Triangle drug trade, that Assistant Secretary of Defense for International Security Affairs Richard Armitage, along with other US government officials, were managing the financial transactions for the US narcotics trade through Australian banks. Col. Gritz was stunned by this revelation. Bo Gritz testified before the U.S. Congress, House Foreign Affairs committee, International Narcotics Control Task Force on June 30th, 1987. He was visiting Southeast Asia's "Golden Triangle" in an effort to locate and free missing POW's. He visited with General Khun Sa who told him that Richard Armitage was one of his biggest customers. Khun Sa did not want to be involved in drug trafficking but he had no choice because of U.S. policy. Col. Gritz states in his testimony

> Moreover, there are serious implications that elements within the U.S. Government are Khun Sa's biggest customers. The facts are that for 15 years U.S. taxpayers through legislative bodies like this committee and executive agencies such as have testified here today, have dumped hundreds of millions of dollars into drug suppression programs within Thailand and Burma which have done nothing but nourish the flow of narcotics from Asia into the United States. The proof is statistically clear. Fifteen years ago the flow of Opiates was 60 tons; this year it will approach or exceed 900 tons. … More shameful are the serious allegations raised by General Khun Sa and

---

761 John Camp, The Sound of Loonies from the Grassy Knoll to the Birthers: Barry Seal: The Derelict Gunslinger (February 14, 2011- http://www.derelictgunslinger.com).
762 John Stockwell, The Pratorian Guard: America's Role in the New World Order (Boston, MA: South End Press, 1991) 22 – 23.
763 Alex Constantine, Virtual Government (Los Angeles, CA: Feral House,1997) 206.

his staff that corrupt U.S. officials allow this travesty and in certain cases are directly involved.[764]

Daniel Estulin recounts in *The True Story of the Bilderbergers* how he received information about *Operation Watchtower* that financed anti-communist activities between 1975 and 1984. This operation also dealt with surveillance.[765] In *Trilaterals over America*, Anthony Sutton details more government involvement in drug trafficking. The DEA Chief Judge Bonner charged the CIA with importing one ton of pure cocaine from Venezuela which was sold on American streets. One thousand pounds of the Venezuela shipment was seized at the Miami Airport. The DEA was ordered to leave the shipment alone because it was imported under the auspices of the United States Government. The Department of Justice knew about the shipment as well as Senator Goren and did nothing. The DEA finally exposed it in a 1993 CBS program. In fact the CIA created an "intelligence network" as a cover for trafficking in Haiti under General Cedras.[766]

John Stockwell reports in *The Praetorian Guard*, that the CIA made a deal with Barry Seal to land a plane in Panama, kick some bales of marijuana out on the runway that could be photographed by satellite so President Reagan could take some pictures to the American Public to convince them that the Sandinistas were smuggling drugs to fund their operation. In reality Senator Kerry's investigation revealed that the Contra's and their CIA managers were involved in drug smuggling. CIA/Contra aircraft were flown into the United States and landed at National Guard and Air Force bases where they could avoid being inspected by customs. Massive amounts of drugs including cocaine were flown into the United States in this way. The Senate Committee headed by John Kerry (D-MA) estimated that 50-100 flights of CIA/Contra aircraft had hauled cocaine and marijuana back into the United States. People in the Contra program were frequently caught smuggling cocaine into this country and got past the FBI and Drug Enforcement Agency with national security passes or telephone numbers from the White House. The CIA intervened on behalf of drug dealers a couple dozen times in the 1970s.[767]

Federal attorneys in Florida were receiving instructions from the Justice Department in Washington hindering their attempt to prosecute drug smugglers, specifically from Attorney General Ed Meese, on the grounds of "national security". Other Law Enforcement officials have had similar experiences. DEA figures reveal that the cocaine importation into the US in 1981 was 12,000 to 17,000 kilograms and by 1987 had increased to more than 100 tons.[768]

---

764 Lt. Cot James Bo Gritz USA (Ret), Statement (June 30, 1987 - http://www.ncoic.co).
765 Daniel Estulin, The True Story of the Bilderberger Group: (Waterville, 2007) 17.
766 Anthony C. Sutton, Trilaterals Over America (Boring, CPA Book Publishers, 1995) 88.
767 John Stockwell, The Pratorian Guard: America's Role in the New World Order (Boston, MA: South End Press, 1991) 67.
768 Ibid, 119.

In our "War on Drugs" keep in mind that the taxpayers are paying dearly to support programs to keep children from becoming addicted to drugs, as well as government sponsored rehabilitation programs for users and for the keeping of drug traffickers who are actually caught and imprisoned. With that in mind, it should really make your blood boil that those who we trusted with public office should have so coddled us and so violated our trust in not only participating and profiting from drug trafficking but lying to us about it, not to mention using children to traffic their illegal wares. None of them have been charged or prosecuted to date for the crimes they have committed. And where is Law Enforcement, but sinking in the mire as well. What we need are people in Law Enforcement, as well as judges and prosecutors who have the courage to arrest an ex-president and or vice president and charge him with a crime. What we need are American citizens who will get behind them and insist that neither politicians nor wealthy blue blooded families nor dirty police chiefs are above the law and shall be prosecuted.

33. Adam Where Are You?

And they heard the sound of the LORD God walking in the garden in the cool of the day, and Adam and his wife hid themselves from the presence of the LORD God among the trees of the garden. And the LORD God called unto Adam, and said unto him, "Where are you?" So he said, "I heard your voice in the garden, and I was afraid, because I was naked; and I hid myself." And He said, "Who told thee that you were naked? Have you eaten of the tree, whereof I commanded you that you should not eat?" Then the man said, "The woman whom you gave to be with me, she gave me of the tree, and I ate" (Gen 3:8-12 NKJV).

The one "no" in paradise was the tree of the knowledge of good and evil which stood in the middle of the garden of Eden. That tree stood for freedom. It wasn't that God gave Adam and Eve the freedom to do whatever they wanted, he gave them a free will and they had to have exercise of that free will. This meant they could choose to obey or disobey. He did not tell them, "Well, you have two options and it doesn't matter which once you choose." No, he specifically told Adam, "Of every tree of the Garden you may freely eat; but of the tree of the knowledge of good and evil you shall not eat, for in the day that you eat of it you shall surely die"(Gen 2:16-17 NKJV). They choose to disobey. Thus, they heard God walking in the garden in the cool of the evening and had to hide because they were naked and ashamed. "Quick, hide! We can't let him see us like this!" And so they hid. Then God said, "Where are you Adam?" Silly question for an all present all knowing God, don't you think? Was he kidding? Really, he knew didn't he? Or did he? No. God does not "kid around". He did not know, because he gave them liberty. They were choosing to hide, so he chose not to know where they were. He asked, "Did you eat …?" He did not know. He chose not to know because he gave them liberty. He gave them privacy. So what God was in effect staying to them, "If you are going to hide from me, I will let you. But I will come looking for you, because though you disobeyed me I still care for you. When I call your name, will you answer? Will you come when I call?"

They were not under 24 hour surveillance.

34. Spying on America and American Police State Part II

"Spying is the fuel of fascism."
Naomi Wolf in The End of America

Warrantless surveillance has always been a tool of fascist governments. This kind of surveillance is not new to America, but it has been kept hidden from the American public. In 1970, at in the midst of the hearings of the Senate Review Committee on Improper Surveillance of American Citizens, Zbigniew Brzezinski, who became the National Security Advisor for President Carter, predicted that a group of elites would dominate and control society using technology. In his book *Between Two Ages: America's Role in the Techtronic Era* published in 1976 he makes the following telling statement, "Unhindered by the restraints of traditional liberal values, this elite would not hesitate to achieve its political ends by using the latest modern techniques influencing public behavior and keeping society under close surveillance and control. Technical and scientific momentum would then feed on the situation it exploits."[769].

In 1992, Julianne McKinney, President of the National Security Alumni, published the report of their investigation of the unwarranted surveillance and electronic harassment of American citizens. At the time of the publishing of the report there were 12 such victims. As the investigation continued the number grew to over 200 victims of electronic surveillance and harassment of citizens of the United States, Canada, England and Australia.[770]

On February 25, 1995, NBC nightly News announced the all encompassing domestic surveillance on Americans and others through the NSA and CIA's monitoring of the global internet.[771] This of course occurred prior to 9/11. In fact one of Bill Clinton's first acts upon entering the office of the President in 1996 was to sign off on legislation that require the makers of computers, cell phones and multiple other electronic devices to install hardware that made it easy for the government to monitor communications through these devices. This act required

---

769 Dr. Nick Begich & Jean Manning, Angels Don't Play This Harp (Anchorage, 1995) 180.
770 Glenn Krawczyk, Big Brother's Recipe for 'Revolution in Military Affairs (June - July 1995. - http://www.ivanfraser.com).
771 Dr. Nick Begich & Jean Manning, Angels Don't Play This Harp (Anchorage: Earthpulse Press, 1995) 180.

a warrant.[772] However, true to form, our government had decided to dispense with the warrant. "Several other recent bills, such as the Anti-Terrorism Bill, have asked for unprecedented and clearly unconstitutional, expansion of police and federal wiretap and surveillance powers". Anyone who has been trained by the intelligence web can hack into your computer and monitor what you are doing. Under the Clinton administration wiretaps went up by 40% greater than under his predecessor George Bush sr.[773]

In an article in Nexus Magazine published in May of 1996 stated

> ...The NSA gathers information on U.S. citizens who might be of interest to any of the over 50,000 NSA agents (HUMINT). These agents are authorized by executive order to spy on anyone. The NSA has a permanent National Security Anti-Terrorist surveillance network in place. ...NSA personnel serve in quasi-public positions in their communities and run cover business and legitimate businesses that can inform the intelligence community of persons they would want to track. ...Individual citizens are occasionally targeted for surveillance by independently operating NSA personnel. NSA personnel can control the lives of hundreds of thousands of individuals in the U.S. by using the NSA's domestic intelligence network and cover businesses. The operations run independently by them can sometimes go beyond the bounds of law. ...NSA DOMINT has the ability to **covertly assassinate** [emphasis mine]U.S. citizens or run covert psychological control operations to cause subjects to be diagnosed with ill mental health. ...spotters and Walk-Bys in Metropolitan Areas. .. Tens of thousands of persons in each area working as spotters and neighborhood /business place -spies (sometimes unwittingly) following and checking on subjects who have been identified for covert control by NSA personnel.[774]

Writing in 1998 Michael Sweeney observed that the powers of the Foreign Intelligence Surveillance Act (FISA) were expanded as a result of the earlier attacks on the WTC and the Oklahoma City Bombings. He observes that recent legislation has already eliminated your right to privacy, your protection form unreasonable search and seizure and your right to a fair hearing. A secret court can authorize the FBI to search your property without your knowledge, take anything they want without notifying you without any obligation to return it, conduct full

---

772 H. Michael Sweeney, The Professional Paranoid: How to Fight Back When Investigated, Stalked, Harassed or Targeted by Any Agency, Organization, or Individual (Venice: Feral House, 1998)182.
773 Jerry E. Smith, HAARP: The Ultimate Weapon of the Conspiracy (Kempton, ILL: Adventures Unlimited Press, 1998) 151.
774 Mark Rich, The Hidden Evil (May 5, 2005- http://www.thehiddenevil.com).

surveillance on you even in your bedroom. They can take further action against you without revealing why. This can be done even if you have only associated with someone the FBI is targeting. To make matters worse should you find an FBI agent in your home and you think he is a burglar and shoot him, you can be arrested and charged with the murder of a federal agent.[775]

Hello! We were still three years away from the 9/11 events that were supposedly used as an excuse to pass the Patriot Act which demolished our Constitution and Bill of Rights. The Patriot Act was about 400 pages long and passed during the panic period in the wake of 9/11. The document which made changes in 15 different US statutes, most addressing previous misuse of surveillance powers by the FBI and CIA, was signed into law by President Bush on October 26, 2001. The act expands government surveillance power but reduces checks and balances which guard the liberties of innocent American citizens. The document was not available for review by our representatives prior to the vote and it was observed by several representatives that it could not have been written between 9/11 and the day it was voted on. It was so long and detailed that it most likely would have to have been written prior to the 9/11 events and was kept in waiting. One of three congressmen who did not vote for the Bill was Rep. Ron Paul, from Ohio. He refused to vote for the Bill because he insisted he needed to know what was in it first and he felt that it undermined the Constitution. He indicated that the Bill had not even been printed before the vote was cast. It is normal procedure that before voting on any piece of legislation, there has to be time for debate and expert testimony from those who will be impacted by it. Normal procedures for voting on legislation were completely suspended for the Patriot Act.[776]

The Patriot Act is alarmingly similar to Hitler's enabling act. The Enabling Act allowed Hitler to permanently bypass some powers of Parliament. It made it legal for the NAZI state to tap citizens' phones and open their mail.[777] The Enabling act mandated the national identity card, created racial profiling, ordered the position of homeland security chief, and resulted in gun confiscation, mass murders and incarceration in concentration camps and curtailed the freedom of the press.[778] The Patriot Act was built upon the FISA of 1978 which permitted surveillance of non Americans and created the secret Foreign Intelligence Surveillance Court. The Patriot Act expands FISA to include American Citizens. FISA imposed limits and a review process on warrantless surveillance and searches due to the numerous abuses by federal agencies of US citizens. However, under the Patriot Act and

---

775 H. Michael Sweeney, The Professional Paranoid: How to Fight Back When Investigated, Stalked, Harassed or Targeted by Any Agency, Organization, or Individual (Venice: Feral House, 1998) 33.
776 Jim Marrs, The Terror Conspiracy: Deception, 9/11 and the Loss of Liberty(New York, Disinformation, 2006) 299 – 300.
777 Naomi Wolf, The End of America: Letter of Warning to a Young Patriot (White River Junction: Chelsea Green Publishing, 2007) 41.
778 Jim Marrs, The Rise of the Fourth Reich (New York, NY: Harper Collins, 2008) 22.

subsequent revisions have resulted in the erosion of many of our Constitutional rights and basic legal procedures that evolved from the Magna Carta.[779]

The Magna Carta, signed by King John of England in 1215, established that all persons have a right to what we call due process. That is you cannot be thrown into jail without being charged and you cannot be held indefinitely. The Magna Carta was strengthened in 1679 with the concept of habeas corpus which states that you have the right to see the evidence against you, face your accuser and also the right to have a hearing in the presence of an impartial judge or jury to determine whether or not you have actually committed the crime you are accused of. These concepts are the cornerstone of democracy. Why do we even need to have these things written into law? Because power corrupts and absolute power corrupts absolutely. Because people in power have the power to deceive and the will to dominate and if not held in check history has proven that they will do so in order to maintain their control over society. Prior to the Magna Karta the King could throw anyone into jail on a whim and deny him legal representation or even the right to know what he was charged with. With the Patriot Act, "The United States is trying to overturn one of the most fundamental principles of Anglo-American jurisprudence and international law. This is a principle that is found in the Declaration of the Rights of Man, in the Universal Declaration of Human Rights, and in the International Covenant on Civil and Political Rights."[780]

> The dangerous aspects of the Patriot act include
> - warrantless surveillance and searches,
> - the ability of the government to tap your phone, read your email and even your post mail without a warrant demonstrating probable cause.
> - the monitoring of religious and political institutions not suspected of criminal activity
> - closed immigration hearings,
> - the ability of the government to secretly and indefinitely detain people without charging them,
> - medical records maintained by your doctor now must be surrendered to the government without a warrant demonstrating probable cause. In the 1930's in NAZI Germany doctors were also required to surrender citizens' private medical records to the state.[781]
> - a gag order imposed upon librarians or other records keepers who have been required to surrender records to the Feds which

---

779 Marrs, The Terror Conspiracy: Deception, 9/11 and the Loss of Liberty (New York, Disinformation, 2006) 301 – 302.
780 Michael Ratner and Ray Ellen Guantanamo: What the World Should Know (White River Junction: Chelsea Green Publishing Company, 2004) 6.
781 Naomi Wolf, The End of America: Letter of Warning to a Young Patriot (White River Junction: Chelsea Green Publishing, 2007) 8.

- prohibits them from telling the party in question that they are being investigated
- the denial of attorney/client privacy privilege for federal prisoners and even denying legal representation to Americans accused of crimes
- the ability of the government to seize personal property and search personal effects without a warrant and without probable cause.
- the ability to hold secret hearings in which the accused is not present to hear the charges and the ability to submit evidence against the charged while those defending the charged are not permitted to see the evidence.

The Patriot act also reversed the decisions and legislation that went into effect as a result of the Senate Subcommittee hearings of the 1970's where it was established that the military and the intelligence community could not surveil American Citizens unless there was probable cause. The watch lists which were outlawed in the 1970's have been established again. These lists are not just names of people to watch. They encompass the whole of one's life. According to the *New York Times*, Vermont Senator Patrick J. Leahy indicated that if you end up on a "watch list" it could keep you from flying or even getting a job. You may never know that you are on a watch list or even why.[782] "Federal Law Enforcement has sent watch lists to corporations containing names of individuals that were not under official investigation or wanted, but that the agency just had an interest in.[783] There are no established criteria for putting any one on a watch list. Somebody with the right connections who thinks you might be a "security risk" can put your name on a list. "Georgetown University Law Professor David D. Cole said, 'If being placed on a list means in practice that you will be denied a visa, barred entry, put on the no-fly list, targeted for pretextual prosecutions, etc., then the sweep of the list and the apparent absence of any way to clear oneself certainly raises problems.'"[784]

Millions of U.S. tax dollars are handed out in contracts to data mining corporations who create these "watch lists" for the government. They create data banks based on "suspicious patterns" of air travel for example. From these data banks they create a "risk assessment" which is tagged onto the name on a watch list. Even if someone only looks like or their name sounds like someone who is of interest to the government that name can be flagged as a *potential* terrorist. The process of putting names on a watch list and cross checking the names of travelers in a data bank is handled by private companies. As of June 2007 the National Counterterrorist Center had half a million names on the list of suspected terrorists. The Automated Targeting System (ATS), which became public in

---

782 Ibid, 97.
783 Marc Rich, The Hidden Evil (May 5, 2005 – http://www.thehiddenevil.com).
784 Marrs, The Terror Conspiracy: Deception, 9/11 and the Loss of Liberty (New York, Disinformatin, 2006) 284.

2006, has made a risk assessment rating of tens of millions of travelers passing through the U.S. The rating is based on suspicious patterns of behavior revealed through commercial data mining. For example, this information is provided by the airlines about "the passenger's history of one-way ticket purchases, seat preferences, frequent flyer records, number of bags, how they pay for tickets and even what meal they order."[785] Surveillance has now become a multibillion dollar industry. Since 9/11 the government has been outsourcing the job of surveillance to independent contractors. This of course created an increase in the number of corporations bidding on government contracts. The budget for independent contractors grew from $32 billion in 2002 to $43.5 billion in 2005. In fact many persons working in the intelligence community can leave their government job one day and start working as an independent contractor the next day for twice the pay.[786] Independent contractors were involved in the Abu Ghraib scandal because the military contracted out interrogation to civilians. The government has created a "security industrial complex" which according to one estimate will be worth $130 to $180 billion by 2010.[787] Now we have a real problem. We Americans love having a paycheck. They are rather necessary. We also enjoy a certain quality of life. Nobody likes living hand to mouth. Americans are now being paid to spy on their fellow Americans. There is a real political incentive to justify what you get paid to do. People become very dependent on that paycheck. They like having their bills paid, their retirement accounts full, and their better homes and gardens. It will happen in any job at any time that the validity of that position is being questioned. Should they actually get paid to do what they do? It is tax payer money that pays them. Has there ever been a job where part of that job doesn't become defending the position itself? Do we ever question the fact that we are paying our government billions of dollars to spy on us while they are cutting social spending, Law Enforcement and Social Security? Hello! How many people do you know who actually have enough integrity to stand up and say, "I quit! Nobody should get paid to do what I do? This is wrong!"

Then there is the community spy initiative called Terrorist Information and Prevention System (TIPS). Operation TIPS was presented to congress in July 2002 by the Bush administration. TIPS was promoted as a tool in the War on Terror. The intention was to recruit persons whose work provided access to homes, businesses and transportation systems such as mail men, utility workers (such as the good old White House plumbers) truck drivers and train conductors. The government was looking for 1 in 24 citizens to spy on their fellow Americans.[788]

---

785 Naomi Klein, The Shock Doctrine: The Rise of Disaster Capitalism (New York: Metropolitan Books, Henry Holt and Company, 2007) 304.
786 Tim Shorrock, Spies for Hire: The Secret World of Intelligence Outsourcing (New York: Simon and Schuster, 2008)113.
787 Naomi Wolf, The End of America: Letter of Warning to a Young Patriot (White River Junction: Chelsea Green Publishing, 2007) 43.
788 Ritt Goldstein, The U.S. Planning to Recruit One in 24 Americans a Citizen Spies (July 15, 2002 - http://www.smh.com.2002).

That would be 12 million and 503 thousand informants in a population of 300 million 72 thousand American citizens. This program was initially disapproved by Congress because Congress did not like the idea of Americans spying on one another. Maybe they remembered the Senate Hearings of the 1970's and the debacle of COINTELPRO. However, the program was approved under the black budget in another form. Thus we have your average citizen trained to spy on and be suspicious of their neighbors. It's human nature to want to feel important. It makes people feel important when they are a part of something. They think they are "serving their country". What the government has done is train roughly 4% of the population in covert operations – that includes safe cracking, lock picking, bypassing security systems, computer hacking, mail tampering, phone tapping not to mention the use of Directed Energy Weapons to drive their targets crazy, rape their victims and cause general physical and emotional mayhem. In other words they have been trained in the fine are of committing a crime without getting caught. Once you train them how to commit a crime without getting caught, you can't exactly un-train them. How then are you going to contain them and hold them accountable?

I am reminded of a television show I used to watch when I was a kid called *Lost in Space*. For those of you who are not old enough to remember, the program was about a family that had taken off from earth in a space ship and had gotten lost somewhere in the galaxy and was trying to find their way back home. Thus episode after episode was an adventure on some other new planet they have managed to land on. What I remember most is the boy named Will Robinson who had a robot companion with him everywhere he went. The robot was extremely good at sensing danger. When he suspected something was wrong he would flail about his arms made of gray corrugated medal and shout, "Danger Will Robinson! Danger Will Robinson!" Our independent journalists and writers have been telling us for years, "Danger America! Danger America!" More than one of those authors has noted the parallels between what is happening in America and what has happened in NAZI Germany and other fascist states. Naomi Wolf observes that most of Germany did not support the NAZIs until they paired citizen surveillance with state violence. Thus opposition was stifled. It began in 1930 when the SS spied on Brown shirts and kept files on them. Masses of citizens were under surveillance which included half a million in Berlin alone. State employees began keeping lists of "asocial" citizens. As a result of these lists people lost their jobs and benefits. People knew their conversations were no longer private and conversations of reports and political leaders were being bugged. People who lived through those years knew that they had been spied on by neighbors, coworkers, fellow students and police. Nannies, maids, office workers were all used as spies.[789] Czechoslovakia and China also used surveillance to crush democracy. Ritt Goldstein noted that

---

[789] Naomi Wolf, The End of America: Letter of Warning to a Young Patriot (White River Junction: Chelsea Green Publishing, 2007) 86 – 87.

the TIPS program will involve a higher percentage of informants that existed in the former East Germany.[790]

All the data mining that is accomplished by those outsourced security systems is used to build a file on every citizen of the United States of America. Those little loyalty cards that you get when you go to the grocery store that you use to get discounts are also used by the government to track your purchases. Those purchases are used to profile you. There is nothing that the United States government does not know about you. This system is similar to the Chinese Dangan file kept by the Chinese government on every Chinese citizen. The file has a record of every mistake you make which the elite might consider an indication that you are a threat to "state security". That file is available to your supervisor and follows you everywhere you go. All your phone calls and emails are logged and all your private bank transactions are recorded in your file.[791]

The enormous Talon (Threat and Local Observation Notice) database was used by the DOD CIFA (Counter Intelligence Field Activity) office to gather intelligence on thousands of US Citizens over a period of six years.[792] Information was passed to the DOD and NSA through emails from DOD undercover agents who attended meetings in churches, libraries and other places attended by anti-war activists who the DOD determined "might" be a threat. Grant Jeffery observes in *Shadow Government* that your private information which is on file with the United States Government is available to numerous policing agencies around the world. Corporate information marketers such as international credit agencies pay foreign corporations to obtain this information which was previously assumed to be private. "This means that untold numbers of strangers now know all about your lifestyle, purchases, tax records, and real-estate holdings". Jeffery also observes that anyone with enough computer knowledge can hack into those files and gain access to your information.[793] This leaves American Citizens open to exploitation by criminals, if not criminal elements within our own government.

Talon was developed by the military to gather intelligence on possible "terrorist" threats. Under a classified order dated July 12th 2005 CIFA (Counter Intelligence Field Activity) office was allowed to collect intelligence on U.S. citizens if there was reason to believe they were somehow connected to international terror activities, narcotics traffic, and foreign intelligence organizations and therefore posed a threat to national security. CIFA obtained information about Untied States Citizens from the NSA and DIA and it turns out that most of them were anti-war activists and the information about them came from monitoring meetings

---

790 Ritt Goldstein, The U.S. Planning to Recruit One in 24 Americans a Citizen Spies (July 15, 2002 - http://www.smh.com.2002).
791 Naomi Wolf, The End of America: Letter of Warning to a Young Patriot (White River Junction: Chelsea Green Publishing, 2007) 83.
792 Tim Shorrock, Tim Shorrock, Spies for Hire: The Secret World of Intelligence Outsourcing (New York: Simon and Schuster, 2008)181.
793 Grant Jeffery, Shadow Government: How the Secret Global Elite is using Surveillance against You (Colorado Springs: Waterbrook Press, 2009) 58.

held in churches, libraries, college campuses, etc. Some of the information in Talon about those people was from emails forwarded to the Department of Defense by infiltrators pretending to be members. The persons on the list were placed there not because they were violent but because they might become so.[794] Once again the DOD is overreaching into an area of "preemptive surveillance" that was common in the COINTELPRO period. Over a period of six years CIFA had developed dossiers on thousands of U.S. citizens using the Talon database.[795]

In 2003 Congress began raising probing questions about CIFA and the Pentagon investigation revealed that 260 records of about 13,000 total records improperly contained information about U.S. persons. CIFA's mission was to set collection standards while protecting the rights or U.S. Citizens. In 2007 the Privacy and Civil Liberties Oversight Board faulted the Pentagon for improper management of the Talon Database and improper and unauthorized collection and retention of information about U.S. Citizens.[796] Retired Air Force-General James Clapper, appointed as the new Undersecretary of Defense for Intelligence, determined in April 2007 that the results of the CIFA Talon database did not merit continuing the program particularly in light of its image in the media and the public.[797]

The most recent step in surveillance control of American citizens is the National ID card. As of December 2009 Americans are now required to carry a National ID card. Most Americans already had a driver's license which doubles as an ID card, but under the Emergency Supplemental Appropriations Act for Defense, the Global War on Terror and Tsunami Relief (2005) every citizen must now carry a National ID card. Not carrying an ID card can result in incarceration. It has standardized state-issued driver's licenses and nondriver ID cards. This act, also known as the Real ID act, has made it mandatory that all state ID's are compliant with federal standards. Not having a real ID card can keep you from flying, being employed and having a bank account.[798] The ID card would be linked to a unique identification number which would effectively link all government data bases together with all relevant information about each citizen. This would also make it mandatory for each citizen to submit his Real ID in order to gain access to health care. The National ID card would eventually replace passports, driver's licenses, voter registration cards, and even birth certificates.[799]

The government also wants to know where you are and what you are doing every minute of the day. In October 2002, Applied Digital Solutions Inc. of

---

794 Naomi Wolf, The End of America: Letter of Warning to a Young Patriot (White River Junction: Chelsea Green Publishing, 2007) 90.
795 Tim Shorrock, Spies for Hire: The Secret World of Intelligence Outsourcing (New York: Simon and Schuster, 2008) 181.
796 Ibid, 178.
797 Ibid, 181.
798 Jim Marrs, The Rise of the Fourth Reich (New York, NY: Harper Collins, 2008) 325.
799 Grant Jeffery, Shadow Government: How the Secret Global Elite is using Surveillance against You (Colorado Springs: Waterbrook Press, 2009) 51.

Palm Beach Florida began promoting their sub dermal personal verification chip, a radio frequency device about the size of the tip of a ballpoint pen that is implanted under the skin which will transmit data to various locations. The device contains a verification number that is read on a scanner and transmitted to a secure data storage sight via telephone or internet. The chip will be used to control access to public facilities such as government buildings, correctional facilities or transportation hubs. The chip will also be used in PC and laptop computers, personal vehicles, cell phones, homes, and apartments. The rational for the use of the chip is to stop ID theft and terrorism. By early 2006, fears of the chip became reality when a Cincinnati video surveillance firm, CityWatcher.com, put the chip in the arms of their employees. It was not mandatory but it set an unsettling precedent.[800]

Using implants such as the Verichip, the National Security Agency can monitor the whereabouts and experiences of millions of people at the same time. Using electromagnetic frequency brain stimulation, electronic signals can be sent to the brain controlling voice and visual experiences of the target. Astronauts were implanted with chips so that their thoughts could be followed and all their emotions could be monitored 24 hours a day. Implanted persons have no privacy then for the rest of their lives. "Using different frequencies, the secret controller of this equipment can even change a person's emotional life. She can be made aggressive or lethargic. Sexuality can be artificially influenced. Thought signals and subconscious thinking can be read, dreams affected and even induced, all without the knowledge or consent of the implanted person."[801] It is important to remember that when our government is talking about surveillance and they are telling us it is for reasons of national security, they are not just watching. They want to control you. These devices were developed not just to watch but to control.

They can turn you into a living breathing surveillance tool. Oh yes, you! They can also use the same device that they use to see what you see and hear what you hear, to make you hear and see what they want you to hear and see. They might decide to "reprogram" your thinking if you happen to disapprove of their agenda. John St. Clair Akwei became the victim of government Remote Neural Monitoring. The device sends signals to the brains auditory cortex which can create auditory hallucinations characteristic of paranoid schizophrenia. NSA operatives can see what the subject sees and they can see visual memory. They can also put images into the subjects brain while the subject is in REM sleep for purpose of programming the subject. John St. Clair Akwei filed suit against the National Security Agency in a DC federal courthouse (civil action 92-0449).[802]

---

800 Jim Marrs, The Terror Conspiracy: Deception, 9/11 and the Loss of Liberty (New York, Disinformatin, 2006) 324.
801 Rauni-Leena Lukanen-Kilde Microchip Implants, Mind Control, and Cybernetics (December 6, 2000 - http://www.conspiracyarchive.com).
802 Alex Constantine, Virtual Government (Los Angeles, CA: Feral House1997) 97.

Echelon is the massive surveillance system operating at Ft. Meade MD used to monitor cell phones, computers and all electronic transmissions from all around the world using keyword search software and a massive data bank. This has raised protests from many European nations though the government has refused to reveal this information to United States Citizens.[803] Echelon and Tempest were originally designed to track Soviet Leaders and the KGB. Echelon was launched by the NSA following World War II. In 1948 five Western nations, including the United States, the United Kingdom, Canada, Australia and New Zealand, entered into an agreement called UKUSA to spy on Russia and its Warsaw Pact allies. It is now being used to spy on American Citizens. The countries in agreement with each other spy on each other's citizens and then transmit the information to their respective countries. Thus they bypass their own legislation about spying on their own citizens. In fact the primary focus of Echelon is on non-military targets.[804] Israel has also used Echelon to spy on Arab terrorist groups.[805]

Echelon is triggered by key words and monitors approximately 90% of all phone calls made from the U. S. overseas or from overseas to the U.S. It is powerful enough to analyze any voice transmission and identify that voice. Your voice is as unique as your fingerprint, so if you call your mother and say, "Hi, Mom. It's me," they can figure out who "me" is even if you are calling from a payphone.

Echelon is headquartered at a U.S. military base on Menwhich Hill in the United Kingdom. It is likely the largest espionage station on the planet. Echelon gathers intelligence from 120 geostationary satellites in earth's orbit. In addition to the satellites the NSA also intercepts using collection platforms from high-altitude military and NSA aircraft, naval vessels, a large fleet of mobile surveillance vans, and the tapping of undersea fiber optic cables. The intercepted messages are transmitted back to NSA through massive undersea cables. Echelon captures and translates incepted conversations on more than 70 languages. It monitors communications from all the European Union, Russia and Asia.[806]

The danger is the use of this device for malevolent purposes. While the United States Government historically had denied the existence of Echelon, an investigation in Europe revealed that Echelon had been used to spy on two European companies, Airbus Industries and Thompson-CSF. This raised objections in Europe that America was using intelligence gathered from Echelon to steal business secrets.[807] Considering that the United States intelligence community is tied to big business

---

803 Jim Marrs, The Rise of the Fourth Reich (New York: William Morrow of Harper Collins Publishers, 2008) 329.
804 Grant Jeffery, Shadow Government: How the Secret Global Elite is using Surveillance against You (Colorado Springs: Waterbrook Press, 2009) 74-75.
805 Jim Marrs, The Terror Conspiracy: Deception, 9/11 and the Loss of Liberty (New York, Disinformatin, 2006) 102.
806 Grant Jeffery, Shadow Government: How the Secret Global Elite is using Surveillance against You (Colorado Springs: Waterbrook Press, 2009) 72.
807 Jim Marrs, The Terror Conspiracy: Deception, 9/11 and the Loss of Liberty (New York, Disinformatin, 2006) 326.

in such an unholy alliance, it is not at all surprising nor unlikely that this can occur. The New World Order does not like dissenters. What would happen if a businessman, who possessed some honesty and integrity, decided to speak out against the abuses of the United States Government? The intelligence from Echelon could easily be used by covert operators to shut down businesses who refuse to cooperate with the NWO agenda.

TEMPEST is ground based. It can read what is on your computer screen, the display of your ATM machine, television set and cash register.[808] It is the weakness in all computer systems that can be intercepted by anyone who knows what hardware and software you are using. Someone sitting in a van within line of sight of your computer can intercept the RF emissions from your hardware and duplicate it on another computer.[809] A key-logger device code named "Magic Lantern," which can be implanted in a computer by a virus-like program records every keystroke on your computer allowing authorities to know your passwords and use them to access encrypted data files. Also deleted files can be recovered and searched for incriminating evidence using a program called Encase.[810]

We have to consider that anything the government can do, a criminal with the right knowledge can also do. The line between criminal surveillance and government surveillance begins to fade with TIPS program when American citizens are hacking the computer systems of targeted citizens for the purpose of silencing those speaking out against criminal conduct sanctioned by the government. In fact in an upside down NWO world, decent citizens appear to be quickly labeled "threats to state security" and are being harassed in a criminal way by people actually "serving" the government.

The government has ways of tracking "criminals". The Veritrack system is a Global Positioning System that is used to track criminals or criminal suspects. The device is worn around the waist and the ankle. Law Enforcement is able to create electronic fences around areas prohibited to those wearing the Veritrack system. It is recharged on a charging base at night and at the same time uploads data to a central monitoring system which allows Law Enforcement to determine if the suspect or criminal has been near a crime scene that day. But what if you are really not a criminal? What if someone just decided you "might" be a threat to state security and decided to track your whereabouts? They can do that without a warrant or without any probable cause. And they can track your children too. The firm Digital Angel has also developed technology that will allow parents to log onto a computer and locate their children instantly.[811] That sounds wonderful.

---

808 Ibid, 326.
809 H. Michael Sweeney, The Professional Paranoid: How to Fight Back When Investigated, Stalked, Harassed or Targeted by Any Agency, Organization, or Individual (Venice: Feral House, 1998)78.
810 Jim Marrs, The Terror Conspiracy: Deception, 9/11 and the Loss of Liberty (New York, Disinformatin, 2006) 327 – 328.
811 Ibid, 328- 329.

The problem being is that it will most likely allow someone else besides a parent to locate that child whose intentions are not so noble. Someone in military intelligence such as Lt. Col. Michael Aquino, for example, may decide he wants to use your child as a mind controlled slave.

Do you like the privacy of your own home? It's not private anymore. The government can use your television set to see what is going on in your home. They can even turn it on at will.[812] Even without a camera in your home, you can be observed. Devices created to allow rescue teams to rescue injured people trapped in a broken down structure or even caught in an avalanche can also be used to watch what you are doing in your home. The Life Assessment Detector System (LADS), can be trained to recognize specific individuals and, thus, to track their movements within a building. The device which is about the size of a flashlight can determine by the unique "fingerprint" of your heartbeat just exactly who is inside the building as well.[813]

You know you already have a geopositional device in your automobile. Isn't it nice that Onstar can unlock you car for you if you lock your keys in your car. They can find you anywhere you go, and what if you don't want to be found? What if they decide to lock you *in* your car??? The capability to remote control your car is also in government hands. One day while I was driving a friend home my car suddenly spontaneously accelerated right before a huge rut in the driveway. I was fortunately able to stomp on the brakes in time. I also noticed one day while I was driving after a severe snow fall that my car "slid" to the side of the road. It didn't really slide. It was remote controlled. Stalkers were attempting to crash my vehicle. Consider what a fascist government can do with you are inside your car. In the process of researching this book I read a few accounts where people mysteriously drove their vehicles over a cliff. The cause of death was determined to be suicide. The person involved was someone who found disfavor in the eyes of someone in the Shadow Government.

With all this surveillance technology you would think the government would be satisfied. But no! They had to put surveillance chips inside your socks and underwear. These Radio Frequency Identification chips (RFID) are implanted in many consumer products including clothing and books or any other consumer product. Thus, when you purchase the item at the cash register with your debit or credit card, that RFID chip becomes attached to your name. That product which you purchased now can be traced anywhere it goes. So you have purchased some Fruit of the Loom underwear with RFID chips which are now attached to your name because you purchased them with your debit card. You put on the underwear and now you can be tracked via the RFID chip in your underwear.

---

812 Alex Constantine, Virtual Government (Los Angeles, CA: Feral House, 1997) 51.
813 H. Michael Sweeney, The Professional Paranoid: How to Fight Back When Investigated, Stalked, Harassed or Targeted by Any Agency, Organization, or Individual (Venice: Feral House, 1998) 80-82.

Wal-Mart has now required 100 or more of their distributors to put RFID chips in their products.[814]

One more item on my list of watching tools is your cell phone. It is no accident that almost everyone has one now. Those of course are equipped with geopositional devices. You can turn it off, but the government can turn it on if they want to use it to find you. Your cell phone can also be used as a microphone. The microphone in a cell phone is used for industrial espionage in stealing trade secrets from a competitor. It can be used in gaining the upper hand in business negations.[815]

Last but not least are those invisible spies hired by the U.S. Government who sneak into your home without your being aware that they are there. The government is working on invisibility technology which can conceal an object that is sitting in plain view. This involves meta material that will not reflect light or bends light around an object so that it becomes invisible. Information available to the public would indicate that this technology is not yet viable but close to being so. Another spy used by the U.S. Government that is also invisible is the "remote viewer". This is a technical term for astral projection, a practice common to those who use witchcraft. Although the term "remote view" does not always involve the spirit of a person taking a temporary trip out of one's body, this does occur. The U.S. Government has contracted with Scientologists and others who practice astral projection. "Remote viewing (RV) is a term of art, describing a particular protocol used in consciousness research. In this protocol a *viewer* attempts to gather sense impressions, and "knowingness", i.e., nonsensorial information about a target."[816] Remote viewing is also another word for Extra Sensory Perception.

The term "Remote Viewing" was created by artist and Ingo Swann, an OT Level VII Scientologist who created the protocol for remote viewing with other remove viewers hired by the US Government to use for military purposes. His partners were laser physicists Russell Targ & Hal Puthoff also a Scientologist and Ed May a nuclear physicist. Former assistant to the Chief of Naval Operations, Stephan A. Schwartz developed a similar protocol which he called Distant Viewing. Steven Schwartz in his research was attempting to determine if Distant Viewing ability was electromagnetic in nature or something else. He read the work of a Soviet researcher Leonid Vasiliev who had eliminated from remote viewing the entire electromagnetic spectrum except for ELF frequencies.

The US Government has been interested in ESP research since WWII when it was learned that the USSR and China had placed a high priority on ESP research. The remote viewing program was initiated out of concern about reports that the Soviet Union was investigating psychic phenomena. US intelligence sources had learned that the Soviet Union was engaged in "Psychotronic" research. Most disturbing were indications that the Soviets were employing psychics to harm their

---

814 Grant Jeffery, Shadow Government: How the Secret Global Elite is using Surveillance against You (Colorado Springs: Waterbrook Press, 2009) 38-39.
815 Ibid, 19.
816 Wikipedia, Remote Viewing (http://en. wikipedia.org).

adversaries using telepathy and even to the point of killing their targets.[817] This led to a visit by two employees of the CIA's Directorate of Science and Technology to Ingo Swan and Hal Puthoff. The visit resulted in a project sponsored and funded by the CIA to the tune of $50,000 with the goal of using psychic abilities to augment U.S. intelligence efforts. The CIA began funding remote viewing research in 1972 at the Sanford Research Institute (SRI) in Menlo Park, CA conducted by Russell Targ and Harold Puthoff. The program began with a few gifted remote viewers such as artist Ingo Swann. Many of the SRI Remote Viewers were from The Church of Scientology. Those receiving training in the program were to use their talents for "psychic warfare." They were required to achieve 65% accuracy and the level was often exceeded. The grant was later renewed and expanded.

A later version of the program conducted at For George G. Meade in MD was Grill Flame in which hundreds of remote viewing experiments were conducted through 1986. Here Ingo Swann developed the standard protocol for remote viewing. In 1984 the National Academy of Sciences National Research Council reevaluated the remote viewing program for the Army Research Institute with unfavorable results. Army funding ended in 1985, the program was redesignated SUN STREAK and transferred to the DIA's Scientific and Technical Intelligence Directorate. Under the DIA the program transitioned to the Science Applications International Corporation (SAIC) in 1991 and was renamed STAR GATE. Edwin May presided over 70% of the budget and 85% of the data collection.[818] Over a period of 20 years $20 million dollars were spent on the remote viewing programs. Over forty personnel served in the program at various times, with 23 remote viewers. Those involved with the team were sure that remote viewers were actually leaving their bodies and traveling to the locations they were describing. They called this "exteriorization with full perception" a phrase coined by the creator of Scientology, L. Ron Hubbard. Both Puthoff and Swann were graduates of Scientology Training Courses in which they were promised by Hubbard that they would be able to leave their bodies at will to perceive remote events. This remove viewing went beyond perceiving events to controlling events and the minds of other people. This was a power called "Thelema" by Ron Hubbard's mentor, none other than black magician Aleister Crowley.[819]

I am experiencing harassment by stalkers and I have experienced the presence of "remote viewers" in my home as well. I have talked to other victims of government harassment who have also struggled with astral projecting spirits. One young man who had been dismissed from military service because he was "hearing voices" told me that astral projecting spirits were trying to smother him to death.

---

817 Jonathan Caven-Atack, The Hubbard Intelligence Agency (August 15, 2009- http:/www.remoteviewing.html).
818 John Pike, STAR GATE [Controlled Remote Viewing] (December 29, 2005 - http://www.fas.org).
819 Caven-Atack Jonathan The Hubbard Intelligence Agency (Dialog Centre International. - August 15, 2009 - http:/www.remoteviewing.html).

This is the age of the New World Order. In this age things are never what they appear to be. The proponents of the New World Order abide by no ethical code but rather ascribe to a "situational ethics". Thus it is okay to lie, cheat steal and commit murder if it furthers their agenda. The term "situational ethics" is a misnomer. There is nothing at all ethical about it. It is another way of saying, "If I am not winning the game the way I want to, I just change the rules to give myself the advantage." The NWO has accomplished in their surveillance having divided and conquered America at last. They have managed to turn American citizens against each other. Thus they have divided and weakened this nation, and a nation divided against itself cannot stand. They know this. That was the idea.

35. Organized Vigilante Stalking

Law Enforcement has developed "policing groups" in every city all across America and Directed Energy Weapons have been put in the hands of ordinary citizens who "stalk" and harass people who have been targeted for various reasons. They are the "non-traditional foes" spoken of in the Pentagon directive.

During the COINTELPRO era, the FBI used unethical and illegal methods of harassing, disrupting and destroying the lives of ordinary citizens who had broken no laws but whom Law Enforcement feared "might" be a threat to state security.[820] The Senate Sub Committee Hearings outlawed COINTELPRO. However, the intelligence community apparently feels it is above the law. They are still using COINTELPRO tactics on American citizens who again have broken no laws. Only now they have at their disposal Directed Energy Weapons to use against these innocent civilians but which cannot be traced to the criminals who use them. Anyone can become a target. The "watch lists" which the National Security Agency used to spy on American citizens who "might" be a threat again were outlawed, but after the passage of the Patriot Act they have become legal again.[821] Ergo, you can be placed on a "watch list" because someone considered you to be a threat though you have broken no laws, and you can be targeted for harassment by these community stalking groups and zapped with Directed Energy Weapons. Targets who have become victims of this kind of criminal activity have little or no recourse because the stalking activity is all covert, and there is little or no hard evidence. However, when victims do have evidence it is generally ignored and the victims are labeled, "mentally ill."[822]

People of primary concern to the establishment are people who have moral values. They want to make changes that people with a conscience won't want to accept. For example using mind control technology to correct and control populations of people and force them into submission might be abhorrent to

---

820 Mark Rich, The Hidden Evil (May, 2005 – http://www.thehiddenevil.com).
821 Naomi Wolf, The End of America: Letter of Warning to a Young Patriot (White River Junction: Chelsea Green Publishing, 2007) 96.
822 Mark Rich, The Hidden Evil (May, 2005 – http://www.thehiddenevil.com).

those of us who have a conscience. In a 1994 publication by the Strategic Studies Institute (SSI) of the US Army War College entitled *The Revolution in Military Affairs and Conflict Short of War* the authors state "Because the authors recognize that Americans have moral values which would 'form significant constraints' in using this technology it would take a 'perceived war for national survival' to soften them up to accept the changes."[823] One of the steps dictators take to push democracies toward a fascist shift is to invoke a national threat. In this case the "national threat" was the 911 attacks.[824] In fact since the 911 attacks there have been many pieces of legislation that have eroded away at the integrity of the United States Constitution. Laws that were put into place to guard your rights as an American citizen have been nullified by the Patriot Act passed in the wake of the 911 attacks. Your home can now be invaded without a warrant and without your consent or knowledge because you were considered a "threat to national security". Your bank account can be monitored, your phone tapped and your computer hacked and your mail pilfered. You can basically be convicted of a crime you never committed, or even knew you were accused of committing. You can be followed everywhere you go. Your bookseller has to surrender of a list of the books you are reading to "officials" who ask. Your doctor has to surrender up your medical records. Your psychiatrist and your psychologist can no longer protect your privacy and neither can your attorney.

You may never know that you are actually being monitored. As long as you haven't done something to upset someone, like speak out against abortion too loudly, or as long as you don't' mind making moral compromises when asked to do so at work and as long as you don't bluster too loudly about globalization or simply upset the status quo, you may never be threatened. If you do you could become a victim like one in 100 Americans today and millions around the globe. Statistics posted on a multitasking website indicate that about 3.5% of the working population of Sweden is subject to mobbing which is organized stalking in the workplace. According to the U.S. Center for Disease Control, 4.5 people per 100 report having been harassed or stalked at one time and statistics from the British government Home Office report 1,900,000 persons in the UK being stalked or harassed at any one time in 2001. That is about 3 people per 100. About %45 percent of them are men. Per the Office of Research Development and Statistics of the British Government Home Office there were roughly 55,000 reported cases of organized stalking in 1988/1999. This figure rose to roughly 220,000 cases by the year 2004/2005. About one in 100 Americans are being stalked by government sponsored terrorist groups.[825] According to Mark Rich, 1 in 24 Americans are

---

823 Glenn Krawczyk, Big Brother's Recipe for 'Revolution in Military Affairs' (June – July 1995 – http://www.ivanfraser.com).
824 Naomi Wolf, The End of America: Letter of Warning to a Young Patriot (White River Junction: Chelsea Green Publishing, 2007) 35-36.
825 Vigilante and Harassment Groups: They're here, they're Real, (May 11, 2007 –http://www.multistalkervictims.org).

cooperating in gangstalking activity.[826] The population of America according to the 2009 statistics from the U.S. Census Bureau is 307,212,123 people. If one in100 Americans are now being targeted for harassment, that would be about 3,072,121 people being targeted for harassment by the U.S. Government. Let me say that the long way. We are talking about three million, seventy two thousand and one hundred and twenty one people. This is what is called a Holocaust.

In 1981 Executive order NO.12333 (December 4, 1981) legalized COINTELPRO activities that were outlawed with the Senate Hearings in the 1970's. It allows for specialized equipment (DEW) or specialized knowledge of the FBI, CIA and all branches of the armed forces to be accessible to Local Law Enforcement. "All are free to mount electronic & mail surveillance without a warrant, & the FBI may also conduct warrantless 'unconsented physical searches' (break ins) ..." The U.S. Patriot Act superseded Executive order No. 12333 which made COINTELPRO tactics legal and authorizes someone to conduct an investigation of you without a real reason or without a court order. That means there is no oversight of agencies with a history of civil rights violations and abuse. There is also no paper trail. According to Ted L. Gunderson 1 in 10 Americans will be recruited to spy on other Americans in some way.[827]

Let me briefly describe how gangstalking manifests and how it operates. The gangstalkers first task is to isolate the victim from family or friends or anyone who may provide support.[828] They begin with the smear campaign that is typically launched through a bogus investigation using a target's family, friends and employers. The objective of the smear campaign is to isolate the victim. The isolation is effected by giving those involved a gag order that deters family friends and associates from telling the targeted person that they are being investigated. Thus those who are being told that the target is being investigated cannot speak to the person who is allegedly being investigated. This becomes an invisible wall between the target and support structures. Those conducting the "investigation" will carry a "case file" which will indicate that the target is "probably" a rapist, pedophile, drug dealer, prostitute, terrorist or racist. Or the "investigators" will say they cannot reveal the cause of the investigation for "reasons of national security". The "pedophile" label may be the most common. Those who become involved in the investigation will be told they are being of service to their country or community thus ensuring their cooperation.[829]

The smear campaign can come from someone who is just pretending to be a concerned citizen or someone either disguised as a public official such as Law Enforcement or from public officials who are also participating. The effect is to discredit the person so that no one will believe anything the victim says when they

---

826 Mark Rich, The Hidden Evil (May, 2005 – http://www.thehiddenevil.com).
827 Ibid.
828 Elenor White, Book Review: Terrorist [Citizen Gang] Stalking in America by David Lawson (May 15, 2007 - http://www.shoestringradio.net/terstalk.htm).
829 Mark Rich, The Hidden Evil (May, 2005 – http://www.thehiddenevil.com).

start to complain about what is happening to them. This tends to have the effect of isolating the individual who may want to draw away from support structures because they are not listening and are responding to the victim in a way that is very offensive. You can avoid this issue by being very discerning. Remember that in a real investigation the investigator is trying to get information and not give it. A real investigator also has to avoid putting ideas into your head so in case you are called upon to testify, your testimony will be considered valid in a court of law. If the investigator says too much and it is determined that he put ideas into your head your testimony could be considered invalid in a court of law. There is also the risk that the information you glean from the questioning may be passed on to the person being investigated which would hamper the investigation and tip off the party involved. If the party being investigated is actually guilty of a crime, being tipped off could tempt the party involved to go into hiding. It is not wise to sign any agreements to keep quiet about what you were told. You could be held legally accountable for alerting the party involved that someone was asking questions about them. If the party doing the "investigation" is in fact a criminal stalker, you don't want to help him in any way. As soon as the "investigator" asks you to keep something secret you should automatically be suspicious. Get his/her name and phone number and if he/she has a badge or a license get the badge/license number. You can call the police to verify that that party is a legitimate investigator.

The goals of the gang stalker include mind control of the victim; [830] to create poison and drug induced psychotic episodes and paranoia, [831] to neutralize dissidents, to keep victims unemployed, induce homelessness, and reduce the quality of their lives resulting in a nervous breakdown and to drive the person to commit acts of violence against themselves, such as suicide, and/or against others.[832] This is done in such a way as that those who engaged the stalkers and identified the victim are protected from being exposed. The actions of stalkers are covert and they have at their disposal the entire arsenal used by the CIA and US intelligence community because it is government sponsored.[833] Their arsenal includes a combination of tactics used by the KKK and those used by the FBI in COINTELPRO combined with the use of chemical agents and Directed Energy Weapons and mind control techniques developed under the CIA's MKULTRA program.[834]

People who become victims have been targeted by businesses and large corporations who have someone they want to get rid of for various and sundry reasons but don't want to pay the cost of firing. These vigilante groups are "for hire"

---

830 Elenor White, Book Review: 1996 by Elenor White (http://www.shoestringradio.net).
831 Mental Health Abuse Psychological Harassment (November 23, 2006 - http://psychologyharass.wordpress.com).
832 Mark Rich, The Hidden Evil (May, 2005 – http://www.thehiddenevil.com).
833 Ibid.
834 Ibid.

for anyone who has the connections and the funds to pay them for their services.[835] A target could have "upset someone". Targets are often corporate whistleblowers. Julianne McKinney reported that during her investigation a large number of targets were single career women who lived alone.[836] Political activists are typical targets, as well as people who oppose globalization. There appears to be a large number of postal employees who have become targets. Many Post Masters have been former CIA employees and Post Offices have become labs for mind control experimentation. Generally anyone who is considered "undesirable" by the elite establishment can become a target which can include the elderly, the disabled and disabled children. Typically, family members of targets can come under attack because the idea is to "treat" the entire family tree.[837] This may be an extension of the old card file system spoken of earlier where "inferior bloodlines" were identified and marked for extinction. This also fulfills the Bilderberger agenda for targeting people for destruction who refuse to bend to the wishes of the established elite.

Those who participate in gangstalking may seem like ordinary people. In fact very decent citizens can be convinced to participate when they are fed very cleverly concocted lies. Someone with a clip board and a lanyard who looks very official will convince anyone. Suites and ties and fake FBI badges can do the trick as well as the "case file". Of course posing as a concerned citizen or local police or sheriff will work too. It is a known fact that the employees of the FBI, CIA and local Law Enforcement have participated in targeting people who have really committed no crimes. As long as it looks official, perfectly innocent people can be convinced to do things they would normally not be willing to do. In fact they may be simply asked to "report" "keep an eye out" which seems harmless enough. But the seed of doubt has been sewn. Community watch groups are also used as harassment groups. They go through desensitization training to soften their consciences so they won't feel bad about what they are doing.[838] They are in effect told very cleverly concocted lies about the individual who they are stalking so they will believe that the target "deserves" what they get.

Some people are bribed into participating and some are blackmailed into participating.[839] Those who recruit participants in stalking gangs have again all the tools available to the US intelligence community because it is state sponsored. That means they have been doing background searches on individuals they want to recruit. If there are any skeletons in your closet that you don't want anyone to know about which could be very damaging to you, it can be used to gain your cooperation in a group harassment campaign. Ex convicts are often recruited

---

835   Elenor White, Book Review: Terrorist [Citizen] Gang Stalking in America by David Lawson (May 15, 2007 - http://www.shoestringradio.net).
836   Julianne McKinney, Microwave Harassment & Mind Control Experimentation (December 1992 -http:llwww.xs4all.nl).
837   Mark Rich, The Hidden Evil (May, 2005 – http://www.thehiddenevil.com).
838   Ibid.
839   Mental Health Abuse Psychological Harassment (November 23, 2006 - http://psychologyharass.wordpress.com).

because they can't find employment anywhere else. These groups operate much like the German STASI who often recruited even family members to spy on one another. It is known that church officials have been used in harassment campaigns perhaps because of course they bought the lie or because they were overzealous and wanted to "keep sinners in line."[840]

Once you have been convinced to cooperate, you will be persuaded to increase your level of participation from "spying" to "harassing". It may seem like harmless harassment to you, but to the one being harassed it is just one layer of a very destructive campaign. Because each person in the group only does a little harassing, they can't be prosecuted for anything.[841]

The victim has been studied well in advance of the beginning of the campaign. Those targeting the individual may actually befriend the target in order to gain his/her confidence so they can learn as much as possible about the person. The target is thoroughly investigated in order to determine what will cause the target to break. Cheryl welsh experienced this while she was a mind control experimentation victim.[842]

Typically the tactics involved in gangstalking include the following;[843]

- Sudden, bizarrely-rude treatment, isolation and acts of harassment and vandalism by formerly friendly neighbors
- Harassing telephone calls, which continue even after the targeted individual obtains new, unlisted telephone numbers.
- Mail interception, theft and tampering.
- Noise campaigns.
- Recurrent confrontations by unusually hostile strangers and comments by strangers which appear intended to evoke "paranoid" reactions.
- Entries into the individual's residence, during the late-night hours while he/she is sleeping, and or during the day when the individual is elsewhere.
- Rapidly deteriorating health, generally of a digestive nature (due to ingesting poisons).
- Sleep disruption/deprivation which is done overtly and electronically
- Vandalism of privately-owned vehicles
- Staged accidents

---

840 Mark Rich, The Hidden Evil (May, 2005 – http://www.thehiddenevil.com).
841 Ibid.
842 Cheryl Welsh, U.S. Human Rights Abuse Report (January 1998 - http://www.mindjustice.org).
843 Julianne McKinney, Microwave Harassment & Mind Control Experimentation (December 1992 - http:llwww.xs4all.nl).

- Isolation of the individual from members of his/her family – virtually assured when highly focused forms of electronic harassment commences.
- Progressive financial impoverishment, brought on by termination of the individual's employment, and compounded by expenses associated with the harassment.

Once harassment commences a target may experience all of the above, particularly intense attack with Directed Energy Weapons and poisoning of food and beverages. Most gangstalking victims who know they are being targeted and know what to expect can guard against some of the tactics. Most targeted individuals will not drink any liquids that were left in their houses while they were out. The attacks are very subtle, such as a violation of personal space, or someone blatantly staring at you. A stalker will invade a targets home and take something stupid such as rolls of toilet paper or one plate from a set of dishes. Targeted individuals may experience recurring car repairs which normally would not be a problem because all cars need repairs from time to time. However, there will be repeated need for repairs that happen too often for it to be what would normally be expected. Many targets give up driving all together which is what stalkers want. This increases the targets level of isolation.[844] Computers are continually hacked and working on a computer can be very hazardous because those who harass may be constantly disrupting your ability to accomplish anything. If the victim complains about any of these tactics, they will appear to be paranoid and targets are typically diagnosed with mental illnesses.[845] Unfortunately The American Psychiatric Associate has virtually insured that this will happen because when they wrote the DSM they included the symptoms of gangstalking in the list of symptoms for paranoid schizophrenia.[846]

Targets are typically blacklisted and are thus unable to find and maintain employment. The government now has "watch lists" which were outlawed during the Senate investigations into COINTELPRO in the late seventies. The Patriot Act made them legal again. Thus these lists are accessible to employers to check for anyone who may be applying for jobs. Some employers even actively participate in harassment of persons applying for jobs with their companies.[847] Julianne McKinney remarks on the impoverishment of those so targeted.[848]

---

844 Julianne McKinney, Microwave Harassment & Mind Control Experimentation (December 1992 - http:llwww.xs4all.nl).
845 Mark Rich, The Hidden Evil (May, 2005 – http://www.thehiddenevil.com).
846 Rauni-Leena Lukanen-Kilde, Microchip Implants, Mind Control, and Cybernetics (December 6, 2000. - http://www.conspiracyarchive.com).
847 Mark Rich, The Hidden Evil (May, 2005 – http://www.thehiddenevil.com).
848 Julianne McKinney, Microwave Harassment & Mind Control Experimentation (December 1992 - http:llwww.xs4all.nl).

The majority of those now in contact with the Project — white-collar professionals — have lost their jobs. Termination of employment in many of these cases involved prefatory harassment by the employer and co-workers, which coincided with the other overt forms of harassment discussed above!

The person whose name ends on a list may never know that they have been listed and therefore have no recourse for appealing. A person's name can be on a watch list even though they have broken no laws and committed no crimes. Most targeted individuals are either unemployed or underemployed. There are literally hundreds of thousands of very employable people being pushed out of the workforce. Attorneys who attempt to help are threatened with the loss of their careers if they do so.[849]

Sadly, local businesses are also participating in harassing victims. They can charge a victim more money than they would anyone else. One person who the author interviewed who is likely a gangstalking victim took his cat to the Vet and the Vet was very rude to him. In addition, the Vet quoted him one price to do what needed to be done, and when the procedure was completed he charged him double what he was told he would have to pay. This is also a typical scenario for gangstalking victims. Local business owners are being told that they are assisting Homeland Security. Homeland Security is again an organization that functions much like the German STASI or the Russian KGB. In fact former agents of the German Staci were solicited by the government to assist with Homeland Security.[850]

One of the problems with the mindset of Organized Vigilante stalking is this idea of "preemptive" intervention. This is the idea that was portrayed in the film starring Tom Cruise entitled "Minority Report". In the movie, "proclears" were able to see if a crime were going to be committed in the future and thus warn authorities. However, the authorities would arrest the "would be" criminal before a crime was actually committed. During the COINTELPRO period groups of law abiding citizens were targeted by the FBI because they "might get violent." What stalkers are doing is committing a crime to prevent a crime from happening. Someone who someone determined might commit a crime is harassed and victimized. If you follow that to its logical conclusion it is easy to see what insanity the whole concept really is. The truth is the stalkers are committing a crime against people who have not committed a crime. If they had they could be tried in a court of law. The truth is also that there is not a single person on this planet that is not capable of committing a crime. We are all sinners. One sure way of making it impossible for anyone to commit a crime is to blow everybody up. Once the planet is cleared of humanity, there will be no possibility of any crime being committed.

---

849 Ibid.
850 Mark Rich, The Hidden Evil (May, 2005 – http://www.thehiddenevil.com).

Considering that there is so much surveillance going on all over the planet, one would think that would be enough to ensure against a crime being committed. Statistically since 2001 crime appears to be declining ever so lightly. However, there are more than 3,000,000 victims of gangstalking in America. Gangstalkers use DEW assault on their victims, they use biological agents, they hack computer systems and are guilty of multiple forms of malicious behavior which goes unreported because Law Enforcement is not permitted to do anything or because the victims cannot prove that a crime has been committed. Most recently when I decided to report my own microwave harassment, Law Enforcement showed up after the second call, they told me to contact the City Council and did not even take a report. When I asked them why they were not taking a report they asked me, "What do you want us to report?" They did however take the license plate numbers of strange vehicles that were constantly parked outside my apartment. Those vehicles subsequently disappeared. The officers gave no indication that they understood what was involved with DEW assault. Covert operations are designed to allow the perpetrators of criminal activity to cover their tracks in such a way that it does not even appear that a crime has been committed. OVS is another covert operation initiated by fascists in the Shadow Government attempting to occupy this nation. Because they are able to deceive the public, it goes unchecked. With such intensive surveillance going on it should really not be at all difficult to prove that a crime is being committed. However, the truth of the matter is surveillance is not about stopping crime and it is not having an impact at all on the crime rate. Surveillance is in place to control people who would rightfully object the crimes being committed against decent Americans by stalkers and criminal elements of our own government. The real criminals are not being watched.

36. The Rule of Law

You might have begun to wonder if there really is any such thing as Law Enforcement in America anymore. It might have begun to dawn on you that if we have federal officials, including Presidents, who have no respect for our Constitution, then having Law Enforcement at the local level might be rather difficult. It should be apparent that there are people who believe themselves to be above the law, or at least have no fear of facing the legal consequences of their actions. Why is that? How is it that we have Presidents and Vice Presidents who feel perfectly safe molesting children, making sex slaves out of women and using both to traffic in illegal drugs? How is it that due process was so lightly thrown aside for the Muslim victims thrown into American concentration camps accused and convicted of crimes they did not commit? And why do we have this parallel criminal "justice" system operating underground victimizing American citizens who have committed no crime while those who hammer them with DEW's, (assault with a deadly weapon) invade their homes (illegal entry), steal their possessions, (theft), spread gossip and slander to discredit otherwise decent citizens, tampering with their cars, (vandalism) tampering with their mail, (a federal offense), poisoning their food and water, and otherwise attempting to drive them to commit suicide (attempted murder) running rampant with no fear of prosecution? You might be asking, why bother with Law Enforcement?

Why indeed? That is an important question, and we must ask it and give it much thought. Why do we have laws – I mean really? From a Christian point of view and a biblical point of view, that is quite simple – people are sinful. In fact all people are sinful. The Scripture plainly tells us "… for all have sinned and fallen short of the Glory of God" (Romans 3:23 NKJV). That verse says two things; 1) We all done it and 2) None of us has measured up to the standard of God's perfect Glory. Not only are we corrupted, but there is a standard by which we are measured and that standard is God – perfect, incorruptible, holy. The law according to the scripture was intended to do one very important thing, to show us how impossible it is for us to be what God is – perfect. "For what the law could not do, in that it was weak through the flesh, God sending his own Son in the likeness of sinful flesh, and for sin, condemned sin in the flesh, that the righteousness of the law might be fulfilled in us, who walk not after the flesh, but after the Spirit (Romans 8:3,4 NKJV). Jesus came to fulfill that law in us. By his death and resurrection we are able to have his indwelt presence in our beings to conform us to that holy incorruptible standard.

But there is a problem. The Bible calls it flesh. Our bodies are made of corrupted stuff. It has desires that are corrupted and a will that is corrupted and conscience that is corrupted. Even those of us who have the indwelt presence of Jesus Holy Spirit still have to wrestle with this corrupted flesh while we are being transformed into God's image. In other words, it takes time. Not everyone has accepted this, and therefore there are people who have not surrendered themselves to the saving power of Jesus Christ so there is nothing to restrain their flesh except – the law. Jesus said, "For verily I say unto you, Till heaven and earth pass, one jot or one title shall in no wise pass from the law, till all be fulfilled" (Mat 5:18 NIV). The scripture tells us that all of creation is waiting in eager expectation of this fulfillment and it groans under the weight of human corruption. "…because the creature itself also shall be delivered from the bondage of corruption into the glorious liberty of the children of God" (Rom 8:21 NKJV).

But you actually feel like you're a pretty decent Joe, don't ya? I'll just bet you can find people in your world who might disagree with that. Truth is we all mess up. And people get upset with us when we do things that disappoint them. We all have a set of standards and they are all different. Some people react pretty strongly to some things that we ourselves don't feel is all that bad. We don't all see things alike. But we all have a tendency to be pretty punitive when people do things we don't like. We have laws because we have to have a stable standard. Laws prevent chaos. They ensure justice is equal across the board. Laws protect everybody. So when somebody does something wrong, we have a law that says, "You can't do that." And we have laws that say, "This is the prescribed penalty for breaking the law." Laws are written when people are thinking and not reacting. They are put down in advance so that when a crisis occurs and people's emotions are charged up, the law prevents overreacting. Emotions can drive us to do things that should not happen in a civilized stable society. Laws also prevent people from having to pay a penalty for a crime they did not commit. Because all people are sinful, it is possible for them to either knowingly or otherwise accuse someone of doing something they did not do. Due process allows for the accused to face their accuser, to know what they are accused of and to have legal defense. Due process ensures that the accused can speak up on their own behalf and eliminates things like coerced confessions and hearsay evidence from being used against the accused.

The law is not perfect and does not prevent crime from happening. It is not possible to create a system of laws that will create a crime free society. One of the reasons why the law itself cannot create a crime free society is that there are people who **wantonly and deliberately disobey** the law but are very good at not getting caught. If laws could make people into decent people, Jesus would not have had to go to the cross and die for us. But we are in this in between place where those who have accepted God's free gift of salvation have not been perfectly transformed into his perfect holy image and those who refused him have not been removed. So we have laws to hold back the tide of evil while God is giving people time to make a choice to accept him or deny him. God is waiting because he does not desire for anyone to perish but that all should come to the saving knowledge of his son Jesus Christ. "The Lord is not slack concerning his promise, as some men count slackness; but is longsuffering toward us, not willing that any should perish, but that all should come to repentance" (2Pe 3:9 NIV).

What we have to understand is simple – we are all very sinful people. We all deserve to die because of the sins we have committed. Many of us don't feel like we are worthy of death. But neither have we stood face to face or eye to eye with a Holy God, so we really have no real idea of just how badly corrupted we really are. We all seem to feel pretty comfortable criticizing our neighbors, but that is a dangerous thing to do when we really have not come to that place of facing our own shame. That is why we have laws. Laws tell us not to do certain things, and they also tell us what we can and cannot do to enact justice on those who have violated that law because we are imperfect judges. ***Laws also prevent the strong from running roughshod over the weak***. That is they stand in the way of the elite establishment who have no respect for life or human rights. People who have power are inevitably going to abuse that power and cause harm to those who have less power. Laws are designed to prevent that from happening.

This brings us to the Constitution of the United States of American and our Bill of Rights. These will do us no good if we don't respect them and defend them. That is what takes courage and vigilance. In order to maintain a civilized and stable society we all have to be on our toes and we have to be willing to defend that Constitution with our lives. When we get lazy, corruption creeps in and we have a situation like what I have discussed in the first paragraph – rampant lawlessness. This also leads to the lawless acts of gangstalkers who are terrorizing innocent civilians who have broken no laws. This leads to secret courts where innocents are accused of crimes that they did not commit and never knew they were accused of committing. This leads to an upside-down criminal justice system in which criminals get away with murder and innocents are tried for crimes they did not commit and where they have no defense against the criminals who are accusing them.

One other thing that I like to think about is the way God designed the Nation of Israel. There are lots of nations in the world and lots of variations in government, but there is only one Nation that had a government that was designed by God himself and not by the people of the nation. That is the Nation of Israel. So when I start to see what is going wrong in American society, I like to compare it with the original Nation of Israel that God designed. They had Ten Commandments. There were actually more than just ten laws, but all the law could be summed up in Ten Commandments. All of them were contained in a few pages of scripture which you did not need an expert to understand. There were not ten gazillion bazillion laws with endless loopholes to exploit. Amazing! There were no jails. If you committed a crime you made recompense. If you deliberately killed someone you paid with your life. If you killed someone by accident you had to go stay in what were called *cities of refuge* and you had to remain there until the Priest in charge of that city died. Therefore, those who were wounded by the death you caused, albeit accidently, were assured that you were being held accountable and life could go on. I also find it also very heartening that those who were responsible for investigating crime and executing justice were the priests. There were no police wearing blue robes and silver badges. Law Enforcement was the priesthood. These were the same people who were responsible for going before God and offering up the sacrifices for the sins of the people. Now I want you to understand this. The sacrifices that were offered didn't really atone for the sin, but they represented the sacrifice that God would make in the future when he offered up his own son as payment for our sins. Hear me. God is the judge. The Priest brings the criminal before the judge and states the crime. The criminal is convicted. But the Judge's son paid the price. Jesus is referred to in scripture as our Great High Priest. He brings us before God with the charge, and he pays the price for our crime.

I want to image this in modern vernacular. Maybe you haven't any run ins with the law other than an occasional speeding ticket. So you go before the Judge and the Cop who pulled me over is standing there explained the charge. You are convicted. You have a stiff fine to pay and you can't afford it. It's too much. So the Cop says, "She can't pay that fine, Judge. I'll pay it for her." Would he do that? Probably not, but that is exactly what Jesus did, and the penalty was death, not a few hundred dollars. The price we would have to pay for the crimes we committed we can never pay. In other words we would be paying it forever in a place called Hell. But Jesus, who conquered death for all, paid the fine we could not pay.

Here is where I have to pause again. There is no one who has not committed a crime against God for which he deserves death. From the scriptural point of view we all deserve to die. Ergo, when enacting justice, we have to keep in mind that we all need mercy, and while I don't necessary feel very merciful toward those who committed crimes against me or some of the victims I have written about, the blood of Jesus applies to us all. There are some pretty hardened criminals in Washington who have hidden some heinous crimes behind the National Security Act and have avoided being held accountable to the law. We can't maintain a stable society and let that go on. In fact God will enact justice on them. The scripture tells us, "Do not be deceived, God is not mocked: for whatever a man sows that shall he also reap. For he who sows to his flesh will of the flesh reap corruption, but he who sows to the Spirit will of the Spirit reap everlasting life (Gal. 6: 7- 8 NKJ). But as horrible and hateful as their crimes are, though they should never be considered above the law, neither are they exempt from the grace of God. The scripture also tells us "Mercy triumphs over judgment".

...because judgment without mercy will be shown to anyone who has not been merciful. Mercy triumphs over judgment (James 2:13 NIV).

37. Operation Zero Population Growth

One of the goals of the NWO is to reduce the world population down to a manageable size. The elite obviously realize that they can't control all the people on this planet themselves. Too many people might actually have enough manpower to fight back. It should be plain that their deceptive tactics are being exposed. They know they can't keep it up for long. Dr. John Coleman, a former intelligence agent of the British MI6 states in his book *Conspiracy Hierarchy: The Story of the Committee of 300* that a worldwide group of elites intend to take complete control of every human being on the planet and to reduce the world's population by 5.5 billion people. They intend to restrict the number of children per family and otherwise limit the population by diseases, wars and famines "... until one billion people who are useful to the ruling class . . . remain as the total world population. There will be no middle class, only rulers and servants".[851]

The NSSM called for reducing the population of the earth by 500 million by the year 2000. Kissinger noted in his report that overpopulation is already the cause of 10 million deaths per year so he was advocating for an increase of the death rate to 20 million per year. Of course the news media was promoting the US policy of population reduction as a positive one, though in strict definition per the UN 1948 convention it was nothing more than genocide. Of course this

---

851 Robin de Ruiter, Worldwide Evil and Misery: The Legacy of 13 Satanic Bloodlines (The Netherlands, Myra Publications, 2008) 19.

is why food aid was provided to counties that complied with the US population control policy.[852]

They want us to believe that this planet simply cannot sustain the number of people now populating the earth. This is a lie. There is more than enough food and space for all the people who live on this planet. It is clear that the reason they want to reduce the population is because they cannot control all the people who live on this planet and they want to reduce the population so it will be easier for them to manage. Or rather, just enough people for them to enslave and not enough people to revolt against their wicked scheme.

War is one of the means by which they intend to reduce the world's population which explains why they keep the United States in a state of perpetual war. They know that hundreds of people will be killed in a war. They don't particularly care if they lose a few thousand soldiers either. An English Major was mourning over the loss of so many troops in the war. Nathan Rothschild stated in response, "Well…If they had not all died, Major, you presumably would still be a drummer."[853] Henry Kissinger made the statement, "Military men are dumb, stupid [and] to be used as pawns for foreign policy."[854]

One of their other methods is the use of disease. Researchers have indicated that the Illuminati have used 'biological' warfare as a method of population reduction. Aids which is a disease allegedly caused by the HIV virus is actually a synthetic form of the black plague created at the bio lab in Ft. Dietrich Maryland. In 1969 Dr. Robert MacMahan of the Department of Defense requested $10 million dollars for the purpose of developing a synthetic agent to which no natural immunity exists. The project was carried out by the CIA Special Operations Division at Ft. Dietrich, MD.[855] Dr Robert McNamara, President of the World Bank approved the funding for the development of this agent. He stated before congress that the world's population was too large to be controllable. Thus he approved the funding for this virus for which there would be no cure.[856] Islamic leaders in Northern Nigeria also claimed that UNICEF provided a polio vaccine that was contaminated with aids. The United States government sent a team of scientists, religious leaders and others to test the vaccine. However, they refused to release the results of the tests.[857]

---

852 Henry Kissinger NSSM 200, II B. Functional Assistance Programs to Create Conditions for Fertility Decline
853 Fritz Springmeyer, The Rothschild Bloodline (July 3, 2009- http://www.theforbiddenknowledge.com).
854 David Icke, Tales from the Time Loop (Ryde, Isle of Wright: David Icke Books, 2003)171.
855 A History of US Secret Human Experimentation (http://www.infowars.com).
856 Antony C. Sutton, Trilateral Over America (Boring: CPA Book Publishers,1976) 78 – 79.
857 Andrew Carrington Hitchcock, The Synagogue of Satan (Austin, Texas: RiverCrest Publishing, 2007) 275.

When people become fearful of these dreaded diseases, they can be induced to get vaccinations to protect themselves. However those vaccinations may actually be the cause of death itself. In the 1990s the World Health Organization backed by the Rockefeller Foundation, the World Bank and the United States National Institute of Health vaccinated of women in Nicaragua, Mexico and the Philippines between the ages of 15 and 45 with a tetanus vaccination that contained human Chorionic Gonadotrophin or HCG which combined with the Tetanus carried a toxoid that rendered the women incapable of maintaining pregnancy. The vaccine was given only to women of child bearing age and not to any men. Because of this, Comite Pro Vida de Mexico, a Roman Catholic lay organization became suspicious and had vaccine samples tested and exposed the vaccine for what it was - a genocidal agent.[858] This was the case of a forced smallpox vaccination which was found to cause many diseases. The vaccination poisoned the bloodstream with animal-lymph. The London Times reported May 11, 1987 that the outbreak of AIDS in South Africa is concentrated in an area where the World Health Organization administered a smallpox vaccination to the population.[859]

Dr. Cornelius Rhodes, a Rockefeller Institute Scientist practicing in Puerto Rico who apparently thought that Puerto Rican's were dispensable, decided to inject a few of his patients with cancer cells. They died of course. He discussed his contribution to the overpopulation problem in a letter that he wrote to a friend that was later confiscated and published in Time magazine in February 1932. He states in his letter,

> ... the Porto Ricans are beyond doubt the dirtiest, laziest, most degenerate and thievish race of men ever inhabiting this sphere. It makes you sick to inhabit the same island with them.... What the island needs is not public health work, but a tidal wave or something to totally exterminate the population. It might then be livable. I have done my best to further the process of extermination by killing off eight and transplanting cancer into several more. The latter has not resulted in any fatalities so far.... The matter of consideration for the patients' welfare plays no role here - in fact, all physicians take delight in the abuse and torture of the unfortunate subjects.[860]

Was Dr. Rhodes tried for murder? No. He was " asked to establish the US Army Biological Warfare facilities in Maryland, Utah and also Panama and was

---

[858] US Co. Epicyte With USDA Funding Developed Seed Corn Containing Spermicide (November 6, 2010 - http://biotech.indymedia.org)

[859] Robin de Ruiter, Worldwide Evil and Misery: The Legacy of 13 Satanic Bloodlines (The Netherlands, Myra Publications, 2008) 78.

[860] Democratic Underground (blog) Octafish, Rhoads INJECTED Puerto Ricans with CANCER cells, Blog March 22, 2005 – April 9, 2011 - http://www.democraticunderground.com

later named to the US Atomic Energy Commission, where radiation experiments were secretly conducted on prisoners, hospital patients and US soldiers."[861]

Abortion is also another method used by the elite to reduce the world's population. Under the caveat of choice they have promoted abortion as a method of birth control. In fact they sent the World Health Organization down to the nation of Brazil to provide abortions to the poor women of the population in an effort to stem the problem of overpopulation. The Brazilian government got word that there were massive sterilizations of the women who were seeking abortions. They made a formal Congressional investigation and found that a shocking "44 % of all Brazilian women aged between 14 and 55 had been permanently sterilized.[862]

The overpopulation problem was addressed in Kissinger's NSSM 200 memo when he discussed using food as a weapon. In fact Monsanto developed Genetically Modified Organisms (GMOs), more specifically, corn seed which was sold to Mexican farmers that contained a spermicidal agent. It killed sperm in the Mexican males who ate the corn.[863]

Famine was another method by which the established elite plan to reduce the world population. One might ask, but famine is a natural phenomena. They maybe could cause diseases with vaccinations. They maybe could create wars which result in many deaths. However, famine caused by draught is something they can't control. However, they can also control the weather. The HAARP research project which is situated in Alaska is an Ionospheric heater which is built on Tesla technology. This technology is capable of controlling weather patterns.[864] If you can control weather patterns, you can induce draught. The Soviets established an electromagnetic grid over North American which researchers believe was responsible for atmospheric changes in the United States. In late 1980, the Washington Post reported a draught that had occurred uniformly across the entire United States. Nothing like this had ever occurred in the history of the U.S. This was an artificially induced Woodpecker Interference Grid phenomenon.[865] Zibigniew Brzezinski wrote in *Between Two Ages*, "The people of the world will give up their freedom to the 'controllers' because there will be a planned famine, or some other serious occurrence, such as a depression or war". He determined that the Old World Order based on Christian values would be superseded by the New World Order beginning in 1989.[866]

Earlier I discussed how the United States among other nations signed the ENMOD (Environmental Modifications) treaty promising not to use weather as a

---

861 Ibid.
862 F. William Engdahl, Seeds of Destruction: The Hidden Agenda of Genetic Manipulation (Canada, Global Research, Center for Research on Globalization 2007) 65.
863 Ibid, 270 – 271.
864 Jerry E. Smith, HAARP: The Ultimate Weapon of the Conspiracy (Kempton, ILL: Adventures Unlimited Press, 1998) 188.
865 Lt. Col. Thomas E. Bearden, History of Directed Energy Weapons (1990 -http://www.mindcontrolforums.com).
866 A. Ralf Epperson, The New World Order (Tucson: Publius Press, 1990) xix – xxi.

weapon against other nations. The fact that they had to sign a treaty of this nature in proof that they in fact have the ability to manipulate the weather for warfare purposes. Long ago a group known as MJ12 was which comprised of wealthy businessmen who were also well connected in the highest levels of National Security had an agenda expressed by then Senator Lyndon B-Johnson who when speaking for the Senate Democratic Caucus on January 7th, 1958, stated, "Control of Space means control of the world... From space, the masters of infinity would have the power to control the Earth's weather, to cause drought and flood , . . . to divert the Gulf Stream and change the climate to frigid...". A document published in August, 1996 by the Air Force presented at a conference titled *Weather as a Force Multiplier: Owning the weather in 2025 discussed* how manipulating the weather and controlling weather cataclysms could be used to the advantage of the military in conflict. The publication acknowledges that the US has signed treaties which would prohibit the use weather as a weapon; however it continued to discuss "weather made to order." As we know that the Soviets already have technology to manipulate atmospheric conditions and cause earthquakes, in reality it is likely that the US has the capability now to manipulate the weather and create storms.[867] The 1996 publication denies this, but if they actually do it would not be the first time they lied to the public. I strongly suspect that the deluge of hurricanes experienced in the southern part of the United States was actually orchestrated by the elite. If you examine what happened in the aftermath you will see that big business benefitted from the storm greatly. Naomi Kline in *The Shock Doctrine* looked at the 2005 Tsunami that hit Sri Lanka. Sri Lanka is a fishing village and the local fishermen had occupied that beach for as long as there was a Sri Lanka. Some businessmen wanted to open up a bunch of luxury hotels on their beaches but could not because the zoning laws favored the fishermen. After the tsunami hit the beach was basically bulldozed. What happened after that is strikingly similar to what happened in Iraq in the wake of the U.S. invasion. The globalists moved in, changed all the laws (it was a crisis situation of course), moved the fishermen to refugee camps and took over the beach. Their luxury hotels sprung up all over the place. The fishermen were of course out of luck.[868] So when one of those "natural" catastrophes strikes, you have to ask yourself, "Who benefits"?

In the scripture when we read of what will happen in the last days, we read of "famines and earthquakes in diverse places". The United States in their ability to control the weather is actually fulfilling Biblical prophecy. Matthew Ch 24:7 says, "Nation will rise against nation and kingdom against kingdom. There will be famines and earthquakes in various places" (NIV). In Luke Ch 21:25 we read, "On the earth, nations will be in anguish and perplexity at the roaring and tossing of the sea" (NIV). That could refer to tsunamis and hurricanes. When Jesus speaks

---

867 Col Tamzy J. House et. al. Weather as a Force Multiplier: Owning the Weather in 2025 (April, 1996 , http://csat.au.af.mil/2025/volume3/vol3ch15.pdf).
868 Naomi Kline, The Shock Doctrine: The Rise of Disaster Capitalism (New York: Metropolitan Books/ Henry Hold and Company, 2007) 394 – 399.

of nation rising against nation and kingdom against kingdom and follows with famines and earth quakes could it not be referring to weather warfare? Prepare yourselves. The scriptures also tell us that in the last days terrible times will come unequalled from the beginning of creation. In fact the scripture says that for the sake of the elect God will intervene and if God had not intervened, not one living soul would be left on this planet (Matt. 22:21 , 22 NIV) So much for the established elite and their Utopia.

38. Global Agenda

Those that are behind the NWO agenda for Global domination have been in the process of manipulating government policy from behind the scenes since before the Constitution was actually written. Those who oppose the United States Constitution and believe that only a certain class of elites is fit to rule would prefer to return this nation to an era where the average citizen did not own their own property and everyone served a group of landlords and royalty. These people were behind the formation of the Trilateral Commission, the Bilderbergers and the Council of Foreign Relations. This kind of thinking originated with the founder of the Illuminati.

Actions taken by the Bush Administration has eroded away at the integrity of the Constitution and which is pushing our government ever so close to the formation of a fanciest dictatorship. The Clinton Administration and both Bush Administrations have pushed legislation and government policy that promotes U.S. domination of global agricultural business. This included development of "genetically modified organisms" including crop seeds which are genetically engineered to benefit U.S. Agribusinesses and force third world nations to become dependent upon U.S. Agribusiness for survival. In addition, via the World Health Organization the U.S. has sent Planned Parenthood and other health care professionals into third world nations to promote "population control."[869]

Holly Sklar Editor of the book *Trilateralism, Elite Planning for World Management* explores the agenda of the U.S. Government for reducing the amount of control U.S. Citizens have over the political process. The phrase, "governable democracy" is frequently used by elites in this circle which communicates their desire to pacify American citizens with just enough control over the political process to keep them quiet.[870] Their motivation is to protect their financial assets in a world market. There is a deliberate and concerted effort by the U.S. Government to eliminate national sovereignty. Robertson quotes Richard Garner, Former Assistant Deputy of State from an article published in the Council of Foreign Relations Journal, "We are likely to do better by building our 'house of World

---

869 Robin de Ruiter, Worldwide Evil and Misery: The Legacy of 13 Satanic Bloodlines (The Netherlands, Myra Publications, 2008) 77.
870 Holly Sklar, Overview (Book Section Trilateralism: Elite Planning for WorldManagement, Editor Holly Sklar, Boston, 1980) 35 – 37.

Order' from the bottom up rather from the top down. . . . an end run around national sovereignty, eroding it piece by piece, is likely to get us to world order faster than an old fashioned assault."[871]

If there were any doubt that our government has a dark diabolical agenda, author and former U.S. Government CIA "Presidential Model Mind Controlled Sex Slave" Cathy O'Brien reported in her book Trance Formation of America of the abuse she experienced at the hands of several U.S. Government officials particularly Senator Robert C. Byrd, former head of the Senate Appropriations Committee. I have referred to her book extensively because it clearly depicts the agenda of the NWO politicians in Washington now manipulating our government. While she was being beaten by Senator Byrd his loose lips gave Cathy some insight into what the NWO is planning. He did not plan on her recovering the memory of her experience. He miscalculated. Senator Byrd described how he would manipulate the Constitution and the U.S. Justice system. His motto was "The only way we can fail is to fail to think of an excuse". He justified mind control as a means to the Neo-Nazi evolution. He also justified manipulating religion to bring about "biblical" world peace. This was also an element of mind control. Byrd declared that the Pope and the Mormon prophet were fully cooperating with the NWO agenda. He also justified drug trafficking, pornography and white slavery as a means of gaining control of illegal activities around the world to fund Black Budget covert activity designed to bring about world dominance which he said would result in world peace. He declared that 95% of the world's people don't want to know what the other 5% are doing who are leading them. He believed in creating a superior race by the use of NAZI and KKK principles of "annihilation of underprivileged races and cultures" by means of genocide and genetic manipulation to breed the "more gifted, --the blonds of the world."[872]

With the kind of evidence presented in this book any believer would want to consider the implications for what we know to be the "mark of the beast". Research on this subject would lead the author to conclude that the "mark" is not just an ink stamp. It will be a small microchip that can be implanted under the skin with a hypodermic needle. Once a person has "received" this mark, they will be able to be remotely controlled by the government.

> Implanted human beings can be followed anywhere. Their brain functions can be remotely monitored by supercomputers and even altered through the changing of frequencies. Guinea pigs in secret experiments have included prisoners, soldiers, mental patients, handicapped children, deaf and blind people, homosexuals, single

---

871 Pat Robertson, The New World Order (Dallas: Word Publishers, 1991) 109.
872 Cathy O'Brien & Mark Phillips, Trance Formation of America (Frankston, 1995) 118–119.

women, the elderly, school children, and any group of people considered to be "marginal" by the elite experimenters.[873]

The device will serve as a tracking device whereby they will be under constant 24 hour surveillance. Their every thought can be monitored, every word spoken recorded somewhere, and bodily functions will also be monitored and manipulated. That the technology to do this is now available is evident. With the amount of money and the kind of priority that the US Government has placed on this kind of research, it is not hard to conclude that this is exactly where our government is going.

It is important to know that a person who becomes aware that they are being remotely influenced is able to resist and withstand the onslaught of abuse, but a person who has the implant chip may not be able to do so. The person who receives that mark will literally be surrendering up his will to the state. He will therefore no longer able to choose to be obedient to God. And the NWO has their own religion that they plan to impose on everybody, in fact by force, as fascists do.[874]

Amschel Rothschild, remember, said that he could control the world if he could control the people's money. Nearly every nation in the world now has a central bank. Those that own the central bank are the Rothschild Banks of London and Berlin; Lazard Brothers Bank of Paris; Israel Moses Sieff, Banks of Italy; Warburg Bank of Hamburg and Amsterdam; Lehman Brothers Bank of New York; Kuhn Loeb Bank of New York; Chase Manhattan Bank of New York and Goldman Sachs Bank of New York. The owners of these banks have controlled the United States since 1914. This information can be found in an article on the web entitled *President Kennedy, the Federal Reserve and Executive Order # 11110* at http://www.apfn.net. A review of *The Bankers' Manifesto of 1892* published online has some telling statements. It reads as follows;

> We (the bankers) must proceed with caution and guard every move made, for the low order of people are already showing signs of restless commotion. Prudence will therefore show a policy of apparently yielding to the popular will until our plans are so far consummated that we can declare our designs **without fear of any organized resistance.** Organizations in the United States should be **carefully watched** by our trusted men, and we must take immediate steps to control these organizations in our interest or disrupt them. ... When, through the process of law, the common people have lost their homes, they will be more tractable and easily governed through the influence of the strong arm of the government

---

873 Rauni-Leena Lukanen-Kilde Microchip Implants, Mind Control, and Cybernetics (December 6, 2000. - http://www.conspiracyarchive.com).
874 Robin de Ruiter, Worldwide Evil and Misery: The Legacy of 13 Satanic Bloodlines (The Netherlands, Myra Publications, 2008) 108.

applied to central power of imperial wealth under the control of the leading financiers. **People without homes will not quarrel with their leaders.** ... This truth is well known among our principal men who are engaged in forming an imperialism of the world. While they are doing this, the people must be kept in a state of political antagonism. The question of tariff reform must be urged through the organization known as the Democratic Party, and the question of protection with the reciprocity must be forced to view through the republican Party. By dividing voters, we can get them to expend their energies in fighting over questions of no importance to us, except as teachers to the common herd. Thus by discrete actions, we can secure all that has been so generously planned and successfully accomplished.[875]

The Bankers' Manifesto was updated in 1934 and says about the same thing with minor modifications. One needs to consider the current state of home ownership in America with home owners mortgaged to the hilt. This is also a part of their plan because they do not believe in the ownership of private property. "The ultimate ownership of all property is the State; individual so-called 'ownership' is only by virtue of Government, i.e., law, amounting to mere 'user' and use must be in acceptance with the law and subordinate to the necessities of the State."[876] The banks begin to offer loans at low interest rates, then the Federal Reserve begins to pull the strings of the economy and people who just bought new homes lose their jobs and go into foreclosure. Thus the bank ends up owning the home. The bank also owns the state. When the state begins to privatize state assets, entrepreneurs begin to borrow money to buy the state assets. Then they begin to lose money because the economy is sinking and the businesses that have been privatized are purchased by the globalists who are controlling the government behind the scenes anyway.

Their plan for global domination is nearly complete.

39. THE FOURTH BEAST

We have already established that there is a cabal of wealthy businessmen worldwide who have decided to steal God's earth from the people he planted on it. We have established that they are not the slightest bit concerned about the welfare of humanity. They mean to dominate by whatever means they have available. They operate with a mindset that they are above the law, and they have been operating in secret for generations. We have also established that these people are fascists. They

---

875 Circle of 13, The Bankers Manifesto of 1982 (November 24, 2008. - http://circleof13blogspot.com.
876 Ibid.

intend to use democracy as a means to an end which is a global fascist one world government in which there are only the elite establishment and their slaves.

What many reading this book may or may not understand is that what we see happening in America and around the world is something that was very clearly laid out for us in the scripture in prophecy long, long ago. In fact, the words of Daniel and Revelation were most likely written on papyrus before there ever was such a thing as a printing press. What I would like to do is highlight some things I have already discussed and look at it from a prophetic point of view.

I have discussed the formation of the International Council of Foreign Affairs which evolved from a vision that Cecil Rhodes had for developing a one world government based on the traditional rule of the English ruling class. The CFR was the American sister secret society to the same organization that formed in Great Britain. There was also one formed for Asian countries. The more contemporary Bilderbergers, on the other hand, desire to submit the sovereignty of the free nations of Europe to a Bilderberger-controlled British-American One World Government.[877] These secret societies have been controlling government policy behind the scenes in America which has in effect overridden the Constitution and the Bill of Rights.

The Bilderberger agenda, furthered by the UKUSA agreement, was signed by the United States after WWII which involved the sharing of signals intelligence between the United Kingdom and the United States and English speaking countries such as Canada, New Zealand and Australia. The original target of the UKUSA agreement was the Soviet Union, however with the end the cold war the emphasis has shifted to domestic surveillance. The aim of the ECHELON surveillance system used to intercept communications of common citizens for purpose of political, industrial and economic espionage in their respective countries.[878]

The tactics that are used by these secret societies to gain control of something that is not rightfully theirs to control involves covert disruption of the lives of individuals and nations. It also involves controlling the weather and the minds of the populace. They have even created diseases in laboratories that have resulted in the deaths of many innocent lives, and they have created chemical agents that do the same. They have orchestrated catastrophes in weather and war where again innocent lives were lost. They have stolen the lives of mind controlled children and adults. They have also manipulated the economy worldwide in an effort to strip people of their wealth.

I would like to compare what is now happening with the book of Daniel. In Daniel chapter 2, God gave Daniel the interpretation to King Nebuchadnezzar's dream. The interpretation involved the prophecy of world kingdoms to come. King Nebuchadnezzar had a vision of a statue with a head of gold. Daniel explained that

---

877 Daniel Estulin, The True Story of the Bilderberger Group (Waterville, OR: Trine Day LLC., 2007) 21.
878 World-Information.org, ECHELON UKUSA Alliance (August 7, 2010. - http://world-information.org).

the head of gold was King Nebuchadnezzar himself. That was the first kingdom. The breast and arms of the statue were silver representing the kingdom that would follow King Nebuchadnezzar's kingdom which would be inferior to his. This was the Medo-Persian kingdom ruled by Cyrus the Great who conquered Babylon in 539 BC. The belly and thighs were of brass representing the Greco-Roman empire ruled by Alexander the Great who defeated the kings of Mede and Persia and came to power in 356 BC. This kingdom was eventually taken by the Roman Cesar Augustus in 31 BC. Daniel identifies Alexander as the first king of this Empire in 8:21 indicating that there would be more kings following him to rule this empire. This kingdom became divided between Rome and Byzantium when the Emperor Christian Constantine moved his headquarters to Constantinople.

In a video produced by Goliath's Sword and directed by Christian J Pinto in September 2007 called *MEGGIDO: The March to Armageddon*, David Hunt, identified the Roman Empire as the fourth kingdom represented by the iron legs of the statue in the book of Daniel. This is probably a commonly held belief among Bible Scholars and there is some precedent for that. Daniel speaks of the ten horns of the fourth beast which corresponds to the ten toes of the statue and says that "in the days of those kings (Daniel 2:44) God will set up his kingdom that will never end." Though I am not an expert on biblical prophecy, if the Roman Empire was supposed to be the fourth kingdom represented by the iron legs of the statue, then something is wrong with the prophecy because the fourth kingdom is followed by Christ's kingdom which will rule over the whole earth and will never end and that hasn't arrived yet. The Roman Empire came to an end in 1806, and the British Empire rose up on its heels. Britain was actually a part of the Roman Empire from about 43 AD till about 410 AD when Roman control of Britannia (as they called it) began to crumble. It was the Saxons who finally repelled the Romans from Britannia in 600AD. The United Kingdom was established in the late 16th and early 17th centuries. At its peak around 1922 it was the largest Empire that had ever existed and it was said that the sun never set on the British Empire. Great Britain ruled over ¼ of the entire world but not the whole world as did the fourth kingdom represented by the legs of the statue or the fourth beast of Daniel's vision. By the end of WWII in 1945 most of the British colonies had been granted independence due to a decolonization effort by European powers (CFR, Bilderbergers etc). Thus the British Empire began shrinking, but it has not come to an end. The fourth kingdom, on the other hand, would encompass the entire globe and would be the most terrible of all the kingdoms crushing its victims and trampling them underfoot. This kingdom is followed by Christ's never ending kingdom.

However, another secret society, the Club of Rome, was established at the Rockefeller estate in Bellagio Italy in 1968 by Bilderberger, Freemason and member of the Committee of 300 Aurellio Peccei, the # 2 executive at Fiat.[879] The Book of revelation speaks of the revival of the Roman Empire in the last days.

---

879 David Icke, The Biggest Secret (Wildwood, Bridge of Love Publications, 1999) 397.

In Revelation 17, John the Revelator sees a vision of a woman riding a beast with seven heads and 10 horns. The seven heads represent the seven hills upon which the woman sits and the beast she rides once was, now is not and will come again. This is interpreted by Bible scholars to be the revival of the old Roman Empire because Rome sits on seven hills. The Club of Rome also divided the world into 10 regions around 1997. The fourth kingdom would be the most terrible of all the kingdoms. Notice that this last kingdom was represented by two legs and two feet bearing ten toes. The feet of iron mixed with clay would be a kingdom partly strong and partly weak.

> The feet and toes you saw, partly of potter's tile and partly of iron, mean that it shall be a divided kingdom, but yet have some of the hardness of iron. As you saw the iron mixed with clay tile. As the toes of the feet were part of iron, and part of clay, so the kingdom shall be partly strong, and partly fragile. The iron mixed with clay tile means that **they shall seal their alliances by intermarriage, but they shall not stay united,** any more than iron mixes with clay" (Daniel 2: 41 – 43 NLT).

It is significant to note that the elite establish their alliances by marrying their children off to one another. However, according to scripture this will not be enough to maintain their alliances. This is the clay part of the statue.

The ten toes are also significant because they are similar to the ten horns of the fourth beast that Daniel had in a later vision. The two legs and the two feet I believe represent the Bilderberger vision of a one world government based on the joint rule of the United States and the United Kingdom or Great Britain. The fact that we have senators and congressmen who were willing to commit an act of treason by singing the Declaration of *Interdependence* swearing their allegiance to a One World Government is significant indication that this fourth kingdom discussed by Daniel here is the United States and United Kingdom One World Government. However, the scripture tells us that is the days of these kings is when God is going to come and destroy that kingdom and those who are faithful to him will rule in a Kingdom that will last forever.

> And in the days of these kings shall the God of heaven set up a kingdom, which shall never be destroyed; and the kingdom shall not be left to other people; it shall break in pieces and consume all these kingdoms, and it shall stand for ever. Inasmuch as you saw that the stone was cut out of the mountain without hands, and that it broke in pieces the iron, the bronze, the clay, the silver, and the gold--the great God has made known to the king what will come to pass after this. The dream *is* certain, and the interpretation is sure (Daniel 2:44 – 45 NKJV).

The stone that crushes that statue is of course Jesus Christ. Psalms 118:22 (NIV) says "The stone the builders rejected has become the chief cornerstone." This verse is quoted in Matthew, Mark, Luke, Acts and I Peter referring to Jesus Christ. It is interesting to me that the conspiracy that has so badly troubled the world was woven and carried out by Freemasons – the builders who have rejected Jesus Christ.

Daniel Ch. 7 describes the vision that God gave to Daniel himself. The vision was the same but described in a different manner. It also pertained to different successive kingdoms represented by beasts. The part of the vision I will focus on is the vision of the fourth beast. The Scripture reads;

> After that, in my vision at night I looked, and there before me was a fourth beast—terrifying and frightening and very powerful. It had large iron teeth; it crushed and devoured its victims and trampled underfoot whatever was left. It was different from all the former beasts, and it had ten horns. While I was thinking about the ten horns, there before me was another horn, a little one, which came up among them; and three of the first horns were uprooted before it. This horn had eyes like the eyes of a man and a mouth that spoke boastfully.... Then I continued to watch because of the boastful words the horn was speaking. I kept looking until the beast was slain and its body destroyed and thrown into the blazing fire (Dan 7:7-8, 11 NKJV).

Remember that the NWO has divided the world into ten different regions which are
- Region 1: The United States, Canada and Mexico
- Region 2: Western Europe
- Region 3: Japan
- Region 4: Australia and New Zealand
- Region 5: Eastern Europe
- Region 6: Latin America
- Region 7: North Africa and the Middle East
- Region 8: Central and Southern Africa
- Region 9: South and South-East Asia
- Region 10: Central Asia [880]

These would be consistent with the ten toes of the Nebuchadnezzar's' statue and the ten horns of the fourth beast. The little horn referred to in Daniel 7 may refer to a leader of the Trilateral Commission. Remember the little horn uproots three of the first horns. The Trilateral commission established a region consisting

---
880 Robin de Ruiter, Worldwide Evil and Misery: The Legacy of 13 Satanic Bloodlines (The Netherlands, Myra Publications, 2008) 302.

of the United States Canada and Mexico, Europe and Japan. The original ten regions established by the CFR divided Europe into Western and Eastern Europe. The Bilderberger Conference in 1996 made plans to break up the nation of Canada separating French speaking Quebec and combine the English speaking part with the United States. They were thwarted by the timely intervention of Daniel Estulin and his companions who notified the press.

Their plan however was to combine the United States, Canada and Mexico into one Nation by the year 2010.[881] The three governments are working quietly without telling their people about what they are doing. An article published online on May 21, 2011 by Bob Unruh of the WorldNet Daily makes it clear that the Bilderbergers are moving ahead with their agenda. The North American Initiative, at it is called, is a plan to combine the three countries into one nation by incriments. An agreement recently made between Barak Obama and the Canadian Prime Minister Stephen Harper bypassed the authority of the US Congress and the Canadian Parliament by executive order creating a "North American Perimeter" which includes the United States and Canada. The agreement was signed ostensibly to combat terrorism but also to facilitate free trade between the two nations satisfying the objectives of the globalists.[882] Estulin notes that combining the three nations is an act of treason as it will annul the Constitution of the United States of America.

The little horn that subdues three kings (also translated kingdom or realm) has eyes like the eyes of a man. Well there is nothing prophetic about a king having eyes. They most generally do. However this horn is different. The eyes, I believe, refer to the massive surveillance now going on in the United States. The Surveillance Industrial Complex is now worth billions of dollars.

In the Bible, the angel spoke to Daniel about the fourth beast telling him that it would be different than all other kingdoms and that it would envelope and crush the entire world (Dan. 7:23 NIV). The little horn is a king who will arise, different from the earlier ones who will subdue three kings (kingdoms or realms) (vs.24) and speak against the Most High, make war against the saints and attempt to change the set times and the laws (v25). The commentary states that the set times refer to times of religious holiday observances such as Christmas, Thanksgiving, or even Hanukah, Purim and the Passover.[883] He will also attempt to change the laws. Those laws might include annulling the Constitution or the laws around the world that have their root in the Christian faith such as the Magna Carta. And Daniel clearly states in vs. 25 "The saints will be handed over to him for a time,

---

881 Daniel Estulin, The True Story of the Bilderberger Group (Waterville, OR: Trine Day LLC., 2007) 222.
882 Bob Unruh, WikiLeaks: 'North American Initiative' no 'theory' (WorldNetDaily- May 21, 2011- http://www.wnd.com).
883 Donald C. Stamps, General Editor and J. Wesley Adams, Full Life Study Bible (Grand Rapids: Zondervan Publishing House, 1992).

times and a half time". This is interpreted by Bible Scholars as being 3 ½ years. Daniel states in chapter 11,

> Those who are wise will instruct many, though for a time they will fall by the sword or be burned or captured or plundered. When they fall, they will receive a little help, and many who are not sincere will join them. Some of the wise will stumble so that they may be refined, purified and made spotless until the time of the end, for it will still come at the appointed time (vs. 33-35, NIV).

After this time (Daniel 7:26) the power of this king will be taken away and he will be completely destroyed *__forever!__* Vs 27 reads, "Then the sovereignty, power and greatness of the kingdoms under the whole heaven will be handed over to the saints, the people of the Most High. His kingdom will be an everlasting Kingdom, and all rulers will worship and obey him." Because I believe that this divided Kingdom is the United States and the United Kingdom and that the three kingdoms uprooted by the "little horn" that arises I believe are the United States, Canada and Mexico, I was concerned about the fate of the United States of America. Most assuredly the ruler will be an American President as America has taken the lead in this "North American Perimeter" endeavor. I had to go back to the book of Daniel and read the passage several times. I believe that the power of the ruler will be destroyed but not the United States of America as a nation. However, judgment is surely coming on the entire world. The Book of Revelation reveals that the nations of the world will surround and attack Israel. This will bring on the final battle of Armageddon. Luke 21:20 -22 says,

> When you see Jerusalem being surrounded by armies, you will know that it's desolation is near. Then let those who are in Judea flee to the mountains, let those in the city get out, and let those in the country not enter the city. For this is the time of punishment in fulfillment of all that has been written (NIV).

Jesus goes on to say that these will be horribly dreadful times. But he says, "At that time they will see the Son of Man coming in cloud with power and great glory. When these things begin to take place, stand up, lift of your heads because your redemption is drawing near" (Luke 21: 27 – 28 NIV).

If what is happening today is a fulfillment of these prophecies in Daniel, then we as believers have to prepare ourselves to face persecution. This is something that Christians in American have had little to do with traditionally. However, Christians are increasingly facing more and more persecution. Christians are being targeted by gangstalkers and other operatives within the government. Michael Sweeney, private investigator and author of The *Professional Paranoid* was targeted by the CIA after he acquired information linking the Watergate scandal and the assassination of President Kennedy. He gave this information to a friend who was a writer but his life subsequently began to fall apart for no apparent reason. He and his wife met with their pastor and prayed about what was happening. God was able to deliver him and he explains in his book into how to fight back when you are being targeted.

Pastors and church leaders are increasingly being targeted and harassed. Pastor Rod Parsley of World Harvest church was recently sued by a former member of his congregation because their child came down with a rash which the parents blamed on the staff at the church. He testified before his congregation that Law Enforcement, the doctors involved who examined the child and Children's Services all testified that the rash had nothing whatever to do with anything the church staff had done. However, the judge refused to allow their testimony to be heard in court at the request of the couple's attorney because it would be damaging to their case! Of course it would!!!! Since when is testimony that is damaging to someone's case not be allowed to be heard in court. That is due process folks. But this is a criminal justice system that is thoroughly corrupted! Rod Parsley was required to pay the couple $3,000,000 in damages or the Judge threatened to shut down the church, the college and the school and take everything that the Pastor owned to pay the damages. The end of the story is God provided the $3,000,000. However, the Sunday offering has been diminishing so that Pastor Parsley has cut his own salary back to what he was making 20 years ago.

In the past year I learned of the shootings of two pastors in the State of Ohio alone. This occurred within a short period of time. The shootings were determined by Law Enforcement to be random acts of violence. I doubt that because it is consistent with a pattern of persecutions against Christians that are occurring across the board in the United States of America. The same year I resigned my job in Knox Co. Ohio, at teacher at the Mt. Vernon High School was fired because he had a Bible on his desk. One of my friends who was also a Christian was fired from her job as a teacher in the Columbus Ohio City School district. Prior to that she felt like she was being targeted for harassment because of her religious beliefs. Remember from the chapter on Directed Energy Weapons that Bill Clinton specifically stated that Christians would be targeted with these weapons. I am being targeted with these weapons. I have also spoken with many other victims of gangstalking who are also being harassed with DEW. While I was watching TV at my mother's home during a holiday visit, I saw Christians on television being depicted at violent, aggressive fanatics. The Mockingbird media is deliberately attempting to mold the minds of the populace to see Christians as villains. This is going to increase persecution and persuade the non-believing populace to comply with their harassment campaign. The Jews were also "villianized" in Germany which aided the government in gaining the cooperation of the German populace in targeting the Jews for destruction.

What all of this means, friends, is that we are being tested and refined by God because he is getting ready to establish his eternal Kingdom over which we will rule with him. God will not forsake us in the midst of our suffering but we have to be patient because we will, even in America, endure much hardship because of our confession of faith. Remember that Jesus Christ went before us on the cross where he suffered and died. We are to hold fast to our confession of faith in the midst of persecution and cling tightly to the cross.

> *He who has an ear, let him hear. If anyone is to go into captivity, into captivity he will go. If anyone is to be killed with the sword he will be killed. This calls for patient endurance and faithfulness on the part of the saints* (NIV Rev. 9-10)

40. The Bohemian Grove, Washington and Witchcraft

While working at the prayer center in my church, I talked to a woman who wanted prayer for astral projecting human spirits who were attempting to invade her home. This woman was quite a prayer warrior herself and this was likely the reason why she was being targeted. In the course of our conversation she mentioned to me that the largest concentration of witches living in the United States live in Washington D.C. The late John Todd, who grew up in an occult Illuminati family stated that he attended the annual witchcraft convention in Washington DC which was attended by many Senators and Congressmen.[884] This did not surprise me. In the course of researching this book, I learned from multiple witnesses that the Washington elite and those around the world in that cabal of people who want to control the world are also heavily involved in witchcraft.

Located in 2700 acres of secluded and guarded redwood forestry in Northern California is the haunt for Washington elites engaged in witchcraft and every form of sexual perversion imaginable. This is place known to many is the Bohemian Grove and those who attend there are known as "Grovers". A 40 foot stone owl, known as Minerva the goddess of wisdom, stands at the center of the worship ceremony. This idol is also known as Moloch – the ancient god to whom the Israelites sacrificed their children.[885] Hegel, who is the mastermind behind the Hegelian dialectic which has been used by the Illuminati to create chaos around the world, was fond of that symbol. The Journal of the Hegel Society of America also uses the symbol of the Stone Owl. At the infamous Cremation of Care ceremony practiced at the Bohemian grove the Priest standing before the owl prays, "O thou, great symbol of all mortal wisdom, Owl of Bohemia, we do beseech thee, grant us thy counsel."[886]

---

884 John Todd, the Illuminati and Witchcraft (1978. - http://www.kt70.com).
885 David Icke, Tales from the Time Loop (Ryde Isle of Wright: David Icke Books, 2003) 335.
886 Terry Melanson, Illuminati Conspiracy Part One: A Precise Exegesis on Available Evidence (August 5th, 2005 http://www.conspitatyarchive.com.

Human sacrifice in America is rampant. Ted Gunderson, experienced in investigations involving Satanic Ritual Abuse, estimated that "there are 3.75 million practicing Satanists and between 50 and 60,000 human sacrifices per year". Human sacrifice is also performed at the Bohemian Grove. In the year 2000 American Talk Show host, Alex Jones, went to the Grove with a hidden Camera and filmed the human sacrifice ritual. He was not close enough to see if the sacrifice was real or an 'effigy'.[887] Cathy O'Brien who was personally at the Bohemian Grove as one of Washington's Monarch sex slaves describes in detail the facility and the activity that goes on there. She witnessed the sacrifice of a young dark haired woman. This was used to intimidate her. "My own threat of death was instilled ... I was instructed to perform sexually 'as though my life depended upon it'. I was told, '...the next sacrifice victim could be you. Anytime when you least expect it, the owl will consume you.'"[888]

Children in the Franklin investigation and Cathy O'Brien testified of being prostituted to multiple Washington dignitaries. On one occasion Cathy O'Brien testified that she saw President George Bush Sr. turn himself into a lizard.[889] She believed he used a hologram. Many in the occult believe themselves to be descended from lizards. Some who have come out of the occult have testified that those who believe themselves to be of lizard decent have to drink human blood to maintain their human form.[890] During their ceremonies, they also create fear in their victims before they kill them. This is because fear creates adrenalin, and they get high from drinking the adrenalin laced blood.[891]

The film of the ceremony at the Bohemian Grove produced by Alex Jones can be seen at www.youtube.com. An article in Wikipedia indicates that this ritual is a "dramatic production". In fact, the film I viewed and listened to did have a dramatic flair. During the ceremony as the fire is lit on the sacrificial alter, a male voice crying out in pain and terror is heard. Is it all drama? There is a huge audience watching the "drama" from across the lake. During the ceremony a character crossing the lake in a boat is dressed in a black robe dipped in blood. He extends one hand out toward the ceremony. The robe dipped in blood is a parallel of the rider of the white horse in the Book of Revelation whose robe is also dipped in blood. This is Christ in Revelation 19:13. So the figure at the Bohemian Grove in the boat is wearing a black robe dipped in blood would be symbolic of the antichrist. According to Alex Jones, the boat rider is beckoning the soul of the sacrificed to come to him. As he does the Priest speaks these words;

---

887 Terry Melanson, Illuminati Conspiracy Part One: A Precise Exegesis on Available Evidence (August 5th, 2005 http://www.conspitatyarchive.com.
888 Cathy O'Brien & Mark Phillips, Trance Formation of America (Frankston, 1995) 170.
889 Cathy O'Brien & Mark Phillips, Trance Formation of America (Frankston, 1995) 165.
890 David Icke, The Biggest Secret (Wildwood, MO: Bridget of Love, 1999) 295
891 David Icke, Tales from the Time Loop (Ryde Isle of Wright, 2003) 311.

No fire. No fire. No fire unless in the world where care is nourished
on the hates of man and drive him from his grave.
One flame alone might light this fire.
A pure eternal flame
At last within the lamp of fellowship upon the alter of Bohemia
We thank thee for thy adoration

Be gone detestable care!
Once more we banish thee.
Fire will have its will of thee.
Be gone dull care and all the winds make merry with thy dust.
Hail fellowship's eternal flame.
Once again Midsummer sets us free.

(At this point screams are heard.)

Every kind of sexual perversion is practiced at the Grove, and it is all caught on tape. According to Cathy O'Brian one of the purposes of bringing Washington elites to the grove to engage in their elaborate sexual fantasies is to get them on film so that they can be controlled by those in power who want to control this country and the rest of the world. They use high tech undetectable fiber optic cameras and fish eye lenses in each of the sexual theme rooms. Cathy was prostituted to many US Government officials and the Mafia in those rooms. She also states that they were heavily involved in drug use there. The Grove is a place where the political elite can party without restraint.[892]

This is the kind of thing that would normally create an internal sense of shame. In the chapter called *The Minds of Men* in the earlier part of this book, I mention that the Illuminati lured people into committing crimes and then used that to blackmail them into cooperation. This tactic was also discussed in the chapter titled *No Place for Our Children to Run*. Thus the Cremation of Care is performed to deaden their consciences while compromised White House Officials are being blackmailed at the same time to force them to cooperate with the NWO. So, they sacrifice yet another innocent soul and commit yet another crime in the process.

Phillip Eugene de Rothschild who spoke with David Icke and is apparently "out" of the whole Illuminati mind control cult was also a witness at the Bohemian Grove rituals. Interestingly he did not finger either the Rockefellers or the Rothschilds as the ones in control, but Allen Greenspan, head of the Federal Reserve Bank. He told David Icke, "Greenspan, I recall, was a person of

---

892 Cathy O'Brien & Mark Phillips, Trance Formation of America (Frankston, Texas: Reality Marketing Inc., 1995) 169 – 170.

tremendous spiritual, occult power and could make the Bushes and the younger Rockefellers cower with just a glance.[893]

The Central Intelligence Agency, which we remember originated when the U.S. Office of Strategic Services and the NAZI SS combined after WWII, has been heavily involved in witchcraft. Edwin Land of the Polaroid Corporation, who has long been involved in the CIA's mind control program, founded the Scientific Engineering Institute at the University of South Carolina. He was involved in "behavior modification" which had its inspiration from the Deaths Head Order of the Waffen SS. In South Viet Nam the Scientific Engineering Institute (SEI) experimented by planting electrodes in the brains of POW's and attempted to spur them on to violence with remote control. When the experiment was finished, the POW's were shot by American Green Berets.[894] The SEI was created by the CIA for studying the occult underground. This institute offered a course in demonology and voodoo at the University of South Carolina.[895]

Lt. Col. Michael Aquino was also inspired by the NAZI SS in the founding of his Temple of Set. The NAZI SS was structured along the lines of an occult order complete with a "high priest" and a ritualized candidacy process. Himmler envisioned his "Black Order" as guardians of the elite Third Reich. In 1933 Hitler and Himmler acquired a triangular shaped castle in Wewelsburg Germany to use for satanic occult rituals. Aquino went in search of this castle and when he found it he had himself photographed there in his United States Army uniform. In the "Hall of the Dead" he performed a ritual mediation, which he called *Wewelsburg Working*, "to summon the Powers of Darkness to their most powerful locus."[896] This experience further inspired his Temple of Set. The Lt. Col. was involved in United States Military Intelligence in the Monarch Project which involved ritual sexual abuse of children. He was one of Cathy O'Brien's mind control programmers.

The lizard angle is a bit troubling. Icke, who is a new ager, believes that the Illuminati bloodlines are actually aliens from outer space that have been ruling this planet for centuries. I would not be persuaded that this is the case. However, in *Tales From the Time Loop*, he makes an interesting observation that in the scriptures, specifically Genesis 6:4, it states (NIV) "The Nephilim were on the earth in those days – and also afterward – when the sons of God went to the daughters of men and had children by them. They were the heroes of old, men of renown." It goes on to say that the interbreeding between the "sons of God" and the "daughters of men" resulted in such wickedness that the Lord was pained

---

893 David Icke, Tales from the Time Loop (Ryde Isle of Wright, David Icke Books, 2003) 309.
894 Alex Constantine, Psychic Dictatorship in the U.S. A. (Portland: Feral House, 1995)18.
895 Marshall G. Thomas, Monarch: The New Phoenix Program (New York: iUniverse Inc., 2007) 40.
896 Linda Blood, The New Satanist (New York: Warner Books, 1994) 207.

in his heart. This resulted in the flood. The commentator of the Full Life Study Bible (NIV) indicates that this marriage was between the godly line of Seth and the ungodly daughters of men that produced such wickedness.[897] There are some things in the Bible that are hard to explain. I am no expert at explaining Biblical mysteries. However, I am not absolutely sure I would agree with the Bible commentator of the New Life Study Bible. It is unlikely that the DNA of Seth's "Godly" line was all that different from the DNA of the ungodly women they choose to marry resulting in the birth of giants. Goliath was one of those giants. Another explanation I have heard is that the "sons of God" refer to fallen angels – i.e. demons. It is known from multiple testimonies that demons do have intercourse with humans. Demons that do this are referred to as a "succubus" or "incubus". If in fact "sons of God" refers to fallen angels, or demons, that would explain the giant size of their offspring as well as the wickedness associated with them. It might also, considering that Satan in the Garden of Eden took the form of a serpent, explain the possibility that these offspring contained the DNA of lizards. A serpent is not a lizard. However, snakes have shoulder bones where arms used to be. In fact, after Satan tempted Adam and Eve, God cursed Satan, the serpent, and told him he would crawl on his belly all the days of his life and eat the dust of the ground. Snakes do taste the dust of the ground in order to maintain their sense of direction, and though they have no arms and legs now, the bones in a snake's body do indicate that they did at one time. There are still children born today with a tail, called a caudal appendage, which has to be surgically removed soon after birth. I will not go into shape shifting here in detail; however it is an interesting read in either Icke's *Tales from the Time Loop* or *The Biggest Secret*.

The Merovingian bloodline, which is one of the Illuminati bloodlines, is said to have come about through the sexual intimacy between a demon, possibly Satan, and a woman. The Frank historian Priscus indicated that the Meorvingians had supernatural powers. Priscus claimed that his mother was seduced by a beastly creature, possibly Satan, so that the beast would live on forever. The Meorvingians may be the 13th bloodline, the satanic bloodline known for their occult skills.[898] John Todd, former member of one of those Illuminati bloodlines testified at a conference he gave in the fall of 1978 that he had seen Satan manifest in physical form, sit and eat meals and have sex with women. His description of Satan is really chilling.

> About seven feet tall, & I'd have to say not just handsome, but beautiful. JET BLACK HAIR, SNOW WHITE SKIN, & THE COLOUR OF HIS EYES, INSTEAD OF BLUE, BROWN OR WHATEVER, WERE A DEEP VIOLET, almost deep purple.

---

897 Donald C. Stamps, General Editor & J. Wesley Adams Full Life Study Bible (Grand Rapids: Zondervan Publishing, 1992).
898 Robin de Ruiter, Worldwide Evil and Misery: The Legacy of the 13 Satanic Bloodlines (The Netherlands, Myra Publications, 2008) 131 – 132.

> And when you looked in them, it was like looking down into the Grand Canyon. It's just bottomless, this power! And believe me, if he ever appeared to you, you'd know you were in his presence.[899]

There is another disturbing fact that I uncovered during my research. This is quite shocking and for many it may be unfathomable. Considering that we have a cabal of people in power who have no scruples of any kind, no sense of right and wrong, and considering the state of modern technology and research, I do not find it surprising or unbelievable. I also find confirmation of this in scripture. We have been for many years hearing about UFO's and alien abductions. I don't believe in either. Research indicates that flying saucers do exist. They are not from outer space and they are not extra terrestrial. They were created by the United States Air Force and NASA with NAZI technology stemming from the work of Nicola Tesla. If you take a glass of liquid and spin it in your hand it creates a funnel. That is called a torsion field. Tesla found a way of harnessing the energy in a torsion field. This was done through what are called Tesla coils which spin around. This is the principle upon which flying saucers are built and fly. People who experienced alien abductions indicate that the "aliens" were NAZIs (see chapter on mind control). This is more mind control experimentation. People have also reported seeing these aliens that they call "grays". I don't believe in aliens! However the logical, albeit horrid, explanation for this is experimentation with genetic manipulation. Bill Hamilton and Tal Levesque (aka Jason Bishop III) reported that there are genetic labs at Dulce AFB with multiple underground levels. They interviewed persons who worked there who reported seeing creatures on one level that were half human and half octopus, a large number of reptilian-humans in cages, and fury creatures that are part human and cried like a baby. There were cages and vats of winged creatures that were part human that were three to four feet tall. On another level there were thousands of part human creatures that were in cold storage. They saw humans in cages that were heavily drugged who were crying and begging for help. They were told these people were being treated for insanity and were instructed never to speak to them.[900] Jason Bishop further describes the activity at the Los Alamos Bio-Genetic research center where they were creating a "slave race".

> Like the Alien "Greys" . . ., the US Government clandestinely impregnated females, then removed the hybrid fetus, (after three months) and then accelerated their growth in the Lab. Biogenetic (DNA manipulation) programming is then instilled – they are "implanted" and controlled at a distance through RF (Radio Frequency) transmissions. Many Humans are also being "implanted" with Brain Transceivers. These act as telepathic

---

899 John Todd, the Illuminati and Witchcraft (1978. - http://www.kt70.com).
900 Jason Bishop III, Dulce Underground Base (December 26, 2010 - http://www.subversiveelement.com).

"channels" and telemetric brain manipulation devices. The network-net was set-up by DARPA (Advanced Research Project Agency). Two of the procedures were RHIC (Radio-Hypnotic Intracerebral Control) and EDOM (Electronic Dissolution of Memory). The brain transceiver is inserted into the head thru the nose. These devices are used in the Soviet Union and the United Stated, as well as Sweden.[901]

If this is true, this is occult science at its worst. We are aghast at such things. Most of us don't want to believe it. There has to be some other explanation. However, a close look at the book of Revelation will reveal that there are several creatures that would appear to be the product of genetic manipulation, not to mention the "Beast" itself.

Christians in America recognize Christian symbols all over Washington DC, but many others see the symbols erected by the occult, more specifically by Freemasonry. The obelisk known as the Washington Monument is one of them. Phallic worship, remember, was a part of the worship of King Balan's people which he detested. He thus forced him people to convert to Talmudism. The obelisk is an ancient Egyptian-Aryan symbol representing the sun and more specifically the phallus which is a symbol of male energy. Obelisks can be found in many places around the world such as at the Thames River in England, in the city of On or Heliopolis in Egypt. The one in Egypt is also known as Cleopatra's needle. There is also one in Buenos Aires, St Peter's Square in Rome, and Central Park in New York (brought from Alexandria, Egypt). The Masons noted in their publication that this obelisk in Central Park was erected "... to praise and adore the divinity of the sun, worshipped by the ancient Egyptians as the source of light and life. It is a representation of the God Ra, or the sun". It also represents Lucifer.[902] Freemasons have deliberately erected these obelisks all over the world because they generate occultic energy. The Washington Monument is the largest Obelisk in the world.[903]

Up until the election of President Regan, all the Presidential inaugurals have been held on the east side of the White house. However, on January 20, 1981 President Regan held his inaugural on the West side and every president to the present, has held his inaugural on West side of the Whitehouse facing the Washington Monument, the obelisk. Those who know that this is a Freemason symbol noted this change with curiosity wondering if Regan was signaling Freemasons all over the world of his allegiance to Freemasonry. David Bay of Old Path Ministries has indicated that this is the case. In fact, he believes this was done in fulfillment of an occultic prophecy from 1492. This prophecy indicated that the

---

901 Ibid.
902 A. Ralf Epperson, The New World Order (Tucson: Publius Press, 1990) 98,100.
903 David Bay, Director, Old Path Ministries Witchcraft in the Whitehouse and in Roman Catholicism (http://www.cuttingedge.org).

leader who faced the obelisk would introduce the man who would introduce the Anti-Christ. "Then, in the late 1700's . . . secret societies communicated that . . . the new America was destined to assume the leadership of the drive to institute the New World Order. From this time forward, occultists looked to American leadership, specifically the President, to fulfill this prophecy."[904]

Freemasons have in fact left their fingerprints all over Washington DC. Albert Pike, Grand Master of the Scottish Rite of Freemasonry, died in Washington DC in 1891. His funeral was held in the Freemason Temple at midnight. A statue of Albert Pike has been erected near the Washington DC police headquarters not far from Capitol Hill.[905] Domed buildings are also a part of the Freemason symbology. Buildings like the Congress Building in Washington DC exist in other places around the world.[906] The Freemason Illuminati symbol, the All Seeing Eye, of course is on our dollar bill and the reverse side of the Great Seal of the United States. The street plan of Washington DC also bears the symbology of the Freemasons. These include the Seal of Solomon, the Masonic compass, the five pointed star, the great owl (Minerva, Moloch), as well as the great Pyramid with the top missing.[907]

The Bible clearly speaks on these things in Romans chapter 1. The Illuminati claim to be the "enlightened" ones. They worship a stone owl, which has the body of a woman and the head of an owl called the goddess of wisdom. This is what the scripture reveals;

> For although they knew God, they neither glorified him as God nor gave thanks to him, but in their thinking became futile and their foolish hearts were darkened. Although they claimed to be wise, they became fools and exchanged the glory of the immortal God for images made to look like mortal man and birds and animals and reptiles. Therefore God gave them over in the sinful desires of their hearts to sexual impurity for the degrading of their bodies with one another. They exchanged the truth of God for a lie, and worshipped and served created things rather than the creator – who is forever praised. Amen (Romans 1: 24 – 26 NIV).

41. Whither the Church?

At church one Sunday I was looking over the pew at a notebook that a sister in Christ had brought with her and on the cover of the notebook was a characterization of a pastor behind his pulpit while beneath him were two women

---

904 Ibid
905 David Icke, The Biggest Secret (Wildwood, MO: Bridge of Love Publications USA, 1999) 199.
906 Ibid, 362.
907 Ibid, 364 – 365.

dancing, presumably before the Lord, with all their might. The caption on the picture read, "Too blessed to be stressed." Once while listening to a radio broadcast pertaining to the recent devastating earthquake in Haiti, a news reporter observed some Haitians, in dire straits because of the quake, standing around in a circle lifting up their hands and singing praises to God. The thought brought tears to my eyes. It is one thing to be singing God's praises in the midst of our blessing, and another entirely to be singing his praises in the midst of a terrible catastrophe.

What concerns me is that the church in America does not see the catastrophe we are facing here in this nation. We have become entirely too wrapped up in redecorating our homes, paying our bills, trimming the bushes and hanging one more stocking on our fireplaces to notice that this nation has been slowly slipping from our grasp. Our sin in the church is complacency. Much of it has to do with the lack of information.

Once I had a dream. In my dream I was grabbing people and dragging them into the church. We were in the middle of a war and I sought safety in the church for myself and those with me. I had people on the floor between the pews on their knees with their heads down to the floor and their hands protecting their heads. "We'll be safe in here" I was saying. But the moment I said that, one entire side wall of the church was blown away and on the other side of that wall was a group of Roman Soldiers on horseback. They began taking people away and conscripting people into service.

I was disturbed about that dream, but I didn't really understand the significance of it until years later when I learned that I was a gangstalking victim and that people in my church had possibly participated in a criminal act. Why? For lack of knowledge. They had been deceived. They willingly complied with what wolves in sheep's clothing asked them to do because they, quite frankly, were not watching for the wolves in sheep's clothing. After four years of research I realized that there were more than just problems with gangstalkers infiltrating our churches, and we have cause to be concerned.

John Hagee in his book Day of Deception makes note that for the New World Order to succeed they will have to rub out the church. The United States of America is the central hub of the New World Order, though it has many "hubs" around the world today. Great Britain is one of them and so is Israel. If in this country we expect to go on with our faith without suffering persecution were are fooling ourselves. However, we will rarely experience an all out attack on the church. That would not be wise for our enemies to do that. They would be soundly defeated. Our enemy prefers covert operations to all out attacks because they are invisible. Though the U.S. media which is owned by the Eastern Establishment is involved in "Christian bashing", most of the attacks on believers will come less discernable ways, and that is what concerns me. Remember the words of the Count de Virieu, "The conspiracy which is being woven is so well thought out that it will be ... impossible for the Monarchy and the church to escape it.[908]

---

908 Jim Marrs, Rule By Secrecy (New York, NY: Perennial Harper Collins, 2000) 241.

Understand that the Hegelian Dialectic which has been the core philosophy implemented by the New World Order, can also be used by Freemasonry in their assault upon the church. Much of the time Christians attribute disturbances within the church as a "spiritual" attack or an attack by Satan. We have not paid attention to the possibility that there are infiltrators in the church that are deliberately attempting to neutralize or control the church. Freemasonry's plot for world control was two pronged. It included infiltration of civil government as well as infiltration of the church. Leo Strauss, Professor of Political Science at the University of Chicago, taught his students that they had to deceive the people to accomplish their secret agenda. He also taught them that this required using the church in a deceptive way to accomplish their goals – which are entirely anti-American not to mention anti Christian. His students became officials in positions of power in our government and many of them made professions of faith but acted in ways that were contrary to anything we would call Christian. Pope Leo XXIII noted that Freemasons were determined to overthrow the religious, political and social order with its roots in religion. However, Pope John XIII in 1962 wrote in *Athanasius And the church of our Time* that Freemasonry has shifted from its intent to destroy the church to using it by infiltration.[909]

We have already discussed the fact that Joseph Mengele, infamous NAZI psychiatrist, was the mastermind behind the Monarch mind control research project that developed mind controlled slaves out of children by deliberately inducing trauma and creating multiple personalities in them. Cathy O'Brien was a Monarch mind controlled sex slave. These mind controlled slaves are used as sleepers and have been planted in every city and state across the land triggered into action by key words and phrases. They are used for various purposes including sex slavery, assassination etc. They never reveal their true purposes because they don't know what they are. Their mission is buried within the multiple personalities that have been programmed into them. Ergo, they can infiltrate your church and no one will notice that there is anything different about them. Monarch slaves are found in places where they can influence governments, churches and church organizations, science, education, finance, media etc.[910]

Many who have come out of the occult have testified that there are people in the church, even in positions of leadership who are actually members of the occult and are in the church to disrupt and control its activity. John Todd, a member of the Illuminati Collins family and former "Grand Druid", indicates that the occult has spent millions of dollars putting their people in fundamental churches all over the United States. They are trained in Christian beliefs and they know how to act like a Christian. "The newest form of blasphemy by a witch towards the Christian God is to sit there & praise the Lord & act like a Christian, laughing the whole time". One of the members of his cult, a woman by the name of Regina, was sent

---

909 Robin de Ruiter, Worldwide Evil and Misery: The Legacy of the 13 Satanic bloodlines (The Netherlands, Myra Publications, 2008) 44.
910 Ibid, 321.

to keep an eye on Jerry Farwell's church. In the church that Todd attended as a believer there were four High Priestesses in attendance who he states had the church in a mess until the leadership took action to correct the problem.[911]

In fact Todd testified that the Illuminati "own" a number of Christian churches. He went to a movie that was a Christian production and he suddenly had questions that he had never had before about Christianity. He wanted to talk to a Christian Pastor but he had to be careful about who he spoke with because the Illuminati "own" the ministers of so many churches. If he talked to the wrong one he could get killed. This happens because the Illuminati have money and pastors, he observes, who are not sold out to the Lord have a hard time turning down a bribe offered of a half a million dollars or more. "In fact, one church I know of got eight million dollars in two years, and another one got ten million dollars in one year! So, they can receive some money."[912]

The scripture speaks to us of the "wheat" and the "tares".

> Another parable he put forth to them, saying, "The kingdom of heaven is like a man who sowed good seed in his field; but while men slept, his enemy came and sowed tares among the wheat, and went his way. But when the grain had sprouted and produced a crop, then the tares also appeared. So the servants of the owner came and said unto him, "Sir, did you not sow good seed in your field? How then does it have tares? He said unto them, 'An enemy has done this.' The servants said unto him, 'Do you want us to go and gather them up?' But he said, No; lest while you gather up the tares, you also uproot the wheat with them. Let both grow together until the harvest: and at the time of harvest I will say unto the reapers, "First gather together the tares, and bind them in bundles to burn them: but gather together the wheat into my barn" (Matt 13:24 – 30 NKJV).

Jesus in this parable clearly indicates that an enemy put the tares in among the wheat. In other words, it was not an accident, it was deliberate and it was done while they were sleeping. While the church was sleeping an enemy planted infiltrators among us who are not believers but are there to disrupt and or control the church to suit the purposes of the NWO. Jesus tells us that we are not to try to pull them out because we might damage the true wheat in the process. In the end at the time of the harvest Jesus will root them out. What this means is that we need to understand that every person who we see when we enter the church is not a believer. They may be actually seeking and we need to encourage that. But they may also be sent there to spy on us and also to manipulate and control us. Understand that these people usually aim for the power centers of any

---
911 John Todd, the Illuminati and Witchcraft (1978. - http://www.kt70.com).
912 Ibid.

organization including the church. Cathy O'Brien in her book Trance Formation of America tells us that a Catholic Priest was in charge of the Monarch Program in a Catholic School where she attended. She was also programmed using religious language. We must be ever vigilante and watchful of the flock because those who want to rule the world know they cannot get away with their scheme without controlling the church.

John Todd, former Grand Druid and member of the Illuminati Collins family, left the occult when he became a Christian. He began speaking out to the church about the occult and its influence on the church. He was arrested and imprisoned on false charges in South Carolina by those who wanted to silence his testimony. This should cause us more than a little concern. We hear of things like this, but few of us expect to encounter this kind of assault because of our faith and involvement with the church. But Todd testified from his jail cell that an underground church was formed in Nebraska because Christians and pastors were accused of child abuse and sentenced to prison on trumped up charges.

> Where we started seeing ... laws about child abuse being put into effect by the federal and state governments without ever being passed as law. Children were being taken from their parents without a chance for the parents to be allowed to speak in the trial. All it took was some child psychologist, "I suspect child abuse, blah blah blah." We started seeing how 90% of the people being tried were fundamentalist Christians, so an underground was formed. It contained Christian survivalists but it contained everyday people also. And all they [the people who had him arrested] wanted was where these safe houses were, where these places of refuge were, what the underground conductors who they were. That's all they were asking me.[913]

John Bevere in *The Bait of Satan* describes a situation that is clearly created by an infiltrator. The Pastor that was over him in the church where he was acting as a youth pastor was deliberately attempting to discredit him in the eyes of the head pastor of the church. Pastor Bevere held his ground and sincerely tried to resolve the conflict between himself and his boss. Eventually, while Bevere was actually out of the country, the head pastor of the church discovered that Bevere's boss was attempting to disrupt and discredit several of the staff in the church and that man was eventually fired. Bevere used the word, "wickedness" to describe what that pastor was doing.[914] This is precisely the kind of covert activity we can expect from those who oppose the church and the Christian faith even inside the church. The danger is that they will ensnare even decent God loving Christians in doing their bidding. It is a fact that there is nothing those of the occult persuasion

---

913 Ibid
914 John Bevere, The Bait of Satan [Book]. - Lake Mary: Charisma House, 1994) 40 - 43.

like better than to corrupt good moral Christians. They seem to take a particular delight in turning Christians into operatives that will do things that no godly person should ever do.

We should not go around accusing people in the church who frustrate us of being "sleepers" or "spies" or "operatives". Sleepers can't help themselves. If we knew how to identify them we could pray for them and minister to them. They are redeemable. Operatives of Freemasonry are Luciferians. They worship Lucifer. They have a worldview that is wholly the opposite of the Christian worldview. Ergo, they have no problems pretending to be Christian and working against us all the time. They can very subtly create dissention in the church. Covert operations are very hard to uncover, but if we are diligent in obeying the scripture when there is a conflict in the church we can avoid being snared by one of their traps. One of the things we can do is not only avoid gossip, but lovingly rebuke those who do. Gossip is one of the indications we can watch for in an operative. They may be working to discredit a member who is being targeted by one of their cult groups. Their attempts to influence are incredibly subtle. When someone is attempting to influence the way you think about someone or the way you respond to them you have to ask yourself what their motivation is. You also have to put yourself in the position of the one being talked about. You have to ask yourself, "What if it were me? How would I feel about what is being said?"

The other thing we have to be watchful of is how they have infiltrated our communities. Again they aim for power centers of any organization. In every community across America you will find Freemason lodges. Many of their members think that they simply belong to a fraternal organization. The true purpose of Freemasonry is actually hidden from the lower levels of Freemasonry. However, people are attracted to Freemasonry because it helps them gain positions and prestige. Once their members are in positions of authority, they are bound by oath to protect fellow Freemasons. They can also make things difficult for Christians employed in community jobs. In the chapter entitled the Minds of Men, I discussed at length Adam Weishaupt's development of the Illuminati including his attack on the Jesuits at Ingolstadt University. He states, "Through the intrigues of the Brethren the Jesuits have been dismissed from all the Professorships; we have entirely cleared the University of Ingolstadt of them."[915] Intrigue is another word for *covert operations*. There are Freemason judges, and Freemason Police Chiefs, and Freemasons are on the boards of social service organizations and in positions of power in our schools. They oppose the church in every way shape and form. They can through covert means remove Christians from their positions. As a church we need to be watchful of this, and we also need to have believers in positions of power to protect our communities. The Church of Scientology uses similar methods as Freemasons, and the founder was himself a Freemason. The

---

915 Terry Melanson, Illuminati Conspiracy Part One: A Precise Exegesis on Available Evidence (August 5th, 2005.- http://www.conspitatyarchive.com).

New Age conglomerate of churches operates in the same way and they are all connected to the New World Order.

Our government is in a fascist shift. We are being spied on and watched everywhere we go. The church is no exception. In fact, the church is going to increasingly become a target. Hitler also made every effort to subdue the church in Germany as he was coming to power. A "Muzzling Order" was issued by Hitler's appointed Reich Bishop, Ludwig Mueller. This decree, issued on July 23, 1933, was designed to bring the German evangelical church under NAZI domination. Thus ministers were forbidden to speak out against controversial or political topics.[916] What disturbs me is that the American church bought the 9/11 lie without question, and without question acquiesced to the invasions of Afghanistan and Iraq. When the scandal broke revealing the abuses as Abu Ghraib, I did not hear one sermon from any pulpit and not one protest in the church for what happened there. All I hear is, "pray for our troops" and "They're over there defending our freedom." It should be plain by this point that we are not "over there" defending our freedom. The New World Order has an agenda and that does not include American freedom. Our troops may be simply following orders, but even that is an expression of complacency when we realize where all of this is leading us.

We have spies among us, and they are not there to simply spy on us. They are there to disrupt and neutralize the church. They will create and have created dissension. They are subtle covert operators who support the NWO agenda. They are targeting members of your church for destruction. Why? For many reasons. They do not target all Christians. They target Christians who are outspoken, full of kindness, or are simply devoted to doing what is right. They target Christians who are swimming upstream in the world, so to speak, those who refuse to bend to the NWO agenda. They choose Christians that they can easily dislodge from the church because there are fewer supports around them. They can subtly spread gossip and rumors, write poison pen letters and deliver them in the name of targeted person. They slowly and deliberately drive a wedge between their targets and any family or friends who might support them. They will worm their way into leadership positions and begin to disintegrate the integrity of the church. Most pastors are worried about church splits and much of the time I see them pointing fingers at "errant" members of the church. Pastors need to be concerned about church splits. But when a member of the congregation begins to finger someone in leadership for wrongdoing, that member is usually not heard and may experience harsh treatment for their willingness to speak out. However, understand that infiltrators usually aim for the power centers of every church, so it is not unlikely that someone is leadership is actually guilty of wrong doing. The scripture tells us exactly what to do when an accusation is brought against a member or leader in the church. If we follow the "Book" when these things occur then we can spare ourselves from being harmed by infiltrators. One other book that would be helpful

---

916 Jim Marrs, The Rise of the Fourth Reich (New York: William Morrow of Harper Collins Publisher, 2008). 288.

in understanding covert operations and how they can affect the church and what to do to fight back is a book called *The War at Home* written by Brian Glick. In this book he describes in detail the works of covert operators in the FBI against American citizens and organizations including the church.

Of course every person in the church who is guilty of some wrong doing is not a covert operative. None of us are perfect, and we should not expect leadership to be infallible either. We are all in need of mercy and grace from time to time, and we need to exercise great caution when dealing with conflict in our churches. One of the other things we need to be aware of is how the covert operators can influence true Christians to actually do something very ungodly to brother or sister in Christ. Covert operatives use real believers to accomplish their mission. Understand that the illuminati still wants to wipe out religion. Think of this. If they can destroy the integrity of a man's relationships in the church by surreptitious influence, that man (or woman) will eventually get discouraged with his or her faith entirely. They may blame God for what happened. They will begin to distrust God. They can become confused about God's true character. I remember one day, before I became aware that I had been stalked in the church, I said to God, "If I had to determine how you felt about me by the way your people treat me, I'd have to say you hate me." Now that I understand what covert operations are about, I am a little stronger and am not nearly as discouraged when people in the church are mistreating me. But this kind of thing can likely be the reason why many people leave the church and give up on their faith entirely. We need to be alert. I think that pastors in our churches take it much too lightly when people leave the church. They need to stop and think about why that is happening and do something about it. God does not simply let his sheep go. He goes after them, and for a good reason. He does not want his sheep eaten up by wolves!

We need to be extremely concerned about mind control. To blithely believe that God, of course, will protect us from this is denial. God gave us a will. We will always have to make a choice to listen to God or listen to another voice. He gave us his word, but so often we let "experts" tell us how to think even when what they say is contrary to the word of God. Remember Eve in the Garden of Eden was a perfect woman. She was sinless and uncorrupted, but she was still faced with temptation. She had to choose to listen to the word of God or listen to another voice. Her choice and the choice of her husband resulted in the entire world being thrown into darkness.

During a field training exercise known as REFORGER about four of my fellow soldiers were sitting on a hill in a little hut with radio equipment monitoring the exercise of "enemy" troops in the valley below them. One of the operators decided to be the "enemy" battalion commander, so he got on the radio and identified himself as such. He started giving orders to a bunch of infantry troops. Those troops had a book with a challenge and password for the day with them. It was proper procedure for them to challenge the one identifying himself as the battalion commander by giving him a codeword. If the one identifying himself as the commander was really the commander he would have been able to reply with the appropriate password. None of the soldiers who spoke to their "commander" that day were willing to stick to their guns and insist that the commander respond with the appropriate password. They were intimidated. Thus our guy on the radio had the entire unit dressed in MOPP 4 gear and so confused that the entire battalion was literally immobilized. MOPP (Mission Oriented Protective Posture) gear is a protective suit worn to protect soldiers against chemical, biological or nuclear attack. It does that well, but it is also horribly cumbersome and it is difficult to function normally when clothed in this gear. Thus is inhibits a soldier's ability to respond in a combat situation. The real Battalion Commander was furious with our team for what they did. It was our job to do what we did. It was part of the training. Actually, the exercise had a prewritten scenario and it was already decided who would win the war. Unfortunately those whose job it was to evaluate each player in the exercise decided that the team that was supposed to win the war actually lost because they did not follow procedure and were therefore unable to function.

My fellow brothers and sisters in Christ, this is exactly what operatives are doing in our churches today. Please hear me. We have the word of God. He tells us what to do. We have a choice to make. We will either listen to his voice or we will listen to the voice of an enemy, and that will determine the outcome. Mind control is a very real and present danger in the church today. It can be very subtle and it can be very direct. Directed Energy Weapons, which we have already discussed, can and I believe have been used to manipulate the mind, will and emotions of believers in the church.

One of the first attacks against me that I later identified as a DEW assault happened while I was attending the Vineyard Christian Fellowship church in Columbus Ohio. I was under attack in that church. There were signs of covert operations that I did not identify until I began to research gangstalking. I was becoming very angry with God and very discouraged. One day I said something to God in anger. It was very wrong of me, but I was under intense assault. I was hanging onto my faith in God by a thread, and I told God so. I woke up at about three in the morning hearing a voice echoing "from heaven" which said, "I will not forgive." I believed that God was telling me he was not going to forgive me, and that meant of course that I was condemned to hell. I was of course devastated. So I began to fast. While I was busy in my office at work, the Holy Spirit spoke to me. His words were a healing balm and a refreshing breeze in the midst of my trouble. He said to me, "Do you really think that fasting will do more for you that the blood if Jesus Christ has already done?" His word sent the darkness in my mind fleeing. His word always will. I now understand that my stalkers were trying to make me believe that God did not want me anymore. They were not only attempting to drive a wedge between my brothers and sisters in Christ and I, but a wedge between myself and God as well.

I am not the only believer to have been assaulted by DEW. In fact I can point directly to an entire congregation in Toronto Canada that I believe was under the influence of electronic mind control. Understand that DEW has the power to influence the thoughts, will and emotions of human beings. Your brain and your entire body is electric and it can be remotely manipulated just as your television can be remotely manipulated. The Clinton Administration had already determined that Christians would be on his list of targets for DEW assault. Bill and Hillary Clinton are among those attempting to push this nation into a one world government.

In 1994, the Airport Vineyard in Toronto Canada began to experience a move to of the Spirit that was quite phenomenal. However, as time wore on pastors of the Vineyard movement international began to withdraw their support. People were actually barking like dogs during worship and howling like roosters. Was that a move of the Spirit? I believe not. John Hagee called it witchcraft.[917] In fact it smacks to me of mind control by those who hate the church and love to mock Christians. Unfortunately, the Toronto church was "asleep". Directed Energy Weapons can be used to manipulate entire populations, so manipulating one small church is not beyond them. They sit behind a computer screen and manipulate people like they are just animated characters.[918] I can just seem them laughing, "Let's see if we can make them bark like dogs!" The reason they can do that is that they can "lock on" to your brainwaves and manipulate you externally. By locking on to your brainwaves a remote operator "...can induce desired states: meditation, calm, even euphoria. Used unknowingly against an individual it is the basic mechanism of Radio Intracerebral mind control . . . "[919] They can inject thoughts into your head that you can believe are your thoughts.[920] If they can thus manipulate your thoughts and emotions imagine what they can do in a church when they begin to externally manipulate the thoughts of people in the congregation in a negative way and create dissention.

> As Flanagan noted in a recent interview is that the HAARP project could be is not only the biggest "Ionospheric heater" in the world, but also the biggest brain-entrainment device ever conceived. According to HAARP records, when the device is built to full power it can send VLF and ELF waves using many wave forms at energy levels sufficient to affect entire regional populations.[921]

Again, if we are listening to the word of God which is written down for us, then we can avoid some of the damage this kind of manipulation can do.

---

917 John Hagee, Day of Deception (Nashville, 2000) 209
918 N.I. Anisimov, Psychotronic Golgotha (1999 - http://www.mindjustice.org).
919 Jerry E. Smith, HAARP: The Ultimate Weapon of the Conspiracy (Kempton, ILL: Adventures Unlimited Press, 1998) 68.
920 John J. McMurtrey, M.S. Inner Voice Target Tracking and Behavioral Influence Technologies (April 6th, 2003 - http://www.Slavery.org.uk).
921 Dr. Nick Begich and Jean Manning, Angels Don't Play This Harp (Anchorage, Earthpulse Press, 1995)139.

It won't do us any good to blithely say to ourselves, "God is in complete control" as if somehow we aren't going to have to worry about any of that. The book of Daniel clearly tells us that the Saints of God are going to be turned over to the antichrist for a period of 3½ years. When Daniel asks Gabriel when all the prophecies will be fulfilled, Gabriel tells him, "… when the power of the holy people has been completely shattered, all these things shall be fulfilled" (Daniel 12:6 NKJV). I had to search Strong's for the meaning of the words "power" and "shattered". What that verse says is that there is going to be a time when the strength of the church is broken. We will have nothing left to fight with. At that time Jesus will return to defeat the antichrist. Some are convinced that the rapture is going to happen before things get really bad and true believers won't have to experience anything horrible. They may be correct, but I don't believe that is what the scripture is telling us, and we should prepare ourselves for a fight.

42. Choose

The Gospel According to Bridget

It has taken me 4 plus years to come to an understanding of the New World Order and how they operate. I have been a Christian for 35 years. I have in my mind begun to perceive the parallel opposite elements of the NWO and the Kingdom of God. Many who read this book may not be believers and many are. However, this is the place where I need to show you the choice you have to make.

Americans are used to the idea of having choices. That includes choices in religion. Christians are most often faulted by others because of our claim that the Christian faith is exclusive. In other words, we say there is no other religion. I want to tackle that sensitive issue here because the choice that we all have to make is a profoundly important one. It is much more important than choosing which flavor of ice cream you want which is how the religious question is often treated.

People choose to be religious because they are attempting to relate to a God that they cannot relate to through their five senses. It is a universal human hunger to find a way to reach out to God. The reasons for that would include the fact that life is difficult, sometimes terrifying and often tinged with emptiness and we need a power that is bigger than ourselves that is more capable of responding to the issues we face than we are. In short we know we need God. Life is too much to face without that higher power. Secondly we have the issue of death to face. The fact that our lives are going to end someday leaves us with a nagging question – what is the meaning of my life? Why do I live at all, and why am I going to have to die? Religion is a way of addressing that nagging question. It also helps us cope with the fact that we have lost people we love through death.

God, however, is not a religion. He is not a man but he is a person. Neither is he defined by religion. He is who he is. He does not change because you change your religion. In Exodus Chapter 3 God calls Moses to go to Egypt and lead the

Israelites out of bondage. Moses asked him what to tell them when they asked him who sent him. God says, "I AM WHO I AM!" He calls himself, "I am" (Exodus 3:14). What a name. There are profound implications in the fact that God called himself, "I am".

It might help to think of your own personhood. You are a person. If people want to get to know you they don't invent a religion. They talk to you. They knock on your door and pay you a visit. Of course you have a physical body. People around you can relate to you through their five senses. God is invisible. We can't relate to him that way.

Let us consider another point. We reach out to God hoping that he is interested in knowing us. We hope that he cares about us. We want him to. We need him to care. In fact the Bible does indicate to us that God is interested in knowing us and he does care about us. In Exodus 3 God meets Moses at a burning bush and tells him that he has heard the cries of the Israelites in bondage in Egypt and he is concerned for them. He has made a plan for delivering them from their misery. In the New Testament he sends us his own son in the form of an infant. He came to us in vulnerability. He put himself in our arms. In Luke 15 Jesus tells us a parable of the prodigal son who left his father taking his inheritance with him. He tells how the father looked day after day after day waiting and hoping that his son would come home. I want you to imagine what that is like. When was there a time in your life when you missed someone you love. Maybe there was a disagreement and you wanted to resolve it. But you had to wait for that person to come to you. When you have an intense longing for someone you are constantly hoping, "maybe today". The father of the prodigal in the parable was hoping against hope, "maybe today." When he finally sees his son coming, he breaks into a run. That is desperate longing. That is hunger. In fact God's hunger for us is much stronger than our hunger for him.

If God wanted to get close to us, if he desired us like we desire him, he would have to find a way to enter our world. The truth is we are helpless unless he finds a way to get to us. This is where the Christian faith parts from other world religions. In the Bible Jesus Christ is the physical representation of the invisible God. He is called the Son of God. God identifies him as his son in Matt: 3:17. He speaks from heaven in an audible voice when he says "This is my beloved son in whom I am well pleased". Jesus says "I and the father are one" (John 10:30 NIV). In John 8:58 Jesus very pointedly identified himself with God when he said, "Very truly I tell you ... before Abraham was born, I am!" Jesus was God's answer to the human craving to get close to him. He came in human form. He came with a message to tell us that yes God is interested in knowing us. Yes he cares about us. Yes he has an answer to the question of death. Jesus did not come to give us a religion. He came to give us God himself. He came to give us life. He came to overcome death for us. He came to tell us that we have purpose in being a beloved child of the creator of the entire universe. He came with an eternal gift of life. "I have come that they may have life and may have it more abundantly" (John 10:10); "For God so loved the world that he gave his only son so that whoever would believe in him would not perish but have everlasting life (John 3:16).

One very important point that Jesus came to make in his ministry is that we are in fact helpless without him. God is Holy. We are sinful. Our sin makes it impossible for us to come to God on our own. In our sinful state we cannot stand in God's presence. In the book of Exodus we read the story of how Moses met with God who used him to deliver the Israelites out of slavery. Moses had a unique relationship with God. He stood face to face with God (Exodus 33:11). Yet even in that relationship Moses did not see God in all his Glory. So Moses wanted to see God in all his glory. God allowed him to do so. But he had to put him in the cleft of the rock and cover him with his hand as he passed by. Moses could only look at his back. For God told him, "No man can look at my face and live" (Exodus 22:20 – 23NIV). In Exodus 19 Moses is instructed to put boundaries around Mt. Sinai and warn the people not to try to come up the mountain because if they got too close to him them would die. Death is the penalty for sin. Jesus is the only way to overcome that obstacle. He died in our place (John 3:16). He is also the only way we can "get to" God. He said, "I am the way the truth and the light. No man can come to the Father except through me" (John 14:6, NIV). In Acts 4:12 (NIV) we are told, "Salvation is found in no one else. There is no other name under Heaven given to men by which we must be saved." John 10:1 Jesus explains that anyone who attempts to get into the sheep pen by any other way other than the door is a thief and a robber. He goes on to say, "I am the gate for the sheep. . . . Whoever enters through me will be saved" (John 10:7, 8 NIV). You have a door to your house. If someone wants to enter your house he has to come in by your door at your invitation. If he attempts to enter through a window or attempts to come through your door without your invitation he is not your friend. Jesus told us he is the door to God's house. He is the only door to God's house and the only way to get to him. The reason for this is that we need a covering for our sin. Jesus paid the price for our sin and therefore when we come to God in Jesus Christ, God sees his son. He does not see our sin. It has been atoned for.

After Jesus was crucified and rose again, he told his disciples that he was returning to his father. Of course having lived through the shock of seeing him crucified and then being filled with the joy of seeing him alive again they were not happy about this. He was leaving them. But Jesus comforted them by telling them that he was going to send them another comforter, the Holy Spirit, who would fill them with power. In Acts chapter two we read the story of how the Spirit of Jesus Christ filled his disciples while they were praying in the upper room. The scripture says that tongues of fire appeared on their heads. Thus Jesus has made a way for us to abide continually in God's presence. When you accept the blood that Jesus shed for your sins and you surrender yourself to Jesus you receive his spirit inside of you. From then on God is always with you wherever you go (Matt 28:20NIV). From then on you have rights as children of God to ask whatever you need of him in the name of his son (John 14:13, John 15:16, John 16:23 NIV).

People addicted to "choice" have a problem with this exclusiveness. This is the issue we have to face. When we invent religions we also invent a god to go with that religion. We invent a god whom we can control and manipulate to do our bidding. It is a part of our sinfulness. We want to be in control. So we invent a god in our own image that satisfies us. But when we come to God we come to him on his terms not on our terms. When we come to God we come to surrender. God is not going to bend to our will. He will not be manipulated or controlled by us. His intentions toward us are all good. He desires what is best for us. Therefore we will often find ourselves in conflict with him because the sin in our "self-ness" resists his holiness. We are willful. We have to be brought to that place of surrender. He loves us completely. He will not use force. But when we get to that place that we understand that we cannot control him we can get frustrated until we learn to relate to him. Even those who love God and believe in Jesus Christ have trouble with that. It is a lifelong process of being transformed so that we are conformed to the image of his son.

He came to save us. Here is where we have to make a choice. He will absolutely not force himself on us. He will save us from the NWO if we choose him. We have to choose to trust him. We have to surrender ourselves to him if we want him to save us. When we surrender, we choose to obey him.

The NWO vs. the Kingdom of God

God laid down laws to guide his people in forming community. Those laws were based on the notion of loving your neighbor. In Exodus Ch 20, the commandments stated clearly are as follows. I want you to see the Kingdom of God and Compare it to the NWO.

- You shall have no other Gods before me.

In the New World Order, the State is God. In their religion, Satan is God.

- You shall not make for yourself an idol in the form of anything in heaven above or on the earth beneath or in the waters below. You shall not bow down to them or worship them.

The Washington Monument is a Freemason constructed edifice that represents the male phallus and also the Egyptian Sun god Rah. At the Bohemian Grove they worship at the feet of a stone owl otherwise known as Moloch. They also practice human sacrifice. From Washington to California and everywhere in between sexual perversion associated with idolatry has covered this land.

- You shall not misuse the name of the Lord your God for the Lord will not hold anyone guiltless who misuses his name.

New World Order cultists use religious language to mind control children thus creating a barrier between them and any belief in God or Jesus Christ.

- Remember the Sabbath day by keeping it holy. Six days you shall labor and do all your work, but the seventh day is the Sabbath to the Lord your God. On it you shall not do any work . . . .

The New World Order would have us slaving seven days a week. Most retail businesses are open seven days a week.

- Honor your Father and your Mother so that you may live long in the land the Lord your God is giving you.

The NWO believes that children are the property of the State. They have passed numerous laws which limit the authority that parents have over their children. One of those laws allows minors to acquire contraceptives and have abortions without their parents consent or knowledge.

- You shall not murder.

They have slaughtered millions of people in their effort to accomplish their agenda crashing planes into buildings notwithstanding. They have no regard or respect for life. Life is secondary to the accomplishment of their ambition.

- You shall not commit adultery.

There is no respect for the marriage covenant with the NWO. In fact, if you don't cooperate with them they may just decide to destroy your marriage. (See chapter on Surveillance and the American Police State Part I.) Marriage also has a way of stabilizing people. They want to destabilize the world and thus marriage is actually a hindrance to their objectives. Adherents to the NWO typically have no qualms with infidelity in their marriages. In fact the Illuminati were instructed that committing adultery was okay as long as you didn't do so with the wife of the head of the order ![922]

- You shall not steal.

They will steal your underwear ![923] They will steal your house! They will confiscate anything you have if it suits their purposes.

- You shall not give false testimony [lie].

They can't accomplish their mission without deception. Therefore they have made a policy to deceive the American public. In fact they have infected the "free press" with their deception. They create secret courts where mockery is made of justice, where they can lie freely in order to accomplish their goals and where innocent people are convicted of crimes they did not commit based on hearsay evidence, coerced confessions etc. They typically indemnify any of their operatives from prosecution by denying any evidence that will convict them while they use false evidence to convict persons who are not guilty of any wrongdoing.

- You shall not covet your neighbor's house. You shall not covet your neighbor's wife, or his manservant or maidservant, his ox or his donkey, or anything that belongs to your neighbor.

They want your life including your job, your car, your house, your marriage, and your children. A man who called into the prayer lines at my church had three trillion dollars in gold and oil investments. However, the U.S. Government decided that it was too much money for any one person to have. Thus anytime

---

922 Terry Melanson, Illuminati Conspiracy Part One: A Precise Exegesis on Available Evidence (August 5th, 2005. - http://www.conspitatyarchive.com).

923 Greg Szymanski, The Evil Lurking Within (July 31, 2005. -http://www.resne.com).

he attempted to get any money out of his account, it was confiscated by the U.S. treasury. The United States Treasury has literally confiscated 6 million dollars from this man and he was living like a pauper.

The foundation of the Christian faith is the death and resurrection of Jesus Christ which is presented in four gospels on the Bible. The entire Bible tells us that man is corrupted. We are sinners. Yes I know I am sounding like a broken record. From the first sin in the Garden of Eden throughout history every human being has "fallen short of the glory of God" (Romans 3:23 NKJV). The Bible clearly tells us what the consequences of our sins will be. "For the wages of sin *is* death; but the gift of God *is* eternal life through Jesus Christ our Lord" (Rom 6:23 NKJV). The Bible also tells us that God is willing to forgive if we are willing to confess. "If we confess our sins, he is faithful and just to forgive us *our* sins, and to cleanse us from all unrighteousness" (1John 1:9 NKJV). The Kingdom of God is about forgiveness. The Bible also clearly tells us that when God forgives us of our sins, he forgets them and remembers them no more. The record is wiped clean. "As far as the east is from the west, *so* far hath he removed our transgressions from us" (Psalm 103:12 NKJV). Therefore when we come to God confessing our sins, he cleanses us from sin. That is he removes the sting of sin from our souls and he forgets that we ever committed the sin. We get a fresh start. In fact the Bible tells us that we get a fresh start with God every day. "This I recall to my mind, therefore have I hope. *It is of the LORD's mercies that we are not consumed, because his compassions fail not. They are* new every morning: great *is* thy faithfulness" (Lam 3:21-23 NKJV). We still have to struggle with our flesh which never gets any better. The corruption we struggle with is in our fleshly bodies. Our task is to overcome our flesh which remains corrupted. We have to come to live by our spirits and not give in to the desires of our flesh. It is a fight, and we win the fight in Jesus Christ. The Apostle Paul speaks of this fight in Romans 7:18 – 25(NKJV) "I know that nothing good lives in me, that is, in my sinful nature. For I have the desire to do what is good, but I cannot carry it out. For what I do is not the good I want to do; no, the evil I do not want to do – this I keep on doing. Now if I do what I do not want to do, it is no longer I who do it, but there is sin living in me that does it. So I find this law at work. When I want to do good, evil is right there with me. For in my inner being I delight in God's law; but I see another law at work within my members. What a wretched man I am! Who will rescue me from this body of death? Thanks be to God – through Jesus Christ our Lord".

God has a perfect plan for addressing the sinful nature of man. It does not include putting him in bondage and blackmailing him into cooperation. However, that is precisely what the NWO is doing. Not only have they everybody under surveillance and not only do they have access to your private life but they intend to use it to manipulate you into cooperating with their profoundly evil agenda. Not only will they search your background to find something they can use to manipulate you, if they can't find anything they will actually set you up to tempt you to do something grossly immoral or illegal and then catch you on film. They are determined to put a noose around your neck one way or another. The illuminati used a system of espionage to spy on all their trainees gaining as much information about them as they could. They also enticed them into committing criminal acts that they could use as blackmail material to gain their cooperation. "With pleasure they see them commit any...treasons or treacherous acts because they not only turn the secrets betrayed to their own advantage, but thereby have it in their power to keep the traitors in a perpetual dread, lest, if they ever showed any signs of stubbornness, their malefactions should be made known."[924]

The Bible is clear about God's intentions to save mankind. Man sins. God made provision for our sins by sending His son to die for us. Romans 5:8 states, "But God demonstrates His own love for us in this; While we were still sinners, Christ died for us" (NKJV). The NWO invites those who have unleashed their passions in horribly sinful ways to the Bohemian Grove every year for the "Cremation of Care" ceremony where they "cleanse" their guilty consciences by sacrificing someone else's son or daughter. In fact, they will not only commit murder to "cleanse" their guilty consciences but they will shed your blood to save their own skin. They have no problems with killing someone who attempts to expose them.

The Christian faith is rooted in love. All the way through the Bible the message is simply this, "God loves you no matter what you do. His love for you will not fail. He will not give up on you. He will not leave you." The book of Hosea, which brings tears to my eyes every time I read it, is the tale of one of God's prophets who had an adulterous wife named Gomer. In fact God told Hosea to marry Gomer knowing what she would do. But God sent him to go and get his adulterous wife and save her from her adulterous life. He rescued her from her own sins. (You won't find the word "codependent" anywhere is the Bible.) The book of Hosea is a prophetic picture of God's relationship with Israel. In Isaiah 54:10 God speak of his unfailing love for us 'Though the mountains be shaken and the hills be removed, yet my unfailing love for you will be not be shaken, nor my covenant of peace be removed,' says the Lord who has compassion on you." The scriptures also tell us how to define love, "This is how we know what love is; Jesus Christ laid down His life for us..." (John 3:16 NIV).

The concept of love has been rejected by the New World Order. The Illuminati believed in keeping people in line by spying on them and coercing them into submission. They didn't care if people hated them as long as they feared them. "Oderint dum metuant, let them hate, provided they fear, is the principle of the government."[925] A former member of the Ordo Templis Oreintes lodge in San Bernardino California, Candace Reos, testified for the Riverside Police in 1969. When she became pregnant she was told by the head of the lodge, Georgina, that she would have to condition herself to hate her child. In fact cult children were

---

924 Terry Melanson, Illuminati Conspiracy Part One: A Precise Exegesis on Available Evidence (August 5th, 2005. - http://www.conspitatyarchive.com).
925 Ibid.

secluded from their parents for training which included being severely beaten and heavily criticized.[926] In *The New Satanist*, Linda Blood writes, "The core message of Satanism is designed to destroy the human capacity for love, warmth trust, and adherence to any moral code, leaving the individual desensitized and out of touch with reality". She indicates that cults deliberately induce psychological and physical trauma in order to destroy a child's ability to form attachments.[927] It is known by those who have worked with foster care children that if a child does not form a loving bond with someone by the time he/she is 6 years old, the child will not develop a conscience. The New World Order is determined to eradicate your conscience. They want people who are willing to lie, cheat, steal an commit murder or do anything they are asked to do. Having a conscience gets in the way of completing their mission. Thus deliberately destroying a person's ability to form attachments or even feel love for anyone is the key. Lunarcharsky, the Russian Commissioner of Education, said: "Christian love is an obstacle to the development of the revolution. Down with love of one's neighbor! What we want is HATE…. Only then can we conquer the universe."[928] Sergei Nechayev, the Russian Revolutionary influenced the Bolshevik communist revolution with his writings. The death toll of the revolution was approximately 42 million. His writings influenced Nikolai Lenin one of the prime movers of the revolution. He embraced a situational ethics which opposed love and human relationships. He wrote

> The revolutionary … despises and hates the existing social morality….
> For him, morality is everything which contributes to the triumph of the revolution. Immoral and criminal is everything that stands in his way.
> The revolutionary must be tyrannical toward others. All the gentle and enervating sentiments of kinship, love, friendship, gratitude, and even honor must be suppressed in him and give place to the cold and single-minded passion for revolution.[929]

In the Bible we are told that God desires to bless us with abundant life. Jesus came to eradicate poverty. Jesus tells us in John 10:10, "A thief comes only to steal and kill and destroy. I have come that they may have life, and have it to the full" (NKJV). He promises to provide all that we need and in Matthew Ch. 6 he tells us not to worry about what we will eat or wear because he promises to provide those things. We are to seek his kingdom first, not riches, but he will provide what we need. God desires for his people to be prosperous. In Deuteronomy 28; 11 he tells the Jews, "The Lord will grant you abundant prosperity – in the fruit of

---

926 Alex Constantine, Psychic Dictatorship in the U.S. A. (Portland: Feral House, 1995)59.
927 Linda Blood, The New Satanist (New York: Warner Books, 1994)104, 129.
928 A Ralf Epperson, The New World Order (Tucson: Publius Press, 1990 274.
929 Sergey Nechayev, The Revolutionary Catechism (1869 -http://www.marxists.org).

your womb, the young of your livestock and the corps of you ground – in the land he swore to your forefathers to give you" (NKJV). That is not an unconditional promise. It comes with obedience to God's will. God set a standard of morality which creates a stabilized society for those who adhere to it.

The New World Order sees poverty as a way of controlling people. They do not want people to prosper because prosperous people have the power to resist. One of the goals of the Bilderbergers was to eliminate prosperity (See the chapter titled "The Council of Foreign Relations..."). One of their goals is zero population growth which will cause the economy to decline. They do not want anyone to prosper who is not willing to submit to their one world government.

Sexual immorality is strictly forbidden in the life of a believer. In Romans 13:13, 14 we are instructed to abstain from sexual immorality and not to give in to the desires of the flesh. Though many Christians struggle with their sexuality and also drug use, the blood of Jesus Christ was offered as the way of delivering people from addictions. Jesus does not desire for us to be addicted. Jesus also clearly indicates that pedophilia is absolutely abhorrent to God. "But if anyone causes one of these little ones who believe in me to sin, it would be better for him to have a large millstone hung around his neck and to be drowned in the depths of the sea" (Matt 18:6 NKJV). There are many who have been delivered from sexual addictions and drug addictions in Jesus Christ. Jesus does not want his people in bondage. "The Spirit of the Lord is upon me, because he hath anointed me to preach the gospel to the poor; he hath sent me to heal the brokenhearted, to preach deliverance to the captives, and recovering of sight to the blind, to set at liberty them that are bruised" (Luke 4:18 NKJV).

The New World Order however advocates for every kind of sexual perversion known to man. Those fleshly desires are nourished at the Bohemian grove and elsewhere. They engage in sadomasochistic violence with unwilling men, women and children. The New World Order uses sex as a way of controlling people. They know they can control people who are addicted. A report written in 1961 by MKULTRA mind control psychiatrists Wayne O Evans, director of the U.S. Army Military Stress Laboratory and psychiatrist Nathan Kline of Columbia University indicated that because meaningful work would only be available for a few in the future, drugs and sex would be an acceptable means of controlling the general populace. They have a philosophical view which severs any connection between sex and reproduction or disease and thus it "… will undoubtedly enhance sexual freedom". They state " … The sooner we cease to confuse scientific and moral statements about drug use, the sooner we can rationally consider the types of neurochemical states that we wish to be able to provide for people."[930]

Mind controllers have used sexual trauma for years to induce multiple personalities in children and they use it also to control adults. Not only are sexually traumatized people more "controllable" but they have managed to tempt

---

930 Jim Keith, Control, World Control (Kempton, ILL: Adventures Unlimited Press, 1997) 57 – 58.

many of our congressmen and senators to live out their sexual fantasies even with children and have caught them on tape. Thus our representatives have been morally compromised and their careers will be destroyed if they do not cooperate with the agenda of the NWO.

Jesus came to heal us of our diseases and the New Testament is replete with stories of those who were healed of their diseases by the touch of the Master. He also raised the dead. The NWO wants to kill off a goodly portion of the population. They want only slaves and slave owners to exist on earth. Thus they have created diseases as a way of trimming down the population. Abortion is also one of their favorite methods of trimming the population. As I have already discussed, they literally sterilized a major portion of the woman in the nation of Brazil. They have sent the World Health Organization around the world to perform abortions on women of impoverished nations, and they have "vaccinated" the same with diseases bringing death. They also created the aids virus to do the same.

This nation was born from people who were tired of the tyranny and slavery of England. They came to this land and forged a path through a very dangerous wilderness to create a nation free from slavery and tyranny. Many of them died in the process. This nation was founded on Christian principles by people who understood the depravity of human nature. They left us with many warnings which I am afraid we have not heard.

The Nation of Israel was rescued from the same kind of tyranny in the land of Egypt. Their tormenters literally put them to work baking bricks in the hot sun day after day. They were beaten and abused and lived on only what they had to have to survive. They cried out in their misery and God heard them. He sent them a deliverer. Because of disobedience, after they left Egypt, one generation lived in the desert before they entered the land that God had promised them. They had to fight to get it, but God was with them. As he promised, he delivered them a land flowing with milk and honey. Joshua was their leader. On the day he sent the Israelites home to enjoy the gifts God had given them he made a speech. It is worth our time to consider what he said to them.

> *And Joshua gathered all the tribes of Israel to Shechem, and called for the elders of Israel, and for their heads, and for their judges, and for their officers; and they presented themselves before God. And Joshua said unto all the people, "Thus saith the LORD God of Israel, Your fathers dwelt on the other side of the flood in old time, even Terah, the father of Abraham, and the father of Nachor: and they served other gods. And I took your father Abraham from the other side of the flood, and led him throughout all the land of Canaan, and multiplied his seed, and gave him Isaac. And I gave unto Isaac Jacob and Esau: and I gave unto Esau mount Seir, to possess it; but Jacob and his children went down into Egypt. I sent Moses also and Aaron and I plagued Egypt, according to that which I did among them: and afterward I*

brought you out. And I brought your fathers out of Egypt: and ye came unto the sea; and the Egyptians pursued after your fathers with chariots and horsemen unto the Red sea. And when they cried unto the LORD, he put darkness between you and the Egyptians, and brought the sea upon them, and covered them; and your eyes have seen what I have done in Egypt: and ye dwelt in the wilderness a long season. And I brought you into the land of the Amorites, which dwelt on the other side Jordan; and they fought with you: and I gave them into your hand that ye might possess their land; and I destroyed them from before you. Then Balak the son of Zippor, king of Moab, arose and warred against Israel, and sent and called Balaam the son of Beor to curse you: But I would not hearken unto Balaam; therefore he blessed you still: so I delivered you out of his hand. And you went over Jordan, and came unto Jericho: and the men of Jericho fought against you, the Amorites, and the Perizzites, and the Canaanites, and the Hittites, and the Girgashites, the Hivites, and the Jebusites; and I delivered them into your hand. And I sent the hornet before you, which drove them out from before you, even the two kings of the Amorites; but not with thy sword, nor with thy bow. And I have given you a land for which ye did not labor, and cities which ye built not, and ye dwell in them; of the vineyards and oliveyards which ye planted not do you eat.

Now therefore fear the LORD, and serve him in sincerity and in truth: and put away the gods which your fathers served on the other side of the flood, and in Egypt; and serve you the LORD. And if it seem evil unto you to serve the LORD, choose you this day whom you will serve; whether the gods which your fathers served that were on the other side of the flood, or the gods of the Amorites, in whose land you dwell: but as for me and my house, we will serve the LORD (Joshua 24:1-15 NKJV).

43. FEMA AND MARTIAL LAW

They are taking us back to a time before there was an America, a constitution, and a time before "We the people..." believed that all men are created equal and endowed with certain inalienable rights because "they" don't believe.

And unfortunately for us, we have never lived in any other way. What we perceive as "natural" was not natural to those who fought and died to give us our liberty. You have to stop and think of what it was that made our founding fathers willing to shed their own blood. Our founding fathers did not grow up in an "America". They did not have a flag over which to recite the pledge of allegiance. They did not until they came here have the right to own their own homes. They could be thrown in jail on a whim and executed for nothing. They had watched family members disappear into the Moloch of the British Empire. They did not get to go to bed at night and sleep peacefully believing that they would wake up in the morning and everything would be alright. They did not have a fat 401K to make them feel secure. All our founding fathers had was a dream and a hope they were willing to die for. And because they could not live forever they passed on their hope and dream to us. And we had better wake up.

Under the Nixon administration the Law Enforcement Assistance Administration (LEAA), an arm of the U.S. Justice Department, met with Richard Nixon, Attorney General John Mitchell, H.R. Haldemann, John Erlichman, and Dr. Bertram Brown, director for the National Institute of Mental Health. At this meeting they developed the National Population surveillance Computer System. The Surveillance system was designed to monitor U.S. Citizens and to create a national police force under Operation Cable Splicer and Operation Garden Plot.[931] Cable Splicer covered California, Washington state, Oregon and Arizona and put them under the command of the 6th Army. Cable Splicer was the model for an orderly takeover of the State government by the Federal Government. Garden Plot was the plan to control the population.

At the meeting a link was forged between the LEAA and the National Institute of Mental Health (NIMH). The LEAA provided funding for 350 NIMH projects which included mind control and behavior modification programs in hospitals, prisons and schools. The Department of Health Education and Welfare was included with a program to screen all children on Medicaid for psychological problems, programs for treating prison inmates with psychoactive drugs, shock treatment for child molesters, psychosurgery for prisoners as well as vomit inducing drugs for prisoners who broke rules and also Anectine, the terror drug for California prison inmates.[932] The LEAA which was originally geared for Martial Law became turned toward mind control and behavior modification.

In November 1974 the U.S. Senate Subcommittee on Constitutional Rights, Senator Sam Ervin and Congressman Leo Ryan who was murdered in Jonestown, were a part of the committee that investigated the LEAA. Subcommittee Chief Counsel Doug Lee read through Cable Splicer documents and determined that it was a model for a takeover.[933] They interrogated Donald E. Santarelli director of the LEAA who announced that the LEAA would no longer provide funds for psychosurgery. Funding continued however.[934] The government publication, "Individual Rights and the Federal Role in Behavior Modification" located on the web at http://www.eric.ed.gov, revealed that the DOJ, VA and DOD among others

---

931 Ibid ,111.
932 Ibid.
933 Jim Marrs, The Terror Conspiracy: Deception, 9/11 and the Loss of Liberty (New York: Disinformation, 2006) 269.
934 Jim Keith, Mind Control, World Control (Kempton, Ill: Adventures Unlimited Press, 1997) 112.

were involved in behavior modification projects without proper accountability. "One such project at Atmore State Prison conducted over 50 psychosurgical operations, which according to Dr Swan of Fisk University, were lobotomies performed on black political activists."[935]

In April 1984 President Regan signed the Presidential Directive # 54 which allowed the Federal Emergency Management Agency (FEMA) to activate a secret national readiness exercise code named REX- 84. The purpose of the exercise was to test FEMA's ability to assume military authority in case of a domestic national emergency. REX 84 was so highly guarded that special metal doors were installed on the fifth floor of the FEMA building in Washington, D.C. The only people that were allowed to enter the premises were ones who had a red Christian cross on their shirt. Col. Oliver North was in charge of the development of REX 84 plans and operations. It was initially designed to coincide with U.S. Military action in Central America and it called for the National Guard and the U.S. Military to be used for domestic Law Enforcement. The Military would be used to take into custody an estimated 400,000 undocumented Central American immigrants in the United States and also black Americans who would be detained at 10 detention centers to be set up at military bases throughout the country". Others included in the round up were "tax protesters, demonstrators against government military intervention outside U.S. borders, and people who maintain weapons in their homes …"[936]

The plan called for the suspension of the Constitution, the declaration of Martial Law and turning the government over to FEMA. The Rex 84 plan was first exposed during the Iran-Contra Hearings in 1987 and reported by the Miami Herald on July 5, 1987.[937] It also allowed for US citizens to be detained in concentration camps without due process. Secretary of State George Shultz also lobbied for a pre-emptive-strikes bill which would allow for listing "known and suspected terrorists" in the US who could be killed by government agencies "with impunity". The strikes would take place on the basis of information that would normally not be permitted in any court of law, such as hearsay evidence and coerced confessions. Listed persons would not be permitted to sue in court to have their names taken off that list.[938]

---

935 Marshall G. Thomas, Monarch: The New Phoenix Program (New York: iUniverse Inc., 2007) 54.
936 Harry V. Martin with research assistance from David Caul, FEMA - The Secret Government (1995- http://dmc.members.sonic.net.
937 Allen L. Roland, Rex 84: FEMA's Blueprint for Martial Law in America (December 04,2010. - December 4, 2010.- http://www.globalresearch.com).
938 John Stockwell, The Praetorian Guard: The U.s. Role in the New World Order (Boston, MA: South End Press, 1991) 20.

As a part of the Rex 84 operation some 600 to 800 secret detention centers were established around the country. An article by Friends of Liberty reveals the locations of many of these camps. Some of them listed are as follows;[939]

- Alabama – Maxwell AFB currently in operation with support staff and a small inmate population.
- Alaska – East of Anchorage in the wilderness that is accessed only by air or by railroad with an estimated capacity of 500,000 detainees. This is a massive "mental health" (aka mind control) facility. Also Elmendorf AFB also in Anchorage and Eielson AFB - Southeast of Fairbanks.
- California – Vandenberg AFB, Oakdale (20,000 capacity), Long Beach Federal Prison (possible deportation point).
- Florida – Elgin AFB
- Georgia – Ft. Benning (Multiple reports that this will be the national headquarters and coordinating center for foreign/UN troop movement and detainee collection).
- New York – Ft. Drum
- Virginia – Ft. AP Hill (capacity 45,000).
- Wisconsin – Ft. McCoy

Operation Garden Plot and Cable Splicer fell under the umbrella of Rex 84. In 1991 the late John Todd, spoke from prison about Cable Splicer and Garden Plot.

> For over twelve years I have said that the goal of the United States government was to activate what is called Operation Garden Plot and its sub-plot Operation Cablesplice. Which was martial law, total military control over all police forces, governments, and so on. I've said that in order to do that they wanted the populace out there to scream at the president that he wasn't doing his job of protecting them from acts of terrorism. And that they were willing to give up their constitutional rights. Now we have seen time and time again in order to stop the drug wars to stop the drug dealers, and all the bloodshed that they are willing to give up Constitutional rights. People are willing to do it. People, when terrorism strikes, are willing to do it.[940]

Ten years after John Todd made that statement from prison, the September 11 events threw into motion a series of events that have decimated our ailing

---

939 Friends of Liberty FEMA CONCENTRATION CAMPS: Locations and Executive Orders [Online] November12, 2004 - http://www.sianews.com).
940 John Todd, John Todd's testimonial while in prison (February 26, 1991 - http://www.kt70.com).

Constitution and severely depleted our civil rights, not to mention have eaten away our protective due processes like acid eats away at metal.

In 2006 George W. Bush signed the Defense Authorization Act in a private ceremony in the Oval office. The act was 1400 pages long. Within those 1400 pages was a little unnoticed "rider" which gave the President authority to declare Martial Law and employ the armed forces including the National Guard in the event of a public emergency in order to restore public order and suppress disorder. The emergency could include a hurricane, a public protest, or a public health crisis. Prior to the signing of this act Martial Law could only be declared in case of insurrection. Democratic Senator Patrick Lehey was the only one who spoke out against this piece of legislation. Normal procedures which would allow Congress the review the bill before it was passed were completely bypassed.[941] This is all seen by Daniel Estulin as a move by the globalists the eliminate national sovereignty and absorb every nation including the United Stated into a one world global market for the purpose of benefiting those involved in the corporate world granting them "profits without restraint". Those of us who oppose them "may be considered a threat to national security and detained indefinitely, with or without evidence, under Patriot and Military Commission Acts. We're all "enemy combatants" stripped of our habeas and due process rights, unless we can prove to be dumbed-down cattle."[942]

All that remains is for there to be some kind of crisis, Hegelian style, probably created by the established elite, to convince us all that Martial Law is necessary for our protection and security. Is that okay with you? Are you ready to give up your constitutional rights for a lie? Are you ready to let local Law Enforcement and the U. S. Military have card blanch for detaining whoever they want whenever they want without legal representation for an indefinite period of time – say just long enough for them to erase your personality and reprogram you to be an obedient compliant robot?

You know, the citizens of Hitler's NAZI Germany gave up a lot of things believing that they would not be harmed. But they weren't thinking about their Jewish neighbors. So they didn't pay attention when their Jewish neighbors just disappeared. Keep in mind that what was done to the Jews during the holocaust was accomplished because of apathy. The church in Germany failed the Jews because they were not watching for wolves in sheep's clothing. Dietrich Bonheoffer was famous for speaking up in favor of the Jews while the church opposed him.[943] Pastor Martin Niemoeller spoke up about the corruption of Germany and the problem with apathy in his own country. His words were published in Time Magazine August 28, 1989. He said, "First they came for the Communists, but I

---

941 Naomi Klein, The Shock Doctrine: The Rose of Disaster Capitalism (New York: Metropolitan Books: Henry Holt and Company, 2007) 309.
942 Daniel Estulin, The True Story of the Bilderberger Group (Waterville, OR: Trine Day LLC., 2007) 380.
943 John Hagee, Day of Deception (Nashville: Thomas Nelson, 2000) 9.

was not a communist so I did not speak out. Then they came for the Socialists and the Trade Unionists, but I was neither, so I did not speak out. Then they came for the Jews, but I was not a Jew so I did not speak out. And when they came for me, there was no one left to speak out for me." In the book *Watership Down* written by Richard Adams, a group of very well fed rabbits living in a great underground cavern seem to simply not notice when one of their members disappeared. Another group of rabbits who had taken up shelter with them were deeply disturbed by what appeared to be a prevailing sense of denial on the part of their hosts. When one of their own members disappeared they investigated. Fortunately they were able to rescue their friend from a rabbit trap, but they discovered to their horror that they were living on a rabbit farm and the farmer was making sure they were well fed so he could kill them and eat them. Their hosts simply refused to face reality though they had a strange wall, a memorial, where they put pebbles whenever one of them disappeared.[944]

Shall we build another memorial, or shall we fight back?

44. Hope

There was a period of time in my life when it seemed that the church was failing me. I had given my life to Jesus Christ when I was fifteen years old. I had been an active member of my church since that time, and wherever I went in my travels, one of my favorite things to do was find a church to worship in. I found great delight in meeting new people and especially those who shared my faith. But at some point it seemed that the church was turning away from me and I did not know why.

Things got the worst they had ever been when I began attending the Vineyard Christian Fellowship. I was at first enamored with that church, but something went strangely awry. I was being ignored. It was a pointed kind or ignoring. I noticed people staring at me. Not just looking at me absently but blatantly staring at me with looks that could kill – and did. One day I asked one of the pastors to pray for me and while he was praying for me he was banging on my head with his hand. I had a migraine and that was not helping, so I asked him to please not bang on my head. He looked at me with disgust, threw his hands up in the air and walked away. I was stunned though I continued to attend there.

I was asked by one of the members to join a missionary team that was planning a trip to Afghanistan. It was something I had wanted to do all my life, and I was excited about the opportunity. But suddenly the leader of that team, who had invited me to go, turned on me as well and was being very rude to me. He eventually dismissed me. I was devastated. I tried to talk to the pastoral leadership about what was going on. I spent a goodly amount of time in the office of the associate pastor who was very kind to me. However, I don't think he really connected to what I was

---

944 Richard Adams, Watership Down (New York: Scribner, 1972, Rex Collins, Ltd).

feeling. Though he was truly a very compassionate man, I doubt that he realized that there was something going on there besides the grumblings of one dissatisfied member. Frankly, I was just one of many fish in a very large tank. I counseled for a while with an LPCC who worked there. She was again very compassionate but it wasn't helping. I was also on the prayer ministry team ministering to others, but honestly felt drained. The atmosphere was so hostile and cold.

I was growing increasingly angry with God and at one point I "heard" God tell me that he would not forgive me. He later rescued me from that devilish deception, but my relationship with God was severely wounded because of the atmosphere in the Vineyard. I was constantly breaking down and crying. I was dragging myself to church on Sunday morning. One day I could not do it anymore so after I forced myself to get up and go to church, I forced myself to walk out of there for the last time. It was three years before I could even drive bye without feeling angry.

I chose another church, Christ Community, and was again very active. But the same kinds of things were happening there that were happening at the Vineyard and I was mystified. I talked to the associate pastor and his wife one evening and simply broke down and cried. There was something very wrong with that occurrence. I was not tearful when I went to the pastor's house. I was discouraged but not in the mood to cry. But before I could open my mouth to speak, suddenly I dropped my head and began sobbing uncontrollably. That experience mystified me at the time because I did not know anything about Directed Energy Weapons. I know now that it was a DEW assault designed by the stalkers to make it appear that I was having an emotional breakdown. The pastor and his wife of course prayed with me, but nothing was really resolved. I eventually bought a house closer to my job and left Christ Community.

During this period of time I was becoming increasingly disturbed by what appeared to me to be a deep apathy on the part of the church. The Bible clearly tells us what will be happening in the last days. In Daniel 12:1 (NKJV) we read, "… And there shall be a time of trouble; Such as never was since there was a nation, even to that time." Believers in Jesus Christ know we are in the last days because that period of time was marked very clearly for us by the rebirth of the nation of Israel. Yet I saw around me people living happy go lucky lives as if nothing could possibly be wrong. I stood in the driveway of my Apple Valley home looking at beautiful flower gardens, the woods and the lake with a deep sense that something was terribly wrong. It was early fall. I remember that moment well. I stood there and I prayed these words, "God what am I not seeing? I know what your word tells me about the last days, but everybody is going about their business as if nothing could possibly be wrong. Even in your church there is something very wrong. But no one I talk to seems to want to hear me. Please show me what it is that we are not seeing."

My job, which I really loved, was becoming difficult as well. I was emotionally sinking and I did not know why. Then I was befriended by one of the upper management in the agency I worked for. We got to be pretty good friends. But unusual things were happening around my house as well. Something was always breaking. One morning the battery of my car went dead. The lights had not been left on. I had not been having any trouble starting my car. There was no reason why my car should not have started. Nevertheless I had to buy a new battery.

Then one night I awoke to the sound of voices coming from my basement. I got up to make sure I was hearing what I thought I was hearing and sure enough there were two men standing outside my basement sliders carrying on a quiet conversation. I quietly dressed in the dark, went into my windowless bathroom with the phone book and my cell phone, shut the door, turned on the light and looked up the number for the local sheriff's department and pre-dialed it into my phone. Then I crept downstairs as quietly as I could and sat down on my exercise bike and waited. In a few minutes I saw the sliders light up like a Christmas tree. There was a very cheap white curtain with foam backing hanging in front of those sliders, and when the man on the other side turned on his flashlight I could clearly see his silhouette on the other side. I dialed the sheriff and in whispered tones explained to the dispatcher what was happening.

When the Sheriff arrived he pulled into my driveway with flashing lights and at the same time I heard someone jump off of my balcony and hit the ground hard. The Sheriff walked around my house and, amazingly, did not find anything. They didn't find any footprints. I wondered why they would bother to check for footprints in dry grass. For that matter I wondered why they would turn on their flashers when they approached my house. It would be unlikely that the prowlers were going to wait around to get caught. There were two officers and they were quite cold, and one of them was more than a little rude. So much for being a public servant.

Over the next couple of months there were about five more calls to the Sheriff's department and invasions to my home, and voices in the attic and things breaking etc. My "friend" at work forced me to have a psychiatric evaluation. I was "diagnosed" bipolar and declared "unfit" for duty. I was supposed to stay home for the next twelve weeks and do nothing using up all my vacation and sick time. It was at that point that I realized that something very sinister was afoot. I subsequently resigned my job.

It was then that I began doing research. God said, "The people who are doing these things to you are very cleaver at coving up their tracks. That means they have had practice. They have done it to someone else before." I went to the library and typed in two words, "psychological harassment". I did not know how else to describe what was happening to me. Those two words opened the door to my understanding of the things about which I have written in this book. It was then that I began to learn about organized vigilante stalking. It finally made sense. The invasions of my home; the voices in the attic; the bizarre behavior on the part of people in my church; my crying fits and what happened to me at work all fit the pattern for a stalking victim. I learned that one in one hundred Americans are experiencing the same thing and that this is a worldwide phenomenon. In 2007

I got an answer to the question that I had asked God, "What am I not seeing?" I continued my research for four years and the results of that work are in this book.

In the midst of learning to fight back, I also learned to lean hard and heavy on God. He was for a while my only friend because all of my family, friends and associates had been deceived by stalkers or others cooperating with them. I continue to be harassed by stalkers on a daily basis. I am under constant DEW assault and am sexually harassed by DEW even when I am in church. Stalkers have no morals whatever. Though my faith has sustained me and I am sure their attacks have abated because of divine intervention they don't want to give up. They are playing a devils game. Stalkers are people who have been deceived at the least and at worst are mind controlled slaves. They have been conditioned not to feel shame or guilt for the things that they do. They continue to get away literally with murder because of apathy and corruption in Law Enforcement, the criminal justice system and in the society at large. The church is not an exception. I have tried very patiently to reveal to people around me that there is something very evil going on in our world, however most I have talked to remain silent and unconcerned. This may be because they have been deceived by stalkers or operatives (tares) among them or because they have been beguiled into signing one of those agreements not to do anything to help stalking victims. The problem is that even decent people can be complacent and they can be deceived. We have been lulled into a false sense of security in this country and it is taking its toll on us very quietly.

Daniel the Prophet clearly tells us the West is going to fall. The scripture tells us that in the last days there will be a great apostasy in the church (2Thes 2:1). This falling away comes because people feel safe and secure and don't perceive the encroaching darkness. People will be in a state of apathy. Because of this they will fail to perceive obvious warning signs of danger. Thus "many will turn away from the faith and will betray and hate each other" (Matt 24:10 NIV). In Matt 10:21 (NIV) we read "Brother will betray brother to death and a father his child; children will rebel against their parents and have them put to death". This betrayal is accomplished by covert operatives who, like tares among us, deliberately and very subtly create dissention. This is exactly what stalkers did in the churches I attended. I recommend reading John Bevere's *The Bait of Satan*. He addresses this issue of offense in the scripture and how imperative it is that we learn not to be offended. Jesus also tells us that in the last days all men will hate us because of him (Matt 24) but by standing firm we will be saved. In Isaiah 4:1 the prophet tells us that in the last days seven women will take a hold of one man and beg him to marry them. They promise to provide their own food and clothes in exchange for his name to take away their disgrace. That verse stands out to me because a large number of gangstalking victims are single women. I have talked to several gangstalking victims who are single women and these stalkers have no scruples. One woman I talked to was a single 65 year old retired woman who was being hammered by DEW in her vaginal area. I have sensed in them a spirit of misogyny, a hatred of women. Mark Rick also has indicated that gangstalkers are driving their victims into sex slavery.[945]

It might be helpful here to discuss what is mean by "covert operations". It is a form of warfare. In a typical war there is a zone that is called a "front". That is the place where the line is clearly drawn between the encampments of the two entities at war with each other. In a traditional war there is a clear dividing line and your enemy is on the other side of that line. Your enemy is clearly distinguishable from your comrades by the uniform he/she wears and the insignia on his/her uniform. Your uniform identifies you for who you are as well. There are clear rules called "The Rules of Engagement", "The Laws of War" And "The Geneva Convention" which clearly outline what is acceptable and not acceptable in combat situations. There are penalties for violating those rules. Of course no real war is ever quite that cleanly, but that is what a traditional war looks like. In covert operations all that is thrown aside. You can't tell the difference between a friend and an enemy and thus covert operations are very risky. There is no "front". Covert operations are run by a situational ethics which amounts to "whatever it takes" to accomplish your mission. The only hard and fast rule would be "Whatever you do, don't get caught." I am firmly convinced that the attack upon the church in the last days will be accomplished mostly by covert means and deception of the saints.

Here is where the dividing line is drawn for believers. Jesus commands us to love our enemies. That has been my biggest challenge. I have not in all my life encountered such raw evil as I have in the behavior of gangstalkers. They put nails in my tire, drain the oil out of my car, tamper with my breaks and even cut my breaks at one point. I did notice that though the stalkers seemed bent on frustrating me, one or two of them might actually have been trying to be nice to me or it might have been someone else trying to combat their destructiveness. Stalkers were constantly tampering with my breaks which were always squealing, but occasionally it appeared as though someone attempted to fix what had been tampered with. Stalkers have poisoned my food and water, broken into my home on almost a daily basis and are constantly breaking things in my house which I have to either replace for fix. They continually hacked my computer while I was working on this document. They were obviously threatened by the contents of this book. Thus they would insert errors such as removing a letter in a word or deleting a word. They messed with the punctuation. They deleted text and changed the way I worded things. They also destroyed one laptop and changed my password on another so I could not use it. They locked my keyboard down a couple of times so that I had to go to the library to work on my research. They destroyed two printers and tried to make it impossible for me to print on the other two. They have hammered me with microwaves and give me a headache at least once a week. On more than one occasion I had a headache that lasted for several days because they would hammer my head with microwaves and charge it up again just about the time the headache was about to go away. I am repeatedly sexually assaulted by their

---

945 Mark Rich, The Hidden Evil (May, 2005 – http://www.thehiddenevil.com).

Directed Energy Weapons when I am in church, at home and while I am working. The last time I called the police on them afterwards I was absolutely electronically raped. All of these things are common occurrences with gangstalking targets. They attack my bowel and bladder functions repeatedly using DEW and once while I was shopping in Kohl's they made by bowels and bladder absolutely let loose. I drive a Toyota Corolla which has barely 200,000 miles on it and they are tearing it apart. They destroyed the heating and cooling system, dropped my muffler twice, and I am sure they have taken Toyota parts out of my engine and replaced them with parts from a less durable vehicle. They also "tapped" my mechanic so that he never really fixes things that I know are not working right. One mechanic put the brake shoes on my car backwards so that my breaks squealed very loudly.

I made it a habit to pray for them daily. However, I would get up from my prayers and sit down in front of my computer to work on this book and they would begin tampering with my laptop making it almost impossible for me to get anything done. On more than one occasion I have given them a piece of my mind, "You wicked filth!" , after praying for their salvation. Stalkers have no scruples and no respect for anyone. There is no right or wrong in their minds. I have told them, "You know, you act by sheer animal instinct. You are not at all civilized. If you want to live that way then go live with the animals in the jungle!" I still pray for them as I wrestle with my own ability or inability to love them. The truth is they never show their faces. When someone physically rapes you, you're supposed to scream, fight, kick, bite, and scratch. The truth is that a rapist may give up when there is resistance. However, when I am being raped by a sex offender using a Directed Energy Weapon and I scream, (which I am often inclined to do) it just looks like I have just lost my mind. You can't see the rapist. There are no bruises and no physical evidence. What pains me is that while I am trying my very best to be the kind of person God calls me to be, thus tyring to love my enemies, my invisible enemies are deliberately trying to find ways to tip me off balance. So they have discovered that I detest them the most when they sexually assaulting me with their sick weapons. Gangstalking sex offenders are hiding their crimes behind a veneer of respectability. I hurt because I get angry with them and I don't want to. I hurt because they are people that God loves and wants to save and I want to demonstrate Christ's love. However, I find it impossible to do with sex offending stalkers who have no scruples and no conscience and who are not being held accountable by anyone. The truth is that they actually punish me for being kind to them. If I speak softly to them and try to be kind they simply turn up the heat and start beating up on me psychologically. I am convinced that that are practicing mind control techniques and Satanic Ritual Abuse that are designed to destroy things in my personality which I value the most – compassion and mercy.

Thus, the NWO has accomplished another feat in dividing and conquering America. It is a lot easier to hate an enemy you can't see. Stalkers sit on the other side of a computer screen and their targets are mere animations on their screens. They do not perceive them as human beings. They on the other hand are invisible.

Their victims cannot look them in the eyes and see their humanity. So loving them is a profound challenge. There are upwards of 12,500,000 stalkers in this nation attacking their fellow citizens. That is 12,500,000 Americans who are committing criminal acts on a daily basis who are not being held accountable for their crimes.

In a nation that is beleaguered with covert criminality everything has become corrupted. American businesses, doctors, lawyers, employers even clergy are cooperating with stalkers. It is even possible that some Christians have become stalkers. This is the result of a massive deception on the part of the United States Government to which all have fallen prey. The NWO has worked for years to desensitize Americans to the suffering of others. The concept of "codependence" has persuaded Americans and Christian America that caring for other people is not healthy. Although the concept may be legitimate in some forms it becomes the catchall excuse for ignoring the suffering and needs of our "neighbors" who Jesus commanded us to love (Luke 10:27). In this regard the concept of "codependence" is not biblical as we understand it. In the world of work we are admonished by our superiors to "be professional". Even in the helping professions the notion that we ought to love people is downplayed and professionalism is stressed. There is nothing wrong with being professional, but Jesus did not command us to be professional. He commanded us to love one another. "My command is this. Love each other as I have loved you" (Luke15:12 NIV). He goes on to say, "Greater love has no one than this, that he lay down his life for his friends" (Luke 12;13 NIV). We are admonished to carry one another's burdens and in this way we will fulfill the law of Christ (Galatians 6:2). The Apostle Paul tells us in I Corinthians 12:26 (NIV) "If one part [of the body] suffers, every part suffers with it; if one part is honored, every part rejoices with it." Jesus says the same thing when he says, "I tell you the truth, whatever you did for one of the least of these brothers of mine, you did for me" (Matt 25:40 NIV). By desensitizing people to the suffering of others, the stage is set for a criminalized society. With the constant proliferation of sexual perversion we have a sexualized, criminalized society. Those who refuse to accept this criminalization and sexualization of our world will likely be targeted by mind controllers, calling themselves behavior management professionals, who will attempt by sick forms of desensitization (such as constant rape by DEW) to force us to accept what is absolutely unacceptable to God.

What should the response of the church be in the midst of this rampant lawlessness? We are admonished in the scripture to stand firm. Jesus has compassion for stalking victims as much as he has compassion for stalkers. One day while I was in my barracks room at Ft. Meade I was despairing over the evil that was happening all over the world and the warnings of scriptures about the last days. I had fallen asleep and when I awoke it was raining. The moment I opened my eyes God said to me, "I cause the rain to fall on the just and the unjust." I have to meditate on the meaning of the word "mercy". God is still in control. He sees all the evil under the sun. He knows the thoughts and deeds of every man, woman and child on the planet. He has chosen to let the rain fall so that both those who live righteous lives and those who live unjust lives can still eat. He cares about us all.

Many stalkers were homeless and were picked up off the street by those that employ them. Being a part of a stalking group gave them a sense of belonging and respectability. Homeless people endure much more than hunger from lack of food. They endure shame and loneliness because of the stigma attached. Some of them came out of prisons and were given the right to be free as long as they cooperated. Prisons have become mind control laboratories and no one is safe there. Many stalkers are Law Enforcement and retired Law Enforcement or retired military. There is plenty of mind control going on in both those institutions. When society has lost the concept of loving one's fellow, the notions of forgiveness and grace are also gone. Thus people become vindictive and exact cruel forms of punishment on people for the pettiest offenses. This is the groundwork for lawlessness. One thing I have noticed about stalkers is that they are absolutely committed to accomplishing their mission, however corrupted it may be. One has to wonder what would happen if all 12,500,000 of them would be as willing to be committed to something positive what a difference that would make.

When Jesus was teaching people to love their neighbors, they wanted to know who he meant by "neighbor". In response he told them the parable of the "good Samaritan". That was a parable that confronted them with their lack of mercy, because he chose as the hero of the story a character that they would have rejected – a Samaritan. Samaritans were "half breeds" or Jews who had interbred with others who had occupied their land. They had thus committed treason intermarrying with the enemy of the Jews. However, in the parable the Samaritan was the one who "loved his neighbor" while other characters who should have been responding to their "neighbor's" crisis ignored it. I have noticed that there are people out there who though they do not share my faith, they still have compassion for mankind and are still willing to face and fight this invisible war. God has a place in his kingdom for people who are willing to fight. So I pray endlessly for them. I deeply desire for them to know my savior. He desires to embrace them.

Law Enforcement is a dichotomy in itself. In a lawless age when the government is up to its ears in organized crime, how do we expect local Law Enforcement to accomplish their mission? When Freemason judges are sitting the bench with an oath to protect their lawless members, many in Law Enforcement may feel like they are spinning their wheels getting nowhere. Not to mention the fact that our NWO infected government knows everything there is to know about anybody so anybody in any official capacity who has anything questionable in their background can and will be blackmailed into cooperation including Law Enforcement. We have an entire society that is snared and trapped like rabbits on a rabbit farm.

For example, I went to the pharmacy to get one of my prescriptions refilled. I was taking two 10mg tablets of a blood pressure medication a day with another medication to treat migraines. I had been taking it for about a year so I am sure of what my prescription was. However the pharmacist gave me 100mg tablets instead of 10 mg tablets. I spoke to the pharmacist at the store and told him he had made an error (big error). He insisted that my medication did not come in 10 mg tablets and so he thought that my doctor meant 100 mg. That should have red flagged me on the spot. If a pharmacist is unsure of what your prescription is supposed to be, he is supposed to call your doctor not make a wild guess! He increased my prescription from 20 mg to 200 mg without talking to my doctor. I insisted he was wrong. He changed my prescription to 25mg tablets, which is what he said I had gotten the last time. That was wrong also. Why didn't he check to see what I had gotten the last time in the first place? I took the 25mg tablets and only took one of them instead of two.

I noticed that the pharmacist's hands were shaking while I was talking to him. What I know now is that stalkers will use many and varied devices to get people, even businesses, to cooperate with them. In this case, the stalker wanted the pharmacist to do something that was illegal. He most probably used blackmail. He would have checked the pharmacist's background and found something that he had done that was either illegal or embarrassing and threatened to expose him if he did not cooperate. In the day and age when the government has unlimited access to any and all of your personal information and have you under constant surveillance, finding something to use against you if you don't cooperate is not difficult. It pays to live a righteous life. It also pays to have a Savior. All of us have done something sinful in our lives. I have too. But Jesus does not intend for those things to be an albatross around our necks the rest of our lives. Jesus shed his blood to free us. Take your sins to the cross. Don't let some bully destroy your life with them.

Those who have a heart to know we are in the last days and we are engaged in spiritual warfare like we have never been in the history of the world need to forge a chain of compassion all across this country. Knowing the truth is the first step. Accepting the truth and putting away fairy tale fantasies about life in America is the next step. Law Enforcement needs our prayers. Imagine what it would be like to know that a young girl, the same age as your own daughter, was being held captive and prostituted by someone to public officials who were likely not showing her any mercy. And imagine what it would feel like if you were told you could not do anything to help – directly. So you did what you could to rescue the girl but what gets put in print is that you neglected your most basic responsibility and in the eyes of the public you're a disgrace. And you have to put food on your table and feed your own family. And you get discouraged and life becomes a game of earning a paycheck. You lose your wind and your fire. What would it mean to you for the believers in your community to reach out to you, pray for you and wrap you in kindness rather than animosity?

Think about the elite. They may remind you of the people on your favorite soap operas that everybody loves to hate. But I am remembering the story the John D. Rockefeller told his son Nelson. His daddy used to let him jump into him arms.

And he loved his daddy and he trusted him until the day his daddy let him fall and hit the ground and told him never to trust anyone completely. The elite do not grow up in loving, nurturing environments. They don't value love. They are mind controlled from their youth and are exploited by their parents for the furthering of the NWO agenda. And they pass it on to their children. I was standing in line at the grocery store one day and I saw a picture of Chelsea Clinton on the cover of one of the tabloids. She was wearing a wedding dress and her blond tresses were piled up on her head. Her smile was radiant. She looked like any bride would look on her wedding day. When her father, Bill Clinton, was sexually exploiting Cathy O'Brien and her minor daughter at the same time, he was being filmed by George Bush Sr. George Bush asked him if he was ready to bring Chelsea along and "open her up". Bill Clinton's response surprised me. He said, "I don't know. I'll have to talk to Hillary".[946] I wondered as I looked at Chelsea's picture if maybe, just maybe, the Clintons might have had enough compassion and love for their daughter to spare her the trauma that so many of her peers had been subjected to. We need to form a chain. We need to stretch out our arms to the elite and their children and wrap them in prayer. We might save some.

What if we created an environment where stalkers could come out of hiding and safely confess their crimes? And what if we could forgive them? And what if we got down on our knees and went before God and repented of our blindness and selfishness, for failing to notice the broken and the wounded in our midst that desperately needed to be noticed. We need to form a chain of love across America of people who know the truth and refuse to surrender themselves to the lie. We need to from a chain around the soldiers who have been used as pawns on the chessboard of global greed. We need to uplift and up hold those who spoke out against what they saw in Iraq and refused to participate. We need to face the truth, examine ourselves, stand before God to be examined and repent. We need to prepare ourselves because God tells us it is going to get worse.

> *For then there will be great distress unequaled form the beginning of the world until now—and never to be equaled again. If those days had not been cut short, not one would survive, but for the sake of the elect those days will be shortened. (Matt 24:21 – 22 NIV).*

Remember that God says what he means and means what he says. When he says "no one would survive" he means there would not be one living soul left on this planet.

The Bible is one solid and sure guide for facing our enemy. It was written by the same God who created us – ergo it is the manual for everything we have to face as God's creation. The prophecies in the scripture have told us what to expect in these last days. American Christians who are hoping to be raptured out of here

---

946 David Icke, The Biggest Secret (Wildwood, MO: Bridge of Love Publications USA,1999) p. 338

before things get really bad may be in for a shock. Jesus clearly told us that the day or the hour of his return is not known even to him. Thus he gave us warning signs to watch for. He did not tell us to sit tight when you see these things happen because we would not be hurt by any of them. We are told in Hebrews 3:6 to hold fast to our confession of faith and stand firm until the end. When we are told "hold fast" it means there is a storm coming.

Here is our hope. This is the last lap. Since the time that Adam and Eve sinned in the Garden of Eden mankind has had to wrestle with evil. We have suffered death and loss, war, depression, famine, disease, poverty, crime of the most hideous forms and horrendous injustice. But there is a better day coming. The earth is ripe for a bath. Jesus is coming back and he is going to destroy all that is unholy in his sight and those who surrendered themselves to him and were washed in his blood have an eternal inheritance and everlasting joy. The Book of Revelation is worth reading for those who have wept many tears.

> *And God shall wipe away all tears from their eyes; and there shall be no more death, neither sorrow, nor crying, neither shall there be any more pain: for the former things are passed away (Rev 21:4NIV).*

45. The Fountain

I think we were in New York State somewhere, my mother and I. I seem to remember Uncle David being there. My Uncle David lives in New York State. It was in the heat of summer. We had gone to a park for some kind of event. We were standing outside a big gate and Uncle David had gone inside to get some information. We were waiting for him.

We were standing near a huge fountain. It was round with a spire in the middle that was probably 10 to 12 feet high. It was tiered inside at the base with the tiers rising like steps toward the middle. I was just a child, I don't remember how old, maybe not 10 years old yet. I just remember looking at the fountain and thinking how much fun it would be to splash around in that clear crystal water. Of course I thought it would probably not be allowed. But it was so hot, and I thought if it was not allowed then someone would tell me. I asked my mother, "Mom, can I jump in the fountain?" I remember she wined that I would get all my clothes wet. I said something like, "I don't care. I'll dry." She said, "Oh, I suppose." So, I jumped into the fountain and swam around with all my clothes on. And there I was just splashing around in this big beautiful fountain. There were other people standing around looking at me. Some of them looked at me and asked "Is it allowed?" Some were children and some were adults. I remember seeing some of them look at each other and shrug. Then all at once they too plowed into the fountain. And there we were, children, adults, with all our clothes on in the heat of the day just having a blast splashing around in this fountain.

Of course it wasn't allowed. So a policeman came along and chased everybody out. But we had had some fun.

The policeman was like a lot of people who are too much concerned about what is proper, legal, politically or socially correct and not concerned enough about what is good. They are the Pharisees in the world. They are in the church and in the world as well. Phariseeism is not a hazard of religion so much as it is a hazard of human nature. Jesus is precisely the opposite of that. Jesus says, "The fountain belongs to me. Come and jump into my fountain and be refreshed."

I was a child. I was not concerned about what was proper, legal or politically or socially correct, but about what would be good. Children have a very uncomplicated way of looking at the world. There are some things that children understand much better than adults because of their uncluttered minds. I have this faith that there are still people with uncluttered minds who have the capacity to lead. They know that non-conformity is not a sin especially if "everybody else" is heading for a cliff! They become radical because they are simple and uncluttered in their thinking. Politics won't persuade them. Fear of losing their jobs or even their lives won't deter them. Fear of disapproval from the extremely cluttered status quo won't stop them. Their vision is clear. They know the difference between right and wrong and good and evil. There are universal truths that stand like pillars of light guarding their souls against the encroaching darkness. They are not afraid of anyone's disapproval. They know this world is passing. They that can hear the voice of Jesus in their hearts and know the one who conquered death for all do not fear even death. No, they fear a cage, and they fear God above all else.

You know what I want. I want you to get in this fountain with me. I want people who are tired and weary of this ugly war to get in here with me. I want Jews, Iraqis and Palestinians to get in here with me. I want stalking victims and stalkers who are tired of the way they have been living to get in here with me. I want Freemasons and even Satanists who are tired of the deadness they feel inside. I want politicians, journalists and Law Enforcement to get in here with me. I want people who have never know what it is like to be bathed in mercy and compassion to get in this fountain with me and stand under the waterfall of God's passionate love for mankind. I want you to know him and the eternal hope that he has to offer you. There is nothing like it on this planet and our hope is always in Jesus Christ.

> "Come now let us reason together" says the Lord, "Though your sins are like scarlet, they shall be white as snow; though they are red as crimson, they shall be like wool." (Isaiah 1:18 NIV.)

> But Jesus said, "Let the little children, come to me and do not forbid them: for of such is the kingdom of heaven" (Mat 19:14, NKJV)

Then Jesus called a little child to him, set him in the midst of them, and said, "Assuredly, I say to you, Unless you are converted, and become as little children, you will by no means enter into the kingdom of heaven" (Mat 18:2,3, NKJV).

The wolf also shall dwell with the lamb, The leopard shall lie down with the goat, The calf and the young lion and the fatling together, And a little child shall lead them (Isa 11:6, NKJV).

Made in the USA
Middletown, DE
01 October 2018